ATLAS

in

ASCENDANCE

America at War

BOOK III

GREGORY C PHILLIPS

Blue M Publishing, LLC - Chicago

Library of Congress Cataloging-in-publication data
Names: Phillips, Gregory P.
Title: *Atlas in Ascendance*
Description: First edition | Blue M Publishing [Paperback], Chicago, IL [2017] | Series: Book three of trilogy set | Contents: *Atlas in Ascendance – America at War*| Summary: The battle lines are drawn, as conflict between the new republic and the USSA is inevitable. The clash is between two different ideologies as well as their military capabilities. In a land so long united by a common people and cause, the ultimate outcome is explosive and traumatic. | Audience Note: Recommended for readers fifteen and older | Language Note: Infrequent offensive language.
Identifiers: ISBN 978-1-945385-02-5 (Paperback)
Subjects: LCSH: sh85001072 Adventure stories| BISAC: FIC031060 FICTION / Thriller Political | FIC055000 FICTION / Dystopian | FIC037000 FICTION /Political | GSAFD: 00000cz a2200037n 45 0 680 Dystopias
Classification: LCC PS370-380 | DDC 813/--dc23

Phillips, Gregory C.
Atlas in Ascendance: America at War, Gregory C. Phillips
Contents: Part four – The New Republic | Part five – War | Part six – The End is Near

ISBN 978-1-945385-02-5 (Paperback)

Printed in the United States of America
www.blueMpublishing.com

Fabulous Book Cover Design by HIP Distribution
Published by Blue M Publishing, LLC, Hammond, IN

Blue M Publishing
6205 Indianapolis Blvd
Suite 100
Hammond, IN 46320

Atlas in Ascendance
BOOK III

Book Summary

In the third and final volume, the United States of America continues to slide into totalitarianism just as the newly minted republic from the breakaway state of Wyoming gets its beginnings. However, a despotic ruler emerges as the USA decays and changes *In God We Trust* to something more in her own likeness. The USA and its constitution become the United *Socialist* States of America - the USSA -- and it no longer wishes to sit idly by and permit Wyoming and other states to secede; rather, it saber-rattles its intent toward war.

The battle lines are drawn, as conflict between the two neighbors is inevitable. The clash of diametric ideologies is at hand, and they ready their armies and navies for combat. In a land so long united by a common people and cause, the ultimate outcome is as explosive as it is traumatic.

*****

Contents

ATLAS in ASCENDANCE - America at War
BOOK III

PART IV THE NEW REPUBLIC

CH 1 It's All in a Name

And so, it had begun.

Soon more states began petitioning to join the new Republic of Wyoming, making it apparent that Wyoming was not alone in its journey. The heavy lifting of creating a new nation could be shared with others, and with their combined resources and determination they could re-create what had been lost years earlier. The freedom bandwagon could accommodate many more riders, but with it would come the need for a new name.

The moniker *Republic of Wyoming* was too provincial, too limiting. It would not do if other states were to be welcomed into the fold. No, with all the new states involved, there needed to be a broader, more inclusive appellation. And so, like the convention that drafted a new constitution, a new convention was held to rename the infant nation. However, this time the gathering was conducted over the SI-net, with 3-D realism that made all feel as if they were interacting with each other in a large hall.

There were hundreds of names proposed, ranging from the *Republic of WyoTexas* to the *Republic of the Central Plains*. It was easy to eliminate most as being either self-serving or down-right awful. One by one, the delegates from pending state applicants and those from within Wyoming, submitted their suggestions, which flashed up on the screens of all who participated.

JC Sumner, who had been elected interim president at the Wyoming independence convention, was asked to chair the naming convention as well. Sitting comfortably with his Cabinet in a virtual-reality room in the Republic's temporary White House in Cheyenne, Sumner addressed those convention delegates online and pressed to establish the ground rules for any decision making.

"We will not make a circus out of these proceedings," Sumner said. "The Naming Committee has received many proposed names, but we must cut-off this phase of the process so that these can be evaluated. We will cull through them quickly and distribute those names we believe warrant consideration for your review and approval. I realize how important this is to all of you; however, as we continue to spend our time debating a name, we neglect much more pressing issues, many of which may ultimately determine our Republic's success or failure long term.

"Therefore, I urge you to make a decision promptly and be flexible so that we can get a simple majority to assent to one name. The Naming Committee will review what we have, and I promise that you will have the final list by eight o'clock tomorrow morning. Votes must be cast within twenty-four hours to be valid. The two names that receive the greatest number of votes will be selected for the final runoff. That will take place the following day. Thank you in advance for your patience."

The Naming Committee reviewed the names and found none to be particularly good.

"You have to be kidding me!" said Oishi Gupta, the president's administrative assistant. "Listen to this one – *Red-blooded Republic*. Are these people serious?" She quickly clicked the delete button and moved to the next one.

"This one is almost as good," said the assistant to the Secretary of Defense, Josh Templeton. "How about *The Ole' Red, White and Blue*?" he said. "That's real original."

The group laughed and giggled as they read the candidate's names. Only halfway through the process they had all agreed that adult beverages were the only way to get through the list. And, by the end of the evening, they were laughing so hard they could hardly breathe.

"Well, do we have a list?" asked Sumner, sticking his head in the doorway at about midnight.

Oishi tried to keep a straight and sober face, but even that was a challenge. "Yes, sir, she answered. I believe we've found five truly awful names for you." With that, the group burst out laughing, and the president merely shook his head, smiled and left to go upstairs to bed.

The next morning, the group was able to get up early and prepare the final list. The list was distributed over the SI-net to all the delegates – the following appearing on all their screens:

> **Republic of American States**
>
> **League of American States**
>
> **Terra America**
>
> **Association of American States**

As had been the case with most things, the feedback from the delegates was swift and scathing. Few were happy with *any* of the choices, and votes trickled in for two or three of them but far from showing consensus or leanings toward any in particular.

"What do we do now?" asked Sumner, sitting with his Cabinet at a long, oval table setup in the room next to his office. Josh Templeton and Secretary of Health, Loretta White, twisted nervously in their red, high-gloss, leather chairs, while the rest watched as their president seemed truly baffled by this seemingly simple issue. "We could spend another three months negotiating a name with each delegate, but this is something not everyone is going to agree on," added Sumner, twisting a black, ballpoint pen around in his fingers.

White leaned forward and spoke first, folding her arms on the table and putting on a face that showed seriousness and determination. "Mr. President, I think we need to make a decision here in this room and let everyone know. It's not the way any of us wanted it, but it looks like that's what it's coming to." "I agree," said Rich Briggs, the Secretary of Commerce. "Let's just agree on something and move on."

"What about … say … the Republic of the Plains," said Templeton. "All the states are from the Plain States of the old Union."

"But what if Florida decides to join us?" asked Ash Nguyen, Secretary of the Treasury, leaning back in his chair and shaking his head. "They certainly won't like being called one of the Plains States."

Sumner could tell that even within his own group finding an answer was not going to be easy. "Then I'll decide," he said, abruptly, raising his voice in frustration. "We'll call it the Republic of American Territories and League of Affiliated States."

Everyone looked at him with astonishment. "Really?" said Secretary White, shaking her head. "That's not going to fly with anyone, sir, with all due respect." Other heads around the table were shaking in agreement.

"I'm sorry, Mr. President, but I must concur with Secretary White," said Shea. "While a good effort, I think the name is too long and cumbersome. But …" she stopped for a moment as if something had come to mind, "… what if you take the letters of your suggestion, sir, and turned them into an acronym?"

"An acronym? What would that be?" asked the president.

"Well … the acronym would be ATLAS. What about the Republic of ATLAS?"

There was silence for a moment as people thought about it.

"I've heard worse," said White, still swiveling in her chair. "But I think it should be The ATLAS Republic."

"It's not great, but it isn't bad," Nguyen added, nodding slightly. "I could live with it."

"We are shouldering the burdens of creating a country that will restore the power and glory of the old USA. We will be the ones who will be the guardians of democracy for the world. It will be a heavy load, but like ATLAS holding up the heavens, we will succeed," said Shea.

"All in favor," said Sumner quickly.

"Aye," replied most in the room.

"Opposed?" None raised his or her hand.

"The motion carries to rename the country, the ATLAS Republic. Meeting is adjourned."

And there it was – The ATLAS Republic. Not only did the country have a new beginning, it also had a new name.

*****

CH 2 USSA in Turmoil

As the ATLAS Republic was waxing, the USSA was waning.

Having been renamed the United Socialist States of America and given a new constitution – *Constitution 2.0* – the old USA seemed to have run its course. States' powers had been minimized or eliminated, their governors and state legislatures increasingly pushed aside in favor of local, but still federal, junior congresses that reported directly to Washington. Private property had largely been seized by the federal government. Large companies, known as GovCo's, were overseen by federally-appointed boards of directors. These companies were allowed to generate profits but only within certain limits. All profits were taxed at high rates to fund the continued growth of social experiments and programs created by the Left. Businesses had begun to shut down or relocate to other countries. The government owned more and more of the nation's economy, but less of it was generating anything meaningful for society as a whole.

Manufacturing and service facilities, once bustling with activity, stood vacant, abandoned by owners who had given up trying to make a better life for themselves and their families in America. In those businesses where the government was able to keep the doors open, layers of staffing had been added and employment rosters had ballooned, increasing costs of production by multiples of what had been the norm. Work that had been keenly honed and choreographed for high-efficiency to meet demand now employed thousands more unnecessary people -- partly to reduce the national unemployment rate and partly to hold down civil unrest. And as the government's nationalized workforce grew geometrically, so too did the number of bureaucrats needed to process the additional paperwork. It was all great for lowering unemployment, which had been hovering around 17 percent. The Bureau of Statistics could finally and legitimately say that unemployment was at just below 5 percent. But the nasty truth was that the low unemployment came at a high, unsustainable price. As production costs skyrocketed, more of the nationalized companies operated at losses as the high costs could not be passed on to paying consumers. These losses caused these companies to require more cash to keep operating – cash that came from Uncle Sam. But for the USSA to have the money to pay these companies to keep them afloat, it had to raise more tax revenue or borrow more and increase the debt. Of course, the higher debt levels meant higher interest payments which also increased the debt ... and on ... and on ... and on it went.

There had been a time when Washington had lauded the high unemployment rate, convinced it was a good thing; after all, free time permitted people to pursue their *dreams* and fulfill their *passions*. However in reality, it only permitted people to pursue sloth and crime. In the major cities, crime had soared 68 percent with violent offenses rising to the point that the states had to deploy their National Guards to keep the peace. That action only pushed violent crime out to the suburbs where people had already gone to flee the problems of the inner city. With few jobs in the cities and rising crime in the suburbs, families were moving back to rural areas, buying farmland

and building new houses. But they weren't there to till the soil or raise crops. Instead, they telecommuted from home via the SI-net. It was an ironic reversal of a geographic shift that had been going on for centuries -- that of people moving into cities for the rich culture and greater job opportunities. Those allures no longer existed. Instead, they had been replaced by staggering property taxes, widespread crime, and corrupt city politicians who were constantly on the take.

Not only did families move out of town – so did businesses. High vacancy rates in the big cities had become epidemic. Deserted buildings were everywhere, ripe for drug addicts, gangs, prostitution, and violent crime. Whole sections had been demolished and left fallow, growing nothing but trash and filth. Several city councils considered returning their urban landscapes over to big farming companies, but instead were forced to form agricultural cooperatives or co-ops under threats from Washington. Co-ops across the country were sponsored by the Ministry of Residential Equality to prop-up the inner cities. However, funding was scarce to support such groups and many collapsed from lack of money.

Another vice that had taken root in most major cities were the burgeoning open-air drug markets. The previous First Citizen of the USSA, Jack Fourier, had succeeded in legalizing all drugs. Prescriptions were no longer required because there were so few licensed doctors to write medicinal remedies. Not only were drugs widely available, but the Ministry of Health and Human Dignity provided addicts with clean needles, free housing, meals and even laundry service. Some got vouchers for weekly entertainment at shows and bars to "ease the transition" back into society for those afflicted. Government-owned opium dens were common, and hashish and marijuana was widely sold in ministry outlets throughout the country. Heavily taxed, the corrosive substances brought in tax revenue and had the dual benefit of keeping the people in a trance-induced state of apathy and depression -- just what was needed to maintain their totalitarian state.

But with the collapse of production and the flight of creative entrepreneurs who had snuck out of the country on forged travel documents, the USSA was mired in a stagnant economy and deteriorating military. Without fresh blood to fuel innovation and advance technology, Washington was forced to rely on its own infrastructure to maintain its military readiness. It was the Ministry of International Policing (formerly the Department of Defense) that began producing military hardware and software out of its own factories. At costs twenty times what the private sector had been excoriated for charging, the defense budget had ballooned out of control. Although there was massive spending, there was minimal effectiveness from those dollars. Falling farther and farther behind in the arms race, the ministry could no longer compete against China, Russia and the Islamic States. There were no breakthroughs in capabilities and hadn't been for years. In fact, the USSA had begun purchasing its technology *from* China and Russia, and that equipment was usually one, if not two, generations behind what these countries were adding to their own arsenals.

On the monetary front, the economic landscape in the USSA was also bleak: extreme inflation, high interest rates, devaluated currency, and loss of worldwide respect dominated the critical issues. America's dollar had not reigned supreme in the world for decades. Due to the $249 trillion of debt, the dollar was no longer considered hard currency, and with the introduction of the UnitedCoin which had replaced the dollar, the USSA was left in a small pool with many other has-been countries, struggling for dignity and respect in a world that had passed them by.

The stark reality was that the USSA had become a second-world country, just as had Britain, France, Germany and the rest of Western Europe. The USSA had succeeded in following in their footsteps down the hilltop and into the dark valley of despair.

*****

CH 3 Reality Lost

There was something wrong at the White House, but no one could put a finger on just what it was. There was no information coming from the executive branch. It wasn't unusual for First Citizen Fourier not to be seen in public for days at a time. After all, he was a busy man, and there were things that he did that he made classified to keep them from the public. News reporters often joked that even his bowel movements were considered top secret. No schedules were ever printed of the First Citizen's daily meetings or travel plans. Yet, when Fourier wanted the news attention and coverage, his team made sure there were cameras everywhere -- from the moment the door to the White House opened to the second Air Force One landed at its destination. All footage was filtered and re-filtered to make sure only the images Fourier wanted to show were given. No other news was allowed. But now, even that coverage had been strangely silenced without explanation.

After three days of mystery, there was a flurry of activity at John Adam's first Washington home at 1600 Pennsylvania Avenue. Notification of an emergency meeting of the First Citizen's Cabinet was sent by encrypted message to all ministers. Recalled from foreign trips and important meetings and events, the ministers and even members of Congress were summoned.

Eventually news of the Cabinet meeting began to leak out from unidentified sources, and although the media was warned not to print anything about what was going on, the SI-net picked up on it.

Rumors Spread that First Citizen Fourier is Dead!

Chaos at the White House as Commander in Chief Believed Felled by Disease!

Chief of Staff Mum about What is Going on at 1600 Pennsylvania Avenue!

The stories spread quickly, and it was difficult for the general press to stay silent any longer. By the time of the meeting, there were press cameras everywhere outside the White House, filming the black, stretch limousines as they filed through the iron gates and passed the white, sentry posts. Hours ticked by; yet, no one emerged. The nation – the world – waited and watched.

Finally, a press conference was called. It was the first in four years, and none of the reporters knew what to expect. The press room at the White House, normally empty except for when the janitorial services in the building were performing their duties, was packed with media-types, all buzzing about what were the latest rumors or conspiracy theories. However, no one claimed to know anything for certain.

Set for three o'clock, the press meeting was soon delayed. Reporters sat impatiently, watching the digital clock on the wall as it clicked past three-thirty, four-thirty, and then five. Finally, just as some in the room were about to leave, Press Secretary Kenneth Beister, came out from behind the blue curtain and walked to the podium.

The seal of the POTUS or President of the United States had been replaced a year earlier with the new symbol of the First Citizen, a Grizzly bear, passive-looking, holding a hammer in one paw and olive branches in the other. Above it on the seal was the narcissistic image of the First Citizen's face, faintly etched into the background as if it were the country's new supreme being – one to which homage would be paid for generations, just as had China's Mao, Russia's Lenin, or Cuba's Castro.

"I want to thank you all for coming today," Beister began, clutching the sides of the podium tightly, as if he were anticipating sudden electric shocks from a wired grid below his feet. "As you may have surmised, there have been developments here in the White House during the past few days. The First Citizen and his wife have taken ill. We are uncertain of the cause of their illness, but we are hopeful that they will be back on the job soon. In the meantime, the Minister of Unity, Angel Ratner, will be assuming the day-to-day duties of the First Citizen until he can return to work."

Ratner came out from behind the same blue curtain wearing a conservative navy, chalk-striped suit and white blouse buttoned to the top. She wore no jewelry and little makeup – her only adornment was a hollow mask of concern which she attempted to wear as convincingly as possible.

"Thank you, Kenneth," she said without emotion, gesturing toward the press secretary. "First, I want to say that there is no need for alarm or concern. We are all certain that this is a temporary condition that will be remedied with rest and medical care. The First Citizen's doctors are here and all believe there is no need to move either the First Lady or him to the hospital as their conditions are not deemed serious."

That was of little comfort to anyone in the room. The mere fact that a minister had to assume the duties of the commander in chief while the First Citizen was ill suggested this was not some minor ailment. The press and the people had been lied to before about things both large and small. In the past, these falsehoods had been explained away; however, they had never risen to this level of severity.

Emboldened by the absence of the First Citizen, a few reporters stood up to shout questions, something they used to do prior to Fourier's election to office. "Minister Ratner, why isn't Minister Griffin assuming the duties of the First Citizen while he is ill?" one reporter yelled. "Isn't he next in the succession line?" Another shouted, "Yes, Minister Ratner, where is the Minster of Tax Enforcement?"

Ratner clamped her jaw, grinding her teeth at the disrespect shown to her and her estimation of her own self-importance. "The tax minister is out of town," she said without hesitation. "We are in contact with him and are apprising him of what is happening."

Another reporter stood up with hand raised. "Minister Ratner, I understand that he attended the White House function just the other night when the president of Uzbekistan was in Washington. Did he leave town after that? We received no notice of his travels."

"Yes, he left the very next morning, but again, he will be returning," answered Ratner, becoming increasingly agitated.

Yet, the reporter persisted. "Doesn't the new constitution require that the Minister of Taxation Enforcement immediately assume the duties of the First Citizen if he is incapacitated? Are you suggesting that the minister too is incapacitated?"

"Yes, otherwise shouldn't he be in charge right now?" asked another journalist.

"Again, the minister is indisposed at the moment and cannot attend to the matters at hand. He has asked that I step-in until he returns. I am in charge right now." These were words that escaped her mouth unintentionally, and they were not lost on the ears of her audience. A coldness instantly fell on those in attendance – a sensation that chilled all to the bone.

"But minister ..." began a reporter, attempting one more time.

At this point, Ratner's calm became stormy. "I *said* Minister Griffin is unavailable, not incapable. Although I am third in line for succession, I am not acting in that function. That is why I am only the caretaker at this juncture. We will keep you apprised of his condition and that of his wife as we find out more from the doctors. That will be all for today." And with that, she turned in disgust and walked briskly out of the room.

The press sat stunned. Too confused to speak, they looked at each other in bewilderment, but were too frightened to voice any discontent within listening range of the White House minions and any eavesdropping devices planted in the press room walls. They left as confused as when they'd come into the room.

Still, the mainstream news wires were filled with the story that they'd been fed.

Fouriers Sick with Unknown Illness; Expected to Return Soon.

First Citizen – Wife: Struck by Sickness.

However, no one believed it. The real story was evolving even more quickly, and it was coming from so called "outlaws" of the SI-net, including the now-notorious GOFLA organization. From deep within the bunkers of GOFLA headquarters just outside of Cheyenne, members were busy trying to find anyone associated with the White House who might have some knowledge – some real knowledge – of what was happening there. From delivery truck drivers to trash pickup personnel, all were sought to get information. But to their frustration, all mouths had been silenced – even some permanently. The new editor-in-chief, Bronson Updike, had found three people dead and five missing who had worked in the kitchen or on the waiter staff during the state dinner for President Safaev of Uzbekistan. Any promising leads from them had ended in a cold, dead end.

Then, after three more days of obfuscation, GOFLA found a source – Margola Vasilik. Left behind to fend for herself, she was embittered by Ratner's treatment after she took the position as Minister of Unity. Vasilik was supposed to get Ratner's job when she moved up, but instead, the deputy minister was passed-over – the minister position given to someone else. Fed up and seeking a safe place to land, Vasilik contacted Sumner directly, who put her in touch with Updike at GOFLA. There she told him the entire story.

Updike used the old-style typing method to create his blogs and did so with rapid-fire precision, as Vasilik recited what she had seen and heard that night at 1600 Pennsylvania Avenue. She said that she had become a close friend of Minister Griffin. Vasilik had cultivated the relationship to counter the overbearing and often frightening and destructive behavior of her boss. Vasilik told Updike she believed Griffin might be a powerful advocate for her if she needed to resign from Ratner's ministry and find another position in Washington.

"So, you said it was at the state dinner that odd things began to happen?" asked Updike, listening to Vasilik's narration.

"Yes," said the former deputy minister, her holographic face white with trepidation. "It was the night of the state dinner in honor of President Safaev. Bailey told me that Ratner was planning something foul. He said he didn't have much information but that she had suggested to him that he could be First Citizen and she Second Citizen if Fourier were out of the way. He dismissed it as a joke, but now I don't think it was. I think Ratner wanted more than Fourier gone. I think she wanted both of them out of the way."

"Do you think Griffin is dead too? Do you think he's still in Washington?"

"There has to be some record of his flight out of the country, if that's what Ratner says happened. Right?"

"Yeah, but we haven't been able to get our hands on anything. They say it's all classified," said Updike.

"You said earlier that it was a plot to poison the First Citizen – that's what Griffin told you."

"That's what he said. Ratner said she had worked it all out and he wasn't to worry. It wouldn't be traceable," answered Vasilik.

"Do you know what the toxin was?"

"No. I never found that out."

Updike sat back into his chair, absorbing the magnitude of what she was telling him. He was having a hard time believing such plots would exist in the highest levels of the federal government. "So, you're convinced that not only is Fourier dead, but so are his wife and Minister Griffin?"

"From what I understand, they've all been dead for weeks. It's been really hard to get any information, but I do know someone in the White House on staff. She tells me the bodies are being kept on ice in a special room in the basement of the mansion."

"So, is Minister Ratner running the government?" asked Updike, still typing.

"Yes. She alone is in charge now."

Updike's conversation with Vasilik was cut short, as there was an unusual clicking noise on the line.

"Margola, are you still there?"

"What is that noise?" she asked, her voice quaking.

"I … I'm not sure," answered Updike.

Quickly his interview ended. "I've got to go," said Vasilik who hung up abruptly.

Updike continued typing to the end of his blog, ending with the paragraph which in part read:

> Will we ever know for sure what happened? Probably not. Very soon, they will have to let us know who is alive and who is dead. But more important than that is, who is now in charge?

The blog post sent shockwaves through the USSA, and civil unrest began almost immediately. The riots began again in the major cities, starting in Baltimore and Detroit and quickly spreading to Philadelphia and Cleveland. Seeing an opportunity, one of Fourier's Cabinet members seized the chance for power.

Dutch Welbourne, Minister of Justice, called a press conference, summoning the obedient coterie of reporters to the Old Executive Office Building next to the White House. The room was packed shoulder-to-shoulder with eager news staffers hoping to get any information on what was alleged from the GOFLA blog. Standing at the podium, Welbourne smiled broadly, thinking he had usurped the limelight from Ratner who hadn't been seen or heard from in days.

"Thank you all for coming," said Welbourne. "I'm sure you have heard the rumors about the situation with the Administration, and I'm here to clarify everything for you. As you know, First Citizen Fourier and his wife, Patricia, had taken ill shortly after the state dinner with the president of Uzbekistan. It is alleged in one misdirected SI-net posting that a member of the Administration staff had come forward with details of some elaborate plot to kill the First Citizen and his wife. I wish to confirm that the First Citizen and his wife …"

At that moment, there was a commotion at the back of the room. Welbourne had posted guards at the grand double doors to prevent any other member of the Cabinet from walking in on the conference. He had given strict orders that they were to be detained outside the room and taken into custody if necessary. As Attorney General, Welbourne had told his Justice Ministry, the Secret Service and Ministry of Internal Inquiry that he had the power and obligation to bring calm and order to a government on the verge of chaos.

Welbourne looked uncomfortably at the ruction at the back of the room. "I think we need more security at the rear entrance," he said, growing concerned over what was happening in front of him. This was his moment – one he did not want disrupted. More guards from behind him ran to help the two sentries who were having difficulty with someone trying to enter. Loud pounding came from the entrance, each time buckling the center where the two black doors met. With all they could muster, six men put their shoulders into the barrier to keep out the intruder.

Welbourne cleared his throat, now more comfortable that the situation was under control. "Now, as I was saying," he began once more.

Then, from a small door behind him came another voice. "No! As *I* was about to say." It was a woman's voice, vocalized with both power and authority. Minister Ratner pushed her way in front of Welbourne and took over the microphone. He looked stunned and helpless, unable to react quickly to a situation that was spiraling out of his control. "I just want to thank the Minister of Justice for calling this press conference for me," said Ratner, approaching the podium and boxing Welbourne out of the way. He merely blinked blankly, his eyes staring right at the overloaded freight train that had run over him at full speed. It held no empathy, no morsel of compassion. It was a soulless spirit, devoid of all goodness and incapable of ever finding it.

"The rumors you have heard regarding the First Citizen and others is untrue, just as Minister Welbourne was about to tell you. In fact, I stand before you with Margola Vasilik, the one who was allegedly quoted in a malicious post that many of you have been discussing. She is here today to refute those claims as lies and mistruths." Ratner turned to Vasilik, who was standing in the doorway behind her and motioned for her to come to the dais.

The thin, wispy young woman looked tired and sullen, worn down by likely grilling from the Unity minister and her henchmen. She slowly approached Ratner and stood before the group. "I do admit to having had discussions with a certain individual about the recent happenings at the White House; however, what was put on the SI-net was ... a blatant lie. This story is a complete fabrication."

"And what is the truth, Ms. Vasilik?" a reporter asked.

"Well, the truth is what Minister Ratner has been telling you -- that the First Citizen has taken ill, and the Minister of Taxation Enforcement is vacationing out of the country," she answered, rather unconvincingly.

"But, no one has said that the tax minister was vacationing," answered the reporter. "What was said was that he was out of the country on government business."

Ratner abruptly cut Vasilik off and gently pushed her aside. "Apparently, you are uninformed then, as the White House has repeatedly said that Minister Griffin is out of the country on urgent government business. We expect him back within the week."

"Where did he go, then?" asked another reporter.

"Uh, he returned with President Safaev to Uzbekistan. They had further business to address based on their discussions while the president was here," she answered.

"So, how is the First Citizen? We have not received any word for at least five days?" came another question.

"His condition has not changed. Nor has that of his wife, I'm afraid. The doctors are still looking after them."

"What plans has the government made in the event that they do not recover?" came a question from the back of the room.

"I don't believe it is appropriate to make any presumptions about their prognosis. We continue to believe they will recover, and there is every indication that they will do so." Then, avoiding any further questions, Ratner concluded the meeting, making certain there was no room for Welbourne to re-exert himself. "I believe that is enough. I'm sure you will have other questions, but the press secretary can answer those later. I will be discussing what my plans will be with Minister Welbourne. That is all." And with that she, Vasilik, and a distraught Dutch Welbourne left the room.

Press Secretary Beister, was not in the room to deal with the bombardment of questions he would have received had he been there. Instead, the room was left empty, except for the reporters who could only look on in amazement at what had just taken place. There were now more questions than ever before.

***

As much as the White House wanted to sustain the misdirection and continue propping-up the now-mummified bodies of the First Citizen, his wife and the tax minister, it could not do so indefinitely. But, by then, Ratner had her plan in place and enough people contacted and threatened into obedience that the lie was no longer needed.

Within another day, Ratner's actions were swift and sure. Welbourne and the other members of the Cabinet were summoned to the White House where they were taken into custody.

The next day, a press release was issued.

> Today, the White House, the Congress, and the country, mourns the loss of a great man. First Citizen Fourier passed away early this morning. His wife, also stricken with the same, unknown disease, passed moments later. The First Citizen contributed much to the growth and success of this country, and his loss is significant.

> We continue to investigate the cause of the malady that claimed the lives of these two great Americans. As such, all members of Fourier's Cabinet have been detained for questioning in connection with the illnesses. There is suspicion that the group conspired to poison the leader of this country for their own gain. Unfortunately, these allegations permeate the entire Cabinet, including the Ministry of Justice and its minister, Dutch Welbourne, who is believed to have master-minded the assassination.

> In the meantime, Minister Ratner, who uncovered the plot, is working tirelessly to find answers. As dictated by the Constitution 2.0, she is working with Minister Griffin until further steps can be taken to stabilize the Administration and appoint successors to the ministries. At this time, the Minister of Tax Enforcement, who is on his way back from Uzbekistan, will assume the responsibilities of the First Citizen once he is sworn in."

Of course, no one believed it. And, a day later, another press release was issued.

It is by every measure a tragedy, but we have learned that the plane in which the minister of Taxation Enforcement, Bailey Griffin, was traveling, crashed upon take-off from the airport in Samarkand, Uzbekistan earlier today. The minister and other members of his entourage, including his wife, were killed. Their bodies will be flown back to the USSA for burial as soon as arrangements can be made.

Therefore, Minister Angel Ratner, the former Minister of Unity, was sworn in as First Citizen an hour ago. She has assumed the responsibilities of leading the federal government. As her deputy minister of Communication, she has chosen Margola Vasilik. Congress is expected to approve the appointment, as all members of the Enlightenment Party have offered their condolences to the families of those lost, and their support for First Citizen Ratner in her efforts to reunite the country after such a unfortunate series of events."

Sumner turned off his computer. He immediately called Shea to fill her in on the news, just in case she hadn't already been notified.

"Well, what do you think?" he asked, as soon as she walked through the door. "I'm sure you heard."

"Yes," she said. "I can't think of a worse scenario. Can you?"

"No, I'm afraid not," Sumner answered.

"So, what does it mean?"

"It means it's time to batten-down the hatches," said Sumner.

"What?"

"It's time. I predict that within a month, we'll be at war."

*****

CH 4 The Inventor

Businesses began leaving the USSA in droves, sneaking over the border and setting up shop in the new Republic. With them came the best and brightest of the citizenry, and not far behind them were other people who wanted work. The intelligentsia and the skilled came into what was once Wyoming to expand commerce, raise the standards of education, construct a sound infrastructure to support growth, and most importantly, develop a second Silicon Valley. A new Economic Enterprise Zone for entrepreneurs was created to promote ideas, inventions, and break down the barriers of the socialistic system that had stymied them for so long. It had been Shea's idea, and one she had fervently supported. With the addition of Kansas, Oklahoma and Texas, the ATLAS Republic had access to fertile farm land and a warm-water port with the imports and exports that it brought – a vital link to the rest of the world.

But both Sumner and Shea scrambled to keep up with the rapid pace of change -- he with the job of assimilating the other states into a cohesive union, and she with the task of making the rest of the government work within the governance of the *ATLAS Constitution*. The long hours were draining her, and although she was comfortable in the small mansion4 of the former lieutenant governor of Wyoming, she missed the life she'd known back in Boston. She still pined for her soul mate, Patrick, wondering where he'd gone and what had happened to him. To her, the joy of seeing a new promise, a new beginning for the country was overshadowed by her personal loss. She only wished he had been able to see the changes she was witnessing and of which she had become a part.

It was late one night. She had come home from the president's office in the newly built capitol in Cheyenne. The president, she and his Cabinet all shared offices in the same facility, making coordination of their efforts more seamless and cohesive. The newly founded Congress held its sessions only a block away, and the Supreme Court was merely one block the other way down the street. The only new building erected was nearly one mile away, on the outskirts of town -- that of the Bureau of Statistics. But that was by design; it was meant to be kept independent from the rest of the government. Yet, there were other reasons for building farther out. They had run out of available land to build other buildings in the heart of the city. The large, pentagonal building – one modeled after the one in Washington – was constructed where land constraint was not an issue. Realizing the importance of intelligence gathering, they commissioned the establishment of an edifice large enough to house a huge system of computers working in parallel. Computer sizes were shrinking as quickly as they had in the early twenty-first century, but that had only enabled more hardware to be packed into the floor plan.

Kicking off her shoes, Shea poured herself two fingers of Stoli Elit vodka and added a full pour of tonic with two squeezes of lime. Plopping down into her French provincial, wheat colored, chenille sofa, she threw her head back and closed her eyes. It was exhausting work, and the pressures were becoming greater and greater. After taking a quick slurp of the clear cocktail, she set her cordial glass down on the oval, walnut end-table next to her and turned on the reading light over her shoulder. On the table, she'd left an autobiography of Andrew Jackson. It had given her comfort, as she'd read about the loss he suffered just after being elected president the first time in 1828. His wife, Rachel, had died within a few short months after the election, never getting to share the White House with her husband. He had been devastated by her passing and had invited his niece, Emily Donaldson to join him at 1600 Pennsylvania Avenue. She would keep him company and manage the hostess affairs of the house. Shea had wondered how lonely Jackson had felt during the time. He had left the Hermitage, his estate just outside of Nashville, to take up residence in Washington, leaving his many friends and neighbors. The Hermitage would always be his home, just as she thought Boston would always be hers.

Shea began reading when her phone rang.

"Hello?" she answered.

"Shea, this is Sumner. We have a major issue with how to defend against the vast military of the USSA. You and I have discussed this often, but now I think it's getting critical that we do something to protect ourselves. With the expansion of our territory, we have more border to protect. I've spoken to the Chairman of the Joint Chiefs, General Ward. He thinks it's imperative that we meet and work out a plan."

"What do you suggest? We need time to develop our own weapons as we can't afford to purchase them from foreign countries right now. Our exports are growing, but it will take a while."

"We don't have a while. We need to develop our own weapons now – or find them lurking in a laboratory someplace, waiting to be discovered. You'll have to meet me tomorrow morning."

"Where?" she asked.

"In Cheyenne. Secret Service will pick you up. We'll be flying to Rapid City, South Dakota."

"South Dakota? They aren't even part of the Republic!"

"They will be," said Sumner.

***

The president's plane landed in Rapid City's small airport and pulled around to only one of five gates at the terminal. A black sedan pulled up, stopping the plane short of the jet bridge and three agents jumped out, motioning the two to get inside. It was a short drive north from the airport where the car pulled over and stopped in front of a red bricked, two-story building sitting next to a large, abandoned warehouse. The planks on the building were peeling of their original crimson paint, and what remained was of a streaky, dark oxblood hue.

Sumner reached for the door handle, but Shea stopped him.

"Where are we?" she asked. "And more importantly, why are we here?"

"As I said, we need a new technology to protect the Republic. My team got a call from an inventor up here. He has developed something they think will give us an edge over the USSA if it comes to an all-out war."

"What is it?"

"I think it's better if he shows us," said Sumner. "I'm having a bit of trouble getting my own head around it."

"Have you met him before? How do you know about all this?" she asked.

"It was a patent application, apparently. It stood out. The Patent Office vetted it with our security advisory team; they said it was remarkable. They went so far as to say it would be a game-changer." Then, he added, opening the car door wider, "Shall we?" He motioned toward the warehouse.

Shea led the way down a narrow, dirt path to the run-down warehouse. It had rusted piece of gray sheet metal that framed the front door. It stood in stark contrast to the rotted wooden boards on either side. For the roof, there was corrugated steel with edges that were ragged and irregular. A circulating fan sat perched in an open window at the end of the building, rattling and squeaking annoyingly each time the belt completed its cycle. Around the outside were weeds, broken pieces of brick and piled stones. The raw, rustic path dusted Shea's black shoes, making the tips look white by the time she got to the door. At first, she wasn't sure whether to knock or just go in, but when Sumner passed by her and pushed on the peeling, red door, she just followed along.

"Hello?" Sumner called, looking around, his eyes shifting quickly from side to side.

Inside the building were its two most prominent inhabitants -- decay and neglect. Cobwebs blanketed the ceiling and doorways and wafted in the air from the pulsating currents of the building fan at the far end. There were once-finished walls inside, suggesting an attempt had been made to outfit an office at some point. Painted a pale green, the faded walls were spotted with water stains from a leaky roof and years of inattention. Although this first room inside was built as a small office, all the usual equipment and *accoutrements* were missing. There were a few dark gray filing cabinets against one wall and papers scattered across the floor, but besides that there was little to suggest that there had ever been a business there – certainly never a thriving one.

"Is anyone here?" Sumner asked, speaking loudly and expecting someone to answer. Still, no one responded.

They continued walking through the abandoned office and out through a door in the back that led into the brick building next door. As the door opened, it squeaked loudly, signaling their arrival to anyone who was working in the back. Although Sumner had instructed his security team to ensure the area was safe prior to their visit, it was still unsettling that there was no one there to offer them even the smallest semblance of a greeting.

Sumner poked his head through the door, glancing around to see if anyone was inside the second area. "Hello? Is anyone here?" he asked again.

A low-pitched voice rumbled from somewhere in the back, obscured by a labyrinth of equipment, wires, strange chambers, monitors, and computers. "Who wants to know?" came the reply.

In the middle of the room was a table with what appeared to be a large satellite dish, but with a broad, round brim surrounding its coned center. Not more than three feet across, the device looked unassuming and harmless. Just behind it, was a gray-bearded man with a matching mane of long, stringy hair making adjustments with a yellow-handled screwdriver. He was tall and broad-shouldered, but somewhat stooped, as if age and life had been hard on him. Looking up from his work, he seemed annoyed that anyone would interrupt him and his project.

Shea gasped, her brain as well as her knees buckling. She braced herself against the wall, trying to hold herself up, but her breathing was fast and shallow. She looked like she'd seen a ghost.

Sumner stood staring at the man huddled over the table. The single-bulb lamp swung gently overhead, casting an eerie shadow over the satellite dish. "Uh ..." Sumner said, stuttering.

"What's the problem?" asked the man, staring at him with piercing blue eyes. "Who are you anyway? I wasn't informed of anyone coming to see me today."

It was Sumner who spoke first. "Patrick? Is that you?"

The man looked confused. "What did you call me?"

"Patrick?" asked Shea, almost afraid to move a muscle for fear the dream might evaporate before her very eyes.

The man stood without answering, blinking at them without any reaction.

Shea ran and thrust her arms around him, clinging to him as if he were the last person on earth who could save her. "Patrick ... it *is* you. You're Okay! You're alive!" She was crying as she clutched his neck and shoulders, holding on afraid to let go for fear she might lose him all over again.

He gingerly put his arms around her, looking lost and distant.

Realizing he was not embracing her in the same way, she stepped back, looking at him perplexed. "Patrick? What's wrong? It's me, Shea," she said.

"I'm sorry," he said, embarrassed. "I have to say that you look familiar, but I just can't put my finger on how I know you. It's my head, you understand," he said, apologetically, "It's not you."

Shea stood in front of him, stunned. "Patrick? You don't know who I am?"

"No," he said haltingly. "My head hasn't been right for a long time. I just can't remember things that happened before about a year and a half ago."

"What happened to you?" Sumner asked, coming closer, his face serious and focused.

"I don't know. I'm not sure what happened. But anything before a year ago, and it's all a blank. I'm starting to remember a few things here and there, but a lot of it is a blur," Patrick said.

"You're my husband," Shea said quietly. "We've been married for almost twenty-eight years ... you ... you don't remember any of it?" Shea choked back tears, realizing the man she had spent most of her life with could now not even remember ever having been married. The wonderful reunion with her long-lost husband was not the moment of which she had dreamed.

"Your husband?" asked the man, standing back with alarm. Then, he said, "What name did you call me?"

"Patrick. Your name is Patrick Disone. You're married to Shea here," said Sumner pointing to her. "You two have been married a long time, and you live near Boston – or you used to, anyway."

Patrick looked at Shea, putting his hand up to her cheek and wiping away her tears. "You're beautiful," he said, smiling at her. "I hoped I'd be married and could only imagine being attached to someone as pretty as you are."

Shea returned his smile, but for some reason his comment didn't help. She sensed it – it was a coldness, a chasm that was between them that had never been there before – even when they had first met. From that day forward, she had always felt close to him – he had been her soul mate. But now, it was gone.

Sumner looked back at Patrick. "It seems we have a lot of catching up to do with you. I'm a friend of yours too. You just don't remember. I'm President Sumner, but you would have known me when I was a U.S., I mean, a USSA congressman. You and I have had some interesting times together. But that's not important right now. Patrick ... your name is Patrick, you know ... what happened to you?"

Patrick put his head down. "I don't know. The last thing I really remember is waking up in a Dollar Six Motel with a splitting headache. I assumed I'd been drinking too much and had a hangover, but the headache didn't go away, and I didn't remember where I'd been drinking the night before. And, oddly enough, I couldn't even remember my own name. There wasn't much I did remember, and I didn't even have a wallet to tell me anything about myself. I've managed to catch odd jobs here and there to pay for my room and board," he continued. "I found this abandoned warehouse and setup shop. For some reason, I'm really good at putting complex machines together using pretty simple stuff you'd find at the hardware store. At least that's what a friend of mine told me."

"A friend?" asked Shea. "Who's your friend?"

He looked at her sheepishly. "I didn't know I was married. I didn't have a ring, and I couldn't even find out where I was from. She helped me with getting an apartment in town. I work with her at the diner."

"You work at a diner?" Sumner asked, incredulously. "You have a PhD. Do you remember that?"

Shea took a few steps backward. This was all too much for her to bear.

"Are you alright?" Sumner asked, noticing her unsteadiness.

"I'm just a little light-headed," she said.

Patrick pulled over a dusty stool, wiping off the dirty, black vinyl with the cuff of his shirt. "Sorry about that," he said. "Here, have a seat."

Shea sat down and lowered her head, trying to regain her thoughts.

"The diner was all I could find without a name or background. Like I said, it's paid the bills," Patrick remarked, continuing his story.

Sumner felt awkward, standing between two people who had been so in love and intimate, now not even knowing who the other was. It had only been eighteen months since the incident, and they'd gone from the perfect, loving marriage to complete strangers. *How random life can be,* he thought.

"So what is it that you've developed, Patrick?" asked Sumner, trying to break the tension.

The man looked at Sumner still not recognizing his friend. "It's odd … being called Patrick and all. I've been wondering for months what my name was. The local police said they had more important things to do than find out who I am. When I contacted the state and, after it was abolished, the feds, neither one would give me the time of day. I was on my own. So, since I didn't know my name, everyone here calls me Johnny G. I don't know why. It just stuck."

"Do you prefer we call you Johnny G, then?" asked Sumner.

"For now, call me Johnny. I'd have to get used to Patrick, if that's what my name is," said the man.

Johnny moved back over toward his lab table and pushed a few tools out of the way so he could get to the rectangular control panel that sat on top. It was dominated by a large, oval video screen. A smaller box to the side held other visual displays with icons suggesting that it linked with the satellite-type dish that lay some distance away on the console in the other room.

"What's that?" asked Shea, trying not to stare at him. She pointed to a large, round, white cone that was suspended from a rafter. It looked like an old-fashioned stereo speaker, except turned inside-out. There was a metal ring around it that seemed detached, yet a part of the cone at the same time. The object was so light, it blew with the breeze, swinging back and forth effortlessly overhead.

"That's my listening device," said Johnny. "I can listen in on conversations of other sounds hundreds of kilometers away, filtering out everything I don't want and homing in on what I do want. It's super sensitive — kind of like a space telescope that can capture only a few particles of light from a distant quasar and filter out everything else. It's quite remarkable."

"In your paper, you say that this machine was capable of burning objects from a distance. Is that true?" asked Sumner staring at another device on Johnny's workbench.

"Not just burning," he said, somewhat offended.

"So, what does it do?" asked Shea.

"It's funny. It seems pretty simple to me. The mechanics and software only took me a month or so to put together. Yet, no one else understands how it works the way it does. It's almost like something in my brain must have been jarred into some strange, but wonderful alignment of some sort. It makes connections that let me think in ways others don't. People around here tell me I'm a genius, but I don't know. It seems pretty nature to me. Was a smart before?"

Shea nodded, fighting back emotions about the way he used to be. "Yeah, you were pretty smart before. You created some amazing things in your day."

"How does this thing work then?" Sumner pressed, moving closer to the dish.

"Well, in layman's terms, I've created a miniature nuclear bomb."

"Nuclear bomb?" asked Shea, alarmed.

"You understand Einstein's equation $E=MC^2$?" asked Johnny.

"Yes," said Shea. "It's the amount of energy given off by a certain mass."

"Very good," answered Johnny, somewhat condescendingly. "You actually listened in science class, then. Because a nuclear explosion is a chain reaction of converting mass to energy. Even the smallest amounts of matter – say a few atoms – can give off huge amounts of energy. It's what the sun does all the time, but under extreme pressure. It converts hydrogen into helium and other elements using fusion. What I've done is the same thing, except twisting gravitons into a field to simulate great pressure without the mass. It uses string theory and ..."

At that point, both Sumner and Shea's eyes began glazing over. They listened but did not understand a thing Johnny was saying.

Finally, Sumner interrupted him. "How do you create enough energy to create fusion? We've built huge machines to try to generate enough power to make fusion happen like that. The only thing that's worked before now is detonating an atom bomb to produce fusion. That's how the hydrogen bomb works."

"You're right. It's taken fission to create fusion. But, now it doesn't. As for the way I do it, well, for now, that's a secret," Johnny replied, smiling like the Cheshire Cat.

"So, it's cold fusion?" asked Shea. "I remember a briefing in Congress about research into cold fusion which has gone on for nearly a century."

Johnny shook his head. "What is important is that this technology be used for good purposes, not evil ones."

Sumner grimaced. "Define good versus evil? That is a difficult question, you know – one that has been debated by philosophers for millennia."

Johnny looked at him circumspectly. "I don't know what you mean."

"Well, what if the opprobrium were the mass slaughter of innocent lives for no reason but to intimidate and coerce the rest of the populace?"

"I'd say that would be pure evil. There is no doubt about it."

"I agree. But what would you say about someone else using some action or force to defeat the ones who had killed indiscriminately?"

"That would be a good thing," Johnny replied.

"Even if those actions resulted in innocent people being accidently killed in the process?"

"You said accidently killed. Do you really mean accidently?"

"Yes. Sometimes things are done for the greater good, but that result in unintentional death and destruction," said Sumner.

Johnny nodded. "I understand, now. Yes, you're right. Sometimes there is the greater good. But to the extent bad things can be minimized in achieving that, then ..."

Shea was still not in the present. Her thoughts were still racing, watching the man she had known and loved be so different and detached. Instead of listening to the philosophical babble between Johnny and Sumner, she got up. "I think I'll wait in the car," she said, walking out of the room.

"Was it something I said?" Johnny asked.

"No. I'm sure she's still just trying to get over the shock of seeing you. That's all." Then, returning to the device, Sumner asked. "When can we have a demonstration?"

"Why not now?" answered Johnny. "Let's go out back. I don't like for others to see the strange things that I can do with this technology. In these parts, they'd think I was a heretic or something."

"They stopped burning witches and warlocks at the stake a few years ago," Sumner answered, smiling.

"Not around here, they didn't," Johnny retorted.

Johnny disconnected a few pieces of his equipment, loaded them on a cart, and pushed it through the back door of the warehouse. The field behind the building was overgrown with tall weeds and littered with rusted old machines, from washers and dryers to toasters and carcasses of trucks and autos. All had seen better days.

Sumner followed him, this time with the two security men that had accompanied them. He let him get several yards ahead before Sumner said: "What exactly are you showing me?"

Johnny turned with what appeared to be a gun in hand. There was a strange look on his face that gave Sumner pause. Instantly, the security team pulled their Glock 44 handguns, and one shouted "Stop right there!"

"Relax," Johnny said. "All I'm going to do is demonstrate my little gadget here. There's nothing to be afraid of."

"No, it's Okay, boys," said Sumner, motioning for his security team to lower their weapons. "Johnny, go ahead. We'd like to see what you have here."

Johnny smiled and asked, "Pick something?"

"Pick something?" echoed Sumner, unsure what he was asking.

"Yeah, pick something from the yard – anything."

Sumner looked around the yard. There was nothing but junk scattered all over the place. He felt that the best test would be something big, heavy and significant. That would prove that this invention would have true military importance to the new Republic.

"What about that old, school bus over there?" asked Sumner, pointing to a faded, yellow shell that had once carried children safely to and from their class building. Its windows were all shattered or completely broken out. The right side was crushed, and the engine compartment abandoned, having long since lost its occupant. The side of the bus bore the nearly illegible words **North Sumner High School**.

Sumner High School. How ironic, thought the president.

"Fine," said Johnny, confidently. "I can do that."

Sumner stepped back a few paces, unsure what to expect. The only thing that gave him comfort was that Johnny didn't flinch, taking no unusual precautions or safety measures. The only thing he said was, "Here, put these on," handing him a pair of dark green goggles.

Sumner complied, and after Johnny slipped on his goggles and adjusted them, he steadied the gray pistol in his hand and pointed it at the school bus -- a distance of some fifty yards. Pressing a button on the grip, he waited as a humming noise started, which grew in pitch and intensity. A small green diode light on the gun gradually changed to yellow, then orange, and finally red, blinking a warning that it was ready. "Okay, here we go," he said. He pulled the trigger.

"I don't see anything," said Sumner, looking for something to come out of the barrel.

Johnny smiled. "You will." He then turned his attention back to the school bus.

A second later there was an immense burst of light from the gun combined with a loud *crack*. The light emitted had shot across the field some thirty meters, causing the tremendous *bang*, similar to a lightning strike. The bus began glowing, quickly going from a dull red to a brilliant white, before there was another popping sound. Faster than Sumner's next blink, the bus was gone. Below where it had been, the grass was burning and smoke was rising in a thin plume. Only gray and black ash remained.

Sumner stood in stunned silence. Had he really just seen what little boys had fantasized over since the days of *Flash Gordon* and the TV series *Star Trek*? Even he had grown up watching science fiction movies that had shown space adventurers pulling out laser guns, or *phasers* as they called them. But never had the technology come close to being able to focus that much energy on something to vaporize it – at least not in a form small enough to carry on your back or in your hand.

"*Wow*," said Sumner soberly.

Sumner walked over to Johnny and stretched out his hand. "Mr. Johnny. If you are willing, the Republic will pay you well for this technology. As you know, we are a small nation, trying to emerge from the shadows of the USSA. ATLAS is up against tremendous odds, especially comparing our military with that of the old USA. We would not stand a chance unless … unless of course we had your technology. Can you see it within yourself to help us? We would greatly appreciate someone like you on our team, working for our cause."

"I'll have to think about it," said Johnny.

"You do know that if any of the ministries in Washington find out that you have this technology they may force you to turn it over to them?"

"It's possible?"

"Sadly, I think so. But I want you to know that we would not do that. We believe in the sanctity of property, especially intellectual property, and the fact that you created this means you're entitled to reap the rewards from it. Our constitution is like that of the old USA. L Our nation was born on the assumption that rights are given by God and are inalienable to mankind. As part of those rights to life, liberty, property and the pursuit of happiness, we firmly believe in capitalism and the rights of individuals to keep what they create. This invention of yours is, well, yours. You may do with as you wish. I only ask that you consider making it available, at a price, to our Republic. What do you say?" asked Sumner.

"I understand what you're saying," said Johnny.

"I just have one question, however," said Sumner. "How many people know you have this machine? It seems like several know that you're working on it."

"Oh, there are two other people who know about it. Besides my girlfriend …"

"So, the three people … Do they have access to or any knowledge of the details of your invention?"

"If I tell you, you're not going to round them up and send them off to some labor camp some place are you?" asked Johnny. He wasn't smiling.

"In the USSA they would do that. We don't do that in the new Republic."

"Okay, then no. No one has any access to the information. Just me," said Johnny.

"So, you keep it locked up?" asked Sumner.

Johnny pointed at his head. "It's all up here," he answered. "No one can get it up here."

"Does it require that big dish and console in there to work?" asked Sumner, pointing to the warehouse where the other pieces were located.

"Right now, yes. But, I've already started on a unit that only requires a power pack – like a large backpack," said Johnny. To get it even smaller will take more time.

"A backpack size right now is good enough. You can keep working on something smaller. Someone from my office will be in touch with you," answered Sumner. "We're going to need several thousand of them within the next three months. What about that?"

Now it was Johnny's turn to smile. "You're joking."

"No. Deadly serious. Can we mass produce these things?"

"Anything can be done with enough time and money. Do we have those?" asked Johnny.

"I can get the money. I can't buy you any more time," answered Sumner.

"Well, one out of two isn't too bad, I guess. When do we start?"

Sumner reached out and shook Johnny's hand. "Thanks. Our country and I thank you."

"What about her?" asked Johnny, looking out toward where their car was parked and Shea was busy looking through her messages.

"She'll come around. She just needs some time to adjust to all this. It's new to her. She'll be fine."

As Sumner and Shea left the warehouse to go back to the car, Sumner put his hand on her shoulder. "Are you sure you're okay?" he asked.

Shea could not gather her thoughts enough to speak at all. The man she had loved, she'd found. Yet, by some twist of fate, she hadn't. It was not he. It was not the person she had adored and who had adored her. Something had happened to his brain when he'd had his accident. Something incredibly wonderful for the Republic; something devastatingly tragic for her. For Shea, she finally had the answer she had been searching for the past few years -- *Yes, her husband Patrick was dead*.

*****

CH 5 Consolidating Power

The railcars had already started coming off the proverbial tracks when Ratner assumed control of the government. She moved quickly to quell any challenges. Having eliminated the top two authorities who kept her from the top spot – Fourier and Griffin -- she was well on her way to solidifying her role as sole ruler of the nation.

The First Citizen had met his death by poisoning, as had his wife. They and others had partaken of the black tea at the state dinner held for the President of Uzbekistan and his entourage. It had been Ratner's and Griffin's plan to put a reactive agent in the tea that, when mixed with apple, would produce a deadly toxin. When apple pie was served unexpectedly at the dinner, Griffin panicked. Yet, it wasn't the apple that had killed them – it was chocolate. Fourier, his wife Patricia, Bailey Griffin, Angel Ratner and others stayed after the dinner, drinking and smoking in the private quarters in the White House. When a tray of chocolate desserts arrived, all were too eager to have some – except Ratner. By morning, all but she were dead. After their deaths, power transferred to the third post in line, the Minister of Unity. After the Minister of Taxation and Enforcement -- the office held by Bailey Griffin -- Ratner held the next position of succession. She was now at the pinnacle – she was the sole survivor and now ruler of the USSA.

However, Ratner was not without her problems. Margola Vasilik had become an unresolved issue for her. Having spoken with people at the White House and learned of the plot she had forged, Vasilik was a liability – a loose end. To appease the ambitious, but naïve woman, Ratner had placated her by making her the Deputy Minister of Defense under Sara Miller Emerson. That had kept her quiet long enough to let the explosive allegations of Ratner's involvement blow over. The news cycle was no more than a week or two, and by that time the public had lost interest in the story, instead engaging in conversations over what dress an Oscar-winning best actress wore out on the town in London the previous night. That new diversion was just what Ratner needed to begin a pogrom of her own. Although Vasilik enjoyed her new position and the marginal power that came with it, her incessant complaining and challenging of decisions was getting old. Ratner had put up with it, but her patience was wearing thin.

Yet, there were other problems awaiting the new First Citizen. The taming of the leaders of Congress was also an issue. However, as for everything, money talked. Ratner's wealth paid for everyone to stay on her side – money that she had taken from EG, Inc. and her inside dealings as Minister of Unity. She had made a fortune selling the patent plans for Lenoir Lab's SECE engine, even though they were incomplete. That sale combined with extortion, bribes and rampant insider trading all created pots of money for her – lots of pots and lots of money. Money was what greased the paths for everyone for everything. No one challenged her authority as long as their money kept flowing.

But she would take a different approach against those she couldn't trust and feared no retaliation. These threats could only be negated through swift but clandestine force. Dutch Welbourne was the first to go. It was easy to plant national secrets in his apartment and arrest him for treason. He was never mindful of spy-craft and especially not aware of any such machinations being waged against him. His only fear came after the failed press conference he tried to hold – his own little attempt at a *coup d'état*. But that fiasco spelled doom for him as well.

Likewise, a raid was conducted on Kenneth Biester's townhouse where child pornography was allegedly found. The news outlets were called to bring in camera crews that recorded footage of his being dragged from his home in front of his mortified family. Another Fourier Cabinet member, Elijah Marcus, Minister of Fair Trade, was accused of selling top-secret, sophisticated computer programs to the Chinese. This was farcical as the Chinese were one or two generations ahead of the USSA militarily and would have had no use for the software. Even Hunter McFarlen, the former vice president of the USA, was arrested on some trumped-up charge, "just in case," as Ratner had said when giving the order.

But one person was more important than all the rest – the Minister of Facts and Statistics, Daniel Cho. He had been a very quiet, unassuming member of Fourier's Administration. More like an absent-minded professor, he came across as introverted and apolitical. However, it was this mild-mannered minister who caused Ratner much angst. Cho had contacts throughout the government, and when he discovered his fellow Cabinet members were being rounded up, he fled. Fearing he would work against her and produce statistics unfavorable to her management of the country, Ratner knew he had to be found and silenced.

Mindful that a powerful propaganda machine had been Fourier's key to success, Ratner enlisted the help of Roger Nelson, the newly appointed Minister of Domestic Policing – what had been the FBI – to find Cho. Partly to test Nelson's loyalty but also to muster the resources she needed, the First Citizen commanded Nelson to "spare no expense and take care of things." Ratner had declared that Cho had fled only because of his many crimes against the government that were just coming to the surface after the death of Fourier. Nelson obliged.

Days later, the country was riveted by a live telecast of the MDP with their helicopters and search lights piercing the night's sky hunting Cho through the backwoods of his native state of New Hampshire. Zooming in for close-ups once they finally flushed him out, the cameras captured the pure terror on his face, his hair disheveled, blowing in the wind with dirt smeared below his right cheek. The government news network caught every second of the circus event, adding subtitles to the images stating that he was "armed and dangerous" even though the pictures showed no weapon on him.

The chase took several hours, and, like a cornered animal, Cho was pushed to the edge of a steep cliff – a craggy rock outcropping known as Death's Gateway by the local community. Circling overhead, the blades of the MDP choppers blew the boughs of the trees and whipped up stray pieces of rock and scrub from around the minister, generating a miniature cyclone that ripped and clawed at him from every side. Cho put his arm up over his eyes to shield them from the glaring spotlight beaming down on him and from the debris that stung his face. His jacket and pant legs bubbled and flapped, like a weather forecaster reporting on a hurricane. The cameras pulled back to give a wide-angle shot, and viewers could hear a person in the chopper order the pilot to drop down closer to get a better angle.

It was then that Cho shuffled his feet backwards to escape the punishment of the winds, lights and torrent of attention. To the horror of all who watched, he stumbled. Waving his arms in the air, he tried in vain to regain his footing, but the strong gusts from the blades rotating above him pushed him ever closer to the edge. Then, he vanished. It was over.

There was no outcry. In fact, the telecast got high ratings and good reviews from the blood-thirsty critics. To most who were already dulled by the ongoing barrage of similar, but fictional, shows on the air, this was largely absorbed as just another reality show. Cho's body was ever shown, so it was as if the entire thing were staged. The MDP helicopters were called off immediately – told to return to base – and the orders to retrieve the remains weren't issued for another three days.

***

But while the threats to her power were being summarily eliminated, Ratner's new role and the perks that came with it were swiftly being embraced. She took full advantage of her lofty position with all its benefits: luxury accommodations everywhere she went, an entire fleet of jets at her disposal at any time, a recently procured executive yacht costing over three hundred million dollars, a staff of thousands, and an unlimited treasury to dish out money and favors to anyone and everyone she needed on her side. Many claimed she had been practicing for such imperialism all her life. She would never deny that. She had always felt she was destined for greatness. With a personal entourage of over fifteen hundred, including security, the First Citizen had become the titular head of new royalty in America. King George III would have been jealous of her.

To name a few, Ratner's retinue included body guards, drivers, secretaries, legal advisors, stenographers, logisticians, photographers, media spin doctors, historians, baggage handlers, communications staff, emergency crews with doctors, nurses, and a full mobile hospital, military personnel with a battalion of five hundred soldiers complete with armored personnel carriers, and a trailer-bound emergency helicopter. When traveling by air, the old Air Force One had been replaced with a brand new 797 MegaJet, referred to as *Citizen One*, and a defensive battle group of nine others, including fighters, decoys and a new NE-8A AWAC air warning and control craft that could detect threats over three thousand miles away, whether launched from the ground, an aircraft, a submarine or from one of many Chinese's attack satellites circling overhead. The only thing the AWAC couldn't detect was an attack initiated from the joint Chinese-Russian military base on the moon, located in the SOS crater, Sosigenes.

"Where are we on those carbon emission fines?" Ratner asked Oscar Tate, of her Ministry of Environmental Protection. He was seated directly across from her in the Cabinet Room. She preferred the physical meetings of all Cabinet members rather than the virtual meetings conducted by the former first citizen. It was unusually warm in the room, and it wasn't long before members were pulling down their ties and wiping their brows with their handkerchiefs.

"We've had no need to issue any, Madam Ratner," answered Tate, who was always deferential and subsuming. "All the fossil fuels plants are closed, and the rest of our heavy industry has been completely nationalized now. Since we own them, we can't exactly fine ourselves."

"Don't be a smart-ass," Ratner snapped, scowling at him. "I know we can't *fine* ourselves. I just need to find more sources of revenue. We have to keep the poor and lower middle class off our backs. They have to be happy enough not to cause us a problem in the streets, yet unhappy enough to depend on us for their survival. Got it?"

"Yes, Madam," he answered, looking down at his electronic notepad.

Just then, two small, young women dressed in black service attire and carrying trays laden with pitchers of ice water and wedges of lemon came through the door. Right behind them was Clancy Holt, the chief of staff. He had been out, minding a problem with the air conditioning unit. "Madam?" he asked, entering circumspectly, "Apparently, they won't be able to fix the AC unit just yet. It will be a few hours before temperatures can be restored."

The environmental minister was grateful for the intervention from the Holt. He stood silent beside him, hoping the new First Citizen would move on to other topics or adjourn the meeting. Ratner looked disgusted at the entire conversation. It irritated her. "Can't you handle it?"

"Yes, Madam, we will continue to work on it," said Holt, quickly exiting the room.

"Let's move on, shall we?" Ratner said, aggravated, but getting back to the meeting. "Now, what about our state's production levels?"

"We have all that information for you," said Marna Coyn, the new Minister of Facts and Statistics, taking over for the recently deceased Daniel Cho. "You can find it presented on your screen, Madam." The relevant graphs and charts popped up on Ratner's screen, and she motioned that the entire presentation should be flipped over to the gigantic 3-D screen that hung at one end of the room. "First Citizen Fourier set a Five-Year Plan for manufacturing output last year. I have a breakdown of steel production, mining, manufacturing capacity and output for autos, heavy machines, consumer products, chemical stocks, agricultural production by major crop type, construction starts, oil and gas production, coal tonnage, lumber harvesting and replanting, mining and imports of critical technology minerals – chromium, cobalt, manganese, bauxite, tungsten, palladium, titanium, platinum, copper and zinc by month and by sector for the past year and compared to the prior year. I also have statistics on labor employment, gross domestic product, inflation rates, debt and deficit levels, interest rates, new job creation, and educational competitiveness. I'm sorry to say that we continue to slide in our world rankings for math and science literacy. We now rank one hundred twenty-fifth, just behind Mexico and Brazil."

Ratner looked at her with contempt. "Why the hell do I want any of that? None of that means anything! It doesn't matter! And anyway, why do I want facts from my Ministry of F**ked-up Statistics?" she barked. "Those numbers are for the pin-heads and the masses, not for us. I only care about the polling numbers and what numbers you are providing the public – not what's really going on. What do people think about things we're doing for them? That's what's important. I don't give a rat's ass what the actual numbers are as long as our story is good."

Ratner's deputy-minister of communications was summoned to the meeting to give the latest polling numbers. Since the death of Fourier, the public had been uneasy about things, which showed in the decline in the overall level of optimism in the country. "It is true," said the deputy minister, "that overall optimism has dropped from 38 percent to 31 percent, but we believe it will rebound once people understand the positions the new First Citizen will be taking to solve this country's problems," he said.

"What are the levels that we will be publishing?" asked Ratner.

"We will show the results as 31 percent very optimistic, 45 percent optimistic, 21 percent neutral, and 3 percent negative."

"What? Why 3 percent negative?" she asked, defensively.

"Well, we can't show 100 percent positive or people would know something is wrong."

Ratner just growled. "What about the numbers for our energy conservation projects, green-house gas emissions that cause global warming, our clinical research grants studying the behavior of primates as they relate to humans, the gross proceeds from entertainment forums, the percentage of welfare and food stamp users, lifestyle vouchers, PUE payments – you know, the perpetual unemployment benefits we give people – voter registration credits, Party member rolls, big donors to the party and such. Those are the numbers I'm interested in," she said, already moving on.

"Uh, I'll have all that for you in the morning, Madam," answered Tate, who was also responsible for those matters.

"Oh, I also need to know what we are doing to keep the lid on those right-wing fringe groups. You know – the ones out west. We have to keep them in check. After that disastrous little incident in Cheyenne several months ago, we can't have another one like it." Then, she paused. "What's going on with their little break-away experiment anyway? I thought it would have collapsed under its own weight by now. That's what I was counting on. Conrad, what do you have on them?"

Conrad James was the new Minister of Justice who had replaced Dutch Welbourne in the post. He was capable, but sometimes strident in his approach to her job. Brilliant, but confrontational at times, he was usually forthright in his reports and advice to his superiors – whether it was wanted or not.

"Madam Ratner, my ministry has reported that the Republic of Wyoming is actually doing remarkably well. They have been quick to establish an infrastructure of government following the old US Constitution and have reinstituted many of the older systems that were in place prior to the Fourier Administration taking office. What they lack are resources for a military or even a reasonable National Guard. Their armaments rely heavily on parts and materials that they can get only from us. We, of course, have withheld all assistance. It should only be a matter of time before they are unable to sustain themselves. They have no access to seaports and their airports can be easily neutralized. However, for that assessment, I will defer to the General Williams." Conrad nodded to her comrade sitting next to her to take the floor.

One of the few positions Ratner had not replaced was that of the Chairman of the Joint Chiefs of Staff, General Shontal Washington. Washington had good rapport with the troops, and Ratner did not want to disrupt that at a time when military support for her was paramount.

Washington rose and began her report, citing the numbers of military planes, tanks, armored vehicles, troop levels, howitzers, rocket launchers, and other armaments her intelligence told her that the new Republic had, or at least she thought it had. "But these are just estimates," she added. "Our numbers are based on what we know Wyoming had before they declared. They have no capability of increasing their military strength without the USSA. They have no relationships with any foreign governments. They have no access to credit, so it's not something we should worry about. They can't pose much of a threat."

"They are soliciting other states to join them," said Roger Nelson, Minister of Domestic Policing. "That could be a problem. We haven't been able to discredit them at this point, so we may have to use force." "Who's running the show out there?" asked Ratner.

Nelson pulled out his own computer tablet and punched a few icons on the flat screen, moving from database to database. The images of the new leaders of the Wyoming Republic popped up on his screen. Among them were Sumner's and Shea's.

"This is the list of leaders we have in our system," said Nelson. "I suggest we put their faces and names on a deck of cards like they did a long time ago when we were looking for terrorists in Iraq and Afghanistan. We can put a bounty on their heads – you know, something like two to three hundred million apiece for the top ones. That should flush them out of their hiding places."

Ratner looked over at Nelson's screen and perused the faces. When her eyes found Shea's, they stopped. "I know her," she said, pointing her finger at the image. "She's the one that fought us on that engine patent. That bitch! That was over a year ago, I think. Yes, it was she and her husband who'd started a company to develop a high efficiency gas burning combustion engine. They kept pushing to get the patent." She laughed. "It's too bad that they were never able to cash-in on it. It was worth billions you know. I wonder whatever happened to that company." Of course, she already knew. It was that sort of rhetoric that she enjoyed.

Not knowing to what she was referring, Nelson just shrugged his shoulders and continued. "I don't know about that, madam. All I know is that she's one of the top people now. She's their Attorney General, I think."

Ratner laughed again, waiving her hand dismissing the entire idea. "Then there's nothing to worry about. She's not worth our concern. But just in case, we need to keep our eye on them. If their little Republic doesn't fold within six months, then we'll go in and shut it down. Otherwise, there's no reason to waste valuable resources on them. No other country is going to recognize them. They certainly aren't going to have any standing in the World Council," she said.

The World Council had replaced the long-defunct United Nations. It was thought that the five permanent members of the Security Council unfairly dictated terms to the rest of the nearly two hundred countries, which were members. Those disenfranchised members rose up and, as a group, threatened to walk out and form their own group. Caving to the demand, the powerful five -- Britain, France, China, Russia and the former United States -- agreed to a new entity, which was called the World Council. In it, the five agreed to fund the entire operation of the Council and make tributes to the World Bank to assist the economies of developing countries. However, the World Council and World Bank schemes quickly turned into a way to funnel money from rich countries into the pockets of the despots and dictators. Russia and China pulled out while Britain, France and the newly constituted USSA remained, agreeing to pump trillions into the reserves of third-world countries. The poor saw nothing of it and continued to starve while their rulers dined on Champaign and black, Beluga caviar.

"Not being in the World Council may be a good thing, Madam Secretary," said James without thinking.

"How so?"

"Well, I ... I was just thinking that the World Council isn't, well, you know, what we'd hoped it would be.

Right?"

"Conrad! Really! They help the poor, for God's sake. How do you expect them to make it without help from richer countries like ours."

James knew not to pursue the argument any further with his boss. She liked a challenge now and then, but only one that was superficial – one that she could win.

At that point, an aide to the First Citizen came in unannounced and hurried over to Ratner, whispering into her ear. She nodded, but said nothing. Then she asked, "Wyoming hasn't sealed its border; has it?"

It was General Williams who chimed in. "They don't have much to seal it with. As I reported earlier, their only military is their national guard with older equipment."

"How many states are involved?" she asked, now paying more attention to what her Chief of Staff was saying.

"There are ten states at this point, but none shows an eager interest in seceding, except maybe Louisiana," said Nelson, interjecting. He was lying but felt the truth that all ten states were scrambling to leave the USSA would be unsettling to his boss.

"Louisiana is just a big swamp anyway," she muttered, dismissing the threat.

"Yeah, I don't see it growing. In fact, we see signs that the states that were thinking of joining are now rethinking their decisions. There are several state legislatures that are meeting to ban any group who favors secession and even prison terms for their leaders," Nelson added.

"Okay, next we have international affairs," Ratner said with disinterest. "Sara, you have sixty seconds to tell me what I need to know."

As Sara Emerson, the minister of defense, or International Policing as it was officially known, hurried through her report, Ratner watched the seconds tick by on the clock in the room. When sixty seconds had expired, Emerson was only partially through her briefing.

"Thank you," said Ratner, interrupting her in mid-sentence. "Now, there is something I need to bring up." Ratner's demeanor changed abruptly. Her voice had dropped half an octave, underscoring the gravity of what she was about to say next, and her face became rigid and stern. "It's come to my attention that someone on my staff has been spreading rumors about me and the death of the former First Citizen."

There were shocked faces around the table, but no one said a word.

"Specifically, they have been saying that I played a part in the death of the former First Citizen. I was really taken aback by the allegation. Of course, I had nothing to do with it, but I shouldn't have to sit here and defend myself. I really don't think that's helpful for any of us, especially for the country, to spread such lies. I also take umbrage at the tone and nature of the comments I've heard being said. This must stop. I am not asking; I'm *demanding*! I will not stand for disloyalty in my Administration. I have always been dedicated to my country and to the service of my fellow man and woman. I have never wavered from that mission, and I won't do so now."

Ratner rose from her chair, somber, rigid and grim. Her hands, clasped at the base of her back, were locked stiffly in place as she walked behind her Cabinet members, analyzing the face of each one as she passed. The tension in the room was thick, as the ministers fidgeted nervously in their chairs.

"Yes, there is one here who is plotting to undermine what we are trying to achieve in this country – what Fourier started and what I am going to finish. That is, the total reconstitution of the country into a Marxist society. We, here in this room, shall be the ones deciding who succeeds and who fails. We will determine who joins our party and becomes worthy of living in comfort and who does not. We will be the ones who judge who lives and who dies." Ratner turned abruptly. There was a sudden flicker of evil in her face as it appeared demonic – even possessed -- for a moment. "It is a power that we cannot take lightly. Therefore, I need to know that everyone is on board with me – that I can trust each of you implicitly. You must be willing to do whatever it takes, whenever it is required. There can be no shirking, no hesitation, no doubt. You must submit entirely to the *Cause*. Can you do that?"

All heads in the room nodded in agreement.

Ratner smiled. "I see that everyone is on the team then," she said, stopping behind the chair of Roger Nelson. "But then, perhaps that isn't true. As I said earlier, there is someone here who is not on my team and is working actively against me. But who is it? And, why would they do such a thing?"

No one moved in their chairs, except Shontal Washington, who remained calm, shifting ever so slightly to pull herself up straighter in her seat. Roger Nelson squirmed. Visibly shaken, he sat with his hands folded in front of him on the table. Uncomfortably, he pulled his tie down farther on the front-placard of his perspiration-soaked white shirt.

"Let me make myself clear," Ratner continues, "I do not and *will* not tolerate any grumbling or defection of anyone in this room. Do you understand? I will not accept challenges to my programs. They are right and meaningful to the people of this nation, whether they understand and appreciate them or not. We must look out for our Party first and the power we wield. We must be absolute in protecting it, regardless of what we must do to ensure it. Without that power, we cannot hope to help those less fortunate."

Ratner moved on, relieving Nelson of the increase in his blood-pressure risk of an embolism. He breathed out slowly and calmly, trying to attract as little attention as he could. The First Citizen was quiet as she made her way along the perimeter of the silk, Persian rug that was the focal point of the room, glancing at each member's empty water glass. Several seconds passed before she broke the silence saying, "You all know the country faces a water shortage. We have endeavored to put in place as many desalination and filtering plants across the country as possible, but we don't catch everything. We can't – we're only the government. We make mistakes too." Then, she laughed unsettlingly and added, "So, I see each of you have had your glass of water; however, I just learned from the kitchen that there was a problem with the potable water today and that it may have been contaminated with a rare toxin. It is tasteless and odorless, unfortunately – at least, that is what I'm told."

Horror struck the group; each letting out a gasp, and many staring at the clear, empty water glass that rested directly in front of them.

Ratner shook her head. "It's really tragic, because I'm also told that you all have only another ... well, twenty minutes or so before the toxin takes effect. The organism will begin breaking down your circulatory system. You will feel sharp pains in your abdomen as your heart, lungs, and other vital organs as they begin to thin and let the blood flow directly into your body cavity. I think they call it hemorrhaging."

"My god, woman! What have you done!" shouted George Ruszkov of the Ministry of Foreign Affairs, beginning to stand up. But feeling dizzy, he sat down immediately and put his head on the table.

Ratner gave him a cold stare. "I haven't done anything, my good man. As I said, there was a problem in the kitchen, and somehow this poison has infected our water supply today. But having said that twice now, it's important that I also inform you that I have the antidote just for such occasions. You can't be too prepared you know," she said with a wicked smile. "So, tucked away on the underside of each of your chairs, you will find a white pill bottle. All you have to do is find it and take the remedy. The crisis will be averted," Ratner said calmly. "There's no reason to panic. You have at least another five or ten minutes."

Immediately, all the Cabinet members leaped from their chairs, frantically searching under their seats, even flipping them over to find the small, white bottle that had been attached. To Ratner it was comical, watching grown men and women acting like children to find a magic potion that would cure their affliction. Having found their bottles, they unscrewed the top and shook out the pale, green pill that would save their lives. Myrna Coyn's hands were shaking so badly she almost dropped her pill on the floor before she could get it into her mouth. Even General Williams, head of the joint chiefs, looked disconcerted and anxious.

"But how do we take the pill if the water is poisoned?" asked Marshall Whitman, minister of Health and Human Dignity.

"If I have to tell you that, then you might as well give me your pill now and hope for the best," snapped Ratner.

Almost everyone in the room popped the little green pill into their mouths and swallowed it dry. Sara Emerson nearly choked on her pill, but managed to get it down her throat after several attempts.

"First Citizen?" asked Conrad James, "I found the white bottle, but there wasn't any pill inside." His face was reddened and sweaty.

Ratner smiled at her Attorney General. "You don't have a pill in your bottle?" she asked in a mocking tone. "Are you sure you're sitting in your regular chair?"

"Yes, I'm quite sure. This is where I always sit," James answered.

"Well, then I guess no mistake was made," Ratner responded without emotion.

"Excuse me?"

"I mean that you say you are in the seat that you should be in, correct?"

"Yes, but I don't have a pill. That's what I'm trying to tell you," said James, looking sicker as the seconds passed.

The others in the room -- their minds clearing of their own panic -- quickly grasped what was happening, and a look of shock came over them. They were frozen with fear for their colleague.

"I know," said Ratner, coldly. "Well, then. I think we've solved this problem. Now, who's next on the agenda to report?"

It was only then that Conrad James also understood. His face drained, and hysteria grabbed him with its bony fingers.

"But First Citizen, it wasn't me! I didn't say anything to anyone!" James cried out. "I swear!"

"That isn't what I understand, minister," she said. "I have heard quite a different story from many others."

"My god! My god! You have to believe me! I wasn't being serious. I was merely joking around. You know how people are. Everyone just likes a good joke now and again on a Monday morning. It wasn't anything, really!"

"No, it isn't anymore, now is it?"

Within the next few seconds, James's body began to shudder, and he bent over, vomiting blood on the floor next to his chair. A red ooze also started seeping out of his eyes and nose, dripping onto the long, beautiful conference table.

"Would you not mess up the table, for god's sake!" shouted Ratner, only glancing at him long enough to see him beginning to convulse. "If you aren't fit to be at the meeting, then excuse yourself."

James muscular contractions became violent, jerking his body uncontrollably. His arms began flailing and his head twitched, twisting it from side to side. He fell to the floor, doubling over in pain, writhing from the agony, as the lethal organism slowly began dissolving his organs from within. "But ... but ..." he began to say. By then, however, it was too late. Blood began pouring out of his eyes, ears, mouth and, it was assumed, every other orifice of his body. His dark eyes rolled to the back of his head, and he collapsed on the floor, a pool of scarlet beginning to accumulate on that expensive, silk Persian rug that blanketed the wooden floor.

"Holt! Get someone in here to remove the trash, will you?" demanded Ratner. "It's so hard to find a good Attorney General these days."

Hurriedly, Clancy Holt ran out of the room to get help. It wasn't long before two muscular Secret Service agents rushed in, but by then James wasn't moving. Instead of trying to resuscitate him, they left to get latex gloves and return, carting off his body as if it were a dead soldier on a battle field.

"Well, I'm still waiting for the next report?" demanded the First Citizen.

It was Roger Nelson, the Minister of Domestic Policing, who was next in line to give his report. He trembled as he held notes that he could recite. They contained information that was the truth – what was really going on, but not what he knew Ratner wanted to hear. He looked over in a state of petrifaction at the empty, bloodied, seat of the Attorney General.

"Well, what are you waiting for?" growled Ratner.

Nelson was short and of small stature. He was usually very assertive, but that was a trait he wished to put on display at that moment. It was made perfectly clear how *not* to survive in the Ratner

Administration. But to make matters worse, he was reporting on the same topic as had Conrad James. It was easy for him to worry that his utterances may lead him to the same fate as his peer.

"Uh, yes, Madam. We have been tracking various rogue groups in the country," Nelson said. "Most have been neutralized through other ministries, like the Ministry of Taxation and Enforcement where we've taxed them out of existence, the Anti-gun and Tobacco Ministry that has thrown just about everyone with a gun in prison, the Ministry of Labor which has fined all non-union workers demanding proof of a union ID card, and the Ministry of Licensing which has revoked operating permits for all right-wing groups or had them arrested for errors and irregularities in their paperwork to the ministries. Others group leaders were detained or their property confiscated for various minor infractions. It's been effective – sending a cold message to anyone else who might try to form a group challenging us."

Ratner smiled, but corrected him. "Challenging *me*, Nelson," she said cheerily. "That's about the only thing I've heard all day that's made any sense. It's good to know that we're making progress on our war against ignorance in this country."

"That's all I had," said Nelson as he meekly slumped deeper into his chair, hoping to be ignored in the larger sea of other ministers at the table.

"Does anyone else have anything to say?" Ratner asked, going back to her computer screen.

No one said a word.

"Alright then. I think this was a very productive meeting. Hopefully, we'll have more like this one," Ratner said as she left the room.

*****

CH 6 What to Do?

Sumner called a Cabinet meeting of his own to discuss the situation. General Ward offered a more in-depth review of the tactical and strategic positions of the relative military forces and the resources available to the ATLAS Republic. In detail, he discussed the pros and cons of several strategies he and his staff had developed to counter the possible threats of the USSA.

After his presentation, Sumner leaned back in his chair, putting his pencil to his lips as if he were about ready to light and smoke it. "Any comments?" he asked, looking at his team.

"It's interesting," began the Secretary of Health and Human services, Loretta White, "that in creating a free and open society that values independence and self-determination, we find ourselves in this situation. But I guess we all knew this might come."

"What situation is that, Loretta?" asked Sumner.

"Possibly having to go to war to defend those things," she answered.

"Yes, I'm afraid we all knew what we were getting into when we took these first steps toward a new democracy," said Secretary Ingram, head of the State Department. "I think we realized there would be a challenge from the USSA – that they wouldn't let us go peacefully. Quite honestly, I am surprised that they haven't reacted to what we've done. Freedom always comes with a price."

"You know," began Shea, "we have an extraordinary opportunity to capitalize on our free-market economic system. Entrepreneurs have been flooding into this country to setup shop and be free to develop their ideas. Of course, they want to make money off those ideas – things that have been *verboten* for so long in the USSA. The president and I just returned from a trip to such an inventor in South Dakota. He has some amazing prototypes that might change the outcome of a war – if we are forced into one."

"It is remarkable technology to be sure, but what we need are defensive strategies and tools," said Sumner. "With the USSA's overwhelming number of weapons, we won't last long if we can't stop what they might throw at us."

"What is it? This new technology?" asked White.

"We will discuss it at another time, after we have briefed our defense secretary," Sumner said, shooting a glance at Josh Templeton. "But, what if we brought together the best creative minds we have to help us build a defensive force – a new technology -- that no one will want to challenge?"

"Like a reconstituted Manhattan Project," said Shea, referring to the US project to build the atomic bomb in the 1940s.

"Yes, except not to build another nuclear device, of course. Rather, to build something that will protect this new country of ours – now and in the future," said Sumner.

"I like the idea," said Ingram, nodding approvingly. His sentiment was echoed around the table.

"Then, Josh, you should work with General Ward and Secretaries Templeton and Briggs," said the president.

"We're going to need a lot of resources for a project of that size," said Briggs, Secretary of Commerce. "If the USSA puts in a no-fly zone and-or naval blockade, we'd be in trouble."

"Then, Lawrence," noted Sumner, looking back at his secretary of state, "I want you to work with the Canadian prime minister, Macdonald, and the Mexican president, Juarez. We need a treaty that allows us to bring imports through Texas and North Dakota. Those are the two border states with those countries. We could get materiel through that way."

"What about the Quebec Prime Minister, Francis Valois?" asked Ingram. "We should inquire with him as well."

"I understand that Quebec is now a separate, sovereign country, but it's is too far east to help us, I think," said Briggs.

"In some ways, but it controls access to the Great Lakes via the Saint Lawrence River and Seaway. If we get them on our side, we would have a waterway through the Great Lakes – at least as far as Duluth. I've been in talks with the former governor of Minnesota, and it seems like we're making progress in moving them into our sphere. I think talks with Valois could be critical if we're able to sign Minnesota into the Republic," said Ingram.

Lawrence Ingram was a reserved, studious man. A graduate of Brown University as an economics major, he got his law degree from Harvard and a doctoral degree in economics from MIT. Considered one of the most brilliant and commonsensical diplomats of his time, Ingram was a coup for the new Republic. Tall and thin, with lanky arms and a Lincolnesque body, Ingram was a mind with which to be reckoned. He was also neither pompous nor egotistical, preferring to work with others and generate new ideas than presume his were the only viable options. His subordinates adored him, his peers respected him, and his superiors felt they couldn't be without him. It would have been easy for him to pursue a presidential position for himself, except he lacked one key element – charisma. Almost deadpan in his demeanor, Ingram preferred the background rather than being front and center. Playing second was fine with him, and it was equally agreeable to Sumner.

"Ah, yes," responded Sumner. "I see where you're going with that. I agree; that's quite astute. So, go ahead and strike up talks with Valois. We may need him on our side."

As the meeting adjourned, Sumner signaled to Shea as everyone else began leaving the room.

"Yes, sir?" she asked, coming up to him.

"Shea, I think it's best if we don't include Patrick in the Manhattan Project," he told her.

"You mean, Johnny, sir?"

"Yes."

"Why? He's probably got more ideas than everyone else put together," she exclaimed.

"Call it a hunch, but I think he works better alone. Let's just let him be ... let him come up with whatever he can on his own," Sumner said.

Shea looked at him skeptically. "You just don't want me working with him, do you?"

"I think it's for your own good, right now, Shea. He's not the man you knew. And, in many ways, you're not the same either. You've gone your different ways and, well, I think it's better for both of you."

"I don't agree, but if that's what you want, then fine," she replied, somewhat defensively.

Shea walked away before Sumner could say any more. He could tell that he'd hurt her even though he hadn't intended it.

At the same time, Shea knew it was a mistake. If there was something Patrick had, and she presumed Johnny did as well, was the ability to manage as well as create. *He would see,* she thought. *He would eventually change his mind.*

*****

CH 7 Annoyance

As Sara Miller Emerson reviewed her reports, things weren't looking good. All indicators showed the USSA economy slowing again. Tax revenues were down; deficits were up; the country's UnitedCoins were dropping in value; unemployment was at 35 percent and rising; and the people who were left were losing faith in their government. Things were as bad, if not worse, than during the Depression of 1929-1941, and all those dismal statistics would affect how much she, as minister of International Policing (Defense), could spend on the USSA's military.

She turned on the huge, thin TV screen that was papered onto her wall and watched as the world's images floated across the glass.

"And in world news, we have unrest brewing in the Middle East as the land, which was once occupied by the former state of Israel, tries to regroup and reconstitute a new country they call Zion. Zionists clashed with Palestinians and Iranians whose lands were also sterilized by the use of neutron bombs decades ago. Experts say that finding a mutually agreeable area to divide for each party is unlikely and is only a pipe dream of those who survived the nuclear attack that killed substantial numbers of the Jewish and Muslim people in those countries Much of the land is still uninhabitable; however, clerics and rabbis are still optimistic that they will be able to reach an agreement and allow their people to return to areas where life is possible.

"In other news, the premier of the New People's Dynasty of China, Xing Jaipong, has signaled his dissatisfaction with the muscle being flexed by the Russians. Since the expansion of the old Soviet Union to retake the countries it held as satellites after World War II, the renamed Russian Federation of States has amassed significant troops on the border with China and what was once Eastern Europe -- now the Northern Union of Islamic States. The Russian expansion back into Belarus, Poland, the Ukraine, Bulgaria, Romania, Moldova, Slovakia and Serbia, plus Finland has made China nervous in recent years. Only the Czech Republic and Hungary have remained outside Russian aggression. China has focused its attention on its new satellites of Taiwan, Indo-China, India, the Philippines, Australia and New Zealand. Yet, the two world superpowers remain wary of each other's intentions. Many experts say both are eyeing the fertile lands of Western Europe, now under control by the mullahs from the Sunni State and the ayatollah from the Jihadist Shia Nation. However, that is mere conjecture. For now, the World Council is meeting to ..."

Emerson turned off the TV, not interested in what the inept and inactive World Council was doing. It hadn't done anything in years, much like the United Nations before it.

Ring, ring.

She looked at the antique phone on her desk. It was a gray phone with a plastic cradle, small handset, and series of square push-buttons numbered from zero to nine; it had never rung during the two years she had held the office. The phone was unique in that it was hardwire-connected with the leaders of many second-tier nations of the world.

Only the First Citizen had a red phone that joined to those of the superpowers, Russia and China, and those of the other two demi-superpowers of Saudi Arabia and Iran, now called the Sunni State and Jihadist Shia Nation, respectively. She was only a lesser pawn in the bigger game of world politics, but she was fine with that.

"Hello, Minister Emerson speaking," she said, just in case it was the president or premier of one of those nations.

"Sara?"

"Yes, who is this?" she asked.

"This is Premier Yamauchi," said the voice, as the diode on the voice digital analyzer turned green, confirming the pattern. Yamauchi was the former head of Japan, which had been absorbed into the mainland of China.

"Yes, Premier Yamauchi. How are you today?" asked Emerson, trying to sound diplomatic and steady.

"What can I do for you?"

"I will be switching to our pre-arranged secure line. Please wait for my contact," he said before the line went dead.

Emerson hung up the phone and waited until a red light illuminated on the gray phone, signaling that advanced, cryptographic algorithms had kicked-in to conceal the nature of the voice communication.

"Yes?" she asked, picking up the line once more.

"Minister?"

"Yes, go ahead Mr. Premier."

"I'm calling to advise you that there has been a breach of security in Japan. Your covert assets here have been compromised, as the Chinese have broken the codes of our underground operations, and, I suspect, yours. During the past twenty-four hours, eighty-one of your agents have disappeared. We have no control over what is occurring. We believe it may be happening all over the world, as I have tried to contact my Nipponese Underground agents without success. If this is true, then many of the secrets of the USSA, the resistance forces in Japan and many of their allies are most assuredly breached. You know what that means."

Emerson began to feel the perspiration beading up on her forehead. Her hands and fingers became cold and clammy, and nausea began to overcome her.

"Yes," she said simply, attempting to maintain her composure.

"China may know the locations of all your nuclear submarines, ICBM mobile missile launchers and other deterrent assets. We have detected that they are changing launch codes on their missiles and possibly re-directing their warheads toward those coordinates. If they are planning an all-out attack, your country could be incapacitated quickly, allowing them to mobilize a massive sea invasion on the West Coast."

"That's quite impossible," said Emerson. "We renounced all our nuclear capability years ago. We no longer have any nuclear subs or ICBMs as they posed an existential threat to our neighbors. We have unilaterally dismantled all projections of power so we're not seen as a 'bullying' superpower in the world. They have no reason to ..."

The Premier chortled uncharacteristically, knowing full well that the USSA had not been considered a superpower for many years. "I see," he said, amused. "Well, in any event, I suggest you contact your First Citizen. The threat is real, and unless your country is willing to take counter measures, you may find yourselves in a war you hadn't bargained for. As for us, if you go down, so will our resistance efforts. There aren't that many traditional nations on Earth anymore."

"You forget about the industrialized countries of South America," said Emerson, challenging the assertion.

"If you think that 250 percent inflation down there has saved them from economic ruin, then you are probably right," Yamauchi said sarcastically. When he had led the nation of Japan, they had already dismissed the faltering economy and crumbling society of the West, knowing it would never come to their defense. However, they still needed the alliance – both militarily and industrially. The world had devolved, and in many ways the Nipponese Underground resistance movement was the last bastion of fighters for freedom left in the world – except for those in Wyoming.

Still, Emerson fumed at the implication, but held her tongue. "I'll convey your thoughts to the First Citizen," she answered before hanging up.

Access via phone or physically to Ratner's Oval Office was virtually impossible. She was guarded by a phalanx of government gatekeepers, and although Emerson held power in her position as the defense minister, she still was only able to meet with her boss once a month. First Citizen had told her that foreign policy bored her and that "People overseas don't vote in the USSA; so why should I care?" Yet, this incident was important, and she felt she needed a way to communicate it to her superior.

"General Williams," Emerson said, phoning the chairman of the Joint Chiefs of Staff, "this is Minister Emerson. I have information from the Japanese Underground about a possible breach of security ... Yes, I was phoned on a secure line ... Yes, it involves certain information that we need to get to the First Citizen ... I will meet you in her office in three hours ... Yes, ma'am." Emerson hung up.

Three hours was a long time for an emergency, but for a meeting with Ratner, it was miraculous that it could be setup that quickly. After the general had cleared all the hurtles of gaining access to their boss, Emerson walked into the Oval Office. The presidential seal that had once been emblazoned in the center of the carpet had been replaced with the symbol of the USSA's new mascot, the bear. The desk by the window that looked out over the Rose Garden was of a modern, glass and steel design – a striking departure from the massive, carved wooden desks that had rested in that same spot for centuries. On the back credenza and suspended from other walls were banks of monitors that gave live feeds from different domestic news rooms, all controlled by her Administration. General Williams, Director Wanda Fredrick, and

Ratner's own deputy minister, Margola Vasilik, were already there talking to the First Citizen, when Emerson walked into the room.

"Director, you were saying that the Chinese have broken our encrypted codes?" asked the First Citizen. "How many agents have we lost?"

"It's hard to say," responded Fredrick, head of the CIA, now known as the International Data Collection Agency or IDCA. "At this point, there are forty-two agents who have not contacted us at the appointed time. Many are in sensitive positions. But what's worse, the system of satellites we use to monitor the activities of all our agents has been scrambled. We believe the Chinese are using their latest EMP device to disrupt our intelligence gathering."

"This electromagnetic pulse, is it something different than they've used before?" asked Ratner. "I thought we added proper shielding to all our satellites to prevent a problem?"

"They've found a way through our shields, First Citizen. They are ahead of us in most aspects of space warfare," said Fredrick.

"Is that right?" asked Ratner, looking over at Emerson. "You're my defense person. It's your job to keep the country safe. What do you say to that?"

"Yes, Madam. They have been ahead of us in that area for some time now."

"How could you let this happen?" shouted Ratner, acting as if it were the first time she'd ever heard of the issue. "I never knew about this!"

"It wasn't under your watch, Madam. It was under Fourier's."

"But you're in charge of defense now, and this should have been fixed!"

"We also haven't had the money, First Citizen. All the money is going for social programs right now." "All the money?" Ratner repeated, challenging her minister.

Emerson backed down at once. "I didn't mean all the money, surely. But a lot of the tax revenues is going to other things."

"Bull sh*t!" said Ratner. "There's plenty of money. We can just print more if we need to."

"Without our satellite network, we're essentially blind," said Fredrick, getting the conversation back on point.

"But don't we have naval assets out in the Pacific?" Ratner asked. "The Sixth Fleet should be patrolling the waters off our coastline there."

"The Sixth Fleet was cut and mothballed three years ago," said the general. "We only have two battle groups now. There really hasn't been any need for more."

"You should have been giving me a briefing of what the Chinese have been doing," Ratner stated, snidely. There had been weekly briefings on all military matters, but neither Ratner nor her predecessor Fourier had bothered to attend. Their briefings were limited to domestic social issues and the potential unrest within the borders, not outside them. The tumult and revolution of the rest of the world was considered of no consequence to their rule. Anyway, they were viewed as having no political advantage, and therefore useless. Resources were limited, and the once-mighty US military was now only an empty shell under the USSA banner. The navy was considered brown-water, not blue-water, meaning it was only large enough to patrol the country's own shoreline – unable now to project a force in oceans far afield.

While the Russians and Chinese had poured trillions into their militaries from 2012 through 2049, the USSA had cut its military budgets to the bone in each of those years, shrinking them by more than 8 percent per year. The Navy had fewer than sixty-three ships, down from over three hundred in the 1980s. The Army enlisted only 51,000 men and women, as compared with the 554,000 in 2012. And the Air Force had only six squadrons of fighters -- old fifth-generation planes of aging capability from the 2010s -- and only one squadron of bombers – the ancient B2 style that no longer had any stealth capability. Many wondered whether the USSA military would even be able to defend its own homeland from foreign aggressors should that need arise.

General Williams outlined what the Chinese had been doing during the previous two years. She said their cyber warfare capability was second to none in the world, able to extract sensitive data from almost any hardened server site and capable of implanting crippling viruses that could not be easily destroyed or eliminated. Their anti-satellite programs had destroyed the satellite networks of India prior to its invasion and had done the same to Japan the following year. They had built five aircraft carrier groups and had over four hundred naval vessels, including, ICBM-capable nuclear submarines, subs with anti-satellite weapons and advanced AEGIS-type cruisers, once solely owned by the USA. Their hypersonic scramjet transport aircraft could land whole battalions almost anywhere in the world within hours. Platform airbases in Earth's orbit provided them the capability of striking anywhere quickly, in addition to their lunar military installation. Advances in detection-technology had enabled them to "see" inside buildings. It was widely thought that they had placed moles throughout the highest levels of the USSA government and many other high posts within Russia, the Sunni State, the Jihadist Shia Nation and the Northern and Southern Islamic Empires.

"What is the possibility of a strike on our West Coast?" asked Ratner.

"It's hard to say," said the general, working off her laptop. She pushed a button making a 3D image of the world appear in the center of the room. "If our satellite network is destroyed, we won't have much of a warning." The hologram showed the positions of the defense satellites circling in orbits overhead.

"I believe it's serious," said Emerson nervously, interjecting. "They could strike quickly, just as the Japanese did at Pearl Harbor, and we wouldn't know what hit us."

Ratner gave her a cold stare. "I think you're exaggerating quite a bit, here, minister. We've seen no other aggression from the Chinese since they took over Japan. They're over three thousand miles away and wouldn't have the capability of occupying America if they wanted to. We're isolated over here – completely protected due to our geography. I'm not concerned."

"Even so, perhaps we can initiate PB&J," the general said coolly.

The First Citizen nodded, seemingly knowing what that program entailed.

"I'm sorry. I'm not familiar with …" said Vasilik.

"And why do you need to know?" snapped Ratner, losing no time to put her in her place.

"Madam," said the general cautiously, "in this case it may be of benefit for them to understand what this program entails."

"Why?" Ratner asked.

"If there's a problem, we may need to coordinate their resources to assist in the containment."

Ratner thought briefly, and then acquiesced. "Go on," she said simply.

At that moment, Ratner's administrative assistant interrupted. "Madam, there is a Julius Ratner on the line. He says it's important."

The First Citizen frowned, not wishing to be bothered. "Can you ask him what it's about?" She returned a moment later. "He says it's about your mother."

"Fine," huffed Ratner, leaving the discussion to pick-up the line.

While Ratner was on the phone, General Williams began describing the program. "You see, PB&J is a top-secret project that we have been working on for years. It was started under the Fourier Administration and has grown steadily under the careful guidance of First Citizen Ratner," she said, blatantly sucking-up to her boss.

"Well, what is it?" Vasilik asked, impatiently.

"We have developed a mutated contagion that spreads very quickly. It is far more lethal than the Ebola virus or the venom of a *Chironex flecken* jellyfish. It kills faster than Sarin gas or Anthrax. We have found a way to introduce the toxin into the food supply of a culture like China or Russia. Once propagated throughout the entire chain, a small amount, say half a kilogram, is enough to kill nearly one billion people."

"Did you say one *billion*?" asked Vasilik, shocked by the number.

"Yes. That would eliminate about 70 percent of China's population and eliminate any threat," said General Williams without emotion. "It would be far better than unleashing one of our other synthetic viruses which we have little control over. This way, we can target the poison and ensure it's contained within the boundaries of the enemy combatant."

"You're saying you would be willing to kill-off one billion people," Vasilik said again, repeating herself.

"Yes. Of course," the general answered. "And you wouldn't?"

"No!" shouted the deputy minister. "I certainly wouldn't!"

Williams looked away from her in disgust. "That's what I figured. That's why we didn't want to tell you."

"So, where does that leave us?" asked Emerson.

Ratner returned to the conversation, looking unsteady and shaken. Is everything alright?" asked General Williams. It was the first time the general had actually seen her boss disturbed by anything.

Stoically, Ratner answered. "Apparently, it's my mother. She's a hundred and twelve and was diagnosed with congestive heart failure."

"I'm sorry," said Emerson, sympathetically.

Ratner sat silent for a moment, thinking. The others didn't know whether to speak or not, but the general finally broke the stillness. "Madam, do have any thoughts on the PB&J program? What are my orders?"

It took a few more seconds, but the First Citizen finally regained her composure. "How many nuclear warheads do I have at my disposal?" Ratner asked, still numb from her phone call.

"What nuclear warheads?" asked Vasilik, again being stunned by the question. "We aren't supposed to have any nuclear warheads. Are there any other secrets we are keeping from the American people?"

"Yes, Margola," said Ratner, now more agitated than ever. "We *do* have secrets, and we *did* keep our warheads! Are you happy, now?"

"No. We're in violation of our treaties with Russia and China," answered Vasilik.

"They kept theirs too, you idiot!" shouted the First Citizen. "Don't you get it yet? The treaties are only for public consumption. It's all for show. It's always been that way. None of the countries abide by the treaties they sign, and they don't expect the other guy to do it either. It's all for the little people to think their politicians are actually doing something to make our world safer. Grow up!"

Vasilik shrunk back into her chair. She was being intimidated, and she realized that Ratner was not someone with whom she wanted to battle. This was a lose-lose proposition, and it wasn't worth the price of admission.

"We need to impose conscription immediately," said the general. "We need all eligible men and women forced into service -- all except those who are exempted, of course."

"Who's exempted?" asked Emerson, incredulously.

"Don't worry," said Ratner. "You and your family are perfectly safe, as are all the other politicians' families in Washington. We have a special exemption where no one we know will have to serve. Basically, we stay here and manage the war while the other poor bastards out there fight it for us."

"And when did that exemption pass Congress?" Vasilik asked.

"It didn't. I issued an Executive Order a few weeks ago when I found that China was building up a presence just off our coastline."

"So, you knew about all this?" asked Emerson.

"No, not all of it. But, I did know enough to issue the order. College won't be an out either – unless it's an Ivy League school, of course. I also put in a provision that a contribution to any campaign fund of more than one million UnitedCoins would also get you exempted. Of course, we only recognize contributions to *our* campaign to qualify. It's just easier on everyone." Then she paused. "But you know, I think I have a better idea. We'll just get our mercenaries from the breakaway states. We'll have them fight for us."

"How will you do that?" asked Emerson.

"We'll invade," said the general.

"Invade our own states? But ... but thousands will be killed!" Vasilik said, alarmed.

"Yeah, probably," answered Ratner. "But they chose this, not me. We'll give them an ultimatum, but then we'll just roll in the tanks. It was very effective in 1956 when the Hungarians got feisty with the Soviets. It worked again a few decades ago when Russia took over Eastern and Western Europe. Tanks are very intimidating against a populace, you know."

"Then, we'll take the able-bodied men and women and put them in military camps. Those who don't comply or we can't change – we'll just eliminate them," said the general.

"You mean killed," said Vasilik, indignantly.

"What do you think I mean?" replied the general.

"We can't allow that," said Vasilik.

Ratner laughed. "*You* can't allow that, Margola? Really? What are you going to do about it?"

"I'll expose you and your plan," she said. "I'll tell the media."

"Okay. If you think that will do any good. They won't believe you, and they won't report the story. You'll only humiliate yourself," she said. "You need to come back to reality, dear."

"We'll see about that," Vasilik said.

"I tell you what. Why don't we all step back a second," said Ratner, suddenly changing her tune. Her face morphed completely, becoming more serious and relaxing to the point of serenity. With eyelids calmly drooping over her black eyes and mouth flattening with tranquil repose, she smiled with a hidden evil. "Perhaps we *are* being too rash in this decision," said Ratner, coolly looking at the general. "Margola, we'll sleep on this one. Let's get back together tomorrow morning at seven o'clock. We'll meet here at the White House and lay out the pros and cons. Perhaps we can see if there is another option for us. This entire Chinese threat has caught us all off guard, and we also have to weigh what the Russians and Saudi's might do."

Vasilik looked at them askance.

"No, really, Margola. I'll call a meeting of the Cabinet members, and we'll re-evaluate this. Would that make you feel better?"

The deputy minister glanced over at the general and then nodded. "Yes, I think that's the least we should do. We should also consider involving Congress."

"One step at a time," said Emerson, trying to corral her subordinate. "As the First Citizen said, let's start with the Cabinet and see where that leads us."

Margola Vasilik left the room, together with Emerson and Fredrick.

After they had gone, Ratner walked over and closed the door, immediately turning to the general. "I'll have my assistant contact the Cabinet and advise them of our meeting in the morning," the general said to her.

"That won't be necessary," Ratner replied.

The general looked at her, puzzled. "I don't understand," she said.

"You will," answered the First Citizen. "But there is something you need to do first."

*****

CH 8 Coming to Grips

Shea returned home. It had been a long day. Her new dog, Enza, greeted her at the door of her residence, her wide eyes gleaming with excitement and her long, auburn tail wagging as if she were fending off swarms of marauding flies. Only five, Enza had been at the local Humane Society for months before Shea spotted her on a spontaneous visit. Her previous owner had been an elderly woman who could no longer care for her. But the spunky Labradoodle was swishing her tail madly, just as she had when Shea had first met her.

"There you go, girl," Shea said, cooing and scratching her behind the ears. "Mommy loves you. Yes, she does."

But, before Shea could get settled, her private phone was ringing. "Yes?" she answered, kicking off her shoes.

"It's Sumner," the president said. "I ... I was going to talk to you about the other day with Patrick, I mean Johnny."

Shea collected herself, calming her nerves and forcing out her professional persona once more. "I think the technology is brilliant. It's something we desperately need," she answered.

"No. What I'm asking is, 'How are *you* holding up?'" Sumner asked, his face on the visual display showing deep earnestness and compassion. Sumner had not spoken with her about their day in South Dakota, since their visit with the quirky inventor — not from a personal standpoint. The shock of his being her long, lost husband had been traumatic for her, and he had wanted to give her some time.

"I'll be alright," she said, with a strained smile, trying to put a brave face on things.

"You don't even lie well," he answered.

"I just need time to think. I just got home, and it's just me and Enza. It seemed like yesterday when it was me and Patrick. It was a better time then," she said.

"And it will be again, Shea. As you say, you just have to give it some time." Then he added, "Perhaps you need a few days off — to rest and regroup."

"Thank you, Mr. President, but no. There is too much to be done. It's a critical time for the Republic. I can't."

"Unfortunately, I have to agree with you. We need you, now more than ever. But, when all this is over, you should take some time."

"When will it be over, Mr. President? I don't see that for a long time. There are just too many threats to our existence, and we have so much rebuilding to do — our economy, the government infrastructure, foreign relationships ... it's endless. I often wonder how the Founding Fathers pulled it off at all."

"It was a simpler time then," said Sumner. "Life is more complicated now."

Mr. President, that is probably the greatest understatement I've ever heard muttered from your lips," said Shea, now smiling genuinely.

Sumner laughed. "Yes, you're probably right about that." His face then grew serious once more. "But, I want you to know that I'm here for you. Anything you need, just call me." Then, he added, "I'm having a small gathering of people to the house tonight. It's purely social – no formalities. I hope you can come." "Sure," she answered.

Shea turned off the screen and picked up her two-jigger glass of Scotch, taking a couple sizeable gulps. *I needed that*, she thought, before returning the container to the coaster. She put her head back into the comfort of her soft leather chair and soon drifted mindlessly into a deep slumber.

When she awoke, she yawned and rubbed her eyes. Groggy and disoriented, Shea thought she'd only been asleep for a few minutes, but when she looked at the clock embedded in the wall of the room, its bright blue numerals read **2:12 AM**.

"Oh, sh*t!" she said, sitting up abruptly. She had slept over twelve hours and missed the president's party. "Call JC Sumner," she said, commanding her phone to dial. It buzzed twice before she said, "Cancel that!" Uncertain what to do, she decided to do nothing and again fell back asleep in the chair.

***

Several days passed before she saw the president again. Both had been busy addressing the urgent needs of the country. It was after a Cabinet meeting when the president pulled her aside, his hand gently taking her by the arm. "Is everything alright?" he asked. "I'm concerned about you."

"There's no reason to be, Mr. President," Shea answered, although it made her feel good that he was so interested in her and her wellbeing.

"Well, I didn't see you at the party the other night. I hope I didn't offend you. I certainly didn't mean to."

"Oh, no. Not at all, Mr. President. Everything is fine. There's nothing to worry about, sir. Really."

Sumner's face softened, the gentleness of his nature coming over him. "Shea, I want you to call me JC."

"No, Mr. President. It's protocol to address you as ..."

"No, I insist, Shea. You and I have a special relationship, and I want you to feel comfortable around me. When it's just you and me, call me JC." Then, he said, "But of course when others are around, Mr. President is appropriate. Is that all right with you?"

"Okay, JC. I ... I'll try to do that," answered Shea, pleased by his words.

"Now, is there anything I can do for you? If you say you're okay. I guess you are then. Well, ..." Sumner now seemed to be stammering over his own words. "Well ... I should let you go. I just want to be sure you are alright. That's all."

"Thanks, Mr. Pres … I mean JC," she said, correcting herself.

As she left the Cabinet room, Shea felt good. She felt more connected than she had in a long time. *Perhaps …* she thought. Then she tried to put it out of her mind. *No. Not now, not yet, not … It's too soon.*

In time, a sense of normalcy began to return to Shea's composure. Beginning to put the rediscovery of Patrick and his amnesia behind her, she began to refocus her attention on helping Sumner run the Republic. But one afternoon, Sumner came into her office carrying a manila envelope.

"What's that?" Shea asked, noticing the package.

"This came in my email. I printed it out. I think you need to take a look." Sumner's tone was flat and cool. There was a slight look of disgust on his face as he unceremoniously dropped the envelope on her desk.

She looked at Sumner wondering why he had delivered it personally. "I assume you want me to open it now?" she asked, as he stood in front of her, his arms folded tightly on his chest.

He nodded.

She tore open the envelope and pulled out the contents. As soon as she saw what was inside, she shoved it back into its protective covering.

"What is it, Shea?" Sumner asked, skeptically. There was a note of disappointment in his voice.

Shea looked at Sumner. There was a sickening ache in her heart. If there had been someplace to hide, she would have sought it out. She wanted to escape, to run away and never come back. The haunting of the past continued to rear its ugly head — first, a husband who no longer remembered her and now this.

"You already know, don't you?" she asked.

"Yes. Is there something you'd like to share with me?"

Shea looked down, embarrassed and ashamed. "Remember we talked about the ministry agent in Belize?" she asked. "Well, we had an affair while I was there." Tears streamed from her face, and she began to sob. Taking a tissue, she said, "JC, there was so much going on in my life then. I was confused. I wanted to find my husband. I ached because I couldn't find the one I loved. There was an emptiness — a void — that I couldn't fill. I guess he was just there at the right place and time. I was weak. It just happened."

There was no change on Sumner's face, but she could tell he understood.

"I miss Maria too," he said, looking away and out a window, as if he might see the spirit of his wife outside. "It's hard."

"Yes," she answered, "it is."

"But there is something in there you should see. It's a note," said Sumner.

Attached to one of the photos was a scrawled missive, which read:

Are these of any interest? For the digital files and all prints, it will cost you money and power. How much of each will be up to you.

An Admirer

Shea shook her head. She could feel her body trembling, reacting violently to the invasion of her privacy and to the blackmail. It was bad enough that Sumner knew – it was quite another for the rest of the country, perhaps the world, to find out. It hadn't been unusual for leaders of countries to have affairs. Even some of the Founding Fathers had been caught in adulterous relationships from time to time. Alexander Hamilton had an affair with Maria Reynolds that nearly destroyed him when it was made public; Thomas Jefferson with one of his slaves, Sally Hemings.

"What do you think I should do?" Shea asked, holding her head in her hands.

"I don't believe this is going to be a big deal. The French have been doing it for centuries. The good news is that only you and I know the truth right now. Everyone else thinks Patrick is dead. If you had an affair in Belize, I don't think people would hold it against you. I really don't think it will be a problem. And, from Patrick's memory loss, he shouldn't have any issues with it either. In fact, it may make his new situation a lot easier for him to deal with."

In some ways that was true. In other ways, it was a final nail for Shea and Patrick ever getting back together. She knew it was over anyway, something that was still difficult for her.

"I think we should see how things play out," Sumner said reassuringly. "They haven't said clearly what they're after in that note. We don't know what they want, yet."

"You're right. Let's wait and see what happens," Shea said, putting off the decision.

After Sumner left, Shea pulled out the envelope's contents once again, and sat in her chair, staring at what she'd found. There in color were eight by ten photos of her and her Belizean lover having sex in his apartment. She couldn't believe someone would stoop so low as to set her up like that. But there it was in front of her for everyone in the world to see. It showed her naked on the bed, her legs spread wide and the handsome, dark-complexioned imposter having his way with her. The look on her face was one of ecstasy, and then she realized the look on his face – as if he were punching his time clock – no emotion at all. She had been duped; she had been made to look stupid and licentious. And, she knew she'd have to pay.

*****

CH 9 Loose Ends

Vasilik drove home and pulled her car into the garage, the door closing automatically behind her. She was concerned about what was going on in the White House and the First Citizen's capricious attitude not only toward the lives and livelihoods of the men and women around her, but to the millions of USSA citizens. *Ratner didn't care,* she thought. *She really doesn't give a damn whether millions live or die!* She had grudgingly accepted Ratner's softening position and willingness to take the matter before her full Cabinet. Although it was unlike Ratner to change her mind, Vasilik would take any small win she could get if she felt she was in the right. Over time, she thought, the First Citizen would understand the consequences of her actions – that people might suffer if the wrong ones were made.

She told the car to close its door and went over to the black-box, electric wall unit to retrieve the short 220-volt electric cord she used to recharge her car every night. The thick cord pulled out of the wall on a loaded spring and pushed easily into the three-prong outlet just behind the passenger door on the car's right side.

Opening the door to the house, she announced that she was home, not expecting anyone to be up or to greet her. Her partner was probably upstairs in bed watching TV and her daughter was likely in her room studying. As a junior in high school, her daughter Amanda was trying to make the grades for a good college; her older son Nathan was off to the University of Pennsylvania, an Ivy League school – one that Ratner had disparaged by telling her that their students wouldn't qualify to get an exemption from conscription.

Vasilik walked to the door that separated the house from the garage and opened it, but then stopped, realizing she hadn't flipped on the battery charger. "Crap," she mumbled to herself. Reversing course, she closed the door and trudged back over to the electric box, its red and green lights showing the system active and ready for use. Putting her briefcase down, Vasilik looked up at the digital screen and pressed her finger on the button marked *Charge.*

The box instantly exploded. Metal shards flew out in all directions, impaling Vasilik's body and slicing through vital organs and other soft tissue. The force snapped her back, kicking her back against her car, where she crumpled to the ground. As sparks continued to sputter off the charging pole, Margola Vasilik lay dead on the floor, her eyes wide open but the right side of her face scorched black, burned beyond recognition.

***

It was seven in the morning when Minister Emerson entered the Oval Office. "I thought we were having a Cabinet meeting this morning to review the strategy against the Republic?" she asked Ratner, who was sitting behind her desk. General Williams was on one of the sofas in the middle of the room, reviewing charts and data on her computer.

"No need," the First Citizen said, not bothering to look up. "It will just be the three of us."

Hesitantly, Emerson came in and sat on the sofa opposite the general and drew out her sliver-screen computer. "And Margola, will she be …"

"No," said Williams. "She was unable to attend, this morning."

Ratner finished what she was doing and rose to join the other women around the steel and glass coffee table that kept the two couches separated from each other. "Good. Now we can get on with what we need to do. We were talking about Operation PB&J, weren't we?" asked the First Citizen.

"But what about Margola?" asked the defense minister.

"What do you mean?" Ratner asked coldly.

"Well, she said she'd expose us if we considered using that platform. It would create further unrest with the public at a time when things are pretty unstable domestically. Don't we want to consider that?"

"Vasilik is no longer a problem," said the general.

"I don't understand," answered Emerson.

"She's dead," said Ratner, bluntly and without emotion. "She died last night at her home. There was an accident in the garage or something. The local police are investigating, of course. Tragic accident, yes. Anyway, we don't need to concern ourselves with her anymore or being *outted*."

Emerson sat stunned. She didn't have to be told what had happened. "I see," she said quietly. "Then, we'll have to send someone to the funeral, I guess."

"Yes, yes. Handle it," directed Ratner. "I'm sure you have a black dress you can wear."

"Uh, yes, but aren't you going too?"

"I'll leave it to you," answered Ratner.

"And make sure you bring tears," added the general, smiling darkly.

*****

CH 10 The ATLAS Underground

"What is it, Oishi?" asked Sumner, glancing up from his work as she entered the room.

Oishi had replaced Randy Marston as Sumner's chief of staff after Marston's sudden and inexplicable disappearance while investigating the oil refinery explosion in Louisiana. Sumner had felt responsible for his fate, having sent him down to follow-up on information that the fire had been deliberately set by one of Fourier's ministries. They were never able to find him. Oishi had worked in the office with Randy and had stayed with Sumner after he'd left Capitol Hill and started GOFLA. Now she was a trusted assistant upon whom he relied for everything.

"There's a gentleman here to see you," said Oishi in her quiet, unassuming voice.

"Who is it? Did he have an appointment? I didn't have anything on my calendar."

"No, he didn't have an appointment, Mr. President, but he said you would know what it's about." "And his name?"

"He said it was Thorne, Kilby Thorne."

Thorne entered the room, dressed as immaculately as he always had. Having been deposed as president of EG, Inc. and kicked off the board of directors once the government takeover of GovCos and other large multinationals in the country was completed, Thorne had left the country to try his hand at running a company overseas. Soon, however, he found that most other "free" countries were under the influence of socialism where capitalism was viewed as an antiquated, failed notion of the past. He wandered from country to country in search of a job – a place where a large, independent company needed an experienced, savvy chief executive who was willing to do what was necessary to get results – but found few of those opportunities left. As head of the largest GovCo organization, he had quashed small, start-up competitors, using Machiavellian tactics to destroy their businesses – including Shea's and Patrick's company. At the time, he had felt no remorse for it. To him, it had only been a means to an end. With the backing of those in government and the halls of power, he had been given free rein to eliminate all opposition without fear of judicial reprisal. In some cases, he had enjoyed Congressional backing through clandestine legislation that provided him tax breaks and exclusive deals by describing qualifying companies in a way in which only EG, Inc., would meet the requirements.

Without finding a position abroad, Thorne had returned to America. Even during the short year, he had been gone, he wasn't prepared for what he saw when he returned. The nation, now called the United Socialist States of America, had deteriorated into chaos. Few worked, and those who did were not productive. Those who didn't were subsidized by massive welfare spending and mountains of federal debt. Traveling to Washington, Thorne hoped to land a cushy, high-paying lobbying job on Capitol Hill; however, there was no longer any need for them. Everything was done through Executive Order, bypassing Congress completely. It was only through his government connections that Thorne had been able to get an exit visa and travel to Wyoming where he took a chance. He had been the enemy before, and now he was returning to ask his opponent for help.

Thorne stood in front of Sumner, the two men eyeing each other, uncertain of the other's intentions.

"So, Mr. Thorne," the president said, after exchanging small pleasantries and listening to Thorne's story, "why should I trust you?" It was a direct, pointed question that even made Thorne wince.

"Well," Thorne said, stammering, "I really see no reason you should."

Sumner smiled. "You know, Mr. Thorne, that may be the first honest thing I've heard you say in a long time." He sat back in his chair, his fingers pressed together as if in prayer. "What is it that you want then?"

"A chance," said Thorne. "That's all I ask."

"What sort of chance?"

"Whatever you think is fitting – appropriate, sir."

"Do you still have connections all over the country – all over the world?" asked Sumner.

"Why yes, of course. But they often have their hands tied. Officially, they are under the thumbs of government leaders, so there isn't much they can do for us."

"Can they provide us information?"

"Why yes. I'm sure they can. It will be sensitive, but it's doable."

Sumner leaned in toward Thorne, assessing the man and trying to determine whether this was a new Kilby Thorne or just someone sent to him from Ratner. He would be hiring a double-agent then, and he knew the risks. "Thorne, I have a new mission for you. This is a bit out of the norm for a civilian, but you have the right background to oversee this. And in case something goes wrong, I don't want the USSA to be able to blame the Republic or use it as an excuse to go to war. Do you understand?"

"Yes, sir."

"Now, do you remember about the French Underground during World War II?"

"Yes, they helped the Allies destabilize the Vichy – German government. They got our servicemen out of the country when they were shot down, and they conducted missions of sabotage, destroying key depots and facilities inside France that the Germans used for their war effort."

"Very good. So, about what I need you to do. We need to form an ATLAS Underground within the USSA -- you know, a resistance movement. I need intelligence – a lot of intelligence. We need to know what they're planning, if anything. Is this something you're willing to do?"

"So, you need someone to spy for you?"

"I think *spy* is pretty strong. I think it's more just information gathering. We know people in several cities too who can help you. You'll need to organize them. You're good at that. But, you'll also need to be discreet. You will report directly to me. Do you understand?"

"When do you need me to get started?" Thorne asked, reaching out his hand to seal the agreement.

"Yesterday," said Sumner.

***

It took months, but over time a series of underground cells were created within the USSA, all with members who were sympathetic to the new Republic. The members had been hand-picked for their leadership and were experienced or trained in covert military operations. Thorne was active in the recruiting of agents willing to cross the line, infiltrating back into states that were firmly wedged into the sphere of the USSA and under the bootjack of the First Citizen.

Thorne was quick to setup a system to convey critical information from the cells to Cheyenne. Unlike the Enigma machine of the 1940s, the existence of the SI-net and other ultra-frequency electromagnetic wavelengths added new dimensions not available before. Encryption had also reached new highs with unbreakable codes that would require millennia to solve even with supercomputers. Although the Republic didn't have all the cipher capability of the USSA, there were non-technical ways to get information where it needed to be. Using these simpler systems, Thorne was able to funnel messages to and from his cells, tracking the movement of USSA troops and materiel near their shared borders. What the Republic lacked was satellite capability – an Achilles heel so significant, that without it, their hopes hinged more on luck than statistical probability.

"So, what's the latest?" Sumner asked Thorne, as he was reviewing the briefing.

Thorne had been giving the president weekly reports on the efforts of his Underground cells. Now, he took off his glasses and rubbed his eyes. "We have twenty-six cells operating in non-Republic states," Thorne answered, pointing to a map that demarcated the border between the USSA and states of the ATLAS Republic. "Here, here, and here," he added, tapping his finger at Washington, Chicago, and New York. This is where we have the strongest cells, and these are key areas. Of course, Chicago and New York are still in bankruptcy, but there are enough civil services going on to keep the cities going. We have people in city halls, police districts, and National Guard units in other cities and states too."

"And what are they telling you?"

Thorne sat back, relaxing the muscles in his shoulders and arms and letting his hands drop to his sides. "It's odd," he answered. "It's as if they don't even realize we've seceded."

"What about Worthington, Minnesota?" asked Sumner.

"Worthington?" asked Thorne. "What's special about Worthington? Do you mean Washington?"

"No, Worthington. It borders with South Dakota, right here," Sumner said, pointing to a map of the USSA. "Joplin, Missouri, near the line here with Kansas and Oklahoma; Moscow, Idaho, of all places, right here," he said, continuing to push his pen tip toward a town sitting on the state line with Washington State, "and Fort Carson, near Colorado Springs, where we thought all along they would make their first move. So, you're telling me they haven't even begun discussions of mobilizing any troops against us?"

"My cells tell me they have begun initial plans to move troops into areas near the Republic borders. In fact, they have started pulling a few troops out of their military base in Fort Carson. It's less than a hundred kilometers from there to the border with us here in Wyoming. The Colorado counties that have seceded are to the east of that, so they wouldn't be a factor in any conflict."

"Do we have a cell in Colorado Springs?" asked Sumner.

"Yes," answered Thorne. "It's under the command of Colonel Jacob Marcus. There are only sixteen in that group; most are civilians, though. Only three are hard-core ops people."

"What did they send you?" Sumner inquired.

"It's encrypted, but they tell me … let me see … yeah, it's right here." Thorne read Sumner the distilled message, which had been embedded throughout a website forum on baby diapers.

> 14Ap, FtCar 4Div est move N wi 6d. Rt87. No heavy/air or Spec.

"What the hell does that mean?" asked the president.

"It means that the 4th Infantry Division from Fort Carson is moving north within six days via state highway 87. There is no heavy machinery moving north with it, nor is there any air support expected. The 10th Special Forces Division is not expected to be involved."

"It doesn't mean it's an attack. It could be just part of a regular exercise."

"Don't know. But to me, it suggests they are finally coming around to some sort of action," said Thorne.

"Well, we need to get General Ward on the line to inform him," added Sumner.

"What about sat intel, sir?" asked Thorne. "We desperately need a bird in the sky. We're operating in the dark right now. What about the Chinese or Russians? Has State begun conversations with either of them?"

Sumner shook his head. "Of course not. Think about it. The Chinese and Russians would love that – to get a foothold in North America. They'd be the first to extract every concession out of us that they could — not the least of which would be to ask for a military base right here in Wyoming. Is that what you'd trade your freedom for?"

"No, sir," said Thorne, adding, "Then what about the Canadians? They have a ring of satellites up there too. It's pretty crowded in space these days. It's a wonder there aren't collisions of these things now and again."

"State has been talking with them about an alliance. The discussions are moving slowly, though. They are reluctant to get involved," said Sumner.

"Well, we need something. Anything we can get would be great, Mr. President," said Thorne. "We're just too vulnerable where we are right now."

"I know, but you and your cells need to continue funneling us information. That, I'm sure."

As Thorne was leaving the room, Shea passed him in the doorway, shocked by his presence. He didn't seem to recognize her, or at least acted as though he didn't. He did, however, smile and offer a salutation.

Shea shut the door behind her after entering. "Why the hell was he here?" she asked, stammering with her question.

"He's working for me," said Sumner.

"Thorne? Kilby Thorne is working for the Republic? You've got to be ..."

"Now, before you go off, I think it's a good thing."

"How on earth can you say that? With all due respect, sir, there's no way you can trust that snake."

"Perhaps not. Yet perhaps he can also be one of our most valuable assets."

"Valuable? You are kidding me, aren't you, sir?" asked Shea. "You can't really trust him. I mean, any information that he's giving you is probably a lie. You know that, don't you?"

Sumner sighed. "Perhaps," he said. "So, to answer your question, no, I'm not swallowing everything he's feeding me. We're checking it through other channels too. However, everything we've gotten so far has checked out."

"So, what is it that he's doing for you ... for us?"

"I can't tell you at the moment. But, soon, I will. You must understand that we don't have many people in this Administration with the reach that Thorne has. He knows a lot of people. He can get to a lot of people. I'd rather keep him on our side if we can. You're familiar with the old saying?"

"Which is?" Shea asked.

"Keep your friends close; keep your enemies closer."

*****

CH 11 Socialized Medicine

Ratner had applauded the forward-thinking improvements made by her predecessor in the area of medicine – at least as long as her family had not been affected. Taking over as First Citizen, she expanded the program, making sure everyone was covered by government healthcare. It was called "Single Payer," and the people were told it would simplify everything, making it easier for doctors and patients. No one would ever have to pay for care again, and life would be … wonderful.

But after a several months of chaos and dwindling finances, a few changes had to be made.

Emergency rooms at hospitals soon required appointments, unless the patient was determined to have a life-threatening condition. It was a one-strike-and-you're-out policy. One visit to the ER with a non-life-threatening condition and the person was banned for life – regardless of their future state. In general, care was given based on decisions made by government tribunals, and these were governed by two unpublicized factors. First, a patient over sixty-five was considered too old to warrant help. It was a simple cost-benefit approach to medicine. Scarce resources meant rationing, and that applied to those with little chance of recovery or who were deemed to have less value to society than the youth of America. The second factor was the nature of the illness. Those with terminal illnesses were doomed. They would get many promises – but no care. In the end, the brutal truth was that terminal cases were best handled by accelerating the inevitable. *Sub Rosa* euthanasia was becoming wide-spread, and the government voluntarily turned its back on prosecuting any cases. *It was in society's best interest*, many in the government said, off the record.

It became the medicine for the *hoi polloi*, never intended for the political elite or well connected. For the masses, twelve to eighteen month waits to see a doctor were routine. Promises of cost reductions from socializing medicine were never realized, and instead of addressing the problems, excuses were given or statistics twisted to adjust reality to what the Administration wanted it to be. Worse yet, mortality rates had risen sharply during the prior decades – the result of fewer doctors wanting to embroil themselves in the low-paying, highly bureaucratic environment of healthcare. Pharmaceutical companies and those creating new medical equipment were controlled by government ministries and produced few new cures or solutions. As nationalized companies, their willingness to take risks, ability to fund research and development, and capacity to attract smart, innovative people had dried up. And even though nothing new was being developed, old diseases – particularly viruses -- were morphing into new, more deadly strains. The potential for an epidemic was growing more real every day.

For any other American, the diagnosis of congestive heart failure or cancer for a woman over sixty-five was terminal. No doctor or hospital would legally be able to take up the case, and if they did help, they were subject to fines and imprisonment.

Most often, the patient's family would just be told to get the person's affairs in order. There were a few countries without socialized medicine, but with carefully constructed catastrophic care programs; these had continued to develop new healthcare solutions. Human hearts and other organs were grown in laboratories and were readily available in these countries. Costs had declined, as companies competed to create more efficient ways of cultivating and harvesting these organs.

However, for Ratner and others in the Administration, they had made sure that healthcare was not a problem for them. They had their own plans, which covered all aspects of their health and that of their family. The only problem was getting the latest treatments in the USSA. Many developed drugs and surgical procedures overseas were still banned in the country, pending decades of additional testing that were required by the monolithic bureaucracies. To get around this, politicians often flew their family member overseas for treatment. However, although it had never been an issue for Ratner and her family, it was now an issue. Given the break-away of the Republic and possibility of a civil war, these countries with more advanced healthcare systems did not want to become embroiled in any of the USSA's issues – particularly a private one involving the First Citizen.

"What do you mean they won't see her?" Ratner screamed at the Canadian deputy minister over the phone. "Tell your minister of health that he *must* authorize it! My mother is suffering from congestive heart failure. She needs treatment!"

"I am sorry, Madam First Citizen," said the woman on the screen in front of her, "We are still evaluating the situation. Our Health Ministry has not yet had time to evaluate your request."

"Not had time!" she yelled.

Ratner had already contacted Russia and China to get help, as both countries had health systems vastly superior to that in the USSA. The health minister in each case had given her the same answer – *We're looking into it, and we'll get back to you.* As for the Islamic States, she had not bothered. Even if they had not regressed in their medical practices, they would not have offered any treatment to an unbeliever.

"Bull sh*t!" Ratner said, undiplomatically. "I want to speak with the prime minister," she demanded.

"The prime minister is out at the moment, but I will leave him a message," said the woman.

Ratner hung up on her. Relations between Canada and the USSA had deteriorated during the years, and the heads of state rarely met together. When Fourier had been president, he had worsened things by revoking the North American Free Trade Agreement or NAFTA, which immediately raised trade barriers between the two countries. The same action had infuriated then President Juan Garcia of Mexico as well, whose country was also affected by the move.

"I need a heart," roared Ratner, "and I need one now!"

The *double entendre* was evident, and no one in her office lost the double meaning of that statement. They all feared her and had come to understand that, unlike the Tin Man, she probably would never find a heart of her own.

*****

CH 12 *Incognito*

The bar was dark, and even though smoking had been banned in the entire state, even outside, the room was filled with thick, billowing gray clouds. It was the rebellious attitude to which some establishments still clung, even though the fines and regulations would easily put them out of business if they were caught.

Thorne pulled his late-model, navy Corvette around the side of the building, letting the vehicle auto shift from *D* to *P*. Not all highways had auto governors strapped to aging telephone poles along roadways, and cars were still equipped to be driven manually by their owners. This was essential in rural areas where things were as they had been for over a century. The bar was secluded, near a small town in Missouri. It was popular with the locals and still hung neon orange, indigo blue, and lemon yellow beer signs from its windows.

The peeling, white door, stood as sentry under the half-lit, flickering neon sign above that read *Danny's Bar and Grill*, with the second *n* in Danny was not working, making it look like *Dany* owned the place instead. Pulling open the door, a plume of silvery-gray smoke escaped into the natural surroundings as Thorne walked inside, letting the door slam with a *crack*.

"Sit where ya' like," said an older woman who was wiping down a table nearby with a damp, red and white wash rag while chatting on her PCD that was pinched between her shoulder and cheek. Her black, matted hair was pulled tight behind her head. She had not aged well, sporting multiple chins and jowls that made her neck look strangled inside her tight, white, waitress uniform. Ignoring Thorne, she casually walked away to continue some conversation on her phone that she had most likely started minutes if not hours earlier.

Thorne picked out a booth in the back where a dangling, red lamp shade was suspended overhead. It was cheesy, but then again, so were most places like that near the small town. He slid across the sticky red-vinyl seat and picked up a paper menu from behind the empty pepper shaker and half-full ketchup bottle that were pressed against the wall. There was even a salt shaker, even though the state health commissioner had ordered all be removed from restaurants for health reasons decades earlier. The same rules had been imposed throughout the country by the federal ministry a year later.

After fifteen minutes, a pudgy waitress with shoulder-length reddish hair that hung straight and uncurled, sauntered over to the counter with an order pad clutched in her fat fingers. Chewing gum, she smacked a few bubbles as she approached, the fat under her arms dangling and swinging back and forth with each step.

"I'll have a glass of Merlot," said Thorne, smiling up at the waitress.

"Merlot?" she asked, not understanding his request. "We don't carry that kind of beer."

"Do you have anything else?" he asked, having hoped there was a full bar someplace in the restaurant.

"Nope. Domestic beer, 'furrin' beer or light beer," she answered.

Thorne sighed heavily. "Okay, so what foreign ones do you have?"

She turned to look back at the kitchen where five bottles were lined up on the counter. "We's got *Heineecan*, *Corona*, *Stella* somethin', *Labatz*, and, uh, *Killuns*."

"But Killians isn't foreign," Thorne answered. The look she gave him could have melted an ice statue. "Okay, then," he continued, "I think I'll just have a Stella. Thanks."

"One Stella. Got it," she said curtly, turning and stomping off in the direction of the bar while snapping her gum all the way there.

It wasn't long before his brown bottle appeared, and not long after that that his appointment showed up. Thorne didn't get up; instead, he sat staring at one of three working TV screens in the place that was broadcasting sports and entertainment twenty-four seven.

"What's the word?" he asked, as the broad-shouldered man joined him, slipping in on the other side of the table.

Colonel Marcus was not your stereotypical drill sergeant of a commander. He was small, quiet and thoughtful. It had been his intellect and keen ability to read people that had propelled him up the ranks of the military. Retired now, he had been instrumental in covert operations in the mountains of Afghanistan and Pakistan in the early days. He peered out through his steel-rimmed spectacles, his deep gray eyes concealing memories of horrible events he had witnessed during his thirty-two years of service.

"We'll assume the ears are on," he said vaguely, referring to the likelihood that there were listening devices somewhere nearby that could and would pick-up their conversation. Even in remote locations, the Red Shirts, the national police force deployed by General Williams, had planted sensitive listening devices around small towns, particularly near local watering holes where the locals would get drunk and most likely have loose lips. The bugs were small and placed inconspicuously inside the establishment while the owner wasn't looking. If certain words were used, the video and audio recording apparatus would trigger, registering every word and image.

"Of course," Thorne replied. "I think that's always a good assumption."

"New equipment has arrived at the office," the colonel said, alluding to military hardware that had been delivered to Fort Carson. "It's hard to say whether it will work. We expect to have a maintenance group check it out and rewire it if necessary." By *re-wire*, he was telling him they would destroy or sabotage it if necessary.

"How many technicians will you have working on it?" he asked.

"There are about twenty-five Kelvin techs being readied," Marcus answered. "I have enough people in the office to let you know if things change. Right now, the equipment may be ready to move within five days. It's likely trucks will take it toward Denver."

Thorne nodded, understanding that twenty-five thousand troops would move north within five days, probably arriving at the border with Wyoming. It was a trip that would only take a few hours, so there would be little warning.

"Do you have anything on any other office?" he asked the colonel, referring to any other part of the country.

"Not at this time," Marcus answered.

"And your girls – how are they?" Thorne asked, this time actually referring to Marcus's older daughters, one of which was married and living in Dallas; the other an attorney practicing law in Washington, D.C. The colonel was worried about the one in DC, as that was the first place the Republic would have to disrupt if things worsened. He'd tried to convince her to leave, but she wouldn't. Her fiancé was there, working for one of the ministries, so her allegiances were skewed toward the Administration rather than those of her father.

"Cora is doing well. She just had another baby -- her third. His name is Joshua; born three weeks ago. He and mother are doing fine. As for Marianne ..." It was hard for him. He loved both daughters a great deal, and the thought that one might be in harm's way was disturbing to him. "... she's still practicing law. Her company is now part of the Ministry of Defense or whatever it's called."

"Do you talk to her often?"

"No, I haven't spoken with Marianne in months now. It's been ... well, you know, difficult. I just hope all this gets worked out."

"I understand," said Thorne, smiling sympathetically and taking a gulp of his Stella.

"And your boss? How is he holding up?" asked Marcus.

"He's busy. Let's just say that. There is a lot on his plate right now, as you can imagine. The home office is buzzing with activity, trying to keep all the projects juggled. There is so much to do in so short of time," he said.

"No, I really can't. It seems daunting to me on your end, anyway. At the branch level, it's a little more manageable, I think."

They chatted on for another hour, taking care not to say something that would be picked up by the monitors. After finishing their drinks, Thorne got up and left, slipping on his sunglasses and pulling his collar up so the facial recognition cameras would have a harder time identifying him.

After Thorne left, the colonel sat watching the TV screen above his head, finishing his beer. He called the waitress over to pay the tab, when two men came into the place. It was obvious who they were. Only the elite Black Corps from the Red Shirt Regiments wore black suits, black shirts and a black tie. Sometimes they were referred to as The Black Suits. These were members of a ruthless group that acted as watchdogs and enforcers for the ruling class. They were feared for their brutality and lack of any sense of justice or due process.

One man had a small, rounded face, and eyes that were narrowly positioned close to his rather large nose. With hair cut to a buzz, his look was as severe and austere as his manner. He walked with a slight limp, nursing some unseen injury to his left foot. His partner was taller, but his black suit was just as misshapen, hanging on him like curtains in a funeral parlor. The look on this second man's face was not as gnarling and nasty as that of his partner, suggesting that he was merely a co-pilot to the lead next to him.

"Do you mind if we have a seat?" asked the shorter man, coming over to the booth.

"No, go right ahead," said the colonel calmly, looking curiously at the men across from him.

"I take it that you are not from around here?" asked the man, not bothering to introduce himself or the other man.

"No. Can't say, I am," Marcus answered, not giving out any more information than he had to. "But, from the looks of it, I'd say the same about you."

Ignoring the comment, the short man asked, "From where then?"

"I'm from Cimarron Hills."

"Oh, you're up by the Air Force Academy, then?" said the man.

Spotting the trap, the colonel politely corrected him. "No, actually, Cimarron is south and east of there."

"Oh, that's right. You are right. You see, I'm not from around here, as you can see," said the man, smiling mischievously. His grin was as dangerous as it was trying to be ingratiating. "Then you work near the Academy, I assume?"

"And why would you assume?" asked the colonel, studying the Black Suit's body language. He could tell there was something awkward about how he was sitting in the booth – at an angle, rather than facing him head-on.

"I just thought you'd work there. You look like a military guy – the short haircut and all."

"No, I'm afraid not," said Marcus, refusing to give up anything more.

The Black Suit sat, staring at the colonel without saying a thing. Smiling and nodding, he waited for Marcus to break the discomfort, but Marcus didn't cave. He returned the smiles and the nods, unwilling to succumb.

Finally, after what seemed like an eternity, the short, Black Suit asked, "I saw you were with someone. He left just as I was arriving. Who is he?"

"A friend."

"How do you know him?"

"Why is that important?"

"It's important to me," said the short, Black Suit, now more threateningly. His smile no longer attempting to mask any suggestion of civility or decorum.

"I see," said the colonel. "Well, he's a friend, just the same."

"May I see your papers?" said the man, sharply, his face stern and stone-like.

"Is that a request or an order?" asked the colonel.

"Give me your papers!" said the man, putting out his hand.

The colonel reached into his coat. At that point, the tall, Black Suit jumped up and pulled out a small, Sig Saur 9mm handgun, pointing it at Marcus. "Slowly, sir!" he barked.

"Hey, I'm only getting my papers, as you asked."

"Slowly, I said!" repeated the tall Black Suit.

Marcus pulled out his USSA passport, his National ID card, and his Travel Authorization Papers or TAPs that allowed him to travel outside a twenty-mile perimeter from his home address. In fact, these were high-level papers that permitted him to travel outside the state of Colorado, but not outside the country; that required a Gold Level that was limited to diplomats and those politically connected. However, these TAPs were forgeries, but they were good ones. He would never be able to get real TAPs – not with his history in military Special Ops. It had become a curse to have served the country, as all ex-military were considered threats to the government and were locked down tight. As for the faked papers, he'd never had a problem using them.

The short Black Suit opened the passport and matched it against the colonel's portrait. Then, he compared the National ID card to the passport and his TAPs. "Why do you have a Bronze Level TAP?" he asked, referring to high level of freedom granted to the colonel.

"My business sometimes takes me outside the Red Zone, the restricted area where I live. I've had Bronze Level status for over a year now," said Marcus.

"What is your business, uh, Mr. Marcus?" asked the man, reading the name from the passport.

"I work for a defense company."

"Name?"

"Hoffman Aircraft."

"Never heard of it."

"SI-Net Google it," said Marcus.

"I'll do more than that," replied the man.

He took out a small device that looked like a large, old-fashioned cell phone. He turned it on and read aloud the information from the papers Marcus had presented. Then he added, "Also, search Hoffman Aircraft and list of employees."

Now the colonel began to worry. As part of his cover, he was supposed to have been setup at the company as an employee, but he had never received full confirmation of this. If the device were hooked up to the National Security Database, which had huge files on every person living in the USSA, including the new Republic, he might be in trouble. Forged papers was a crime punishable by life in prison, although more and more, they were just making these people disappear, as they couldn't afford to keep them incarcerated. The device spoke back. It was a soft, soothing woman's voice, which would determine his fate. "Hoffman Aircraft was owned by Lockheed Martin, prior to the industry's nationalization by the Ministry of Fair Trade. It manufacturers sophisticated guidance systems for missiles. The employee list includes ..."

When the voice began with the A's, the short Black Suit interrupted, "Stop, no, lookup "M" for Marcus, first name." He stopped for a moment to look it up. "First name, Jacob."

Marcus held his breath but acted calmly, as if nothing was of concern.

"... our database shows no listing for a Jacob Marcus."

Marcus didn't move. The Black Suit smiled. "I thought so," he said, removing his own gun and directing it toward the colonel under the table.

However, training had taught Marcus not to panic. Instead, he took a slow, deep breath and let his mind work.

"Thanks, Jane," said the short Black Suit, signing off from the device.

"She didn't find me because I wasn't an employee," said Marcus, trying to buy time and confuse the issue if he could. "I was a contractor, so I wouldn't be listed as an employee. Those are two different lists and two different data bases."

The short Black Suit looked skeptical. "Jane, please check the contractor list at Hoffman Aircraft."

"Checking contractor list," said the computerized woman's voice. It was several seconds by the time she responded.

Meanwhile, the colonel had pulled out a six-inch, switchblade knife from his bag that sat next to him on the booth cushion. He held it in his palm, blade exposed and ready to slam it into the man's leg under the table, hopefully close to an arterial artery.

"Results from the contractor list at Hoffman Aircraft shows ..." There was a pause of three or four seconds while they waited for her to come back on the line. "... that there is a J Marcus listed on the register," said the woman.

"Can you be more specific?" asked the man. "What other information is available?"

"No other information is available. He worked at the facility for two years."

"Worked? Or do you mean works?"

Again, Marcus tried to remain calm.

"Worked. His last assignment was apparently marked as completed."

"When?" asked the short, Black Suit.

Marcus tightened his grip on the knife handle and began to raise the point of the blade to within inches of the man's groin.

"September fifth."

"September fifth of this year?" asked the man.

"Yes, September fifth of this year."

Marcus retracted the knife blade and pushed it up into his sleeve, concealing it from view.

"It's only August fourth," answered the man, disappointed. He thought he'd nailed the colonel, but even he wouldn't pull the trigger on someone without more evidence against them. It was clear there was a problem with the database information. Marcus's contract had another month according to the records. It was hard to tell who was connected with whom, and if the Black Suit erroneously messed with the wrong person, he would be the one facing a fierce inquisition and possible prison time.

"You are correct," answered the woman, not realizing the mistake.

"Fine," said the short, Black Suit, withdrawing his gun and shoving it back into its holster. He handed the passport and other papers back to the colonel. "Here," he said, giving no apologies.

"Am I free to go?" asked Marcus.

The Black Suit didn't reply. He merely got up and motioned to the tall Black Suit to go. Both quickly left, letting the entry door smack against the frame. Climbing back into an unmarked, black sedan, they unceremoniously sped away.

Marcus began breathing again. Worried now, he realized there was someone in his cell that he couldn't trust. No one knew of his meeting, except those in his cell. It was very possible that all the information he'd given Thorne had been a lie. He'd been given most of it from trusted people inside his group. However, now he realized they could no longer be trusted. Worse yet, it would undermine his own credibility with Cheyenne. As a colonel, his name and credibility were everything.

Then, a second thought crossed his mind. There was another who knew about the meeting, and that was the man with whom he'd just met.

*****

CH 13 Contingency Plans

During the next three weeks, things grew worse. The mole had broken the communications with several other cells, revealing the whereabouts of those cells and some of their members to the regime in Washington. Marcus was shocked at the rapidity and ruthlessness of the crackdown. He had gotten a message through to Thorne about what had happened to him after he left the restaurant, and his boss had seemed to understand the implication.

Nothing they could do would prevent the purge going on with other ATLAS Underground cells. First it was the Seattle, Washington cell. The commander there, Major Douglas Foster, vanished from his home in the middle of the night. His wife and daughter were unharmed, but were told by the alleged kidnappers that they would never see their family member again if they spoke to anyone about the break-in. Little did they know, they wouldn't see him whether they did or not. Next was the Chicago cell. The commander had managed to escape his home as the Black Suits broke in, but his second in command was not as fortunate. She was pulled over on the highway and stuffed into an ambulance. Neither the cell commander, nor Thorne had heard from her since then. And the latest was the forced entry into Colonel Marcus's home. They destroyed the house looking for evidence, but he had ensured there was nothing there to link him to the Underground. He assured Thorne that they'd gotten nothing and that his connection with the Republic and with Thorne was still secret.

But these attacks on the cells had struck a dagger into the underground movement. Sumner just hoped they would not be fatal. The Republic needed the cells now more than ever. It lacked the fire power, satellite surveillance and other assets of the USSA, and the only way to survive was to stay one step ahead and use superior strategy and tactics. It had worked throughout history. Underdogs, confronted by superior opponents, had come out on top using a different paradigm or different approach. It would be the same for the Republic. They only had to find it.

Sumner took Thorne aside, into an office that adjoined his own. "Thorne, have we made any progress in finding the mole in Colorado Springs?" he asked. "I see it's been devastating to our efforts in other cities across the USSA. They've managed to destroy many of our cells."

"Not yet, sir," responded Thorne. "But, we will. It's just going to take time." His air was one of steadiness, yet detachment.

Sumner understood full well that they might never find out who it was. Back in the 1940s and 50s the British had a double agent at the highest levels within MI5. It was only later, in the 1960s that Kim Philby was identified as the traitor. By then, he'd already boarded a plane and was living in Russia, safe from the reaches of British officials and their justice. The information coming in from other cells was now at a trickled pace from what it had been earlier. They didn't have to be told that it was all because of the lack of trust within the ranks. They didn't know who they could trust and who they couldn't. A message to the mole could result in their death or someone else within their cell. Each cell was a family unit. They worked side-by-side all day and sometimes all night. They had each other's back — or so they thought. The mere fact that there was one amongst them who could not be trusted tore at the very fabric of what made the entire system work. That had to be mended quickly. Without that, the ATLAS Underground was doomed.

Regardless of the intel from the cells, Sumner and his Cabinet had to assume that the USSA was preparing to go to war against them. With the opening of their economy and elimination of most taxes, tariffs, trade regulations, and the structuring of laws to promote specifically the talents of entrepreneurs and innovative companies, the ATLAS Republic was thriving. But with that freedom was the age-old problem of allowing in saboteurs and infiltrators bent on destroying what they were trying to build. Sumner had beefed-up the FBI to its maximum capability — to ferret out miscreants and other organized groups or plants from the USSA who would destabilize their government and operation. They had designed an elaborate screening process to catch most imposters, but there was always a chance of someone slipping through the cracks.

Sumner held weekly meetings of his Cabinet, and with Shea at his side, he ran a tight ship, demanding status reports on new initiatives to gain a military advantage from strategy and unique weaponry. A thriving manufacturing base had been wooed into supporting their cause, allocating much of their production output to the military effort. The population also understood what was at stake, willing to sacrifice luxury items and even some staples, allowing the government in Cheyenne to stockpile them for the long-haul. A USSA-imposed embargo on them, sealing off their Gulf of Mexico ports, was expected at any time.

"How is our copper and tin production?" asked Sumner, directing the Cabinet meeting. "And when will we have a sufficient six-month stockpile of circuit boards from our electronics manufacturing?" His Cabinet secretaries each came prepared with their answers, giving him the information he needed or telling him they'd follow up to get the data.

Most important was the concern over water supplies. The Great Lakes and other major waterways were largely in the hands of the USSA. Portions of the Mississippi and Missouri rivers were under Republic control, but if the USSA cutoff these areas of access the shortage would be more ruinous than running out of oil.

"What is our contingency plan for water?" Shea asked, looking over at the head of the joint chiefs of staff. "Our aquifers will only last about eight months if we get into an all-out confrontation with them."

General Ward opened his computer and pushed a button, projecting a 3D map into the center of the room. The outline of the old USA showed prominently, with an Earth-shot rendition of the ecosystems of each region. He touched a point near Chicago, bringing the entire Great Lakes Region into fuller view.

"As you can see," Ward said, before clearing his throat, "the territory around Lake Michigan is under the secure control of the USSA, as are all the other Great Lakes;

however, as we all realize, not only is Lake Michigan a source of fresh water, it is a strategic stronghold. The USSA, of course, has many air assets it can project from there, but any ground troops could also be launched in greater numbers from bases around the lakes. Next would be the Mississippi River," he said, zooming into the portion just north of Memphis, Tennessee. "Here is where the areas controlled by the USSA and those by the Republic meet. Unfortunately, it is possible that the regime could dam the Mississippi north of this point to cut off vital fresh water to the south – the area under our control. This is a major weakness for our position."

"That would take some time to build," said Ash Nugyn from Treasury.

"They wouldn't do that anyway," said Loretta White. "That would flood the entire Midwest region, killing millions."

For a moment, there was silence in the room. Everyone was contemplating what had just been said.

White spoke again, amidst the quiet. "I'm serious. Ratner may be dark, but she's not that evil. She wouldn't do that to her own people – surely, not."

Ward frowned and shook his head. "No, not to *her* own people – to *our* people. To citizens of the Republic."

"I think the general is right," said Sumner, stepping in. "To her, we are no longer Americans. Hell, even if we were Americans, I doubt it would matter. No, we are more alien to them than the Russians or Chinese. We *are* their enemy now. We have to understand that."

"My god," said the secretary, in a murmur under her breath. She stared at the president as if he had sentenced her own family to the gulag.

"It is troubling to consider, but they have the technology and the capability of damming up the mighty Mississippi," answered Ward. "My estimates are that if the river were bottled at the convergence of the Ohio and Miss Rivers at the tip of Illinois it would flood an area larger than Lake Superior, covering two-thirds of Illinois, the eastern half of Missouri, and much of Iowa. St. Louis would be entirely underwater, as would thousands of other, smaller towns up and down the river. The impact downstream towards Louisiana would also be devastating, as the fertile land of the south would turn arid, and it is possible the Gulf of Mexico could rush back into the void where the delta from the river runs into it, killing all marine life that thrive on fresh and brackish water."

"How would we stop it?" asked Sumner.

"We would have to rely on our Underground to let us know what is being planned," said Ward. "We have to keep this network open and operating. If sabotage is necessary, then we'll employ it. Dams are easily breached if necessary, and harder to rebuild. However, the rising of the waters would be quick, and we'd have little time to react." The general looked at Ingram, as if shifting the weight of the world upon his shoulders.

"I understand, general," said the Secretary of State, attending the meeting. "We will try to get whatever information we can from our Canadian friends. Unfortunately, recently they've been more close-lipped about what's going on, particularly after they shared the manufacturing data of the USSA with us."

"Why do you think that is?" asked White, dusting off a speck of lint from her jacket coat.

"We think Ratner is putting pressure on them," said Ingram.

"Like what?" asked Nugyn. "Do we have any proof of that?"

"Yes, actually," said Sumner. "It appears our friend in the White House has secretly threatened Prime Minister MacDonald using old, mafia-style tactics. I was informed that the prime minister's youngest daughter was cornered by a man just outside her school. The girl's bodyguards were neutralized and she was told that if her daddy cooperated with the American Republic that he and his buddies would be

back to kill her and the rest of her family. They are still investigating how access was gained to the little girl and why the Canadian Security Intelligence Service agents were so easily eliminated."

There was quiet in the room. Each person was reflecting on the implication – that if Ratner was willing to kill a prime minister and his family, what else was she willing to do? Worse yet, what might she do to them and their families?

"I think I understand," said Loretta White.

"We all understand very well … too well," Sumner answered, empathizing with everyone sitting around the table.

*****

CH 14 Manhattan Project

Their first meeting was held inside a small lecture hall traditionally used for first-year psychology students at the University of Texas in Austin. Had the university administration known the true nature of their session, they would not have been pleased. Austin, unlike most other parts of Texas, was a healthy repository of liberal thinking within the state. A group dedicated to defending and possibly saving a fledgling democratic, capitalistic state would have been an anathema to them. Yet, fifteen highly entrepreneurial, brilliant innovators from different industries and walks of life sat in the same room, united under the same cause.

To keep her identify clandestine, Shea had registered under the name of Mildred Peabody with the university's Events Department. She had laughed at the name that one of her assistants had come up with on the spot. "Mildred Peabody?" Shea had answered her. "Are you kidding me? Couldn't you come up with a name a little less sexy?" Her assistant had come back with other names, like Edith Winterthorp and Elsa Tinkleberry but it was Mildred Peabody that had eventually won in the vote count.

"Thank you for coming and participating in this project," said Shea, opening the meeting and looking out over the intelligent eyes staring at her.

The attendees sat before her in seats as they had undoubtedly occupied as college students years, if not decades, earlier. The men and women covered the demographic spectrum, from Asian to African, from PhD to college drop-out, and from young to old. Their commonality was in their innate ability to create something from nothing and in their remarkable levels of intelligence. None was stupid – far from it. One young scientist in the group had become a tenured professor at Princeton at the age of nineteen. His field, simply put, was M^2-theory – the still unresolved *Theory of Everything* that would, physicists hoped, describe how everything in the universe worked. At age sixteen, he had proved mathematically the theoretical existence of multiverses and the existence of twenty-six dimensions, rather than the eleven that had been previously thought. However, the concepts were so difficult to comprehend, that few on earth came close to wrapping their heads around what Dr. Lin had derived. The theory had been named M^2 to replace the previous M-theory concept widely viewed as the most promising at the time. The joke was that neither the M nor the M^2 monikers actually meant anything, except possibly "mad."

"In many ways," Shea began, "the project we are about to embark upon is like the Manhattan Project begun in 1942 that, as you know, led to the development of the atomic bomb. It got its name from the thousands of people who worked on it in secret in Manhattan at Columbia University and other sites around the city. All told, five thousand came and went from these buildings without anyone else knowing about what it was that they were doing. And, of the 130 thousand who worked on it, most didn't know the objective.

"In this day and age, things are different. We have nanotechnology, synthetic computing, AI robotics, and other technologies that have replaced humans. However, you are here because there is one thing we have yet to reproduce digitally – creativity and innovation. I'm sure it will happen eventually, but for now we have you," she said, smiling and gesturing to the fifteen people in front of her.

"Like the Manhattan Project, this will be *above* top-secret. Also, like that project, our goal is to create a system that will enable the ATLAS Republic to survive an all-out attack from the USSA or any other power in the world who wishes to destroy our new nation. Given the military capabilities at the hands of those who wish to do us harm, this will be a daunting task. As you can imagine, we have limited resources. But what we lack in strategic assets, we make up for in something else we've created – freedom and independence. ATLAS is a place where we can dream big dreams; think unthinkable thoughts; and create that which is thought unattainable. We are unchained in this new Republic. We have revolted, and we will rise to achieve the impossible. That is what we encourage ... no ... we pray this group will be able to do – the impossible. Your charge is to dream, think and create that impossible. We are all counting on you.

"Now, are there any questions?" she asked.

One hand went up. It was Dr. Lin.

"Yes, Dr. Lin?" Shea asked, expecting some erudite question which she would have no possibility of answering. "Please keep it as simple as possible, as I am only a layman here," she said with a smile.

"Okay, Attorney General Disone. I'll try," he answered. "What's for lunch?"

After the laughter subsided, the group met together to brain storm, coming up with unique and, sometimes, absurd remedies to the monumental task facing them. They would continue their discussions for the remainder of the week, narrowing their ideas down to three they felt had the greatest potential for success within the confines of the budget with which they had to work.

The list was received in Cheyenne, where Shea reviewed it. Her eyes brightened as she read the major headings of each topic. There was little that she understood within the detailed text of each idea, but she would leave that to others to decipher.

Sumner called her later in the day to find out what options had been proposed. "So, is there anything good in the bunch?" he asked.

"I think you'll be pleased JC – very pleased," she retorted.

*****

CH 15 Johns Hopkins

The First Citizen's mother grew weaker each day, deteriorating rapidly during the span of just three weeks. Her decline alarmed Ratner, who became more and more desperate to find a synthetic or lab-grown heart. Finally, through illicit connections in South America, she managed to smuggle in a synthetic heart that was fabricated in China. It arrived in cryogenic suspension at Johns Hopkins Hospital in Baltimore, a mere forty-five miles from Washington, D.C. As the doctors were on the government's payroll, it was not hard to encourage them to overlook the illegality of their surgical procedure to install the new heart. The procedure lasted a mere two hours, and while Ratner was not present, she did contact the hospital once the surgery was completed.

"So, how is she doing?" the First Citizen asked, with concern. It was rare to see this stone-cold woman exude any emotion, especially one of caring or tenderness.

"We believe she will be fine," said the doctor. "Everything went smoothly. She should be up and around the hospital halls in no time."

Ratner visited her later that day, getting off the elevator accompanied by six Secret Service personnel. The entire wing of the hospital had been emptied of all patients so the mother of the First Citizen could be left undisturbed. These patients were stuffed five and six to a room – those normally intended to hold only two at a time. Even contagious patients were forced into rooms with others rather than be left in hallways to infect everyone in the hospital.

A nurse opened the door for Ratner so she could enter the hospital room. It was expansive and was filled with flowers. White roses were her favorite, and they filled nearly every space available. In front of her lay her mother, sitting up in bed but taking little notice of who had arrived. Finally, as her daughter approached, she glanced over at her. "It's about time you came," said her mother with a surly edge.

"How are you, mother?" Ratner asked, taking hold of her fingers. "You look good for someone just out of surgery."

"I've been out of surgery for several hours now," said her mother, her mouth turned downward in a perpetual frown.

Ratner looked like her mother in many ways. Both were small and almost frail-looking. Both had been born with chestnut brown hair. They shared rounded faces, a turned-up nose, a high forehead, and a lack of any earlobe that connected their ears to their heads. But even more striking were their coal black eyes that sat heavy and sallow within their faces. Whatever morsel of emotion she held within her, the leader of the USSA had gotten it from her father rather than her mother. It was unlikely that Ratner's mother had ever felt any love or tenderness for her mother as her daughter was showing for her. It was not hard to see where the family gene pool was concentrated.

"I know," said Ratner. "I came as soon as I could." She motioned to one of her attendants who produced some more roses in a crystal vase and a box. "I got you something, I don't know if you'll like it, but ..."

"Well, what is it?" asked her mother, rolling her head towards her daughter.

"You'll have to open it," said Ratner, handing it to her. The box was a shiny, made of silver with a matching bow.

"Jewelry?" her mom asked.

"Well, yes, but it's something you don't have. I thought you might like it. It's from South Africa. There are only three in the world. You can wear it on a night out sometime."

"I can't open the box. You'll have to do it," said her mother, pushing the box back at her.

The First Citizen coaxed the sides of the small, silver box and popped off the top. Inside was a black, velvet bag with a drawstring. Ratner loosened the cord and pulled the mouth of the bag open. "Open your palm, mother," she instructed.

Her mother feebly held out her palm, and Ratner let the precious contents drop from the bag. Out fell a short, platinum necklace chain studded with large, emerald-cut diamonds. The diamonds encompassed the entire chain with the exception of one large, rather ugly stone in the center.

"What do you think?" asked Ratner, watching her mother's reaction with anticipation.

There was little movement in her mother's face but she looked over the item with the scrutiny of a microbiologist peering into a microscope. "It's dreadful," she finally answered.

"Really? Dreadful? That's all you can say?"

"Yes, dear. It's dreadful. What the hell is this lump of concrete in the middle here?" asked her mother.

"Mother, that's a stone from the Chinese Mars mission that just returned. I had to bribe some people pretty high up over there to get it. It's one of only twenty pieces in the world. You should feel special."

"Looks like a rock to me," said her mother, dropping the precious bundle back into the box and tossing it on the hospital stand next to her bed.

Ratner should have been used to this abuse. She'd suffered under this disapproving matriarch for her entire life, and the rejections never got easier. She had hoped that by becoming the leader of the country, she would finally garner the recognition and attention that she'd always wanted from her. But, it was obvious that even that had not been enough.

"Alright, mother. You go ahead and get some sleep. I'll come back tomorrow. Hopefully, you'll be in a better mood," said Ratner, kissing her mother on the forehead before leaving the room.

But, overnight, complications arose, and Ratner's mother had a violent response to medications given to her by the government-funded staff. Most medications were prescribed by computers and administered robotically. These systems, once the gem of the world, were now grossly antiquated. Lacking the resources to maintain them, they had fallen into a state of disrepair. The irony was that although Ratner had spent hundreds of thousands of taxpayer dollars to procure a new heart for her mother, she had not realized how much the entire medical system with the country had degraded.

When Ratner learned of the complication, she rushed to Baltimore, ordering that her VH-3E helicopter be readied immediately. She arrived only thirty minutes later at Johns Hopkins, rushing through the front door of the wing where her mother was being treated.

"What's going on?" Ratner asked a doctor who was standing in the doorway to greet her and take her upstairs.

"Her heart stopped, Madam. They're just trying to get it going again," she answered, matter-of-factly, as if it happened every day to the mother of the First Citizen.

Ratner watched from outside the room as they worked on her mother, giving her jolts of electricity to get her heart started again, and injecting a stimulant drug into her IV to prevent heart arrhythmia.

"Come on, Ms. Ratner," said the doctor in the room, giving the heart another jolt. "Come on. You need to come back to us, Ms. Ratner. Come on!" The body jerked again, as the Joules of electricity pulsed into her body.

Ratner couldn't see the heart monitor, but she could hear it. It was morbidly monotone, indicating no pulse or life. "What are they doing? Tell them they have to get her heart going again. Whatever it takes. They'd better get that started!" Trembling from nerves and fear, she looked on helplessly through the clear glass, her mother's body lifeless in the bed. Waiting only a few more minutes, Ratner pushed aside an aide and barged into the room.

"You'd better get her back!" she screamed, getting a surprised look from the doctor in charge who was readying the machine for another jolt.

"We're doing everything we can, Madam," said the physician in a controlled, flat tone.

As her mother's heart refused to beat, Ratner's was beating at a torrid pace, and she could feel the perspiration wetting her temples and dripping down the sides of her cheeks. She wiped them off with a towel one of the attendants gave her and promptly threw it back, expecting it to be disposed of for her. "Mother, come on!" she mumble to herself. "You can't leave me! You can't!"

For the next hour, they tried more electricity, stimulation drugs and direct heart message. Finally, the doctor put down the paddles. She looked up and saw Ratner, pale and shaking, at the edge of the bed. "I'm sorry, Madam. We gave it all we could. We just couldn't save her. She's gone."

"No! You have to keep going! I don't care how long it takes. I want her back!" demanded the First Citizen. "Get back at it!" she shouted.

They spent another twenty minutes repeating all they had done earlier — still without success. Finally, Ratner's chief of staff, Clancy Holt, took her by the shoulders and helped her out of the room. Ratner didn't cry, but instead, sat on a bench just outside the room, somber and emotionless.

"Do you want to stay or go, Madam?" Holt asked her, sitting beside her, but afraid to touch his boss or give her any comfort.

"Take me back to Washington," she answered. "I've got work to do."

But that was not the end of the episode. The fury of the First Citizen could not be exaggerated. Back at the White House, she exclaimed, "I want every doctor involved, every nurse, every practitioner, every orderly and every scrub fired and put in prison! I want this hospital closed down — every lab, every surgical room, every closet shuttered! Then, I want it bulldozed and anything that's combustible burned! Do you hear me!"

When the Minister of Health and Human Dignity tried to intervene to calm things and ask the First Citizen to rethink what she was doing, the minister was also fired.

Johns Hopkins University Hospital — in compliance with her Executive Order -- was burned to the ground.

*****

CH 16 Tracking Johnny

The dark clouds of war were beginning to gather on the horizon as Sumner granted Johnny a significant sum from the limited state treasury to develop a more mobile version of his phaser weapon. After only a month, Johnny had devised a prototype to be used on tanks and a smaller one for Humvees. However, he still had to shrink the platform even more to create the handheld version Sumner wanted. Johnny had one month to make that happen, and then he'd have to demonstrate it in front of the joint chiefs.

Johnny flew to Cheyenne to give an update to General Ward and others on the status of his project. Things were progressing, he told them. But, he needed more time, more money or both. They told him he could have more money and help, but not more time. He had only two weeks left. The date was fixed; the demonstration etched in stone. He had to produce or they would abandon the experiment, he was told. Refusing more people to help him, Johnny said he would meet the deadline — somehow.

"And you believe you will be able to prove the capability of the new mobile platform?" asked General Ward looking at Johnny's own test results.

"Yes sir. I have been able to reduce the equipment's footprint to something a little larger than a backpack. The power source for this is hydrogen capsules," said Johnny, holding one up. It was no larger than a .38 caliber bullet, with a stainless-steel casing. "There is enough mass, approximately three grams, in one of these to generate the energy needed to obliterate an entire army, including tanks, howitzers, mobile missile systems, rocket launchers, armored personnel carriers and infantry fighting vehicles. Calculated, it's approximately the amount of energy from a thirty-two-kiloton warhead. Calculated, it would be ..."

"I'll take that as a yes," said the general, interrupting. "We just need to prove the technology, Johnny. You can understand that. So, have the backpack system ready for the demonstration within two weeks. "If it works as you advertise, you will be lauded as the next Einstein. You'll be rich and famous."

"It's not about the money," said Johnny, his face rigid and unemotional. "It's about our survival." Johnny said, body more pronouncedly stooped than Shea had ever seen it before. "It's about the survival of all of us — throughout the world. The threat of a nuclear holocaust must be eliminated. Using this laser technology, we can detonate those warheads too, before they ever reach us."

General Ward reported Johnny's progress to both Shea and Defense Secretary, Templeton. "He says he can deliver."

"Do you believe him?" asked Templeton, unconvinced.

Ward thought for a moment. "You know," he answered. "Yes, I believe I do."

"If there is anyone who can, it's Patrick … I mean Johnny," said Shea. "The man I knew is still inside him. I know he'll pull through for us."

"And one more thing," said Ward. "He doesn't even care about the fame and fortune that will come from his invention. He really doesn't care."

It was odd that a man who had once been such a proponent of a free and capitalistic society would be so unaffected by the possibility of wealth. However, as Shea thought about it, *What was wealth without freedom and family? It was, indeed, all about priorities and what was important in life. Perhaps his memory loss and the trauma of whatever he had gone through had caused a realignment within him. Yet, at this point, both were threatened with the real possibility of having neither.*

After a few days, Shea got a call.

"What are you doing?" said Johnny, obviously infuriated over something.

"I don't know what you're talking about, Johnny. What's the problem?" she asked him.

"You know perfectly well what the problem is. You're watching me! You've got me under surveillance. There's someone outside my apartment right now. I can see them down there, sitting in their black sedan eating dinner out of a drive-through paper bag."

"Johnny, we don't have anyone watching you. I swear. Now what exactly do you see outside your apartment?"

Johnny looked out the second story window of his apartment, slowly pulling back the maize-colored curtains. "Like I said, the car, it's just a plain sedan – black, four-door."

"Can you tell me the type of car? Or can you read the license plate?"

"It's black; that's all I can tell," said Johnny.

"Let me call you back," said Shea, hanging up and dialing another number. "Director Hawkins, this is Attorney General Disone," she said, speaking to the head of the FBI. "Did you send men to monitor John Johnny? Is he being watched?"

"No ma'am," Hawkins answered.

"He claims there's a black sedan outside his apartment. Men are watching him."

"What color did you say?" asked the FBI director.

"Black."

"No, we use gray, anyway. Gray SUVs – not sedans"

"Who uses black sedans then?" asked Shea.

"Could be anybody. But it's definitely used by the Ministry of Internal Inquiry – their FBI," said Hawkins.

"That's the USSA, then."

"It could be."

Hanging up, Shea called Johnny on the other line; his image coming up and floating in mid-air. "Johnny, you're sure the car is black? It's not gray?" asked Shea, attempting to reconfirm.

"It's *black*!"

"Johnny, look outside now and tell me exactly what you see."

"A black sedan with two ... uh, well, no. There isn't anyone in the car now," he answered, with a startled surprise.

"Johnny, you have to get out of your apartment. Those aren't our men. I don't know who they are, but they don't belong to the Republic."

There was a knock at the apartment door, but it sounded more like the banging of fists. "Mr. Johnny, this is the apartment sup, Mr. Leonard. I need to come into your apartment and check some plumbing problems that were reported downstairs."

"Sh*t!" whispered Johnny into the phone. "What the hell do I do?" he asked.

"Mr. Johnny! I must insist that you open this door right away. The plumbing problem is severe, and unless we fix it others in the building will be affected. Mr. Johnny?"

But there was no hesitation. The sup never finished his sentence. Instead, there were three shots fired outside his apartment door that went through the door, shattering a vase on a table and chipping off wood from a chair nearby. The door ruptured as the entire jam splintered into pieces, and two men in black suits rushed in. Behind them lay the apartment superintendent, his body crumpled over in front of the entrance and blood spreading from an unseen wound somewhere beneath him onto the floral-patterned carpet outside in the hallway.

The Black Suits looked around, guns drawn, but the room was empty. Seeing the open window at the far end of the room, they rushed over to it and scanned the alleyway below for any movement. There was no one in sight.

"Briggs, he's down there someplace. You need to find him. He can't get very far," said one of the men, talking into his watch-sized PCD. Both rushed out of the apartment, jumping steps to get down to the bottom and continue their pursuit. Minutes passed before the black sedan screeched its tires, roaring away down the street. Eventually, these noises died away, leaving nothing but the slow, metronomic ticking of an old-fashioned wall clock over the faux fireplace in the den.

A few moments later, Johnny came out of the closet where he'd been hiding behind some clothes piled up against the wall. He waited a few more minutes and then took the stairs down into the basement where there was a door that exited into a small, hidden alley between his building the one directly behind it. He took nothing with him except a small, dime-sized storage disk. But that was all he needed.

***

Republic men picked Johnny up not far from his apartment. He had been careful not to keep any secret documents at his apartment except for the dime-sized file keeper he had attached to his keyless car entry fob. He knew his apartment would be completely destroyed by the Black Suits looking for him once they figured out that he'd never left his apartment. There was no reason for him to go back.

"So, you think there's been another leak?" asked Sumner, after his briefing.

"We don't know, sir. All we do know is that there were few who knew where Johnny was living. Fewer knew what he was working on," said Templeton.

"What do you know about Johnny's girlfriend?" Shea asked, her arms crossed defensively. The question came across more like an accusation than a question.

"Johnny said they'd just met at a diner. It was in Sioux City, apparently, before he moved on to Rapid City to setup his laboratory," Hawkins said, defending his background-checking procedure. "We went to Sioux City and checked it out – where they stayed, who their friends were, where they worked – all of it. There were no irregularities."

"Where is she from? What kind of family does she have? Where did she go to school?" she asked, peppering him with questions.

"Whoa! Slow down!" said Sumner. "What's all this about? Do you think she's passing along secrets?"

"Maybe."

"Or is this personal?" asked Hawkins.

Shea clenched her jaw. She wasn't looking for a fight, but she wasn't about to start one either.

"I think you should take a deep breath, Shea," said Sumner, coming to her defense. "We're only trying to find out who could have passed along the information."

"So, what *do* we know about her?" Shea persisted.

"Her dad was a farmer, and they lived not far from Sioux City. She'd lived there her whole life. Her mother died when she was little. I think she said she was only twelve when it happened. She has two brothers, both older. She told agents that one lives in Atlanta, and the other in Washington. She talks to the one in Atlanta once a week or so. The other – not so much."

"What about the one in Washington? He may have ties to Ratner and the Administration?"

"We've done a thorough search and found no ties between him and the Administration or anyone else of influence there. He schedules cars for the RTS, the Robotic Taxi Service, in town."

"But there must be more going on here. Information is being passed along multiple avenues, not just from this project. We have the Underground Cells too. It's not Johnny's girlfriend. Rest assured of that," said Sumner, offering reassurance.

Shea was still dissatisfied but wasn't going to press the issue any further.

Meanwhile, Sumner ordered that Johnny be secured behind the fortified walls of National Security Administration building. Sumner had also insisted on moving all his experiments and prototypes from the warehouse in South Dakota to Cheyenne. Johnny had protested, but after the incident at his apartment, he had little recourse but to watch as the trucks arrived to move his prized experiments. He was less than happy, and it showed in his work. Rather than making huge strides in the lab, his progress after that point was measured only in small incremental changes.

When asked about his readiness for the joint chiefs meeting, Johnny would only say, "I'll be ready when I'm ready."

Sumner had asked Shea to contact him and try to smooth things over, but even she found it difficult to reach him. "Are you worried?" Sumner asked her, wondering whether Johnny would come through for them.

"No, Patrick is fine. He'll deliver, if he said he would," she answered.

"Patrick would come through, but will Johnny?" asked Sumner.

For that, Shea had no answer.

*****

CH 17 Digging Deep

The mole had still not been discovered, but information Thorne said he had received from two of his commanders suggested that it was either in his Colorado Springs unit, the Chicago unit or that in Washington, DC.

Colonel Marcus had sent a series of disinformation bulletins, hoping that something would circulate back from the USSA side of intelligence gathering. He had gotten a "hit" on one of the communiqués that suggested the Republic had captured a NORAD ICBM silo in North Dakota, one of many intercontinental ballistic missile bases still operated by the USSA's North American Aerospace Defense Command Center. In fact, these were supposed to have been dismantled many years earlier by the Fourier Administration as part of its unilateral disarmament program. Russia, China, and Saudi Arabia had taken little notice, and had resumed building mobile missile launch platforms instead. At the time, the dismantling had been made public with much fanfare about how the USA was leading by example in world peace efforts; however, only two of sixty-one sites were touched.

"What do you have for me?" asked Thorne, on a secure line.

"It's either my number three commander or my personal attaché," said Marcus.

"Talk to me," said Thorne, stiffly.

"Major Brathwaite has a stellar record. He served in the conflicts in the Middle East and in Asia. He was never awarded a meritorious honor for his special ops group capture of a high-level Islamic Al Qaeda operative in 2035, which he deserved. But he's demonstrated his loyalty to us by infiltrating the Air Force base here – Peterson – and obtaining top secret documents for us about the movements in and out of the base together with changes at NORAD headquarters there. As for my attaché, Sergeant Major Tullis, I really can't believe he would turn on us either. He's young – only twenty-six – but he's single and has no outside family around here. He's quiet, but has always executed missions that were given to him. Sir, I just don't know."

"Why do you think it's one of those two, then?"

"I only gave the intel about the NORAD facility to those two individuals."

"No one else?"

"Not other than the head of the cell in Washington, D.C."

"Max Burger?"

"Yeah, Colonel Burger."

"I've known Max Burger for years. He and I used to spar regularly when Congressional appropriations for EG would hit a snag. He was hard-nosed, but fair. I just can't see him ..."

"I don't know, sir. The problem is we don't have any hard evidence either way. We have to find out for sure. At this point, we need to go with another round of disinformation. We have to know."

"You're right," Thorne replied. "You have the green light. Do as you need to."

Thorne ended the call but was still uneasy about things. Swiveling around to his desk, he said, "Computer, pull up all information you have on Colonel Marcus."

"Researching Colonel Marcus," answered the computer. It took a few moments before his screen was full of reference points. The first was Marcus's personnel file from the Republic's Top Secret Database. His digital picture showed the colonel as he had been some ten years earlier, apparently not having been updated recently. Thorne scanned the pages for anything unusual before coming to an obscure entry in his personal webpage – one he had taken down just before the Republic had declared its independence from the USSA. In part, the entry read:

> Jack recently returned from a trip to Nagoya, Japan, where he consulted for the New People's Dynasty. Japan, having been overrun by China during the closing days of the Sino-Nipponese War, is in the process of being turned into a governorship and may be renamed, Eastern China within the next few years. Mr. Marcus has experience in organizing military units and understands the Chinese methods for deploying troops for offensive and defensive purposes.

In another reference, he found:

> Samuel and Jessica Marcus were married June 2, 1993, in St. James Church in Roxbury Mass. Sam met his future wife at a Socialist Party fund raiser, and they dated two years prior to their union.

> Samuel and Jessica are Jack's parents. He also has three brothers – two older and one younger. The eldest brother is also a member of the Socialist Party, and is still a card-carrying agent of the organization.

Thorne threw his chair back, shaking his head. "Crap!" he said to himself. "How could we have missed this?" His next action was to make a call. "Mr. President, this is Thorne. I need to talk with you."

*****

CH 18 Diplomacy

"Send it," said Ratner gesturing for the message to be sent. "This should get their attention," she added.

The message was delivered via satellite coupling and beamed down to all cell phones, satellite TV sets and any other electronic devices using satellite technology. Consequently, millions of citizens living within the Exclusion Zone -- the label the Administration attached to the ATLAS Republic -- received the following message.

BULLETIN: To All Living within the Exclusion Zone --

It is with anguish that we deliver this message to all those misled republic citizens who have been brainwashed into believing that their current leaders are acting in their interest. We can assure you that they are not.

Were you aware that your leader, JC Sumner, was having an affair with his attorney general and that there are serious questions about his involvement in the death of his wife who died on their ranch last year? Were you aware that together Sumner and Disone are secretly plotting to strip you of all your rights? They are building prisons at a dizzying pace to incarcerate anyone who opposes them. Did you know they are planning to initiate a war against the USSA, to conscribe your sons and daughters, to sacrifice them in an unwinnable war, and for what?

As we speak, they are scheming to create some excuse – some reason -- to go to war against the USSA. Think about it. How will your small country fight against the power and military might of the USSA, the nation that won three world wars. If they try, millions will die. Is that what you really want?

All these things are true. So, stop it now, before it's too late! Rise-up and revolt against the people who are deceiving you. Take back your lives and your rights and demand that your leaders abandoned their reckless ways and return to the security and protection of the Motherland. The USSA represents safety for you and your family. Don't let Sumner's and Disone's self-serving affair destroy you and your children for generations to come.

Very truly,

Those Concerned for Your Wellbeing

The message spread like wildfire, copied and recopied throughout the Republic. People got scared. Was this the ultimatum they had feared? Were these things true about their leaders? Who could they trust? It sent everyone in the Republic into an uproar – just as Ratner had planned.

Within a day, Sumner got on the Republic's private version of SI-net with a live video bulletin addressing the message the First Citizen had dropped onto his citizenry. It had been her attempt to destroy his cause without firing a shot. Pragmatic and calculating, the move was smart, and Sumner had to have an equally effective retort.

Presenting himself in a starched white shirt, dark suit and patriotic red, white and blue tie, he sat behind a desk and addressed the people, just as U.S. presidents had since the time of JFK and LBJ in the 1960s.

"My fellow Americans," he began, having memorized his speech, "By now most of you have received or heard about the message distributed to the people of the Republic by the current First Citizen of the USSA, Angel Ratner. In it, she claims, among other things, that as leaders of this sovereign country we are intent upon enslaving our masses and leading you into a war against the USSA – a war that she claims we cannot win. She has also made many other allegations about me, the Attorney General, and others that are patently untrue.

"I am sure that to a large extent, my address to you tonight is unnecessary. It has only been a year since we broke away from the chains of the USSA – those that once enslaved us. The lies and treachery of their leadership then are not forgotten today. Their motives are clear, and so are ours. They have always stood for big government and less personal freedom; we, on the other hand, declared our independence from their tyranny, much as Washington, Madison, Jefferson and others did from their tyrants, the British.

"Yet, our Republic and the USSA share one thing in common; we both wish to avoid another Civil War. No one wishes to revisit that dark event that nearly destroyed America over two hundred years ago. Some seven hundred, fifty-eight thousand died in that conflict. That is something that should never happen again.

"But we have lost many of our own already in the current battle against oppression by the First Citizen. Those in the Cheyenne statehouse were among the first to die for our cause – our belief in freedom. Personally, I lost my wife, Maria, not to my hand, but to criminal agents from the USSA. So, for the sake of those who have already given their lives, we cannot abandon our mission. We cannot let those who now subjugate the people of the USSA be able to once again claim dictatorial rights over us.

"It is likely that the USSA may create an event that will try to provoke us into a conflict with them – they would like nothing more. Instead, we wish only peaceful coexistence. Neither side should seek the destruction of the other.

"At the same time, if threatened by force, the ATLAS Republic will defend herself. The USSA must understand that. We will fight. We will defend our sovereignty. And, we will be the ones who will emerge victorious if this is the road they choose to take.

"But, I wish nothing but harmony between our two nations – a continent where independent countries can agree to disagree and can work with each other for mutual benefit, rather than mutual destruction.

"May God bless you, and may God bless the ATLAS Republic."

It was brief, but most thought it sincere and effective. The SI-net blogs lit up after the speech, calling it one of the greatest by a politician in a long time. Others called it Churchillian.

Unwilling to back down, Ratner pressed on. She continued her barrage of allegations, each time ramping up the rhetoric. Her charges ranged from the serious – that Sumner had several illegitimate children from various women he'd worked with while in Washington – to the ridiculous – that China was secretly masterminding and financing the entire ATLAS Republic movement. To Sumner's credit, he addressed each allegation as it came, not letting Ratner or anyone in her regime gain the upper hand. Yet, he felt he should also try diplomacy. During these exchanges, Sumner sent Lawrence Ingram, his Secretary of State, to Washington to visit with Ratner's Minister of Foreign Affairs, George Ruszkov. Ingram returned but with more questions than answers.

"Mr. President," Ingram began, "I tried to make it clear that the Republic is no threat to the USSA and that we only want to co-exist in peace. Ruszkov raised the points that our secession was illegal and that other states within the USSA are being bullied by us into leaving the USSA union. I told him we were doing nothing of the sort. However, he wanted me to agree to reject all applicants into our Republic as a first step toward establishing peaceful relations with them."

"What did you tell him?" asked Shea, sitting across from Ingram in the president's office.

"I told him I would have to confer with the president before I could respond to that," answered Ingram.

"Did he agree to stop beaming propaganda and lies into our country?" asked Sumner.

"I asked, but he refused to answer my questions. His position is that we are without portfolio – that I held a sinecure within my government. He made it quite clear that they have every right to take whatever actions are necessary to rejoin us with their dominion."

"So, where does that leave us?" asked Shea.

"I asked for a treaty," said Ingram. "It's what we agreed to before I left. I presented the points verbally, going through each one and telling Ruszkov that each matter was subject to discussion and refinement."

"I don't see how he could argue against that," said Shea. "It's something that will let them save face and let us avoid a costly war that's in no one's best interest."

"He pressed me again on not admitting any states to our Republic. He said that would be a direct act of war against the USSA and would result in immediate action on their part," said Ingram.

"What type of action?" asked Sumner.

"He wouldn't say."

Sumner thought for a moment, glancing out the window at the small courtyard just behind his official residence. Spring had come, and the birds were chirping loudly trying to attract a mate. "I just don't trust her. I don't think you can get a signed agreement with Ratner and believe that she will uphold her end of the bargain," he said, not looking back at the group.

"But what's the downside of an agreement?" asked Ingram, trying to salvage his work.

"Disarming and putting ourselves at the mercy of the Ratner Administration," said Sumner, coldly. "That's what they will ask for next after we give up admitting new states. They will want our complete and utter surrender before any shots are fired. Then, we may find ourselves the object of a wrath unseen on this continent in centuries. You thought taxation was high before? You believed we had no rights before? You really think we will escape this without prison or perhaps execution? Think again."

"I suppose so," Shea responded. "I just wish we were dealing with people of integrity. We've all seen what Ratner can do to those who disagree with her or pose a threat."

"I think they will stand up to their side of a treaty, if we sign one," Ingram said. "I got a good feeling about that from Ruszkov, despite his gruffness. I think that's the image Ratner wants him to present, but I've known George for a long time; that's not who he really is."

"That's what Stalin thought he was getting when he sent Molotov to negotiate a deal with Hitler in 1939," said Shea. "It resulted in an agreement for sure – the Molotov-Ribbentrop Pact, which lasted less than two years before Hitler violated it and attacked Soviet positions in Poland in 1941."

"I looked into his eyes and, I think he is someone we can work with," Ingram continued to protest. "I think he can persuade Ratner to be reasonable with this. He's part of her inner circle. He's got her ear."

"How do you know that?" asked Sumner. "Is that what he told you?"

"Not exactly. But, I think I'm a good judge of people," said the Secretary of State. "He's their number three person. He seemed to know a lot about the inner workings of Ratner's Cabinet and how she works with them."

Sumner grew suspicious. "I'm still not sure. I think we have to be careful with this." He paused, thumping his index finger against his temple. "I tell you what. I will authorize you to continue discussions with Ruszkov to see what agreement you can forge. But, I will withhold any support until I see there are clear signs they might comply with something to which you might agree."

During the next several weeks, Ingram flew back and forth from Cheyenne and Washington, D.C. holding meetings with subordinates to Ruszkov, never talking with him directly. This was not a good sign, but Sumner permitted it. Then, after exhaustive discussions, Ingram returned with what was to be the final outline for a treaty. His plane landed back in Cheyenne a day earlier than expected, and he hurried back to the president's house for a briefing. His demeanor was not happy.

"Mr. President, we were not able to reach an agreement," began Ingram, looking tired, his eyelids sagging and his left eye twitching from nervous fatigue.

"What happened?" asked Sumner, with a note of surprise and disappointment. "I thought we were close to something that would work for both of us."

"We were blindsided," Ingram said meekly.

"By what?" asked Josh Templeton, also in the room for the briefing. "My department provided you all the intelligence we had on them. We knew where their weaknesses were."

"They asked for money ..." said Ingram, "... lots of money." He shook his head. "I thought we could wrap it up ... we were close to a final draft when that word came in from outside. It was sudden – happened just like that," he said, snapping his fingers. "Ruszkov read a note that was slipped to him and then everything just unraveled."

"How much?" asked Shea.

"Ruszkov said Ratner wanted money for damages caused by our separation from the Union. If we paid her, she'd let us walk."

"They're the ones who caused the damage!" said Shea, insulted at the idea. "They've killed our friends; they've killed family; and almost as bad -- they've destroyed what was the greatest nation in the history of the world."

"How much do they want?" asked Sumner, solemnly.

Ingram fell silent.

"Lawrence, how much?" Sumner repeated.

"Ruszkov said Ratner wants ... one trillion United Coins."

"What?" said Sumner, believing he'd heard it wrong.

"One *trillion*," Ingram said again, annunciating and elongating the last word.

"She's mad!" said Shea. "No country on earth has resources like that." "That's like two hundred trillion of the old US dollars, right?" asked Templeton.

"Yes," replied Ingram.

"That's the entire amount of the USSA debt! She wants us to pay off the entire debt of the Union – a debt they've amassed over the last three hundred years," said Shea.

Sumner looked down. "Obviously, it was a ploy to torpedo the treaty," said the president.

"But why even start the negotiations then?" asked Templeton, scratching the side of his head.

Ingram responded, "To score political points, I think."

"Yes," added Sumner. "Ratner can claim that she negotiated in good faith and that we were the ones who pulled out of the talks. It will make us look like we don't want a diplomatic solution."

"So, what happens now?" Shea asked, looking at the other men in the room.

Templeton cleared his throat. "I'm afraid, I may have an answer to that, but it's not pretty. We've been tracking the military movements of the USSA using intelligence we've gathered from our friends to the north – Canada. They've shared with us intel they've gotten during the time we've been negotiating. It's clear that Ratner has been using these weeks to build-up its manufacturing capability -- military hardware, missiles, bombs, and chemical weapons. They've begun stockpiling petrol, critical alloys and other resources they will need in case of a prolonged war with us. When Canada asked about this, the Ratner Administration told them that it's all routine and they are merely responding to developments elsewhere in the world."

"Bull sh*t!" said Shea, surprising those in the room. "That's crap, and everyone knows it."

"So, what's our counter?" asked Ingram.

"We stall," said Sumner, crossing his arms and lowering his chin in contemplation.

"What will that do?" asked Ingram.

"Buys us time to continue working on our projects – those of Johnny and the Manhattan group. It's obvious that they are at the point they need to be for a first offensive or they wouldn't throw us this curve ball to derail the negotiations. They don't need any more time, but we do. We need to take a lesson from history. First, we need to build up *our* manufacturing capabilities in the event of conflict. Second, like I said, we need those new technologies, and third ..."

They all waited for Sumner to finish his sentence.

"... and third, we need a France," said Sumner.

"You mean, we need France?" asked Shea, trying to correct him.

"No, we need *a* France. Just as the colonists needed a major power to be on their side against the British in 1775, we need a major power to be on our side if it comes to that."

"Who is that going to be?" Ingram asked.

Turning back to Ingram, Sumner said, "Lawrence, where are we with discussions with our neighbors?"

"Mexico is a no. Canada – well, I'm not sure. They have been willing to work with us, but they're being careful right now, trying to straddle the fence."

"What will it take to pull them over to our side?"

"What do they want? What do they need?" Shea asked.

"Land? Money? What?" asked Templeton. "Certainly not a union with us."

"Why not?" asked Ingram. "They've always felt like the stepchild."

"Yeah, but that was then; this is now. Now, we're the stepchild and they've become the grownup."

"True, but would it be so bad if we were all one unified country – equals in every way?" asked Ingram. "I think you've been smokin' something," said Shea, dismissing the idea.

"Perhaps, but it's worth a try. Lawrence, see what you can do. If it's not that, then you'll have to come with something else. Keep me in the loop," said Sumner.

"I'll do my best, sir," said Ingram.

"You'll have to do more than your best, Lawrence. You need to make this happen. We're all depending on you," answered Sumner.

Ingram looked around the table. All eyes were on him, and he felt the pressure. "Yes, Mr. President. Consider it done."

*****

CH 19 The Potty Wars

Although talks had stalled in the negotiation of a peace between the two countries, the propaganda wars had not. Not only did the USSA increase the number and frequency of its threatening notices to the citizens of the Republic by flooding the SI-net with blogs, posts, and streaming broadcasts, they also intensified their attacks on the Republic's leaders. Almost anything could be digitized and modified to look a certain way, especially if it were slanderous or licentious. Entire videos were aired portraying Sumner and Shea in various sexual activities using computerized graphics and, in some cases, avatars. They were disgusting and crude. Shea quickly lost her concern over the photos with her Belizean lover; these new, manufactured ones were far worse.

Although no one in the new Republic wanted to watch these revolting scenes, many did so out of morbid fascination. When told *not to look*, it was human nature to do just that. Over time, the antics grew bolder and the outrageousness of each was designed to top that which had come before. To Sumner's and Shea's dismay, it was having an effect. When polled, more than half of their citizens had seen the photos, and while they didn't believe they were authentic, they held negative views of their two leaders.

It wasn't until the distribution of a full-length feature film called *Fornocopia,* commissioned by Ratner through the government-owned film studios of Paramount and Columbia, that Shea's spirit was finally broken. She rushed into Sumner's office, demanding that something be done.

"I won't tolerate this anymore!" she yelled, throwing down on the president's desk a snapshot of the movie poster that was circulating throughout the SI-net. "What are you going to do about it?" she said, her mouth and lips contorted with rage.

"What would you like for me to do?" asked Sumner, calmly. "There isn't much I can do, unless you want me to put through a gag order, an Executive Order, like they do in the USSA, shutting down free speech and the SI-net. Is that what you want?"

Shea gave him a look that would have withered any ordinary man. But, the president didn't shrink from what he'd said.

Shea crossed her arms, tucking her hands in tightly to the nooks of her elbows. "Damn it, JC! You know what I mean!" she said. "This has to stop! They're killing our reputations and our integrity. People are starting to believe this sh*t!"

"I understand your concerns, Shea. I really do. But really! What do you want me to do about it?"

Shea sat, pouting. "I don't know, but this just isn't right."

"No, it's not – not by any form of decency in what was once our civilized world. But it isn't the way it used to be, Shea. This is part of our world today though."

"But if we don't fire back, they'll keep on doing this. We need to fight them on this. We need to fight fire with fire, as they say."

Sumner thought for a moment. "You know, maybe it has gotten to the point we need to respond to this childishness."

"You may call it childish. But when it's a tactic that works, it's called *effective*," Shea said sarcastically. She could tell that Sumner didn't care for her backhanded remark, and she quickly apologized. "I'm sorry, JC, ... I was out of line."

"No, perhaps not," he answered her. "You know, things were actually not much different back in the nineteenth century. Do you realize what some of those presidents endured? First, you had the knockdown, drag-out election of 1800 between Jefferson and Adams, both of whom hated one another. Jefferson's people said John Adams was a hermaphrodite, neither a man nor a woman, while Adam's backers said that people's homes would burn, wives would be violated and children would die if Jefferson were elected. Then you had Jackson and John Quincy in 1824. People for Adams claimed Jackson's wife Rachel was a 'confirmed adulterous' and a 'dirty black wench.' Jackson's supporters claimed Adams sold his maid as a concubine to the Czar of Russia. When the votes were counted neither Jackson nor Adams had won a majority of votes in the Electoral College, so the House decided the race. Henry Clay asked for the secretary of state position if he could deliver the election to Adams, which he did. It wasn't until 1828 that Jackson got his revenge and won against the incumbent Adams. Similar accusations were thrown during that race too. The sad thing was that the race, in some ways, broke Jackson's wife Rachel, and she died before Jackson could take office. But there were other acrimonious fights, like Garfield's campaign in 1880 against Winfield Scott Hancock. In that contest, there was a mysterious letter, the Morey Letter, that surfaced making Garfield look bad just before the election. It was a forgery and almost torpedoed his chances. I could go on, but you get the picture."

"So, do you expect me to just sit and take it? That's what you're telling me?"

"There is always a time and a place, Shea."

"Is now the time and place?" she asked, her eyes seeking an answer in the depths of her boss.

Sumner smiled. "I think now is the time and the place. But, I'll leave it up to you to figure out the how. Just make sure it's not traceable back to us. You're right, we have to fight with fire. I hate doing it, but unfortunately, that's just the way it works these days."

"I'll take care of it, sir," she said, returning the smile.

But before Shea could coalesce her strategy, she got a call from Sumner. "Do it!" he said angrily. "Destroy them. Do what you have to do. The gloves are off!"

"What happened?" asked Shea.

"I'll send it to you," said Sumner, more agitated than she'd ever heard him.

Shea waited for it to come onto her computer, and when she saw it, her jaw dropped.

Truth Revealed!! – Maria Sumner Slave Holder & Child Abuser

Sumner's wife Maria held slave children in her basement and abused and tortured their first child, leading to the girl's unreported death. Maria was never brought to justice because of Congressman Sumner's connections on Capitol Hill. Sumner paid off three federal judges and other lawmakers to keep her out of jail ...

Shea couldn't stomach to read any further. Several manufactured pictures accompanied the blog, showing Maria in an orange, prison jumpsuit and having a nasty, smirk on her face, together with images of children with bruises and scars all over their bodies. It was hurtful to Sumner, striking him at his most vulnerable point. Maria was as near sainthood as could be said of a person – kind, generous, and loving to a fault. She had been murdered by USSA assassins at her own ranch, and now those same people were not too low to try to destroy the only that was left – her legacy and reputation. The president had loved her dearly, and her loss had been devastating to him.

Shea didn't know how to respond. All she could do was write *I'm sorry* in a message back to him.

To say hers was a subtle counter attack was like referring to Pearl Harbor as a minor, inconsequential skirmish. Shea launched what she felt was appropriate in the circumstances. To others, it was a nuclear strike. Either way, it was effective.

"Send it," said Shea, instructing her assistant to coordinate the release with backdoor channels that could never be traced. Like those issued from the USSA, the bulletin could not be firmly attached to anyone; it was only by reasonable deduction that one would think it was either promoted by the USSA or the Republic. However, what was a strength was also a weakness, and it was that which Shea exploited.

BULLETIN: To All Living within the Exclusion Zone --

It is with even more concern and urgency that we deliver this message to all republican citizens. We have been sending all of you warnings for weeks on what is going on in your fledgling nation. And, we have been telling you that your leaders are getting ready for an all-out ass sault of the USSA. All these things are true.

But even worse, Sumner and Disone are planning far deeper plots – those which will go down in the annals of history for being fetid and coarse. In the next several bulletins, we will advise you of these horrific acts and what you can do to protect against them.

The first is unisex bathrooms. That's right, we said it – the "U" word.

Sumner and Disone are plotting to order all bathrooms closed and remodeled as unisex toilets. There will be no hiding from this order – it will affect public and private restrooms alike. You will be forced to share a bathroom with someone of the opposite sex whether you like it or not.

Even stalls will not be marked male or female – they will merely have the unisex symbol: ⚥

In addition, Sumner and Disone will be establishing a tribunal to review all complaints of violating the order. This commission will form task forces to enter your private homes unannounced and check to see that even your home bathrooms are marked with the aforementioned symbol. Violators may face life-in-prison terms or worse.

Again, we bring you this and other warnings to help you make your decision whether to support your two leaders. We believe the choice is obvious.

Our next bulletin will address another forthcoming Executive Order that tragically will affect millions of other republicans: pet flatulence. Please stay tuned.

Very truly,

Those Concerned for Your Wellbeing

The phone rang on her desk, and she knew it was the president. She was afraid of what he would say, but to some degree she didn't care. Her conscious was clear. She did what felt thought she had to do – what she thought the president had wanted her to do. *If it were too much, then it was in the eye of the beholder,* she thought. She had no regrets, even if he was calling to ask for her resignation.

"Shea?" came the familiar voice and the image of the president's face hovering over her desk. His face was stern and seemingly stolid.

"Yes, JC?"

"I …" he began.

"If you are asking for my resignation, I will give it to you, sir. However, I want to defend myself by saying that feel that what I did was justified. I was not intending to provoke a war or a conflict, and in the end I did not. What I did was not traceable back to us, as you requested, so I don't see any reason you should be upset."

"I'm not," he answered.

"You're … you're not?" she asked, surprised by the response.

"No, I'm not. I think you did a good job on this one. We were not implicated, and it's been ruinous for the Administration. I understand that Ratner has been fuming about it for days now. Besides … they were hilarious. I believe it's turned the tables on them, making them all look like fools. After your bulletin on pet flatulence, their warnings lost all credibility. It completely emasculated them and blunted their attack. Well done."

Shea smiled and breathed deeply once again. She could feel her heart pounding in her chest and continued taking slow, easy breaths to bring it under control. "Thank you, JC. I ... I'm glad you agree."

"Well, I do have some encouraging news too," Sumner said, now smiling. "I just got a notice from the polling group. Our popularity numbers have been falling as you know – what with the barrage of negative propaganda coming from the USSA. However, I think she's over-reached now, and your latest ploy has done a lot of damage to her. Today's numbers show a decided turnaround. People are fed-up with the tawdry and outrageous allegations being hurled from their side and they no longer believe anything they read in the bulletins. The numbers show that 85 percent of our people don't believe a word of it. Another 9 percent aren't sure, which leaves just 6 percent who really do believe their garbage, and, frighteningly, what you wrote as well. So, thank you."

"You're welcome, JC," said Shea, a small surge of energy coming back into her being.

"I think we'll weather this thing," said Sumner. "I believe we're on the other side of it."

Shea smiled. It was the first time in weeks. Again, there was a twinkle in her eyes as he looked at Sumner.

"You were right, Shea," he said. "At a certain point, you do have to fight back. What's important is how you do it."

"That means a lot. Now all we have to do is win the broader war." "Let's hope it doesn't come to that ... the war part, that is," said Sumner.

"I agree, sir," said Shea.

"But if it does, I'm glad I've got you on my side," he added.

*****

CH 20 Trust in the Devil

Sumner sent a request to the Republic's Congress asking for war powers to prepare the nascent nation for a conflict with the USSA. These were quickly granted after a closed-door hearing was held with congressional leaders, disclosing the Canadian intelligence that had been gathered regarding Washington's moves to ramp-up USSA war-time manufacturing capability. In a unanimous decision, the Senate voted to give the president authority to do what was necessary to protect the nation. However, just as the 1973 War Powers Act of the old USA had stipulated, this power would sunset within sixty days and would require congressional renewal for the president to continue deployment of troops.

Sumner then called a Cabinet meeting to reassess the Republic's preparedness. He was fully aware of the flagging efforts with Johnny's phaser, and it was too early to determine the status of the Manhattan II Project. Therefore, he was putting more hope on other measures in process to equip the military and place assets strategically where they would be needed most in the event of a crisis.

"Well, Mr. President, we are having difficulty in getting the necessary raw materials to build certain systems. In addition, our international credit rating has not yet been established, so it's hard for us to buy weapons from Europe and China. Russia has agreed to sell us weapons and extend credit but the prices and rates are usurious. Canada has extended credit, and we are purchasing military armaments from them, but ..."

"I don't want more *buts*, Secretary Templeton. I'm sorry -- it's your job to get us what we need to defend this country! Given what we're up against, we can't accept any 'I tried's.' I won't accept it – not now!" said Sumner, huffing at his defense secretary. It was the first time he had expressed genuine anger in a Cabinet meeting, but the pressures were mounting. The threats by the USSA were growing, and either the Republic prepared or they would face annihilation.

"Yes, Mr. President, but it all takes time. You can't expect us to ..."

"Yes, I do!" said Sumner, cutting Templeton off. "I expect a lot, I know. But so do the people of this Republic. They expect us as their leaders to protect them. That is our number one function. If we can't do that, then we aren't doing our jobs and shouldn't be in office."

Sumner sat back in his chair, thumping the table with his fingers. He contemplative and seemed distracted, but everyone soon found out why.

"I was approached several weeks ago by a person whom many of you know. This was someone who was on the dark side of things in the USSA for a very long time and created a lot of problems for many of us. He told me that he's changed and that he wants to be on the right side of things this time -- not the wrong side. Many of you will say that he can't be trusted – that he was always under Ratner's thumb and always will be. That may be true, but in this case, we need someone who has run a major operation and is capable of getting us the results we need. He is working on another project for me, but I feel it is necessary that he also become responsible for making sure that we meet our production quotas, production quality goals and integration of all our military needs with the production supply line. When you knew him, he was CEO of EG, Inc., one of the largest companies in the world until it was taken over by the USSA bureaucrats. His name is Kilby Thorne."

There was a collective groan throughout the room. Shea wanted to speak up, but she had already spoken her mind with the president and didn't feel it would be productive to raise her objections again in front of the group.

"As I said, many of you will object, but ..."

"I too find it hard to believe that you would welcome such a fox back into the henhouse like that," said White, outspoken on nearly every subject.

"I agree," said Nugyn. "With all the other problems we have and you've decided to bring another on board. I can't quite understand it."

Sumner took a deep breath and closed his eyes for a moment. Then reopened them and said frankly, "If not him, who would you put in the position to fix all the problems we're having with our war production effort?"

"What about Shea?" asked Ingram. "She could handle it."

Shea shook her head. "Thanks guys, but I've been nursing this thing along for months now and doing my job as Attorney General. I just don't have the time. But, more importantly, I don't have the experience, nor do I have the worldwide connections that Thorne has. He can get us things I can't. He knows people I don't. He's ..." she stopped, pursing her lips, "... he's the right person for the job. If we can trust him, that is."

It was Templeton of the defense department who was obvious in not speaking up. He was the one who had failed in the war-time production effort as anyone else. Shooting down the proposal of Thorne would have been detrimental to him. Besides, like Shea, he had enough to do over at the newly erected Pentagon building.

"We already have one mole in the organization," said Ingram, chiming in. "I guess another won't hurt." Sumner frowned. He didn't appreciate the sarcasm and tone of Ingram's comments.

"No disrespect, Mr. President, but I just don't think it's wise. We have no way to monitor what he's giving our enemy," said Ingram.

"We will bug his phones and monitor his comings and goings. Will that be sufficient? That's about all I'm able to do." Sumner glanced over at Jay Hawkins, head of the FBI. "That will be your added assignment, director," he said. "Just don't let him out of your sight or sound."

"Yes, sir," he answered.

"Now, if that's everyone's biggest compliant of the day, I'd like to get back to work," said Sumner with unusual gruffness. Getting up from his chair, he left the room briskly and let the door close with a *thump* behind him.

***

Thorne was immediately thrown into the role of directing the materiel buildup. As the new director of war procurement, his task was to convert private sector manufacturing into public sector production for the military – something the country had not seen since the 1940s and World War II. Thorne pressed the president to issue an executive order requiring every business to contribute to the war effort. Those that disagreed were allowed to close and move elsewhere, retaining ownership in their land and facilities. However, they were not allowed to produce on their own behalf.

For its part, the ATLAS Republic promised payment. To some business owners it was a vacuous promise. They believed they would never be paid for their services, just as did factories and shops during the Revolutionary War. Of course, businesses of the current time had good reason to be wary – they had lived through the broken promises of payment by the bankrupt USSA government. Many companies went broke waiting to be paid by Washington for goods and or services rendered. However, in general most businesses in the Republic were willing, through blind patriotism, to offer their services on the basis of a simple government IOU. They had sacrificed much to leave the USSA, and they were willing to sacrifice a little more.

Rather than turn all production over to federal bureaucrats who knew nothing about business or production, Thorne brought in many of his old managers from EG to oversee the manufacturing of goods for the war effort based on in-depth analysis of what was going to be needed and when. Various forts submitted purchase orders and justifications that were issued to procure armaments. Operations was expected to fill them on time and within budget. Those companies that could not meet those requirements were dropped; those that met their goals were given more orders. The result of the free market exercise was that more materiel was created within the span of six months than had ever been created before in the history of the world. Not since WWII had so much in munitions and conventional weaponry been developed. The gulf between technology companies and manufacturers -- between creativity and manufacturability – had been successfully bridged. Now it was only a matter of importing the necessary raw materials to keep it going.

Prototypes of fighters, bombers, land artillery, navy subs and offensive cruisers and carriers were developed using 3-D printers. In addition, web-viruses, EMP satellite killers, and other types of computer and electronic warfare were perfected. Cyber-attack capability was readied, and defenses against such attacks installed. The only pieces missing were Johnny's phaser and the Manhattan initiative. These were kept under wraps to prevent leaks that could be devastating to the Republic's chances in a war. Only a few knew of their existence, and then, even fewer knew how and when each might be used. One person who was deliberately kept in the dark on these initiatives was Thorne.

By the end of June, Thorne had delivered impressive numbers to Sumner. "Yes, we have the production numbers for the previous quarter," said the procurement director, motioning toward the chief statistician who headed that branch of the government.

Thorne went over the numbers as they came up on the screen in front of the president and his Cabinet. "We've produced four hundred advanced, sixth-generation fighters during the quarter. That's a total of twelve hundred in total. Bombers total sixty-five for the B-4 model and fourteen of the more advanced B-4b."

"The B-4 and B-4b are both drone bombers, correct?" asked Sumner.

"Of course, sir. We haven't had a human flying a bomber aircraft for some time," answered Thorne.

"Go on then."

Thorne went on spewing statistic after statistic. "Rifles, pistols, ammunitions, armored suits, com devices with computers, and all other infantry field equipment are on target for meeting quotas. We should have enough by the end of the year."

"And what if war breaks out before then?" asked Shea, not trying to be difficult, but her question was the white elephant in the room.

"We'll have to accelerate our production," said Thorne.

"And what about soldiers?" asked Sumner, now looking at Templeton.

"We have readied plans for conscription in the fall, if not sooner. This is something I don't want to suggest, but I see little choice but to prepare for it. It may be inevitable."

Sumner cradled his chin in the palm of his hand. He knew what Templeton was saying was true, but he hated the thought. "How many robotic soldiers can we get our hands on?" he asked.

"Unfortunately, we don't have any within the boundaries of our Republic, sir. The closest facility that has those is in Yuma. I believe they have over one hundred thousand, but they would be under the control of the USSA."

"And if we must go with a human army, how many do we have of eligible age and capability?" the president asked.

"I believe we would be well short of 500,000, sir."

"What about training? How long will that take?" asked Sumner.

"About six months, Mr. President."

"A year is too late. It is likely that the USSA will invade before then. So, perhaps we need to begin conscription now and begin training."

"Yes, sir. I agree, sir."

"But we need a backup plan, Templeton," said Sumner. "We have to assume that we won't be able to prepare our troops in time to confront an onslaught from the USSA. Where again did you say those robotic soldiers are stored?"

The rest of the meeting was used to review war strategies drafted by the generals. They were numerous and considered countless scenarios that had all been fought on computer simulations to determine a win or loss. War simulations had been going on for ages, and in the current era, it was only a matter of strategy – most times avoiding the expected, and going with the unexpected. The USSA would be doing the same. Sumner, however, was counting on the fact that they would be using more antiquated machines and software than those of the Republic. This was another advantage of an open, capitalistic society – the quantum leaps forward in software and hardware designs by entrepreneurs.

Days passed; then weeks. Yet, nothing more came out of Washington. There was no violence, no incursion, no invasion. No longer were there even any threats being disseminated. It was eerily quiet.

Still, the military commanders of the Republic watched nervously, their Def Con position unwavering at Level 2, the second highest. Templeton went about his normal routine but obsessively checked his PCD for any urgent messages. Meetings with his defense department and National Security Agency came and went and so did those with the president. But, there was nothing to report from the USSA. Worse yet, all information from Thorne's Underground cells had completely dried up – the effects of continued leaks from the still-unidentified mole.

Shea was in continuous communication with the people involved in the Manhattan Project as well as

Johnny's small crew of scientists. It was odd for an attorney general to lead such efforts, but both Templeton and Ingram said they were too busy with other things to get involved. *Anyway*, they had said, *Shea knew the participants better than anyone else. Why, just based on that, she was* clearly *the best one for the job.* The truth was that both were afraid the projects were doomed to failure, and neither wanted their names attached to them.

"Something must be up," Shea said, talking to Johnny in his lab one cold morning in early December. "The First Citizen is too strident not to follow-up on her vow to destroy us."

Johnny shook his head. "I don't know. I don't remember, of course, much about her or what she's capable of." He took another bite from an egg-salad sandwich he'd ordered. It was toasted and pierced with toothpicks wrapped with green, plastic tassels. The sandwich sat, resting peacefully on a white paper plate, minding its own business except for the long, green pickle with which it shared the space.

"Well, how is it coming?" she asked, sipping on her sweet iced tea and peering over his shoulder.

"It's coming," he answered, pushing the dill pickle to the side of the plate.

"What do you mean by that? You are supposed to finish your handheld prototype for the Jt. Chiefs meeting next week. You'll be ready for that demonstration, won't you?"

"Uh, no. Probably yet," he answered, nonchalantly, continuing to work on equations on his computer.

"You won't have your prototype finished?" she asked, trying to remain calm.

"No."

Calmly, she took another gulp of tea. "That's a problem. Don't you think?" she asked rhetorically.

"Not really," he answered, still not biting on a serious conversation.

It was then that Shea began to get a little exercised. She grabbed his chair and swiveled it around to face her. Her demeanor had changed instantly, the fire ignited in her eyes and in her soul.

"Johnny! Do you think this is some kind of game? Do you really believe that you have all the time in the world to do whatever you damn well please?"

He looked at her with a blank stare. "I don't see the problem," he asked her.

"Well, I do," she answered soberly, shaking her head. "I … I just don't understand you! How can you say this is not a problem, Johnny? We have troops out there relying on this new weapon of yours. If we can't have it ready when they go into battle, they will be slaughtered. They will die, as we don't have any weaponry right now to compete against what the USSA has. Sons and daughters will spill their blood on American soil because you didn't seem to think this is important or that there is no urgency to it all. You disgust me!"

Johnny sat staring at her. He no longer wore a white lab coat, and sat in his blue jeans, crimson and sage flannel shirt and oxblood colored cowboy boots. She wasn't sure he heard her or if he did whether, even then, he understood what she was telling him.

Shea reached out and seized him by the shoulders, shaking him. "Johnny … Johnny … are you even in there anymore?"

"I hear you," he answered in a monotone. "I just don't know why you have to get so excited about it."

"I just told you, Johnny! We have a responsibility to the young men and women of our Republic who are willing to give their lives for us. Doesn't that mean anything to you?" Shea was losing patience and hope. Now she was wondering whether there was no more Patrick left inside this man she used to know. If not, then perhaps the cause was lost before the first shots had even been fired.

"I see," he answered, showing a modicum of emotion with what she had confronted him. "Perhaps, then, you are right in what you're saying. I must admit that I have been focused on the science of it all, making sure that we've advanced the concepts I've presented in the most scientifically enlightening way possible. I was seeking to create something grand – a complete shift in paradigms with things that had never been done before. I guess I lost perspective of my foundation over which I was building my dreams."

Shea said nothing. She didn't have to. What she'd said was beginning to sink in, and for that she was heartened.

"It isn't just about the science, is it?" he asked.

"No, it's about winning a war. It's about keeping our freedoms. It's about being able to speak our minds, argue our point of view, disagree with our leaders, and associate with whomever we want. It's about practicing whatever religion we want or not worrying about being arrested in our own homes for violating someone else's view of political correctness. It's all those things. Don't you agree?"

"Yes," Johnny answered, without hesitation. "It is. I am beginning to understand, and I will make sure a prototype is ready for next week."

Shea took his arm and squeezed it. Smiling she said, "Thanks. The Republic ... I ... thank you." Then, she gave him a kiss on the cheek. It felt good to her.

Johnny spent the next thirty minutes going over all the details that needed to be fixed. Shea absorbed them, just as she had when they were married. She synthesized all of it and boiled down the complexity into a few simple issues. "So, it's a matter of connecting the modulator core to the bridge element. The form factor is so small that you need new technology to make that happen. Is that what you're saying?" she asked.

"Uh, yeah. I guess," said Johnny, surprised at her methods of deduction.

Shea grinned. "I think it's something you should talk to Secretary Templeton about. He has a company that is providing him with echo reverberation technology and they are using similar methods to connect two pieces of hardware."

"What about production?" Johnny asked her. "You're going to need tens of thousands of these devices. I've never worked on that scale before, and I really don't know how to go about it."

Shea knew that while she was good at identifying key problems and focusing an organization's attention on fixing them, she was less familiar with managing massive projects involving thousands of workers, sourcing agents, and processes. Neither Patrick nor she had done those things when they had run their company. All the production of their engines had been outsourced.

"John, I'm afraid I'm not going to be of much help to you. However, I do know someone who might be."

Reluctantly, she decided it was time to advise the president that someone else should take it over managing the project, and it wouldn't be someone that the former Patrick would have been pleased to work beside. Shea only hoped that this was an area too in which Johnny had lost all recollection. It would be better that way – better for him and better for her.

***

The next day, Shea marched into Sumner's office. "JC, I have something I need to tell you," she began. Sumner looked up from his desk. "What is it Shea? Nothing serious I hope."

"Yes, sir. It is."

"Okay, let me have it. What's on your mind?" Sumner put down his pen and pushed his pin-cushioned leather chair back from his desk.

"I think Thorne should assume managing the production of the phaser units. I'm still afraid he can't be trusted, but if there is anyone who can run the production program, it's him."

"I see," said Sumner, pushing his reading glasses down on his nose. "Well, perhaps it will make the decision easier if I told you that I've just received information that Ratner has given orders to the Ministry of International Policing to attack our Republic. Do you believe that could be true?"

Shea looked down at her feet and sighed. Running her fingers through her hair, as if to reactivate her senses, she said, "Yes, JC. I'm afraid I do."

*****

CH 21 Third World

The economy of the USSA had been in tatters for years, even before the constitutional change from the USA to the new socialist power that ruled with an iron fist. During those years, from Presidents Rios and Fourier to now First Citizen Ratner, Washington had addressed its budget shortfalls by printing money – a euphemistic way of saying they incurred huge amounts of debt to fund their welfare programs. This debt was owed back to those who bought the Treasury bonds issued by the Ministry of Bursars to fund it all. Eventually, this money had to be paid back to those creditors, but all the government did was borrow more from others to pay back earlier investors. It was a Ponzi scheme of the first order, and it had worked for over a century – until now. Now, the USSA government was being pressured by the New World Order Bank – the second iteration of the old World Bank -- to reduce its spending. The world's currency of choice had long been changed from the US dollar to the WorldCoin as agreed among the major world powers of China, Saudi Arabia, Iran, and Russia. The US had lobbied hard against the change; however, it no longer held any clout, and its efforts failed.

In the meantime, the US dollar was expected to be devalued 90 percent as the country's national debt of 103 trillion dollars exceeded by five times the nation's annual production output or GDP. US debt was reduced to *junk* status which meant the federal government had to carve out more of its budget to make very high interest payments to investors. Without the promise of high interest payments, no one would buy the USSA debt for fear of not getting repaid – the risks of default were just too high.

But when the USA became the USSA, the Ministry of Bursars issued an edict stating that US coinage would be changed from the US dollar to the USSA UnitedCoin, and that the smallest usable coin would become the *UC1* UnitedCoin. All prices would be rounded to the nearest UnitedCoin. The initial exchange rate was set at one UC1 for every US$100 and the UC1 was to be devalued 90 percent against other world currencies. It was the redenomination of a currency in crisis. The bottom line was that American currency was devalued. It was now worth less than it was before, and that wasn't good.

To the average citizen of the USSA, the effect was devastating. The cost of all foreign imports shot up to stratospheric levels. The price of bread rose only from five dollars per loaf to eight, but for olives imported from Italy, the cost increased from UC2.50 per six-ounce jar to UC230.00. Consequently, the demand for olives tanked as did that for virtually all other import goods.

For those few who ate olives or used olive oil it was hard, but for every American who bought any type of apparel, it was ruinous. Virtually all textiles and clothing were imported from overseas. Most manufacturing capabilities had disappeared from the shores of the United States decades earlier. Cheaper labor in Asia coupled with increasing union demands for higher wages and benefits in the US caused nearly all clothing makers to abandon facilities in America and build them or outsource them overseas. As a result, the price of a shirt that normally cost thirty US dollars, now cost three hundred. Designer shirts were no longer accessible at all to anyone but the ultra-wealthy, going for more than two thousand.

Yet, that wasn't the only change. The new coins in denominations of UC1, UC5, UC10, UC20 and UC50 had symbols of bears, flags, hammers, doves, and other meaningful images, while the paper money began at UC100. The pictures of the Founding Fathers were considered taboo and were replaced with other, more relevant personages. Washington on the US$1, Lincoln on the US$5, Hamilton on the US$10, Jackson on the US$20, Grant on the US$50, and Franklin on the US$100 were all replaced. The new UC bills had Barak Obama, the forty-fourth president, on the UC100 bill; Martin Luther King, Jr. on the UC200; Maya Angelou, poet, on the UC500; Caesar Chavez, activist and union leader, on the UC1000; Eugene V. Debs, leader of the Socialist Party of America in 1912 and founder of the American Railway Union, on the UC2000; Niha Awad, executive director of the Council of American-Islamic Relations, on the UC5000; and Shirley Chishom, first African-American member of Congress, on the UC10,000. Plans were underway to print higher denomination bills, if they should be needed.

However, few in America even realized who the new faces were, and didn't really care. They were just fresh, new slick bills that made them feel richer. It was always better to have a Shirley Chishom worth UC10,000 in your wallet than one of an old, white guy like Alexander Hamilton even though they were worth the same. It was only when they went to the store to exchange those notes did they realize they were no better off or in fact worse off than when they had held the 10 dollar note of Hamilton. Instead of paying US$3.00 for a gallon of milk, as they had decades earlier, a single gallon jug now cost them the equivalent of US $296.00 or nearly three Obama UC100s. Cans of soup that once sold for US $2.30 now sold for US $215.00 per can or over two Obama UC100s. Cars, when you could find one to buy, cost a minimum of US $2.1 million for a compact, no-nonsense coup, and once-private homes no longer existed for sale, long since seized by the government. But that mattered little, virtually no one but the political class could afford the black-market price of nearly US $44.2 million for a small, cramped, two bedroom ranch. The number of Shirley Chishoms needed to buy it wouldn't fit in an overstuffed suitcase.

Yet, every effort was made to deceive the public. Units of measure were changed – cut down into much smaller increments to obfuscate the reality of hyperinflation. Gas was longer sold by the gallon; rather, it was sold by the deciliter or one-tenth of a liter. This was the equivalent of 0.026 gallons. It was no longer the era of 23 cents per gallon of gas as experienced in the 1950s and 1960s. The price of gasoline had skyrocketed – not because of a shortage, but because of the devaluation of the US dollar and taxes and fees, including the 85 percent surcharge imposed to curb its use. Adjusted for inflation and taxes, a gallon of gasoline should have cost US $4.56 per gallon. Instead, it actually costs consumers US $827.00 per gallon. But when it was sold by the deciliter and in UnitedCoins, the price only looked like this on the station signs out front: *UC*

0.22 per dl. There was only one other small problem – one couldn't find any gasoline to purchase.

As a result, people bought electric cars. This proceeded well until the coal power plants were closed. Then, new restrictions on charging cars were implemented, allowing it only between the hours of one and four in the morning. Poaching from power lines and neighbors' trunk lines was widespread when brownouts and blackouts began to strike the major cities. Without power, vehicles couldn't be charged and people were stranded. Worse yet, truck drivers were often held up at gunpoint and stripped of their precious batteries. Left stranded, it took them weeks or months to get goods to their final destination.

Eventually, the minister of transportation stepped in and issued an edict stating that rationing would begin immediately. As in the 1970s, people were designated a certain day of the week when they could charge their vehicle. Electric charging cards were issued and could only be used for vehicle charging on certain days as approved by the government, such as every other Monday for the lower classes or all days – these cards referred to as Gold Cards – for the political class and wealthy. This, of course, only led to card theft and the selling of cards on the SI-net and the black market.

Anarchy ruled. Local police departments had been disbanded and replaced by Washington's internal police force, the Red Shirts. Directed by the Ministry of Unity, the Red Shirts were a band of brutal thugs who struck fear into the locals, but did nothing to stop local violence. Disruption and chaos were their allies, as the citizenry – bereft of their right to bear arms – were defenseless and forced to rely on the Red Shirts for protection. Most found that their protection was up for sale too – the more paid to the provincial Red Shirt captains the better the protection.

With the economy in free-fall, Ratner took action. Much like her predecessor, First Citizen Fourier, she imposed stiff tariffs to keep out lower-cost, better-quality foreign goods. Domestic factories that had closed were reopened for a short time after the duties were effectuated. TV's, electronics, autos, and other goods, previously and exclusively made in countries with low wages or higher levels of technology saw their prices shoot-up overnight. Longer term, some foreign companies attempted to open their own plants in the United States to produce those items; however, when they found costly fees, licenses and other barriers erected by the government as well as the interminable delays and bureaucracy involved, they canceled their projects and withdrew their investment.

But USSA factory production did not rise as a result, either. Trading partners retaliated against the USSA with high levies of their own, while domestic consumption fell-off from high unemployment rates and shoddy domestic workmanship. People refused to pay high prices for things that would fall apart with in a year. Instead, they either did without or found other alternatives.

As production levels continued to fall, Ratner could not allow the unemployment rate to rise, so GovCos kept workers on the payroll even though they did little or no work. Costs again rose as there were fewer units manufactured over which to spread the burgeoning payrolls, and with that prices were again raised by the companies. This in turn caused consumers to buy less, so fewer units were made, so costs increased, so prices rose, so on … and on … and on the cycle went. The hamster was churning furiously on its wheel, but it had not moved an inch. It remained in the same cage, with the same bars, with the same master. It was only more exhausted than ever before.

Without the ability to suck more money from the populace, Washington turned to the New World Order Bank – the place where third-world countries had gone for decades to feed from the money trough offered by rich, industrialized nations as a palliate for their sense of self-immolating guilt. Now, the USSA found itself in the same category as many others from Africa, Southeast Asia and South and Central America – as second, if not third-world nations. Had it really come to this?

***

It had happened nearly sixteen centuries earlier. By 476 CE, the great Roman Empire of five hundred years was at an end. Although threats from northern tribes such as the Vandals and Goths contributed to it, there were unmistakable internal factors as well. Military spending to maintain order in distant, conquered lands and profligate spending by the government racked up huge debts for the treasury. The emperors raised taxes to fund these ventures. As taxes rose to lofty levels, the rich left, creating a vacuum of wealth, taxes and capability within the empire. Business merchants and farmers also stopped their trade, as the taxes outstripped what they made in total. All things were taxed, including land, crops, animals, slaves, and luxuries. In addition, during the two hundred years leading up to about 235CE, silver content of the coinage fell from purity to one percent. This devaluation enabled emperors to coin more money to pay soldiers and workers at less cost. But as more people were thrown into poverty, others who were politically connected lived well. Paying little or no taxes, the political elite held marble palaces, enjoyed fine wine, and had stables of slaves at their bidding. To placate the masses, emperors offered free entertainment, such as at the Coliseum and amphitheaters, and subsidized staples, such as salt, wine, bread, oil and pork. As prices spiraled upward, more became impoverished. In 302CE, Diocletian ordered all prices to be frozen to prevent an uprising. This only created shortages of crucial goods, leaving shelves barren and people even more irate. But government corruption also contributed to the downfall. Incompetent, self-serving emperors, sycophantic senators only seeking enrichment from their office, and lower level politicians readily accepting bribes and tributes, eroded public confidence. Finally, forced to starve the military of resources, emperors turned to mercenaries to wage their wars. The lack of money for weapons, men, and loyalty, left the legions and their leaders to seek their own power. Some joined the barbarians later to sack Rome or attacked Roman outposts on their own. In any event, the Roman army, a once awed and powerful force, had been reduced to a shell of its former self.

Shea closed the book. It was an antique she had stored in her closet since her father had passed away and left his entire library. This was a book that she had intended to read but had never seemed to find the time. Now, she sensed it was important.

She yawned, stretched her hands into the air and then pushed away from the desk. Before she turned off the light, she glanced back at the cover – *The Rise and Fall of the Roman Empire by Edward Gibbon, together with a Review and Analysis by Arthur Perkins.* A cold chill entered her bones, and she shook her shoulders, as if it would cast away the demons of history. Her father had always told her that empires were both raised and destroyed – that none lasted forever. Like all things, they had births and they had deaths. It would only be a matter of time, he had said, before the American experiment ended. What he wasn't sure of was whether it would be from some foreign invasion or through internal self-destruction. They were now finding out the answer.

Oh, how history doeth repeat itself, she thought.

*****

CH 22 Moral Dilemma

Canada had long been a stepchild to the old United States. Lacking the industrial might and population of its southern brother, it had always been in the shadows of the US superpower status. However, decades of change in both countries had inverted that equation.

After years of watching the USA in decline, devolving into the USSA, Canada was playing a more active role in world affairs. In many respects, it was a world leader within the ranks of Russia, China, and the Islamic States. With foreign exchange surpluses, low taxes, and a new, business-friendly economic environment, many businesses had moved to Canada from around the globe, especially from the USSA. This continued until laws in America were passed, halting the "brain drain" and banning companies from relocating there. But, these companies only shut down operations entirely and re-incorporated in Canada under the same name.

Rich in natural resources, particularly oil, coal, and natural gas, Canada offered new companies many advantages. Opportunities abounded, as they once had in the United States. Certainly, the business climate was more restrictive than the salad days of the middle twentieth century, but it was far from what it had become in the USSA.

Still, the one thing Canada lacked was significant tracts of arable land. With such a cold climate, less than five percent of the land was available for farming; thus, reliance on the United States and its wealth of tillable land throughout the Plain States and Midwest had been vital. Since foodstuffs were one of the few things the USSA was able to export prior to the schism with the Republic, Canada had maintained a close relationship with its southern neighbor. However, now that the Bread Basket of the USSA had largely split off into the ATLAS Republic, things were different.

Ingram flew to Ottawa to meet with the Canadian foreign minister and minister of agriculture. These meetings were substantive and amiable, like three old fraternity brothers gathering for a reunion thirty years after graduation. A later meeting with Prime Minister MacDonald was more direct, yet still cordial. After his meeting, Ingram felt he could bring Canada on board with the new Republic — at least to recognize them as a sovereign country. This would place Canada at odds with the USSA. But with the abundance of food generated by the Republic's Plain States, it would be hard for the prime minister to rebuff the region that was now feeding his own people.

"I think they understand what we are trying to do," said Ingram in a secure conference call with Sumner. "It's not a sure thing, but we are making progress."

"And what about the Québécois? Are they willing to consider an alliance?"

"They say they won't support either side in this right now. Their prime minister specifically told me that they want to remain neutral. Bovier said they want no part of a schism between the states. 'They will not be drawn into it,' he said to me rather coolly. On the other hand, Prime Minister MacDonald seemed sympathetic to our cause. I think there is room for negotiation there."

"Well, get MacDonald's backing – however you have to!" said Sumner, frustrated at the lack of a deal. "This is too important to us. We have to get them as an ally, even if you have to stay up there for the next three months, Lawrence, then do it."

"Yes, sir."

Sumner hung up the call, as Shea came into his office. "Oh, Shea, I'm glad you're here. I've got some things to go over with you."

"What's wrong?" she asked, situating herself on the love seat opposite two guest chairs in the middle of his office. She crossed her legs and opened her tablet computer.

"It's Canada. They're not taking sides. It's what I expected, but I really held out hope they would come into the conflict as our ally in all this. It's not that they are being cold to the idea – quite the contrary. The prime minister has been very engaged with us, offering military intelligence, extending us credit, and increasing purchases of wheat and corn to help us with our financial imbalances. He's also committed that he won't allow the USSA to use any of his bases to launch attacks against us. The one thing he won't do right now is recognize us as a sovereign country."

"Why not?" Shea asked.

"They don't want to provoke the USSA. The relationship with Ratner and the Administration has frayed, but I'm sure he doesn't want it to sever completely. Canada still needs certain key imports from them, and the USSA gets most of its rare alloys from the mines in Canada."

"Britain did that during our Civil War," said Shea. "They walked the middle ground with the North and South, even though their textile mills were hurt badly by the lack of cotton imports from the South.

Likewise, the South was hobbled by the lack of currency coming back from England. The British knew the North had the military and manufacturing advantage; they just weren't sure about the North's military leadership."

"Was that common," asked Sumner, "that foreign powers chose neutrality in such circumstances?"

"Well, throughout history, when there have been internal conflicts within countries, those on the outside have been reluctant to interfere. They want to be on the winning side when it's all over, and if they choose sides too early, they could end up with the short stick. Look at the US Civil War. Both Britain and France stayed out of it. They didn't take sides. The same was true for the Russian Revolution of 1917, and the French Revolution of 1789. Now, it's true the Allies sent in forces to help the anti-Bolsheviks try to put down the rebellion, but there wasn't much effort put into it."

"Didn't the French Revolution lead to several wars with neighboring states?" asked Sumner. "I don't believe it was just all an internal conflict. I think it spilled over, if memory serves me."

"Yes, but the European powers largely stayed out of the revolution itself. They weren't drawn in until Revolutionary France, emboldened by toppling their monarch and centuries of such rule, declared war on its neighbors."

"Okay, let's assume you're right and other countries stay out of our conflict. That doesn't help me much," said Sumner. "In fact, it makes things worse. Without foreign help, we're sunk."

"I understand, sir," said Shea, pushing a lock of her hair back behind her ear. "Well, there have been many wars started with a triggering event, as you know. But these have also had the effect of pushing countries to align themselves with one side or the other much faster -- as it did in the Spanish-American War and Nazi Germany."

"Are you suggesting that I fabricate some ruse for war like what Hitler did or which was created around the sinking of the USS Maine in Havana Harbor?" asked the president, uncomfortable with what he was hearing.

"No, sir," Shea answered quickly. "I'm only saying that unexpected events can shape things in ways we cannot foresee. I'm not suggesting that we create them intentionally."

Sumner sat silently, ruminating on the ideas floating through his head – ideas that were conflicting to his very nature and core. Yet, would it be so terrible to contemplate such a thing? When backed into a corner, animals lashed out at that which is attacking them. Yet, are we merely animals – beings no better morally or ethically than the lions in the savannah or the vultures that hover overhead, circling for their next meal? The president tried to shove these thoughts from his mind, yet they continued to carom back. His struggle had always been between good and evil. But what if the only way to defeat evil were with other evil ... a lesser evil? Was there such a thing? Could one justify an evil, immoral act by saying it was less deleterious than not acting?

"I know what you're saying, Shea," said Sumner, his spirits dampened. "I understand fully. These are the tough questions that all presidents have had to face in one form or another. It comes with the office, I'm afraid."

Shea nodded, without expressing an emotion or any other opinion. "It is a lonely job, sir. That's what I've read."

"It is indeed," answered Sumner.

***

It was several days before Shea was able to get another meeting with Sumner. She still had not informed him of the slow progress with the two major technology projects upon which the Republic's survival might hinge.

"So, where are we on the Johnny project and Manhattan II?" asked Sumner, more melancholy than Shea had ever seen him.

"I just don't see us finding a panacea from Johnny or the Manhattan scientists any time soon, sir," reported Shea with a disappointed tone in her voice.

"Go on," said Sumner, his voice trailing off.

Shea looked at him carefully. This was not the man she had known for the previous few years, the one who had led the breakaway from the USSA and the one who had willingly taken the reins of the Republic to guide it into its own destiny – to carry on the legacy of the United States of America through the rest of the century and, hopefully, into the next. No, this was a man who was distracted, drained and perhaps now even showing fear. He had never shown that side of himself before – to anyone. It worried her, not only for herself, but for the Republic at large. They needed him strong, now more than ever before. Now was not the time for him to lose his compass or his will.

Yet for now, she stayed the course, addressing the matter at hand. She would also keep her thoughts to herself until it came to a head and something had to be said or done.

"I heard the tests are scheduled soon," said Sumner looking blankly at Shea, but not seeing her. "Johnny is making good progress. Is that right?"

"Yes and no, sir. Johnny told me that he's working on a larger machine – the size of a howitzer or tank. It will generate enough power to liquidate a battleship, cruiser or even an aircraft carrier."

"Well, that's good news," he answered, his voice perking up slightly.

Shea was tempted to leave it at that, but knew that would not help in the long run. "It's true … that's good news. We need a weapon of that capability in our arsenal," she answered, "but, work on the handheld device is going nowhere, I'm afraid. Johnny is no farther along on this than he was three weeks ago. He's taken his eye off the objective, I'm afraid. I believe I've got him refocused, sir, but then there is the matter of manufacturing and producing the things. That's not Johnny's strength, nor is it mine." "Thorne?"

Shea's mouth grew tight, as if she'd just sucked on a green lime. "I … I hate to admit it, but yes. We need someone with global manufacturing experience to pull this off. Just as we've given him charge of the other munitions procurement systems, I believe he should run this as well."

"I see," said Sumner.

"I know it's putting more power in the hands of a person we're uncertain about, but what other choices do we have?"

Sumner took a deep breath, turning once again to look out the rear window. It was becoming more and more frequent, as if he were trying to escape from his current reality and had no other way to achieve it. "If you're going to the casino, you might as well put it all down on the table."

Shea hated gambling, and she disliked the analogy, but she accepted it all the same. "Yes, sir. So, you agree?"

"Barring other options, I'd say yes. He's not shown disloyalty to me or the cause."

"Not yet, sir," said Shea without thinking. Sumner turned back toward his attorney general. There were more wrinkles around his eyes and across his forehead, making him look more like an aged prune than ever before. Shea wished she hadn't added those last comments and quickly spoke to make amends.

"Sorry, sir."

"What about Manhattan II? How is that progressing?" Sumner asked, continuing to probe.

"That's the other issue. I think Dr. Lin is stuck as well. However, his is fixable. I think we just need to have Johnny work with him. The Manhattan Project issue is one of theoretical and applied physics – both areas where Johnny is a genius."

"But what about the project's team? How are they going to react to someone from the outside coming in at this late date? Don't you think it might undermine their cohesion? Aren't you worried about the team accepting Johnny into their fold?" Sumner asked with his usual depth of understanding.

"I don't know," Shea answered, not having thought about those aspects. "It's something I'll have to consider if we roll John into their situation."

"He's also not the most easy-going, friendly person," said the president. "He is likely to ruffle feathers."

Shea thought for a moment. "I've got some ideas," she said. "I can make this work."

Sumner's mouth upturned only slightly, almost imperceptibly, but it was enough of a smile for Shea. She took it as a win for her … for him … for the Republic. Perhaps, just perhaps, there was hope after all.

*****

CH 23 Tally of States

With the deepening division between the Republic and the USSA, states were being forced to take sides. The states that remained with the USSA were still numerous even though their governors and state legislators quickly and facilely capitulated to the threats coming out of Washington. Others who were unwilling to submit and be subjugated under Ratner's dictatorial demands, called emergency sessions.

Even though their state governments had been disbanded by the new *Constitution 2.0* adopted by the USSA, these states were ignoring it, choosing to continue following the protocols of the first constitution. In a growing chorus, more and more were defecting to the Republic. At secession conventions, the legislators voted unanimously to join ranks with the rebels from Wyoming.

However, that was before the ultimatum issued by the First Citizen.

> *Be it known to all those former states that believe they can disregard the Constitution of the USSA and unilaterally decide to disengage from our Union – you are mistaken! You may not and you cannot secede! If you choose to go down the path of secession, then you are hereby warned that we, the USSA, will not tolerate such action and will any and all means necessary to stop it. Any measures taken to leave the Union will be met with force. We will compel you to remain, as legally you are obligated to do so. We will send troops to suppress any uprising, and we will punish those whom we find are traitors to the Motherland.*

Before the proclamation, twelve states had begun efforts to defect from the USSA; now all had suspended their petitions for statehood. Wyoming stood alone once again.

Without other states joining it, Wyoming was isolated in the middle of the continent. It was not close to any major body of water to receive vital imports and raw materials to fuel their budding technology industry. With Canada and Mexico sitting on the sidelines, the Republic was naked and defenseless. Establishing a corridor to water was essential.

"What do we have?" asked Sumner, sitting at the head of the Cabinet Room table. "What states have expressed interest, which ones have backed out, and which ones can we salvage?"

"Mr. President," said Ingram from State, "originally, we had the states of Kansas, Oklahoma, Arkansas, Louisiana, Mississippi, and Alabama along the Gulf Coast; Georgia, South and North Carolina to secure the southern Atlantic Coast. We have secured the northwest counties in Colorado which will give us unfettered access through Kansas, even though we continue to work on Nebraska. To give us access to the Great Lakes, Indiana was leaning our way, notwithstanding Chicago and the northwestern counties of Lake and Porter in Indiana which would be lost, of course. The leaners were Texas and Florida – two critical states – but we were making real progress in bringing them in. Ohio was also in play for us – this would have helped if Canada and Quebec would have come onto our team. Other states like North and South Dakota, Iowa, and Idaho were within days of signing, until the threat was issued."

"So, who are the low-hanging fruit here?" asked Sumner. "Which states can we pull back in with a little persuasion? We need to regain momentum. We need to restore a trickle of water from the stream in our direction once more."

"We need Texas and Florida to have any real chance at a water route," said Josh Templeton of Defense.

"One step at a time, Josh. I agree, but as I said, we need to create momentum again, and the best place to start is with those we can most easily bring back into the fold," said Sumner.

Ingram turned on a map of the old Continental US and projected it into the middle of the table. The map had three primary sections outlined with a black line encircling each. The first was the line drawn around Wyoming which was colored in bright crimson; the second highlighting the borders of states or just counties that had agreed to sign the pact before withdrawing. Filled in with a medium rose color, these would likely require the least work to repatriate. The third outlines were for those states that were going to be harder to reach and convince – these remained white. All other states were marked in gray as being difficult or impossible to move out of the USSA column.

Sumner rose and ran his fingers over the rose-colored states. "I think we have a shot at getting all of them. Where are we with those?" he asked Ingram.

Ingram ran down the list of strongly supportive states, and briefed the group on his conversations with their governors and key legislators. "… and in Nebraska," said Ingram, finishing his presentation, "the governor there, Governor Al Butler, is old school. He doesn't like what' happened any more than the rest of us, but he's got a weak legislature who's not willing to back him. Butler is a Marine, a colonel from the Special Ops Command. He doesn't take any sh*t from anyone, and he wants our help in convincing the state house that joining us is in their best interest."

"What if we gave them a demonstration of our phaser unit?" asked Templeton. "That's technology that would make them see we can defend ourselves and them against what the USSA can throw at us."

"I don't know," said Shea. "What about the secrecy of it? If we tell them, then everyone will know, including Ratner."

Ingram glanced her way with skepticism in his eyes. "Shea, at this point, we should assume Ratner already knows and is working on her own version."

"I also believe that at this point, it is in our best interest to let others know we have this weapon. It may do two things – one, it could do as Templeton suggests and show we are strong enough to defend ourselves and two, it may reinforce to Washington that it will not be so easy to engage us in conflict. They will suffer significant losses if they try," said Crawley from CIA.

"If we get these others back on board quickly and get the tide moving again in our direction, I think Texas and Florida will see they need to get on the train before it leaves the station," said Shea.

"But that would also mean, building a navy of our own," said Templeton. "Getting those ports along the Gulf Coast is critical, yes. But if we can't defend them, then there's no point. The USSA's navy isn't what it once was, but it's still strong enough to disrupt our shipping lanes. We need some deterrents in the water."

"Which country would assist us in building some? ... some war ships?" asked Sumner.

Well, it's not like the good ole' days when the South used Britain to build its ships during the Civil War," said Shea, bringing in the historical perspective.

But otherwise, the room was abnormally quiet. "I can see that this is a problem for which we don't have an answer," said Sumner, disappointedly. "So, it looks like it's Josh's job to figure out one. Templeton, this is a high priority. We need some answers."

"Yes, sir," said the Secretary of Defense.

Sumner pushed back from the table, straightening his tie and pulling down on the suit sleeves that had ridden up on his forearms. "Okay, people. Let's get cracking on this. We don't have much time to get our country back."

***

Sumner went back to his office, motioning for Shea to follow him. They went into his office and began calling.

"Let's start with the governor of Texas, Miriam Sanford," asked Sumner.

"Yes. I assume you have the number?" asked Shea.

"Yeah. Let's see what we can do," responded the president.

The line rang, and the governor's assistant picked up. "Governor Sanford's office," she answered.

"This is President Sumner and Attorney General Disone from the ATLAS Republic, we'd like to speak with the governor."

"Let me see if she's available," responded the assistant, talking in a high voice.

There were no visuals, only audio, and it took several seconds before the assistant's tinny voice came back online. "Hello, President Sumner? No, I'm sorry, the governor isn't available right now. But you may leave a message."

"I see," said Sumner. "I only wanted to let her know that we have information on USSA troop movements near Texas that may be of interest. However, if that isn't a priority for her, I understand. Please let her know and that she can reach me anytime. She has my number. Thank you."

Sumner hung up, as Shea looked at him. "What information?" she asked. "We don't have any information on military movements of the USSA."

"She doesn't know that," answered Sumner, smiling. "But I imagine she will call."

Sure enough, after an hour, Oishi announced that they had a call. "I'll take it," said Sumner with an air of ubiquity. "On screen," he instructed the computer. "Miriam, it's so good to speak with you again. It's been over a year since we last chatted."

On the screen was the visual of the state's governor. Sanford was not smiling. Her fat, pudgy face was bounded by thin wisps of highlighted hair pulled back into a braid that clipped to the back of her head.

She wore heavy eye makeup with thick, black mascara and gray eye shadow, giving her an ominous appearance. "JC, yes, so good to talk with you as well," she answered as cool as it was disingenuous. "But you understand that we aren't supposed to be corresponding. It's a violation of USSA law. However, what is it that I can do for you?"

"Miriam, it appears that you've moved your state toward an alignment with the USSA. Is that right?"

The governor sat up straighter in her chair, clearing her throat before she spoke. "I really don't know what you're referring to," she answered. "As you know, most decisions are made in Washington these days."

"Yes, but we all know that you and the people in the Austin statehouse still make the ultimate decision whether your state remains within the USSA or votes to secede. Isn't that right?"

"That is a decision that the state house speaker and senate majority leader make together," she answered. "They have voted and elected to stay with the Union, JC. You know that."

"Yes, but they would not have made any decision without your input – as the chief executive officer of the state."

"This has nothing to do with you," the governor sniped.

"It does when it comes to your revoking your initial commitment to join the Republic?" asked Sumner.

"We made no such commitment, and you know it."

"How much did she offer you, Miriam?"

"What?"

"How much did Ratner offer you to keep Texas within the USSA? I heard it was close to 42 billion in aid and another 2 billion to be split between you and Davidson, your house speaker. Is that right?"

Sanford's face grew red with rage. "How dare you …"

"Oh, I don't dare to do anything, Miriam. I know you, and we have intelligence that traces those specific payments that were made. So, do you still deny it?" Sumner had nothing, but he knew Sanford, and he knew he wouldn't be far from the truth. Apparently, he guessed right.

"You know it doesn't matter what you do, JC. I'm immune from prosecution here in the USSA. Ratner will see to that."

"You are if you trust the First Citizen. But you may not be immune to the wrath of your fellow Texans?" asked Sumner.

"Are you threatening me?"

"I can make sure that every citizen of Texas knows what you've done. Then, you'll need to flee your precious state before they arrest you and string you up. Knowing Texans the way I do, it won't take them long."

"The people here have no power," said the governor. "They can't touch me."

"They're only one of a few states whose citizenry threatened anarchy if they were forced to turn over their guns when Fourier tried to confiscate them a few years back. It got ugly in your state if I recall. Eventually, you had to ask Fourier to back down."

"But he didn't back down. You know that too," said Sanders. "And don't expect Ratner to either."

"I don't," said Sumner. "But you didn't enforce the new laws either. You just looked the other way. You let your people keep their guns because you didn't want to get strung up someplace. Isn't *that* right?"

"We enforce all the laws of the USSA," said Sanders smugly. Her eyes narrowed as the intensity and emotion began building once again within her.

Sumner crossed his arms in passive repudiation. "So, you'd stake your position and your family's safety on that, would you?"

"What are you saying?"

"I'm saying that your popularity will drop amongst the masses – people who … still carry guns. That doesn't worry you?"

Sanders bit the inside of her cheek, clenching her teeth tightly together to prevent saying something she might regret later. "If I join your Republic, Ratner will invade the state," said Sanford. "We can't defend against that."

"Seems to me, that she may do that anyway. You see, I have you covered on both ends. I can also leak to Washington that you're conspiring against Ratner at the same time you're taking her money. That's a double no-no. She will not only invade, but you may be the first one dragged behind a military truck with a grappling hook stuck through your body. Not a pleasant thought."

Sumner could be brutal when he had to be, and it was time that he met fire with fire. Pulling punches now would mean the collapse of their nation. They had worked too hard to let that go.

"What do I get if I join your little band of merry men?" Sanford asked, with disdain.

"It's not just men, governor," said Shea, interrupting "There are a great many women involved in this endeavor too. But while I share the president's views, I do understand the predicament in which you find yourself. You only want what's best for the people of Texas, and you're afraid they will suffer at the hands of a brutal, dictator if you choose wrong."

Sumner gave a thumbs-up sign that was out of view from the phone's camera so Sanders would not see it. It was a classic good cop-bad cop setup, which Shea picked up on without being asked. She had assumed the good-cop roll to help Sanders out of the corner Sumner had put her.

"Governor Sanders, we really do want Texas to join us. We believe we can offer you and your state the freedoms and benefits you will never get with Ratner. Your citizens will love you for making such a bold, courageous move, and your name will probably go down in the history books of Texas as one of the greatest."

Even Shea had to laugh inside. Her attempt at toadying up to the narcissistic governor was instantly evident. Sander's features softened, the rigidity of her skin relaxed, and her breathing seemed less labored and stressed as Shea concluded her remarks.

In turn, Sumner backed off in his assault. "I didn't want to upset you, Miriam, but you and I both know the stakes are high. We need you, and you need us. Together, we will prevail. We will succeed in creating our own independent country apart from the USSA, and we will grow to become what America used to be – the greatest nation on the planet. If you get involved, if you bring Texas in, you'll make certain that your state gets favored status. If you wait, and come in later after the USSA collapses, you will just be one of many."

"It doesn't look like I have much of a choice," said Sanford, fidgeting for the first time.

"Sure you do," said Shea. "You can do what's right for you and your state, or you can ignore the obvious and march down a path where they're already started posting yellow, diamond warning signs."

"It's a path that will only lead you all off a cliff, Miriam. It's up to you."

Sanford looked away from the camera, as if there were some other unknown person in the room. She waited for a response or signal before giving one to Sumner. "Send the paperwork. I'll convene the legislature. We'll get the secession papers going. You will have free and unfettered access to the state of Texas. We will join your Republic."

Sumner smiled. "Thank you, Miriam. I knew you would see the benefits of aligning yourself with us." The line disconnected and Miriam's picture vanished from view.

Shea glanced at Sumner. "*Wow,*" she said. "And she didn't even ask about the USSA troops on her border."

"No," said Sumner. "We've known each other a while. She must have known that was a ruse. But in the end, it worked. Who's up next?"

"Who do you know in Tallahassee?" asked Shea.

***

Flying to Tallahassee, Sumner and Shea were picked up by the Florida governor's limousine and hurried off to the mansion. There were no butlers or house servants to greet them at the door, as they had expected. Instead, the governor himself, Jimmy Mason, came to the door with a big smile on his face.

Jimmy was a good-ole-boy who had grown up in the rough and tumble world of politics. He was young, only thirty-three, and the youngest governor in the country. Stocky and stout, Jimmy's belly was one of the first things they noticed as they shook hands with him. His double chi and broad shoulders made his five-foot-ten-inch frame appear much larger than it was. His complexion was ruddy, and his hair an Irish red, combed straight back with a little bit of added gel. With this fat, chubby fingers holding a two-olive martini, he looked relaxed and comfortable in the large house, holding onto what remained of the reins on the third most populous state of the Union.

Hello President Sumner. And you must be the Attorney General, Shea Disone is it?" he asked, almost whimsically. "We've been lookin' forward to seein' you both. Mama has been talkin' about you nonstop today," he said. Then, peering over his shoulder, he shouted, "Mama! Your guests are here!" His eyes returned to his guests. "She'll be right down," he said, apologetically. "May I get you somethin' to drink?" he asked.

The governor's mansion was on an expanse of land some ten blocks north of the capitol building. With its six, majestic white pillars in front and ionic capitals, the red-bricked dwelling was a landmark in downtown Tallahassee. The second-floor balcony wrapped neatly behind the front columns, and the two wings offered administrative and entertainment facilities for the governor to carry out his official duties as executive of the state.

However, the inside of the mansion had not been renovated in over thirty-five years. State revenues had been tight even though Florida had enjoyed a growing population and tax base. The formal, federalist furniture looked more at home in a presidential museum in Washington than a southern estate. It looked nothing like the image the governor presented to the public or to his guests. Gold ornate picture frames held old oil paintings captive on the walls, and the wall paper looked faded and worn. There was a musty smell, which came from the high humidity and age of the room's fixed inhabitants.

"Come on back to the sitting room," said the governor, motioning them through the more formal living area. "Don't mind the stuffy areas up here. I never use 'em. Since I'm not supposed to change anything up here, I just leave it be."

Passing through a wide archway, the three entered a brightly lit sunroom, surrounded by towering windows that let in the beauty of the back gardens. A bright, canary yellow with white trim, the room exuded joy and freedom. In the center was a low, wide fountain of four tiers made of weathered iron. The sound of water spraying out the top and then rushing down the rocky ledges gave a tranquility that was addicting. There was plenty of sitting space in the area, and Sumner and Shea made themselves comfortable on one of the many soft floral sofas positioned along the wall.

One of the house attendants, dressed in a dark suit, white shirt and black bow tie, hurried over with a pleased expression on his face and asked them again if they wished something to drink.

"That martini looks good," said Sumner, pointing to the governor's drink.

"Just a sweet tea for me," said Shea, shaking her head.

"So, Mr. President, it's been a few years. Hasn't it?" said Jimmy.

"That it has, Jimmy," answered Sumner. "I think the last time I saw you, you were still in the Florida state legislature – senate majority leader, I believe."

"Probably so. That place hasn't changed too much over the years. It's still a knock-down, drag-out sort of place. If you need reassurance and support in what you do, the state capitol is not the place to be. They'll cut your legs out from under you and then force you to walk home."

"Sounds like several other places I've worked before," said Sumner, smiling. "But that's what I wanted to talk to you about."

I suspected as much," said Jimmy. "It's about the state's petition to join the Republic, isn't it?"

"Yes, I'm afraid we were very disappointed when you decided to retract that petition. It caused quite a stir in my office, you know."

Jimmy took a sip of his martini and then lifted the red, plastic pick, sucking one of the olives off the skewer. "I do understand what a position that put you in," he answered, putting the other stuffed, green olive back into the glass and swishing it from side to side. "But I couldn't fight my legislators. They went to battle over this one. I just didn't have the ammunition to take them on. You understand."

"Come on, Jimmy," said Sumner, leaning forward. "Was it that you didn't have the ammunition or you just didn't want to do battle over it? Is your position that precarious that you don't have the political capital to get something like this done?"

Jimmy blinked awkwardly, not liking the sound of the words, but then shrugged it off. "Listen, Mr. President, there are certain things going on that are underminin' everything I do now. As you know, the feds have stripped us bare. The states just don't have the clout anymore to do much of anything on their own. It's been headin' in that direction for quite a while. You know it as well as I do. Anyway, the house and senate both decided they didn't want to pour anymore gasoline on the fire. They felt if they did, they'd lose their pensions and every other perk they'd earned during their terms in office. There's no fight in 'em – Ratner's declawed every last one of them."

The attendant returned with a white, porcelain platter decorated with bright pink hibiscus flowers upon which rested three glasses – two martinis and a sweet tea, the latter poured into a large glass tumbler with a lemon wedge sitting atop.

Taking the martini from the attendant, Sumner took a sip and put it down on the round coffee table in front of him, next to the other martini which still held a quarter of its contents. "How much fight is left in you?" Sumner asked the governor pointedly, narrowing his eyes as he spoke his challenge.

The governor smiled uncomfortably and nervously shifted himself in his chair. "I'm sure you might come to that conclusion too, but it isn't so. I assure you Mr. President. I want what's best for Florida. At this point, the legislature has decided that staying with the USSA is in its best interest."

"And you agree?" asked Shea, coming into the conversation.

Unwilling to give an answer, Jimmy merely retorted, "As I said, I must vote with the legislature on this one."

"What if I told you that Texas and ten other states are moving forward with their secession plans to join the Republic? Would that change your mind?"

"When did this happen?" asked the governor, sitting up straighter than he had earlier. He uncrossed his legs and put his elbows on his knees. "I understood that no other states were going with you."

"You thought that Ratner's little scare tactic had forced the others to turn tail. Is that it?" Sumner asked. "Something like that."

Jimmy, Jimmy. You disappoint me. I thought you were made of better stuff than that. I thought you were one of the tough guys – one of the John Wayne types down here."

"Not even you are that old to be citing John Wayne now, Mr. President," Jimmy said chuckling, his belly jiggling from his own joke.

Sumner laughed. "I suppose you're right about that. No, I didn't know Mr. Wayne, as he was before my time. But what I can tell you about the man is that he stood up to his own beliefs. He wouldn't let anyone bully him if he thought his cause was right and just. Same with Clint Eastwood. Both men were icons of bravery for their causes during their time. They didn't let the Left push them around, and neither will we. As a well-known news reporter once said, 'This nation will remain the land of the free only so long as it is the home of the brave.'"

"Do you believe in freedom, Governor?" asked Shea, studying his reaction.

"Of course," Jimmy answered.

"Then, will you help us? Will you join our team? Are you willing to fight back against your legislature? Willing to convince them that our cause is noble and that freedom is worth the struggle?" she asked.

Jimmy looked down at his polished, black loafers, moving them about with random anxiety.

"What we have to do, Jimmy, is hit them where it hurts – their pocketbooks," said Sumner. "We have information that several of your legislators have taken money directly from the bursar's office in Washington."

"Bribes?"

"Yes. It runs in the millions of UnitedCoins, so it's not chump change. But because of interstate commerce laws, they have made deposits into state-owned banks. The money is still in this state."

The light bulb went off in Jimmy's head. "And you want me, as governor, to freeze their accounts."

"Yes. If you put liens on the accounts, we can force them to reconsider their alliances. Of course, we will also petition them on the facts of our cause and the likelihood of our success," said Sumner.

"I'm not sure that's a good approach," said Jimmy. "I don't know how you are going to survive a battle with the USSA."

"Neither did General Washington and his Continental Army. They faced the greatest military machine on the planet at the time, didn't they? I cannot disclose much, but I can tell you that we have some of the best minds in the world working on a defensive strategy. Several look promising, and we should be able to deploy them soon. We expect them to work, and when they do, they will render the forces of the USSA useless."

"Useless? You're exaggerating."

"We don't think so," commented Shea. "These are truly ground-breaking inventions – ones that may tilt the balance of power within the world from the most powerful militaries to the most vulnerable – or at least equalize it to some degree."

Jimmy fingered the red, plastic pick again and slid the other olive off and into his mouth, chewing it before knocking back the rest of his first martini. He smacked his lips again and stood up. Putting out his hand he said, "Mr. President, when do we get started?"

*****

CH 24 Manhattan II

Just outside of Ames, Iowa, there was a massive building complex that was constructed during the period from 1942 into the 1950s. It was known as the Ames Project, and its leader, Frank Spedding, developed a process to reduce the cost of packaging uranium to be used and refined into plutonium, the fission material of the atomic bomb. It was there that a team of scientists worked in seclusion to take their idea and develop it into a workable prototype.

Of the fifteen men and women who sat in the classroom at the University of Texas in Austin, fourteen remained. The one exception was Collier Forsythe, who took ill while at the meeting and was hospitalized. His family had a long history of Type 2 diabetes, and although the illness could be completely controlled, it still could not be cured. The remaining group reconvened in Ames to begin work on what they hoped would be the salvation of the Republic – something that would defend them from the nuclear and non-nuclear arsenals of the USSA.

The idea they had submitted was made as a joke as they had brainstormed the options in Austin. It had been Dr. Lin's idea of a comical submission – to embed it within the list of other, far more practical possibilities. When the group received word back from Cheyenne on the project that was selected from those proposed, their first reaction was to laugh. However, when they were told that it was, indeed, the project the Administration wanted pursued, their carefree approach turned somber.

"But, we were only kidding when we submitted that as a possibility," said Dr. Lin. "We weren't serious about being able to do it. There's no way we can do that!"

"Is it within the laws of physics?" Shea had asked, looking at him over the tops of her glasses.

"Well, I believe it is, yes. But that doesn't mean we have the technical capability to ..."

"Then find it," she had remarked to one of the smartest people on earth. "If there is any group that can, it's this one." And with that, she had walked out of the room, leaving the fourteen to stare at each other in disbelief.

"She is kidding," Pamela Tokarov had said. "Isn't she?" However, Shea had not been joking. So, it became their directive to construct a defensive energy field around key targets as large as twenty kilometers in diameter. The field would be akin to an upside-down bowl, blocking anything from penetrating its shield and destroying lives or property within.

Tokarov herself had PhDs from Harvard and MIT with her area of specialization the study and analysis of dark matter and dark energy that she had located within the universe. A young physics major, she had been top of her class as an undergraduate, but her work had been stymied by the lack of funding and importance placed on it by Washington. "Frivolous" it had been called. She was relieved to find work with Dr. Lin who was greatly interested in the effects of dark matter and energy and potential interactions with other energies discovered within the framework of eleven dimensions. Russian by birth, she had grown up with two tiger parents who had pushed her to the breaking point. School had been an outlet, but even there they had put enormous pressure on her to succeed. However, now they were disappointed in her. Her father had told her that by moving to Wyoming and joining the Republic, she had dishonored the family's honor. However, she had ignored him, choosing to join Dr. Lin and his idealistic plans to create a system that would defeat the six-hundred-pound gorilla of the east – the USSA.

"A shield of that size and magnitude will take a tremendous amount of energy," Dr. Lin had remarked. "I'm not sure how we can generate enough sustained energy to give adequate coverage or force."

"Pulse it," Tokarov had answered. "You know, nanosecond micro-bursts of, say ten to the twentieth joules of intense energy to create a curtain, in effect."

Dr. Lin had been impressed. "Yes ... that just might work. But how, in God's name can we generate even *that* much energy?"

The group labored over the physics and science of creating enough energy to accomplish this. Through the sheer gray matter of the minds of those involved, they determined that even less energy might be required if they used micro-bursts staggered at long intervals. At one one-thousandth of a-second intervals – an eternity in physics – the pulses wouldn't require as much power, but would be able to destroy almost anything, like an ICBM, that might come through the energy field area at over eight miles per second.

Shea visited the Ames facility with Josh Templeton and General Ward to view the program's progress. As they got out of their cars, they noticed the energy of the people hurrying to-and-fro among the six independent buildings of the complex. Everyone seemed to be in a rush to get to their destination, carrying their computers and sometimes odd-looking equipment that had no recognizable purpose or function. As for the buildings, they were deplorable. Not having been renovated since their abandonment back in 2018, the ramshackle structures exhibited signs of age and decay. The red-bricked buildings with limestone trim, arched, blue windows and large, globe wall-sconces were a Romantic revival architecture of the early 2000s that was dated; however, from the central headquarters on the campus, there was a vitality and life that transcended the archeological appearance of their brick-and-mortar facility. This was the hub -- the brain of the organism that reached out to other dwellings nearby and kept them enriched with thought and promise.

The three diplomats walked up the limestone stairs that were guarded by two tall, brick pillars with old-fashioned lion figures roaring atop each. Behind these immobile, but statuesque creatures was a battery of armed guards and checkpoints. The center, as well as the operation, was considered top-secret -- high enough on the list to warrant protection from level upon level of security. Both the ex-governor of Iowa and the local mayor of Ames were aware of a secret project there but were only informed that it was to develop a new generation of farming machinery. It was a deception to keep one of the most sensitive projects as clandestine as possible; yet, it was deception just the same.

"Yes, I'm Attorney General Disone and this is General Ward and Secretary Templeton from the Republic. We're here to see Dr. Lin," said Shea, expecting the visit to have been thoroughly coordinated. It was a surprise visit; however, at the very highest levels of each group, people had to know.

Disone, Ward and Templeton each presented credentials to the guard who scanned them with holographic light and asked that they step forward for retinal scans. Once those tests were passed, they were buzzed through to the inner-sanctum – the nerve center for all activity at the laboratory. This was ground zero.

Dr. Lin came promptly down the hallway, clicking his heels as he traipsed across the hardwood floors. His small, thin frame, bony appendages, and near-robotic movements, showed an almost android formality to his demeanor. His face was narrow and gaunt, with straight, black glossy hair, thin lips and ovular, black glasses that were too large for his face. He smiled and extended his slight, almost feminine hand to greet the visitors.

"So glad you could come," he said, bowing slightly, either out of habit or uncomfortable with the social formality required with foreign dignitaries. "We've been expecting you. Why don't you follow me?" He lifted his pale, thin arm and motioned for them to follow his procession down the same hallway he had just traversed. The hallway looked like an old university office row with tenured professors' offices lining each side. Old oak doors and high, transom windows overhead greeted the visitors, allowing only a trickle of light from within the offices to cast down on their faces. The corridor was a nostalgic walk for the three visitors who had spent many extra years pursuing graduate or law degrees.

Halfway down the hallway, Lin said, "Now, just turn to your right. That's right. It's room number 239 – an *apropos* number, don't you think?" alluding to the atomic number of uranium.

Lin tried to push open the door, but it wouldn't move. Then, he said, "Oh, yeah. I forgot." He placed his hand on the white pad just outside the entrance.

"Passage Granted," came a disembodied, soft, feminine voice across a speaker overhead, together with words displayed in red.

"After you," said Dr. Lin, as he gestured them through the door.

They all entered a rather cramped laboratory -- smaller than what they had expected. For a project that would create a machine capable of producing energy spreading over twenty radial kilometers, it seemed rather simplistic and unimposing. Still, the room was over twenty meters wide and fifteen deep, with ceilings that rose two full floors above them. Inside the space lay shiny-new, metal equipment of all shapes and sizes, with wires and cables wrapped around and through nearly every one of its square meters of volume. Some connections were so thick with cables that it was difficult to see if there was any equipment underneath the morass. In the center of the room was a doughnut-shaped contraption of some size, taking nearly two-thirds of the length and width of the room. It too was full of wires running up and down and left and right.

At the far end stood a glass chamber – a small, dome-shaped structure, with a tiny dot, hardly discernable, floating just beneath its apogee.

"What's all this?" asked Shea, pointing to the doughnut and what looked like a glass menagerie in front of them.

"That's what you're here to see," said Dr. Lin. "This is ... well, for the lack of another term ... a tokomak of sorts. We used these to project particles at near-light speed and smash them into other particles, creating immense amounts of energy. However, this one is different. You see, at the end there in the glass, we are able to create and contain a quantity of anti-matter through our experimentation. As we accelerate positrons at near light speed, we smash them into a few Moles of antimatter to generate huge amounts of energy. This energy is focused through these magnetic fields to form an impenetrable force field. It splits the array of energy into an umbrella, which can blanket an object, making it impervious to outside forces. The energy is modulated in nano-bursts to maintain the intensity and minimize the need for continuous bombardment. We only need a small amount of antimatter to create a field that will last long enough to be able to infuse new antimatter into the system and sustain the reaction. It's a functional system."

"I'm not sure I followed all of that, but it sounds impressive," said Secretary Templeton. "Can we get a demonstration?"

"Most assuredly," said Dr. Lin. "You'll need to wear these goggles, however." Lin pointed toward a row of thick, midnight blue lensed glasses carelessly thrown into a white box on the corner of the table. Each of the visitors quickly grabbed a pair, securing them to the bridges of their noses.

Lin called over three assistants who took their stations at the control panels at several different pieces of equipment that were concentrated in one corner of the room. Another assistant, wearing a blue smock and matching slippers, looked over a series of displays closer to where the antimatter was positioned inside the clear cage.

"Proceed," said Dr. Lin, giving all a quick nod of his head.

Instantly, there was a low hum and a small vibration that gradually faded away. After a few more seconds, there came a burst of light shooting downward from atop the glass dome and striking the small dot inside the chamber. The light stream was a pale pink when it immerged from the doughnut, but turned a fiery red and then a marigold orange, after colliding with the antimatter. Those flamboyant colors streamed down from the spot of antimatter like tendrils from a pulsating jellyfish. This light oddly bent, as if part of a watery stream, re-directed by boulders or stones blocking its path at the top of the dome. The energy traveled to the outer membrane of the glass dome, forming a distinctive umbrella-like shield.

"That's incredible!" said Shea. "It really works!"

"Impressive," said the general. "I never thought it was possible."

"Nor did we," said Dr. Lin. "Only after we were able to extract enough antimatter were we able to generate the energy we needed to create it."

"Will it deflect missiles and other projectiles?" asked Templeton, anxiously.

"All we know is that this model is effective ... as a mosquito killer," said Lin, laughing to himself. However, when no one else was amused, he went on. "What I mean is that it's so small that it will destroy small things that fly into it, but we don't know much more. Theoretically, if the ratios were to hold, it would destroy incoming missiles, yes."

"What do you mean, if the ratios hold?" asked Shea, still looking at the luminous dome that was still perfectly formed in front of her.

"Increasing the effectiveness of the model by thousands of times is quite another thing. Although the principles are the same, the energy level will need to be much higher to sustain a twenty-mile diameter safe zone. We are still experimenting with modifications to this method to do this, of course. But I think it will take a total paradigm shift in thinking to get there. We just don't have a clear idea about it at this point."

"What do you need to get there?" asked Ward. "We have limited resources, but we can see what we can do."

"If I knew, I would tell you," said Lin. "Right now, I can't." "Well, we need this sooner rather than later, doctor," said Shea.

"We're doing the best we can," said Lin.

"I'm sure you are. But sometimes we need even more, if that's possible," answered Shea. "The USSA will not wait for us to complete our work before they decide to attack us. Therefore, we have to have something ready within three months."

"Three months!" cried Lin. "There's no way it will be ..."

"Doctor, I wish I could give you more time. But we don't have it. I know you can do this. We all have confidence in your ability," said Shea with a reassuring smile.

The three left as they had come, and all three left with the same nagging thought. *Can the doctor really pull this off or is it beyond him? Is it beyond anyone?*

*****

CH 25 DemoCap

While the economy of the ATLAS Republic waxed, that of the USSA waned. The shift in prosperity couldn't have been more dramatic. Even with the travel restrictions and then outright ban on gaining travel documents within the USSA, its remaining smart, entrepreneurial and talented professionals found ways to get across the border into the Republic. More and more jobs were being abandoned in the former USA, at least in the private sector. The Enlightenment political party continued to attract a following, but it was out of survival, not out of any love for the party. One either worked for the party and the government – whether directly or through GovCos -- or got handouts from an array of programs, from basic foods to weekend entertainment – whatever was necessary to placate the masses.

With the outlaw of profits and nationalization of businesses, most shop owners and plant managers either moved out to the rural areas to plow a field for their own family's dinner table, or secretly emigrated elsewhere. Brain drain was also a problem. The USSA government did everything it could to hire the smart ones out of the universities and into government, paying them with the special perks usually bestowed only on those in the reigning Enlightenment Party. Some took the jobs, but many left anyway, finding bigger paychecks and more challenging career opportunities awaiting them in Canada or the Republic, where there were fewer restrictions. The top pay in the USSA was UC 99,999 under the law. In Canada, graduates were easily making the equivalent of UC 600,000 and more. So, the drain continued unabated.

Incensed by the trends, Ratner forced new legislation to stop *all* citizens from leaving the country unless they obtained a special dispensation from the Foreign Ministry. Travel, which had been governed by one's Travel Authorization Papers (TAPs), now required additional authorization from the Foreign Ministry. It made it illegal for anyone to leave the country without a special endorsement on top of their regular TAPs. Those of the Enlightenment Party received the *Green* Endorsement automatically. All other citizens had to request it; most were denied. None of this stopped the exodus.

As for the Republic, President Sumner made it clear to the ATLAS Congress that it was not pass frivolous, meddling legislation to impede the growth of business within the fledgling country's borders. He told them they should focus on sensible controls to ensure that air, water and the environs were not abused and that public life was not threatened; however, the red tape and financial penalties and punishments of the USSA were to be avoided. Although companies that willfully and wantonly polluted were prosecuted, standards were scaled back to levels that created balance between human needs and environmental factors. "While I do not sanction carte-blanche or laissez-faire capitalism, neither do I support the strangling of the golden goose," he had told them. "We must create a framework for open, transparent competition in commerce. No one should be repressed by others with more power and money. At the same time, after establishing a level playing ground, we must people take responsibility for their own destinies. Government must not interfere."

As a result, the role of capitalism came roaring back into vogue. Those in the Republic understood that a thriving business community meant a thriving society. As Sumner had articulated, it didn't have to mean that the strong trampled the weak. Instead, it meant that the strong created opportunities for the weak to improve their fortunes, while at the same time leveraging the capabilities of a well-educated and skilled labor force to accomplish their objectives. It could be a win-win for both, if viewed that way by both. Such outcomes were always better in the long-run for everyone. Such a symbiotic relationship -- where each benefited from the other – was the optimum solution. Punishing one over the other would not improve the sustainable fortunes of the parties together. Those businesses that treated their employees and customers well thrived, while those that didn't failed. It had almost become a business axiom. Still, the word *profit* and the realization of the same by these businesses meant that *all* classes of the population improved their lots in life. It wasn't a rich versus poor paradigm. It was a you-help-me and I'll-help-you paradigm -- and that was a good thing.

Barring a war or other major incident, elections in the new Republic were scheduled within the year, and Sumner had begun his campaigning. He was the odds-on favorite, but there were no guarantees. Sumner's only competition was Erin Petrovsky, a well-meaning, but left-of-center state representative from Wyoming. She was organizing the New Congress Party to compete with the New Freedom Party of Sumner's. As promised, elections under the constitution were scheduled for the first Saturday and Sunday in November, rather than the first Tuesday, as it had been for over two hundred years.

During Sumner's second week of stumping, he visited Oklahoma City, paying his respects at the memorial where 168 people lost their lives when an insane militant and accomplice detonated a truck bomb in front of a federal building in 1995. Later that day, he addressed a huge crowd that had gathered at the Alfred P. Murrah building to recognize the fiftieth anniversary of the bombing. In his speech, Sumner extolled the virtues of the capitalistic system and the proven ability of that system to grow an economy and enrich a society at large.

"My fellow Americans, I stand before you today, working to help you rebuilt a nation, a culture, a society that was nearly extirpated by a government intent upon crushing the hopes and dreams of its citizenry. My attorney general and her husband were a prime example -- starting a company that developed high efficiency combustion engines in a country called the United States of

America. Even then, it was difficult to succeed in any new business, but they were able to do it. They called their new engine the SECE, and its design was remarkable for its fuel efficiency and low cost of production. It all sounded like a perfect solution and an obvious success story. However, that dream was killed by the USSA, crushed like those of thousands if not millions of others.

"However, her dream is being realized in the ATLAS Republic which we have built. We have created a society and economy that embraces the entrepreneurial spirit and encourages risk taking. The government doesn't take sides – instead, it lets the free market do that, and, like other things, the best product or service will rise to the top. It's capitalism at its best.

"In this case, our Republic has used the SECE engine to build high-efficiency engines for our military vehicles, extending our petroleum supplies and making fuel logistics easier. We also use it in state-owned vehicles, lowering the cost of running the fleets and creating the trucks, buses, and cars that run in our government. It saves us millions each month.

"All this has helped us build the economy of this nation. Our growth rate of 8.4 percent is extraordinary. Compared with the USSA's recessionary rate of 3.5 percent and the negative 1.2 percent for the rest of the world, we're doing quite well.

"At the same time, we haven't turned our backs and let business run roughshod over the rest of society. There are norms; there is behavior that is acceptable to a modern society and that which is not. Government in its role as protector must work in concert with business – not as a coconspirator and not as an antagonist. We won't ignore misdeeds by business consortiums cornering the markets for themselves using intimidation and unethical behavior to force smaller companies out of business. However, we will not suck profitable companies dry with onerous taxes and paperwork just because they are doing something right for their customers."

This last comment got a hearty laugh from the group.

"We will not allow big business to dictate terms to us. Further, we will do everything we can to ensure that competition is fostered at every level of commerce, and to an extent, every level of government. Government must account for how it spends taxpayers' money. There must be effective metrics in place to show it is using those funds wisely, and when government can't provide the services efficiently, it outsources those to private industry where they should compete for the opportunity."

To this, Sumner received loud, boisterous applause.

"You see," he continued after the plaudits subsided, "it is also important – no, it is critical – that we keep multiple parties within our electoral system. This is another form of competition – one that competes in the world of ideas for the vote of its people. One party rule means a totalitarian state – period. It will crush free speech, free religion, free press, and free life wherever and whenever it is allowed to happen.

"The original *U.S. Constitution* did not provide for political parties. These were invented by Jefferson and Hamilton – the Democratic Republicans and the Federalists, respectively. They fought like brothers. Yet, the country grew stronger because of it. It is the way in which we can voice dissent; a way in which we can challenge each other to do better; a method to ensure we have the opportunity to evaluate competing theories and policies and decide on what's best for us – for our nation.

"Just as democracy requires at least two parties, capitalism requires the balance of opposing forces. Here I underscore the term balance. Capitalism must be tempered by robust competition and a level playing field. There cannot be a motif that protects GovCos from government laws or, on the contrary, benefits unfairly from those laws. The premise of Too Big to Fail is false, just as is the thought that free markets only reward the rich and punish the poor. Balanced free markets – ones that temper business freedom within the confines of democratic and capitalist, or what I call DemoCap, axioms will prosper. These DemoCap laws are: Transparency, Competition, Merit and Spiritual-Reality. Let me explain.

"First, business and government must be transparent in the way they conduct business or pass laws. Full disclosure about relationships and details of transactions when there may be a conflict of interest are essential. Of course, there are always matters of national security or proprietary secrets that must be preserved, but those must not be used as a guise to cover-up surreptitious activities. Such action must be prosecuted and punished severely in the courts.

"Second, there must be competition at all levels. Competition is the great equalizer. It is what has driven America to achieve more than any other country on the planet. It may be considered creative destruction, which is unsettling to many, but it is what drives the engine of ingenuity and progress in this nation. Without it, we would stagnate like the USSA.

"Not only should we have competition in commerce, as I have noted we should have it in government. We should demand that if our government cannot provide services to its citizens at a cost that is less than that in the free market and as good, then it must outsource those activities to the private sector. Government should be held to performance standards just as we hold business to them. For business, it's measured in profits. For government, it should be measured in consumer satisfaction, as measured by votes, and cost-effectiveness, as measured by law.

"Third, rewards must be merit based. This is different from the concept of equality. Equality suggests that we treat everyone the same, regardless of whether they perform well or not. It is a Marxist view, where the strong carry the weak. Ironically, often times the weak – protected by laws -- take advantage of the strong. Forcing the strong to give up what they've worked hard to achieve is not an answer. It only weakens the strong and, more importantly, impoverishes the weak. It does nothing to strengthen the weak, but merely makes them more dependent on government and handouts, not less.

"Our voluntary system of charity has worked marvelously well for centuries, and more incentives for the wealthy to establish foundations and give to such causes would ensure funds are spent on truly worthwhile things.

"Therefore, people should earn based upon what they produce and contribute to society based on the value perceived by a free market. Such merit should not be judged based on color, race, gender, ethnicity, creed, sexual preference, or any other factor. One should not get preferential treatment because he or she is black or white, brown or gray, green or pink. It shouldn't matter.

"Fourth, spiritual-reality. What is this? The first part, spiritual, comes from the Latin *spirare* or to breathe and *tus* or to act. Therefore, the act of living is inherent in the meaning of spiritual. A wider perspective includes the notion of a person's soul, sacred religions, or even more generally, ethical and moral considerations. It is what we hoped or wished the human spirit really was – pure and untainted.

"However, there is a second element – reality. This is the human condition, directed by lower-level, primal principles. It involves the understanding of human nature as it is – not what we wish it to be. Darwin outlined the evolution of biology in his opus primus, On the Origin of Species, first printed in 1859. Since then, most have come to accept that man has evolved from lower-level species to his present-day form. Unfortunately, with that evolution comes baggage – greed, lust, arrogance, jealousy and a multitude of other more extreme complexes that are occasionally exhibited by people. When these are the prominent traits of people we've elected to office, our society suffers. They will not change just because we wish it. Such behavior changes when there are requisite benefits and punishments to either encourage or discourage such actions. This is why we have laws; this is why we have government. But it does not mean that we need a government that controls every aspect of our lives – from the time we rise to the time we sleep. Our system of laws has expanded exponentially since Ten were given to Moses. We now have thousands if not millions of individual laws that protect us from each other and from ourselves.

"Are there those who are altruistic and need no encouragement to do the right thing? Yes. Are there those who, despite encouragement, will never do the right thing? Yes. Will we be able to protect all the people all the time from every conceivable danger or transgression? No. At some point, we must give people independence to choose their own path whether to succeed in life or fail. It's called individual responsibility, and it originally formed the bedrock of our old USA. It is not the duty of the government to ensure happiness, to ensure success, to ensure equal distribution of wealth for all. No, it is the government's responsibility to protect its citizens' lives, to protect its citizens' liberties, and to create a society in which they may pursue their dreams. Nothing more, and nothing less."

To that, those gathered before him stood on their feet, applauding furiously. The noise level was deafening, and the group began to chant "Sumner! Sumner! Sumner!"

"Whether you're an agnostic or atheist you have some level of spirituality – believing in humanism or perhaps some fundamental virtue or truth. Spirituality is the glue that holds mankind together. It gives us purpose. Without it, we have nothing.

"So, with that I again thank you for working so hard for the Republic. Although we may have dark days ahead, I believe we will have many more glorious ones as well. We must believe in ourselves and in God or our own truth and never give up. It was once said, 'we can have life without freedom, but not freedom without life.' I would say it differently – we can only have life if it comes with freedom; otherwise, it is no life at all. Thank you."

Numbering in the thousands, the group rose to give him an ovation that he would remember. His heart filled with warmth and gratitude as he smiled and waved his appreciation. *Perhaps it is all worthwhile,* he thought. *Perhaps they really are grateful for all the hard work we're putting in to make this thing work.*

Sumner stepped off the podium and began walking toward the side stage, when someone came running up to him. "Mr. President," said the voice. It was his newly promoted Chief of Staff, Oishi Gupta. "I have an urgent call for you. You need to come with me." Gupta led the president and two Secret Service agents to a backroom where they could project the 3-D image of the caller into the room without others eavesdropping.

"What is this about?" asked Sumner, the look of worry, etched across his forehead.

"You will be talking with Secretary Ingram," said Gupta. He will be available … now."

Ingram's stern demeanor flashed as an image into the room, his mouth downturned as if he had dropsy. His eyebrows nearly met in the middle, as he puckered his mouth before beginning to speak.

"Mr. President?" Ingram began.

"Yes, Lawrence. What is it?"

"I'm sorry to interrupt you, but I need to inform you that there has been a development, sir."

"What? Where?" asked Sumner, his heart skipping a beat as he listened intently.

"It's Ratner. I think you should come back to Cheyenne immediately."

*****

CH 26 Phaser Test

It took another three weeks before the large backpack-sized prototype was ready, and Johnny proudly carried it to the front of the audience that had gathered at the Wyoming National Guard firing range just outside of Cheyenne. In attendance were Shea, Secretaries Templeton and Ingram, General Ward, the Joint Chiefs and their direct reports. While progress with the Manhattan II Project was proceeding more slowly, Johnny had vaulted ahead, resolving his most vexing problem of shrinking the fit-form of the phaser into a handheld device.

Dramatically dressed in military camouflage, complete with helmet, black high-top boots, and tinted goggles, Johnny appeared happier than Shea had ever seen him. He was glowing in what was to be his shining moment. This would be his legacy – how historians would memorialize what he had done in his life.

Dropping the backpack on the ground and kicking it just to show how rugged it was, Johnny raised his arms to motion for everyone's attention. "Now, if I may begin," he started. "I'm glad all of you could attend my little demonstration today. This project has taken months of preparation and, I must say, many of my brain cells to solve complicated technical issues that arose during my experimentation. However, I'm pleased to tell you that I've come up with a very workable unit that will serve you well in the field."

Johnny picked up the cloth bag, imprinted with the deep forest colors of green, brown and black that swirled in amorphous forms on its surface. "This is the fusion core reactor unit," said Johnny pointing to the heart of the camouflaged satchel. "It weighs about twenty kilos, although I think I can shave some of that off. It's connected here to the phaser's magnetic and triggering units." With that, he produced a black, pistol-like gun with a chocolate brown, umbrella-shaped cone on the front, coiled with crimson and gold wires winding back toward the grip. From the bottom of the grip, a black cord – something that looked like a thick extension cord – extended to the underside of the backpack. The entire unit didn't appear heavy, but was bulky and cumbersome.

Johnny slipped on the backpack, shoving his long arms through the two loops and balancing it between his shoulder blades. Unwrapping the kinked extension cord, he held the pistol in his large, meaty palm.

"In front of me is a pile of old laboratory equipment. This unit will, in laymen's terms, incinerate the equipment. Neither the backpack nor the pistol will get hot. As you will see, both will remain cool to the touch. The phaser will focus a beam of intense energy generated from the miniature fusion reactor inside the backpack to mere picometers in diameter, bombarding the equipment and creating a chain reaction within the molecular structure to vibrate the atoms to the point of vaporization. Notice the sequential dissipation of the matter as the beam heats the atoms to incendiary temperatures."

Johnny held up the pistol, but stopped. "I admonish you to use your goggles at this point, otherwise, you may suffer permanent blindness if you look directly at the beam." He didn't have to repeat himself, as all of those in attendance hurried to grab their protective gear.

Johnny pulled his own dark green shades down over his face and pulled the trigger. Just as before, there was a very low humming noise coming from the backpack; then, a moment later a bright yellow light shot out of the pistol, illuminating the pile of equipment for less than a second, making it glow with enormous intensity. There was no sound or movement in the target, it just grew brighter and brighter on its own. Then, it all happened in an instant -- a loud *bang* or *pop* ending in a mini-explosion, showering sparks and fragments of metal in all directions. It was like a rocket during a fourth of July celebration shooting up into the air and exploding into a dazzling array of flares falling to the ground. All in the room shuttered in amazement and looked on where the equipment had once rested. Now, only a black pile of dust remained, with a steady, smoky plume rising into the air overhead.

The generals, normally a staid bunch, reacted with *oooh's* and *aaah's* in amazement as they marveled at the science fiction project that had come to life for the first time in recorded history.

"Was this what you were expecting?" asked Johnny, confidently, grinning from ear-to-ear.

"That was spectacular," said one of the generals, his mouth agape in wonder and awe.

Johnny's face continued to smile, the upturned corners of his mouth giving away some secret he'd been hiding during the entire show. "Well, if you thought that was amazing than what do you think of this?"

He pointed the pistol at an old, full-sized M1A1 tank that was sitting nearly a quarter mile away, its turret beginning to show signs of rust from disuse. The yellow beam of light again flashed from the barrel of the gun, cutting a straight-line path over the distance, striking the tank's lower back track. It disintegrated in less than a second, dropping the backend to the ground with a *thump*. Johnny pulled the trigger two more times, each time hitting a different part of the tank and making that part disappear as well.

"Even better, right?" he said eagerly, enjoying the spotlight and the success. "But what if I told you there's no need for this backpack?" He now pointed to the satchel on his back as if her were a supermodel displaying new cookware in an advertisement.

There were gasps in the crowd. Stunned by what they had just witnessed, none could imagine that one man could possibly invent an actual, working phaser, the size and capability that they had grown up seeing only in the movies. It was impossible.

Johnny disconnected the cables and removed his backpack, opening it to show there was nothing inside it but rocks. He dumped the primeval remnants out on the ground and kicked a few with his feet. "Like I said, I don't need the bloody backpack. All I need is this," he stated, holding up the pistol-like device that had disintegrated a multimillion-dollar tank. Johnny had become a showman, and he was very good at it. But what made it special was that he was able to deliver on what he promised.

Walking over to General Ward, Johnny thrust his hand out holding the pistol but safely pointing it toward the ground. He smiled and nodded to the general, suggesting that he take it. The general looked apprehensive and, at first, was reluctant. Then, Ward summoned his courage, gingerly taking the weapon and looking it over with a keen eye. "What do I do?" asked the general, still afraid to activate something as deadly as he'd seen.

"Here is the safety," said Johnny, showing him how to work it. "It works just like any other pistol in that way. With the safety on, it won't fire. The next model will incorporate the person's fingerprint ID, and monitor his vitals, matching those to what is stored in the embedded computer chip. Only when all those match up, will the person be able to fire it."

"How soon can I have two thousand units?" asked Ward, eager to get his hands on them for his troops.

"That depends on how much the Republic is willing to sink into production efforts," said Johnny. He turned to Shea with a raised eyebrow. "You would know that, right?"

Shea had still not told Johnny about Thorne's involvement, and she felt that this was not the time to bring it up. "Of course, John. We will be coordinating that immediately now that we know you've got something that works. I'll inform the president right after we leave here."

As they left, Shea wondered how she would break the news and what his reaction would be. Hopefully, he wouldn't remember that part of his life and the villain Kilby Thorne had once played in it.

*****

CH 27 Directorate Control

The constitutional decree was issued jointly by the Executive Branch, now referred to as the Directorate, and the Supreme Court, whose members had been paid off to concur with its provisions. Once the millions in UnitedCoins had been deposited in Swiss accounts for the Justices, the decree was sent to the People's Congress for a rubber-stamp endorsement. This was not just a crisis for democracy – it was the final and complete overthrow of a system of government. It was the final triumph of a revolution, begun and won without a shot being fire.

And so went the shift in power from a *trias politica* – a balance among the three branches, namely the executive, legislative and judicial – was narrowed by two. The separation espoused by Montesquieu, and put into practice by Washington, Madison, Jefferson, and Hamilton had suffered its final, mortal blow. The internal war of ideas had ended with a sad whimper, rather than a cataclysmic battle. There was no procession or parade. It was all handled over during a weekend, in the dark of night. Virtually no one knew, and that's just the way First Citizen Ratner wanted it. Now, only the Directorate made any difference; it was the sole arbiter of justice, and of life and death.

Executive Order 49666, issued in obscurity, finally found its way to the surface and was revealed with stark and brutal force. It started with the Governors' Conference, scheduled for August 6-7 in Phoenix. Just as the conference convened, the USSA Attorney General Nate Ericson sent in troops that swarmed the conference center downtown and blocked all exits. The brigade commander walked into the office of the meeting organizer and ordered that the meeting be canceled. When she had initially refused, he raised his M16A7 rifle and pressed the muzzle into the soft side of her temple.

The governors weren't initially told why their conference was terminated and why the paramilitary group was holding them inside. Instead, they were informed that they were being protected from a potential terrorist plot and that the meeting was shut down. Each governor had been escorted from the center back to the hotel and then followed to the airport to ensure they had all departed. The following day, each governor received a hand-delivered letter from Ericson that read:

Dear Governor:

The federal government of the United Socialist States of America has declared a state of emergency with respect to its debt obligations to debt holders and other matters confronting this great nation. Under such conditions, it is necessary for us to enact martial law. Henceforth, the Directorate of First Citizen Ratner will assume all responsibilities previously held by the People's Congress and Supreme Court. Urgent matters in today's fast-moving world require immediate action – something the old three-branch form of government could not manage effectively. In addition, we can no longer afford to run multiple branches of government. Such redundancies of government functions are impractical at the federal, state, and local levels. Therefore, I have proclaimed the following constitutional changes:

> *1.   Your state, commonwealth, county, parish and all other local government bodies shall be disbanded immediately, and all authority and jurisdiction turned over to the Directorate and its local branches.*
>
> *2.   All agencies of these government bodies shall be dissolved, and their functions assumed by the corresponding federal agency of the Directorate.*
>
> *3.   Your role as executive of your state or commonwealth is hereby terminated as of the date of this notification.*
>
> *4.   All judicial functions shall be turned over to federal courts, now run by the Directorate.*
>
> *5.   All state, commonwealth, county, parish, city or other laws are hereby invalid and superseded by those of the federal government. To the extent there are no such federal laws in place, the Directorate will issue such laws to be obeyed in all the previous states.*
>
> *6.   All national and state guards and militia units shall be absorbed into the USSA military structure according to the branch of service.*
>
> *7.   Any other functions, such as police, hospital, education, park service, sanitation, public transportation, agriculture control, corrections facilities, environmental protection and labor fairness, among others, shall also be directed to the corresponding federal agency.*

It is unfortunate that such measures are necessary; however, we believe this is merely a temporary measure to help us right the wrongs of past administrations and the mismanagement and irresponsibility of the opposition party when they were in power.

As First Citizen of the United Socialist States of America, I appreciate your cooperation with this decree, which is historic in correcting the fatal flaws that were inherent within the rigid and unyielding framework of our former constitutions. We live in the modern era – one that requires rapid decision making and the ability to change course quickly as dynamic and fluid conditions require.

Only now will we be able to move forward as a people and a society. Only now can we realize the greatness of this marvelous land.

With warm regards,

First Citizen Angel Ratner

Although the governors were in an uproar, there was no coverage by the media outlets. They knew they had to defend Ratner and her actions, lest their licenses to report on the airwaves (TV, radio, or SI-net) would be revoked immediately by the Ministry of Transparency and Communications. So, nothing was done. Independent news groups and SI-net blogs were summarily shut down once the letters were circulated to prevent adverse spin on the story. The following day's *New York Times* headline was indicative of most:

Ratner Brings Efficiencies and Fresh Reasoning to Complex Governing Structures

Shea never picked up a *New York Times* paper, but someone sent her a discreet email urging her to do so. She read it carefully, intent upon understanding what was happening in the USSA. *The time is right*, she said to herself. *We have to act while the hammer is coming down on those we've left behind.*

She got on the phone to the president informing him of what was going on. He told her to contact Thorne, saying that it was time to mobilize the Underground, regardless of the plant within the organization.

Thorne began instructing his loyalists to stage marches throughout the USSA, starting with the big cities. The first one was organized in Washington, the second in Chicago. Others followed in Boston, Philadelphia, Atlanta, and Richmond. Colonel Marcus was all too eager to initiate the social media blitz to notify people of the protest. It required persistence and ingenuity to avoid the government censors, but he had figured out a way.

The marches had to be assembled quickly. Electronic bulletins of the marches were broadcast less than an hour before the protests started, intentionally giving the Red Shirts no time to coordinate a counteroffensive. To make it more difficult, the rallies were only an hour in length and were over before the Red Shirts had time to put them down. Several times, TV cameras crews showed up to cover the negative side of the demonstrations. Although hostile, the coverage was exposure none-the-less, and it was widely distributed. People saw that others were as dissatisfied as they and were acting on it.

"This is Cassie Jurgenson reporting for *TV 7 News Chicago*," said the tall, leggy young blonde woman appearing before the camera with her mascara running slightly just below her right eye. There was a light drizzle as the cameraman panned the crowds behind her, showing the protestors pumping signs up and down with their fists.

"Behind me is a group of protestors who have come to Daley Plaza, where the former city government operated. They say they are marching against recent news that Washington has declared null and void any further actions by state governors, their legislators, and the courts. The Executive Order came down from Ratner's Administration earlier in the week, stating that all legislative, executive and judicial authority previously held within the states is now under the purview of the federal government."

Behind her were several protestors wearing button-down shirts or nice blouses of various colors and patterns and either khaki's or modish jeans. They looked professional or at least well-educated – the types not ordinarily seen in such rallies. Each marcher was peaceful, holding up placards and posters decrying the heavy-handed actions of the Directorate.

But when the camera light went on, signaling that the broadcast was live, the reporter shifted to another group quite unlike the vast majority of well-dressed protestors at the demonstration. These activists were pushing and shoving the others around, purposefully bumping them and trying to intimidate them. Dressed in sweatshirts, some with slogans that were disgusting and offensive, others with pictures that were equally revolting, these young people were unruly and riotous. Devoid of any sense of decorum or rule of law, they gathered in packs, disrupting and creating chaos. These were groups that were paid by authorities to discredit the entire protest. It was part of the strategy to turn public opinion against the march – against those who were defying the Administration.

These were the thugs to which the camera now pointed -- and pointed exclusively.

"As you can see, these people are very vocal about their position against First Citizen Ratner and what, they say, she's done to America. Let's talk with Tom here … Tom, why are you marching today?"

The reporter thrust her microphone up to the man's mouth, nearly making him gag on the projectile as it pressed toward his head. His eyes were glazed over, obviously overcome by the effects of some substance he'd taken earlier, and he wobbled and staggered, trying to regain his balance.

"I … we … I mean … it's just wrong. The whole thing is bad, man. You know, really bad!"

"What is it that's wrong, Tom?" asked the reporter, trying to keep her subject on track.

"The whole thing … it's all wrong!" he answered, looking around in a daze. With eyes half closed, he took his hand and ran it through his hair, pushing it back on the sides. "It's just messed up! The whole damn thing is just f*ck'd up!"

"So, what is the issue you're protesting against? Why are you here?"

"I dunno, man. I heard the government was doing something bad to us again. So, I showed up. All I want is for everyone to love each other, ya' know! Just love each other. That's it. When the cosmic rays of Myra come down and fill your body you'll understand. You'll see how glorious life can be. Myra is the goddess of all of us, ya' know. She's the bomb, man. She's … well …" The man turned his face, his attention span disintegrating by the second.

Cassie turned to the person next to him. He was equally disoriented and appeared as though he had just drunk a fifth of vodka or smoked three joints. "And you, why are you here today?" she asked him, again pushing the microphone forward.

The man wasn't even able to look at her or the camera, his face just kept trailing off, becoming distracted by other things going on around him. His mouth agape and drooling at the corners, he mumbled something incoherently.

"I'm sorry, I didn't catch that. What did you say?" pressed the reporter.

"Uh, well … ," he finally blurted out, slurring his words. "Uh, I … "

"Yes?" she asked again, milking the absurdity for all it was worth.

But the man started to swing his arms wildly, hitting her microphone and then knocking her over. She fell into the cameraman, pushing him to the ground and causing the shot to go awry. Everyone at home saw the folly of what was happening, but they were confused as well, waiting for the reporter to catch her breath and conclude the broadcast.

Disheveled and disoriented, the reporter got back to her feet and hurried to end her ordeal. "As you can see, this group is out of control. They seem not to understand why they're here or what they're doing. That goes for just about everyone I see around me. This is ..."

Suddenly, another man, this one well-dressed and coherent grabbed the microphone and began speaking. "What she just broadcast is not true," said the young man with short, brown hair combed to one side. His face was angular and serious, and the intensity of his commitment shown through his eyes like a beacon in a fog. "The morons she just interviewed were hired to disrupt our protest. They aren't part of it at all. This entire news cast is a ..."

The reporter wrestled the microphone away from him, and quickly signed off, "This is Cassie Jurgenson, reporting for *Channel 7 News*."

After the bright, halogen light on the camera went off, the reporter put down her microphone, pushing aside the articulate man who had tried to discredit her report. But without saying a word to him, she instead turned on the other two apparent bums whom she had interviewed. "What was that?" she yelled at one of the men. "You made me look like an idiot!"

The two, wild-eyed men laughed and smiled at each other. "We were only doing what you told us to do," said one of them, now perfectly normal.

"No you didn't. We told you to look and act like druggies. I didn't tell you to rip knock me to the ground!" Her voice was raised and piercing.

"I thought that would give it a more realistic effect," said the second man, only marginally disappointed in their critique.

"Whatever," said the reporter, "just don't let it happen again on the eleven o'clock airing. Okay?"

"Yes, ma'am," said the man. "But we need to get paid half up front before the next show – like you promised."

"Go over to the news van. The guy over there will give you your money. But you'd better be back here for the late newscast," she warned.

Cassie was, indeed, the same Cassie that had bravely smuggled out the video images from the massacre in Springfield, Massachusetts a year earlier. After giving the footage to Sumner at GOFLA, she had lain low for months trying to create another identify and another way to make a living and survive. With help from GOFLA, she was able to recast herself as another news reporter, moving up quickly until she got her job in Chicago. She loathed what she had to do, but it put bread on the table and wine in her liquor cabinet. Deep down, she felt like a traitor, but she only hoped another opportunity would come her way where she could make a difference.

"Okay, boys, let's wrap it up here until we're back on the set," said Cassie, directing the news crew in the van. Just then, seven armored personnel carriers roared into the plaza followed by two tanks and nine Humvees. USSA Red Shirts jumped out carrying M16-A5 and A7 rifles and wearing belts across their chests with thousands of additional rounds of munitions. The camouflaged M1-A4 tanks rolled into position and pivoted their 120 millimeter canons toward the frightened crowd. The crowd of thousands backed away, not knowing what was happening.

The captain in charge of the squadron stepped out of his Humvee and hoisted his megaphone. "Disperse your protest or we will have no choice but to engage. Then, he pointed his rifle to the sky and began firing off shots into the air."

To Cassie, this was déjà vu. She had seen this play acted out in Springfield and understood that there were even fewer restraints on the Red Shirts now. She already knew how the play would end, and it wouldn't be a happy one.

"Let's get out of here!" she screamed at the camera crew. "Throw your cameras in the van and ..."

Shots began to ring out as protestors ran to get out of the way. In the first volley, twenty bodies fell to the ground, bleeding from fresh wounds to the chest and extremities. A few others were hit directly in the face and died instantly. The red stain of blood began flowing freely onto the tan cobblestones that blanketed the plaza in front of the ex-city government building.

Cassie sat behind the wheel of the small, azure blue news van parked along the curb, hoping no one in the military group would spot them. She trembled, petrified, as she watched the carnage once again unfold before her eyes. *I just can't take this again,* she thought. *I just can't!*

She started the van and slowly began to pull away, hoping the gradual withdrawal would go without notice. But as she peered out her side mirror, she saw one of her cohorts with his camera hanging out the side of the van still taking footage.

"What are you doing?" shouted Cassie, shocked at his temerity. "You'll get us all killed!"

The camera man put his finger to his lips and continued filming.

"I told you to stop! Really! Now!"

Another series of rapid fire shots from the M-16's echoed like the staccato popping of popcorn in a hot skillet. The bullets ricocheted off nearby car doors, one hitting an older gentleman in the shoulder, driving his body backward. His bald head struck the pavement in silence, but the damage was done. A corporal ran up to him, putting his rifle muzzle to the man's head and pulling the trigger. The Red Shirt didn't hesitate killing an innocent citizen – it seemed all too easy for him. After firing off a second round for good measure, the young soldier stood up, spotting Cassie and her cameraman. Unshaken, the cameraman held his camera capturing the scene and filming the soldier as he walked toward them menacingly. "Put it down!" yelled the soldier. "Put it down now!" he roared.

The cameraman sat defiantly inside the van, unmoving. "I'm part of a news crew. I have every right to film what I see here."

"Not according to the high command! This is a classified op. You can't film it. Now put down the camera!"

"Put it down," whispered Cassie, her lips quivering. Panic struck her, and she stomped on the gas pedal to get away; however, the van stalled.

The cameraman continued his defiance. "You'll have to kill me I guess," he told the soldier, taunting him.

The single shot rang out, but it was buried in the sea of other crackling sounds bouncing around the plaza. No one paid any attention – except Cassie and the other men in the van with her. She watched in horror as the bullet passed through her colleague's head – entering with a small red dot, but coming out the back spraying chunks of flesh and membrane on the white, interior walls of the vehicle. Blood spattered all over her light gray pants and trench coat, and she screamed as the camera fell to the floor along with its owner. Both lay shattered and irreparable.

Cassie restarted the van and floored the accelerator, overriding the automatic pilot, and speeding away. The force of her action tossed the other crewman in the back around like a child in a blow-up bouncy house. Careening the wrong way down a one-way street, she swerved left and right to avoid crashing into other cars and pedestrians. But as soon as they were several blocks away, she pulled the van over to the curb and slammed on the brakes. Bent over with her elbows stretched out across the wheel, she began sobbing, pounding the console and biting the knuckles on the back of her hands. Cassie couldn't bear to turn around and see the remnants of her cameraman. She'd seen this type of death before, and it haunted her to that very day.

"Cassie," came the weak, halting voice of the other crew member, "we have to get back to the studio, you know. We have to show the producer what we have here."

Cassie didn't move, her body riveted to the steering column.

"Cassie, did you hear me? We have to ..."

"Yeah, Steve, I heard you!" she said with misdirected anger. There was a long pause before either spoke again, and it was Cassie. "You know they won't touch it – the film, I mean. There's no point in taking it to them."

"I don't think that's true," said the crew member. "This is a major story. It's a bloody disaster. They *have* to cover it."

"They won't. I'm telling you right now," she said, releasing her death grip on the wheel and pulling herself up. She wiped the tears from her face, not caring whether it smeared her mascara. She was done with that – she was finished with all of that. She pushed the button on her three-point harness to free herself and opened the door, grabbing her satchel as she stepped out.

"Where are you going?" asked the crewman. "You have to take us back to the studio."

"Here," said Cassie, throwing him the van activator. "Drive yourself. I'm done."

The crewman watched as Cassie walked away at a quick pace, but not one that would draw any undo attention to her or the azure van. Once more she was trying to escape the tentacles of a brutal and repressive regime. *But this time,* she told herself, *I'm not getting involved. It's just not worth it.*

Steve started up the van and sped back to the studio, carrying with him the dead body of their companion. But once inside the parking garage, he coldly left it, instead hurrying to the editing room where he knew the producer would be reviewing the footage for the night's broadcast. Pushing his way into the room, he found the producer huddled over the viewing screen making comments to the production assistant.

"What the hell's this?" said the producer, startled at the unwelcomed interruption.

"Sir," Steve began, "I've got some footage you need to see. It's from the protests down at Daley Plaza." "Leave it on the table. I'll review it after I finish this," the producer said gruffly.

"But sir, it's something we need to get on tonight's broadcast. You should look at it right away. It's our lead story. The Red Shirts massacred a bunch of people down there just a few minutes ago. They shot and killed our cameraman, Ted."

"I said leave it on the table," repeated the producer. But when Steve didn't move, the man got heated. "I told you to leave it! Now get out! I've got other film to review."

Steve left the case containing the video chip on the table, prominently sitting where it wouldn't be forgotten or lost.

That night, Steve watched the new cast with his wife, expecting to get a call from the producer or even the president of the network congratulating him on obtaining the story of the day, if not the year. When the six o'clock news came on, the two sat on their sofa at home, watching their wall monitor.

As the news anchor opened the show, he smiled and said:

"Good evening. Tonight, we start with ..."

"Here it is," said Steve. "This is our stuff right here."

"... we start with the latest actions of the school board which has voted to increase the pay of local teachers by twenty-two percent this year in response to city-wide strikes during the previous school year. Chicago school children have not attended school for six months - since last March. Most schools graduated all students anyway even though they did not finish their grade's curriculum."

"What?" cried Steve. "What's with the school board? We had a massacre out there today. Where's that?"

Next, the anchor turned to another story, this one about workers striking in Oak Park for increased benefits and shutting down the town. "We have a reporter out on the street covering the latest developments of this story. Nina Simpson is there with our exclusive coverage. Nina?"

After twenty minutes, the downtown massacre had not yet been reported, and both Steve and his wife sat in disbelief. Finally, after the weather and sports, the anchor came back to wrap up the broadcast. "... And our final story comes from Daley Plaza, where protestors attacked local police, injuring many police officers and disrupting traffic all afternoon. State guard units had to be called in to restore order and many of the hooligans were later charged with disobedience, attacking police officers, and other crimes. The First Citizen's spokesperson said these were the kinds of *anti-patriots* that were destroying the nation. 'Left unrestrained,' said the Minister of Affirmative Justice, 'they would be happy to bring the country to its knees and destroy everything we, as a people, have worked so hard to build over the years. *They* are the reason the country is facing hardships right now,' said the minister. 'The criminals were placed in detention pending arraignment scheduled for tomorrow.'"

The anchor turned in his chair to face another camera and said, "And that's the news this day. We hope you had a good one and that you'll join us again tomorrow. Good night."

Steve picked up his coat off the back of a high-backed, wooden chair in the family room and threw it over his shoulders.

"Where are you going?" cried his wife.

"To get things straightened out!" he yelled back, slamming the door behind him.

Steve reached broadcast headquarters and ran up the steps that led to the executive suits. Finding the door that had a plastic nameplate reading *General Manager*, he swung it open unannounced.

Bart Clemons, General Manager, looked away from the TV screen he'd been watching – one of many screens that he tracked every night to assess his competition in the time slots. His long, narrow face had a look of surprise on it. With eyebrows that ran together in the middle of his forehead and his shaggy, dark, curly hair, he looked somewhat Neanderthalish, although his family pedigree was anything but that.

"Can't you see I'm in the middle of something here!" Clemons snapped, annoyance evident in every element of his face.

"Bart, what was that broadcast all about in there?" Steve said, not caring at this point what might happen to him for speaking out. "We had exclusive video of a government massacre downtown – they killed our cameraman and other innocent bystanders for God's sake, and you can't even show it on the air?"

"We covered the story. What's your problem?" said Clemons, crossing his arms and setting his jaw rigidly.

"What's my problem? You twisted the story to make it look like the protestors were attacking the police and troops. You even said that the troops were just defending itself! That's crap, and you know it!"

"I don't know that," Clemons answered. "And apparently neither do any of the other media outlets. They all aired the same angle of the story."

"You're all lying! You're all conspiring together on this!"

Clemons's demeanor didn't change. "That was the story, Steve. We stick by that."

"I was there! I saw what happened. Were you there? No! You only see things from the comfort of your black, leather chair here, while sipping on a brandy in your own corner office overlooking the Chicago River … But then, I'm sure you're paid not to see anything other than what they want you to see."

Clemons sat, now folding his arms readying for a confrontation. But instead of engaging, the corners of his mouth turned up, like horns on a steer. "Yes, of course," he answered. Reaching over to his phone, he tapped a key and said, "Margie, would you ask Dom and Freddie to come up here. Steve has something for them, and they need to go back to the editing room for a while."

"There," said Clemons, "does that make you feel better?"

Surprised, Steve let his armor melt, and he lowered the metaphorical sword he was about to wield in front of his manager. "Well, I guess that would be fine," Steve said. "I just want to be sure you tell the American people what really happened out there. If you do that, then I'm good."

"No problem," said Clemons, as the two husky men came into the room. "Please take Mr. Estrado to our new editing room. The producer will meet you there to handle things."

Later that evening Steve's wife called the station. "Hello, this is Tina Estrado. Is Steve still there? He hasn't returned home yet. I was wondering if he is still working?"

"No, I'm sorry, Ms. Estrado," said the night-shift guard. "He left about two hours ago."

Steve never made it home.

*****

CH 28 Dark Clouds

"Mr. President," said Ingram, speaking as directly and unwaveringly as he could, "I'm afraid I have some bad news."

"What is it, Lawrence?" asked Sumner, bracing himself.

"The USSA is preparing for war," said the Secretary of State.

***

Shortly after midnight one day later, encrypted information came into the headquarters of the Republic's Intelligence Agency (RIA). Decrypted, it read:

> **Bulletin** – USSA troops amassing on the border of western Illinois down through Arkansas. Word from the White House late tonight stated it was a military training exercise. Republic forces should be put on DefCon1 alert.

Sumner immediately contacted his chairman of the Joint Chiefs and reviewed the scenarios and defensive options.

"We have only two mechanized divisions along our eastern front with the USSA," said the general, talking as if they were revisiting the battle plans of the Allies during WWII. "The USSA appears to have moved seven divisions toward the border, positioning them for what … we don't know. I would advise …"

"General," said Sumner, looking at an aerial photo obtained from Canadian intelligence of the possible points of attack just across the Mississippi River, "what are the chances this is just a diversion. What if they are planning an assault elsewhere?"

"It could be, Mr. President, or perhaps they aren't intending to attack at all. Many times, an enemy will test the defensive measures and countermeasures of an opponent before fully committing to an assault."

"How will we know which they are doing? Perhaps they are merely trying to provoke us into starting the fight. That way, they can claim to the world that we were the aggressors."

"I wish I could tell you," said Ward. "It could be any of the above at this point."

"General, I need to know which of these is most likely and what our countermeasure is going to be as soon as possible. We have no time to lose. Run the computer simulations or whatever else you need to do. The scientists working on our Manhattan II program have put together an extraordinary computer system – it's first rate. Let's make use of it. I want probabilities factored into each scenario as well. Use game theory too, if you have to. Ratner was a big proponent of that arcane science. It is likely she will use that in her calculations or miscalculations."

"Yes sir," said the general, getting ready to leave.

"And general, I want your analysis within the hour."

The general looked ashen at the unreasonable request. "I'll do my best, sir."

"No, general. I need it within the hour. If they unleash their arsenal on us, we won't have any time to defend ourselves, much less muster a counteroffensive."

"Yes, sir."

*****

PART V - WAR

CH 29 Ratner's Ruse

Sumner sent his two mechanized divisions to the west bank of the Mississippi River to counter the troop movements of the USSA. Within a few hours, the potential confrontation de-escalated with the USSA withdrawing some of its troops. However, later that day, the First Citizen issued a statement which read in part:

Although there are several states that have announced their intention to secede from the Union and there has been an active revolt going on inside of the state of Wyoming for some time, these acts are illegal and non-binding upon the federal government of the USSA. As such, the USSA does not recognize any state's desire to withdraw from the Union and will take all measures necessary to ensure that the Union, as constitutionally established, will continue unaltered. Just as the sixteenth president of the previous union stated in his First Inaugural Address, quote "I hold that in contemplation of universal law and of the Constitution the Union of these States is perpetual ... It follows from these views that no State upon its own mere motion can lawfully get out of the Union; that resolves and ordinances to that effect are legally void, and that acts of violence within any State or States against the authority of the United States are insurrectionary or revolutionary, according to circumstances."

Therefore, all states contemplating any such illegal action should immediately cease and desist from all activities that violate their constitutional obligations as states of the federal union. If such measures are not withdrawn, such states shall face the consequences imposed on them by this government. These will be extreme and decisive.

It was an open threat, and Sumner knew it. He also sensed that the rhetoric would soon escalate as well, and he preferred to take no part in it. Yet, with the USSA declaring war on the Republic, he had no choice but to take all precautions to prepare for the worst.

But what happened next, even he could not have foreseen.

Cameras were rolling as the First Citizen appeared in a studio with a green background to give her State of the Citizenry address. It was something required by the old Constitution, but had been in accomplished in written form starting with Jefferson up to the time of Taft. Wilson restored the direct form of communication, when he addressed Congress on the floor of the House in 1913. However, times had changed. There was no longer a Congress and no longer a requirement to give such an address. However, it was still an opportunity for the leader of the country to look good in front of his or her people – to get positive air time.

Using the studio, the White House could choose the venue they wanted to make up, displaying it behind the First Citizen just as they did in making the fantasy embodied in the movies. As if she were really speaking in front of the Capitol building, the screen behind her superimposed a huge gallery assembled to listen to her every word, making her appear bigger-than-life.

Ratner stood at a podium setup in front of the green screen, looking relaxed and in charge and wearing a dark gray suit buttoned high at the collar. With her black hair pulled back in a bun, she resembled a modern Mau Tse-tung. On either side of her stood two USSA flags, their colors of green, orange and black in stark contrast to the red, white and blue that citizens were used to seeing when the country was governed under the rules of the old USA. An applause track was added to overlay on top of the other visuals to make it sound as if there were a huge crowd on the DC Mall in front of her watching and listening with earnest attention.

"Good evening, my fellow comrades," Ratner said, her head still while her lips moved and eyes scanned the prompter in front of her. As the piped-in applause track was dialed down in the control room, her mood changed to one that was as somber as it was austere. "I appreciate the applause and the recognition of the great job that my administration is doing. We have been working hard to ensure that the American people are safe and prosperous. But tonight, I want to make the American people aware of a clear and present danger – the so-called Republic. We have been working for over a year and a half to mend fences with the rebels who are attempting to break away from our beloved country. Negotiations and discussions were initiated by my State Ministry and, although these efforts were met with contempt and resistance by the Republic, we were making progress. However, these talks abruptly broke off earlier this week when the leaders of the rebels demanded that we turnover our national treasury to them. They also demanded annexation of our states of the Dakotas, Iowa, Nebraska, Illinois, Colorado, Montana, Idaho, Utah, and Missouri.

"We found these demands repugnant and unacceptable. When we tried to appeal to their sense of reason we were categorically rebuffed. That is when our communication collapsed. Worse yet, we discovered that the Republic has spies operating within our borders, conspiring to blow up monuments to our heritage like our White House and Capitol buildings, as well as kill our own citizens. We gained knowledge that the Republic was plotting to kill thousands at this year's World Series. It is a terrorist act, nothing less, and we must take action to protect our denizens.

"They are domestic terrorists ... terrorists who threaten the very existence of a Union that has been together for nearly three hundred years. We have faced this menace before – in 1860 when the southern states brought civil war upon the country to preserve the evil of slavery. Much in the same way, the Republic is threatening for reasons that are as nefarious as those of the Confederacy two hundred years ago.

"But make no mistake about it, these people are dangerous. They are a black, dark force within America, and unless they are stopped and brought back into the fold of our Union, they will continue to ..."

At that moment, shouting was heard in the distance and the camera cut to a man at the back of the crowd behind the First Citizen, waving a pistol and firing off two shots, neither of which landed close to the First Citizen. The sound was amplified so that all could hear him yell, "Viva la Republica!"

Quickly, Capitol security forces surrounded the man and tackled him, disarming him and then dragging him away from the Capitol building steps. He continued to scream obscenities and cry out for the cause of the Republic until his voice faded in the distance, drown out by the raucous and roar of the crowd. Ratner was sprawled on the floor, motionless. The camera zoomed-in on her body as it lay on the ground. Several assistants ran into the scene to attend to her and check to see if she was still alive.

Seconds ticked by with the attendants talking frantically amongst themselves and the audio cut – creating tense, unsettling moments. Finally, the body moved, her hand trembling beside her side and her legs twitching under her. As the seconds passed, Ratner moved more and more, reassuring all who were watching that she was not instantly killed. Eventually, she sat up and then was helped to her feet, wobbling unsteadily as she rose. As she stood, the camera focused on a red spot on her blouse, right in front and just below her heart. Once the photo was registered, Ratner cried out in pain and fell back to the floor, collapsing as she clutched her chest. White House security moved in quickly and carried her off the podium in full view of the cameras, her eyes closed and face pallid. However, once off the set stage, she opened her eyes and whispered to one of her assistants, "Did they get all of that? How did I do?"

"Yes, madam, I believe the entire country saw it," said the assistant. "You did a marvelous job. Quite the actress, you are."

"Good. Now take me to GW Hospital in Georgetown to make it all seem genuine," she said as they lifted her onto a gurney and into an ambulance that was already stationed outside the building, waiting for her.

Indeed, most of the nation was gripped by the apparent violence on the television screen, and the mainstream media covered the story nonstop for days, investigating the shooter and the "critical" state in which they imagined their First Citizen.

"This is day three after the senseless violence that everyone witnessed on the steps of the Capitol as First Citizen Ratner tried to deliver her annual address to her people." The news anchor's voice was halting, almost quivering. "Her speech was interrupted by a domestic terrorist, now known as Clyde Quinn, a known sympathizer with the Republic. Mr. Quinn has ties to the upper levels of the Republic and is a personal friend of JC Sumner, the leader of the outcast band."

Of course, none of that was true, but no one was going to contradict the allegations, especially as they came directly from the White House.

"Mr. Quinn apparently obtained forged travel documents and passes to gain entry to the State of the Citizenry Address from someone within the Republic. It is clear that it was his mission to assassinate the First Citizen. As of now, we don't know whether he was acting alone or as part of a larger conspiracy. We also don't know who was orchestrating this act -- whether it was by the Republic military or by Sumner himself. "As for our First Citizen, Madam Ratner is recovering from a gunshot wound to her abdomen. We don't know how severe the injury is, but we understand that she lost a lot of blood and was in great pain when taken to the emergency room. We will keep you advised as we get more information. Of course, our hearts and prayers go out to our First Citizen and her family."

The coverage continued throughout the rest of that day and into the next. By then, reports were dribbling out of the hospital that her condition had worsened, then improved, then worsened again. The news outlets hoped this would go on for several more days, as their ratings improved with each change. However, by the fifth day, the rouse was over, as someone inside the hospital leaked that the First Citizen was no longer there.

"This just in," said the news anchor, "First Citizen Ratner improved greatly overnight and was awake and chatting with assistants this morning. Doctors believe that she will be released later today. Doctors also indicated that her wounds would have no lasting effect on her health or ability to carry out her responsibilities as leader of the free world."

It was ironic as she was never injured and was never the leader of the free world. There was little free world left in the world, and the USSA was far from the beacon of hope for freedom and liberty it once been – a torch it had carried long and steadfastly for over two centuries.

Meanwhile, Ratner was in the Oval Office listening to the coverage and reveling in the adulation. "Yes," she said into her intercom, reacting to her secretary's notice that her minister of International Data Collection, once the CIA, was there to see her. "Send her in."

Wanda Fredrick came in carrying a black, leather case containing her computer tablet and sensitive, critical information. The use of the terms *secret* and *top secret* had been abolished, as government information was *all* considered that "of the people." However, the reality was that *more,* not less, information was kept from the populace than ever before. Virtually all of it was considered secret now.

"Madam Secretary," she said coming over to her and pulling out her tablet. It immediately opened and projected a hologram of the map of the North America on her desk. The minister pointed to the outline of the Republic in the center of the country. It highlighted not only Wyoming but other states leaning toward or already involved in joining the rebellion. The new territory cut in half the two coasts of the USSA, an image at which Ratner had loathed to look during her short time in office.

"We have to act now," said Ratner. "The story line of my attempted assassination by members of the Republic is fresh in the minds of the people. They're all whipped up, just as we planned. And, that Kwan guy, or whoever it is, you've taken care of that?"

"Quinn, madam. Clyde Quinn. We've made the payment to his family. It was only an estranged brother, so his execution won't cause anyone a problem."

"Good. And now that I've recovered," she said chuckling, her eyes sparkling with evil delight, "it's time to make my statement."

"Yes, I've already alerted them that you will be addressing them again from the steps of the Capitol – to finish your address, madam. I told the media that you would complete your State of the Citizenry Address at that time," she answered.

"Screw the address," Ratner shot back, "We both know what I'm going to do."

"Madam?"

"It's time to go to war!"

*****

CH 30 State of the Citizenry

The War Powers Resolution, adopted by more than two-thirds of Congress in 1973, was intended to limit presidential power in committing American forces into combat for extended periods. The Resolution permitted the president to send troops into conflict for up to sixty days without congressional approval; however, since its adoption, the resolution had been largely ignored.

The First Citizen knew she was not bound by its provisions, as it pertained to the old United States of America. However, she did understand that by presenting her case to the people, it would help garner public support for her and what she was determined to do. Besides that, she needed a distraction. She needed something that would take people's minds off the deteriorating economy and falling of real standards of living throughout the USSA. Since the new *Constitution 2.0* had passed, the average American had seen his standard of living decline by 18 percent. This was realized in just twelve short months, and the rate was accelerating. It was a path that could not be sustained without an uprising, and Ratner knew she had two choices -- either avoid the rebellion or prepare to crush one when it came. For now, she chose hoped to avoid it.

"I stand here today to complete the State of the Citizenry Address that was so violently interrupted nearly a month ago," she began, again speaking in front of a green backdrop that was filled in with pictures of enthralled onlookers on the steps of the Capitol. Behind her were a row of armed guards dressed in khaki fatigues and assault rifles; farther behind them was a row of USSA flags – the green and orange stripes symbolizing the seven continents and five oceans that united all countries of the world, and the black ellipse with the single orange star in the center, representing the one federal government empowered by the energy of the secular universe around it. "But, I shall finish it this time, despite the on-going threats we face today as a society and as a nation," she said, raising her voice and showing strength and determination.

To that, the special effects crew gave her a standing ovation, showing throngs of people cheering and whistling, both on Capitol Hill and down the length of the DC Mall. Ratner smiled weakly and waved gently, putting her hand across her side and clutching the edge of her ribcage. This act was written specifically into the screenplay for the day's action scene to remind people of the near-mortal wound she had suffered at that very same podium weeks earlier.

"But there has been much that has transpired since I first began that speech. The world – this continent – is a far more dangerous place than it has ever been. In the nearly three hundred years since this country was founded, only once before has this nation been at war with itself. And that war cost us over six hundred thousand casualties. Do we really want to go down that road again?

"I don't want to, nor do you. However, the state of Wyoming has incited this -- has provoked this. They are the ones that sent an assassin here to this very stage to kill me. They hoped that by silencing me, they would silence the country and those who only want a united nation. None of us wants to see families divided. None of us wants to see hatred brewing and exploding between family members. All of this could have been avoided. Unfortunately, we have discovered through our superior intelligence agencies that there are additional plots being hatched by the leadership of that state – plots that intend to create more violence, more acts of terror, not only on the government, but on you, my people." To a few, the injection of the term my people was strange; to others, it was missed entirely. "They are planning to bomb grade schools and nursing homes, hospitals, shopping malls, theaters, sports stadiums and 3-D senso-round gaming facilities. Cowards – yes. But they are also terrorists. They are coming for you, for me, for all of us.

"They are anarchists who have been against our empathic mode of governing from day one. They reject helping others less fortunate than they are. They are the unfeeling, uncaring rich, who have left states where compassion and outreach were hallmarks of those states' mission. Sitting in their big houses and behind their big desks, with billions in their bank accounts, they live comfortable lives. It has always been we, the enlightened ones, who care about our fellow women and men. We are the ones who have given the shirts off our backs for the homeless and the starving. We are the ones who are the protectors of the children, the aged, and the infirmed.

"No, those in the Republic want to restore the practices of the twentieth century regime of Nazi Germany. They will put everyone who doesn't meet their standards in concentration camps -- everyone who doesn't agree with them; everyone who looks different than they, and everyone who believes in a different god than they. All will be put into camps. And no, they don't call themselves the Aryan race. They use other terms and code words to cloak their evil intentions like patriot, neighbor, friend, humanitarian, and others. They say they are the compassionate ones who will lift up everyone from poverty. They lie. They say they will raise the level of the entire ocean of prosperity and everyone will partake of it. They lie. They say they will create jobs and prosperity. They lie. They claim they have the answers to all our problems. They don't.

"My fellow Americans, with what we know about their intentions and plans and the ruthless attack on me a month ago, I am declaring war immediately on the rebels of Wyoming. It will be a short skirmish, nothing more. Their plans to destroy us will be thwarted, and their ability to attack our people will be eliminated. They will be brought back into the fold, into the Union, and we will then renew our attention to solving the real issues of this great country – the gap in wealth between the rich and the poor whom they enslave. That is the wrong we need to be fighting. That is the real war we need to wage.

"Thank you, and may the human spirit guide us all."

*****

CH 31 The First Salvo

Sumner watched and listened pensively as Ratner delivered her encore performance of the State of the Citizenry Address. This time, he was prepared for almost anything – from special effects blowing up the Capitol building to an alien spacecraft flying in low overhead and beaming her directly on board. The latter would have been more of what he hoped would happen, but he thought both unlikely.

But what he hadn't anticipated was the brash, direct declaration of war from Ratner. Her accusations that the Republic had been behind her assassination attempt had been largely bluster, and he expected another shoe to drop – some larger fabricated incident involving an attack on a government building or public event, not unlike what Ratner had perpetrated in Cheyenne. But the declaration of war shocked even him.

Sumner, Secretary Templeton and General Ward had worked through various plans to defend against possible invasion routes the USSA might use to re-occupy the territory. None were good. Two things were holding them back: any buffer zone created by new states joining their cause and the development of game-changing technology – both were taking longer than expected. Now, they had run out of time.

"Put the Air National Guard on Def Con 2, immediate threats, and the Republic Army on Def Con 3, high level of threat," said Sumner, his angst-ridden face showing signs of strain. "We've just learned that the USSA intends to take action against us. So, we must assume an invasion will be coming soon." He stared blankly at his Cabinet, which he had convened in an urgent session.

Sitting at the head of the table, the president held his arms out straight, palms down on the surface, as if concerned the massive piece of furniture would levitate on its own accord. He was pale and weathered, his face sagging under the immense weight of the decisions he was expected to make. Even his starched white shirt and striped, silk tie of several shades of blue were not in their usual state of perfection. One side of the tie's knot was lower than the other, making it askew under his collar.

"How soon?" asked Shea.

"We don't know," answered General Ward. "As the president said, we must assume the worst – that it is eminent, yes. We will be positioning our ground troops at key, strategic points around the state."

"And the outlook?" Shea followed-up.

Sumner's expression was grim. He shook his head and sighed. "If we only had a few more months," he said, "we'd be able to amount a credible defense. But as it stands, our forces are lacking. But, I think we need to hear from Secretaries Ingram and Templeton. Men, what do you have for us?"

Templeton started, leaning in on the high-gloss, tabletop surface and clasping his hands in front him. "We have intel from Canada that the USSA Army, several divisions worth, are moving from Minnesota, pouring into Iowa and South Dakota. Another division is in Colorado moving northward to us, and yet another is being shifted from Utah into the southwest corner of our state. Their mobilization has begun. Although we see ground troop movements, we see no aerial activity at this time. As a precaution, we have ceased all our commercial and military flights inside and outside the state as well."

"Mr. President, I do have news that I haven't had time to share with you yet, but it is of some importance. I was just notified of it before coming to this meeting. May I?" said Ingram, apologizing for not having advised the president before introducing the information.

"Let's hear it, Lawrence. What do you have?" prompted Sumner. "At this point, we're all in this together."

"We are being flooded with calls from governors of the states who are being invaded by USSA troops, demanding that we let them join our Republic immediately. They tell us they aren't willing to go into bondage – that, as one put it, 'King George must be defeated,'" said the Secretary of State.

Sumner pushed back from the table and put his hand to his chin in contemplation. "Interesting," he said. "I would have thought just the opposite."

"I as well, sir," said Ingram. "But apparently, they have taken as much as they will take – just as we had."

Sumner breathed out a long, noticeable sigh of relief and smiled briefly. "Thanks, Lawrence. I needed to hear something good today."

"Who has petitioned us?" asked Nugyn of Treasury.

"I think we've got our corridor to the Gulf," Ingram said cautiously. "In addition, we've provisionally signed Louisiana, Mississippi, Alabama and Florida. With the seaport of Houston, that would give us New Orleans, Pascagoula, and Miami. However, we don't yet have Jacksonville, Savannah or Charleston, as they are farther up the coast. All governors are willing and able to give us access to their state and National Guard units and any other resources we need."

"Outstanding," said Sumner, cheering up. "Now, what are our contingencies?"

"Sir?" asked Ingram not understanding the question.

"The contingencies?" Sumner repeated, "We know Ratner will react most unfavorably to the defections of her states. But how will she react, and what can we do about it?" Sumner was always pressing others to think beyond the here and now, even when the here and now just happened.

At first, there were blank stares, but quickly Templeton cleared his throat to speak. "Mr. President, as far as a navy, we do have access to those ships that are currently moored at the naval bases at Corpus Christi, Pensacola, Pascagoula, Panama City and Key West. Many may resist their ships being seized, but we are making such arrangements as we speak."

"How many ships will we get?" asked Nugyn.

"From our intel, it appears that we will not get that many, but we should have three cruisers, nine destroyers, twelve attack submarines, three guided missile subs, a frigate and various support and amphibious craft. We don't have all the details as of yet," said Templeton, rattling them off from memory.

"Very good," said Loretta White, impressed with his recitation.

Eeee-ooo, eeee-ooo, eeee-ooo!

Cutting through the air like a knife through chiffon pie, the sound was deafening. Tall and strategically-placed air-raid towers, which housed enormously powerful speakers, sent their warnings across town and into the surrounding counties, as if tornados had been sighted in the vicinity.

Eeee-ooo, eeee-ooo, eeee-ooo!

"This is not a drill," said the robotic voice, reverberating off the walls inside the Cabinet room. "I repeat, this is *not* a drill. Proceed immediately to a designated air-raid shelter. I repeat, this is *not* a drill. Proceed immediately to a designated air-raid shelter."

"What's going on?" asked the president, jumping up from his seat.

"Sir," said Templeton, looking at his PCD. "It looks like our radar has picked up incoming missiles. We must hurry, sir. They've given us thirty-five seconds until impact."

*****

CH 32 No Fly

One of the first things President Lincoln did when prosecuting the war against the South was to impose an embargo around their major seaports. Since the North lacked a robust navy, it had to focus its fleet on blocking the few ports that provided lifeblood sustenance to the southern cities and the war machine of the Confederates. Among those ports were New Orleans, Pensacola, Galveston, and Mobile along the Gulf of Mexico, and Savannah, Norfolk, Wilmington and Charleston on the East Coast. Although not wholly successful, the number of ships running the blockade fell from one in ten to one in three by the end of the war as a greater number of ships were deployed and improved interception tactics were used.

What Lincoln did not have to worry about during the 1860s was a Confederate airlift to evade the blockade and provide needed materiel and supplies into strategic southern areas. But Ratner did. She could impose a naval embargo all along the coast, or at least as far as her meager navy assets would allow, but she wouldn't be able to stop any resupplying by air, unless …

"Do we have the no-fly zone in place yet?" asked Ratner, questioning General Shontal Williams as they reviewed their plans for putting pressure on the Republic and forcing them back into the Union. Both Williams and Sara Emerson had been called to the Oval Office for a tongue lashing, and while they were there Ratner had ordered Clancy Holt to join them and share in the abuse.

"Madam, we are …" Williams began.

"That was not a question open for discussion, general! It demands a yes or no answer. Now which is it?" "Not yet, madam."

"Not yet! What the f*ck is wrong with you people? Do you think this is amateur hour? We have a threat to this Union, and you're f*cking around with getting an embargo. I need a no-fly zone. Now what's so hard about putting that in place, eh? Now get it handled. Got it?" Ratner waved them off, dismissing them unceremoniously.

After the meeting with the First Citizen, Minister Emerson held an *emergency* meeting with advisors, including the deputy ministers of the Navy and Air Force, National Intelligence Agency, National Security Agency, the Air and Army National Guard chiefs, Defense Intelligence Agency, Defense Logistics Agency, National Recon Office, Defense Threat Reduction Agency, the National Geo-spatial Intelligence Agency, as well as agencies from the Ministry of State, including the Bureau of International Security, Bureau of Political-Military affairs, Bureau of Democracy and Human Rights, the Ministry of International Policing, the Office of National Intelligence, the Office of International Counter-intelligence, the USSA Institute for Peace, the Ministry of Environmental Protection, and another dozen or so agencies that had been created during the previous four years of the Fourier Administration. In addition, someone from the Panama Canal Commission attended, just in case there was some aspect of the discussion that applied to it. Some one hundred and fifty people squeezed into an auditorium to discuss what needed to be coordinated to enforce an embargo and create a no-fly zone. At the initial meeting, they agreed only to a calendar of future meetings. In typical government fashion, it took three more months to agree on a course of action. In the end, the final series of meetings lasted five days and – and agreed they couldn't do it. But at least, Emerson would not be accused of excluding anyone.

"So, what do we need to do?" asked Emerson, with Williams and Holt in her office. It was the original three whom Ratner had been asked to *make things happen*. "We couldn't agree on a course of action. I couldn't get everyone on board."

"All we need is a no-fly zone over Wyoming," said General Williams. "Why is that so hard to do?"

"But you've got to coordinate it with ..." began Emerson.

"Bull sh*t!" said Williams, "I give an order, and I get it done!"

"But the Ministry of Panama Relations has to be made aware and agree, just in case ..."

"In case what?" the general screamed. "We'll deal with it."

"Not if Ratner disagrees. And you know what that would mean," said Emerson, defending herself.

Williams was quiet, looking at the other two in the room. "Well? What are our choices?"

All were afraid of the First Citizen. They knew what she was capable of doing.

Finally, they all agreed. "I'll arrange it with the National Guard units of the states surrounding Wyoming," said Williams. "We'll impose the no-fly on our own."

"How long will that take?" asked Holt. "You know Ratner wants this thing done as soon as possible." "Give me this afternoon. It should be in place by tomorrow," said the general.

*****

CH 33 Truth or Fiction

As with all things, the concept was easy; the implementation hard. Even Michael Lin, one of the smartest scientists on the Manhattan project, if not the country, struggled with a way to generate the power needed to protect a small city from incoming missiles or from the invasion of troops. It was a simple matter to form a barrier around a small model; it was quite different on a large scale. Oddly, it was the inverse problem that Johnny faced with his phaser project. Rather than miniaturizing something that was powerful, it was enlarging something to be as powerful. The theory had been mapped by Lin and Tokarov, deriving abstract calculations on multi-dimensional planes creating mathematical techniques never contemplated before. Still, it hadn't been enough. The other ten scientists and industrialists left on the team were unable to create a working model that was even one one-hundredth of the size needed. It was frustrating and elusive.

Lin threw the computer tablet across the lab, not even watching as its sliver-thin shell shattered into a thousand pieces. "Damn it!" he roared. "It's just not right! It can't take that much energy to make this happen. We'd need forty, nuclear reactors generating the equivalent of voltage at full-power, pushed through a cable no larger than an old, twisted-pair coax to make it work. And that's just to deliver a plasma screen of a single arc around the circumference of the shield."

"Relax, Michael," said Tokarov, her words trying to be soothing. She was fifteen years older than he, and had more maturity dealing with other people on teams and in the laboratory. "We'll get this. It just takes time."

"You heard what Disone said! We don't have time. We have to get this thinking working!" he said, pacing in the room, his head held low and his shoulders drooping. "We're just missing something -something right in front of our faces. I can just feel it."

Lin turned to her. "Can't you understand that?" he remarked, gruffly. His patience was wearing thin. Youthful, energetic and driven, Lin wanted to make a difference with the new Republic. He carried the weight of the world on his shoulders whether it was deserved or not. In this case, there was some truth to his concern. It was an enormous challenge – one that had never before been coaxed from the equations and reality of physical law. But, then again, neither had the problem of a nuclear weapon been resolved until the first Manhattan Project. Sumner had given him – them – an immense burden, and Lin didn't want to let anyone down.

Rather than deal with his bad mood, Tokarov let her eyes drift back onto her computer screen. Without agreeing or disagreeing with his question, she chose to ignore it and began making quick, sharp strokes with her electronic pen, forming yet another algorithmic function for the computer to solve. Then, she shook her head and pressed the *Erase* button, starting over again. Finally, not hearing anything more being directed at her by her boss, she said, "I don't know what else to tell you, Michael. You have to deal with this --- it's your issue. The rest of us are coping the best we can, but we can't cope with you throwing a tantrum everyday about how unjust this entire assignment is and how it's unfair to ask anyone to come up with a solution in such a short amount of time ... Just deal with it!"

But when she got no response, she looked up to see where he was. In fact, he was no longer in the same room, having left to either complain to someone else or to jump back into things once he's blown off enough steam.

Tokarov sighed and brushed her dark hair away from the side of her glasses, tucking it back and under a beret she had clipped-in earlier. Walking through the various lab rooms, she finally found Lin sitting at a lab counter, staring at the small, scale model they had used a week earlier to demonstrate the potential of their device.

"You know," she said, approaching him, "I know you don't want any help, but I think it's time to ask ... you know."

Lin's head snapped up immediately. "Help? Who can help us with this? There isn't anyone on the planet that can work with the stuff we're dealing with."

"Johnny," she said abruptly.

There was a look of pained realization in his face. Then, it softened. "Oh, hell no!" he said. "I don't need help, and I certainly don't need it from *him*!"

Tokarov moaned. "Michael, is this about you or about the future of the nation?"

Lin bit his lip. The comment angered him, but it struck a nerve.

"Michael?"

"Yeah?"

"Did you hear what I said?"

"Yeah! I heard you. I heard you, Okay!" he protested.

"Well?"

Lin couldn't bring himself to answer. He was proud — sometimes too proud.

"You know I'm right," said Tokarov, persisting.

"So."

"Then call Johnny. He may be able to help you."

Lin still wouldn't budge. Tokarov waited for his response, but then rolled her eyes, giving up. "Fine," she muttered to herself. "Do what you want. You will anyway."

An hour later the phone line in another laboratory buzzed.

"John? This is Michael Lin. I'm on the Manhattan Project. I was wondering if you would have some time?"

*****

CH 34 Bunker

The first explosions shook the president's office, ripping pictures from the walls and books from the shelves. Chandeliers swung and dust fell from the ceiling like the winter's first fine snow shower in November.

"Get to the bunker!" shouted Oishi, directing all the Cabinet members to the recently-built cement structure that had been excavated quickly and was still under construction.

The entrance to the bunker was a narrow, dimly lit hallway with cement walls, gray and rough, and low ceilings. At the end was a foreboding black curtain that hid the small, tight elevator that connected the surface to the underground refuge. There was none of the usual mahogany paneling, marble inlay and other refinements to which those in government were accustomed; rather, the elevator looked more like a maintenance elevator with its metal sides, simple, straight pieces of bar steel for a railings, and a floor that was still covered with construction paper to protect the nicer, stone finish from the heavy, steel castors of the electronics and telecommunications equipment that had not yet been installed in the rooms below.

As the Cabinet members hurriedly shuffled down the hallway toward the elevator, more missiles hit their marks outside. Ingram was thrown to the ground before he had gotten half way to the elevator shaft. Tumbling onto his side, Ingram threw up his arm to offer a counterbalance, but only managed to catch Loretta White on the heel, sending her flying to the floor as well. Dust began pouring down on them from the exposed beams overhead as the shelling continued, the bombs landing on various government buildings in and around the president's mansion.

Shea stared at the single elevator door and then at the other seventeen people standing, waiting to be rescued from the nightmare going on outside by the single, solitary lift in front of them. "How are we all going to get on there?" she asked as the doors opened.

"We aren't," said Oishi. "It's a high-speed elevator, but only six can get on at a time. We'll have to make three trips."

"Get on!" shouted Sumner, as a rocket hit the presidential west annex, a building adjacent to the one they were in. Sumner pushed five of his Cabinet members into the elevator and then Oishi.

"But Mr. President, I need to direct ..." objected Oishi, putting her hand on the president's arm and pushing back in resistance.

"I'll do that," said Sumner. You're getting on." He didn't hold back and forcibly pushed her into the elevator as the doors were closing.

The underground room trembled again and again as if Wyoming were being hit with a magnitude eight earthquake. Once again as the bombs fell and shook the walls around them, Shea and others huddled by the elevator door.

"Stay close to the door," said Sumner. "There's more structural support over here."

But even as the words left his lips, an explosion ripped through the narrow corridor, engulfing the group as the dust storm swirled around them.

"Is everyone alright?" asked Sumner, trying to see through the murky fog.

"Shea! Shea!" came a voice out of the sooty veil.

When the dust had settled slightly, everyone saw Shea's crumpled body on the ground, a large piece of concrete lying nearby. Sumner rushed over to her and lifted her with his hand, feeling a gooey wetness from behind her head. He pulled his hand away and gaped at the heavy crimson streaks that covered his fingers.

The door to the elevator swung wide.

"Get her on the elevator," ordered Sumner. "We have to get her downstairs where we have medical supplies."

General Ward and Templeton helped Sumner lift Shea's limp body into the opening and lay her on the creased and soiled construction paper. "You three get on, and get her down there!" said Sumner, motioning for three others board quickly.

"But we only have four of us on here," said White, looking around inside.

"There's no more room," said Sumner, seeing that Shea's body was taking up more room than expected.

The door closed once again, delivering the next passengers to safety hundreds of feet below. A few minutes later, the doors reopened, revealing a floor that looked as if it had been sloppily painted with a cheap, broad brush using bright red hues. The red stains were haunting, showing elements of drops and smears and using the body of the attorney general as a palette.

"Get on people!" said Sumner pushing the rest of his group onto the lift.

"But there isn't enough room for all of us, Mr. President," said Templeton. "You need to go down!"

"He's right, Mr. President," said General Ward. "You must be saved. You *must* get on, sir."

There were seven left to descend, but room for only six. "No, general. You go on. I'll be fine," said Sumner. He took the general by the sleeve and began to shove him in. But the general sidestepped the attempt, and Sumner lurched forward, missing his intended subject and stumbling into the elevator. At that moment, another missile above struck the President's House – this one, a direct hit. Striking the center where the president's office and Cabinet room stood, the rocket ripped through the roof, spewing forth a ball of fire and shrapnel that obliterated everything in its path. Directly below, the ceiling began collapsing in on itself, unable to support the weight of three floors that had fallen in on the old, wooden beams laid almost two centuries earlier. These seemed to be the last vestiges of hope for those trapped within.

As the matted steel elevator doors gently closed, and the sounds and violence of the growing holocaust within the corridor grew quiet. There was no sound inside the compartment as it descended through earth and rock, except for the electric hum of the motor spinning the wheels and tethers that were lowering all inside to safety. Sumner got up off his knees, where he'd landed after being manhandled by his Joint Chiefs chairman, and dusted off his soiled pants.

After forty agonizing seconds, the doors groaned as they opened, revealing the rest of the group which was sitting or standing near a corner of the Receiving Room. Only twenty by twenty, the Receiving Room was large enough to accommodate up to thirty people and provision them for as long as six months. The supplies were stored in other store rooms adjacent to the Receiving Room. Also attached to the underground complex was a kitchen, sleeping quarters, meeting rooms and two Situation Rooms with high-tech communications equipment that was resistant to EMPs or electromagnetic pulses and sophisticated hacking efforts. As for the storage rooms, they were still being outfitted, with metal shelves that had not yet been fully assembled and many foodstuffs still sitting in their original shipping containers. Water was stored in sturdy, blue plastic bottles, awaiting use in case of emergency.

"Where's the general?" asked Oishi, as the president got off the elevator.

"Up top," said Sumner, exercised. "He didn't make it on the elevator." Sumner urgently punched the button for the lift to return to the surface, but it seemed to ignore his commands. "What's wrong with this thing!" he shouted, pounding even harder on the control panel. But the display overhead read: *Lift Disengaged.* Spotting the message, Sumner said, "What's the problem with this damned thing? I've got to get back up there!" He kept thumping the *Up* button to send him to the surface; yet, it continued to defy him.

Templeton moved into the elevator with him and looked at the screen, pushing the same button. "It's not activating. It's supposed to disengage if the electricity is out upstairs and there's damage to the elevator shaft."

"You mean we can't go up? What about the stairs?"

"A bomb destroyed the staircase, sir. They are completely blocked. No. I'm afraid we're stuck," said Templeton.

"And the general?"

"I don't know. At this point, there's nothing we can do but wait."

*****

CH 35 Unauthorized Access

"Colonel? We just got word that there's been an attack on Cheyenne. We should have gotten that information out of our Washington cell, but I haven't heard anything from them. It looks like troops are being redeployed out of Fort Carson and possibly an air assault from Schriever Air Force base there in Colorado Springs. But, you're in that loop too! Your cell in Denver should have known about it. Why didn't you say something about this? It's something you should have reported! What's going on with your cell there?" Thorne asked, speaking over a secure line. He was clearly irritated — even irate over the lack of intel he was getting.

"I heard the same," said the colonel, "but only within the last hour. I don't know why we didn't learn of it earlier. It's something I need to investigate on my end. That's all I can say."

"That's not a good reason," said Thorne, not accepting excuses.

"I agree, sir. But I will figure it out. You know I will. Now, is there any word on casualties in Cheyenne?" asked Colonel Marcus, hoping to move off the accusation.

Thorne hesitated, then said, "Unfortunately, they hit a lot of our command and control, knocking out our com center in Cheyenne. We don't know what the condition those are in at the moment. I've been trying to reach the Defense Secretary and the Chief of Staff, but they aren't picking up."

"What about the mole? Have they found him or her?"

Looking sterner than ever, Thorne's demeanor became even cooler. "No ... but then again, have you?" For the first time, there was a hint of indictment in his delivery.

Taken aback, Marcus answered, "No. We still haven't found the mole, sir. I've been watching, listening, trying to find it — even planting false information to flush him or her out. But I've got nothin'."

"You know we've lost three cells already – fifteen people executed by Ratner's regime. They were good people, colonel. Damn good people," said Thorne.

"Yes, sir. I knew some of them too. But this is a war, sir. We will lose some – often our very best."

"That's why I'm telling you this, colonel. It's top secret, and I know that I can trust you."

There was no hesitation in Thorne's delivery, but still, Marcus wondered whether this was a disinformation plant to see if he were the mole or whether it truly was top secret. The colonel waited, interested to hear the nature of what was about to be presented to him. "You know you can trust me, sir," he answered.

"We have been trying to get information on it for weeks now. It is the most tightly guarded secret in the Administration, and so far, no one has been able to find anything on it. Given the secrecy, it must be something big. To date, Ratner hasn't been able to keep her team's mouths shut about many things."

"Other than the attack in Cheyenne today," quipped Marcus.

"You're right about that. That one was a surprise. We should have had intel on that, but something failed us along the way. It's something that Secretary Templeton and I have to figure out. But in the meantime, I need you to get information on something called Barbosa – Operation Barbosa. It may have something to do with equipment being imported from overseas. What my people tell me is that it's a game changer on their end. Could it be China who's sold them something? Or maybe Russia? We don't know, but I'm worried about it."

"I may know a way to get at that," said the colonel. "But it will be risky."

"Go on …"

"Sir, I need authorization for a break-in," asked Marcus, boldly.

"A what?" asked Thorne with shocked surprise. "You're joking."

"No, sir. I heard that the minister of International Security was expected to visit Norfolk, Virginia next week. There was something about a shipment coming in to port there. As you and I both know, the minister doesn't just go to a port to oversee something unless it's big. It was all vague and top secret. If I can break-in to the ministry, we have a chance of getting that information," said the colonel, explaining.

"How in the hell are you going to do that, colonel?" Thorne asked, leaning forward, his face now closer than ever to the wall mounted screen and camera in his office.

"I have a plant inside the ministry. If I can get her to disable the security tomorrow night, we'd have thirty minutes to get in, find the files, take a copy of them, and get out. She'd be there to show me where I might find them. She's got a high security clearance, so most things are accessible to her."

"Why don't we just try to hack into the ministry files?"

"Things above top-secret are never kept on-line, sir. They're kept the old-fashioned way – on paper in a safe."

"Who's going in?"

"It will be me, Georgia, Issa and Williams. Three will go into the building while one will standby outside and monitor our activities via VPN, letting us know what's happening. It will be quick and clean."

Thorne hesitated. "I'm not sure," he said. "I think I need higher clearance for something like that. I'll have to get back to you, colonel."

"We don't have much time, sir. If we do this, I need to have a green light by midnight tomorrow. Can you get me that?"

"I'll get back to you," said Thorne, not saying whether it would be prior to midnight.

"Midnight? The building is undergoing a maintenance shift and the computer software will be down for an upgrade," Marcus asked again. "But it will only be down for an hour."

"I'll get back to you," Thorne huffed.

"Okay, but just so you know. My team will have to be ready to move within minutes of your approval, otherwise, my plant won't be able to disarm the security. We'll have to abort the mission." "I got it, colonel. We'll be in touch."

***

Colonel Marcus looked at his watch. It was an old fashion Swiss-Army time piece, but it still was accurate to the second, every four years. The digital dial read 2345 or 11:45 PM – only fifteen minutes before the drop-dead time when Marcus needed an answer before calling off the mission. Only fifteen minutes before the security circuit would be temporarily disabled by his collaborator while she made the software upgrade inside. Certain security staff were also out sick that day, and the building management had not been able to find anyone to replace them between the times of 12:00 AM and 1:00 AM.

The colonel waited until his watch showed him 2355; then, he made his own decision. He texted a cryptic message into PCD, *"U-2 ready?"* The message appeared immediately on the PCD screen of his second-in-command, Georgia Tallis.

"U-2 ready," was the response.

"U-3 ready?" "This was the computer manager inside the building.

"U-3 ready."

"On command," messaged Marcus.

Marcus waited patiently, keeping his eye out for anyone coming up on them just outside the loading dock on the backside of the building. Wearing heat-absorbing, black fatigues, Marcus and his team were nearly invisible to infrared cameras. With a heavy layer of decalescence cream on his face, the colonel remained motionless, crouching behind a mound of white Styrofoam wrapping materials that had just been discarded outside the ministry compound that day.

As his watch clicked to 0000, the colonel heard Issa and Williams file in behind him, ready to go. There was only a two-minute window for stage one to get through a small, but secure, gate that protected a drainage tile that led to the inner core of the building grounds. Once inside, they would have the remainder of the hour to find Agent X, as Marcus called her, and get the documents on Barbossa.

"Go" was the simple command Marcus sent to release the genie from the bottle, knowing full-well he would not be able to put it back.

The gate clicked open, and the three commandos hurried through, placing anti-magnetic tape over the locking mechanism to prevent it from trapping them inside.

"Let's go. We don't have much time," shouted the colonel, running toward the narrow drainage tile that was less than three feet high and covered with overgrown brush.

Sinking to his knees, Marcus climbed in, feeling the cold, wet dampness of the runoff flowing unabated from the ministry grounds which were higher in elevation. Crawling on their elbows and knees, they finished the fifty-foot obstacle quickly and pulled themselves out the other end, muddy but exhilarated.

Their hearts pounding, they all had been trained to control their emotions lest they cloud their judgment or reaction time.

Marcus stood up to survey where they were. "The point of ingress should be twenty meters that way, but we have to go around that dock to avoid the cameras," he said pointing to the access tunnel to the shipping and receiving dock. At that moment he stopped and looked at his PCD. It read:

Project cancelled. Boss did not approve.

The colonel snickered to himself. *Ya' gotta love the government,* he thought to himself.

Marcus waved his small squad onward to get inside the tunnel before being spotted. Only thirty feet inside, they stopped at the corner of one section of the foundation, where there was a ribbed, steel grate just large enough for a well-trimmed body to squeeze through.

"Here we go," said Marcus, removing his high-torque screwdriver. Within seconds, all screws were backed out and the screen pulled off and leaned against the stone wall. He glanced at his watch again – 0013. They were running behind schedule already.

"Go!" he said in forceful, whispering tones. He tried to remain calm; yet, even with his experience, the colonel's heart rate jumped as he watched his team inch into the duct and disappear inside. They were completely defenseless – their only way out was back the way they'd come. Again on their bellies, they made their way through the maze of ductwork with Williams leading the way. He had a map of the inner workings of the heating and air conditioning system loaded into his PCD and was watching his device as they crawled, following the twists and turns designated by the mission plan.

Finally, they found the end of that ducting branch, and Williams drilled out the screws keeping the grate secured to the other side of the wall. Pushing the grill work inward and then moving it aside, Williams turned around with a broad smile. "We're in!" he said with pleasure.

By the time everyone had pressed their bodies through the hole, Marcus was locating his spy inside the building. Within a few minutes, they were in an abandoned hallway walking toward one end, when a figure appeared suddenly.

"Don't worry," said Marcus. "It's X."

He approached her with outstretched arms, taking her in and hugging her as if she were his long-lost daughter. "X, how are you?" he said.

Tiny and thin, she weighed all of ninety pounds, perhaps less. Yet, with her four-inch heels, she managed to achieve a height of only five feet, three inches. "Hi, Marcus. And these must be your accomplices," she said with a straight face.

X was pretty. Her long, auburn hair flowed down her back and curled around and under her left arm. The light from the overhead green eco-bulbs was purposefully dim to save energy, so it was difficult to see clearly, but her face appeared youthful and full of vitality. X's features were striking, with a thin face, long eyelashes, and petite nose. Her dimples were barely visible, and then, only discernable when she made a wry or dry remark.

"You all look like you've dressed appropriately for the occasion, though," she said, her dimples showing again. "Alright, well, we can't stand here all day, so let's get going."

Walking briskly down the dark corridor, she passed only a few doorways, as all were executive suites that took up large sections of the building's floor space. At the end of the hall was a small elevator. There she stopped.

"I can't get on the elevator with you," she exclaimed. "They would know instantly it was me, as I have to wear this biometric badge at all times when I'm in the building. You aren't wearing one, and they didn't plan their system to consider someone being this far into the building not having one. So, you can go up the elevator without being caught. But at the top floor, it'll be different when you get off. You'll be just outside the minister's office. There are cameras and detection monitor everywhere. You'll need the gift I sent you," she said, looking at Marcus.

"Yeah, it took me by surprise, that's for sure," said Marcus. "I won't ask who or ..."

"It's an organically grown one that is a clone of the minister's. Don't ask me how I got it.

"I won't," answered Marcus. "But you're sure the docs are in the office there?"

"Yeah. There's a safe inside the inner sanctum — inside his room. You're other gift should help you at that point."

"Got it," said Marcus. As she left them, there was a look of affection in his eyes, but he brushed it aside. "Take care of yourself, X."

X didn't look back as she walked back down the hallway; however, she did wave and blow him a kiss just before she turned the corner at the corridor's end.

The elevator was fast and efficient as it sped through the unseen shaft surrounding them. There were no floor numbers or buttons on the wall of the steel box within which they rode. The silence inside was strange and unnerving, as most of them had experienced during wartime, just before a battle.

The doors opened, and lights in the hallway flashed on, brilliantly illuminating every square inch of the outside lobby area.

"What do we do now?" asked Williams, nervous at seeing the search light beaming outside the elevator, strobing up and down the corridor like a prisoner of war camp.

Marcus reached in his backpack and pulled out small, pistol-like device with a canister attached. Aiming it like a rifle, he pointed it at a camera hidden up into the corner of the hallway and pulled the trigger. A powerful, thin spray of black paint shot out the end, engulfing and sticking to the entire lens, like honey in a comb. With machine-gun deployment, the colonel nailed the other five strategic camera positions he had memorized from the information provided from X.

"Okay, it's clear. Let's go," said Marcus, tilting his head for them to go through the doors.

It wasn't hard to find the office of the minister. The double doors were massive, embedded in the middle of the hallway with no other doors visible, except the maintenance doors at the other end. But the minister's doors were special. Imported from Germany, they were allegedly the doors rescued from the Krolloper, the Opera House used after Hitler burned down the Reichstag in 1933. Made of heavy oak, they held deep insets framed by ribbed molding and within each was the symbol of the Hindenburg government – the Weimar Republic. It was odd indeed – the USSA using symbols of the black eagle from Nazi Germany – but it was only one of many things that made little sense in the *new* America. Alongside the oak door was six-by-six-inch glass panel, inset into the wall. There was no marking on it or other indication of its purpose.

"Is it a retina scan or fingerprint scan?" asked Issa, watching Marcus evaluate the device.

"X said it was retinal."

"Do you trust her?" asked Williams.

Marcus squinted and scrunched up his face in disgust, recoiling from the accusation. He didn't bother to answer, but instead continued with his plan. The colonel set his black pack down and unzipped the top section. Then, he reached in and pulled out a clear, plastic bag.

Issa spotted it and began to react violently, starting to heave whatever contents she had in her stomach.

"Don't!" warned Marcus. "Issa, you have to control yourself!" He opened the plastic bag and pulled out the eyeball, which dripped with a slimy, clear, viscous fluid. The eyeball had red capillaries running from the white corneal part in front to the rear where the optic nerve would have attached. The retina, itself, was a chestnut color, with striations of blacks and other shades of brown intermixed, as if swirled together with an underpowered blender.

"That's truly disgusting," said Williams, also backing away from his commander.

Marcus took the orb and held it up to the retina scan by the doorway. The scanner took its time to evaluate the surface of the eyeball and the unique signature of capillaries and blood vessels in the back to confirm its owner. The machine's computer processor continued assessing the article presented for an unusually long time. Then, its red spider web-like overlay of images re-scanned the eyeball. Finally, there came a digitized voice that sounded through the unit's speaker – "Uncertain Result. Please present eye for repeat scanning." The voice was intended to be an Australian woman's voice, but sounded more like one from South Africa.

Williams and Issa sat deathly still, nervously watching Marcus regroup and recompose his wits. Again, he steadied his hand and presented the eyeball, placing it into the full view of the scanner. All watched as the red light shot out from the lens embedded behind the glass panel and wrapped itself around the surface of the ocular globe. Comparing every capillary and other blood vessel to those on file, the process was laborious with older software such as this one. The scanner went silent for a full minute, shutting off its diode lights and digesting what had been presented. Williams and Issa held their breaths while Marcus watched the display screen.

"Confirmed," said the disembodied voice, together with the green words that appeared on the screen.

For a brief second, they heard a mechanical sound, as the lock unlatched from its harbor. Marcus pushed on the door, and it gave way, revealing the inner sanctum of the minister's lair.

Phew! exclaimed Williams, breathing a sigh of relief. "Two down, and ..."

"*Shhhh!*" scolded Issa, putting her finger to her lips and giving him an angry glance.

The general quarters inside the compound were expansive. Not only did the minister have seven administrators, each had her own suite off to the side of the carpeted pathway that led to the minister's private office. Only the receptionist desk was in an open area, and that was as big as the Oval Office in the White House. They hurried past the receptionist desk and the other offices on their way to the closed doors at the end of the runway.

When they got there, Marcus glanced all around the door frame. "I'm sure there has to be some lock here someplace," he said, searching for something that would indicate the door was secured. "Do you see anything?"

Williams and Issa studied the frame carefully while Marcus walked back down the hall, examining the walls and floorboards in great detail. Moving his hand from picture to picture, he jiggled each to see how it was attached. Finally, he came to one that felt funny to him. "Wait a minute," he said, speaking softly. "This one doesn't feel quite right." He took off his glove and slid it all along the picture's frame until he could feel five buttons hidden on the bottom, invisible to all who passed. "Sh*t!" he said.

"What is it?" asked Williams, now facing him.

"There's a coded lock on the underside of this picture frame. I'm sure the buttons have to be pushed in exactly the right order to unlock the office."

"Let me see," said Issa. She knelt and looked under the frame. "Ah, you're in luck, colonel. It's simple, and the wear pattern on the frame confirms it."

"What's that?" Marcus asked.

"For a government bureaucrat, the easiest way is the only way." Issa swiped her finger quickly, tripping each button in rapid succession. Instantly, they heard the private office door unlock. Issa smiled. "See."

"But how did you know they swiped that way and not the other way?" Williams asked, scratching his head.

"I guessed," she said, laughing.

"Okay, you two, let's get in and out," said Marcus.

Marcus tapped his PCD. "U-2, this is U-1. How's the weather out there?" he asked.

"U-2 here. Weather is calm. No wind. Fair temperatures, over."

"Roger that," said the colonel.

As Marcus entered the minister's room, he was distracted by the size and spaciousness of the cavern within. The office had rare tapestries from the medieval times and oil paintings from various centuries decorating the walls, the latter ranging from a Caravaggio and a Rubens to several pieces by Monet, Renoir and Degas.

"These must cost a small fortune," said Williams, looking on in wonder. "How could he have afforded these?"

"I'm sure he didn't buy them. He probably extorted them. That's what they do now – they threaten the billionaires with jail time unless they turn over priceless art or jewelry. It's how they get rich." Marcus glanced at the mission time on his PCD. "Bloody hell," he mumbled to himself. Then, in a louder voice, he said, "We have to find the safe and get out. Let's get a crackin'. You need to find a hidden latch that will open a secret vault in here. Don't touch it when you find it. I've got to use this decoder to read the digital password and enter it. It's a real-time system that requires you to put in the exact code at the precise time it gives you. The latch is probably something that looks like something else – you know, like a bookend or a knick-knack that seems out of place."

"You mean like this?" asked Issa pointing to a black, computer mouse on the desk.

"Why is that unusual?" asked Marcus. "We used to use those all the time."

"*Used to* ..." said Issa. "*Nobody* uses those anymore. Everything's voice command now."

"Not for me," said Marcus. "I still you one."

"You're a dinosaur too," said Issa, irreverently, but only joking.

Marcus pressed the right button on the mouse, and a door on the rear credenza popped open, revealing a black safe inside. "Ah, yes," the colonel said, putting his palms together and swishing his hands back and forth rapidly. "This is an old-fashioned fingerprint reader, just as X told me."

Issa backed away from her boss. "Colonel, you don't have parts and pieces of a finger in your little case there, do you?"

"Not exactly, lieutenant." But Marcus did reach into his satchel. He pulled out another container; except this one held a variety of latex finger tips. He chose one and slipped it over the end of his index finger. Reaching up toward the safe, he swiped it past the small, narrow slit that he presumed read the ridges and indentations of surface presented.

Nothing happened, so he tried again. Still nothing happened.

His finger trembled as he pressed the fake prints against the scanner one more time. Marcus watched as the fake print he pushed against the glass caused the system to display the word *Processing* on the small, black screen he hadn't even noticed, but had been mounted just beside the heavy, steel door that kept him from getting inside.

"Come on," muttered the Colonel impatiently, knowing that every second the system took to evaluate the prints was not a good sign.

The red word changed to green and the word *Confirmed* before unlocking the door. Weight sensitive panels had been installed inside the safe floor and would record any addition or deletion from what was intended to be stored inside. If programmed, the safe would set-off the alarm anyway if another code were not entered to permit the person accessing the safe from removing or depositing something into it. Marcus knew the type of safe and worried that it may have been coded that way. If so, he would only have sixty seconds to figure out the ten-digit code – something virtually impossible. However, consistent with Issa's observation, most bureaucrats were lazy, and he assumed at that point that no pass code had been entered.

Nervously, he lifted an envelope that sat quietly, undisturbed on top of the pile within. The weight screen flashed in green iridescent numbers above the safe "33.485 ounces" and then in red numbers " -6.238 ounces" indicating the change in weight. Marcus held his breath once more. If the screen began flashing, it meant it had been armed. If no, then no pass code had been set.

The waiting was interminable. But after fifteen seconds, the numbers flashed off, leaving a pristine, black screen that soothed anxieties and restored the colonel's heartbeat to something closer to normal. For the next minute, he flipped through the stack inside the safe, pulling out documents and scanning them quickly. Eventually, he found what he was looking for – one marked "Barbossa"

He didn't bother to read it; he didn't have time. Instead, he laid it out on the floor and took digital scans of all the pages. Then, he replaced the documents and closed the safe door.

"We got it. Let's go," said Marcus, securing the safe back into its concealed, hiding place.

But as he closed the lid on the safe, he heard a voice on his com. "U-1, this is U-2. The weather's turned from beautiful to a three-flag hurricane. Winds at sixty knots, and rain coming down like there's no tomorrow. We need to evacuate, over."

"Details?" asked Marcus. There was nothing but static on the line. "U-2, details?" Still no answer. "U-2, do you copy?"

"What's happened?" asked Issa.

"Don't know, but something's going on. We have no choice but to go out the way we came in," said Marcus.

"There is another way, colonel," said Issa.

"That's suicide!" said Williams. "We'd never get out of here alive if we go that way."

"Colonel, you said X told you of the other way out of here, right?" asked Issa, looking away from Williams.

"Yes, but ..."

"Well?"

The colonel threw the scan disk into his bag. "Let's go," he said without indicating what his decision was.

All three hurried back down the interior corridor and stopped at the door just short of the main hallway outside. Marcus cracked open the door, but saw no one coming and heard no sounds. "Come on," he said, motioning with his right arm. As they closed the door behind them, the security box on the door chimed twice. Then the voice said, "Enter exit code."

"Exit code?" said Marcus, riddled with anxiety. "X didn't mention any exit codes."

He punched in a series of numbers hoping to buy himself some time, but the system responded promptly, "Invalid code. One more attempt permitted."

"Crap!" said the colonel.

"What are you going to ..." began Williams, but he got his answer before he finished the sentence. Marcus took his fist and smashed the display, cracking it and sending pieces of it to the floor. The display suddenly changed underneath the spider web of shattered fragments. "Processing" it read.

"Oh, bloody hell!" shouted Marcus. "Come on."

It was several seconds, perhaps minutes, before the high-pitched screeches pulsated through the air and vibrated the walls. Cameras setup in the corners of the hallways perked up with their red diodes coming alive to film the intrusion.

Issa began to run toward the elevator doors, but Marcus stopped her. "That's a death trap for us now," he said, pulling out his pistol. "We have to go out the back. There's a loading dock there we can use. It has multiple exit points. And there is always a set of stairs to every floor in case of fire. That's code, you know."

Williams and Issa ran behind him, finding a janitorial stairwell and hurrying down the flights of steps to the basement. There they dashed toward where the dock had appeared on the colonel's hologram. On a metal placard beside one of the doors was a sign marked **B137: Waste Disposal**. Marcus grabbed the handle and pulled. It didn't move. He yanked again, but it seemed locked from the outside.

Subtly, beneath the piercing sounds of the alarms and the blinding flashes of lights from the hallway strobes, came the sounds of doors opening and slamming, and then footsteps.

"They're coming," said Marcus, grim faced. "Lock and load." He checked his .45 pistol and groped around his belt to ensure his backup clips were within easy reach. "Williams, you cover the rear, but stay with us."

Williams put his hand on Issa's back but had his pistol drawn and pointed behind them as they shuffled down the corridor toward the next available door. The footsteps grew louder until it seemed only seconds away. "Ready your weapons," admonished Marcus.

As soon as the first armed soldier rounded the corner behind them, Williams fired. The shot hit the man in the forehead, dropping him like a fifty-pound barbell. The next man dodged and weaved as he came out, avoiding the next bullet from William's gun. But Issa turned too and followed up with a quick volley of her own, striking the second man in the left side of his face.

Marcus kept moving, grabbing door after door, until he found one that would yield its guard. "Move!" shouted, Marcus, pointing through the doorway and toward a row of laundry containers stacked up against the wall on the far side.

Security forces poured into the hallway behind them, running perpendicular to the escape route and immediately opened fire, sending a spray of lead down the narrow opening. But, by then, all they could see was a door slowly closing off the corridor where the fugitives had fled. The squad ran to the door, but stayed to its side so they couldn't be seen or shot through the hollow barrier. The lead soldier counted on his raised hand, putting up three, then two, then one fingers before clutching his fist and ripping open the door, running inside. The room was empty.

Marcus could feel his pulse racing. He was trying to keep his breathing under control, but it was hard. He had to stay calm and think clearly. This was what he was trained to do, but he also knew the odds. Unless they could get the door at the back of the linen room open, they were fodder for the machine guns bearing down on them. The other soldiers were still two rooms down from where they were hiding succumbing to the faked exit he'd quickly staged by opening another door in the hallway to buy them time. Pushing a button on his holograph, he studied the blueprint of where they were – the red dots showing their exact location in the basement. The hologram revealed a door out of that room – somewhere.

Marcus looked around. *There's no door here?* he thought to himself. *Is my hologram right?* Yet, it was clear on the diagram. But where was it? All he could see were blank walls.

"I don't see it," said Marcus. "Can any of you see a door out of here? My floor plan says there is one!"

"I don't see anything, colonel," said Williams, getting overly excited. He was beginning to panic, but Marcus calmed him.

"Settle yourself, Williams," scolded Marcus. "We'll only get out of here if we remain calm."

Within seconds they heard the door to their room open, and circumspectly five soldiers, rifles drawn, ran in taking immediate, defensive positions.

Marcus, Williams and Issa made more deliberate movements – quiet and precise – to avoid being heard or seen. They still had to find the exit. Unwilling to stay still and wait while the security men searched the entire room and finally found them, they scoured the walls and cautiously moved soiled linens to locate the hidden doorway.

It was one such pile that stubbornly wouldn't move, and when Issa pushed on it, the tower toppled over, making a huge crashing noise as the heavy, folded towels hit trays and buckets tucked away behind a table.

"Crap," mumbled Issa, as she saw the stack fall. But there was nothing she could do to stop it at that point. The damage had been done.

Shots rang out, spraying a nearby wall and filling it with black holes in a random pattern. Williams and Marcus returned fire again and again, their shots keeping the enemy at bay. But in front of Issa was the sought after door. Broad, yet unremarkable, it was their gateway to freedom, if they could get it open.

"Go through it, Issa. Open the damned thing!" shouted Marcus, continuing to fire.

Issa grabbed the handle and pulled, but the door didn't move.

"Try pushing on it!" yelled Williams.

She leaned in with her shoulder, but that much force was unneeded. The door swung open immediately, and she fell through it, as if she were taking a pratfall on a comedy show. Yet, she gathered herself and came back out, her gun raised and ready to engage the fight.

"Get outta here!" Marcus shouted to Issa. "You have to find the way out the back."

The initial gunfire drew other members of the assault group into the fray, carrying M-16Gs and pouring through into the room. Quickly, Marcus and Williams were outnumbered. Marcus motioned for Williams to go next. "Go!" the colonel yelled, as he laid down another line of fire to cover for his compatriot. Again, there was fierce return fire, breaking the glass of several washers, striking the walls and blowing out many of the overhead florescent lights which shattered and showered glass onto the floor. The colonel saw Williams disappear through the doorway, and began firing again, hoping to make his own escape.

Marcus let loose a fierce barrage of bullets and ran through the open doorway, slamming it shut as lead whizzed over his head. He picked up a crowbar that sat beside the floor and wedged it under the door, straining as he pounded it in as tightly as his muscles would allow. Another bullet blasted through the door and passed by his right ear; this time, he could feel a trickle of warm blood sliding down the side of his face. Turning to run, he heard the gunfire continuing, carving the door into pieces.

Behind him, Williams and Issa were trying to get another passageway open. Williams wrenching on the door knob, while Issa had her gun pointed at it, ready to shoot. "Just blast it!" shouted Marcus, nodding to Issa to take care of the impediment. Williams stood back, and Issa shot up the handle and lock. The door unlatched easily and swung open.

Issa ran out. But just as she vanished into the open darkness, there was another battery assault as the attackers splintered the remainder of the door, preparing to burst through.

"Go Williams! Get through the door now!" shouted Marcus pushing him along.

But Williams called out. "Sh*t!" he bellowed. "I'm hit," he said clutching his chest. A bullet had penetrated the wall and struck him, passing just behind the protective vest he was wearing. "I can't breathe," he said struggling for air. "I can't breathe!"

Marcus bent over him to see where he'd been struck when two more rounds came through the wall as the SWOT team behind them tried to dislodge the door from the crowbar. Both rounds pushed Marcus forward, hitting him in the back but neither going through his KevlarX vest, a paper-thin version of Kevlar. He slammed against the door in front of him before regaining his senses. When the colonel looked back down at his patient, he saw Williams's eyes still and unmoving. Blood was coming out of his mouth, and his body was limp. Marcus felt for a pulse, but the heart no longer sustained him.

As Marcus tried to lift Williams's body, he was struck once more, this time by a slug ripping through his shoulder, and he clutched it in pain. Issa came back through the doorway. "We have to get out of here, colonel," she said. Then, she looked down at Williams. "Is he?" She stopped, unable to mouth the words that were on her mind.

"Yeah, he's gone, Issa. We have to get him out of here," said Marcus, continuing to try to lift the body, but now with a damaged shoulder.

Issa raised her head. "They're almost through the door, colonel. We have no choice but to leave him," she added, glancing down at a friend who was no more.

Marcus grabbed onto Issa's arm, and she helped him out onto the shipping dock. Behind they left their friend and comrade who was no longer able to help them, just as they were no longer able to help him.

The soldiers stormed through the door and quickly spotted the second opening, stepping over and on Williams's body to get to it. But once they got outside, they found only an empty landing, except for the material goods that had left out from the previous day's shipments. It was as if the intruders had never been there.

Issa quietly put the water drainage grate back in place above her. The tunnel back to the outside world had been just as wet as it had been when they'd entered; yet, freedom was freedom, and they would gladly take it over rotting in a USSA prison for the rest of their lives.

"Colonel?" asked Issa, tugging on him. His body had suddenly grown heavy, almost impossibly so. "Colonel?" she asked again.

The colonel's eyes were closed, and his body unable to transport him any farther. "Come on Marcus!" shouted Issa, pounding on his chest. "You can't leave me now. Not you too!"

*****

CH 36 Return to What's Left

They could hear the dull, heavy thuds overhead, as if giants were again walking the earth and each step was another quake on the surface. But with each rumble, their hearts sank further and further, visualizing the total and utter destruction of all they cherished above ground.

As the bunker air conditioning had not yet been connected, the Cabinet members sat with sweat dripping from their faces. Balancing on benches made from the five-gallon drums of powdered milk, dried eggs, and other staples and spanned by left-over construction planks, they waited for silence.

Sumner and Oishi sat beside Shea as she lay on the floor, a white cloth tied around her head that covered a square, first-aid bandage they'd found in one of emergency kits. Shea was groggy, but her injury was not life-threatening – only a deep laceration into the left part of her skull. It continued to ooze, bleeding through the cloth, but she would recover fully, except for a bad headache.

Around Cheyenne, the attack had targeted communication towers, which were all knocked out; but there were three *SAT*-phones with linkage to one of several Canadian satellites orbiting in geosynchronous orbit overhead. Sumner had just gotten off a call with the Canadian Prime Minister, and his Defense Secretary was talking to General Moore, who was next in line after General Ward.

"What does it look like up there?" asked Templeton, holding the phone to his ear. "Do you have someone on their way over to the bunker to restore power to the elevator shaft?" Templeton listened intently and then nodded, saying "uh huh" several times as he eyed Secretary Ingram, who sat next to him. "Okay, so we can't expect anyone for another hour – and that's if the air strikes stop. Is that what you're telling me? … uh-huh … uh-huh."

"How's she doing?" asked Loretta White. She looked down on Shea with sympathetic eyes, pushing her hair back from her forehead and smiling. Loretta smiled at Shea as her eyes began to focus once again.

"I'll be fine. I'm tough," Shea said softly, then chuckling to herself.

"We all know you're tough," said Sumner. He wasn't overly concerned, but he asked Loretta to grab a blanket and cover Shea just in case she was suffering from mild shock.

Then, Sumner glanced at Templeton. "What's the general telling you?" he asked.

"Uh-huh. Okay, then. Thanks, general. Hopefully, we'll be out of here soon. Let me confer with the president and get back to you." Templeton hung up the phone, putting the rather large, soap-bar sized device down on the table. "It's pretty bad up there," said the Defense Secretary. They haven't destroyed everything, but there are a lot of buildings that have been reduced to piles. Life is at a standstill. Our anti-aircraft guns have shot down ten of their fighter-bombers, and for now, they've gone back to their base – presumably in Colorado Springs."

"Does the general want to respond? To retaliate?" asked Sumner. "Was that his question to you?"

"Yes, Mr. President. He asked if you wanted to respond to their attack?"

"What type of response is the general or you recommending?"

Templeton pulled on his pants, bringing them up higher on his waist and tucking in his white shirt so it wasn't billowing over the top of his black, alligator belt. "The general suggested we launch a counter attack, striking the Air Force base in Colorado Springs and …"

"… and what?"

"And the Air Force Academy just north of there too. He thought it would send a message and be a symbol of our resolve, sir."

"No, I won't bomb non-military targets – even if it is indirectly related to the war effort. And what is the likelihood of our aging fighter-bombers getting through to the Air Force base there? What planes would we use – those F-37 fighters from our National Guard units?"

"Yes, I'm afraid so, sir."

"They wouldn't make it even close to that base without being blown out of the sky. I think our best course is not to respond, Templeton. We can play on world sympathy and generate support – that includes military support as well. But the general should be alert to a possible second wave attack. Make sure he's on that."

"Yes, sir."

Templeton phoned the general and gave him the news. It was clear from the tone of the conversation that the general was fine with the decision and would take the appropriate measures to watch for any second wave. Since they had the benefit of Canada's satellite network, getting an early warning of such an attack would be much more forthcoming, especially with the damage inflicted by the USSA on civilian life in Cheyenne.

It was about an hour later when they heard electricity go on and some auxiliary compressors above them begin to whirl and rumble to life. Shortly after, the cables on the elevator were drawn taut and the SAT-phone rang. Templeton answered, listened and nodded his head. He turned to Sumner and said, "We're up and running again, sir. We can load people onto the elevator for extraction to the surface."

"Let's get Shea on the first run, Josh," instructed the president. "She really needs to get to a hospital."

It only took ten minutes to make the trips up and down the shaft to get all the Cabinet members out, and on the last run, the doors opened to reveal to Sumner all that he had feared. He walked out and gasped at what he saw. "Oh, my god," he said, looking around. "There's nothing left."

A colonel who was already directing the clean-up effort saluted the commander in chief as he exited the bunker elevator. "At ease, colonel," said the president. "Can you tell me about casualties? What's happened to the mansion? To the government buildings? To Cheyenne and the people?" he asked.

"We don't have an accounting yet, sir. We're still working on that. But I can tell you that hundreds have died – perhaps thousands. We don't know."

"And General Ward?" Sumner asked the colonel.

"I'm sorry, sir. But we found the general's body just outside the elevator when we arrived. We've removed the heavy concrete that fell on top of him. He was dead almost instantly."

"He was a hero, colonel. He sacrificed himself for the rest of us – a brave man."

"Yes, sir. He was always that way. Brave to the end."

As Sumner looked around, he saw a burned-out shell of the building that was once the presidential mansion. The entire roof had collapsed, and two of the four walls – those on the north and east sides were in complete ruin, blackened by fire. The smoke was thick, but a stiff breeze was blowing it easterly toward the downtown area of the city.

Sumner took out his white handkerchief, unfolded it and put it over his face, coughing from the oppressive roils of soot, smoke and dust that were spinning in the air around him. But squinting, he could make out the remnants of furniture, lighting fixtures, and other office articles interspersed among the shards of glass, wood, and twisted metal that lay everywhere, like some morbid, nouveau art sculpture that might be seen in a contemporary museum.

In the distance, he could hear the wailing sirens of ambulances running up and down the desolate streets of town, picking up the injured and rushing them to the hospital. As for the dead, there was little reason to rush them anywhere anymore. That grisly part of the clean-up would have to wait.

"Bastards," said Sumner watching it all unfold around him. "We will not get even, but we will make it painful for them if they try this again." He could only hope that his Manhattan team and Johnny's project were near perfecting their systems. It was obvious now more than ever that they needed both – one to protect themselves against such attacks in the future and one to make it costly for the USSA to try an aggressive frontal assault of that kind again.

But for now, he hurried to the hospital to see about Shea. He had a lot on his mind, but something that never seemed to escape him was his attorney general. She had always been special, and every day he realized it more and more.

The hospital was packed with patients. They were in the halls in gurneys, in waiting areas, even in the parking lot. The scene was from an apocalyptic movie, with bandaged, bleeding and hobbling people all trying to get help. Many were moaning, some screaming and others silent. It was those who were silent that needed the most help – either severely injured or dying or ... perhaps already dead.

Sumner's heartstrings were pulled tight. They were on the verge of breaking as he watched families crying over others who were struggling for life or where life's struggles were over. His anger grew, but he kept his emotions in check. That was his role; that was his responsibility as leader of the new Republic.

Sumner entered Shea's room, one she insisted upon sharing with someone else. She hadn't wanted a room at all, but the doctors feared a concussion, so they wanted to keep her overnight. The president approached the bed and sat next to her. He smiled warmly, his eyes softening as they met hers. "I just wanted to be sure my favorite attorney general was doing alright," he said, taking her hand and caressing it tenderly.

She felt the softness in his touch, and returned his smile. "It only hurts when I laugh," she said, trying to get a laugh out of her boss. And she did.

"So, don't laugh," he answered, parrying her comment.

She started to answer him, but he interrupted, ",,, and don't give me anything about being able to play the piano either. 'Cause I know you don't play."

This time she laughed, but then put her hand to her head in pain. "Don't' do that!" she protested lightly.

"Okay. I won't. I have to get back, but I just wanted to check on you. Glad you're feeling better," Sumner said.

"JC," she said to him as he was leaving, "thanks for coming."

"No problem. It was my duty."

"I hope it was more than that," she said, waiting for an answer.

"It was."

*****

CH 37 Bad News

Sumner was in a meeting, listening to a briefing from his Director of Wartime Production and others on phaser manufacturing issues when Oishi came in and circled around the far end of the table before coming up to the president's seat. She whispered something in his ear and then handed him a folded note. Sumner took the note and separated compressed halves, reading its brief contents.

> **Bulletin**: *Operation Assobrab has been terminated. Four missing – presumed dead. No productive result.*

The Assobrab mission was a humorous way to reference the search for Barbossa documents, by creating a semordnilap, or word spelled backwards. However now, with such somber news, he showed no emotion.

"Mr. President? I asked whether you thought the fourteen-week production cycle was fast enough for us," asked Thorne.

It was apparent to Sumner that Thorne had not yet received the same information about his team and their mission or he would not have been so calm at their meeting. Yet, it was not the time nor the place to raise it.

"Uh, I'm not sure I heard the question," said Sumner, trying to refocus on the meeting.

"Fourteen weeks, sir. I believe that production schedule is much too long," said Templeton.

"Yes, yes. I agree. We need to do much better than that, Thorne. You have to bring it in within the six-week timeline we discussed at length last week."

"But, Mr. President, with all due respect," answered Thorne, now feeling the heat. "It just isn't possible to ..."

"Anything is possible!" snapped Sumner, out of character.

Others in the room could tell that Sumner was upset by the news – whatever he had read in the note.

Thorne stopped his presentation, looking lost and aimless. "I don't know what to say, Mr. President," he said finally. "Would you like me to continue or just stop here?" he asked, looking away from his graphs and charts.

"Uh, yes. I think so, Thorne," Sumner answered, out of sorts. "But you'll need to excuse me. Thorne, you need to come with me." The president got up and left the room, obviously shaken.

It was a major blow to the cause and even more, personally, to Thorne. His Underground army was in shambles. Outside the makeshift, new Cabinet room – intended to be a temporary replacement for the on bombed out earlier in the week – Sumner pulled Thorne aside and filled him in on the news.

"Talk to me, Thorne," said Sumner. "Tell me what happened."

"I don't know, sir. The unit went before we gave them the go ahead."

"I wasn't aware there was a mission, Thorne. So, what was all this about?"

"You were in the bunker, sir. We couldn't reach you, and I didn't want to make the call. So, I told them to stand down on this one. Apparently, they went ahead with it before receiving my message."

"I see," said Sumner. He felt uncomfortable with the answer, but didn't pursue it.

"So, the team went in and must have had some problems. There were three teams, actually. One was the look-out; the second, the inside contact, and the third, …"

"They were the ones we lost," said Sumner.

Thorne hesitated. Then said, "Yes. I suppose, they were. That was the team that went inside the ministry."

"Tell me about Barbossa."

"If I could, Mr. President, I would, but we don't know. That's why Colonel Marcus was so intent on getting into the facility – that's where the intel was supposed to be."

"How did he hear about it?"

"We have a source inside the facility. She alerted us and helped us with the mission. She said there was something big brewing – some big project they – the USSA – was working on. Marcus just wanted to get in and get out. You know - just bring back that info so we would know what Barbossa is. He died a hero, sir."

"Yes, absolutely. But, of course, we won't be able to …"

"You're right sir. It's a secret mission. It's just sad that we won't be able to give him – his wife – a purple heart or medal of honor. He deserves it."

"Yes, he does."

"Is that all, sir?" asked Thorne, licking his wounds.

"We need two things. First, you need to come up with another plan to get that intel. We need to know about Barbossa. And two, I need a report on where we are with your Underground. I don't like the fact that we haven't found that mole yet."

"Yes, sir."

But before he walked away, the president stopped Thorne, raising his hand requesting one more moment. "What do you think happened? – to Marcus, that is?" the president asked.

"Apparently, we don't know, sir. You have all the information that we've been given thus far. I guess we'll have to wait for more details."

"What's your hunch?" pressed the president.

"May I speak freely, sir?"

"Of course."

"I do believe he must have been undermined by the mole. It was a pretty well-planned mission. I know Marcus too. He's thorough. I just can't imagine something going so wrong."

"What about our source? Is she still there?" Sumner asked.

"Yes, but we'll have to get her out of there sooner than later. She's not safe. But we have to wait a while when it will raise less suspicion. Now, they'll be reviewing everyone who was in the building that night, including her."

"What's her name – the inside agent?"

"I don't even know, sir. Marcus wouldn't tell me," said Thorne.

"I understand. Keep me in the loop," Sumner said.

Sumner walked back to his temporary office shaking his head. *Would anything go right?* he thought. It seemed like nothing was at the moment. *I need to lead these people out of this,* he said to himself. *They're looking to me. They trust me to save them and our country. I can't let them down. I just can't!*

*****

CH 38 Johnny's Help

It had been a bitter pill, but Lin had swallowed it for the good of the Republic. Johnny flew out to meet with him and with Pam Tokarov to discuss the status of their work and the issues they were having. The initial greeting between the men had been stiff and formal, with both needing to defend their egos and their reputations. Initially smiling, the two soon slid into a shouting match over the theories being used to develop the foundation of the shield.

"No! You can't do it that way! You have to have the wave property define the energy levels required," said Lin, crossing his arms and turning his head away from Johnny.

"But that's the only way you can obtain synchronization of the power modulator!" retorted Johnny. "There is no other way!" His face was reddened with rage and indignation.

"Boys, boys!" shouted Tokarov, stepping between them. "You aren't listening to each other! You're talking past one another." She looked up at the clock on the wall. "It's six thirty. Why don't we go out and have a nice dinner together. We can disconnect from this and talk about something else for a while. We'll come back at this in the morning."

Johnny looked warily at Lin, and Lin reciprocated. Neither man trusted the other, even though, in many ways, they were both very much alike. Moreover, they needed each other.

All three left the building, registering their fingerprints in the front lobby scanner as testimony that they were leaving for the day. The system blurted out the automated valediction, "Goodnight, Dr. Tokarov. Have a nice evening," addressing the customized message to each as an index finger was removed from the scanner box. Out in the car, neither man spoke to the other, nor did they look at each other. Arms folded, and faces staring out opposite sides of the car window, it was immensely awkward and uncomfortable for all.

Thankfully, the drive to the restaurant was short, and the car turned into the lot, pulling into a slot as directed by the auto's internal guidance system. Inside they were seated at a booth toward the back as Tokarov had requested, to avoid disturbing other patrons should another argument ensue.

Taking the leather-bound menus, Tokarov passed them to the two belligerents, neither of whom looked at her. As for Tokarov, she couldn't wait to get the waiter's attention, eager to get a drink in hand before the fireworks began in earnest.

"Can I get you something to drink?" asked the waiter, a portly, middle-aged man with husky, black mustache and long sideburns. It looked as though he hadn't smiled in years, a condition either enforced by restaurant management or self-imposed.

"I'll start with two shots of vodka," said Tokarov with a mischievous grin, "and a plate of smoked salmon." She turned to the other two and said, "The salmon is what we call a *zakuski* in my country – in cleanses the palate."

"I don't care about the salmon," said Lin, recoiling from the request, "and I don't want anything to drink. We have to work tomorrow."

Tokarov put her hand on his arm and said sternly, "Michael, if you don't relax tonight and try to get to know each other, there won't be a point of going into work tomorrow."

The waiter returned with a platter of six shot glasses, each sweating profusely. After placing the smoked salmon down, he positioned the two ice-cold shots in front of each person. Lin and Johnny just stared at them not knowing exactly what to do.

"The first toast I will make," said Tokarov, raising her glass and pushing it toward Lin and Johnny, "is to the success of our project. May the Republic reap the benefits of our mutual trust and camaraderie. May we be able to work together to put egos aside and put others before ourselves. And may we be able to come up with a god d*mned solution to this problem!" Then she knocked back the contents of the glass and slammed the empty container back on the table with a pronounced *bang!*

"Well, ..." she said staring at the other two. "You're both already one behind me. Drink up!"

Johnny and Lin picked up their glasses and poured the cold, clear liquid down their throats. Johnny didn't blink, but Lin grimaced, twisting his face into contortions that made Tokarov laugh. Johnny smiled, but Lin didn't think it was very funny.

"What are you laughing at?" Lin asked his partner.

"You drink like a pansy," she said to him. "You'd be laughed out of the bar in Russia."

"We're not in Russia," he retorted.

Tokarov ignored him. "You know, I'll do the next one too," she announced, picking up the second glass – this time waiting for the other two men to do the same. After they'd grudgingly clutched the jet fuel in their hands, she said, "And, as a second toast, I'd like to say that I hope we can become true friends. This project is going to need that out of us, and I think we're all capable of burying the hatchet without placing it into the skull of our compatriot."

"That's called a mixed metaphor," said Johnny.

"Okay, then," said Tokarov, "to mixed metaphors!" Again, she took the shot and banged the glass on the table. This time both Lin and Johnny followed suit.

Two hours later, the waiter came over to their table and interrupted. "I'm sorry to disturb you, but this is last call. We are shutting down the bar now. Would you like anything else?"

Tokarov was giggling and sipping her drink, while Johnny was laughing at a joke Lin had just told.

"Mister waiter," said Tokarov, slurring her words a bit. "I think we'll have one more round for ole' times sake. And, I suppose, the check."

"Very good, madam. Will there be one check or three?"

"Four," said Lin, his eyes glazed and a quirky smile on his face. "I now see four of us. So we'll need four checks."

Everyone laughed, with Johnny nearly in tears, slamming the table and chortling so loudly he was drawing attention from the other tables. "Just one," he answered. "You can send the bill to Uncle Sumner. We can thank him for tonight's festivities."

"Here, here!" said Lin, raising his glass as if it had been another toast.

The waiter left, and Tokarov slumped back into her seat. "I wonder who's going to drive us home," she said slowly and deliberately.

"Why?" asked Lin, rolling his eyes trying to keep them focused.

"'Cause, we've all had a bit too much to drink, I'd say," she answered.

"Hey, as the Rolling Stones used to say, 'We're not back in the USSR' lady," said Johnny, winking.

"The Stones? It was the Beatles, Johnny. Wow, I guess you really did lose your memory," said Lin, laughing. Even Johnny chuckled at this one. "That's what I've been telling everyone!"

Tokarov calmed her giggles and put on a straight face. "This has been fun," she said. "I think it's helped break the ice a bit. Hopefully, it will help us all work a little better tomorrow. What do you think?"

Johnny smiled. "I think you're flippin' nuts if you think I'm going to be in any shape to come in to work tomorrow. So, I'll agree with you. There should be absolutely no problems!"

"Very funny, Johnny. No, I'm serious," said Tokarov.

There was a moment of silence before Lin broke it. "Yeah, Johnny's not such a bad guy. I think we can work together."

"Good," said Tokarov. "Then put your boxing gloves away tomorrow, or whenever you come in, and let's get this thing done."

***

The next day, Tokarov was in the lab by seven fifteen, while Johnny strolled in at eight o'clock. Lin didn't stagger in until nearly nine thirty, claiming that he had to drop off his daughter at school. Even though it looked like he'd had a rough night, he was smiling when he came in.

Before they had a chance to get started, the phone rang.

"Dr. Lin?"

"Yes?"

"This is President Sumner. How are you?"

Lin instantly stiffened, never having had a direct call from the president before. "I am fine, sir. What is it that I can do for you?" His transformation from hung-over lackey to astute professor was remarkable and almost instantaneous.

"Dr. Lin, we've been watching your progress closely, and we believe you are doing a fine job. However, ..."

The president's voice was direct and unwavering, and Dr. Lin waited for the shoe to drop. He suspected something was afoot.

"... we want you to work with Dr. Johnny on your project. We believe both of you – together – have great ideas and can make this work."

"Yes, sir. We will be working together. I think his input will be valuable."

"Dr. Lin, Dr. Johnny will be running your Manhattan II project going forward. Do you understand? It's nothing personal. We just need to achieve faster progress on your work."

Dr. Lin tasted the bitterness of the pill he was being given. "I see, sir."

"Please, Dr. Lin, we believe you are a splendid scientist. We just hope you and Dr. Johnny will be able to work through your differences for the good of the Republic. Can you do that?"

"Yes sir," said Lin.

"Good. I knew you could. Now, we expect great things soon from you. Please press on and get us what we need out of your fine work."

"Yes sir. Thank you, sir."

"No, Dr. Lin. Thank you."

Lin hung up the phone. He was disappointed, but he understood. He had not been able to make the progress he had hoped for – progress he had promised Sumner in the first place.

Lin turned to Johnny who was on the other end of his laboratory table working on abstruse equations for the project. "I thought about what you said, Johnny," Lin said, sitting down in front of both Johnny and Tokarov. "I think you're right, except with a small tweak. If we take that wave theory and use it with the photon compressor, then add ten to the twentieth joules to the output amplitude, I think we may be on the right track."

At first, Johnny frowned. However, as he thought about the previous evening and their working relationship, his smiled. "Dr. Lin. I think you're right. Let's try that."

"Call me Michael," said Lin, with a grin.

Johnny reached out to shake Lin's hand, as if meeting him for the first time. "And I'm 1Johnny," he said with a smile, "but you can call me Johnny."

*****

CH 39 Colonel Marcus

They limped through the thick weald, down a trail guarded by the towering, wooden oak sentries whose only duty that night was to hide the escape of the two intruders. Marcus was losing blood, his shoulder damaged by a bullet as they were fleeing the Ministry of International Security. Issa was doing all she could to support him, her arm around his waist and offering her shoulders for him to lean against as they stumbled along. Several times he fell, dizzy and disoriented, but she made him press on.

"Come on colonel! Push yourself. You can do this," she barked.

They pressed on until they reached a main road. It was dusk, and the rain began pelting them from the above, turning the pavement into a slick, shiny ribbon of concern. They sat, waiting as the wetness soaked deeper into their clothes; the cold pressed farther into their bones.

"What's happened to major Tallis?" asked Marcus, referring to their lookout.

"I don't know," said Issa, shivering from the cold. "I can't reach her."

Issa sat close to Marcus to stay warm, keeping her hand on his shoulder to keep some pressure on it as they waited for someone to drive by. "It's only going to be a few more minutes, colonel. Someone will be coming soon. I just know it."

However, it was more than an hour, and no one had passed. Issa felt his wrist for his pulse – it was weak and thread, but there was little else she could do. Being religious, she did the only thing she knew to do - prayed. She put her hands together and looked to the heavens, searching for help.

Whether her prayer was answered or it was just serendipity, she would never know; however, a sound could be heard coming from just over the hill, and one light popped over the crest as it grew brighter and closer. Issa jumped up and started waving, both arms high in the air as if the vehicle wouldn't be able to see them just off the side of the road.

It was a white, Chevy pickup truck with only one headlight shining. It was traveling slowly, so when Issa stood in the middle of the road, blocking the way, she was in little danger. The truck pulled over to the side and stopped, rolling down the passenger window.

"What's up?" asked an older man inside. He was unshaved, wearing a white, cowboy hat and talking with a single toothpick dangling from his mouth.

"Can you get us to the hospital? This man is injured. I'm helping him," said Issa, intentionally being vague about what had happened.

The old man looked Marcus over, noticing that his eyes were shut and he was barely able to sit up. He also saw the dark stains on his shirt coming from his shoulder.

"Well, I dunno …" he said, "I don' like to get messed up in stuff like this." He shook his head and began to roll up the window.

"Please," Issa pleaded, looking helpless and needy.

"Fine," said the old man, shifting the toothpick to the other side of his mouth. "But, you'll need to get in the back. And, make sure he doesn't bleed all over the inside of my truck!"

Issa went to Marcus and helped him up, but when they got to the back of the truck, the colonel wasn't able to lift himself up and in.

The old man inside, huffed, threw the shifter into park and got out, shutting the door behind him. He grabbed Marcus by the hurt shoulder, making the colonel groan in pain. "Sorry, bud," said the man, looking more closely at the shirt. "He's been shot, miss!" said the man more excitedly, as he figured out what the injury was.

"It is?" said Issa, acting dumb. "Oh, my!" Her performance was weak but enough to convince the old man.

The cowboy rolled his eyes, but succumbed. "Fine. Let's jus' get him on aboard. You two can figure out all of this later. But, don't expect me to come into the hospital. I'm jus' gunna' drop you off. That's it!"

The truck bumped along the road, moving only slightly faster than it had before it had stopped for them. The rain continued to come down, sometimes pouring, sometimes drizzling, but all the time making the trip more and more miserable.

Issa had started to nod-off by the time the old man saw the lighted sign for St. Francis Hospital Emergency Room, and the truck turned off the exit and headed south to where the blue hospital sign directed him. The truck lumbered onward, following the arrows pointing to the assistance, but by this time the colonel's breathing was short and shallow.

The old man pulled the truck up, but steered clear of the emergency room entrance. "I can't take you up to the door. I can't get involved in this," he said. "You'll have to get out here."

Issa helped slide Marcus's limp body off the bed and onto the pavement. As the raindrops splattered his pallid face, she ran to the building and through the automatic sliding glass doors. Within a minute, two nurses and a physician ran out with a gurney and lifted the colonel onto it, shuttling him back inside.

Time passed slowly, and Issa did everything she could not to watch the digital clock on the wall in the waiting room. Keeping her mind off things, she flipped through the television channels, finding little of interest. After being subjected to a channel on eighteenth century Afghanistan cooking, one on the plight of lower-upper class Muslims in the Saudi Kingdom, and yet another on the possible extinction of cockroaches should climate change return, Issa turned the box off.

The next thing she knew, she was awakened by a doctor wearing a white lab coat and black, electronic heart and lung analyzer hanging from his neck. His head was wrapped in a white turban, and he had a long, thick, coarse black beard.

"Ma'am?" he asked, tapping her on the shoulder.

At first, she was startled, but then realized it was the hospital's emergency room doctor.

"Doctor?" she asked, trembling, worried about what he was about to tell her.

"Did you come in with the patient?"

"Yes," she answered.

"Are you a relative?"

"No. I'm just a friend."

"Well, we're going to have to contact the police department on this, ma'am. He's been shot, and we have to report all incidents to local police."

"I understand."

"You will have to stay as well, as they will want to question you. You'll have to wait here," said the doctor, without sympathy or comfort.

"How is he?" she asked.

"I can't tell you," he answered. "You're not a relative."

"You can tell me how he is. I'm the one who brought him in, after all. You just can't tell me any ailments or other conditions he has," she retorted, knowing the laws.

"Fine," huffed the doctor, who, as a government employee, was used to having his way. "Your friend is stable. He lost a lot of blood, but we're giving him some now."

"When will he be able to leave?"

"Not until the police have questioned him. Then, it will take a day or two before he's strong enough to be discharged – if he is discharged."

"What do you mean, if?" asked Issa.

"If the police don't arrest him for something he's done wrong," answered the doctor, condescendingly. "Now, if you'll excuse me, I have patients to attend to."

Realizing she didn't have much time, Issa waited for the doctor to vanish through the double doors to the critical care unit before she got up. The waiting room held only one other person, and he was sound asleep on a row of chairs in the far corner. When the corridor to the emergency rooms cleared of nurses hustling to and fro, Issa shuffled quickly through the same set of double doors through which the doctor had just passed and began looking for the colonel. Luckily, he was in the room nearest to the exit, his eyes shut and chest rising and falling methodically with the help of a breathing machine. Into his arm was a clear tube, taking out blood and filtering it through an artificial blood regenerator machine next to his hospital bed.

Issa slipped into his cloistered alcove and drew the cheap, plastic curtain across his bed. "Colonel! We need to go. Colonel, can you hear me? It's Issa."

Having been an emergency medical technician before joining special forces, Issa knew how to disconnect the machine and change the settings so it wouldn't set-off any alarms at the nurses' station. "Come on, colonel. You're coming with me," she said, helping him out the hospital bed.

She grabbed his clothes and then repositioned his arm around her waist, just as they had when they'd left the ministry building. As she pulled back the curtain, she made sure no one was nearby before walking him down the hall away from the double doors and over to a stairwell exit. There, they rested for a moment while the colonel came to and caught his breath. His red blood count was higher, but still not normal, and he was weak from dehydration and lack of food.

"We'll get something for you once we're out of here," said Issa, helping to lift him back on his feet and down the two flights to the first floor.

"But you should have seen the look on his face when she came to the bar ..." was a male voice she heard just outside the first-floor exit door. Issa hadn't yet opened it, and they crouched down so the people outside wouldn't see them through the glass slit just above the knob.

"... yeah, that must have been a pisser for him. Don't you think?" said a second man, laughing.

"You taking the elevator or should we take the stairs today?" said the first man, putting his hand on the door knob.

Issa took a breath and held it. Her heart raced, and she pulled the colonel closer to her to make sure he didn't fall and cause a commotion.

"Ah, I've got my hands full with this cafeteria plate," said the second voice. "I'm going to be lazy and take the elevator. You can use the stairs if you like."

Issa waited, hoping the handle wouldn't move. It didn't. Instead, the elevator bell sounded and apparently both men got on as she heard the door close.

She rose and peered through the glass. Seeing no one outside in the hallway, Issa opened the door, trying to act normally, like someone just helping a patient exercise in the corridor after a surgery.

Before long, both were outside and moving as quickly as they could away from the hospital. Issa checked her PCD and saw that she finally was getting service again. Her battery was down to 2 percent, so she made the call immediately. "Hello, Mr. Thorne? This is Issa Gomez. I've got a wounded colonel with me. We need your help."

*****

CH 40 Second Wave

"Shea, it's Sumner. How are you feeling?"

Shea had recovered quickly from her traumatic experience and the concussion, and there had been no lasting effects. Within a few days, she had been back to work — much against her doctor's orders and those of the commander in chief.

"I'm fine, JC. I told you before, I'm fine."

Sumner looked at her skeptically but had no choice but to accept her assessment. "Good," he said, "but I still think it was too early for you to jump back into things."

"JC, really! We've been over this. I'm fine. Trust me on this one, okay?"

The president took a deep breath before he started in again. "Shea, there have been other attacks. You need to come to my office as soon as you can. Are you alright to ..."

"Mr. President!" she exclaimed.

"Shea, just come over."

"JC, can you tell me where they've attacked?" she asked, holding the phone in her palm, trembling. "Are they coming in through Nevada or Minnesota, as we thought?"

"No," said Sumner, "they've infiltrated our air space and are bombing our manufacturing plants in Kansas, Alabama and North Carolina. We've suffered damage to several factories there that produce munitions, rifles, and tank turrets. A facility that made truck engines and transmissions was also hit, but not much more at this point. But the worst of it was along the Gulf Coast. They bombed our refineries near Baton Rouge and Houston, and struck our stockpiles of diesel fuel and oil. We'll be able to rebound, but it will take time to rebuild. We're going to be crippled by the fuel shortage. We're hopeful we can be back up and running within three days."

"Who controls Alaska and their oil at this point?" asked Shea. "They're not part of our Republic, yet."

Sumner smiled. "As of today, they are. I just heard from the governor there. They want an expedited approval process to align with us."

"Prudhoe oil," said Shea, referring to the vast amount of oil under the Prudhoe Bay Alaskan wildlife reserve. The Alaskan pipeline had split the country divisively during the 1980's, and it had been shut down in 2037, as environmentalists had convinced Washington to end production. This was done despite the fact that the pipeline had brought thousands of jobs to Alaska, helped make the US energy independent, and had created an explosion of the reindeer and musk ox populations, as the warm oil in the pipelines had encouraged mating, rather than retarding it. Still, those who were shrillest on Capitol Hill got their way in the end, and the oil flow was stopped.

"Yes, Prudhoe oil. The state began drilling again last week in defiance of the law. We will get the oil within a few months as it comes down through Canada. The problem is, when they extended the pipeline, they ran it through interconnected pipelines in Alaska and Alberta into Montana."

"So, we have Alaska in our column, but not Montana. I see the problem. Any chance of getting Montana to come over?"

"None," said Sumner, flatly. "They've been sipping from the tainted Kool-Aid cup of liberalism too long." "Any other options?"

Sumner looked on thoughtfully. "Yes. Calgary, Alberta has been working on a secret pipeline for over a year. It would come down through our border with North Dakota. They just couldn't get it approved because of Washington. Now, we can. It will only take a month to bring it across."

"Excellent," said Shea. "And the oil shale in Texas and North Dakota? How is the fracking of the Bakken, Eagle Ford and Permian Basins going? Can we get that too?"

"Absolutely. That was resurrected instantly, once Texas came back on line with us. Even though fracking was outlawed over twenty years ago, it didn't take long to get the rigs back working. That and Alaska will be our lifelines," said Sumner. "But there's something else."

"What?"

"We're under attack, and we don't have our phasers ready for our troops to defend us. Thorne is working on it, but it's taking more time than we thought. So, we need to get those robotic soldiers out of the military warehouse in Yuma. The Arizona governor has secretly okay'd it as long as we get in and out within the next five days. I've alerted Templeton. He's contacting Thorne to see what he can do with his Underground cell out of Phoenix. It will take a lot of assets to move one hundred thousand of those things in that short of time."

"It's impossible," said Shea. "I'm no military expert, but I don't see how you can accomplish that."

"Come over here so we can discuss it," said Sumner with a beckoning grin.

In less than an hour, Shea had arrived at the secure hotel where Sumner was staying as temporary quarters. The mansion in Cheyenne had been destroyed, and they were still trying to figure out where he would live until something else could be built. Josh Templeton and General Moore were already there, and the president got right down to business. "So, what do we know from the attacks?" he asked Templeton.

"Sir, the bombings may only be the beginning. The assault was halted again, mysteriously, just as the first one was. There has been no destruction of any of our military bases or other military targets – just a focus on our production capabilities. Command and control systems have been hardened from EMP attacks and as you know, they are buried deep underground and hard to compromise. We are concerned about sabotage and terrorism from within — especially the mole situation within the Underground system which has still not been fixed."

"Have we sent our fighters up against their bombers?" asked Sumner.

"Sir, F39s and F42s have been sent up to attack the bombers, but these are sitting ducks for the F47s that the USSA has. If we could only get our hands on the new J-35 Chinese fighter or the S-39 Russian one, we'd be able to take them down quickly," said Templeton.

"There's no chance of getting those," said Sumner shaking his head. "The best we can do is get our hands on some of Canada's latest fighters, modeled after the sixth generation, Chinese Shenyang J-33."

"But what about the shields over our major metropolitan cities?" asked Shea. "When will they be ready? Has Thorne been able to get them out of prototyping and into something we can use?"

"No. I guess the power drain from them is significant, "said General Moore. "They've decided that changes have to be made again to lower the power demand. Right now, this defense could only be used when bombing runs are detected and then all power grids would have to be redirected to the shields. They said even then, it might not be enough power to make the system work. And even it if did, Johnny said we wouldn't have any ability to counter any attack as the dome of the shield would prevent surface to air countermeasures. We have no satellites of our own and, as you know, we need to rely on Canadian and Australian orbitals. Only Australia has hardened, combat satellites."

"We need those robotic soldiers out of Yuma," Sumner said, reaffirming the need. "How do we do this?"

"We know the robots are housed in modular storage units," said Moore. "There are about a thousand robots per unit, so it only requires pulling out a hundred modules. If we can fly in ten of our heavy-lift, CH-57B Rhino choppers in there to pull out those pods, we can get all of them in …"

"… ten trips," said Shea. "Pardon my surprise, general, but that sounds … well … absurd?"

Sumner gave Shea a disapproving look, but nodded his head. "I'm not sure I would characterize it that way; however, …" he paused, searching for words, "… I must agree. That won't work. You'll need to do better than that gentlemen."

"We'll have to reconsider this," said Templeton. "There are no good options right now. We'll have to get back to you."

"You'd better not think about this too long, Josh. We have five days. That's it," said the president.

As the group started to leave the presidential suite, Sumner clasped his fingers around Shea's arm. "Would you stay for a moment?" he asked her.

"Okay," Shea answered. But then, as she watched his face, she asked, "Is there something wrong, JC? You look annoyed, or something."

Sumner's face softened. "No, not at all. It's just that ... Shea, I ... in the bunker ... we were all worried about you. I was worried about you. Seeing you lying there ... your head injured ... I just realized how important you are to me."

Shea smiled. "I appreciate your concern for me, JC. I feel I have a great responsibility to this country, and ..."

"Shea," said the president, interrupting, "I do mean this country, of course, but ..."

"... but what, JC?"

"Also to me, personally." Sumner stopped and looked away, gathering himself up again. "Anyway, I ... well ... I care for you."

Shea gazed passionately into his loving eyes. "I care for you too, JC," she said, mimicking what he'd told her.

It was a magnetism, an attraction, that was as irresistible as it was improper. Both still had feelings for their first loves; yet, each had different reasons why those could never again be fulfilled. The two were strong individualists, independent and opinionated. While, at the same time, they shared a common, fundamental and moralistic belief – that of the freedom of the human spirit to pursue its dreams. Together, they had the Herculean task of cobbling together a second America – a second chance at "getting it right." And the people of the Republic looked to them for their leadership to show them the way. They were entrusted to fulfill that charge. But there was also this chemistry between them. It was something that had been there, deep down, from the start. Now, each day, it grew stronger, and the more time they spent together, the greater the feelings became.

Shea felt it, as if her body were being pushed from behind by some mischievous cherub trying to get her in trouble. Each of them drew closer, inch-by-inch, like a slow-motion replay of a critical moment at a sporting event. Closing her eyes, she waited with breathless anticipation for warm, moist lips to touch hers – to engulf her desires and her passions.

Yet, that same cherub suddenly sounded in her inner ear and whispered things she did not want to hear, but had no choice but to listen. She opened her eyes and pulled back, putting her finger on Sumner's lips as he had also been leaning toward her.

"We can't, JC. We just can't," she said with a regretful pout. She looked away from him and wiped a tear that had begun to gather in the corner of her eye. "JC, I care for you so much too. But you and I both know this is not the time. We just can't do this right now. You understand?"

Sumner slumped back and drew a long breath. "You're right, Shea. I was only thinking of myself and of you – of us. We do have bigger responsibilities." Then, he moved toward her once again, gently and circumspectly. He took her hands in his and caressed them tenderly. "Well, if nothing else. I just wanted you to know how I feel about you."

"I know," she answered him. The smile on her face would stay with her the rest of the day … the rest of her life.

*****

CH 41 Blockade

Just as they had expected, Ratner moved swiftly to impose a blockade of the entire Gulf Coast, leaving the Republic relying on what few ports they had on the Atlantic seaboard for imports of critical wartime materiel. Ratner felt it would be more difficult for the Republic to move supplies from the Atlantic states than those from the Gulf Coast. Years earlier, Charleston Bay, South Carolina, had been dredged to allow the big tankers and cargo ships to enter from Europe. Like the other recent additions to the Republic, South Caroline had joined out of fear of the totalitarian ways of Washington. It was one of the few ports to which the Republic could still gain access, and Sumner knew it was only a matter of time before it too would be threatened with closure.

The president's other concern was that of USSA submarines. Although the submarine fleet had once held over ninety vessels, the number had shrunk considerably due to the lack of money and the lack of will to field and supply a military presence. All of the *Ohio-class* intercontinental ballistic missile subs had been scrapped unilaterally by Enlightenment Party edicts. This was done in the belief that the world would follow their lead and dismantle their own nuclear arsenals. They didn't. The reduction of the attack submarine fleet was made because the term "attack" was deemed too provocative and the Administration at the time felt it was a destabilizing tool in the world, rather than a constructive one. Therefore, the sixty-one attack subs in the fleet were mothballed – all except six *Virginia-class* units that were intended to prowl each coastline in the event it were threatened.

Another favorable event was the dismemberment of the naval surface forces. As with the submarine fleet, the number of surface ships had been drastically curtailed, turning a once-powerful blue-water navy into a junior-varsity brown-water coalition. The USSA only had one carrier group, and its flagship, the aircraft carrier *USSS Obama* was in port in Roanoke, Virginia, undergoing repairs. It was a repeat of the fall of the British Empire during the previous century. Once a mighty naval power, the British squandered their fortunes and influence after decades of social re-engineering. In the end, it left them with little defenses, no ability to sway opinion in the world or guide the direction of events. It had become a vassal of the Islamic state, enslaved by clerics and religious fanatics who had eventually brought that once-great nation to its knees without firing a single shot.

For the president, a partnership with England, or with any of the European nations for that matter, was no longer an option. The twentieth century had long since been relegated to the pages of history books. He had to act as if he were on his own.

***

The 253,000 ton merchant ship *Santa Clara II* steamed out of Havana Harbor hoping to reach Tampico, Mexico to deliver fresh produce from Cuba within the three days scheduled. It was a relatively simple route, straight across the Gulf of Mexico, just skirting the north end of the Yucatan Peninsula.

Taking turns on look-out, the crew performed other chores on board – washing down the decks, painting, securing equipment and cargo, inspecting lines, repairing and performing maintenance work on engines and machinery used on the ship as well as keeping up the living quarters. The engineering crew that worked on the power plant hailed a staff of twelve, while the stewards crew, including the cook, was composed of only five. The rest were general hands – mainly able seamen, but also a few less experienced ordinary seamen.

That day, the winds were light, blowing out of the northwest at four knots with the waves not managing much above three to five feet. Skies clear, with the exception of a few puffy, white cumulous clouds dotting the azure canopy, the voyage was as routine as one might expect in the tropical waters of the south. As the boat rocked gently from side to side, sea gulls played on the deck, hopping and flitting about in circles in frolicsome rants that were entirely ignored by the men on board. Instead, the Santa Clara chugged on, cutting its own path through the steel blue waters, the light crashing of the waves against the hull and the metronomic rocking from side-to-side lured the men toward falling asleep rather than doing their work. The salt spray of the sea occasionally leaped up and over the bow when the ship would dip into a trough and resurface, but the cooling of the misty spritz was a refreshing break from the relentless heat of the sun overhead.

"How are we doin' with that rope, Hatchet?" asked Pendleton, the boatswain or bo'sn, giving one of the ordinary seaman the evil eye. "I've been watchin' and you've not been workin' too fast. The heat bucklin' your brain?"

Hatchet was one of the ordinaries, a young seamen not more than three months out of high school. His real name was Anthony Petronelli, but the men just called him Hatchet. He never knew why; it was just one of those things. He'd always loved the sea and wanted to go into the USSA Navy, but his leg had been broken in three places as a kid – an accident when he fell off the roof of the family barn – and the Navy had rejected him. Yet, he persisted and convinced his widowed mother that the merchant marines was the place for him. So, he signed up. He was in it for a three-year stint and was just learning the basics of working on a big ship.

"Yes sir!" Hatchet said without thinking. "I mean, no sir!"

"Which is it, Hatchet? Yes sir or no sir? It can't be both."

"No, sir!" replied Hatchet.

"Was that no sir to my question that it can't be both or that the heat's bucklin' your brain?"

"No, sir, that the heat's bucklin' my brain, sir," said Hatchet, trying to work faster. He took the three-inch diameter rope and began splicing it onto another.

"Okay, that's what I thought you said," said the bo'sn. He moved on down the deck, looking for other seamen to pick on. It was his nature to be difficult, but at the same time, the men respected him. He'd been sailing for decades, and he knew his stuff. For each trip, Captain Sewell always requested that Mack Pendleton be assigned to his ship, and he always was.

Pendleton climbed through the hatch, down the ladder to Deck One, where he usually stopped-in the mess to see what the cook was planning for supper. "So, how're we a doin' today, Bibbles?" said the bo'sn.

The cook was a crusty old tig, who'd didn't like it when the crew came around when they weren't supposed to, either looking for food or favors. But Pendleton was different. He was an old friend, whom Bibbles always looked out after. In fact, Bibbles and the bo'sn were in a group of five who played poker every night – every single night – from the time they got off their shift to the time they hit their bunks. Neither man had made anything or lost much from the exercise – they mainly just took turns taking each other's money and they giving it right back the next night.

This time, as was usual, Pendleton's was a harmless visit -- only after the menu. But then if he could weasel a morsel now and again that was fine too.

"I ain't got nothin' for ya'" spat Bibbles. "You'll have to wait for supper." It was like the cook to give the bo'sn a hard time now and again just to keep him in line.

"Aw, come on there Bibs. You have to have some left overs or somethin' don' ya?"

"I tell ya' I got nothin' Mack!" Bibbles said, whacking the fatty piece of hindquarter with his cleaver.

"Alright then," said Mack, "I hear ya." But the bo'sn took a couple golden brown tater tots that had just come out of the deep fryer, still sizzling and crunchy.

"Hey! I saw that!" shouted Bibbles after him, but Mack only smiled, waved and disappeared back down the passageway. "Damn him," the cook mumbled under his breath.

The day continued uneventfully into the afternoon, as the men fought dehydration with periodic stops for water. The humidity levels were high in the Gulf during the summer and the crew got little relief on deck. There was little shade, and even if there had been, the bo'sn would have made sure the men had no time to enjoy it. And there was no air conditioning aboard, except for the ship's captain. Although his quarters were just as cramped as every other space on the ship, he, at least, had air conditioning.

As the ship sailed on, the sun sank lower in the western sky, passing through several banks of clouds that were growing more billowy and dark. By now, deeper, longer-lasting shadows cloaked the ship's deck, giving temporary relief to the working crews that were about ready to take shifts eating in the galley.

Hatchet finished with his rope splicing and stood up to stretch. He looked out over the midnight blue depths of the sea, and watched as two seagulls floated gracefully across his field of view. He thought of how serene and peaceful it was out in the middle of nowhere, far away from the chaos and turbulence of the mainland.

But his eye caught something in the water not far from the starboard side of the ship. It was a white crease in the dark waves, out of place from the natural crests of white that crowned the rolling currents sweeping from bow to stern.

Hatchet took out his small set of digital binoculars – the pair his mother had given him as a birthday present before he left for duty – and pushed them up against the bridge of his nose. Pushing the rocker button to adjust the focus, he let the device zoom in and out until the blurred image was replaced with some crisp and clean. He squinted … and then squinted again. What appeared in his view looked like a watercolor painting with swirls of blue, white and black. But what it also had was a white, bubbly streak down the center, something Hatchet had never seen before.

"Jake? Take a look at this," he said to a mate who was coiling rope just down the deck. "Something seems to be streaking our way."

Jake came over and took the binoculars, but by that time he almost didn't need them. What he saw froze his blood. "It's a frickin' torpedo, man!" he yelled.

Jake jumped up and ran to the closest com box to alert the captain. Hatchet sat motionless, unable to move as he watched the first torpedo miss the ship by only a few feet, passing harmlessly behind the stern and continuing off the rear port side

"Captain!" said Jake excitedly, "we're being shot at! I mean, there's a torpedo headin' right at us!"…

"Where?" asked the captain.

"Off the port side, sir. About eleven o'clock, sir."

"Disregard and get back to work sailor," yelled the captain, not believing what his sailor was saying.

Jake looked out over the side of the ship, but no longer saw the wayward torpedo. "You didn't see anything?" Jake said, obviously repeating what the captain had told him. "Yes, sir. I'll get back to work, sir."

Jake hung up the mike and shook his head. "Did we really see something or was it just our imagination?" he said to Hatchet.

"I dunno," answered Hatchet. "Being out here sometimes can play tricks on your mind I guess."

Another mate came down from the deck that held the controls and helm, obviously hearing what Jake had said on the intercom. He was smiling and laughing as he descended the stairs.

"That was a good one, there Jake. Have you guys been smokin' something down here on deck?" asked the second mate, still grinning and stopping to light up a joint of his own.

"Sh*t no!" answered Jake, embarrassed and defensive. "Both of us saw it. Right Hatchet?"

Hatchet motioned again toward the same side of the ship and said, "You just watch out there again. They'll send another since the first missed us! You just watch for it."

The second mate took the binoculars and again looked out the starboard side. He perused the sea, and smiled again. "There's nothing out there that ..."

"What?" asked Jake.

The second mate's face was still and expressionless.

"What do you see?" asked Hatchet.

"Uh, it's a ..." started the second mate. "Sh*t!" he shouted.

The torpedo plowed through the water at breakneck speed, just under the surface but close enough to stir up a thin streak of foam behind it.

The explosion was massive, ripping through the center of the ship and sending metal shards everywhere. The *Santa Clara* lurched to the starboard side, throwing all the crew on their faces and sending a fireball up and over the side of the ship. The sea looked as though Poseidon was trying to vomit them out of his domain, rejecting their peaceful request for quiet and peaceful passage to their destination. Hatchet flew across the deck and struck his face against a bulkhead. He staggered to regain his balance, stunned and disoriented. Bleeding, he pressed his hand against the side of his temple to stop the stream of crimson now dripping off chin.

The ship's deafening emergency horn sounded with seven quick bursts, followed by a long, mournful wail. Then, the captain's voice came on with the command, "All hands to emergency stations. All hands to emergency stations. This is not a drill. I repeat, this is not a drill."

But the ship was already starting to list badly on the port side where a gaping hole had been created by the torpedo. Water was rising fast, flooding all decks below and edging its way up toward the main deck.

*Sh*t!* thought Hatchet. *We're goin' down!* His mind was a blur of confusion, but he remembered he was to report to E-103 if there were an emergency. At the station he would find a lifeboat and a crew probably already preparing for the evacuation.

Grabbing a life vest from one of many bulkhead storage compartments, he slipped the hard, orange preserver over his head and strapped it across his chest. Then, he stumbled onward, slipping on the slick, wet deck boards, and following behind two other shipmates who were also headed to the same point of rendezvous.

"E-102 ... E-103," he said to himself as he moved toward his assigned spot. He looked up onto the boom that held the lifeboat, but the boat wasn't there.

"What?" said a shipmate in front of him. "Where the f*ck is it?"

"Must 'of gotten blown off the stay when the torpedo hit us," said the other mate.

"What the f*ck do we do now?" asked the first, looking at Hatchet.

Hatchet moved back toward E-102, but there were several other shipmates already trying to ready the boat. It was hanging from just one boom – the other, badly damaged and unable to support the lifeboat any longer.

"Can we help?" asked Hatchet.

"No!" said someone who was inside the life boat trying to untangle one of the ropes. "Now stay back while we …" *Crash!*

A second explosion completely separated the bow from the rest of the ship as another torpedo reached is target. Hatchet and the others were hurled forward into what looked like a scrum heap. The life boat broke away from the boom and plunged into the sea, sending the man inside flying into the turbulent waters below.

Now, the water was rushing at them from the bow and they clung to whatever they could to keep from sliding toward it. Hatchet wrapped his arms around a mechanics box that was welded to the cargo lift on the ship. But he could see the waters racing toward him like some heartless sea monster ready to

devour him and his friends without feeling or remorse. He pulled himself up, trying to climb to higher ground and away from the maw of death that was rushing toward him. Clutching the rungs on the ladder, Hatchet pushed upward, making his way toward the top of the com tower.

The water rushed up, covering his ankles, knees and then thighs. Hatchet clung to the ladder with all his strength, fighting the force of the sea to rip him from his only place of security.

"No! No!" he cried out, fighting against the icy fingers of death.

But those fingers reached up and ripped him from the ladder, pulling him down and under their shroud of blue – his spirit, lost forever.

***

Sumner got the urgent message:

> *Mexican merchant ship, Santa Clara, sailing from Cuba to Mexico accidently torpedoed by USSA submarine. All lives lost. Incident developing.*

*****

CH 42 Operation Barbossa

"And what are the casualty counts in Cheyenne?" asked Ratner, looking over a report given to her by the Chief of Staff.

"There were 373 killed, 1204 wounded, as best we know, First Citizen. Those are unofficial numbers, but we believe they're pretty accurate," said Clancy Holt, looking over the top of his glasses.

"Were you able to kill Sumner and his little band of merry men?" she asked, now directing a question to General Williams.

"No, madam. We believe we were able to kill my counterpart, General Ward. We believe he was killed in the shelling."

"Well, I guess that's better than nothing," retorted the First Citizen. "But it doesn't deter me from making our next move."

"Excuse me, First Citizen? What exactly is your next move?" asked Williams, caught off guard.

"Invade, of course. We must take over their territory. We need boots on the ground inside that rogue state. It's not going to get done by just bombing them, for god's sake. We have to invade now!"

"Which invasion plan do you want to go with, then?" asked Williams. "We've been discussing an array of options, and ..."

"I don't care what you do, general. I just want those bastards smashed, destroyed, annihilated. I want them crawling back to us on their bloody, maggot-infested hands and knees. Do you understand me?" Ratner said with voracity. "I want no sympathy given to any of them. In fact, we will make examples of each of them by parading them naked through the streets of Washington, then treating them the way they used to back in the old days."

Washington looked nervously at her boss, her eyes flitting between the Chief of Staff and Ratner. "The old days?"

Ratner smiled. "Yes, the good ole days when people were disemboweled while still alive, their entrails burned in front of them, and then drawn and quartered – pulling off each arm and leg and dragging the head and torso through the streets of the capital city."

"When did they do that?" asked Holt, horrified at the thought.

"As late as the fifteenth and sixteenth centuries I believe. That's that they did in Europe. That will teach others not to mess with me – not to mess with the USSA."

There was an evil darkness that came over her countenance as she spoke, as if she had been possessed by a black wraith from Hell. Her face shriveled and her invective words were ejected from her mouth like barbs shot from a harpoon.

"Where's this coming from all of a sudden?" asked the general, shocked at the discussion.

Not understanding that the general was addressing her comment on how Republic prisoners would be treated, Ratner said, "Your blockade is a disaster, Williams! It's not working. Our first air strike didn't scare them. We killed a few, but a few is not enough. The only thing that will get their attention is a full-scale invasion. I've made my decision. Now, it's up to you to carry it out."

Williams was not afraid of a fight on the battle field, but she was afraid of one in the Oval Office. "I see," she said backing down. "And, where and when do you want this initiated?" she asked.

"Where do you think, you moron!" Ratner answered, coldly. "The Republic! I just got through saying that, didn't I? And when? I want it now, of course. How soon can the troops be mobilized to strike?"

"As soon as I'm able to get the heads of the armed forces together to execute our plan, madam," she said in reply, bowing slightly. "Am I dismissed?"

"Yes. Get on this, general, or I'll have you drawn and quartered!"

After General Williams left the room, Ratner looked at Holt. "Well, what's the status of Barbossa? Do we have a prototype yet?"

"Yes, madam. But, I'm not sure it's ready for the battlefield."

"Not sure?"

"Uh, well ... "

"Well what? You either know or you don't," snipped Ratner.

"It's not ready madam," said Holt.

"Now that we have that settled, I want it deployed next week. We're invading in seven days."

"But ... but, they won't be ready, madam!"

"You have seven days to produce twenty thousand of them, Holt. You'd better get busy."

"Yes, madam."

Holt left the office shaking. He was unsure whether to run and defect or whether to see it through. It didn't take him long to decide. *She'll find me, wherever I go,* he thought. *There's not much point in trying to leave.*

Back at his desk, Holt called the minister of international policing. The phone rang and Sara Emerson picked up, her face coming up on a small screen built into the wall of his office.

"Clancy, what can I do for you today?" asked Emerson, giving him her full attention.

"Yes, Minister Emerson, I just received word from the First Citizen about executing an invasion of the Republic. I'll be calling a joint session of the staff to go over our invasion plan and need you there. She also wants us to use Barbossa."

There was silence on the other end of the line and the image of Emerson seemed to freeze on the screen. "I'm not sure it's a good idea," she answered coldly. "We just got the plans three weeks ago and the prototype isn't really ready for production."

"I know, but she insisted that it be used. She wants twenty thousand units available within seven days."

"You're joking, aren't you Holt?" said Emerson, without smiling.

"I wish I were, minister. But no, that's what she demanded."

"That's impossible. You and I both know that."

"Yes, we know that but we also know that the word is not in her vocabulary. So, I propose we get, say, a thousand produced as they are. We'll put them in the field. She won't know whether it's one or twenty-one thousand. She won't care as long as they work."

"That's the other point. We can't be sure of that either," said Emerson. "We weren't given all the details of how to make them -- just some."

"Some is better than none, minister."

"Alright then. We will execute Operation Barbossa. I will make the meeting arrangements on my end. You call the heads of the joint chiefs. We'll meet in my office within the hour." The minister hung up the phone. She sighed and opened a drawer on the bottom of her credenza, lifting it slightly to pull it out to its full extent. She took out a silver flask and unscrewed the metal top, pushing the mouth up to her lips and taking a sip. "Sh*t!" she said aloud, putting the flask back up to her face and making swift work of two more gulps before recapping the top.

She got back on the phone, this time calling her adjutant, Lt. Colonel Chaffey. "Yes, colonel, the White House has confirmed the initiation of Operation Barbossa ... when? ... immediately ... Of course I realize what that involves ... Did I check the initiation codes? ... These will be transmitted to you within the next few minutes on Charley Bravo Three." The minister listened for a moment and then reacted. "Colonel, you were chosen for this very moment. We believed you would be able to handle this. If you're not, then ... Yes, I am sure that the White House is aware of the consequences of this action ... Yes, I said the initiation codes for the operation will be forthcoming ... the First Citizen is expecting much of us, I realize that, but that's our duty, sir ... I will get back to you on further orders, colonel." Emerson sent the codes to the lieutenant colonel to validate what she was saying, her voice wavering as she punctuated the alphanumeric series with the word "Send."

The meeting with the Joint Chiefs of Staff was chaotic and, at times, cacophonous as the chiefs wanted to understand the reasoning behind Ratner's rash decision to invade and to use their newest weapon, even though it was still not ready. Everyone felt it was uncertain whether such a series of strikes and the use of the weapon would be effective. Their troop movements could not be hidden from the view of satellites. Minister Emerson had knowledge that the Republic was getting satellite data from some foreign country but didn't know which one. And even Ratner knew better than to attack the spy satellites of the major powers of China, Russia and Saudi Arabia. Even the lesser powers of the Islamic states had spy satellites orbiting and monitoring troop movements inside the USSA. It would not be difficult for the Republic to get that information passed along.

A few hours later, Emerson got a call from Lt. Colonel Chaffey. "Minister, we seem to have run into a snag with the Barbossa unit. It won't be ready in time."

"It must be ready in time. There are no alternatives."

"But, it doesn't work right now."

"Make it work," insisted the minister, regurgitating the commands of the First Citizen.

"But ..."

"I don't accept excuses, colonel. *Make* it work."

"I'll have to contact the inventor, then," said the lieutenant colonel.

"Then contact him."

"But he lives in the Republic, ma'am."

"Listen, if we have to involve Johnny, then we have to involve him. Got it?"

*****

CH 43 Righteous Sin

Issa got Colonel Marcus to the safe house, but Thorne's emissary had to rely on back roads to get there. All main highways and state roads were sealed off between Wyoming and Colorado, as the dispute between the USSA and the Republic escalated. Sumner had asked Bronson Updike, director of GOFLA, if he would go. Not being directly affiliated with the ATLAS Republic, Updike could not be accused as a spy or linked as quickly back to Cheyenne. Driving all night, Updike finally made it to the safe house to meet them and plot next steps.

"Do you think he needs more medical treatment?" asked Updike, looking at the dressed wound of the colonel's shoulder.

"I'm fine," barked Marcus, irritated at the special treatment he was being given. The tough soldier just grunted, as they continued to look at him. "Just get me assigned to another mission, and I'll be on my way," he said wincing as they attempted to sit him up on the couch.

"Take it easy, ironman," answered Updike. "You're in no condition to run out of this place just yet." He turned to Issa and asked, "Were they able to remove the bullet?"

"It was a clean shot, sir. The bullet exited through the front of his upper chest without hitting any bone or organs. He was lucky."

"I'd say so," answered the director, sitting back on the torn, cyan-striped sofa. "We just need to get you both back to Wyoming. Do you think you can make the ride? I had to take horse paths to get here, and god knows where I'll have to go to evade them going back. I brought one of our heavy, duty jeeps, but there isn't much room to have him stretch out in back."

"I said I'll be fine, Bronson," said Marcus. "Just get us out of here. But before you do, there's something we need to show you."

Marcus nodded to Issa to retrieve the data chip they had stolen from the Ministry of International Policing. She came back and handed the fingernail-sized, black node to Updike. "We think you should see this before we go anywhere," she told him.

Thorne attached it to his PCD and told it to run the data through his decrypt program. "I assume this has something to do with Barbossa?"

"Yeah, and you're not going to be happy," said the colonel.

Images of Ratner with her team came into clear view on the screen. They were sitting around her desk, on the phone with someone whose picture was not being shown on the hologram.

"I'll turn it up," said Issa, as it was hard to hear what they were saying.

"So," said Ratner in the video, "You will provide us the blueprints and technical specs we need to manufacture the weapon?"

"Yes," said the voice on the other end of the line.

"I know that voice," said Updike. "But, it can't be ..."

"I'll give you that, if you promise not to use it for aggressive purposes. It is only to be used for defensive measures – in case the Republic uses its weapons to destroy non-military targets. You cannot use it against civilians or unarmed military personnel. Is that clear?"

"It's John Johnny!" said Updike. "I'm sure of it. He's working on some top-secret project for President Sumner. Why is he talking to the USSA?"

The video continued to roll.

"I think we can give you our assurance that we will not use the phaser in any first strike capacity. We will only use it as you request - as a last effort to protect our citizenry. We are, after all, a peaceful people,

Mr. Johnny. We have not sought to use military force against the state that has rebelled against the Union. The USSA has only tried to use diplomacy to bring Wyoming back into the fold with its community of other states. Surely you understand that?"

"Of course. That's why I'm offering you this technology. I believe that only by having a balance of power in the world can we hope to have stability and peace. If only one side has such superiority, then it destabilizes everything and makes it much more likely that there will be war. It's not unlike MAD during the Cold War. Mutually assured destruction prevented the US and Soviet Union of ever starting anything. Too many innocent people would have died – millions, perhaps. It's something a civilized society – an enlightened society – would never think to do."

"We couldn't agree more, Dr. Johnny," said Ratner from across the room.

"Good. That's exactly what I wanted to hear," said Johnny. "Then we have a deal. I will send you the information electronically over encoded lines. You can then produce the phaser as a deterrent against aggression and other such acts against your nation."

"We look forward to your transmission," said Ratner, pushing a button and shutting off the conversation. But, the video continued, showing the group of three shifting in their chairs as the First Citizen spoke. "Well, that was easy," said Ratner, with a dismissive look on her face. "How naïve is this guy anyway? That's not the way the world works – never has. She who has the power makes the rules, right? I guess he never learned that in his pin-headed physics class. And even better -- we didn't have to fire a shot at them."

"This certainly is a game changer," said General Williams. "We can use the weapon to bring the Republic back into the Union and to protect us against any aggression by China or Russia."

Ratner scowled. "You don't get it, do you," said Ratner, "Bringing back the renegade states is nothing. It's a mere blip on the data screen. But that's why I am where I am. You two have no vision for what's possible here. We're not defending anything. No, we're going to *expand* our nation. We have to be thinking about absorbing all of Canada and Mexico into the USSA. In fact, why stop there? Why not take Central and South America? There will be no stopping us with this technology. Countries will shrink before us. Like the Republic, we won't have to fire a shot and they'll surrender to us."

"But the Republic also has it," said Emerson.

"They'll never use it," answered Ratner. "Sumner and his people would never unleash this on us, just as we never unleashed a nuclear weapon against anyone after Japan in '45. You see – like you – they don't have what it takes either to dominate someone else. They aren't made of the same stuff I am. I won't hesitate – not at all."

There was an eerie silence in the living room of the safe house as Updike turned off the viewer. He took a deep breath. "My god. What has Johnny done?"

"I was thinking the same thing," said Marcus. "Why would he do this?"

"He's a traitor!" said Issa, with contempt and anger.

"It appears so," said Updike. "You're right, though. I need to get this back to Cheyenne as soon as possible. Can you travel?"

"I'm ready to go, Brandon. Just say when," said Marcus.

"Well, then saddle up."

***

The trip back was grueling, as more roads had been closed. Using Canadian intelligence, Updike was able to avoid all the roadblocks and patrol units moving up and down the border. It took nearly a full day to travel what would otherwise have been a three-hour trip from just north of Colorado Springs to Cheyenne. But once back in the capital, Sumner and Templeton were apprised, and both expressed shock and dismay over what they heard.

"Could there be any mistake here?" asked Sumner. "Could this video have been manipulated to make it seem that Johnny was betraying us to derail our project with him?"

"It's possible, Mr. President. We've sent the original to the lab here in town for analysis. If it's a fake, we'll be able to tell it," said Updike.

"In the meantime, what is your recommendation?" asked Sumner, putting his hands in his lap and rubbing them together nervously.

"We have to worry about what he's giving us," said Moore.

"What do you mean?" asked Sumner.

"Well, he could be undermining our own efforts too. Is the phaser something that will actually work? Or is it something that will help our enemy – like signal our location with GPS tracking information, for example, so the USSA knows where our troops are. There could be a hundred and one ways that this technology is aimed to hurt rather than help us. And, there's another problem, Mr. President."

"What's that?" asked Sumner.

"Johnny was also working with the Manhattan team. He's gotten his hands on their technology too. We have to assume that the USSA is aware of what we are trying to build there as well."

"Sh*t," exclaimed Sumner. "I forgot about that?"

"Yes, remember that Dr. Lin was having problems minimizing the energy footprint of the shield in order to make it large enough to build over an entire city. We encouraged him to contact Johnny for advice." "And?"

"Apparently, Johnny was able to help him. Lin didn't report any problems to us. It seems like things are proceeding more quickly now."

Sumner shook his head in despair. Everything they'd been working toward was, again, at risk. And there was no way to be certain what the USSA knew and what they didn't. The only thing for sure was that they had the plans for the phaser and could have someone else look it over for signs of deception. The question was whether the USSA was also building a shield?

"Let's have Johnny come in," said Sumner. "I have some questions for the mad scientist."

Johnny arrived in the afternoon and was escorted by two marines into Sumner's office. He was under the impression that it was just a routine briefing on the status of his project, but when he saw guards posted on the outside of the president's office he knew something had changed.

"Johnny, please have a seat," said Sumner, gravely, motioning for him to come in. The president was not alone. Also in the room were his secretaries of state and defense, Ingram and Templeton, respectively, and his CIA director, Meredith Crawley, and General Moore. Intentionally, Sumner had not invited Shea to attend, not wishing to upset her or to cause Johnny to be less than forthright in his answers.

Nervously, Johnny sat, his eyes darting amongst the participants in the room. He fidgeted with a blue ballpoint pen he was carrying, clicking it over and over again in agitation. Crossing his legs, he tried to appear more at ease and realized his nervous habit was annoying the others seated around him. He stopped clicking the pen and tucked it away inside his coat pocket, awaiting the next act of the unfolding play. Yet, no one said anything to him. Instead, they either looked down at their computer pads or stared at him as though he carried the Ebola virus.

"I'd like you to watch something that came to our attention," Sumner said finally, activating the video. The image began in Ratner's office with her speaking on the phone with the unseen caller.

Within a few minutes, Johnny cleared his throat nervously and shifted in his seat several times, not able to find comfort anywhere. He watched as the damning evidence was presented. When it concluded, he cast his glance down at his lap, either in embarrassment or saddened by the remarks made by the Ratner's trio after the call ended.

"Well, is there anything you'd like to tell us?" Sumner asked, giving Johnny a cold stare. He pushed away from the desk and motioned for the guards to come in. They entered and took their positions beside the door.

"I can understand why you might be upset by what you see here," said Johnny, looking up to engage the president.

"Yes, I am," said Sumner. "But I'm hoping you'll give me another reason why I'm seeing what I'm seeing. I hope you won't tell me that it's a fraud and that you never said what's on this tape, because we've had it authenticated."

"No, I said what I said," answered Johnny, with only a touch of remorse. "But you have to understand ..."

"What is it that I have to understand!" shouted Sumner, in an outburst that was unlike any those in the room had ever witnessed out of him. "That you *betrayed* us? That you lied to us? That you sold us out? How much money did they give you for the technology?"

"Nothing. They gave me nothing."

"I don't believe you, Johnny. You gave it to them for something. Now how much was it?"

"It wasn't because of the money," he began. "It was for a very good reason. Two, actually."

"How could there be a good reason? You gave sensitive, critical information to our enemy. That is a federal offense – a treasonous offense -- and, it's punishable by death. Did you know that?"

"Yes. But ...," said Johnny, trying to make his point. Sumner wouldn't have any of it.

"No, you're missing my point," snapped Sumner. "You gave our enemy the technology to destroy us – to destroy other countries on this planet. Do you realize that you've put that technology into the hands of a sociopath?"

"I did not," said Johnny, "give them the technology. I mean, not really."

"But you did! You said right in the video that you were giving it to them."

"But do you know what I gave them? No. You're only speculating that I gave them the functioning prototype data and plans, right?"

"Well, yes."

"I didn't," said Johnny, shaking his finger at them all. "I'm not as stupid as you may think, nor am I as naïve. The end of that video was no surprise to me. I know who Ratner is. I know what kind of monster she is. I also know that she's been working diligently to obtain our plans for months. She's got a mole network, as you know, but it goes beyond your Underground. She's got moles in the government too. And, by offering her this information, we bought time. She's called off her dogs on stealing the plans of our phaser – for now. She thinks she has them. But, what she really has is a hollow shell – a model that would be no more effective at highlighting a conference presentation than shooting down a drone or missile in mid-air."

"How do we know that for sure?" asked the general.

"You don't, I guess. You'll just have to trust me."

"Trust you? How can we trust you now? We were completely unaware of your little scheme until today," said Templeton.

"I didn't know who I could trust anymore," said Johnny. "I don't even know if the mole is in this room with us."

There was an uncomfortable chill that came through the room with those words. Subconsciously, if not overtly, members of the group began thinking of their peers seated around Johnny, wondering if any were, indeed, a spy.

"That's enough," said Sumner, now angrier than ever. "I won't have you sewing threads of discord throughout my Cabinet and Administration, Johnny. I won't have it!"

"I'm sorry that you feel that way, Mr. President. I just call them as I see them."

"No, you don't, Johnny. You are self-serving – calling it the way it's most advantageous to you." Motioning for the guards, Sumner directed them to cuff Johnny. "Take him away. I don't want to see his face again." The tall, stout marines led Johnny away, pushing him through the doorway and closing it behind them.

Sumner looked at those around him. "Well, we could try him on charges of sedition. But, in the middle of everything else going on, I think we just indict him and let him sit in prison until we have the time and resources to pursue this."

"Or, we could let him go," said Ingram, not having spoken up yet.

"Let him go? Are you crazy?" said the general. "He's a spy. We execute spies, Mr. Secretary."

"What if he's telling the truth? What if he did give them harmless plans. What if there are spies in our labs and in the Administration? What if there is a mole right here, right now, in this room?"

"Lawrence," said Sumner, trying to assuage and calm the waters, "he's only saying those things to disrupt us – to pit us against ourselves. It's a classic maneuver by a desperate prisoner with no other means of escape."

"But what if he is right?" persisted Ingram.

No one spoke up, willing to challenge or affirm what the secretary was suggesting.

"We'll have to come up with something," said Sumner, diverting the discussion. "Perhaps for now, we will hold him under house arrest, confined to his laboratory grounds. He won't have any contact with outsiders, including his immediate team and especially that of the Manhattan group. It's an unfortunate turn of events, but we have to address it and make sure it's contained."

"I agree, Mr. President. Let's watch him carefully and see things unfold. We'll know soon enough whether he's telling us the truth or not," said Templeton.

*****

CH 44 Total Totalitarianism

At first, the consolidation of all state functions into those of the federal government ministries resonated with the populace, which was tired of the cutbacks in government services brought about by the huge federal debt. Ratner had sold the idea based on the trillions to be saved by collapsing all state and local functions into the federal government. As with all her ideas, there had been overwhelming support by the media, Congress, and others in DC. It was state, county and municipal officials who cried foul, but after receiving large severance deposits in their bank accounts and promises of hefty increases in their pension funds, they quickly backed off to support the measure. The fat severance checks went out the very next day.

But the euphoria of the idea quickly wore off. School system funds were cut, class sizes doubled, teacher pay reduced, and buildings closed. Teachers were not upset, as they too were promised a shorter school year and school day, pay throughout the year, and promises of even higher pensions and expedited priority when standing in line for healthcare services. The only casualties from the education overall were, of course, the children.

Drivers' license bureaus were phased out, as all vehicles were required to be auto-piloted or people forced to use mass-transit. No cars were allowed inside major cities, except those of politicians and their families.

Of course, local policing functions had already been subsumed by the Red Shirts, directed by the White House. Likewise, the judicial system at the state and local levels were eliminated and replaced by federal courts.

As all offices were essentially federal, there was also no need for state oversight of elections. This too was transferred to the new USSA Bureau of Professional Certification in Washington. With this, professional licensing was centralized in the federal house, and was broadened beyond those in the fields of medicine, law, engineering, accountancy, and architecture. New licensing was required for receptionists, janitors, anyone in the food and beverage business – from cooks to bottle washers, business managers of all kinds, cashiers, and even parents.

To have a legal child, one was required to pay a fee and obtain a license. Basic courses in first aid as well as diversity and tolerance were required. If a child was born without proper registry of a parent, then the child was taken into protective custody by the state where it could be properly raised. State schools were already indoctrinating all children in the socialist ways and benefits from a "benign ruler" policy.

But, there were many other changes and shifts in function from state to federal, all coming quickly and deliberately. In most cases, rather than the size and scope of government decreasing, it increased. More areas needing government intervention were found with the reshuffling, rather than fewer. The capabilities of the states and municipalities were found to be "corrupt" and "lacking" in taking care of the neediest of their citizens. As a result, more money was spent, not less, and deficits grew even more rapidly than before.

Those few left in society untouched by skyrocketing taxation were now forced to do so, and, a new banking industry was created for it that loaned money to people to pay their taxes. Ironically, these loans were guaranteed by the government.

Taxes on all things increased, including income, estate, gasoline, property, liquor, sales, services, phone calls, television programming, water, electricity, gas, and other things already under the thumb of taxation. But new taxes were also created, covering financial transactions including all deposits and withdrawals from banks and purchases and sales of investments. Taxes were also imposed on miles driven, donations to religious institutions, and food purchases. Energy usage at all levels was taxed, and carbon emissions credits, used for decades, were no longer fungible between businesses or countries. Even estimates of the air breathed and sunlight used per family were made and taxes imposed on that basis. But the greatest burdens were the penalties imposed on things *not* done by people or families.

Fines were slapped on those who used politically incorrect language, did *not* contribute to certain charities, did not own a PCD and pay taxes through its use, violated common decency laws by wearing things deemed inappropriate, did not purchase a specific balance of fruits and vegetables during the year, did not drink or consume water per the guidelines, were overweight, did not exercise at least three times per week, etc. All of these actions or inactions resulted in steep fines and penalties. The sentence for not paying the fines was imprisonment or home confinement wearing an ankle tracking bracelet. Of course, the number of items considered luxury goods increased ten-fold, qualifying them for the luxury tax of 65 percent. New items added to the list were potatoes, bicycles, tennis shoes, and television sets.

Further crackdowns were made on those trying to travel within the country. All travel, except for the political class, was restricted and when it was granted was taxed at 82 percent. No travel authorization papers were issued to anyone else for any purpose.

Lastly, the First Citizen issued a proclamation regarding the naming of cities within the USSA. Immediately, the name of the nation's capital would be changed. No longer Washington, D.C., named after a racist slave holder, the new name would be Sitting Bull City. Likewise, any town within the USSA that was named after a slave-holding president, or any other offensive person in the history of the country was to be changed. People's feelings had to be considered, and all names were to be reviewed by the newly created central body – the Ministry of Enlightened Affairs. Not only would it rule on the names of towns but also on what additional words and phrases, if used, could be prosecuted.

These changes were mandated throughout every system in government and, most importantly, they would be forced on those least able to discern truth from fiction – the children. Children as young as six were charged with un-PC crimes and taken from their guardians for parental negligence. Placed in ReLearning Camps, these misguided children were reprogrammed using the old Soviet and Chinese communist systems of indoctrination, Ratner mandated that the education system for all students – K through college – be reformed with a focus on rewriting history and ensuring that problem solving and independent thinking were eliminated.

The Ministry of Truth and Educational Programming issued new curricula to all schools across the country. New text books were sent to grade schools, middle schools, high schools and even colleges – both public and private – to ensure "the proper education of our children" and to force "the consistency of education across all socio-economic and racial groups." One example cited was that the new history books contained nothing of the Revolutionary War or the *Declaration of Independence*, deemed too inflammatory and dangerous – possibly promoting unstable, radical thinking. The books also failed to mention George Washington, Thomas Jefferson, Benjamin Franklin or any other Founding Father. Instead, the books covered 1775-1776 by spending multiple chapters on:

- The struggles in India against the tyranny of British white men. The strong-handed acts of the East India Company in forcing the British government to send troops to protect the company's interests in India.
- The belated acts of Catherine the Great of Russia in trying to free the serfs of the country – people she had subjugated for years and only under pressure from those enlightened of the citizenry did she decide to act.
- The acts of bravery by the women of the revolutionaries in defying the British. As colonial women, they led the charge for independence, showing the men the true path toward freedom.
- The catastrophic hurricane that killed over 6000 in Guadalupe in 1776, caused by the beginnings of the Industrial Revolution. Smoke pouring from coal fireplaces in England also contributed to the first signs of Global Climate Change in that year.
- The Illuminati was formed.
- Phi Beta Kappa fraternity, a pagan organization without purpose or mission, was formed in William and Mary.

And so went the revision of history and of what the government would now do for the people. With new-found trillions "saved" by closing of all levels of government below the federal level, the Directorate went on another spending spree – dolling out goodies to their own comrades and giving enough scraps to the rest of the unemployed and unmotivated populace to maintain the peace. Votes were no longer required, but a calm and peaceful society was. Turmoil and upheaval were the biggest dangers facing 1600 Pennsylvania Avenue, it would distribute whatever opiates were needed to keep the people stupid, drugged and unaware.

However, despite these efforts, turmoil still seemed to be brewing.

The prospect of civil unrest scared the Administration, as flashbacks of Tiananmen Square in China and Tahrir Square in Egypt decades earlier were on their minds. Before the protests in Springfield, Massachusetts, there had been a brutal crackdown in Russia, when then-President Putin sent tanks to crush a rebellion in Estonia; this was after he had sent troops to take back Poland. All these incidents had resulted in massive protests by the people against their governing rulers, and all had ended in the deaths of hundreds or thousands of people. In each case, the federal, controlling government had resorted to opening fire on innocent civilians. Throughout modern history, the outcome of most rebellions was one of suppression. Either the ruling power released brutal force to destroy its opposition and remain ensconced in power or the military stepped in with a *coup d'état* – either to take advantage of an opportunity or to prevent the outbreak of complete anarchy. Within the USSA, Freedom Party events were being held secretly in basements and garages, fearing savage beatings by the Red Shirts or even directly by Enlightenment Party thugs. However, more and more frequently, those in the party threw caution to the wind and held the meetings in open-air markets, churches, and other public places. Some brazenly taunted the authorities to "come and get them."

Unfortunately, that is exactly what they did.

In response, the militant Enlightenment groups ratcheted up their attacks. They became startlingly more violent and abusive. The attacks – once small physical altercations – suddenly became full-scale military maneuvers that made going to the meetings all but suicidal. As meeting sites were torched – sometimes with people inside them -- family members kidnapped or killed, and eventually children tortured before the eyes of their own parents, the message sent was clear. *Don't f*ck with authority!*

Finally, the *dénouement* and the nation of the USSA quaked.

"I'm Lester Brandt, sitting in for LaToya Trinidad," said the surrogate anchor for the NNB, the National News Bureau, that was already on thin ice with the Administration for its coverage of the story.

"Tonight, we have the heartbreaking conclusion to a story we aired last week, about the Minority Leader's family and the apparent abduction of his eight-year-old son. We warn our listeners that the following story may be too graphic for some viewers, so you may wish to look away and turn down your volume for the next three minutes while we go live to Myron Zwybek in Washington, Myron."

"Yes, good evening, Lester," said the reporter, dressed in a khaki trench coat and standing in front of the Capitol building. "Even though Congress has been out of session for the past five months, members have been active in their home states. The consolidation of the state and local governments into the federal system has not resulted in any increase in workload in the Legislative Branch as most of this effort was absorbed by the Directorate. However, the leaders of Congress are still involved in the important matters of the nation. One such leader, Senator Drexel Warren has been very outspoken and critical of the Administration's handling of the Wyoming matter. Early last week, he organized a march in Washington to protest the alleged attack on Cheyenne. Although some reported that the USSA was behind the attack, none of that has been confirmed. White House involvement has been vehemently denied by the Ratner Administration."

The reporter continued. "Shortly after that rally, the Warren's eight-year-old son, Jamie, went missing. He was last reported leaving school during the day without approval. His classmates told us that he just *vanished*. Unfortunately, we now know that the young boy was murdered, and unspeakably, his severed head was mailed to the family residence, arriving early this afternoon. It is a gruesome affair, and one that suggests ..."

Suddenly, the NNB went off the air with the live feed pulled. Screens riveted to the story instantly turned black with dead air filling in the audio space.

But on another channel, the USSA-operated, nationalized news channel, the story was quite different. Broadcasting on the SI-net and lower-level SAT channels, the USSA-News station anchor began with:

"Tonight, here in Washington, DC, we have another incident of unrest and civil disobedience that has led to a personal tragedy. Witnesses say that at about eight o'clock last night, members of a right-wing extremist group called the Freedom Society gathered to plot the violent overthrow of the city's mayor and the council. The leader of the group is allegedly Senator Drexel Warren – of the very same Warren family that has claimed their son has been missing, and perhaps kidnapped, for the past two days. The police have been investigating and following up on information given them by reliable street informants. Exclusively on USSA-News, we have confirmed that early this evening about a hundred members of the senator's secret society assembled at the Wings of Gabriel Unitarian Church on the south side. These were certainly one percenters, as they came dressed in their Zegna ties, Brioni sport coats and handmade Berluti Italian lace-ups. Most looked as though they'd come directly from their million-dollar penthouse suites or their plush investment banking offices downtown. When the Red Shirts arrived, they found the cult standing in a circle, chanting demonic phrases and holding candles. In the middle of the floor was a pentagram drawn with black paint and an unopened box. Neighbors had complained of guns being brought into the church, and strange black smoke coming from the windows. The commander of the Red Shirts told USSA-News that they found a box in the center of the floor drawing. When they opened it, they found ... well, we can't tell you what was in the box due to the horrific nature of this crime. However, we will tell you that based on what was found in the box, it was confirmed that the senator's young son is dead. Senator Warren and his wife were arrested immediately and are being held without bond."

The anchor shook his head in disgust and added, "This is just another tragic example of what we have come to see more and more. It is these fringe groups that must be monitored and in most cases, outlawed before something like this happens. It is essential that we act quickly and decisively to arrest and imprison these groups before they have any chance of doing heinous things."

"This is Roger McCoy reporting for **Channel 9 News**."

The very next day, the Freedom Party was outlawed by the First Citizen. It was an executive order – the way nearly all the laws were made anymore. Citing the Freedom Party for inspiring criminal actions by societies like the Freedom Society, the

Administration shut them all down. All members identified with the party were arrested and imprisoned with no dates scheduled for their trials. Their families and extended families were also incarcerated. Children were encouraged to tell authorities if their parents had anything with the Freedom Party. At first they asked the offspring to produce letters, words, pictures or anything that might implicate someone. Eventually, even this ruse was dropped, and merely telling authorities about suspicious behavior was enough to be condemned. In addition, the Directorate had another stunning announcement: July 4 would no longer be celebrated. Instead, the nation would recognize May 1 as its new holiday -- to be known as *Humans Day*. It was intended to rejoice over the nature and goodness of the human spirit.

The ease by which she had crushed her opposition only empowered Ratner more. There was a rush of adrenaline from being able to dictate who did what, when and how. She no longer had to explain herself to anyone. Her grip was absolute. Her opinions not questioned. Her power unchallenged. Anyone crossing her at this point was never seen or heard from again.

Shangri-La, Ratner thought, this must be what it is like to be in paradise.

But no one else felt her euphoria. Instead, they all suffered under her brass-knuckled regime. But Ratner was still not pleased. *What more can I have? I can have my way with anyone and anything, whenever I want. What is it that I want that I don't have?* She smiled to herself. *Everything*, she considered. *I want it all — to be the most respected, yet feared person in the world.*

*****

CH 45 First Blood

As for the Republic, it still needed a navy, an army, a defense.

Fearing retaliation by the Administration and believing that the USSA would easily prevail in any conflict against the Republic, all the major defense contractors had remained in the USSA with their headquarters firmly planted near Sitting Bull City, D.C. None had been willing to risk dealing with, let alone moving to, Wyoming. Rather than a curse, this reluctance had been a blessing for the new nation. Instead of being challenged and possibly put out of business by the members of the government-military complex, many entrepreneurial upstarts and small contractors were thriving and able to fill the void and fulfill the Republic's needs. In the process, they developed remarkable and innovative solutions to military logistical problems and combat weaknesses.

Among these companies was Reliant Technology, a company based in Dallas, Texas. It had developed MegLev transports that used the weak magnetic field of the Earth to create a counter force to levitate small trucks and personnel carriers, eliminating the reliance on oil for fuel. This remarkable technology was being expanded to many other types of weaponry in the military arsenal. Another company, MZ Inc, had created a heat seeking bullet -- a miniature Sidewinder missile -- that would travel a certain predefined distance before engaging its heat seeking protocols and targeting an enemy soldier. There were others inventions too: bee-sized surveillance drones to large, B-4 drone bombers and F-53 drone fighters, nanobot infusions to keep troops awake for weeks at a time, implanted computers with retinal displays, a Kevlar-like film that could be applied to cover the entire body and create camouflaging, cloaking fields. Also, with great potential was the dramatic improvement in robotic soldiers, which were nearing human-scale intelligence and mobility in laboratories in Wyoming. However, since these advanced robots were not ready for production, Sumner ordered the "acquisition" of more antiquated models housed by the USSA in Yuma, Arizona. It was a decision that had been hard for him, but, as he was told, "war was war." Capturing those units would deny the enemy their use and fill a temporary gap in the Republic's troop strength at the same time.

However, Arizona was a state on the fence about whether to join the Republic. Certain parts were for secession; other parts were staunchly aligned with the USSA. It was a state with a split personality, but as Washington tightened its stranglehold on the states, the balance of the decision was tilting toward the Republic.

As for technology within the USSA, all Ratner could do was use existing sources inside the country – the same military conglomerates that were now owned by the government and run by bureaucrats. Imagination and creativity had been snuffed out and replaced with outdated methods and technologies that were safe, reliable and consistent. Innovation was considered too risky for civil servants in career positions who valued their jobs over all else. Few were willing to approve a project that might fail and jeopardize their comfortable, well-paying, chocked-with-benefits, government pension. Instead, no one was willing to go out on a limb, and weapon systems languished in perpetual states of development and second-guessing.

But even with more advanced technology, the Republic was fighting a battle of numbers. The USSA had hundreds if not thousands more of everything necessary to wage a war, and losses on the battlefield would quickly decimate the Republic's ability to defend itself. Sumner's best hope was that he could avoid a ground confrontation with the USSA altogether.

But that was not to be.

***

"Cassie?" said the editor in chief for the *Laramie County News*, "we need you to go to Cheyenne and cover a story about the military buildup going on in the Republic. We just got word from the Republic's Department of Defense that our Congress and the president have just appropriated billions for new weapons systems they claim are defensive – that are supposed to deter the USSA from attacking us. You need to find out whether that's true or whether it's just a smoke screen for an offensive attack."

Cassie Livingston had just gotten the job at the *Laramie County News* after months of searching for work. No news agency in the USSA would touch her after she had been accused of absconding with incriminating videos of the Springfield massacre. Word had purposely been leaked amongst the major news agencies about her involvement in the distribution of the tape showing innocent people being gunned down by the Red Shirt thugs that day. She had landed a job in Chicago for a time, but the curse of being at the wrong place at the wrong time or right place at the right time continued to plague her.

She had not been able to get a job since. So, she had traveled west to Wyoming to be amidst the *enemy* – those she had been told were evil, those who would sacrifice their own children to get ahead in a capitalistic society.

Even though she disagreed politically with what she thought the new government was doing in Cheyenne, she did appreciate a free press. She was able to report what was actually taking place, and her stories were printed. That was more than she'd gotten in her prior two jobs. A free press was why she had gone into journalism in the first place – not to push someone's agenda -- but to tell the story of what was actually going on in the world and in a way that everyone could understand. She felt her duty was to print the positive and the negative, the good and the bad, and the beautiful and the ugly, regardless of whose agenda it served.

But as Cassie drove to Cheyenne to see what she could find on the weapons appropriation, her favorite talk show radio station -- something banned in the USSA – was discussing the recent attack on Cheyenne.

"... I'm not sure there's enough information for us to know whether it was the USSA that was involved in ..." began a caller, before suddenly being cutoff.

"We are interrupting this station's programming to bring you a breaking story," said an announcer, not one Cassie was accustomed to hearing on that dial number. His voice was steady and authoritative, flowing on with a stream of words like he was reading the local weather forecast. "There is a report of major military operations just west of the Black Hills National Forest in South Dakota. People in that area tell RRC news that thousands of USSA military vehicles, including tanks, APCs, and other weaponry are rolling through small towns in the area heading west in the direction of Wyoming. Again, this is a breaking story. We will continue to broadcast updates as we learn more about what is happening in that area. Now back to your regularly scheduled radio programming."

Cassie pulled off the side of the road, trying to decide what to do. *I have to go there,* she thought. *That's where the story's going to be. To hell with the military appropriation.*

"Autopilot?" she said, speaking to the car's onboard computer.

"Where would you like to go?" answered the computer voice, a male one with a British accent that Cassie had selected from a long list of options.

"Take state road eighty-five north," said Cassie, calmly.

"To what city?" asked the computer.

"I don't know. Just drive!" said Cassie, curtly.

"How far?" replied the computer.

Cassie hit the autopilot override button, turning it off and flipping it to manual. *If you aren't going to help, then get out of the way,* she thought as she pulled back onto the highway.

***

Sitting along steel benches inside their armored personnel carriers, or APCs, were twenty, armed marines with camo-body armor, arm band computer screens, and hand-held phasers. Behind the marines were amassed a hundred tanks, and over five thousand troops. It looked intimidating, and it was meant to be. The men and women were among only three such units that General Williams had been able to put in the field with the phaser technology, and they had been given specific orders – vaporize everything and anyone that crossed their path. They were to leave nothing behind.

"Alright, men," said the first lieutenant from the 4th Infantry Division, 1st Stryker Brigade unit, shouting to the small, unique company of soldiers he had been chosen to command. "You're going to be using this new weapon. It's extremely lethal, so you have to use caution. I realize you haven't been fully trained on it, but it's a simple aim and shoot mechanism. All phasers are set to kill, so anything you hit will disintegrate. We are to take no prisoners. Therefore, anything that looks like an enemy should be liquidated. Is that clear?"

"Yes, sir," came the chorus from the men and women as they sat inside their APC, looking up at their commanding officer.

Startled by the lack of any resistance at the border between South Dakota and Wyoming, the lieutenant ordered the APCs to continue humming along the road, streaking south along state road eighty-five toward Cheyenne, only two hundred miles ahead.

Moving at over sixty miles per hour, the massive assault force pushed everything off the road that wouldn't get out of their way. Cars lay in ditches everywhere as drivers froze, panicked at the sight of a seventy-ton M1A4 tank barreling down on them or drove off the roads themselves.

"Where are we headed, lieutenant?" asked one of the men inside the APC.

"Can't say, marine," said the commanding officer, chewing gum and fingering his phaser.

"I sure hope it's not Cheyenne," said another marine. "That's where my wife's family lives – just outside of it."

"Marine," said the lieutenant, giving him a stiff glare, "you'll do as you're ordered. You got that?" "Yes sir," shouted the marine back to him.

"And if I tell you to fire on your wife's family and children, you'll do it with a smile on your face. Got that!"

The marine didn't respond, but nodded sullenly.

An hour later, they began roaring into the sleepy town of Lusk, a town of not more than seven hundred people. Flat with only a few e-charging stations where old Phillips 66 and BP gas stations used to be, the town was remarkable and unremarkable at the same time. It was remarkable in the way it had preserved the rural, slow-paced lifestyle so cherished during the nineteenth and early twentieth centuries. However, time had not been kind to it, as the population had dropped by nearly eighty percent over the years. The only stores left downtown were the small grocer and parts shops that still serviced the people along highway twenty. But other buildings that used to house a large machine shop, a feed storage facility and a ranch equipment rental store, had long since closed their doors and boarded up their windows.

The cavalry streamed into the town, hardly realizing that it had entered a populated, commercial area. On either side of the once-bustling downtown were quaint, red-and-tan-bricked buildings. Many had signs in the windows reading *Last Chance! 85% Off Sale!* or *Going-out-of-Business Sale! Must Sell It All!* in black and orange lettering, even though their shelves had been empty for decades. Parked along the curb were pickup trucks in various sizes and colors – holding hay bales, antique or junk furniture, rusted farming equipment, and even one with an old cola vending machine strapped to the back. Quiet and strangely peaceful, the downtown was reminiscent of a long-abandoned mining town that had seen its last ounce of gold leave on horseback years earlier. There were no people out, as one might have expected on a Tuesday morning, even in the smallest of rural towns.

But the young lieutenant didn't give it a second thought. Rural America was weird, he thought, no matter how you looked at it. It was better off bulldozed and turned into a national park of some sort — something to amuse the city folk, anyway. As he approached a major intersection, he looked over at a building on the corner with the sign **Rawhide Drug Co**. It advertised pharmaceuticals for citizens, but it too was closed.

"Men, get out here," the lieutenant ordered. "I want to be sure we're not ..."

Just at that moment, a rocket propelled grenade or RPG hit the APC that had stopped just behind them, blowing it up and sending pieces of shrapnel everywhere. The troops inside the lieutenant's APC heard the shards bounce off the side of their vehicle as though they were sitting in the middle of a ferocious hailstorm. Sliding aside the armored plate on his outside viewer, the lieutenant took a look to see what was going on. All he could see was a ball of fire and smoke from the destroyed unit that had pulled up behind them. It looked like the topper on an oil well that had just ignited.

"Sh*t!" cried the lieutenant, his moxie suddenly melting. "Go! Go!" he now yelled at the driver to get them out of the crosshairs of the ambush.

The APC started up again, but another RPG struck the front, instantly killing the driver and turning the carrier into an instant death trap.

"Get out!" shouted their leader, helping to pull the pins on the rear hatch and letting the heavy, uranium core door fall with a *thud* to the ground. The troops ran out the back and scrambled to shelter next to the drug store, fingers on their phaser triggers.

More RPGs came flying in at them from other parts of the town, destroying even more of the mechanized group's hardware. Inexperienced and insufficiently trained, the lieutenant had stopped the caravan in the center of a convergence point, making them easy targets by Republic National Guard troops defending their turf. The first exploded APC had blocked passage for the rest of the brigade, but the brigade colonel in charge quickly ordered the forward Abrams tank to push it aside and forge ahead. But without air cover, the troops were sitting ducks for air attack, which is exactly what the Republic unleashed on them.

Swooping in from bases in Cheyenne, the National Guard attacked main street with a squadron of older F-37 fighters, a flight of A-10-IIIs and a single AC-130B Spectre gunship. Laying down a curtain of lead, the air assault ships began destroying the tanks and mobile howitzers that were quickly trying to get into defensive positions just outside of town.

Two A-10s flew in low, bearing down on two Abrams M1A4 tanks, spraying shells at ten thousand rounds per minute. Modified as giant tank-killing drones, the A-10s flew pilotless, only by computer linkage, spotting the tanks and firing when they got a lock. Piercing the turret skin, the shells exploded inside the tank, ejecting the body of the navigator from inside the machine. The rest of the tank burst into flames when the magazines caught fire. But just behind the tank was an M6c anti-air mobile defense system, sporting TOW 6 and SuperStinger missiles. The TOWs burst out of their housings, streaking around toward one of the A-10s which was banking to make another run. From out of nowhere was a stream of fire from an F-37, which detonated the TOWs before they could reach the A10. It all happened within seconds, as computers took over the automatic firing mechanisms of the weapons systems.

The lieutenant scrambled out of his APC just before it was struck with an AGM 165 anti-tank missile. He hit the pavement as the top blew off the carrier unit, killing the driver and one other crew member inside.

"Take cover, men," shouted the lieutenant to his men who had taken up positions next to the drug store. "Fire your phasers at will. Destroy the in-coming aircraft and any RPG nests you find in the buildings down here."

His men obeyed, checking their phasers to make sure they were set to the *Kill* position. Then, they leaped out into the fray, targeting their weapons on everything and anything that moved in to threaten them. ***

Cassie saw the contrails of the missiles in the otherwise blue sky just ahead. She wanted to get another good story, but now she worried if she were getting too close to the action. She didn't want to be in the middle of an attack as she was in Chicago or Springfield.

It was clear there had been engagement up ahead, but unlike the days of the revolutionary war, when reporters and townspeople could watch battles from a nearby hilltop, confrontations of the twenty first century spanned hundreds of miles. Anyone within that sphere was a target or, at the very least, could become collateral damage. Either way, if you were shot and killed, you were dead – there was no ambiguity.

Undeterred, she kept driving north toward Lusk, watching the streaking planes overhead and the release of surface to ground missiles which vanished over the horizon, ending with a towering roil of white billowing smoke and followed, many seconds later, by a *thud* or *pop* of an explosion coming from the target. She pushed the accelerator to the floor and began passing more and more cars and trucks rolling by on the other side of the road, fleeing the tumult to which she was headed. As she drew nearer, the car shook from the vibrations each time a missile hit its mark.

Finally, she saw a small, green road sign that read: *Welcome to Niobrara County* with a slogan, *Where all the nice people live!*

Lusk was not far away.

*****

CH 46 Orders Approved

Even before the initiation of ground attacks against the Republic, Sumner had approved Plan B in the event of outright war. Recruiting and training troops took time, and the military and National Guard camps were full of new recruits. But it would be months before they would be ready for the battlefield. For now, the Republic had to rely on already trained troops in the National Guard or those in the USSA forts to defect and come over to join forces with the Republic's army.

Filling the gap between what they had and what they needed required a special talent – the talent of one injured, but recovering Colonel Marcus. Marcus had relied heavily on his second in command and newly promoted First Lieutenant Issa. She had saved him during the mission in Colorado Springs and had encouraged him during his convalescence. But that was weeks ago, and time was not willing to wait for Marcus to heal or the dangers from the USSA to recede.

It was Thorne again who contacted him with his next mission.

"Yes, colonel," said Thorne, "I realize that this mission is even more dangerous than the last, but if there is anyone who can pull it off, it's you. We have complete faith in your ability, Marcus."

"There's faith, and then there's insanity," Marcus replied, after learning about what it entailed. He was not one to shirk from danger, but he was also realistic about the likelihood of a mission succeeding. He had been on missions that had low probabilities of success and miraculously come out alive, and he'd never turned down a mission that he thought would be difficult. However, this one seemed to be a suicide mission with next to zero percent chance of being executed.

"I realize it appears daunting," said Thorne, "but ..."

"You want me to go into a heavily defended USSA fort and steal one hundred thousand robotic warriors for our use on the battlefield. And you tell me I only have seventy-two hours to do it. That's not insanity?"

"You'll have heavy transport helicopters and other equipment, unlike what you had in Colorado Springs," said Thorne, repeating what he'd been told by Templeton.

"But *one hundred thousand units*? How many can you put inside a Rhino?" he asked, referring to one of the big, heavy-lift helicopters.

"The robots are in modular storage units, and there are about a thousand per storage container," said

Templeton. "A rhino can lift one or two storage units at a time."

"You'll never be able to extract that many units that way," said Marcus. "It would take fifty trips by helicopter. It ain't gunna happen that way – that's for sure." He thought for a moment, tapping his fingers on the table. "A train," he said finally, as if it came to him in a dream state. "A train." "What?" asked Thorne, not sure he heard him correctly.

"I need a train -- one with fifty flatcars and two engines. We'll double stack 'em."

"But how will you get a train in there?"

"That's why you asked me to do it, Mr. Thorne. Isn't that right?"

***

The plan was simple, yet complex. Bring in a train, haul out one hundred thousand robots. It was easy – in theory, anyway. However, the devil was in the details.

Sumner provided the technical, electronic, and other manpower needed, while Marcus provided the creativity and genius of execution. Thorne and Templeton only stood by and watched as the master agent did his magic, putting together the team and assembling the resources.

The long train was brought in from various stations throughout Arizona, a state leaning toward joining the Republic. Serial numbers were carefully changed to those of recorded military flatcars and the two diesel engines were increased to three linked electro-diesels to pull the heavy load through the lower range of the Rock Mountains that stretched into southeast Arizona and southern New Mexico. Clearing enemy territory around the hostile town of Tucson and then into the completely USSA-entrenched territory of New Mexico, the train was to enter the newly declared Republic state of Texas and the safety of the southerly town of El Paso.

"Hello, this is Margaret Snyder. I'm the assistant to Army Vice Chief Harold Simmons, here in

Washington. I will be sending over an order to transfer some weapons systems from your facility to Schriever Air Force Base. It is an urgent matter, but we will follow all protocols for the request. Thank you."

Oishi got off the encrypted line, after impersonating the vice chief's assistant. It had been made possible by the work of a crack crew of computer hackers that had broken into the highly-sensitive and protected procurement line used by the USSA Army. Fabricating the credentials of the sender had been difficult, but was accomplished with new software developed by an entrepreneurial group known as TechWiz, Inc. out of Oklahoma City.

"You know we still have to send live, digital images and retinal scans of the Vice Chief. I've scheduled that at thirteen hundred hours today. Will you be ready?" asked Oishi, instructing a member of the hacking team.

"Yeah, boss lady," said one of the young technicians. "It's all ready to roll. You just call it, and we'll do a hologram with the vice chief's medical snapshot. It's like shootin' fish in a barrel," he added with a pleasured grin.

Their overconfidence did nothing to strengthen Oishi's certainty that they had all their bases covered. However, she had been told that they were the best at what they did, and to that point they had succeeded in their mandate. She sighed and rolled her eyes. "Just make sure it's all ready on the encrypted line by thirteen, okay?"

The appointed time arrived, and the robo-call came in as scheduled. "Order confirmation validation in process," said the monotone operator at the other end of the call. The visual screens went up and the holographic image of Vice Chief Simmons displayed in a remarkably life-like manner. "Submit to remote retinal scan," said the operator.

The hologram moved toward a simulated scanner and the red lines of the machine sped across his eyeball. He blinked realistically and then sat back in his chair.

"Scan confirmed," said the operator. "Now, please confirm the order as presented to this office for execution."

The hologram began speaking, but halfway into the dialog there was a garbled sound, as if the hologram had belched. "Excuse me, sir. Would you repeat that?"

The hologram was rewound, and it started as if nothing had happened.

"I confirm that my order to transfer one hundred thousand X6-YF2 robotic field units is to be delivered to Schriever AFB no later than four, October – to arrive no later than *(garbled word)* -one hundred hours," he said again.

Quickly, the techno-nerds working for the Republic scrambled to fix the problem before the ruse was detected. They inserted the word, *sorry*, and then re-ran the last sentence one more time. "... sorry, to arrive no later than twenty-one hundred hours."

This satisfied the operator, and she went on to validate other aspects of the transmission, including the vice chief's security code and other elements the team had obtained from the USSA database they had hacked online.

"Thank you General Simmons. We will process your order."

The verification was completed, but the mission to get the robots was just beginning.

Templeton knew an order of that magnitude would go further up the chain of command, and he was prepared for it. Working on holograms for the army chief of staff and even the Minister of Defense, or what the USSA termed the Ministry of International Policing, were already in progress and near completion. Monitoring SI-net lines and phone lines to capture the verification of the order at these levels was going to be tricky, but here they received help from China, which monitored all incoming and outgoing transmissions throughout the government of the USSA.

Three days later the Chinese alerted Templeton that the web address and phone line of the army chief of staff had been triggered. Oishi and her trio of technical wizards were notified, and the contact was diverted to their own private server and holodeck green-room stage at the headquarters of TechWiz, Inc.

"Call for General Vegas. This is Colonel Pickering in Yuma. General, I've received an order from your vice chief, General Simmons, dated September 27, to move one hundred thousand robots to the Colorado

Springs air force base. I want to confirm this order, general."

The hologram swiveled its illusionary chair and the figure sitting within it looked gruffly into the camera. "This is highly unusual, colonel. You are asking that a commanding officer verify the order of one of my subordinates -- someone of rank above your grade? Are you questioning a superior's orders, colonel?" The hologram of General Vegas was stern. She was known as a ball-buster, and she'd been in the military her entire adult life. Growing up in a military family, she'd seen all sides of army operations – except real battle.

"No, ma'am. I am doing nothing of the sort. I am only wanting to verify that ..."

"Well, then there is no need to verify it if it is coming from a superior officer. Isn't that correct?" The hologram was being digitally manipulated by Terik, the lead technocrat, but under the direction of Oishi who had worked with both the chief and vice chief and understood their backgrounds and idiosyncrasies. The hologram then began to wave-off colonel in a dismissive gesture for which Camilla Vegas was known.

"No disrespect, ma'am, but given the scope of this order, I need you to verify it personally."

The hologram re-engaged and stared at her inquisitor. "Fine," she said curtly. "What do I need to sign?"

"I'll send it now. You'll need to apply your digitized signature."

"Send it," she said, shutting off her screen.

The request came over the line but was intercepted like the rest of the communication. Terik applied the highly-encrypted code that was changed almost continuously and returned it over the same line. Nothing more was heard from the colonel.

"Where are we with the train?" asked Templeton, overseeing the entire operation.

"We have thirty-seven of the flatbeds completed, sir," said Thorne, pleased with the progress. "Colonel Marcus has been directly involved."

"We need to have all finished by Friday," said Templeton, not pleased with the state of affairs. "There can't be any more delay in this. We need those units on the front line. The USSA has already attacked. We'll have to modify their servo controls and memory once we get them in, but that's about all the time we'll have."

"This Friday?" said Thorne, surprised with the new deadline. "But we've been talking about sixteen more days! Since when has that changed?"

"Since this morning," said Templeton. "Ratner's invasion at Lusk has changed everything. Without those robots, we won't be able to defend our borders."

"How many divisions?"

"Four, so far."

"Okay then," said Thorne. "We'll have the robots delivered within three weeks. I'll let Colonel Marcus know."

*****

CH 47 New Strategy

Initially, it had been just Wyoming, Idaho, Nebraska, Kansas, Oklahoma, Utah and the northeast counties of Colorado that had broken away. However, *the plague*, as the Directorate now referred to it, had spread to other states outside this area. The next traunch of defectors included Louisiana, Mississippi, Alabama, Georgia, North and South Carolina, and Indiana, except for the Lakes Region, which vowed to rise up against the rest of the state if forced to secede. The governors of each state had already announced their strong support for what the Republic was doing and, in short order, they left the Union to join the ATLAS Republic. None of this was crippling to the Union until Texas and Florida fell into line. At first, the Texas governor said she would go it alone, as the state had back in the 1830s. However, after the solicitation from Sumner and Shea, she was convinced that joining with the new Republic was in their best interest. Florida too joined after the personal touch and promises made by Sumner and his Administration.

Seeing these two giants fold into the new nation, Arizona, Tennessee, Kentucky, West Virginia and the southwest portion of Illinois, all declared their independence from the USSA. North Dakota and South Dakota were still on the bubble, but both were leaning toward their support for and allegiance to the Republic.

But the schisms that were developing within some states did not end with Illinois and Colorado. Long-simmering bitterness between large liberal metropolitan areas -- which tended toward the socialist model -- and the more conservative rural countryside spilled over into states that had remained on the sideline. In quick succession, Washington, Oregon, California, and Pennsylvania all fractured – fragmenting into portions that no longer wanted to live with each other. Downstate areas were tired of paying for the largesse and welfare programs of the big cities, getting nothing in return.

In all, thirty states or new states formed an alliance with the ATLAS Republic, including last minute defections from Arkansas, Nevada and Missouri.

None of this made Ratner happy.

***

There was stunned silence in the room. The First Citizen couldn't comprehend what had happened to the force she had sent to neutralize the Republic's token force at Lusk -- one expected to defend the most direct route to Cheyenne, the new nation's capital.

"What … what the hell happened?" she stuttered, in disbelief. "I can't f*cking rely on anyone to do anything right! You send out what you think are your best people, and they can't f*cking get it done! What the f*ck is wrong with you!" she snarled, lashing out at General Washington.

"I don't know, Madam. You ordered that the phasers be used, and ..." began Ratner's chairperson of the Joint Chiefs.

"I did nothing of the sort. That was your decision general. I merely *suggested* we use them. You were the one who put them out on the field! You're the one who's supposed to know what's going on with our R&D efforts and the status of our weaponry. How could you let this f*cking happen?"

Ratner turned back to the screen, her face red with rage. "Play it again," she barked.

Her assistant touched a few buttons, and the system went back to the beginning of the segment, showing various views: from the lead tank, from an armored personnel carrier and even a ground shot of one incoming F-37 fighter. Once again, the screen showed the onslaught of missiles coming in from the fighters and then the A-10s and C-130 gunships arriving to begin their assault on the troops below.

Several explosions erupted from direct hits as the Republic's National Guard were effective in first stopping and then destroying many of the armaments in the USSA formation. Without being challenged in the sky, the USSA forces on the ground were naked and vulnerable. But this was supposed to be equalized by Ratner's phaser battalion, which was tasked with neutralizing *all* incoming threats.

The pictures showed the ground lieutenant giving the order for his men to arm their phasers. Each man took aim at the incoming attackers. "Fire at will!" the lieutenant had shouted.

At first, the images showed the tips of the phasers glowing a brilliant red as they had done during the trials Johnny had staged for Sumner and his generals. Within a few seconds, there should have been a blinding light bursting from the pistols and striking the fighter jets and gunships before they glowed and disappeared into a waft of white smoke. Instead, the glow from the pistol enveloped the whole gun and then, like a deadly contagion, traveled up into the bodies of the soldiers, liquefying them within seconds. Each disappeared in a dusty cloud that drifted away to join the tumbleweeds and prairie dogs of the surrounding landscape.

"What happened?" Ratner asked again, fuming. "All my elite men are dead — vaporized – how?"

"I'm not sure," said Washington, nervously.

Ratner pushed a button on her desk, but said nothing. Two armed guards came into the room wearing white and black MP bands around their arms. "Take the general to lockup," she ordered.

Washington looked at Ratner with astonishment. "But Madam, I had nothing to do with ..."

"... with this failure? Really. You were in charge, general. You've been in charge of this entire debacle. Now, I'm taking it over. I've had enough of your incompetence. It will be done my way now. We're getting rid of the phasers. Johnny has betrayed us. I will have his head soon enough. No, we have to break-out the old standby – something that has sent the fear of god into man from the day it was perfected."

"What's that?" asked Holt, watching as the guards escorted the general out of the room.

"You've heard of Fat Man and Little Boy, haven't you?" she asked him, looking at him over the tops of her glasses.

"You don't mean ..."

"Do you have a problem with that?" Ratner asked, challenging him.

"Uh, no, Madam. I just think that perhaps it may be a little premature to resort to that measure. Don't you think? I mean, creating a mushroom cloud over Wyoming, well ..."

"Yes, it's time. The Republic has or will have working phasers soon. Ours don't work. It's better to have an aggressive offense than play defense. This will put them on the defensive; that's for sure."

"True, but you'll be wiping out major parts of the country! Parts that you'll never be able to regain. They'll be barren and useless for decades, if not centuries, due to the radiation. The cost of clean-up will be enormous."

"Shut up, Holt!" Ratner shouted. "Who said we'd clean it up, anyway? They made this mess; now they'll have to clean it up themselves. But, I have another job for you, Clancy, and you'd better not screw this up, or you'll be joining the general."

"What is it?"

"We have to destroy their will to wage war. We must cut them off at the knees – deflate their sense of patriotism and their belief that they can win this thing. We have to do something they would never believe we were capable of."

*****

CH 48 A Once-National Treasure

Cassie had seen the destruction of the USSA brigade at Lusk first hand. Stopping on the outskirts of town, she had seen the shells of burning tanks and APCs — casualties of an aggressive defensive attack by air cover from the Republic. Hundreds had been killed, and many more injured. Yet, few from the Republic's side had been directly involved. Drones had been used to attack the USSA troops. Only a few soldiers had been deployed around the main street area to fire shoulder-launched missiles and a handful of others positioned as snipers to pickoff troops as they left their mobile transport vehicles.

She had watched as the USSA brigade had retreated across the state line into South Dakota. Cassie taped as much as she could on her portable video recorder and captured her thoughts on what she was seeing as things unfolded. Driving her old, beat-up red Malibu at a cautious distance behind them, she followed the disjointed and disorganized group of soldiers as they headed back toward Ellsworth air force base just outside of Rapid City. However, up ahead she saw the line of equipment come to a complete stop near Hot Springs. There was no movement at all for hours, and Cassie had to hide her car behind a small grove of trees flanked by a large digital billboard for the Express Inn & Tavern in Rapid City only twenty-three miles away. After an hour of waiting, she started her car to head back to Wyoming but stopped when the line of military vehicles showed signs of moving.

In front of them, coming in from the east, she could see a huge, rippling curtain of dust, like an approaching sandstorm often seen in the Sahara. Perpendicular to her southern route, the cloud of dust cut-off any view beyond. *Must be reinforcements,* Cassie said to herself, watching it unfold. By now, it had become more than just a dust storm. Popping out of the swirling confusion was a column of fresh, new troops and heavy artillery that was moving toward the new frontline. Most likely, it was for another attack — but this one was not undermanned and undersupplied like the last.

Streaking overhead were war planes with USSA markings — a fighter squadron flying in low, just above the hill tops. It banked over the deployment below and scrambled north, away from the route which the rest of the ground forces seemed to be taking.

I wonder where they're *headed?* thought Cassie, taking film of everything that was going on around her. Although she wouldn't see what happened for another twenty-four hours, she would hear the result and see another series of black plumes in the distance. The devastation of that event would be replayed on television and the SI-net for years to come, scenes that would haunt her for the rest of her life.

***

"Yes, First Citizen, I understand," said the general with the security phone pressed up against his ear. "I will prosecute the war as I would any other. They are traitors to our motherland and they deserve no special treatment. Yes, I concur… of course, madam … we will … We are doing everything we can at this time, but I realize more is needed. We will be executing our mission as you direct it."

The new Chairperson of the Joint Chiefs, General Amir Hussan, was used to the grilling from Ratner, but previously he had been sheltered from her withering tirades by his boss Shontal Williams, who was now in prison. He continued to listen attentively to his commander in chief, and then said, "Yes, First Citizen, we will carry out your orders." He put the phone down nervously.

Standing in front of his desk was General Camila Vegas, Chief of Staff of the Army, and General Samuel Winston, Chief of Staff of the Air Force.

"Well, we have our orders," Hussan explained. "You heard the First Citizen. We have a mission to carry out, so let's get to it."

Vegas stood in numbed attention before him. "Yes, sir," she answered with an unsure salute. "But, may I speak off the record, sir?"

Hussan looked up at his colleague without sympathy. "What is it?"

"Sir, I must admit to having difficulty rationalizing the slaughter of fellow Americans in this campaign.

Our mission is to preserve, protect and defend America – not wage war against it. And, this order ... well ... it's almost too much to understand. Why ..."

"It is not for you to understand, general," said Hussan. "Personally, I think the nostalgia for history in this land makes me sick. I applaud the move by the First Citizen. It's the first step to eliminating the grotesque distortion of the accomplishments made in this country during the previous three centuries. We are finally getting somewhere here. Of course, I would prefer to see more involvement of the Islamic movement, but that is not my call. We have an order, and we will obey it. Besides, it is not the view of this government that these civilians are truly Americans anymore. The Ministry of Justice now considers them enemy combatants of the state and therefore should be treated as enemies of the state."

"But ..."

"General Vegas, you have expressed your opinion, and it is duly noted, off the record. There is no more than can be done. Now, you have a job to do."

"No more than can be done or that will be done?" asked General Vegas.

General Winston started to speak, but hesitated.

"Well, apparently you have something to say as well?" Hussan asked, glancing over toward Winston.

"If I may, sir. I understand that we have a duty and oath to follow the commands of our senior officers and of the commander in chief. However, when those commands are contrary to the ..."

"... to the what, Winston?" Hussan barked. "Are you suggesting that my command and that of the First Citizen are contrary to the best interests of the country?"

"Uh, well, ..." he muttered.

"Then ... perhaps you should join General Williams in her new accommodations. Would you like to do that?"

"No, sir," said Winston.

"What about you Vegas? Do you have any problem with this?"

Vegas hesitated but saw there was no point in continuing the discourse. "No, sir," she said before saluting.

"Is that all?" Winston asked flatly.

"You're dismissed," Hussan answered, looking down at the computer screen on his desk.

Both generals saluted him and left the office.

It was General Winston's task to communicate the grim news to his bombers. Not trusting encoded messages, he wanted to speak directly to the commanders in the field. Otherwise, there was a chance they would not believe him and would ignore the order as some far-fetched joke.

When Colonel Thomas, commander in charge of the bomber squadron, got the radio call from the Air Force Chief of Staff, he was taken aback. "What?" said the colonel, incredulously. "I don't believe I heard you clearly, sir. Are you saying ..."

"You heard me right, colonel. You have your orders," barked the general.

"So, you want me to ..."

"Yes," answered the general brusquely. "These are orders directly from the Oval Office. Now I expect them to be carried out." And with that, he hung up.

The colonel stood in shock. He wasn't sure he could bring himself to carry out the order. Yet, if he disregarded it, he would most certainly face a court martial for insubordination and sedition. He called to his second in command, Major Lewinsky and repeated the order. The major too recoiled in shock and asked for corroboration. But when the colonel ordered him to conduct the mission without further discussion, the major saluted, just as the others had done, and barked, "Yes, sir."

When the major left the facility, Colonel Thomas punched the bombing coordinates and other information into the computer which would encrypt them before sending them on to the bomber squadron. In this case, only one B-2C bomber would be necessary to complete the mission.

It wasn't long before they all heard the old, lumbering B-2C bomber flying overhead at low altitude coming in from the Ellsworth base only a few miles away. Its roar only began to crescendo once it flew over the national forest – the Black Hills National Forest. The first pass was made without commotion or incident. However, five minutes later, the bomber returned shaking the building as it flew higher overhead.

"This is Bravo Zulu four, five, seven," said the bomber pilot. "Bearing to three, two, five, over."

"Roger that, Bravo Zulu four, five, seven," answered air control. "Target is twenty-three clicks on same heading, over."

On the bomber pilot's wing, just off his starboard side, flying within a quarter mile of his plane were four escort fighters, F-37s. They were to ensure no enemy craft came near the expensive bomber, nor any surface-to-air missiles coming from the ground. But they were also there for another reason – secretly instructed to complete the mission if the bomber pilot failed to do so.

"Bravo Zulu four, five, seven now on heading three, one, nine."

"Roger, that ... at marker one eight, trim to three, zero, four, over."

"Roger."

The colonel watched on the wide-field radar screen he had at his command center deep within the National Forest. He saw the one large dot and four smaller dots on the screen moving toward their designated target. This was the first time he hoped his birds would fail in their mission, but he realized that would not happen. The men were too well trained and disciplined to miss their objective.

"Target in sight," said the bomber pilot. "Confirm the mission is a go. Repeat, confirm the mission is a go."

There was a moment of silence.

"Control, please confirm," said the pilot, nearing the point when he had to unload his bombs or miss the target. "Ten seconds to drop," said the pilot. "Please confirm."

"Mission is a go," said the com.

"Roger that," said the pilot. "Confirmation received. Mission is a go."

The bombs fell, gliding toward their destination. It had taken fourteen years to build, beginning in 1927, but only seconds to erase. The explosions in the distance were profound and startling.

The colonel had never cried in his life, and he was not going to then, but he was close. His throat tightened and his eyes watered. He could only imagine what the rocky outcrop of the memorial outside looked like now.

Cassie also felt her car shake as the bombs fell in the distance. She had no way to know where they were falling or why. But as the ground trembled around her, it was as though the earth were shuttering too – distraught over what had just happened.

Cassie headed north toward the smoke. It must be inside the Black Hills National Forest, she thought. Perhaps it's just a forest fire or some munitions exploding and caught the surrounding terrain on fire. She could feel the vibrations of the ground as she drove, the inside of the car's console rattling each time she heard a corresponding thud and saw more plumes of black rise from the forest floor.

Over the horizon to the west were dark plumes of another sort. Billowing up quickly, a mass of cold air was headed toward her, causing an upheaval in the air currents and forming towering cumulonimbus clouds. Deep and black, the clouds grew more menacing by the minute, rushing across the previously clear and blue sky with wanton abandon.

Perhaps Mother Earth is unhappy with us, Cassie thought, looking at the unusual formations in the sky and wondering if, at any time, one might begin swirling into a funnel cloud before her very eyes.

As the storm hit, it blended seamlessly into the black smoke that was hovering just above the trees, obscuring most of the hills and the rocky outcroppings that were scattered throughout that portion of the forest. As the winds picked up, the heavy rains began to pummel the ground and beat an irregular pattern against her windshield and rooftop. Soon, the water fell from the sky in buckets, bringing her visibility to near zero and forcing her to pull off the side of the road.

Cassie sat in her car, her windshield wipers pushing off the droplets at a furious pace, but she was still unable to see anything. "Radio, next station," she commanded the auto computer, but the radio only kept scanning with success – the numbers flitting across the screen in increasing magnitude before it cycled through and back to 88.7. For the next twenty minutes, the rain pelted her car.

Finally, the assault from the heavens began to lighten and the darkness thundering away, like part of herd of wildebeests moving on to greener pastures. The spattering of drops grew less ferocious, and the clarity of her surroundings coming into greater focus. As the black and gray haze began to disperse, Cassie began to make out some outlines.

Getting out of her car, she slammed the door and brushed off the few droplets of rain that were still falling onto her sage green jacket. Looking up, she gasped. "Oh, my god!" she said aloud. "What have they done?"

The mountainside finally revealed its wounds, and she fell to her knees. The iconic sculpture of the four presidents was gone. Mt. Rushmore was no more.

The face of Washington was obliterated, with a deep, pocketed depression where the Mk-85 JDAM bomb had pummeled the smooth, white granite surface. To the right of the first president was an irregular, jagged piece of rock that had once been the silhouette of Thomas Jefferson. The only discernible feature of that likeness was a waft of curly white stone that had framed the left side of his head as a locket of hair. To the far right of the structure was the partially intact nose of the sixteenth president, Lincoln, and his trademark whiskers. But the rest of his face was missing, having cascaded down the mountain slope into a heap at the bottom of the valley below. In the center between Lincoln and Jefferson was the sole portrait of Theodore Roosevelt. Although deep lacerations and gouges were noticeable in the face and forehead, the stone image was largely intact. He alone remained of the once-magnificent tribute to four of the country's greatest presidents.

A tear dripped from Cassie's cheek. There was nothing now that could be done. The awe and inspiration of this great monument was no more. *****

CH 49 Impossible Mission

The train moved slowly along the tracks toward the military base. It was odd that a military base had a direct connection to a commercial rail line, but such was the case with the one in Yuma. Of the fifty flatbeds needed, Marcus had only been able to come up with thirty-five in the immediate area and in such short notice. But then too, since he was only able to arrange a single, turbine-driven locomotive engine instead of two, he would not have been able to pull the weight of fifty cars anyway.

Clicking and clacking down the twin bands of steel track, the train rolled on, past Tacna and then through Fortuna Foothills, just outside of Yuma. Ahead of the train was Colonel Marcus, riding in a sand-colored Humvee with forged papers and credentials. Wearing the uniform and carrying the identification of Brigadier General Armstrong Tanner, Marcus sat shotgun with his aide-de-camp, Issa Gomez, also receiving a "promotion" to major.

Their Humvee slowed as it approached the first of three guardhouses setup just outside the perimeter of the military base. Although small and flimsy-looking, each guardhouse was reinforced with thick concrete and steel to repel armor piercing shells or improvised explosives. High, gray barriers that could be raised and lowered were controlled from within the shelters to prevent possible terrorists from ramming vehicles filled with explosives through the gates.

Issa drove up to the first checkpoint and rolled down her window, handing over both digital IDs and the holographic order confirmation. Marcus didn't even glance over at the guard, but acted as if he were reviewing documents on his tablet computer in the passenger seat.

"Sir, please state your business here," said the guard in a flat, direct tone.

"We are here to oversee the transport of certain cargo out of the base. The order is attached with the documents you were just given. Put it through the computer to verify it," said Issa coolly.

"Wait here," said the guard, shifting his M-16A6 rifle on his shoulder. It took a few minutes, but soon he returned handing the chips back to Issa. "Verified, major. You may proceed," he said, saluting and stepping back into his air-conditioned hut.

Issa continued on another thirty yards to the second checkpoint, where two guards came out – one with a metal detector, the second with an explosives-sniffing German Shepherd. They scoured the vehicle and asked to see inside, checking for anything that could detonate. Having cleared that spot, they moved on to the third and last point of detention, where they were grilled about the nature of the visit. The guard called the procurement office to verify that the transfer had been properly approved. Of course, this verification would occur at several more steps before they would be able to remove even a pencil from the property.

Following the signs, Issa directed the Humvee to the shipping and receiving office where more paperwork had to be completed. Digital orders were once again verified and compared with those on file.

"An order of this size, requires the base commander to approve it," said the master sergeant of unit supply.

"It has already been duly approved," said Marcus. "My commanding officer, the Vice Chief of Staff has even approved it. I see no reason for any more delay." The irritation from so many challenges was beginning to take its toll on his cool demeanor.

"I understand, general, but ..."

"If you must, then fine. However, let's get going. I must catch a plane to Washington yet this afternoon."

"Yes, sir," said the master sergeant. He then picked up the phone to confer with the base commander. "... I see," said the sergeant. "Well, may I reach him in route? ... Oh, alright, then." The sergeant put down the receiver and stared blankly at the general, unsure what to do next.

"Well?" asked Marcus.

"Colonel Pickering is not on the base right now," said the master sergeant, showing confusion about how he should handle the situation.

"That's not acceptable, sergeant. We have to move this cargo out today!" shouted Marcus, intentionally escalating the incident.

"Sorry, general. I'm afraid that ..." replied the sergeant, handing the digital chips back to Marcus.

Marcus got on his PCD and phoned Templeton directly, acting as if he were contacting Washington. "I'll need General Simmons to get on the line to speak to a sergeant here in Yuma," he barked. "We may have to adjust his rank if he can't assist a brigadier general with a critical redeployment of military assets. Can you arrange for that? I need to talk to him immediately!" Marcus projected the image from his phone into a holographic picture that floated in front of him and the master sergeant. It took several minutes, but the image of General Simmons came on line. At first the connection was weak and the people at TechWiz were unprepared for such a call. It was clear Templeton had told them to "handle it" and make it as if the general were really addressing whoever he needed to at the base.

"What's this about?" scowled the imaginary character of Simmons. "I'm in the middle of a meeting with the First Citizen. She's not appreciative of the interruption."

"I have a master sergeant here in Yuma who does not wish to fulfill your order, general," said Marcus. Everyone in the military knew Simmons. He was an old icon of the glory days of the US military and ready to retire any day. Marcus then turned to the young sergeant. "Is there something you'd like to say to General Simmons?" he asked.

At the sight of Simmons, the sergeant's face blanched and his hands began to tremble noticeably. "Uh, well, General Simmons, sir," said the sergeant, standing up and saluting awkwardly. "I'm only following base protocol, sir. I was told that for all orders over …"

"Young man, there is something you have to understand. An order from a major general outranks that from a colonel at your base. Do you understand that?"

"Yes sir."

"Did you learn the different positions within the army in boot camp?"

"Yes sir."

"Do you remember that a general is above a colonel?" "Yes sir."

"Then, I suggest you get General Tanner what he needs. Do you understand?" asked the hologram.

"Yes sir."

"And I really don't want to hear back from you again. Is that understood?"

"Yes sir," the sergeant responded, nervous about how his resistance might affect his future in the Army.

The screen went black, and the master sergeant busily entered the codes and information to make the transfer. "I think this is what you need, general," said the young man, handing Marcus a small, gray transponder the size of a lighter that gave him authorization to transport the robots.

"Thank you, son. Now, I just need to bring this train into the yard here. Please make sure we don't have any more problems with this. Okay?"

The young man got on the line and contacted the other facilities within the base, alerting them of the order and clearing the way for the shipment.

The locomotive engine was driven by an advanced steam turbine. Housed in a shiny, new silver skin, it glided effortlessly along the tracks, slowing and then stopping just in front of rail entrance to the base. It would take hours for the cars to be cleared for passage into the compound, and Marcus took the time to scout the base and locate the robots he'd come to steal.

The master sergeant had assigned a corporal to escort them around the base and show them where they would find the robotic soldiers. Taking an electric golf-cart, the three pulled up outside a large corrugated metal warehouse that looked like it resided in an inner-city ghetto than a military base. With windows cracked or showing only remnants of jagged shards sticking out of the frame as well as white paint peeling in long strands that fluttered in the desert wind, the warehouse hadn't received the attention that the trillions of dollars the USSA spent on defense would have suggested.

"Here we are, sir," said the corporal, hopping out of the cart and marching up to the padlocked door. He pressed the old-fashioned key into the rusted lock and turned it, letting both the lock and chain fall to the ground. Then, he grabbed onto the steel bar and pushed it as far as he could to the side, coaxing the sliding door to move. Once it started, it gained momentum and rolled easily toward its stopping point before banging against the opposing wall.

The inside of the warehouse was stacked floor-to-ceiling with railcar containers, each twelve meters long and three meters high. Together, they looked like a patchwork quilt of color — cinnamon, tangerine, violet, scarlet and auburn — one that never repeated its pattern.

Marcus assessed the task ahead of him and sighed deeply. He realized it would take too long to extract all the containers, and he didn't have the flatbeds to carry everything out in one trip. However, like every mission he had ever been assigned, he would figure it out.

"Let's get the forklift trucks in here to start moving these containers," said Marcus, taking charge. He wanted things staged so when the train arrived inside the base and pulled up next to the warehouse everything would be ready to load.

"Oh, but sir, we'll just use the overhead cranes for this. We won't need forklifts," said the corporal. He pointed upward toward two massive yellow beams with heavy-lifting winches attached.

Marcus smiled. Those would do. Those would do very nicely, he thought.

It only took an hour, and the train moved through the gates, clicking and clacking over the uneven steel tracks that split off into several different directions after it was inside. One of the tracks passed directly through the robot warehouse, simplifying and speeding the loading of the robots onto the flatbeds.

"I only have six hours to get these loaded, corporal. We have to be efficient about this," said Marcus, tapping his watch. The corporal saluted and left to make sure they had all the personnel needed to fill the general's orders.

The loading proceeded slowly at first. Immediately, they had problems with the two overhead cranes. After an hour, both had broken down while lifting the heavy containers, but it was due to the lack of maintenance rather than from the weight of the containers themselves. Finally, after nearly four hours, the cars loaded more quickly using two of the base's twenty-ton forklifts. A loader would move to a stacked car and insert its giant prongs into the side. Then, pushing some black-handled levers in the loader's cabin, the operator would lift the containers into the air as easily as a child would stack wooden alphabet blocks for play, placing one on top of another to fill a flatbed for its ride north. This went on for three more hours -- more than the time Marcus had allotted.

As the minutes passed, Issa became more anxious. She didn't like it when they were well outside the pre-established boundaries of a mission. There were enough uncertainties in any charge; they didn't need to create more problems on their own.

"General," said Issa, addressing Marcus under his alias, "we really need to go."

Marcus agreed, but wanted to get as many of the units as he could. "Just two more cars. That's all. Just two more."

Issa shook her head and closed her eyes. "But, sir …" "Two, major," retorted Marcus, holding up two fingers.

"Yes, sir," answered Issa, feeling it was a mistake.

The mechanized game continued – containers plucked from their resting places, rising into the air and being lowered into positions on the railcar. It was a large metronomic exercise that was enough to lull anyone watching to sleep. But not Issa. After another hour, she said urgently to the general, "We must go now!"

Marcus looked at his watch and realized they were six hours past their scheduled departure time. "Yes, I think you're right, major."

Marcus went to the corporal and explained that due to his timetable, he would have to halt the loading and retrieve the rest of the containers at a later time.

"As you wish, general. You will need to come with me to fill out the appropriate paperwork," said the corporal.

"Major, would you attend to the paperwork while I have a discussion with the train engineer?" asked Marcus, glancing behind him at his second in command.

"I'm sorry, sir. But as you were the one submitting the request yourself, you will be needed to sign off on the paperwork. Please, if you'll come with me, sir," said the sergeant, holding out his arm to direct the general back toward the procurement outpost.

As Marcus walked away, he gestured to Issa to talk to the engineer. She knew what he needed without having to ask.

At the procurement office, Marcus waited while the master sergeant prepared the change order. It required several different documents and multiple signatures to document that fewer containers and robots were being transferred than originally requested and planned.

"Yes, yes. That is fine. We will make the base ready for his arrival," said a private first class who was taking messages in the next room. "Will the general be needing anything special? … No? … Alright then, I will convey the message to the commanding officer … Oh, Colonel Pickering is *with* the general. I see, then I'll let the captain know. Thank you, sir."

The private walked briskly out of the room and started past Marcus, carrying a black folder in his hand.

"Private, is the colonel arriving soon? I was scheduled to depart immediately, but I would like to see him if he is going to be here, say, within the hour," said Marcus, not really intending to visit with the colonel, but rather hoping for information on how much time he had left before they might be discovered.

The private was unsure whether to answer the question as he was told strictly not to tell anyone anything about the colonel's whereabouts unless specifically instructed by the colonel himself. "Well, I …" he muttered. "Sir, I am not supposed to …"

"Son, you're talking to a general," said Marcus, again having to point to the star on his epaulet.

The private squirmed, unsure of what to do, but then said, "Colonel Pickering and General Simmons are arriving from Phoenix by helicopter. They should be here within the next twenty minutes. I'm to make arrangements for their arrival."

*****

CH 50 War Room

With the attack on Lusk, the ATLAS Republic was now in a full-blown confrontation with the USSA, and Sumner sat with his war council for the first of many daily war briefings.

"Where are we?" Sumner asked, raising a half-filled cup of black coffee to his lips. He put it back down on an alabaster coaster and adjusted it so that it was situated perfectly in the center.

General Moore cleared his throat and began speaking. "Mr. President," he said in a low, serious voice, "I'll be frank. We will not be able to prosecute a war against the USSA for more than two or three weeks. We do not have the materiel or the depth of critical resources needed to manufacture the quantity of weaponry and munitions required for a prolonged campaign. In my briefing, I give the numbers. Of those, you can see that the troop strength of the USSA stands at 624,350. Although this has been significantly depleted over the years – the chart you see shows that the old US had 2.1 million active military in 1991 and even 1.3 million as recently as 2015 – their number is still far above what we have. By contrast, all our National Guard troops, together with local militias, account for 122,780. The quantity of tanks, mobile mortars, and other heavy artillery comes to a ratio of seven-to-one in their favor. Small arms are equally one-sided. Now, as far as air force strength, they have a one generation advantage in technology and a five-to-two advantage in the number of available planes. Support craft and refueling units are comparable, however.

"The one thing we have to rely on is the potential for our technological breakthroughs to compensate for the lack of numbers. We just need time. If we had another three months, it would make a huge difference. We would be able to bring online a lot of systems that would eliminate their quantitative superiority. As you know, we have two groups moving as quickly as possible to develop war-changing technologies. You've already witnessed the first one – John Johnny's phaser. This technology neutralizes much of the USSA's firepower if properly deployed and used. The manufacturing of these units is well underway."

The general turned to the group, his demeanor stern and unchanging. "Mr. President, that is my report.

Are there any questions?"

There were a flood questions, and the general did his best to answer them. None were critical of how things had been handled, but rather pushed many "what if" scenarios to anticipate actions and reactions by the USSA. After Moore covered all the details, Josh Templeton asked about the status of Dr. Lin and the defense shield team. "How is Manhattan II progressing?" he asked. "Have they been able to break through their distance limitations?"

"Mr. Secretary, I understand that they are making progress. But, that is all I know," answered the general. "Things have been hampered a bit by the sequestration of Dr. Johnny."

Shea looked over at Sumner. "Mr. President, do we have any more on what information John gave the USSA? It seems that his gambit worked, right? The phaser units used in the Lusk operation exploded, crippling that effort and setting back their phaser program weeks if not months."

Sumner listened quietly until his attorney general had finished. "It does seem that what he told us was true. We have no reason to doubt him at this point."

"Then why not release him from his confinement?" she asked. "Why not let him resume his work with the Manhattan team?"

The president tightened his lips and glanced around the table. It was evident that he was still not convinced of Johnny's total innocence, even though his story had proved true. "Well, I'm just not certain that ..."

"We really need him back in the lab with Dr. Lin, Mr. President," echoed Templeton. "With Johnny, I believe they can get the job done in the timeframe we need. Without him, I'm not so sure."

Sumner smiled and fingered the earlobe-shaped handle on his coffee cup. He was not showing gladness over the situation, but rather understanding. He knew they were right.

"We do expect more attacks along our borders," said General Moore. "We have obtained satellite imaging from our friends in Ottawa that show troop deployments and movements along the Republic's eastern borders. In the south, particularly around Texas, we expect an assault sometime soon. The USSA needs to cutoff our access to the Gulf. We still have supply boats coming into port in Galveston and New Orleans. Our supply lines all the way up to Wyoming are stretched. Our air force has been effective in shunting enemy fighters and bombers from attacking convoys – at least so far. But this may not hold."

"What about message intercepts?" asked Shea, having received information on this from Johnny.

"Excuse me?" answered the president, surprised at the question.

"Message intercepts – you know, decrypts of USSA messages. I understand that we have had some success at this. Can you explain?" asked Shea, returning her attention to the general.

The general shifted his eyes uncomfortably to Sumner, as if requesting permission to explain. Sumner nodded subtly, giving his blessing.

"Well," said the general, shifting his weight back to his right side. "If I may, Mr. President?"

"Go ahead," said Sumner, speaking as if the cat had already been let out of the proverbial bag. "I would go into it, but I'm afraid game theory and probability was never my strong suit."

"Nor mine, Mr. President. But, I'll do my best," said the general. "You can imagine that a massive amount of quantitative number crunching is necessary to crack today's encryptions. The number keys used are in the hundreds of digits in length, making the permutations in the quintillions of possible combinations. However, I can tell you that we are using the latest theorems of quantum computing and quantum entanglement at the subatomic level to decipher them. The equations are more than most humans can comprehend. That's why I leave that to the cryptologists, quantum physicists and mathematicians."

"So, is that a yes?" asked Shea, jokingly.

"Yes," said the general with a rare smile on his face.

The meeting continued but when Sumner adjourned it, Shea again brought up the question of Johnny.

"Mr. President, we still don't have an answer regarding Dr. Johnny. Will you approve his release so he can work with the Manhattan team?"

Sumner didn't like being put on the spot, but when forced into a corner he would give an answer. "Yes.

Let's get him back with Lin. We need that technology as soon as possible."

After the meeting, the president got an urgent call. It was from Thorne.

"What is it Thorne?" asked the president, back at his desk.

"Mr. President, there's been another attack. This one is in New Orleans. The port has been shelled by four squadrons of USSA fighter-bombers, we presume it was the Second Bomber Wing coming out of their Barksdale base. The attack was so quick and unexpected that we didn't have any time to coordinate a counter-attack."

"What are our losses?" asked Sumner, solemnly.

"Total casualties are over two thousand. Two-hundred twenty confirmed dead. The port is destroyed. We won't be able to use it for quite some time. Our Army Corp of Engineers says six months to get it fully operational. Partial usage may happen within two months, if we're able to get the materials and there isn't another strike." "What about Galveston?"

"No news on that port, sir."

"We need to send more anti-aircraft batteries there. We also need a quick response squadron to counter any threat to that port. At this point, we can't afford to lose Galveston."

Sumner got off the phone and swiveled his chair to look out the rear windows of his office. The executive mansion was far from being rebuilt, but he had access to the former governor's place until then.

"Mr. President?" It was Oishi's voice and image coming through on the intercom. "Your attorney general is here to see you."

"Send her in," Sumner replied.

Shea stepped inside the square room and approached the melancholy commander in chief.

"JC, I just came to apologize for putting you on the spot. I didn't mean to ..."

"Don't worry about it, Shea. You did what we needed to have done," he answered, still staring out the window.

"What is it JC?" she asked, noticing his detachment.

"This war -- it's only going to get worse before it gets better, you know. We will lose good men and women in the process too. They are all sons and daughters, brothers and sisters, and in some cases mothers and fathers of someone. It just pains me."

Shea put her hand tenderly on his shoulder. "I know. But for the sake of our future, we have no choice. No one said freedom was easy or free."

"This is true. But it's not *their* fault. It's not the fault of those who are dying. The people who caused this mess are the ones who escape the tragedy and death. They send others to die for them, just like I have to."

"But they fight for their children to live in freedom, JC. They do it for themselves too. It's not completely one-sided. They will reap the benefit, if ... when we come out the other side of this thing."

"So, you're saying it's the poor bastards that die for the other side that are the real ones getting screwed."

Shea hesitated, thinking about the disturbing idea he had posed. "I wouldn't like to think of it that way, either," she began.

Sumner stared at her with intelligence and insight. "How else would you characterize it then? Isn't that the raw truth of it? The group on the side of righteousness dies for a noble cause. That of malevolence dies in ignominy and with dishonor. Or does it depend on who wins?"

"I would like to think that righteousness always wins in the end," Shea answered.

"Sure, we'd all like to think so. But that's not how life works, is it? Sometimes the dark forces win out, don't they?"

"Not in the long run. I believe in the long run, the virtuous will triumph over the debauched. Good will conquer evil."

"For the sake of our nation, I hope you're right, Shea," said Sumner.

"JC, you can't think that way! You just can't! I realize things haven't been going that well for us, but never defined other great leaders in history. Churchill never threw up his hands and said 'I guess we can't beat the Germans, so I'd better surrender now.' Lincoln never lost faith, even after nearly all his first generals – from Winfield Scott to George McClellen and Henry Halleck – were abysmal failures, he never gave up hope. I could go on with others."

Sumner looked into her eyes, seeking answers. "So, you're saying great leaders look past what is necessary in the short run. They see the endgame and believe the ends justify the means? Don't both sides do that? Great leaders can stand for good *or* bad. Being a great leader doesn't mean that you only stand for the good."

"You're right. But you are a great leader and a good one too," she said. "You have a good heart. You always have." She smiled at him affectionately and put her small, soft hand on top of his.

The president leaned forward and took her hand, holding it between his two larger, coarser ones.

"We make a good pair – the two of us," he said smiling. "Don't you think?"

Shea returned the smile, but pulled away her hand. "Yes, but as we've discussed …"

"I know," he answered. Then, he stood up suddenly and took her by the shoulders. "I know what I have to do."

"What?" she asked, looking surprised at his action.

"If I'm going to lead this country, I need to be willing to sacrifice, just as I'm asking of those sons and daughters I'm sending into harm's way."

"I don't understand," said Shea, her face showing puzzlement and stress.

"I'm thinking about your reference to Winston Churchill. Did you know that whenever the air raid sirens would sound in London, he would go to the rooftop of twenty-one Downing Street and peer out over the city to see where the bombers were coming from. He would force himself to watch the destruction of the bombs falling on his city so that he would not become detached from the horror of what his people were going through. He stayed in London. He didn't hide in the countryside in some bunker. He wasn't afraid." Then, he added, "I'm doing to Galveston tomorrow."

"Galveston? Why Galveston?" asked Shea, not having heard the news from the general about the possible attack there.

"Because that's where my troops are. I'm the commander in chief. That's where I need to be."

Shea shook her head. "I don't know what you're referring to, but if something is going to happen there – you shouldn't go. It's too dangerous."

"Great leaders lead, Shea. That's what is necessary now." Shea put her arm around him. "I want to go with you, then."

"No, I need you here," he answered.

"Why? You have everyone else here. I'm coming with you. If you can be stubborn, so can I."

Sumner sighed. He knew it was true. She was as hard headed as he was.

"No, Shea. I almost lost you once. I'm not taking that chance again. That's the end of the discussion." However, Shea had other ideas.

Shortly after leaving Sumner's office, Shea got on the phone. "Oishi, this is Shea. Please book me on the president's plane tomorrow for Galveston."

*****

CH 51 More than Friends

The Republic's militias were no match against the power of the USSA military once the Ratner's forces were fully engaged in the battle with proper air support and supplies. Consequently, the Republic's troops guarding its borders quickly fell back as enemy Abrams tanks, M113 armored personnel carriers (APCs), M2 Bradley infantry fighting vehicles (IFVs), Ground Combat Vehicles (GCVs) and some M1128 Mobile Gun Systems (MGuns) rolled down the state highways and into what was once Wyoming. This time, there was no lack of reinforcements, as thousands of troops were sent in to secure the land, cities, and infrastructure as the wave of force smothered everything in its path.

Where the next major skirmish would break-out, after the ill-fated and half-hearted attempt at Lusk and the more successful bombing of the Port of New Orleans, was uncertain. General Moore thought it would come directly from Colorado, just south of Wyoming – a move that would cut off supply lines to the northern states from the southern states of Texas and Louisiana. However, he did not rule out the possibility of another port bombing in Galveston, Houston, or Corpus Christi in Texas or outside the area at Pascagoula, Mississippi, Mobile, Alabama, or even Tampa, Florida. Given the pattern of the attacks, Moore gave the Republic at least a week to prepare.

However, it came sooner than he thought.

Air raid sirens sounded again in the major towns throughout southern Texas. Cities in the other newly-enjoined states were put on high alert, as the USSA's sole naval battle group entered the Gulf of Mexico and steamed toward Texas. Canadian satellites confirmed the deployment.

Sumner had decided to inspect the Galveston port and the military personnel stationed there. Defensive positions were still under construction after the recent assault on New Orleans. Although it didn't take long to build bunkers, several had been started but remained unfinished.

When the sirens began blaring in Galveston, the president's the *chargé d'affaires* of the port operation burst into the meeting where Sumner was holding discussions. "Mr. President, we must get you to safety," said the major.

"In just a minute," said the president, putting his finger up to request more time. But as soon as he saw Shea coming up behind the major, his eyes widened, and mouth opened. "Shea?"

Shea stepped into the room, walking passed the charge d' affaires and taking a place at the table. "I told you I was coming," she said, without giving him another look. "I was tucked away in the back of your plane. You just didn't notice."

Their building, which resided next to the port, began to shake as cruise missiles from the offshore navy fleet began pelting the harbor and the heavy lifting platforms used to load and offload cargo. Hundreds of feet high and wide and made of high-grade steel, the platforms were extremely rugged but were not built to withstand the impact of two kiloton Tomahawk missiles coming from the three destroyers and two heavy cruisers in the battle group off the coast. AGM-159b-JSSM cruise missiles fired from F-47 fighter-bombers were able to target critical choke-points in the harbor, strangling all movement in or out. Creating a reign of terror, the heavy blasts decimated the longshoremen's rigs, spraying pieces of the cranes, warehouses, storage tanks, and other critical equipment far and wide.

"There's no time to argue about that now," said Sumner, angered by her defying his request. "Let's go."

Running to the armored limousine, both Sumner and Shea jumped into the back before the car took off.

"Major Healey?" said Sumner, contacting the *chargé d'affaires*, "It would be better if we didn't have an entourage. It will only draw their attention to us. Break off the rest of the team. Each needs to go its separate way. That's an order."

"But Mr. President ..."

"I know what I'm doing, major. Now break off the entourage now."

"Yes, sir."

The cars and trucks behind the black limousine peeled off in different directions. The limousine in which the two Republic leaders rode was merely an assault hardened SUV rather than a stretch limo, which made it easier to hide amongst the rest of the Galveston population.

Bombs continued falling in and around the port, one exploding only a few hundred yards from the SUV as it tried to make its way out of the port area. The sound rocked the truck and sprayed stone and cement across the hood and top.

"Sh*t!" said Sumner, cursing uncharacteristically. "That was close!"

Another explosion lit up the road in front of them, blowing two cars out of the street and collapsing a warehouse on top of the street. Fire erupted from a burst gas line, spewing out fierce flames and dense, black smoke that fell as a curtain across everything it touched. Heavy chunks of the building blocked the way out, heaped up in a pile higher than the second floor of the building next to it.

Shea shook as she watched the destruction going on all around them. "How are we getting out of here?" she stammered.

"Backup!" shouted Sumner, directing the driver.

The driver threw the SUV into reverse and stomped on the gas, burning the tires and leaving a thick layer of rubber on the asphalt. Sumner punched into the navigation system to get the address of the local safe house, and the navigation system complied. "Taking over command of vehicle," said the computer, locking out the driver and executing its 911 protocols.

The SUV sped down a winding maze of back streets to avoid open main roads, switching lights as necessary to permit their fast exit from the war zone. Within a few minutes, the vehicle had slowed and merged onto the highway going in the opposite direction of other cars that were trying to flee the city under siege.

"Arrival at safe house in eight minutes," said the computer.

Shea sank back into her seat and put her head on Sumner's shoulder. "It will be okay, now," he said, stroking her hair. "Everything will be alright."

The SUV pulled into a public parking garage of a large commercial office building that had a hotel attached at one end. The complex was well known in the area and held many large conventions during the peak winter season when businesses scheduled meetings in the south to avoid the harsh northern winters.

"It's right over here, sir," said the driver, taking them over to what looked like a small, shabby, maintenance elevator. There were no signs on it or other markings and the area was littered with cigarette butts and globs of black flattened and stuck on the cement all around.

The elevator door opened and the driver motioned for them to get in. He reached in and pushed the button for BB2 and pulled back. "I'll be available when you need me, sir. Just ring."

The doors closed and the tiny chamber jerked slightly as it descended into the depths below ground. It was unusual to have any structure underground in that area due to the highwater table, but that was, perhaps, why it was made into a safe house. When the doors opened, the two walked out into a small, but well-appointed apartment, complete with modern-design furniture and lighting, but no windows.

"Well, I guess this is home for tonight," said Sumner, starting to walk through the entryway room.

Shea put her hand on his arm. "JC? Thanks."

"For what?" he asked, turning toward her.

"Everything. I feel safe with you. I know we all do."

He smiled. "That's my job," he answered her.

She could feel a deepening emotion inside of her, as if everything were somehow alright just because of the man standing next to her. Yet, there was something more. It was a feeling she hadn't sensed since the days of her marriage to Patrick. She loved this man – this smart, caring and empathetic person who had guided all of them out of the wilderness of the bondage. Shea looked into his eyes, and she saw the same feelings toward her – ones of caring and affection.

Sumner leaned toward her and kissed her lips. They were soft and warm, pliant and moist as a baby's cheek. She responded, pushing her mouth onto his and kissing him ardently, stridently, with a sudden impulse that surprised even her. He pushed her hair back and caressed her neck and then her shoulders, sliding his hands lower.

Wrapping his arms around her, he began kissing her passionately, taking her body and pressing it up against his. He moved her over to the large, overstuffed sofa and laid her down on its wide cushions, shifting himself on top of her as he began unbuttoning her blouse like an excited, over-hormoned, high school boy. Tearing open her white, silk chemise, he found removed her bra and began to give her breasts the attention that they craved.

For a moment, he paused to catch his breath. "Are you sure?" he asked, hesitating.

"Yes, I'm more than sure," she said not wanting him to stop and pushing his lips back onto her nipples so she could again feel the pleasure of his soft and sensual caresses.

It was a magical moment, and one that lasted the entire evening.

***

Ring, ring

"What is it?" asked Shea, rolling over in the bed next to Sumner.

"It's my PCD," he said, reaching out and taking it off the nightstand.

"Yes?" asked an exasperated Sumner, reluctantly moving off the bed.

"There's urgent news from Yuma," said Templeton on the other end. The video feed had not been engaged, so the only piece of the transmission that either side received was the audio portion.

"One moment," said the president, moving to retrieve his pants and shirt from the high-backed chair in the room.

"We just got information from our cell in Phoenix. Our colonel has managed to gain access to the military base in Yuma where the robots are stored."

"That's good news, Templeton. Nice work."

"Well, there's other news as well. The commander of the base and General Simmons are about to land there. The colonel and his lieutenant are trapped inside. There's not much we can do to save them at this point, sir. I'm sorry."

"I understand," said Sumner, putting down the phone.

"What's wrong?" Shea asked, now sitting up in bed, her breasts sticking out above the covers.

"It's the mission to get the robots out of Yuma. They've been discovered. I'm afraid we've lost them."

*****

CH 52 Trapped

It was hard for Marcus not to let alarm spill out into his face, but he managed it. "Twenty minutes? Good!" he exclaimed, putting on an insincere smile. "It will be great to see the colonel and the general. It's been some time."

The young private saluted and turned away, leaving Marcus little time to find Issa. When he found her, she was holding a computer tablet, marking off containers as they were being loaded onto the train. Making long strides, but not trying to draw undo attention to himself, Marcus approached her and pushed her tablet away from her attentive eyes. "We're done. Shut it down. Secure the train, and let's move out," he said sternly.

"What's wrong?" Issa replied with a puzzled expression.

"The base commander and General Simmons are landing in fifteen."

"Fifteen hours?"

"No, fifteen minutes!" said Marcus, forcefully, but still whispering.

It wasn't a matter of whether they would be caught while they were on the base. It was only a matter of how they would get themselves out. And at that point, Marcus didn't have an answer.

Issa hurried to the train conductor and explained that there had been a change in plans – that they would be moving out sooner than expected. When asked how much sooner, she had only said, "Now." Meanwhile, Marcus had gone to the warehouse office to begin filling out the necessary departure paperwork.

"But, this says you've only loaded twenty-four containers, general. Are you sure you have all you need? The order says you are to pick-up thirty-five?" said the young lieutenant.

"Yes," answered Marcus, making things up on the spot as he needed, "it appears the weight of the containers is much greater than we anticipated. I've been told by the engineer that it will put too much stress on the turbine engine if we load any more. We'll have to break up the shipment into several more stages, I'm afraid. You understand how these things are."

"Of course, general. This will take a few hours to process – the change that is," said the lieutenant.

"Thank you, son. But in this case, I'm afraid I'll need expedited handling of the matter. You see, I'm expected in Washington by eighteen hundred hours, and I need to catch the next hyperjet out of Luke. Can you handle that?" Marcus was referring to Luke Air Force Base near Phoenix, easily several hours from the Yuma base.

"I'll do what I can, general. But you know the regulations on this kind of stuff. It takes an army to make changes these days."

Marcus laughed at the joke, but it took the lieutenant a second to realize he'd made it himself. "Good one, son. Now, get on it. That's an order."

The last container was secured onto the train bed, and the others were redirected back into the warehouse when three choppers appeared, coming in low from the northeast. It wasn't hard to spot them – the desert terrain made it difficult to conceal anything from visual confirmation. Only the latest attack helicopters had cloaking devices, but these were mere transport choppers and didn't have them on board.

Issa looked up at the approaching whirlybirds. "General," she said to Marcus, pointing,

"Yep, major. It's show time," answered the colonel. The train began moving out as personnel on the base orchestrated the process. At the same time, other men and women in uniform readied the helipad for the arrival of the general and base commander.

It seemed like an eternity for the train to gain speed, chugging slowly, pushing the heavy load toward the high, thick steel gates at the base. Marcus had been successful in getting the lieutenant to call base security and get the gate lifted for the train to exit. The switching plates shifted and the steel-reinforced barriers swung open to allow the locomotive's engine to push some units through. The first of the train beds had cleared the perimeter by the time the first chopper landed.

"Come on!" said Marcus, under his breath, a nervous twitch developing over his left eye. Issa and the colonel jumped into their Humvee and headed toward the vehicular gate on the southeast corner of the base. There were three sets of guard stations, mainly to prevent unauthorized personnel from gaining access into the base; however, there was only one that guarded the way out. When leaving, vehicles were only required to show papers at one before the exit gate was retracted.

More train beds had made it passed the base wall when the second helicopter landed, its blades spinning furiously, creating a miniature sand storm. But there were still eighteen cars still inside the perimeter, connected together in a race against time and discovery. The turbines strained to get up to maximum torque and push the remaining railcars ahead of it. It was agonizing for Marcus and Issa to watch from their Humvee, like giving birth without sedation. Issa drove up to the check point and cranked the window down as she approached.

A third helicopter landed carrying the colonel and the general. It didn't take long for the long, beige door to pop open, lowering itself onto the swirling sands below. First out was the general, dressed in full uniform, hopping out onto the hot sands and holding his hand over his face to protect himself from the swirling, biting sands all around him. Right behind him was the base colonel, carrying a black, leather briefcase.

General Simmons walked several yards to get away from the deafening noise of the engines and the blinding spray of the sand before turning back to the colonel. He looked around and then pointed to the train moving out of the base. "What are you moving in or out with such a big train?" he asked.

The colonel shook his head, not remembering the extraction order for the robots. "I don't know general.

I don't recall any large deliveries or shipments this week. I'll have to check with logistics."

"Papers," said the guard at the gate, holding out his hand and staring sternly at Issa.

Issa handed over the electronic chips that held the forged identities for Marcus and her. They had passed scrutiny the first time, and she expected no problems the second time. Still, both watched nervously as the train continued to move past the perimeter just behind their position. It was still interminably slow in gaining momentum, and as each car cleared the barrier the suspense built. Achieving ninety-nine percent success in getting the train out of the base would be no success at all. It was all of them or nothing, and they still have twelve cars to go. In her rearview mirror, Issa noticed the landing of the third helicopter and the two men who had gotten off. "They've landed, general," she said, squirming in her seat.

The guard returned but without the chips.

"Is there a problem?" asked Issa, stifling a sense of panic.

"You'll have to wait here for a moment. We're having problems reading your documents," answered the guard. The man went back into the guard house and closed the door.

In front of them stood a self-retracting, concrete barrier four feet high, reinforced with super-hardened steel. It would stop a seventy ton Abrams M1A4 tank dead in its tracks even when traveling at forty miles per hour. Marcus sat up, looking for other points of egress in case the worst came to happen. He too began to worry. The intense heat of the desert day was approaching one hundred degrees, and the tenseness of the situation was mounting – both were causing sweat to drip from his cheeks, moistening his collar and tie and to roll down the back of his neck and soak into his uniform.

"Major?" asked Colonel Pickering, holding his military-grade PCD to his mouth, "what's going on with the train I see leaving the grounds?"

"Just a minute colonel," answered the major, from inside the logistics building on base. "I'm trying to pull up that information now. One moment, sir." But the system had been operating sporadically during the morning due to the high heat. Just as the major was about to get in through the firewall, the system went down. "I'm sorry, colonel. We've been experiencing problems with the system all morning. Let me try again."

The major punched in his credentials again and scanned his finger print. "Let's see here," he said. "Yes,

I'm showing ... Oh, crap! ... Sorry, sir. I apologize for the outburst. The system just went down again."

"I don't give a sh*t about the system!" shouted the colonel. "Can't anybody tell me what the f*ck that train is doing? I didn't authorize any train this week!"

"Yes, colonel. It will just be another minute or two. I'm told that the system will be up again, and I'll be able to give you that information," said the major, unwilling to violate protocol and tell the colonel anything but that which was memorialized in the sacred army database.

The colonel waited for another fifteen seconds before hanging up. "General, I'll take care of this. Why don't you go on into the officers' lounge and make yourself at home. I'll join you in a few minutes."

The guardhouse door at the exit was still closed, and Issa could see the sentry on the phone talking with someone back at the base. "What do we do, colonel?" she asked Marcus, reverting back to his official rank. "I'm not liking this."

The look of abject fear was in her eyes. She was brave, but she also knew how they would be treated if they were discovered. The USSA had said that it always complied with the Geneva Convention protocols for the treatment of prisoners, but everyone knew that was a lie. They routinely tortured their prisoners horribly to extract information from them. Most times, the terrorizing resulted in physical disfigurement, mental breakdown or death.

"What are we gong to do, colonel?" Issa asked, with terror on her face.

"I don't know," said Marcus.

*****

CH 53 Collaboration

Dr. Lin threw down the transceiver unit and watched as it bounced along the counter top, finally coming to rest just before falling off the end. "Crap!" he shouted in disgust. "Why can't I figure this out?" he said aloud.

"Dr. Lin, is everything alright?" Pam Tokarov asked, hastily pushing open the door to the laboratory.

"Yeah, it's fine," said Lin. Then he stopped, shaking his head. "No, actually, it's not fine. It's just not working! I can't get the equations right to compute the energy level and resistance correlations required to maximize the shield energy output from the fusion reaction. Within limits, we need to increase the efficiency of the reaction to maximize the energy field, while at the same time, minimize the footprint of the device to be able to setup a ring of linked mechanisms all around the area to be protected. I'm just not able to make the balance work out right."

"Let me see," said Tokarov.

She had been working with Lin for quite a while, and when Johnny was summoned to assist, there had been ill feelings between Lin and Johnny. Now all of that had passed. Lin was relying more heavily on Johnny to help him solve the vexing questions to which they needed answers to make the shield functional. But, even together, they had yet to break down the barriers to its implementation.

Pam studied the esoteric equations. There were pages and pages of them, and determining whether and where there was an error would take time. But in this case, flanked by an exceptional former student and some luck, Lin's oversight was discovered with quick dispatch. "Here," said Tokarov turning to the second page. "Isn't there a minus sign missing? Shouldn't it be *negative* cos x squared right here?"

Lin took off his glasses and pulled the computer tablet closer. He squinted, his eyes narrowing and his forehead buckling like an over-ripened tomato. "Hmm," he said, not yet willing to capitulate. "Let me take a closer look."

Pride often got in his way, especially when it came to an attractive young woman who challenged him intellectually. At first, he had found her off-putting – both overly assertive and bossy. However, each day, she had found a way to soften-up his hard, outer shell. However, this was the first time he had been faced with being corrected by a subordinate, and she was uncertain how he would react.

Lin looked carefully at the line and then took out of piece of paper and pencil, re-writing parts of the equation in quick, deliberate strokes. Moving his lips as he wrote out each symbol, he finally stopped and put down his pencil. He looked up at her without saying anything and without giving her any facial reaction.

"Well, am I right?" she asked, her eyebrows raised in eager anticipation of the verdict. "Come on. Come on now, Dr. Lin. What is it? Am I right?"

Lin broke out into an uncontrollable smile and chuckled. "Yes, Miss Perfect Pants, you are correct," he said before he too began to laugh.

"I'm sure you would have seen it. You've just been distracted lately," she said, grinning but not too broadly.

"Yes, yes," answered Lin, still lighthearted. "I'm sure I would have. But thanks for speeding up the process."

It was a rare plaudit from the cerebral scientist. But what was even more unique was his jocular outburst and ability to accept correction from someone else. It was difficult to say which was more remarkable – solving the equation or Lin's personal transformation.

***

Work continued on the larger shield weapon, but the long hours and stress from the unrealistic deadlines given them, were taking their toll. Each day, Cheyenne called with questions about his progress. When Lin didn't give them the answers they wanted to hear, they turned belligerent and even more unreasonable. It wasn't Shea who was stepping up the pressure, but rather Templeton and his Department of Defense. While Lin understood why they were becoming more frenetic in their pleas and demands, he could only do what he was capable of doing within his own limits. His life was his work -- it personified him and defined him. For days Pam had difficulty reaching Dr. Lin, only to find that he was in his apartment in the dark and in his bedroom, unable to move out of bed. *Acute melancholia* is what the doctor diagnosed. But this was just a fancy term for the fact that he was – depressed.

"Dr. Lin? You have to come out of your room. I understand what you're going through," said Pam, knocking gently on his door, "but you have to come out and talk about it. I feel the same way. I feel like my whole world was turned upside down ... Dr. Lin?"

She heard some movements inside the room, and finally the door opened a crack. "Go away," he said.

"How could you understand? You haven't worked on things like this your entire life as I have."

"Well, actually, since I'm much younger than you, you would be right," she said qualifying what he'd said. Lin started to shut the door on her, when she said, "Dr. Lin, I'm sorry. I didn't mean it that way. You know what I meant."

The door began to open again, very slowly. Once it was halfway ajar, Lin stuck his head into the gap to see her and then shut it again quickly.

"Michael, come out. Let's talk."

This time, Tokarov opened the door and saw Lin standing there in his gray, cotton robe and black socks. His jet-black hair hadn't been combed and was sticking out in all directions. A week's worth of beard had begun to take over his face, attempting to hide the dark and sallow eye sockets that had replaced the once rosy and exuberant ones of his youth. He was only thirty-six years old, but he looked ninety. Dressed only in the gray, MIT-labeled gym trunks Tokarov had given him as a gift earlier that year as a competitive joke, he backed up against the iron bed frame and sat down on the edge, defeated and spent.

She took him by the hand and nestled next to him, looking into his forlorn face that only partially blocked the glare from the LED bulb that glowed from the tall, antique pedestal lamp that he'd oddly placed next to his bed instead of a nightstand. As she gazed at the haggard face before her, Lin could only glance down at his stocking feet. Neither said a word for several seconds – seconds that seemed like hours.

Finally, Tokarov broke the silence. "Michael, you're putting too much pressure on yourself," said Pam. "I know … we know how important all of this is. But you should realize that you're not alone with this. You have a team to help you. You have us." She smiled, earnestly and squeezed the four fingers she clutched in her palm.

"It is my responsibility, though," Lin answered. "The computer systems, the equations, the prototypes – they put me in charge of it all. They put their trust in me to get the job done, and I haven't. I haven't been able to figure it out!" Lin shook his head, moaning as he talked.

"Did you learn nothing from all that work?" asked his assistant.

"What do you mean?"

"Did you learn nothing from the years of education, of trial and error, of prototyping, of error discovery – it's all part of the process. You know that."

"But we don't have the time," said Lin. "We're up against the clock on this one – unlike every other experimental undertaking I've been involved with."

"But did you have the talented team around you that you have now?" she asked, trying to build him back up.

Lin looked back down at his socks. "No," he finally answered.

"A few days ago, you were working on an equation and you hadn't been able to solve it. It had to do with creating enough energy to create the umbrella effect – the iron curtain, if you will. Do you remember that?" she asked him, putting her other hand on top of his.

"Yes, of course," he said, staring blankly at her.

"Do you remember what the problem was? Why it didn't work?"

"You found the missing negative sign in the equation. It should have been *negative* cos x squared," he said.

"Right!" she exclaimed. "Do you see how using the rest of the team will help you get to where we all need to be? Not one of us can do this by ourselves. We need each other. Together, we will find a solution. They did it in 1940 – the first Manhattan team. If they can, we can."

The strain on Lin's face began to loosen its grip. He pulled her closer and said, "You've always been a rock of support, Pam. I'm so lucky to have you." His sad eyes met hers, and she didn't look away. She wanted him as much as he wanted her.

She moved her body closer to him on the soft, baby blue sheets that were pulled back from the white, fluffy pillow. "Michael, ..." she began.

But Lin took his hand and placed it behind her silky black hair and pushed her head toward his. He kissed her thick, full lips, and felt the warmth of her skin on his. Pam did not resist. She didn't want to. Putting her arms around his neck, she eagerly accepted his advance.

Her fervent, quivering lips and soft touch aroused him quickly, and his gym shorts couldn't hide his excitement. Pushing her back onto the bed, he began kissing her tender, vulnerable neck, making her close her eyes as the emotion of the moment pulsated over her entire body. His touch was like magic, each finger igniting a sensory overload of heat and passion.

"Michael, ..." she began, with an ersatz protest, "... are you sure we should ..."

"*Shhh*," he answered, between kisses. "Unless you really want me to stop."

Pam said nothing more. She laid her head back, letting him sweep over her body, unbuttoning her blouse and caressing her inviting nipples. She groaned, undulating her body against his and holding his head against her breast as she took in the growing ecstasy. Her head was spinning with pleasure, a tidal wave of joy that she hadn't felt for a long time.

***

"Michael, does this mean you're going into work today?" asked Tokarov, raising her head from the luxurious pillow on the bed.

Lin turned back to her with a smile on his face, "Not for a while," he answered. "I was going to make you some breakfast first."

She returned the smile. "Fine, as long as you aren't using expired eggs or some other artifact you've been harboring in your refrigerator for months," she said with a laugh.

Lin chuckled. "I'll just make sure I scrape the green mold off it before cooking."

He started to leave her, but instead turned and walked back to the bedside, kissing her on the lips.

"What was that for?" she asked, still glowing from the long, erotic night.

"Thank you," he said.

She looked at him with a feeling of surprise and regret. "Thank you?" she repeated, suddenly embarrassed.

"No, no. I didn't mean it like that," he said quickly. "What I meant was that you're so special. You're such an incredible woman. I ... I've got such deep feelings for you, Pam."

Seeing that he was struggling for words, she thought about helping him, but decided not to. Instead, she lay staring at him and waiting.

He too was hoping that she would save him, but when he realized there would be no lifeline, he added,

"I ... I really do think I'm falling in love with you."

She smiled at him. "Now, that wasn't really that hard. Was it?" Then, she leaned forward and gave him a deep and memorable kiss.

*****

CH 54 Advantage Ratner

The news was not encouraging. After days of aerial bombardment of critical manufacturing, supply and military control facilities, the USSA's ground troops had moved in from all directions, taking large swaths of territory. Reverting back to traditional arms rather than attempt anymore new technologies, Ratner had superiority in numbers on her side, even though the chronic lack of spare parts and the ability to obtain them fast enough made uncertain what equipment was available for use day-to-day.

The First Citizen's main battle force was the Third Corp, which bore the brunt of the assaults. Splitting its mechanized brigade into smaller battalions, the Third Corp struck the Republic at its most vulnerable points. Rolling infantry fighting vehicles, such as the aging M3 Bradley, together with M109B self-propelled howitzers, M1128 Mobile Gun systems, M1129 Mortar Carriers, infantry carriers, logistics support vehicles and other combat units, were used to throw as much hardware at the problem as possible – initially to much success. While ground attacks were mounted from the east due to the flat, prairie terrain coming in mainly from Nebraska, the USSA launched aerial sorties from mobile bases in the west, due to the Rocky Mountains that made moving land troops more difficult. Bombing sorties from F-39 fighters destroyed many of the heavy industry, manufacturing facilities in Nebraska and farther afield in Alabama. National Guard units in Texas, Oklahoma and Georgia were able to keep the USSA air fleet at bay, at least over their states' manufacturing zones. These locations had quickly converted existing commercial capabilities into wartime efforts under the direction of the Republic's Congress. But it was Lincoln, Omaha, Birmingham and Montgomery that were hardest hit by the attacks, virtually crippling their ability to contribute to the war effort.

As USSA ground forces swept in behind the aerial attacks and the shower of howitzer and mortar shells, Sumner's worst nightmare was beginning to materialize in the flesh. The war, now only into its thirty-first day, was closing in on him, and his dream to defeat the tyranny of the First Citizen and the forces of the USSA that threatened the entire American population for so many years was in jeopardy.

"Mr. President," said Templeton, giving Sumner his daily briefing before a session of the Joint Chiefs, "the situation continues to deteriorate as USSA forces occupy key strategic positions within the Republic." Templeton produced a hologram of the Gulf Coast with dynamic images of the fire and carnage in and around various ports – stretching from Galveston to Pensacola. "As you know all too well. Here," the Defense Secretary said, pointing to Galveston Bay, "our oil supply depot, which was buried deep underground, was hit by bunker busters, and the oil refinery, here," he added, moving his marker to a place just north, "was leveled by laser-guided ordinance. We used optical disruptors to confuse the incoming bombs, but we only managed to knock out sixty-five percent of them. Drone strikes have been a regular occurrence throughout the Republic, as Predator X attack drones have been successful at evading our TPQ-57 radar systems."

Sumner shook his head, his mouth and lips were tightened to the point that only two pale, thin slivers were visible in front of his clenched teeth. "What about the phasers? Are they ready to deploy?" he asked.

"I don't know, sir. Johnny tells me that he just needs a little more time," said Templeton.

More time!" shouted Sumner, pounding his fist against the desk. "We're out of time, Josh!" Sumner bit the back of his hand, realizing his outburst was not helpful. He quieted himself for a moment before continuing. "How many do we have produced from the manufacturing facility?" he asked, more in control of himself.

"We have only two hundred units produced," said Templeton. "And another three thousand in production."

"I want them deployed," said Sumner.

"But Johnny says they ..."

"Is he saying that because they are going to blow up on our troops or because he's a perfectionist?" asked Sumner.

"He's a perfectionist, Mr. President," said Shea, chiming in. "He always has been and always will be."

"I agree, but let's ask him directly if there is any significant risk to deployment. You must put it in terms of life and death. He must know how critical it is that this roll-off the assembly line."

"Yes, sir," said the Secretary of Defense.

***

Templeton pulled Shea aside immediately after the meeting. "Shea, I need to have a word with you," he said, clipping his silver tablet pen inside his jacket pocket.

"What is it Josh?" she asked, but then, looking at his face, she shook her head. "Oh, no. You want me to ask John about the phaser don't you?"

Templeton smiled. "You are very sharp, you know that?" he said. "But, yes. I was wondering if you would contact him. He's been so defensive about everything lately. I assume it's because we've burdened him with the phaser and the shield projects together. I think it may be too much for him."

"It may be," replied Shea, "but he'll never tell you that. He'll just suck it up and keep working."

"So, would you ask him?"

Shea sighed. "I suppose," she said, "but you owe me one, Josh."

"I owe you more than that. I'm just glad you're not keeping count."

In the back of her government car, Shea phoned Johnny to follow-up on her promise to the secretary.

"John," she said, getting through. "How are you? This is Shea."

"I'm well," he answered, as if he were n the middle of something.

"I hope I'm not interrupting, but ..."

"As a matter of fact," he began, "I was just ..."

This will only take a minute, John. I promise. What I wanted to know was how you're doing? How are you making it through all this pressure that's been put on you? Are you okay?"

"Yes, of course. I'm fine. You don't need to worry about me. I can handle things."

"Good. I was concerned because I heard that Dr. Lin hadn't been at the laboratory for several days. Is everything alright with him?"

Johnny didn't immediately answer, and by the pause she could tell that everything on that score wasn't proceeding smoothly. "Uh, I think he'll be fine. He just needed to take a few days off. He's been under quite a strain lately, as you can imagine."

"Yes, of course, well if there is anything I can do, just let me know. But there is one other thing, John..." "Yes?"

"The secretary has asked me to inquire about the phaser units. He wants to deploy them." She had dropped the bomb quickly, hoping to catch Johnny off guard and get him to commit to releasing the units for field use. "I'm sure they're ready to put into battle, aren't they?"

"I just need a little more time to tweak them," said Johnny, hedging his answer.

"John, you must understand where we are in the war. We need those units. If we don't put them in the field of battle within the week, we could lose the entire war. Do you understand what I'm saying?"

Again, Johnny was quiet.

"John, is there something you're not telling me? Is there something wrong with the phasers – something like what happened to the USSA troops?"

"Oh, God no!," he said quickly. "Nothing like that. I intentionally miss-wired those units by giving Ratner the wrong blueprints. They had no hope of working properly. No, the hundred or so we have produced should work fine. It's just that ..."

"Just that what?"

"I don't know how long they will last in the field. They haven't been tested for ruggedness. I don't know if they will stand up to one day or three hundred days in the trenches."

"We don't fight in trenches anymore, John."

He glared out her, not seeing the mischievous smile on her 3-D holographic face.

"You know what I meant!" he snapped, without any humor.

"John, calm down. I was only trying to … oh, never mind," she said. "But if we want to use them, they're functional, right?"

"Yeah, they're work like a champ. There should be no problem at all. The only thing you need to do is set the self-destruct mechanism inside them so if they are lost in battle or taken by the enemy, they can't reconfigure them to work with their troops."

When can you have that done?"

"Well, it will take a few days to …".

"John, let me rephrase the question. Can I have them by Friday?"

"Well, I'll have to …"

"John, I'll make this simple. I need them Friday. If there is a problem, you'll have to answer to Templeton. Now, you really don't want to have to do that, do you?"

"No."

"Good," Shea said, nodding her approval. "I'm glad we could work this out. Thanks, John."

Shea clicked the call to an end and the image went black. *I just hope I'm right about this one*, she thought.

*****

CH 55 Invasion

Ratner's major military offensive against the Republic wasn't to begin for another week after the bombing of the ports and the limited attacks made from Nebraska and by aerial bombardment of key manufacturing facilities that supplied critical weapons and materiel to the rebel force. Under the direction of General Amir Hussan, the USSA readied a three-pronged attack on the Republic. It was to be a massive invasion, using all the primary and reserve units he had at its disposal. Attacking with overwhelming forces had been the hallmark of the military policy of the USA in the late twentieth and early twenty-first centuries. However, when the USSA was overtaken by China and Russia in military capability, its superiority, let alone supremacy, was all but erased. When questions began arising whether those countries had achieved military parity with America, most knew the position of the USSA as a superpower and as a leader in the world was over.

Yet, with forty divisions mobilized on the three fronts, the USSA could still defeat a smaller, less significant force in its heartland. All Ratner had to do was give the go-ahead. However, she hesitated.

Waiting for perfect weather, the perfect alignment of forces, the perfect element of surprise and other factors, she dithered. The optimal time came and went. Her forces became lethargic and soft. The scene was reminiscent of Lincoln's frustration with George MacClellan during the Civil War, except the roles were reversed. This time, the generals were pushing the president.

And as the conflict protracted, other nations around the world became nervous. A clear victory for Ratner was becoming less and less certain, and as the war lengthened without any decisive action from Washington, foreign countries began to hedge their bets.

The first shortages to occur were oil and gas. As most of the oil and gas reserves in the old USA were now in Republic-controlled lands, the USSA had to look elsewhere. Canada had large reserves, but it had been the first to declare neutrality in the feud. In the beginning, the Northern Union and Southern Union of Islamic States – from England to Turkey to Morocco – had supported the USSA. With oil-rich fields in the North Sea and the Middle East nations, they were able to satisfy the needs of Washington, whether in peace time or during war. Even Russia had been supplying oil and gas from their Siberian operations. However, with the advent of war and the uncertain outcome, these resources had been cutoff. Smelling blood in the water, these empires saw their opportunity to put the final dagger into the heart of an old adversary – America. It had always been the Devil of the West – the Evil Empire to the Muslim faith. It was opportunistic, but then again, everything was.

As oil dried up – no longer finding its way to the refineries near Philadelphia and Los Angeles – the USSA began to feel the stranglehold on its economy and capacity to wage war. Rationing began in earnest, as the Administration forced its people to sacrifice for the greater good of the country. As winter approached, there was concern how many families would heat their homes. Reliance on wind and solar had never been able to keep up with the growing demand for energy within the coastal walls of the nation.

As unrest grew and demonstrations became more frequent, Ratner's team warned her of the coming storm. It was urgent, they said, that she take action, and it couldn't come too soon. Therefore, Ratner finally decided to move. "We will crush them, this time," said Ratner, looking at a 3D holographic map of the terrain. The images were displayed real-time hovering above the surface of the table. All in the room watched as the units moved along visible tracks toward Wyoming.

General Hussan was on a secure line, giving orders to his generals. They could see the units moving millimeter by millimeter on the grid. Each division was represented by a red rectangle on the map and within it the designation of its division type and number. Across the map, scattered in strategic points of assault were red blocks within which were the codes "1st ARM" for First Armored Division, "2nd INF" for Second Infantry Division, "101st AIR" for the Hundred and First Airborne Division, and others.

Ratner watched eagerly when the first shots were fired. Leaning against the table, she delighted when the table lit up with simulations of what was happening, as if she were partaking in a simple arcade game. Republic forces had moved into defensive positions and had established strongholds of hardened outposts. USSA bombers, although once stealthy, were now detectible by Republic radar systems created by young software quants and entrepreneurs.

"We've got them now," said Ratner, her eyes gleaming with delight. "This shouldn't last long."

The First Citizen and her generals watched intently as a squadron of B2C bombers flew toward their targets inside of Wyoming. Their objective was to eliminate the radar systems of the Republic and open up the territory to unchallenged attacks and bombing.

Sparkles of light scintillated the air over the map as the simulated squadron dropped hot chafe to disrupt heat seeking missiles that might be targeting them as they approached. Steadily the three flights of four small winged ovals, flying in formation, moved onward toward Cheyenne.

Suddenly, there were flashes of intense light coming from the surface of the map upwards toward the planes. In quick succession, each winged oval turned from black to orange and then vanished without a trace.

"What the hell happened?" shouted Ratner, confused by what she'd just seen. "Where did they go?"

"I don't know Madam," said General Hussan. "Let me contact the major general in command of the division."

***

The Republic's infantry battalion leader, Lt. Colonel Wilfred Smith watched the feeds come in from various sources above and beyond. "Confirmation?" he asked, listening to the narrative given to him by his majors and lieutenants in the field. "Do you confirm the elimination of the bomber squadron, over?"

"Yes, colonel, we confirm their elimination. We had four phasers trained on each of the incoming birds. It took about eight seconds before they began glowing; however, that was long enough before the fuselage turned orange and then exploded, over."

The colonel grinned. "Excellent news, major."

"I am concerned about the intermittency of our radar, though. It seems to be fading in and out. Is there a problem that I'm not aware of on your end, over?" asked the major.

"No, Foxtrot Three, I don't have an issue here. I'm wondering if there's some interference there some place. Are there any AWAC's overhead, over?"

"Not that we can tell, colonel. But we can see there are massive troop movements coming our way. The dust storm is tremendous in front of us, even though I'm sure they're using suppressor systems. Do I have authorization to engage, sir?"

"Yes, engage at will major," said the colonel. "You're on your own. We can't risk air coverage given the disadvantage of the generation of fighters we're up against. It's up to you to balance the ledger on this one. Good luck."

"Roger that, colonel."

The major hung up with the colonel and barked out orders for his phaser company, designated as F-3, to get back into their APCs and head east to confront the on-coming divisions of the USSA. He was confident in the new technology to be able to hold back the threat to an extent, but at the same time, to expect his eighty men to fend-off a division of ten thousand, was ludicrous by the standards of modern warfare. Even with such advanced technology, the odds were not in his favor.

"Men," he said calmly, addressing his company, "we are greatly outnumbered. But we do have this unique and amazing technology that will help us even the score. We cannot take that for granted, however. We are vastly outnumbered and are considered the underdog in the battle to come. However, just remember the three hundred Spartans and how they held-off the Persian king Xerxes. It was an epic battle, but although the Spartans lost that conflict at Thermopylae, they won the war. Today, we will win the battle *and* the war. *Let's go kick their ass!*"

Within a matter of minutes, low flying A10 IIIs came in for an attack on the column of advancing Republic personnel carriers. The barrage of lead put down gave the APCs little chance to stop and disgorge their troops. The first two APCs were struck and exploded into a ball of fire, mangling both machines and the men inside.

"Sh*t!" said the major. "All stop!" he shouted, as his men jumped out of the vehicle and sought shelter.

At the same time, two Abrams M1A4 tanks leaped over a barrier in the distance, crushing it beyond recognition and stormed toward them at over sixty miles per hour. The seventy ton monsters were within gunnery range, and lowered their turrets to engage.

"Focus your fire on one thing," said the major. "That's the only way we'll bring enough energy to neutralize the threats. The power from one phaser isn't enough to destroy something that big by itself. Now, you've all been trained on these, so you know what needs to be done."

His lieutenants began shouting and pointing to targets overhead and in the distance. On their count, the beams of the phasers from their platoon were directed at their greatest in-coming threats.

"Fire!" shouted one lieutenant, showing his fist as the final number of his countdown. Four brilliant orange beacons of light sprang from their sources and illuminated the thin underbelly of one of the A10s. It was hard to maintain their aim at such a fast and low-flying attacker, but they were able to keep the beams focused long enough to watch the glow spread to the entire plane before it blew up.

The other A-10 flew past without firing a shot, banking sharply as if the pilot were desperate to avoid the same fate as his wingman.

"Now, let's take out these tanks," said another lieutenant of the company.

Just as had the other lieutenant, the platoon leader had his men target the two tanks that were barreling toward them. All of a sudden, one tank reared back on its tracks from a recoil and a burst of smoke puffed out of the turret. A second later, there was a whining sound as the shell flew past them and struck a low-lying hill, creating a huge explosion and immense crater behind them.

"Man!" shouted one of the men. "That's one m*ther-f*cker of a weapon."

"Fire!" yelled the lieutenant, after rebounding from his couched position.

Another four orange beams instantly discharged and struck the front plate of the tank. However, with heavy armor on the front side, the tank seemed unfazed by the strike. Instead, it picked up speed, readying itself for another shot.

"It's not working, lieutenant. It's not doing anything?" cried out one of his corporals.

"Stay steady men. Keep your beams focused," ordered their leader.

The tank fired another shell, this one erupting with a hundred feet of the platoon, the shock wave knocking several off their feet. This disrupted the phaser fire, but still two of the troops kept their weapons locked on target, with a third added by the lieutenant's own pistol.

Now, easily within range to destroy the entire platoon, the Abrams readied its third shell. "Ready for launch!" shouted the gunner within the tank.

"It's still not working, lieutenant. We have to get out of here!" yelled the corporal, wiping the sweat from his forehead. His head snapped around to see whether his platoon leader was about to call them off, but he only found the determined face of someone hell-bent on destroying that tank.

"Hold your positions!" shouted the lieutenant, gripping his pistol all the tighter.

"But they're ready to fire again!" said the corporal, twitching with fear.

"I said, hold your positions! Continue firing!"

By this time, the other two members of the squad had regained their footing, although a bit wobbly. Still, they were able to re-engage, turning back on their weapons and concentrating the power of two more streams of energy.

"Ready, aim, ..." barked the tank commander.

But before they could launch the shell, the front of the tank melted away, igniting the shell stores cavity and blowing up the deadly, turreted monster. Fire erupted from the top of the vehicle and quickly consumed all inside.

Moments later, the second Abrams suffered the same fate, as another lieutenant in the battalion followed suite, ordering his men to concentrate their fire in the same place and the same way.

Lt. Colonel Smith received the news and quickly scattered his men to take up high positions along the side of the road and pick-off the tanks and other mechanized weapons as they streamed into Wyoming. One by one, APCs, tanks, mobile howitzers, and other vehicles were turned from a desert sand color to tangerine orange and then to dust.

***

"What the f*ck is going on!" shouted Ratner as her map lit up with merciless destruction and the disintegration of nearly an entire division. Even as the black ovals on the map and those hovering in the air just above the surface began disappearing from view, the First Citizen threw up her arms in excited hysteria. "They're being massacred, for god's sake!"

General Hussan scrambled to issue orders to his major general, who was already reeling from the instant turnaround in his fortunes. But, as he was talking on the hardened, secure phone line, Ratner ripped it from his grasp.

"General! What's going on there? What's happening?" she said, her eyes ablaze with anger and disgust.

"First Citizen?" asked the general, surprised to be talking directly to the commander in chief.

"Who the hell else do you think it is?" she quipped coldly.

"Uh, I was just telling the general that we underestimated when they would have full production units of their version of the phaser. Apparently, they have working models in the field and they are blasting our assets out of the sky and our tanks off the roadways. It takes several beams to breach the skin of one of our tanks, but they're able to do it."

"Can't you defend against them? Can't you roll over them before they have a chance to fire on you?"

"We tried an all-out assault, but they managed to destroy everything. Our men now won't face them without some sort of protection – they're just getting annihilated out there," said the general.

"I don't care what's happening. You have to keep rolling into the state! You have to take Cheyenne! I want boots on the ground in Cheyenne!"

"But Madam, we'll lose tens of thousands of men and equipment," said the general.

"Either you proceed, or I find someone who will. Got it?" she roared.

"Yes, ma'am," replied the general meekly.

In the end, the USSA lost eight A-10 IIs, nine F-39 fighters, forty-three aging APC M113B vehicles, sixteen newer Stryker IAVs, three AH-64C Apache helicopters, four M1134B Anti-tank GMVs and six Abrams M1A4s, along with dozens of support trucks and supply vehicles. But the human casualty figure was more stark. It was only because the field general disobeyed orders by ordering a withdrawal that more lives were saved. The number killed totaled 791; those injured, 2373.

The field general was brought before a military tribunal and convicted of disobeying orders, gross negligence and misconduct shortly after the battle concluded. He and four other officers were then summarily court-martialed and later shot.

*****

CH 56 Escape I

Marcus waited impatiently, looking nervously through the window of the guard shack at the sentry studying the computer screen, presumably waiting for the system to reboot.

Meanwhile, the base commander had just entered the logistics building and had gone directly to the first lieutenant in charge.

"Lieutenant? What's the nature of the train outside? Is there some delivery that I'm not aware of?" asked the base colonel.

"Oh, Colonel Pickering, it's the transfer order we received and you signed off on approving the movement of our robotic soldiers that we had in storage. The general has been overseeing this operation."

"General? Who is that?" asked Pickering.

"Uh, it's a … General Tanner, sir. He gave us his authentication and his approved orders. Everything seemed in order."

Pickering instantly remembered having been informed of the transfer from higher ups in the chain. In fact, he recalled General Simmons being part of that authorization. "Yes, yes. I do recall now. Carry on, lieutenant."

The colonel left the logistics group and strode across the courtyard of the base toward the officers' lounge where he wanted to catch the general and show him around the base.

The minutes passed, and the train, which had been moving at a snail's pace earlier, had now picked up considerable steam, chugging away and pulling the remaining flatbeds and their cargo out of the base.

"There, colonel," said Issa watching the train closely, "the train has left the station. At least we were able to get that out of here before being discovered."

"Maybe so," said Marcus, "but if they figure things out soon, they can easily stop the train and detain us.

The only chance we have is if they don't any time soon."

"But first, we have to get out of here, colonel," insisted Issa.

Marcus only nodded. He didn't need to confirm the obvious. And, looking at his watch, he knew their time was quickly running out.

***

The colonel reached the officers' lounge and opened the door. It was a flimsy, spring-loaded screen door and it slammed shut as soon as he released the handle to go inside. He glanced around the bar area, searching for General Simmons, but when he didn't see him, he asked one of the first lieutenants sitting at a table, drinking a cool one after his shift was over.

"Son, have you seen General Simmons? He was supposed to have been here to meet me?" asked the colonel.

The lieutenant jumped up from his seat in surprise at the question and after saluting his commanding officer said, "Yes, sir. He was here for only a few minutes. Then he left with the major. I think they went on a tour of the base, sir."

"Thanks, lieutenant. Do you know which way they went?"

"Yes, sir. They walked out the back, toward the mess hall, sir."

The colonel left, quickly following the direction given to him by the lieutenant. The mess hall was not far from the lounge, and he hoped he would catch up with them before the major volunteered areas that were not yet ready for a general's inspection.

In the mess hall, the major and general were standing by a row of tables, chatting away.

"All handled," said the colonel, coming up to them. "Everything is fine."

The general looked at him puzzled. "What are you referring to, colonel?" he asked.

"Oh, I was commenting on the train that was leaving the base. I had forgotten that you had approved the transfer of the robotic soldiers out of the base. It was a large requisition, but I understand the need for these on the front lines based upon what's been happening lately."

"Transfer? What transfer?" asked the general.

"The transfer that you requested, sir. You asked for all our robots to be transferred. I can't recall the base, but you said you needed them right away, sir."

The general shook his head. "I didn't order any transfer, colonel. I don't know what you're talking about."

Now it was the colonel's turn to scratch his head. "I was on a conference call with you, sir. I saw you on the screen. You approved the transfer. You don't remember?"

"Colonel, I would remember something like that. Listen, I don't know what's going on, but I can tell you right now that I authorized nothing of the kind. Do you understand me?"

***

Finally, the guard opened the shack door and moved toward the Humvee.

"It looks like you're good to go," he answered, motioning them to move out. "Here are your docs. I hope you had a good visit, general."

Marcus smiled and gave a quick nod. "Yes, quite nice," he said, before giving Issa the go-ahead to move proceed through the exit gate.

Issa threw the Humvee into gear and revved the engine. The vehicle jerked, but finally caught the gear and accelerated rapidly out of the base. In the rearview mirror, Issa could see the sentry going back into the guardhouse and picking up the phone. Reactively, she stepped hard on the gas pedal, and the Humvee lurched, gasping for air in the hot climate and taking in as much of that and gas as it could.

"What's happening?" asked Marcus, turning around to view what she was seeing.

"I'm not sure ..." she began, but then said, "Colonel, I think they're on to us. The guards just jumped out of the shack and ..."

Crash!

The rear window blew out of the Humvee as a bullet whizzed through the cabin. They heard two more shots fired, but neither hit the truck.

"Sh*t!" Issa cried out.

"Are you hit, lieutenant?"

"No, sir, just shaken a bit," she answered.

"We have about five minutes before they'll dispatch the helicopters to find us," said Marcus. "Five minutes to find shelter."

"There's nothing out here?" said Issa, "There's nothing to hide behind?"

Marcus looked at the maps he had. "Turn off the road here," he directed, pointing to the side of the highway. Issa pulled the Humvee over and put the shifter into Park. "Let's go. We'll have to hoof it from here."

Issa jumped out of the Humvee, as did the colonel, but before they left, Marcus turned and pulled out his revolver, putting one slug into the rear wheel tire. "Why did you do that?" asked Issa, as she watched the tire quickly go flat.

"To make them think we got off because of a flat tire. They'll think we will be hiding in an amongst the scrub brush or walking near the road to catch a ride out of here."

"But they'll have dogs too, won't they?" asked Issa.

Marcus pulled out a can and sprayed the area around the Humvee and where they'd walked. "This will deaden most of the scent," he said, "but not all. It will confuse the dogs enough that they'll wander a bit before picking up any smell farther down."

"Down where?"

"There," said Marcus. "Let's go. We don't have much time."

Together, they ran down the embankment and into some farmer's fields just off the highway.

"Where are we going?" asked Issa, running to keep up with the colonel. His strides were longer, so she had to double her pace to keep even with him.

"The Gila River runs through here," he said. "That's why there are crops along this stretch. But sometimes it's completely dry. Let's hope there's plenty of water in it for us. It would make things a whole lot easier."

Marcus led the way, cutting through fields and backtracking once in a while to confuse the dogs further. The river wasn't far away, and when they found it, both of them grinned. "Water," said Issa. "That's the best thing I've seen all day."

"Me too," said Marcus. "Let's go across and see how deep it is. If we need to, we can hide underneath the surface. But for now, let's get to the other side to kill off our trail. The dogs will have a really hard time smelling us across the river."

Issa went first, trudging into the water which only came up waist high as she pushed to the other side. There wasn't much of a current, so crossing was easy. Only thirty feet across, the shallow currents put up little resistance as the two waded over to the other side.

"Does your PCD work?" asked Issa, tapping on hers but getting no answer.

Marcus pulled his out and turned it on. "You know they'll be able to track us if we leave these things on. Turn yours off if it's not working. Let me try mine."

The colonel punched in a number and then a code, waiting to hear something on the other end of the line. In the distance, they heard the sounds of helicopters coming down the highway after them. Not far behind, they could see a long procession of base vehicles, with at least two Intermediate Fighting Vehicles (IFVs).

"Get down," said Marcus, pushing Issa back into the water.

Issa crouched down under the current, barely visible below the water. At the same time, Marcus tried to reach Cheyenne.

"Anything?" asked Issa.

Marcus shook his head. "Not yet," he answered. "But someone has to be there. They have to."

The helicopters drew closer, and then, spotting the abandoned Humvee, landed a short distance from it.

Moving up the river, Marcus continued to try to reach his command base, the Department of Defense. He let if ring and ring, almost hanging up, when someone on the other end answered.

"Yes?" was the only response. It was a top-secret line, and the person on the other end was cautious when answering, making certain not to give away any information.

"Mission Yankee 469 Bravo 7," said Marcus, speaking slowly and deliberately. Then, he added, "Clearance Xray Zulu 97."

"Roger, Bravo 7," said the woman on the other end, with the signal bouncing off a Canadian telecom satellite. "What's your Alpha Oscar?" she asked, referring to the area of operation.

"11 Sierra Quebec Sierra 6738 2105. I repeat 11 Sierra Quebec Sierra 6738 2105. Code 9, over," said Marcus, giving them the military MGRS coordinates of their position. "Also, repeat. Code 9, limited time, over."

"Roger that ..." It took a minute for the woman to locate them on the MGRS-USNG map, but once she found them she came back. "Uh, repeat, your Alpha Oscar, Xray Zulu 97, over."

"11 Sierra Quebec Sierra 6738 2105, over," Marcus said again.

"That's ... behind the line, sir?"

"Roger."

"Extraction urgent, over."

"Roger, Bravo 7. Unable to dispatch in that area at this time. Will keep you advised. Good luck."

"Roger," said Marcus as his final words.

Issa looked at him, steadying herself for the answer he was to give her. "Well?" she asked.

"They said they'd get to it," he said, lying to her. He wanted to keep up her spirits, and telling her there would be no help arriving wouldn't do either of them any good. "We just have to lay low and wait – probably until after dark. I'll try them back again then to check the status."

In the distance, they watched as the APC opened and let out six armed soldiers carrying M-16s. From another MP or military police SUV came two flak-jacketed MPs with their German Shepherds. Quickly they picked up the scent and led their keepers to the edge of the Gila River, where, as Marcus had hoped, they lost the trail. It wasn't long before the bank was filled with troops scouring the area for them. Then, too, they came to the other side of the bank and continued their search.

However, Marcus and Issa had found a rocky cove which carefully protected their position from view. They knew that eventually they could be found there, but with some luck, the search parties would continue up and down the river away from their position until after nightfall. It would be then that they'd have to make their move.

With the bodies crouched down and only part of their nose and face sticking up out of the water to breathe, the two remained as motionless as possible for the next four hours. With no reeds or other devices to use for breathing tubes, they had little choice. But, behind rocks, they were not easily spotted as long as they kept their composure and their positions.

Darkness finally came and with it the chance to escape.

Marcus and Issa watched carefully for any remaining signs of troops in the area, and when they were confident none were lurking nearby, they slowly and quietly left their hiding place and crawled through one of the furrowed farm parcels that bordered the river. It was slow and painstaking, moving only a few feet at a time, but it was likely that there were spotters on the lookout for them in that vicinity.

After two hours, they had made it across the farm tracts and were out into the arid, unirrigated land that constituted the vast majority of the acreage in southwest Arizona. But at that point, they had little cover to hide themselves. Luckily, there was only the wispy sliver of a waning crescent moon beginning its trek through the night's sky that provided any light.

"There's a wildlife refuge not far north," said the colonel. "We might be able to get a chopper in there to pick us up."

"We'd better hurry, then," said Issa. "The sun will be up soon."

More than twenty kilometers north, the border to the Kofa National Wildlife Refuge was indistinguishable, and it was only because of the colonel's GPS unit that they knew they were inside the park. Yet, there were no trees or other areas to hide there either, as it was nearly as open and rugged as the ground they had just crossed.

"This is Mission Yankee 469 Bravo 7, over," said Marcus, hoping the same woman would come back online.

"Roger, Bravo 7. What's your Alpha Oscar now?" came the familiar woman's voice.

"Kofa, command. We need extraction, now," said Marcus.

"Got a bird in the sky close by, Bravo 7. Did it just for you," she said with a little joy in her voice. "Give me your NG number, over."

"7055 6580," said Marcus, abbreviating the USNG number. "What's your ETA?"

There was quiet on the other end of the line, and Marcus feared he's lost her. "Command? Are you there, command?"

Still no answer.

"This is Bravo 7, come in command. Are you there, command?"

After struggling to regain contact, the woman's words came back over the line. "Roger, Bravo 7. Sorry for the disruption. ETA is ten. Repeat, ten."

"Ten what," asked Issa. "We won't make it out alive if they can't get here for ten hours."

But it wasn't that long. They heard the muffled rotors of an RAH-66C stealth chopper climbing just over a nearby mountain range.

"Light your flare," ordered Marcus, as he directed his attention toward the approaching sound.

Issa did as she was told and cracked the top of the flare stick she had brought with her from the Humvee. Its goldish-red glow pierced the blackness of the surrounds, bringing wanted attention to their location. The helicopter quickly approached and created a dust storm around them as it blew the loose sands of the desert around them like an unleashed cyclone. Popping on its strobe light, the chopper blinded them with the searing illumination.

Marcus shielded his eyes, but pushed Issa toward the bird as it landed. As they approached, the door began to open and only then did the colonel see the markings on the outside: Army of the United Socialist States of America.

*****

CH 57 Look What I Found

The first five months of the war had strained every fiber of the Republic's economy. Sumner and Shea had dedicated their entire arsenal of the treasury and efforts toward it. It was a life and death matter. And during the early stages, even though they led with confidence, deep down they had doubts. The first battles they had won out-of-hand, by their superior tactics or technology. Capitalism and entrepreneurship had enabled them to leap ahead of the USSA and develop weaponry that would have taken decades for their adversary to create through government grants.

However, the web of industry in the Republic was porous and spies had infiltrated, stealing many of their secrets. These secrets were being reverse engineered or reconstructed to create comparable equipment in some, but not all, areas. Still, by rewarding those who could think and imagine, the new nation was able to stay ahead of the USSA in the technology race.

At first, there were small phaser pistols, then phaser rifles, and then, more recently, the phaser howitzer – a large weapon, capable of destroying planes, tanks, even destroyers and cruisers, with single pulses of high-intensity energy. To date, the USSA had not been able to crack the code on that technology. But they had developed defensive shields made of material weighing less than 5% of what that natural elements would have weighed. These shields were comparable to those developed by the Republic, most likely stolen from the original designs. These shields made it more difficult for the phasers to penetrate the hulls or sides of assault vehicles. However, Johnny had been up to the challenge and had changed the frequency of the laser and its intensity, overcoming the shields and setting the Republic back on course for defending its existence.

However, defending its turf soon became a moot point for the Republic. The USSA made it clear it would not be stopped by superior technology, but rather deployed military techniques from the Middle Ages – throwing men and what few remaining military robots they had at the problem. Hurtling division after division into the maw of its technologically superior combatant, the Republic became an incinerator of death for the attacking forces.

But that was not the only tactic used. Computer EMP attacks began, as the USSA began trying to knock out the circuitry of the devices. Johnny again was called up to develop shielding from these attacks. Next was an escalation of the Atlantic and Gulf coast embargos using the USSA's submarine fleet. There were only a few nations brave enough to supply the Republic with materials for the war effort. At first it was only Australia and New Zealand. However, after the first invasion by USSA troops in Lusk, other countries began funneling supplies surreptitiously to the new republic.

Finally, there was the Battle of Trinity Bay, as it became known, that shifted the tide. It was an accidental encounter, not one that was devised or planned. The USSA had sent a fusion submarine into Trinity Bay, just outside of Houston, to destroy oil refining capabilities there. Although dependency on oil had declined, it was still the primary source of fuel for both sides, and the Republic understood that under no circumstances could these refineries fall into Ratner's hands.

During one USSA mission, the submarine USSA Chomsky, had moved into the Channel that fed Trinity

Bay on the way out to the Gulf of Mexico. From here it could the refineries in and around Houston's heavy industrial areas and shut down the great harbor. It had tried to fire off its battery of six neutron bombs, intending to shell the plants and create a nuclear fall-out to deaden the area for years to come. The missiles were to lift off from the surface of the submarine and strike refinery plants both east and south of the city of Houston. Instead, the submarine encountered problems with its firing mechanism and was detected by Republic forces patrolling from the air. Laser-guided torpedo-bombs, dropped from two AH-1AC Viper helicopters struck the sub's aft but did not sink it. The captain ordered all hands to abandon ship, even though he alone stayed on board, expecting to scuttle it.

But as Republic speed boats approached, the captain was electrocuted on his bridge by an arcing caused by a short during the scuttling routine. His body was found slumped over his periscopic imager, his blackened and shriveled finger still on the scuttle button.

On board were sophisticated encrypting and decrypting devices that were used by USSA command to convey orders. Not unlike the discovery of the Enigma machines by the British during WWII, these devices were gold. It was true that encryption had reached an unprecedented level at the time, but still, each side had to have the ability to decrypt and unlock the code from the other. Public keys and 1024K bit encryption were the norm, and generally were regarded as unbreakable. Supercomputers run in parallel with sophisticated protocols and algorithms had been tried to coax information out of the raw data, but nothing had been successful.

The machines were brought to Johnny to analysis. Unlike the mechanical methods used during WWII, the encryption was all set within the software.

"What do you have?" asked Shea, coming into Johnny's lab with Templeton and General Moore right behind her.

Johnny put away his latest phaser prototype and pivoted the computer screen toward his visitors. He pushed a few buttons on the computer keyboard and up popped a screen with symbols that appeared completely meaningless. They looked as though they came from the Intergalactic Star Fleet Command and created by some alien species.

"What you see here is what the USSA ciphers look like as we receive them," said Johnny, pointing to the strange icons. "The symbols that represented one thing a billionth of a second ago will mean something else a billionth of a second later. It would be virtually impossible to keep up with such changes. However, with the software retrieved from the sub, I was able to reverse engineer the algorithms and the keys. As a result, I can make it look like this."

He pushed a button on the computer and the screen refreshed, showing the symbols turning into English words.

"Wow," she said, her eyes fixated on the scrolling words in front of her. "But how did you parse the symbols and meaningless words into something coherent?"

"That's what the software did for us. It could screen out the superfluous data and cull it down to something meaningful. However, we still need to correlate some words like mission code names and other things. Your spies can get that for you."

"Spies? That's a word I haven't heard in a while. You don't have any spies, do you Josh?" she asked, turning to her compatriot with a smile.

"Of course not," he answered in kind.

"I'll run it through the departments," said the general.

Templeton took the data fob back to the Republic's CIA headquarters to have it matched against intelligence they had on military activities planned or in progress from the USSA. He knew it would take a few days to cross-reference and validate the information shown on the decrypt, but the sooner he could get an answer, the better.

***

It was late the next afternoon when Shea got an urgent message.

> *Stop by my old lab. I've got some important information.*

It was from Johnny.

Shea had other appointments, but she canceled them to have a video call with Johnny from his old, rundown warehouse building.

"What do you have for me?" she asked, staring at the mad scientist via the holographic image of him sitting on a stool, surrounded with the most sophisticated security system available. In the background stood two MPs with assault rifles – the result of Sumner's order to have round-the-clock military level guards.

"I found some other information on that computer we pulled from the sub. I don't know why it was on there, but it was not encrypted and was easy to patch together." Johnny punched in some numbers on the keyboard in front of him and hit Enter. Immediately, a map of the Republic sprang onto the screen with red, blue and yellow dots scattered throughout.

"What am I looking at?" she asked, bewildered at the chaos she saw in front of her.

"The blue dots mark the Republic's Underground Cells in the various cities now controlled by the Republic. The red dots indicate those cities where the Underground Cells were wiped out by USSA forces.

"What are the yellow dots then?" she asked.

"Those are the areas in the USSA where we still have Cells operating."

"I don't understand. What's the purpose?"

"If I overlay the cells with the movement of certain Cell members, I find that there is one who stands out. Look here," said Johnny, punching in some more keys and pulling up a picture on the screen.

"Oh, my," said Shea. "That looks like ..."

"Yes, it is," said Johnny, cutting her off. "The picture was on the computer as well. It appears this is the mole we've been looking for. This is the person who has had contacts inside the USSA and has been transferring information on our missions. So, as you can see, I am not the person you are looking for, Shea."

"I never thought you were, John."

"Is this person still active in our Cell Underground?" "Yes. As a matter of fact, they're on a mission right now."

"There's a PCD number here too." Johnny began to dial it.

"What are you doing?" asked Shea, watching him.

"I want to see if ..."

"No! Don't! You'll just tip the person off that we know. Shut it off now!" Shea shouted.

*****

CH 58 Escape II

Marcus froze by the side of the chopper door, but it was too late. Two rifles were trained on them both, and arms reached out and plucked them from the desert sands.

"Sit!" said one of the two armed men, motioning with the muzzle of his rifle for them to take a seat behind the pilot's chair.

Quickly the other man put down his gun and took plastic zip-ties to cuff their wrists and ankles together so they couldn't move.

Just at that moment, a PCD device sounded.

"Who's is that?" asked the man still holding his rifle.

Both Marcus and Issa looked at each other and shrugged.

"Where is it? Where's your PCD?" asked the other man. He searched the uniforms of both officers and pulled out their PCD's. One had recorded a recent, single call. Getting confused as to which phone he had gotten from which prisoner, the man asked, "Who's phone is this?" and held up one of the two devices.

"It's mine," said Issa, unusually calmly. "But it isn't what you think. I'm with you. I work for the USSA."

Marcus snapped his head to the side to look at his number two. His mouth was open, and he was in shock. "Issa? It was you?"

"Yes, colonel. It was ... *is* ... me," she said coolly, giving no signs of regret or remorse.

"But why?"

"For a lot of reasons, Marcus. My family has been a member of the communist party for years. It was never picked up on my background check. But, I really didn't think much about it until I was approached by the USSA ministry telling me they would turn me in if I didn't help them. At first, I didn't want to, but soon I fell in love with my handler and he began paying me a fortune to spy for them. It was a win-win. When I finish with this mission, I'm getting out. He and I are going to be married. That's a pretty good reason to me, colonel."

"But men and women have died because of you," he said with a blank look on his face.

"They've also died because of you, colonel. So, who is any guiltier than the other, eh? I don't think it's you who can cast stones right now."

Marcus hung his head, his mind swirling with all the things he had told her that were confidential and missions that had gone wrong, and ... the list was endless. He sighed. Feelings of betrayal and despair flooded his body and a sense of deep guilt stabbed him in the heart. *How had he not seen it? How had he not sensed that something wasn't right with her – that she could have been the mole?* He now blamed himself, just as much as he blamed her.

"What are you going to do with me now?" he asked, looking up at the marine.

Issa held out her hands in a gesture suggesting that they cut them from her, but the soldier didn't move.

"Well, you can contact General Simmons back at the base. He knows all about me," she said, still reaching toward him.

The soldier leaned over toward the pilot and said something into his ear. The pilot nodded. Then he spoke with the co-pilot for several minutes, apparently either trying to contact the base or getting other information about their passengers. Finally, he came back, still holding the M-16.

Without warning he grabbed the handle to the door and slid it open. The rush of air nearly blew him off his feet, but he kept them planted. As everything inside flew in circles toward the back of the chopper, the soldier shouted above the roar of the winds, "Get up!" and pointed to Marcus.

The marine helped Marcus to his feet and pushed him toward the open door. He understood what was about to happen, but he had prepared his entire military life for just this moment. He stumbled and was about to fall out, when the soldier pushed him. Marcus closed his eyes.

The colonel felt his left shoulder hit the side of the helicopter, and he fell back into a pile of hard, life preservers. He opened his eyes only to see the soldier moving over toward Issa, whose face had turned from glee to bewilderment. "I don't understand," she said.

The marine reached down and grabbed her wrists, yanking her up and out of her seat. Just at that time, the chopper banked hard, and the soldier released his grip on her. Marcus watched as her body passed by his, her mouth open in horror, and her arms flailing in an attempt to grab the rushing air. Yet, her fingers slipped between the invisible molecules of ether and she vanished into the darkness of the night.

Rubbing his head, Marcus expected his turn was next, and he braced himself. But, instead, the marine slammed the chopper door closed and pulled out his knife. The colonel took a breath and waited for the blade to slice through his sternum and into his heart, hopefully making quick work of things. However, the knife blade flashed up and between his wrists, cutting loose the bonds that had imprisoned him.

"I ... I don't understand either," Marcus mumbled in dazed confusion.

"We're not from the USSA, sir. We're Republic Army. We just use the USSA symbols when we go into enemy territory so we have less of a chance of being shot down."

"What about her?" asked Marcus pointing toward the now-closed door. "How do you know for certain that she was a spy?"

"We didn't at first," said the soldier. "But after what she told you, I confirmed it with the higher ups back in Cheyenne. They had just cracked her case and found that she was a double agent."

"But you didn't have to kill her. We should have brought her back with us to face charges?"

The marine put down his rifle and began cutting off the ankle bracelet from Marcus. "I understand, colonel, but there are a few things you need to know. First, we are desperately low on fuel. We've been out here flying for a long time hoping to pick-up your signal and bring you back. We don't have enough to make it back to friendly ground with all of us on board. Either she went or we all went. Second, they would just put her in prison or execute her anyway, right? She would be disgraced and so would her family. This way, if you like, we can all act as if she were a hero and no one needs to know any different. She died a hero's death, then. Isn't that a better story?"

Marcus thought about it. He knew it still wasn't right to push her out of the chopper, but he understood. "Is that what Cheyenne told you to do?" he asked.

"No, they said, use your best judgment. We want you to come home safe. We all wanted to come home safe, colonel. We all have families, ya' know?"

"Yes, son. I know."

*****

Ch 59 Maple Leaf Mishap

At first, the new shields used by the USSA were effective, but with Johnny's phaser adjustments, they quickly became useless. So, Ratner switched to another tactic, surprise aerial attacks from multiple fronts, forcing the Republic to dedicate its limited phaser weaponry to one area or the other.

The best angles of attack were from the northwest and southeast. Since Idaho had entered on the side of the Republic, that left Montana and Utah a open threats and borders to the ATLAS Republic and its existence. Heavily fortified and defended, the direct southern border with most of Colorado had a team of phaser battalions stationed there. To the east, even though South Dakota and Nebraska had already pledged allegiance to the Republic, the flat and open plain still posed a tremendous threat and opportunity for a massive invasion from that direction.

"What!" exclaimed Templeton when he heard the news.

The Defense Secretary was not accustomed to surprises, but when he found out that the USSA had posited troops on the northeastern front border in Montana, he was agitated. Satellite imagery from Canada had shown troop buildups on the southern border in Colorado; so, he thought that the attack would be directed from the southern border. However, he was quickly coming to the conclusion that it was only a feint. This was serious, and he had to act quickly.

"Get me the president," he screamed into the phone.

Moments later, Sumner came on the line. "Yes, Josh. What is it?"

"The USSA has gotten passed our ground and Canada's space radar systems. They were identified on the northwest border, not far from Cowley, sir. They could cross into Wyoming and move down state quickly."

"How did they manage that? We have recognition software that should have picked up the images!" said Sumner.

"They must have a cloaking mechanism, similar to what we use. I ... we didn't realize they had it.

Someone must have leaked it to them. Their troops only came into view a few hours ago."

Sumner was quiet for a moment. "Call Moore. See if we have any available phaser battalions to airlift into the arena."

"Yes, sir."

The next call was to the general.

"General Moore, we need a battalion of phasers air lifted into the northwestern sector of the state. We have confirmation of USSA troop buildups there in readiness to launch an all-out assault on positions we have. As you know, this is one of the least fortified areas of our border. How soon can we get them there?"

"Mr. Secretary, I don't have any free units. The others are guarding other parts of our border and key areas within other Republic states. If I pull them, it will leave those industrial areas vulnerable to attack. I don't think we want to do that. This could be a feint. Did you think of that?"

"Yes, general, but …"

"I strongly urge you to be calm and use caution here. If it is a distraction, we will only set ourselves up for utter ruin. Our entire industrial base must be preserved, sir. I'm sure you agree."

"Don't you have anything for us to use?"

"The only thing I have is a prototype of a new howitzer phaser. We call her Big Bertha."

"Send her in," said Templeton.

***

Republic troops were also being stretched too thinly to move any into the gap. So, General Moore ordered the deployment of the military robots that had been transferred from Yuma. The train had been able to avoid detection as it wound its way through the mountains of lower Arizona and reached its destination of El Paso, Texas. Once in Republic territory, the units were rapidly transported to different fronts to be assembled and activated. Ten thousand of the sixty thousand units shipped out to Cheyenne where they were readied for duty.

As they stood before the brigadier general in charge of the brigade, the robots were nothing like what the general expected. When told he was getting two brigades of soldiers, albeit mechanized ones, he imaged them to be standing tall and carrying rifles. Instead, he quickly realized what they meant by "early models" and "advanced prototypes."

Row after row of soldiers spread out in front of him, but these were not standing on two legs. Rather, they were upright, but driven by treads like a miniature tank. Between the tracts was a metallic, torso-like post that rose up to a round, silver globe atop. There was no face on the globe, but it was ringed with eight small camera lenses that it used as eyes around its head to detect aggressive actions and spot enemy combatants. From the torso sprung four rotating arms, each holding a different weapon to be used based on the circumstances – ranging from a simple M-16-type rifle to a full anti-tank FGM-148e Javlin missile.

General Warren Croft barked the orders to the first lieutenant and his team that sat by the command computer and their many monitors that gave them direct feedback on the positions and movements of all ten thousand of the robots. Some of the screens were visuals as seen by the robots, others were charts and matrices showing the exact grid positions of each one and its remaining munitions. Quickly, the lieutenant placed at the ready, separate corps of the brigade at critical entry points just inside the northwestern border. He gave instructions to his team to keep a close eye on the horizon to spot the advances of any USSA forces.

At the last minute, six old U.S. Stallion helicopter landed and dropped its rear door, allowing two hundred men, armed only with radios and phasers to jump out. The phaser units were fresh off the production line, and the men, fresh volunteers from their bases to help where they could.

The last bundle off one of the helicopters was a large, square container, carefully protected and sealed in a dark-black, impact-resistant package.

"What's that?" asked Croft, relieved by the backup support of the phaser unit, but puzzled by the additional and mysterious container that arrived with it.

The lieutenant looked at the strange carton. "I don't know, sir. I wasn't even aware of the phaser units coming in."

Then, one of the soldiers came over and saluted the general. "General," said the major, carrying his own computer tablet under his arm, "we have to take assemble this XRBT-457."

"The what?"

"The XRBT-457, sir. It's the latest phaser unit from the skunkworks. They say it's capable of vaporizing an aircraft carrier."

"No sh*t!" said the general, in awe. "Well, hell, son. Let's get this sucker put together!"

The assembly took time, and the general left it to the major to supervise it. Unfortunately, the war was not going to wait for them to finish.

***

"What are we looking at colonel?" asked General Croft.

The colonel looked up at him, taking his eyes off the monitor screen. "Canadian intel says the USSA has over 35,000 soldiers, 550 tanks, 430 pieces of artillery, portable drones, missiles and other weapons they are bringing to bear against us across the northwest border - -right along here." He turned his monitor so the colonel could see it.

"Put it in hologram mode," said the colonel, waving at him that he could move it back.

"On 3-D, now," said the colonel, punching a few more buttons. The image of the Montana – Wyoming border appeared in real time, showing the elevated terrain and the highways and byways that bisected the land. "There, right there!" said the colonel with a modicum of excitement in his voice. "You can see them. They're amassing at two points – first at Cowley, just inside the border, not five clicks from here, and Parkman, just off I-90. That was the obvious gate into the state, but we didn't think they would use it. Apparently, we were wrong."

"How many troops at each point? Can we tell from the images?" asked Croft.

"They're using cloaking to make it difficult to see clearly, but the software upgrade for our radar cuts through a lot of that. It looks like ..." the colonel peered closely at the images as he applied several filters to screen out the interference. "... I'd estimate they will initiate the attack at Parkman to try to draw our troops over there, but the main force is right here ... right in front of us, general."

"How many?"

"Nearly 30,000 troops, 400 tanks, and other vehicles are right here," the colonel said, using his index finger to point down at the ground. "The smaller contingency is over at Parkman. It's enough to worry about over there, but if you move the robots there and keep the phasers here, we may have a chance." "How much time do we have, then?"

"It's hard to tell, general."

"Yes, I quite understand." The general turned and grabbed his PCD which was tethered to a secure line. "Move these robots to Parkman immediately," he ordered.

"What about that black container, sir?" said the colonel, listening to the conversation.

The general looked on as the major and his team were deeply involved in assembling the pieces to make XRBT-457 work. "Leave it here," he answered. "It will take them some time to get it in working order. I don't want to disturb them."

As the last choppers flew in to pick-up the robots for transport to Parkman, the colonel ran to the general, bristling with worry. "General Croft, I'm seeing movements in Montana. I think they're starting their assault."

"Are the phaser corps ready?"

"Yes, sir."

"What about that XR whatever ... the 457 unit. Is it setup?"

"The major just informed me that it is, sir."

"Where is it?" asked the general looking around.

"It's using cloaking, sir. You can't see it right now."

Croft looked even more closely at the landscape, believing he could find some ripple in the air or disturbance in the view. But, he only shook his head. "Pretty good, colonel. I can't see a thing."

"You won't until it needs to fire, sir. Then, it has to decloak. It's like the Romulans in those old *Star Trek* movies, ya' know."

"No, I'm afraid I don't. But perhaps after we're finished with this little battle, I can brush up on them." Croft ordered all troops to be on the highest alert.

Major Jefferson stood in front of his brigade. He looked nervously at the strange device he held in his hand, something that looked more like a toy a young boy would play with in the backyard of his home than a lethal, killing machine. He'd trained with it, and in the safety of the firing range and calm conditions it worked well. Yet, this was not the same. The winds were brisk and the sun's rays were beating down on them, making their defensive suits that much more intolerable.

Now getting their signals from the two man-less drones that circled overhead, the major watched the lights on his armband scanner to see where to direct his force's attention.

"How long?" asked his first lieutenant, standing beside him.

Without looking up, the Jefferson replied, "I figure that within the next fifteen to twenty minutes we should see the enemy, right there," he said pointing into the distance. Using his binoculars, he could still not see any signs of the enemy even though he could "see" them through his feed from the drone overhead.

"Why don't we fire on them now?" asked the lieutenant. "We could easily take out a large number of them before they fire a shot at us. They're only ten kilometers out."

The major shook his head. "They're still in Montana. They haven't violated our sovereign space yet. Montana isn't in our Republic. If we fire on them, it's provocation. They'd be justified in invading us. We have to wait."

"But they invade us before, didn't they?" asked the lieutenant.

"Hey, I don't make the rules, lieutenant. I only follow them. I don't want to end up in some military court under a general court martial, do you?"

"No, sir."

Usually, if they allowed the enemy to get close enough to see them on the ground, the battle would already be lost. However, Major Jefferson and his men wore the latest camouflage gear which reduced the chances of being seen by the USSA's less advanced infantry. It wasn't the cloaking technology used on the XBRT-457, but it did help reduce their signature on the enemy's satellite systems. Instead of appearing as a company of 250 marines, they might appear as a platoon of only 50 or a large squad of 25.

Jefferson said nothing, but motioned with his hands to hold fire. They had been instructed to initiate shooting only when they determined major artillery or the infantry had crossed the state line from Montana into Wyoming, violating the Republic's national border.

Overhead was a brilliant blue sky, the sun shining as if it were going to be a peaceful, serene Easter Sunday without a care in the world. There was no inkling or foreshadowing of violence which patiently lay within a latched cage, waiting to be released into the hearts of those men aligned on either side of the border. As if anticipating the release of the wicked beast within the cage, the prairie was quiet. There were no signs of life other than the men standing apprehensively in their battle formations. The prairie dogs, red-winged blackbirds, black-tailed jack rabbits, and gray wolves had vanished, all taking refuge underground, in caves or high aloft in the few trees that dotted the land.

Minutes passed, and there was no sign of the enemy. Worse yet, it appeared from the drone images that they had not violated the Republic's territorial space. Jefferson punched out an encrypted message back to headquarters – one that was bounced through at least twenty servers located throughout the Republic command centers. He waited and then quietly received and read the reply.

Cottonwoods will bloom within sixty. Prepare your hoes for weeding.

Signaling the message to his men, the major readied his weapon, taking it off safety and checking the power module to ensure it was charged and ready to go. His heart beat quickly as he wated – bracing himself for the coming storm.

Then, there was the roaring sound of tanks approaching fast. Jefferson re-checked his holographic imaging device. It still showed no change in the enemy's position in Montana, either troops or machinery. Yet, all the same, they were there – in front of him.

Although even older stealth technology had made tanks difficult to see and even more difficult to hear, no one in the Republic believed the USSA had the technology to improve on it. Only a mass imaging magnetometer could pick up their traces from afar, and the field commanders had not been equipped with them. With the increase in tank speed to over eighty kilometers per hour, it could rapidly cover enough ground to surprise the adversary before they had time to react.

Popping over the distant hill, the first rank of five tanks flew across the ridge line, blowing past the state and national border within seconds. Speeding toward them, the tanks were within sight, but not within phaser firing distance. For that, they would have to be closer – much closer. It was all that Jefferson and his men could do to restrain themselves from firing their weapons and giving their enemy intelligence on their distance limitation.

"Steady, men," said Jefferson quietly.

Each had their pistols drawn and nervously waited for their commander's signal. Jefferson himself could feel his heart beating rapidly. It was stressful enough when he was on a mission with equipment with which he was familiar. If anyone were killed or captured, they had been instructed that their phaser would automatically enter a disintegration routine so that it wouldn't fall into enemy hands. Of course, that also meant that if they were only injured, the weapon they were using to keep them alive would also be their death warrant. Nothing would remain after disintegration but a heap of black ash.

By now, there were not five tanks barreling down on them, readying their guns, but fifty-five, and another one hundred surfacing over the horizon behind them. It was an intimidating show of force. Jefferson thought quickly, going through the numbers. *If I need four to five men training their phasers on a single tank for up to a minute or more to destroy just one ... we're dead,* he thought. *There's no hope.*

"Hold your fire, until I ..." said Jefferson.

But from behind them came a huge red stream of light, far greater and brighter than anything they were capable of generating from their handheld units. It burned a hole in the air between the soldiers and their targets as quickly and easily as a cartoonist scrawls a new frame in a magazine. There was no sound, no high-pitched warbling noise like that shown in the movies. It was quiet – if not disquieting at the same time.

Jefferson crouched, stunned at what he saw unfold. The red beam glowed on the front of the M1A4 Abrams tank bearing down on them, bounding over undulations and mounds in the pavement. The red zone spread quickly, the circle growing to encompass the entire turret and cannon. Then, they dissolved, particles dissipating into thin air and blowing away into the wind. It only took a few seconds. The power was astonishing.

Moments later, the major ordered his troops to open fire as well, training their phasers on the other Abrams in the column, before they'd had a chance split off in formation. One by one, the tanks glowed hot red and then dissipated into thin air, with only a waft of gray smoke rising from where flesh and metal had once coexisted. Combined with the XBRT unit, the power of all the phasers quickly dispatched the massive assault launched by the USSA.

The other tanks stopped, frozen in their tracks as communication buzzed amongst them about what this new and grave threat was facing them. They had heard about the smaller phasers, but knew nothing of the XBRT.

Within minutes, attack helicopters from the USSA showed up – Apache AH-84s with robotic flight control streamed over the hills behind the other enemy troops. They were unmanned, but lethal. Armed with heat seeking Hellfire 8B missiles and night-vision technology, they could go virtually anywhere and see anything – almost anything. The Apaches opened fire on the phaser company, ripping apart everything in front of them using its 35mm Gatling guns strapped to their side pods. The bullets sprayed flora and fauna alike, strewing debris in clumps everywhere in their path. By the time they'd roared past, there were scores of dying and wounded Republic troops on the ground, shredded or grazed by the lead.

"What's happening?" shouted Major Jefferson, shocked by the sudden appearance of the helicopters. He'd taken his eye off the monitors and not noticed the swift, surprise attack by this secondary force. "Apaches, sir. Five of them armed to the teeth."

"Order the troops to boost their camo to maximum. If they can vanish from those birds, they may buy enough time to get out of there," said the major.

After the choppers flew by, they banked sharply, coming around for another assault.

"Radio the colonel!" shouted the major. "He has to target that big laser thing on those choppers."

The major got on the radio with the colonel and listened, watching the Apaches complete their turns and begin their next strafing run.

His heart began beating faster as he anticipated what would happen next if he didn't get help." But as he remained on the line one Apache broke off from the rest and bore down on his position, coming in low and aiming all its guns directly at his command post.

Jefferson handed the mike over to his lieutenant and targeted his phaser on the approaching gunship. He aimed, careful to strike the heart of the cockpit area where the robotic computer operator sat. The major squeezed the trigger, and a thin, orange stream burst from the pistol-like device, and struck the chopper's glass, at first bouncing off, but then soaking it in. "Come on!" said the major impatiently under his breath. "Come on! Let's go!" At first there was no effect on the large bird, but he shouted to his staff sergeant to aim for the same plane. Together they trained their laser dots at the same place on the canopy, and soon the light pierced the shell and began eating through the robot pilot's skull.

But, bullets started cleaving the air, spewing from the black, hostile monster that threatened to destroy the commander and his company of troops. Jefferson could see the lead striking the ground and causing the dust to spray up in clouds as it tapped the earth like a violent hailstorm approaching on a mission of death.

"Hold it steady, Miller!" he yelled at his sergeant. "You can't move that beam off more than a dime's width or it won't penetrate!"

The river of bullets was within fifty meters of them, then forty, then thirty – coming right at them.

"Where's the colonel?" screamed the major, keeping control and maintaining focus and still waiting for an answer from his lieutenant at the com.

… now twenty-five meters … twenty … fifteen …

All of a sudden, another ball of orange light appeared on the chopper, this one far larger than the ones produced by their small phasers. "Thank God!" said the major.

The XBRT had locked on to the Apache and quickly its presence was felt.

… ten … five

The Apache exploded into fragments, but most vaporized before they hit the ground, falling as pieces of black, charred ruin to the earth.

"Major, we've got company behind us right now at six o'clock," said the sergeant, raising his phaser to aim into the sky.

Jefferson turned around, but before he could engage with his own phaser, the larger XBRT machine had already targeted the new bogies and within a few seconds, each fifty-million-dollar bird had vanished. Johnny's new device had eliminated an entire squadron of highly sophisticated attack helicopters – a crippling blow not only to the USSA air command, but also to its ego.

After that display, the entire battalion of tanks and armored vehicles that had been grinding up the pavement to invade the Republic was in full retreat. They had no idea what weapon had just been used to annihilate them, but at that point, they didn't care. They only knew they had to escape or suffer the same fate.

"Nice work," said Jefferson, taking back the com unit from his lieutenant.

"Thanks," replied the colonel. "I had a lot of help." He looked down at his own phaser and then over at the massively powerful XBRT, and he was struck with awe and fear.

*****

CH 60 Breakthrough

"Mr. Watson, come here. I want to see you," said Dr. Lin calling Johnny on a private line. He had chosen those specific words as those were the ones Alexander Graham Bell had used to summon Thomas Watson in 1876 when he spilled battery acid while trying to develop the telephone. Although Johnny was several hundred kilometers away instead of in the next room, he understood the coded importance of the communication.

"You've done it, then?" asked Johnny with anticipation.

"Yes, Dr. Johnny. We have succeeded. I'd like you to visit so we can demonstrate it for you."

Johnny arrived in less than six hours, his plane landing on the tarmac in Cheyenne and a private car waiting there to whisk him off to Lin's laboratory. Hustling through the front door, Johnny burst into the new, cavernous testing area quickly finding Drs. Lin and Tokarov conversing in front of a large holographic monitor, going over data output from recent experiments. The space looked like it came right out of a NASA testing facility with nearly ten acres of land under roof. The walls rose high on all sides without interruption and were joined together by a humongous geodesic dome with each triangular piece fitting perfectly in place over eighty feet overhead.

"Well? What do you have?" asked Johnny, eager to hear. "Show me your data."

"We'll do better than show you the data, John. We will show you the Dome."

"The Dome?"

"Yeah. Watch this," said Lin. He pulled up a control monitor on the screen and used the touch controls to set the experiment. Then with a few presses of icons on the screen, a soft, but high-pitched tone sounded and then began oscillating up and down the scale. At first the changing pitch was slow and deliberate, but then it grew faster and faster. At the same time, there was a discharge of plasma energy from metallic cones situated in a broad circle on the floor of the research space. The energy began building on the tips of each cone until the note oscillation became so fast it sounded like a single, but cacophonous pitch. When that happened, the light on the ends of the cones glowed a hot orange color, ready to explode like an active volcano poised to spew billions of tons of magma into the sky.

"It should happen ... now," said Lin.

Although it didn't happen at that very second, it was six seconds later when the cones discharged, shooting streams of light and energy into the air at a slight angle less than perpendicular to the floor. The bands bent inward, curving toward some unseen apex at the top of the laboratory space. At this point, Johnny could tell how large and how high the curtain of energy spread. He estimated it to be more than sixty feet in diameter and forming a parabolic cone with a perigee some sixty or seventy feet in the air.

"Very nice," said Johnny, impressed with the progress. "That's great, Lin. It looks like we're almost there," he said, intending it as a compliment.

Dr. Lin pouted. "Almost there?" he said.

"Yes, quite," said Johnny. "Now we only need to bridge the size from this to one that will protect an entire city."

Instead of continuing to sulk, Dr. Lin smiled broadly. "Oh, Dr. Johnny, but we have, sir. We have. Come with me."

The three of them left the testing lab and walked out the back door where there was substantial acreage to conduct larger experiments of various types. Passing through the door, Johnny asked, "So, how big have you been able to make it?"

"You shall see, Dr. Johnny," said Tokarov. "We think you will be pleased."

Outside there was a small white pavilion that sheltered a control center, complete with video monitors and other devices, presumably used to measure the inputs, outputs and throughputs of the experimental machine. Surrounding the center were thick sheets of an indeterminate clear, hard polymer some as thick as six inches -- clearly an attempt to keep those inside the structure safe from errant beams or wayward electromagnetic energy pulses.

Tokarov took her seat behind the controls and began punching instructions into the computer, initiating a sequence that would give them the demonstration they wanted Johnny to see. "This will only take a second," she said, smiling as she pushed through the protocols.

Finally, she turned and said, "If you are ready, you'll need to put on your goggle shields. They are right in front of you." Both Lin and Johnny complied, and as she placed her own over her eyes, she pushed two bar-like handles on the console, forcing them to the top of the panel.

As before, there was a soft, but high-pitched tone which began vibrating up and down. The slow fluctuation picked up speed until its sound was an audible blur.

"Where are the cones?" asked Johnny, looking around for the same pylons that were used inside the test facility.

"Oh, that's our real surprise," said Lin. "We don't need them."

"You don't need them? Then how ..."

"You will see," said Lin, patting Johnny on the back.

Dr. Lin pointed upward overhead where there was a faint black object hovering hundreds of feet in the air, far out in the middle of the field behind the building. As the noise grew louder, they could see the saucer-like object with a cone shaped flange protruding from its underside begin to turn deep red, then orange and then a brilliant, canary yellow.

"For this one you may want to use the noise cancellation headphones as well," said Tokarov, as the noise levels grew. Her dosimeter showed readings of seventy-eight decibels, but the numbers were rising, quickly passing eighty, eighty-five, ninety and then ninety-five. Once the noise rose above one hundred five decibels, Johnny and the others put on their ear protection.

When the cone on the bottom of the saucer discharged, the energy release was massive with streams of light and energy flying outward in a circle and bending down toward the ground in a huge arc, like the sparkling arms of an exploding and scintillating fireworks shell after it had delighted its audience below with its colorful magic.

"Wow, that's really something," said Johnny, looking on in amazement.

He watched as the beams spiraled downward hundreds of feet before striking the ground, causing the grass to sizzle, but not catch fire.

"You've been able to centralize the beam and use nano-pulses, then?" asked Johnny.

"No, we had to use femto-pulses – one one-millionth shorter than the nano-pulses," said Lin. "They cut our energy requirement significantly."

"Impressive. Congratulations. You'll have to inform the president and Josh Templeton as soon as you can."

"There's only one problem," said Tokarov.

"What's that?"

"We estimate it will cost a cool trillion dollars to make enough of these to meet the Defense Department's requirements. And you realize since the Republic is on the gold standard, that trillion is hard currency, not the phony bills printed by the USSA."

"Yeah, but that may not be a problem anymore," answered Johnny. "I have a feeling we'll have access to additional funds from our neighbor to the north."

"Montana?" asked Lin.

"No, Canada."

*****

CH 61 Misguided Intercept

There was only silence on the secure sat-com device in the Pentagon.

"Come in Delta Six; I repeat, transmit your GPS data. We are not picking up any signals. We are also not picking up any activity on the ground, either through our satellite images or via our central software bank. We need to know your status, Delta Six. Come in."

The silence was highly unusual. Even the satellite overhead that would have taken pictures of the goings-on of Delta group was not functioning. The USSA brass was blind.

"Come in Delta Six," said General Hussan, once more.

This time there was some sound on the other end, like muffled voices.

"Come in Delta Six," he repeated.

"General," said a strained voice. It was his lieutenant general on the ground, General Saxby. "We have ..."

"Saxby, come in."

"General, we've had an incident."

"What?"

"We've had an incident."

"What kind of incident?" Hussan asked again.

At that point, the communication again became choppy.

"Give me geo-overlays on this hologram," ordered Hussan, asking the techies to show other aspects of the battle scene not normally revealed or needed.

"Geo-overlays, general?" asked one of the techs.

"Give me terrain detail, weather conditions, and aeronautical data," he snapped.

Instantly, the tabletop showed those reveals. But there were no signs of the army division that he had sent to invade Wyoming from central Montana.

"Delta Six, come in," the general said.

Ratner entered the room without knocking or other means of announcing her presence. Hussan noticed her entrée and sat up in his chair – now more nervous than ever. "What's going on?" Ratner inquired.

"I don't know First Citizen," said Hussan turning toward his boss.

Just then, the distortion and static over the surface of the battlefield cleared, and everyone in the room could see the USSA's mechanized division in full retreat, heading north away from the border with the Republic.

"Why are they retreating?" asked Ratner, indignant over the apparent cowardice of her army. "I want them attacking, not running away!"

"General?" asked Hussan, again on the sat-com. "Why are you in retreat? I repeat, why are you in retreat?"

There was no answer over the phone.

"Send in the fighters … the F-39s general. I want them bombed into oblivion. Do you understand? I want them bombed!" shouted Ratner, looking at the deterioration of her invasion team.

Within minutes there appeared on the holographic image four black ovals in a tight formation and streaking across the landscape toward the point of incursion for the USSA troops. But then, the static and distortion returned to their map. It was difficult to see exactly where the fighters were and what was going on below them.

"Can't you fix that?" asked Ratner.

"We're trying First Citizen," answered one of the techs.

Intermittent clarity appeared and disappeared, but nothing that allowed them a clear view of the conditions on the ground.

"What's that?" asked Ratner, pointing to the blip on the map in front of them. It was a white oval just above the black ovals that represented her fighters.

Hussan shook his head. "I … I … I'm not sure … Madam," he said looking at his battle-plan. We have Apaches in the area, but they aren't that large and don't fly like that. This is flying much faster and at a higher altitude."

"Is it a new type of attack fighter from the Republic?" asked Ratner, nervously fidgeting with her fingers.

Again, the image went in and out, but it appeared that the white oval was closing on the F-39s, and quickly.

"What are you going to do?" asked the First Citizen. "We can't let them shoot down our fighters."

"But I don't know what it is, Madam."

"It's a threat, isn't it?"

"I … I'm not sure. It looks like it, but …"

Ratner pointed her finger at her Chairman of the Joint Chiefs of Staff and waggled it at him. "I need someone in command who can be decisive, general. I need someone who can make decisions. If you can't, then I'll get someone who can!"

Hussan turned white, but nodded his understanding. "Yes, of course, Madam," he said. Then he turned back to his sat-com. "Foxtrot Juliet Four, this is command. Do you read, over?"

It was the commander of the fighter flight of F-39s who finally responded. "Yes, command, I read you, over."

"Major, can you get a visual on a bogie north of your position. I can't tell how far right now. Perhaps three hundred kilometers, but it appears to be closing on you," said the general.

"Negative," said the major. "I don't show anything in USSA airspace that's close to our position, sir."

"There has to be something up there," said the general. "I can see it on my screen. You don't show anything on your active radar?"

"No, sir."

"Roger, major. Keep a watch on it."

"Yes, sir. And what's our target for this mission?" asked the major.

"You're to destroy the Republic's command center in Cowley. I'll send coordinates."

"Roger, that," said the major, signing off.

The general knew he had to do something with the white oval that was still coming in and out of the images they were receiving. "Minot, come in," he said, referring to the Minot Air Force base in North Dakota.

"Yes, general," said the voice on the other end of the line.

"Connect me to the base commander, Colonel Hollings ..."

After several minutes of discussion with the colonel, Hussan had said all he was going to say. "Colonel, you have your orders. Now, carry them out."

"Yes, sir," said the colonel, "but you have my direct statement that I disagree with this decision, sir." "You have your orders, colonel," said the general.

"Yes, sir."

Two minutes later, Ratner and Hussan watched their hologram which was still not able to give them clear pictures or images of the area. But, what they could see were two small black dash-like forms streaking out of the Minot Air Force Base and heading toward the white oval. Flying at nearly Mach 6 or forty-five hundred miles per hour, the missiles covered the distance to the white oval in less than six minutes. They saw the two dashes intercept the oval and an enormous fireball result just above the map. Then, there was nothing. All three images disappeared.

"I guess we got it, First Citizen. The threat has been eliminated," said the general, calming his nerves.

Ratner left without saying anything, slamming the door behind her.

***

"Madam? It's the Canadian prime minister. He's on the line for you."

Ratner waved off her assistant and commanded the phone to answer and show MacDonald on her screen. "Mr. Prime Minister," said Ratner, smiling, "what do I owe the honor of your call today?"

MacDonald's face was red and enraged. His balding pate and sagging jowls were equally engorged with anger and fury. Although wearing a dark, gray suit, white shirt and red tie dotted with small maple leaves, the prime minister's hands trembled as he sat at his desk.

"What is the meaning of the USSA's action this afternoon, First Citizen Ratner?" he said, trying to be as placid and diplomatic as circumstances would allow.

"What do you mean, John?"

"You know very well what I mean, Madam. You shot down one of our commercial airliners this afternoon. We've traced the missile trajectories directly back to your air force base in Minot, North Dakota. Two surface-to-air missiles were fired from the base at 15:35, striking Air Canada flight 3403 bound from Ottawa to Calgary just thirty-four kilometers west of Swift Current, Saskatchewan. All one hundred fifty-five passengers and crew on board were killed."

At this moment, Ratner's face turned color or rather drained of all tint and tone, revealing a white, paleness not at all becoming of her. For the first time, she was speechless, unable to move or speak. Yet, her mind swirled with questions about what had happened and why her general had made such a tragic mistake.

"You must be mistaken," said Ratner, attempting to deny the charge. "We would not knowingly down a Canadian commercial jet. Why would we do such a thing?"

"Why indeed, Madam?"

"I really have no idea what you are talking about. I have not been briefed on the incident, John. I will need to look into the matter before I can make any comments. But, I assure you that the USSA was not involved in the accident."

"It was no accident. I assure you of that," said the prime minister, not showing any signs of being pacified by her answers.

"Well, we will have to see, won't we," said the First Citizen. "Now, if you'll excuse me, I must return to a most urgent meeting that I was attending. We will get back to you as soon as we know something more. Good day, Mr. Prime Minister."

Ratner hung up the line on the leader of Canada. She realized it was an abrupt and unfriendly end to the call, but she could see no more point in engaging in allegations when she knew nothing about what had happened.

"Get me General Hussan!" she screamed at her executive assistant.

*****

CH 62 Canadian Response

"Mr. President," said the Canadian prime minister, "I have tried to reach First Citizen Ratner for two days now, and I can't get a direct response. All I get from the White House is that the incident is of no concern to the USSA. They disavow any responsibility and claim it was likely a mechanical problem as the plane flew from Ottawa to Calgary."

"Prime Minister MacDonald, it is unfortunate that they are taking that position," said Sumner, on a conference call. "As I've told you the past two days, we are engaging our Underground Network to see what information we can obtain for you. We certainly have appreciated the support you have given us these past several months. What we know is what you've already confirmed – flight 3403 was bound from Ottawa to Calgary and was heading due west when, at three thirty-five in the afternoon, it was struck by one of two PAAC4d – advance Patriot missiles fired from Minot Air Force Base. The plane went down thirty-four kilometers west of Swift Current, Saskatchewan, but scattered over a 1.25-kilometer area."

"Ottawa air traffic control confirms there were no problems at takeoff, and we have the dialogue between the pilots and the tower," said the prime minister. "The Canadian TSB has recovered the black box, but we don't have an analysis yet of what information it contains."

"Do you believe they intentionally shot down the aircraft or was it a mistake?" asked Sumner, pressing the tip of his pen up against his lips.

"… that, I can't tell you, sir. It appears to me that they were trying to shoot down one of our national guard planes which was also in the area but mistook the commercial liner for it. I'm not sure how, but that's my guess. I'm getting a lot of pressure here," said MacDonald. "The people here want answers for the one hundred six Canadians and forty-nine others who were aboard that flight. I have none to give them."

"I … I don't know exactly what to say," Sumner answered.

"Nothing to say," said MacDonald. "JC, if it's okay to be on a first-name basis?"

"Sure. I feel like I've known you for years, John," said Sumner, earnestly.

"JC, relations between Canada and the USSA have been deteriorating for years. Fourier wasn't much better than the current one. It's frightening to Canadians to watch as America has plummeted into a black hole of decay. I never imagined it would become as moribund as it has."

"John, that is why we seceded. The people of Wyoming couldn't live any longer under the totalitarian boot of Washington. Their rule had become stifling, oppressive. Elections have not been free here for a very long time. With the ballot manipulations, the complicity of the media, the ignorance and apathy of the voters, government handouts by incumbents – it was all too much to bear for democracy to withstand. In the end, democracy was sacrificed to the avarice and greed of the political elite."

"That is sad," said MacDonald. "I too worry about things here in Canada. We began going down the same path, but somehow avoided the pitfalls that befell your country. The only issue we continue to grapple with is the secession of Quebec some years ago. That nearly tore our nation apart as you recall."

"But you were able to do it without bloodshed. That's remarkable," said Sumner.

"Yes. We let them vote. We let them go. It was their choice."

"As I wish Washington would let us go – peacefully. But they didn't."

"No," MacDonald responded. "And worse yet, they've involved us."

"What is Canada going to do?" Sumner asked, showing deep concern. "Of course, we encourage you to join us and our cause. We are better united than fighting them separately."

The prime minister smiled. "You are right about that," he said. "I just don't think the Canadian people are in the right mind to go to war over this. However, time will tell. It depends on how Washington plays it going forward, I imagine."

"Well, keep the communication lines open. We would be very pleased to learn that you have decided to declare that we are allies."

MacDonald signed off the call, as Shea entered the room.

"How was the meeting?" she asked, seating herself next to Sumner's desk.

"We'd all feel better if Canada joined us in this fight. Yet, at the same time, I don't want Ratner to escalate things by causing more death and destruction across the border to the north."

But Ratner had more surprises in store for the two leaders, which they would learn about all too soon.

***

As promised, other things would intervene.

The buildings of the Department of Defense just outside of Cheyenne had been tightly guarded for months under fear that infiltration by USSA spies would try to pierce security and obtain information on Johnny's project or that of the Manhattan II team. Layers upon layers of encryption and firewalls had been put in place and elaborate detection systems installed to ensure no microchips or other devices were smuggled out of the building complex.

However, there were leaks. The USSA was somehow getting small bits of information from sources inside the Republic. Sumner was concerned and was continually peppering his secretaries for any information they had on a potential mole. He figured it was the same mole that had slipped information concerning the Underground cells to the USSA Ministry of Internal Inquiry.

On the other hand, foreign espionage of the USSA by the Republic was another matter. It was far easier to obtain top secret information from willing conspirators disillusioned with the loss of freedom by the current Washington regime. They faced death if caught, but more and more were willing to sacrifice if it meant being paid and giving their families a better life. These informants would contact people they knew in the Underground, who would relay the information through Thorne at GOFLA to Cheyenne.

All sorts of news would flood in, and it was up to the CIA Director, Meredith Crawley, to make sure it got vetted and filtered, running it through scores of computer databases that would process it in real time and give a binary go or no-go recommendation for the upper levels upon which to act.

It was early in the morning, when an urgent, encrypted message came in from the Chicago Underground Cell. Thorne read it and his face grew cold and pale. He sat down, shaking his head. "This is what I was afraid of," he said to himself. "It's going to start. It's going to happen. And there's nothing I can do to stop it."

Thorne re-encrypted the message and forwarded it to Templeton at the Defense Department. **Urgent,** it read**. President must be notified immediately.** Minutes later, there was a knock at Sumner's door.

"Mr. President, we have news that is of the utmost importance for you."

"Come in, Josh," said Sumner, sitting up in bed, yawning. "What is it?"

"Sir, an airliner that took off from Cheyenne airport thirty minutes ago was shot down over Minnesota."

"My God!" said Sumner, now leaning forward as if he had leaned against a hot stove pipe. "How did it happen?"

"My assets in Chicago tell me that USSA antiaircraft guns that had been repositioned on our border during the night mistook the airliner as a threat. The pilot did not communicate with ground control and orders were given to shoot it down."

"Did all perish?"

"All told, there were two hundred fifty-three on board, including the crew."

Sumner sat up in his chair, pondering what he'd just been told.

"Sir, what would you like us to do? Shall we retaliate?"

"No. Get me General Ward on the phone. I want a briefing in my office in thirty minutes."

Ward came in after twenty-five, as did certain other key Cabinet members, including Ingram and Shea. They sat down around the large, oval conference table, only occupying a small number of the seats that were usually readied for the senior members of the president's Administration.

"There's been an incident, of which you've already been briefed. There is still no news from Washington on this. Ratner has not issued any kind of statement as of yet, nor have any of her other ministers. Our intelligence tells us that it was an accident, or at least made to look like one," said Sumner. "General Ward will give us more details. General."

General Ward stood up and smoothed out his tan jacket and pants before he began. There were so many ribbons on this uniform that it looked like it could have been cut from a makeshift, multi-colored quilt. The general presented the facts as he knew them. Not having had time to prepare a presentation, he merely read notes that were prepared by his staff.

"So, in conclusion," he said, "we can only assume at this point that the incident was a mistake by USSA ground forces. However, we can't take a chance of another airliner being shot down, so we've prohibited any air travel over any part of the USSA until further words are exchanged between the two governments and clarification is gained. Until further notice, all flights from the USSA into the Republic are prohibited as are our flights into their air space. Are there any questions?" he asked, looking up from his notes.

"General?" It was from Secretary of Commerce, Richard Briggs. "Do you have any reason to believe this is the first salvo of hostility by the USSA?"

"Not at this time."

"But we haven't heard anything from the First Citizen on this. Why do you think that is?" asked Shea.

"I've sent a message directly to the White House, but there's been no response," said Sumner.

"She doesn't recognize us as a sovereign state, so she probably won't answer you," answered Ingram.

"It's a protocol thing."

"We may need to use backchannels to get information," said Templeton. "That would circumvent the formality."

"I agree. Lawrence, why don't you take care of that. In the meantime, let's see if she makes some announcement or there is some media outlet brave enough to pick-up the story."

"And if that doesn't happen?" Shea continued. "Do we have a backup plan?"

"We don't have any backup plan at this time," said the general.

"You don't have a plan B? What if this is their first salvo? What if this is the beginning of … of war?" asked Shea.

General Ward stopped and looked over at Sumner. Sumner rose from his seat and proffered his opinion. "In light of the fact that this incident happened merely ninety minutes ago, we have not had time to formulate a plan B." There was anger in his voice. "We will be working with the general on plans B, C, and D during the next few hours."

This was the first time as president that Sumner had expressed anger publicly, and Shea had felt the discomfort of being on the receiving end.

***

Sumner convened a meeting of his Cabinet to discuss the war. It had not been a full-fledged assault as they had anticipated. Many believed this was intentional, as the USSA would not want a "scorched earth" policy which it would have to rebuild after the war. Rebuilding Europe after WWII had cost billions under the Marshall Plan; that was something the USSA could not afford without going bankrupt. Therefore, keeping as much of the Republic in tact as possible, while at the same time inflicting maximum pain at strategic pressure points seemed to be the option of choice.

This was good for Sumner and the Republic. Yet, the President knew he couldn't win the war on his own and he would certainly lose it in a war of attrition. The USSA had instituted a naval blockade of the Gulf, even though supplies were coming into some ports in Louisiana, southern Texas and Alabama. Parts of Florida where smaller ports were not blockaded were also bringing in valuable metals and materiel.

Sumner called the Canadian Prime Minister to express his gratitude for the tacit support through the pipeline and the use of satellite and other facilities. But, his ultimate goal was to begin moving Canada toward an alliance with him. He needed Canada and/or Australia in the war on his side. They were the remaining powers who shared the libertarian views. It was true that Canada had been splintered by the secession several decades earlier by the Quebec Province; however, the rest of the country had rallied and had leaned more heavily to the right, and had prospered. Meanwhile, Quebec had languished, following the socialistic practices of its Franco cousins.

"Prime Minister, it is good to talk with you again. As you know we are becoming embroiled in a *tet-a-tet* with our USSA compatriots. As I am sure you are already aware, the USSA has provoked a conflict with our Republic, striking air bases deep in our own sovereign territory. The incident that the First Citizen cites as our transgression last month was instigated by their Administration. We have proof that the attack was coordinated by her internal intelligence agency. We had no part in that, I assure you."

"Thank you, Mr. President. Our intelligence agencies are also looking into those allegations. Their results are inconclusive at this time. But, I assure you that Canada wants peace on the North American continent," said the PM for Canada.

"As do we," retorted the President. "But, we cannot allow the USSA to draw the Republic back into a union that is oppressive and, may I say, totalitarian in its approach to its states. We fundamentally reject the ways of the USSA and the new Constitution that has been consecrated. We will not live by those principles. Those are not the principles enumerated by the Founding Fathers of our original Constitution of 1789. Madison, Adams, Monroe, Hamilton, Jay, Sitting Bull City — all of them believed in God. Even Jefferson who is demonized as a deist believed in the Almighty. But now — now, the nation of the USSA has shunned all affiliation with the Almighty. It is blasphemous now to suggest otherwise. Within the new Constitution, ideas and principles are fine, as long as they conform to those of the elites — those in power. And they have destroyed the education system to such an extent, and replaced it with such propaganda of the wonders and virtues of Marxism that the general population blindly accepts it. That's all they have left. They can no longer buy votes with handouts and social programs — they don't have the money any more. You understand."

"Yes. Our sister Province, I mean, the nation of Quebec, has fallen into the same trap. They have tried to initiate talks to re-unite our peoples, but the debts and increasing difference in standard of living is making that increasingly problematic."

"It sounds like what we read about in the unification of East and West Germany back in the twentieth century," said Sumner.

"Precisely. That is exactly where we are. The debts from Quebec and the welfare society are enormous. We can't fund them without destroying our own culture and standard of living. This is going to be a difficult time for us."

Sumner paused. "We are in a difficult time too," he said."

"I know," said the PM.

"Can you help? We need technology — military technology. We need planes, troops, materiel."

"I am sure you do, Mr. President." The sound of his voice was not promising.

"We expect the USSA to implement embargos, financial freezing of our assets, and other measures to force us to our knees. They don't want to destroy us — just move us back into their orbit of influence." "Yes. We believe that also."

"So, what can you do?"

There was prolonged silence on the other end of the phone. It seemed interminable, yet, in fact, it was only less than a minute. "It is not a good time in Canada right now for us to commit anything more than moral support for you. We do not wish to embroil the nation and its people in your conflict. The support by the Canadian people is not there, Mr. President. I cannot, in good conscience, send our boys and girls into harm's way in your defense. I just don't have the support."

Now it was Sumner's turn to pause. "You are facing difficult times in Canada. Ottawa is struggling with unification. However, the fate of your neighbor to the south is at stake. If we fail, then you may face a socialistic threat from the south for some time to come. Many times in history, a socialistic society becomes militaristic and the government becomes totalitarian. We already see the totalitarian nature of this Administration."

"That may be true, but they have not been a threat to Canada."

"Not yet."

"Mr. President, we Canadians empathize with your plight. We went through secession several years ago.

333

We are just not prepared to get involved at this time."

Sumner calmed himself. "I understand, Mr. Prime Minister. We will continue to discuss this matter with you. I am sure that at some point you will be persuaded. But, I realize that it is not yet that time."

"We wish you well," said the PM.

"Thanks for your time."

Sumner hung up the phone. Shea had listened to every word. It was discouraging to her.

"Don't worry," said Sumner, watching the expression on her face. "Things will change. I know they will. We will win them over at some point."

"You're right," she said. "Things will change. I just hope they realize the change sooner rather than later.

We need their help. We need planes, tanks, personnel carriers, ..."

"Yes, we do. But it will come. Be patient and aware. There will be a time and place. There always is."

She was hopeful, yet concerned. *What if Canada came around, but came around too late? It was all timing – sometimes even days mattered.* "And Australia? Where are they? What has the Prime Minister said there?" she asked.

Sumner smiled in his usual optimistic way. "I think we can turn them too," he answered.

"So, they are about in the same place as the Canadians," she said flatly.

"Yes. Right now, they are."

"Let's just hope they come closer, quickly," she said, as she left the room.

Sumner put on the proud and positive face, but even for him it was hard. *I have to wear my big-boy pants every day,* he thought to himself. *That's the job I signed up for.*

*****

CH 63 Ratner and the World Council

Realizing that any action against Canada would force world opinion against her, First Citizen Ratner decided to go on the offensive and address the World Council body in Brussels via satellite, which had replaced the United Nations in New York.

The New World Council was reformulated with those third-world countries being given equal status with the industrialized countries at that time -- the USA, Russia, England, France and China, plus Germany, India and Japan. Representation and votes were based on population, rather than military or economic muscle. As a result, the new powers of Canada and Saudi Arabia had elected not to participate. Neither contributed to the operations of the group and neither had a seat at the table. It had mattered little. The WC or "Water Closet" as many sarcastically referred to it, had no power and no influence. It had quickly devolved into an institution of bickering amongst the developing countries to see who could siphon off more of the world's wealth for their own purposes. Generally run by kleptocracies, these countries merely ensured that their ruling class got their fair share of the bounty. Trillions had been redistributed from the industrialized nations to the poorer ones through climate change taxes, energy credits, water redistribution vouchers and other schemes. Each was a method to punish countries of economic might and give their wealth to those who were too corrupt to develop it on their own. And in the end, nothing had changed in the world. No lofty, altruistic causes achieved what they purposed themselves to represent. All that had resulted were that people of the industrialized world were taxed more and pushed to a lower standard of living — all so the rulers of the corrupt banana republics could steal the wealth and have more to suppress their own peoples.

To this end, First Citizen Ratner rose from her chair to deliver her key note speech to the body. Her image appeared prominently on the huge fifty-five foot, square screen that was anchored to the front of General Assembly Hall at the WC.

"President Ab Saud 'il Basim, World Council representatives and distinguished guests, I am pleased to address this august body today with very urgent matters that affect us all and will continue to affect our nations until we can root-out the fundamental, causational factors that have led us to the current state of affairs.

"The schism that has formed within the USSA — that between what is known as the Republic and the United Socialist States of America — is only emblematic of a far greater issue that threatens to overtake and overwhelm other nations of the world — your nations. What you may see as an isolated incident or a parochial matter within my country, is nothing of the sort. This is an issue that will spread quickly into your countries if it is not stopped. And unless the lid is placed back upon the bubbling cauldron of unrest, it will spill out into your own neighborhoods. The unrest is contagious — as evil and lethal as Ebola **or** Marburg hemorrhagic fever **and** we cannot let that happen.

"It is up to all of us to stamp out bigotry, racism, and hatred of others at every turn. Political correctness is vital to a civilized society. We must have control over the discourse and the words our people use. Only in this way, may we protect those who are most vulnerable in our society – those who cannot defend themselves. We must be the guardians against those more wealthy and powerful who seek to oppress the poor of our nations.

"But that is what the state of the Republic spouts as their principles. They seek capitalism where those with money and power can starve the poor, wringing every last farthing from the working-class person who toils and aches from the long hours and horrific working conditions. They are given no choice in the Republic but to serve their new masters. This is unjust and cannot be tolerated.

"The Republic also seeks complete freedom for their citizenry – allowing them to intimidate and bully others by their speech. Those who are forced to listen to such berating tones suffer terribly – afflicted by the scathing words and implications that are just as harmful as violent deeds. But they don't stop at their own borders. It is they who are stirring the pot in my country and soon, in all of yours -- bringing that pot to a rolling boil.

"They must not be allowed to spread their hatred across the globe as they've stated they wish to do. Just as Nazi Germany had a dream of Aryan Herrenvolk or Arian Master Race, so too do those of the Republic. They want nothing more than to impose their white, supremacist views on every other country. It's racist and it's despicable!"

At that point, Ratner got a standing ovation from the third-world countries seated in the large hall. They dominated the assembly by a factor of eight-to-one over the industrialized nations.

"You must understand that the old USA was founded on the principles of slave holders and religious zealots. They believed that the white man should rule the country. Initially, there were no safeguards in the US Constitution to protect African Americans who were enslaved en masse. These were acts of the Founders that have no defense. As a result, we had to abandon the premises of the old Constitution and replace it with something founded on the concept of fairness and equality for all. These principles are fundamental to everyone – everyone should have the right to have wealth and be happy. It shouldn't matter what color their skin is or what sexual orientation they have. Human kind is sacred. Everyone matters and everyone should be the same."

With this, she got another roaring round of applause from the assembly and the gallery. Her tone and her remarks struck the right chords, as she knew they would.

"However, today, the USSA has a renegade territory that does not subscribe to those ideals. As I made clear, it believes in the greedy, corporate, capitalistic way that rewards the rich and punishes the poor. Unrestricted business leads to the pillaging of the poor, the raping of the country for its resources, and the amassing of great, undeserved wealth by the very few. Only a handful realize the benefit from such a society – and they realize it in the form of vast fortunes. In fact, ninety-nine percent are worse off from it. That leaves the one percent who become the billion and trillion-airs. These are the ones who steal, cheat and lie to their workers and to the people of my nation, extracting as much out of them as they can while delivering little in return.

"This bourgeoisie, as Marx so aptly identified them, are not icons of greatness, virtue and decency. No, these are criminals. They deserve to be arrested and brought before the People's Justice – a justice meted out by their peers; a justice delivered by those they have trampled upon, suppressed and brutalized. The rich are the ones who will become the poor and the poor will become the rich."

Again, there was tumultuous applause.

"But our dream of a world where all nations can share in the wealth cannot be realized unless we are willing to stand up to the tyranny of the Right. These groups are the new Nazi's of the twenty-first century. Their brand of 'freedom' must be stamped out; it must be eradicated before it is permitted to spread.

"If we don't stop it, then what are we leaving behind? What are we leaving for our children to inherit? It's all about our legacy and our children, is it not? And no, I am not referring to the one percenters' children. No. I am talking about 99 percenters' children, and in some countries here, 99.99 percenters' children. I will and I will continue to stand up against the one percenters and their governesses, their silk robes and their silver spoons. Bathed in material excess, these children have no perspective as to the poverty, the depravity, and the squalor that our children must endure. Struggling for survival, our children feel joy in getting a fresh cup of water to drink or a few grains of rice to eat. Compare that with the servants and entourages that are lavishly and ostentatiously thrown in our faces by the billionaires of our countries.

"Well, no more!"

The assembly rose to their feet once again. This time the applause lasted a full minute, and Ratner basked in all the glory cast her way.

"That's why we must address the current war within the continent of America. It is the rebellious one percenters who are trying to overthrow my government and our impoverished 99 percent. The struggle of poor against the rich has continued for centuries and it's time it ends! We have no option! We must fight for our survival. No one else will fight for us. Without the power of the government, the poor have no chance. Without the government and its vast resources, we are unable to even the playing field with the rich and incapable of destroying them before they wipe us from the face of the Earth. We can't … we won't allow it!

"Therefore, not only must we fight the Republic. We must fight all those who support them. If we don't support and defend each other, we are lost. They will band together as they always have. Together they will strengthen and become even harder to defeat. We must not allow this either! We must sever the bonds between them now! We cannot wait!

"That is why I ask your support in dealing with the rebellious Republic and all countries that come to their aid. There are many nations colluding with them and against the USSA. They aim to destroy us, and if they succeed, your countries will be next on their lists. They look to global hegemony. They look to rule the world and force each of you into servitude. That is their endgame. That is their mission ... We cannot let them succeed. Thank you."

There was no doubt on anyone's mind that she was referring to the Canadians. It was a masterful speech, and by large measure it succeeded in one respect — it garnered her worldwide support, at least with the 90 percent of countries that controlled the WC. And, whether that would translate into monetary or military support was yet to be seen. At the very least, it would put pressure on the other 10 percent to follow suite.

"Nice job," said Holt, her chief of staff, who was waiting for her to finish.

Ratner smiled. "Yes, I thought my performance was quite good. I believe they bought it."

"Yes," said Holt, "I think they did."

*****

CH 64 Break with Reality

The war was going badly, and First Citizen Ratner was concerned. The last few battles had resulted in the defeat of her highly decorated and respected USSA Marine forces, ones that had once been the envy of the world. Lack of training, equipment, and a collapse of morale in the face of constant social tinkering had left the corps in shambles. Requirements to have the right mix of genders, races, sexual preferences, and other criteria before constituting an army unit had brought the process to a standstill. These standards had all but neutered the military and made it difficult for it to present a defense, not to mention any offensive capability. Those units that were constituted were largely dysfunctional, as anyone not meeting the basic criteria for a position was not removed; instead, the criteria were lowered so the failing individual could pass. Initially, this had resulted in the unnecessary deaths of thousands of USSA forces, while those of the better-qualified, rebel Republic had been minimal. Total deaths to date: USSA 17,833; the Republic 1,245. Other casualty numbers were similar: USSA 58,555; the Republic 2,211.

However, when the first few campaigns went poorly and the losses in battle mounted, Ratner abandoned all vestiges of waging a "human" as opposed to an "Inhuman" war. The gloves quickly came off, shifting dramatically toward the cruel and barbarous end of the spectrum. Ratner's new orders were to minimize losses. If a commander had excessive casualties, he or she could be court martialed convicted and executed. As a result, those who were inept or cowardly in battle were often just shot by their commanders rather than endangering the rest of the squad, patrol, or platoon.

Yet, the White House kept Congress and the public in the dark with how it was prosecuting the war.

Citing the number of USSA deaths at only 833, with 2555 casualties against those of the Republic at 17,245 and 58,211, respectively, the Administration lied. Thus, the First Citizen was still able to claim the moral high ground, telling everyone that America was fighting a "just war" and that she would seek war crime charges against Sumner and the Republic once the conflict was over and the USSA had claimed victory.

"I am leader of the fair world, so why do you question me?" Ratner spat back at her new chairman of the Joint Chiefs of Staff. General Hussan had been replaced by General Althea White, a four-star general who had grown up in South Carolina and been promoted through the ranks to serve on the Joint Chiefs of Staff as Chief of the National Guard Bureau. Now she led it.

"You mean the *free* world," said the general without thinking.

The anger in Ratner's face made the general step back. She exploded in rage, "No! I mean what I say! Leader of a *fair* world! Life is nothing without fairness! That is what this nation was founded on – the notion of fairness for all!"

The general noted the wild, exuberant waving of Ratner's hands in the air, the thick gold bracelets dangling from her wrists and the large bands of diamonds that encased several rings on her stubby fingers. White was also not oblivious to the ornate tapestries, drapes, furniture, rugs, and paintings that graced the First Citizen's new office. She had ordered and gotten a new wing built at the White House for her new Oval Office, some five times larger than the old one. The old Truman Porch had been torn down and the monstrosity built off the back to replace it on the South Lawn. Dwarfing the rest of the White House, the appendage was known as the Angel Addition.

"Yes, of course," Clancy Holt quickly interjected, helping cover for the general. "We understand, perfectly."

Then, Ratner directed her next comments to her chief of staff. "And all those monuments out there," she said pointing to the Washington monument, "they're vestiges of slave holders and of malicious, imperialistic wars. We are a better people than that. They must go. I want them torn down immediately and replaced with icons of justice and equality. We need images of triumph and victory too – something the people can rally around as we fight our war. How can I wage war when the people are constantly reminded of our sordid past – of our failures as a nation?"

"Yes, First Citizen," said Holt, nodding energetically. "I agree with you."

"We are now Sitting Bull City, and yet we have no monuments to that great leader," she began. "So, I want Lincoln pulled out of his throne at the memorial and replaced with Sitting Bull," she demanded. "The Jefferson statue needs to go too. That must be replaced with a statue of Obama, the great statesman of modern times. Of course, all the speeches and words in all the monuments must change too. They have to be from these people." Then, she waggled her finger. "But if you see something in one of their speeches that doesn't comport to our message to the people, then we'll have to change those words too. Do you understand me?"

"What about the Washington monument, Madam? What will go there?" asked the general.

Looking off into the distance, like a ship's captain searching for land over an expanse of water, she said finally, "A giant statue of the Winged Victory holding a sword in one hand and a scythe in the other. You know something larger than the one in Volgograd, Russia – the one named *The Motherland Calls*. Something around three hundred feet would be acceptable."

"We will issue your Executive Order on this, First Citizen," said Holt, cowing to her demands.

"And where are we with the building of the National Center for Islam where Mt. Vernon used to be?"

"Coming along. I believe it should be finished later this month."

"And I see the National Archives building has been demolished and the founding documents of the USA burned?"

"Yes. The Smithsonian Socialist History Museum will be going up on that plot of land near the Capitol within the next few months."

"You do have the original copy of Karl Marx's *Communist Manifesto*? I assume it has been secured for the museum?"

"Yes, Madam."

"Good," said Ratner, pleased with the progress. "Now the only thing we have to do is raze the Capitol and Supreme Court buildings and we'll be finished."

"Yes, Madam," said Holt with Stoic indifference.

The First Citizen got up from her desk and walked around the perimeter of the grand, round Persian carpet in the center of her office, replete with the USSA colors; it sat astride three white leather sofas and several other leather arm chairs. Now pacing from one side of the room to the other, Ratner held her hands firmly on her hips.

"Now what are doing with Canada?" she asked, looking at neither the general nor Holt nor anything else in particular.

"The prime minister has been calling daily since the incident. We've been telling him that you're unavailable, but the calls keep coming in. How much longer do you want us to …"

"They *will* find out that we shot down that airliner, you know. It won't be hard to pin that on us. And although I've turned world opinion against the Republic and the Canadians, I don't know how long that will last. If Canada comes in on the side of the Republic, we may be in trouble."

It was now General White's turn to interject. "Madam, you are quite right. We've analyzed the potential for Canada entering the war against us. Our computers put the likelihood at fifty-four percent. If they do enter on the side of the Republic, the chances of the combined efforts of the two nations defeating us are sixty-three percent."

"Sh*t!" said Ratner. "And why were you waiting to tell me this?"

"I was going to, but it hadn't yet come up on our agenda."

Ratner snorted and rolled her eyes, as if she didn't believe the excuse. "What else do you have for me?"

"We have already confirmed that the Canadians know full well how the incident occurred and who was behind it. This is no longer a mystery, Madam."

"So, we need to appease them, I guess," said the First Citizen, still striding back and forth across the room. But as she uttered these last words, she moved rapidly back to her desk and retook her seat. "What if I propose giving them Montana?" she asked, out of the blue.

"What? Why would we do that?" asked Holt, startled by the declaration.

"Why not? It would pacify them for the time being, and it would allow us time to finish off Wyoming and the rest of the Republic. Once the other states are firmly back into the Union, we can declare war on Canada. Then, after they're defeated and absorbed into the USSA, we'll get Montana back."

The general stood dumbfounded. "What are you saying – that we will go to war again after we finish with the Republic?"

"I'm telling you that not only will we not let them have Montana, but that I'm going after their entire f*king country. I'm going to annex Canada."

"You can't do that. We don't have the military or the finances to do that."

"Once we have the new military technology of the Republic – the advanced phaser systems – we can do anything we want. Taking over Canada will be just the start. Nothing will be able to stop us. Hell, we can begin marching south too."

"You mean Mexico?" asked Holt.

"Not only Mexico, but Central and South America, damn it!" Then she stopped and stared at her chief of staff. "What's your problem Holt? Don't you have the stomach for this? We have a unique opportunity right now. We won't be able to keep this technology to ourselves forever. Eventually others will have it and our advantage will be gone. We have to strike now!"

The general knew those ideas were mad, but she dared not say it. The USSA had neither the money nor the public support to mount such draining and far-flung campaigns. The war with the Republic alone was proving to be a hard sell to the citizenry, forcing up taxes and creating hard times for most – times far worse yet than even those seen during the Great Depression of the 1930s. So, instead of engaging, the general said nothing.

"I want battle plans drawn up for the invasion of Canada," Ratner said, turning her back on the general once more and looking out again over the nation's Mall. "And, I want an armistice drawn up with Canada to buy us time. You know, like the Molotov-Ribbentrop Pact between Germany and the Soviets during WWII. We'll see then what we have to give up, at least temporarily, to keep them out of this war. Whatever it is, it won't matter in the long run. We'll get it back from them after we take them over."

"Yes, Madam," said Holt, obsequiously. "Will that be all?"

"Yes, now both of you go take care of things. I want the treaty ready to go by the end of the day tomorrow. Then, I want our Minister of Foreign Affairs to present it to MacDonald."

Both the general and chief of staff left the Oval Office, closing the door quietly so she wouldn't be disturbed by its sound.

Holt looked at the general and started to speak, but General White shook her head. "Don't even say it," she said as she continued walking away.

***

One week later ...

Ratner waited nervously in her office for word from George Lytel, her minister of foreign affairs. With her were Clancy Holt and General White, along with the minister of international policing, Sara Miller Emerson. Finally, the red phone rang, and Lytel's face appeared on screen.

"Madam?" Lytel began.

"Well, speak up, Lytel, we can't hear you," she demanded. "What's happening up there?"

"I'm afraid, it did not go well, Madam."

Ratner raised her eyebrows, anticipating more from her minister. She was just about to interrupt, when Lytel started up again.

"I was given only thirty minutes with the prime minister. We exchanged pleasantries. But when I began introducing the idea of a treaty between us and initiating dialog on how we might work together, he stopped me. He held up his hand and asked me about the shooting down of his airliner."

"We talked about that. So, what did you tell him?" Ratner asked.

"I told him what we discussed. I told him that we were unaware of anything coming from our side. We were still looking into it, but that we were not aware of any missiles being launched, and certainly there were no orders given for it."

"And?"

"And, he didn't believe me. He said bluntly that he had information that there were two missiles fired from Minot Air Force Base and that the black-box recorder confirmed that the plane was brought down by them."

"I see," she said. "Did he say what they were going to do about it?"

The minister's face looked cold and edgy. The corners of his mouth turned upward in nervous angst and his eyes darted to the side, avoiding direct engagement with his boss.

'Lytel, what did he say to you?" Ratner asked, again."

"He said that unless we come clean and confess our involvement in the incident that he would instruct his Parliament to declare war on the USSA. He said they would immediately ally with the Republic."

The First Citizen laughed, yet no one could figure out whether she was chortling from anxiety or because she was merely amused.

"He's bluffing," said Ratner. "They won't risk it. It's not significant enough to create a war between our two nations."

"What would you like for me to do?" Lytel asked, shrugging his shoulders.

"Get another meeting with him," she answered.

Lytel shook his head dramatically. "No, he made it abundantly clear that he would have no more conversations with me or anyone from the USSA until we admit our involvement."

"Fine!" said Ratner, indignantly. "Then come home. If they won't play ball, then we'll have to proceed with destroying the Republic before turning our attention towards them. Canada will get what's coming to it soon enough. As for MacDonaold, he's not going to do anything for a while. These things always take time."

***

Two days later ...

"Madam? We're tracking six squadrons of fighters and one squadron of bombers that have appeared as threats on our radar." It was her minister of International Policing, Sara Miller Emerson who had contacted the White House and been patched directly through to the First Citizen.

"Where are they coming from?" asked Ratner.

"Canada, Madam."

"Are you sure?"

"Yes, quite sure."

"Are they in USSA air space?"

"No, but they are flying along the border near us – very near the border just north of Montana."

"On screen," said the First Citizen, shouting at the computer to pull up the visual feed of the radar screen that her minister was getting.

Hovering in the middle of the room was a curved, bent circle with a map inserted inside. Segmenting the map were yellow, crisscrossed grid marks, each with a number and letter. Moving across the grid network were the six groups of small dots and one with larger ones that the minister was reporting. Everyone in the room watched as the clusters advanced, methodically inching westward in an uncertain trajectory. As the dots passed from one grid section to the next, the disquietude grew.

"Should we scramble our fighters?" asked General White. But her point became moot as suddenly the dots veered sharply, turning southward and crossing immediately into USSA territory.

"They are now officially in violation of USSA airspace, First Citizen," said the minister. "We should scramble our fighters."

"Yes," said Ratner, emphatically.

Within a few minutes, black dots surfaced on the matrixed map, appearing just west of Minot Air Force Base in North Dakota. Quickly, the USSA fighters swept inch by inch toward an intercept point with the Canadian air force.

"What do we know about their bombers?" the First Citizen asked the general while still staring at the 3D map in front of her.

"They are new models developed by the Canadians based on the Dassault Mirage bomber. Just as the old B-1 bomber was completely reworked into the stealth B-2 decades ago, so too was the old Mirage bomber. The latest version is the Mirage VI b2. According to our database, it has a range of six thousand nautical miles and is capable of carrying up to eighty, two thousand-pound, class Mk84, GB-37 bombs. Top air speed is just over Mach one or six hundred knots. Cruising ceiling is forty thousand feet. The …"

"Okay, enough," said Ratner, waving off the general. "But are they nuclear capable?"

The general looked at the First Citizen with a cold sober face. "Yes," said the general without emotion.

There was quiet in the room as if a large scorpion was sitting on the table ready to strike at anyone who made a sound.

"So, what action should we take?" Ratner asked finally, shifting her gaze quickly from minister to minister.

General White looked uncomfortable in her chair, shifting to one side and looking down at her computer to avoid eye contact.

"General?" That was the word from her boss that White was hoping not to hear.

Instead, the general deflected. "How much time do we have before the bombers near our air force base in Montana?" she asked her aide de camp, Major Stanton.

"Five minutes, fifty-four seconds until Malmstrom AFB, general."

White looked at Ratner. "Madam, what are your orders?"

It had all happened so suddenly, so unexpectedly. To shoot down the incoming planes would solidify a war on a second front. The USSA was coping with the superior weaponry of the Republic, struggling to find ways to overcome the disadvantage. To add another front to the north would make things all that much more difficult. However, not to shoot them down would make them appear weak and strengthen the Republic's position even more.

"Send up fighters from our Malmstrom base to intercept, then. They'll be much closer," said Ratner.

"Can't, First Citizen. You removed all fighters from that base last year. We have much of our strategic communications there now," said the general. "That's our central command and control center for the north-central states. Once SAC was closed from Barksdale base in Louisiana, it was distributed among several bases, including Malmstrom."

"Why the hell did we pull defenses away from a strategic command post?" Ratner fired back.

"Don't know, First Citizen," said the general, even though she knew full well it had been one of many stupid decisions made by the "all-knowing" Administrations of Fourier and now her own boss.

Ratner scowled at the general, but then said, "Get a hold of the Canadian prime minister. Get him on the phone immediately."

Holt instantly began calling Ottawa, but after waiting a few minutes he looked at Ratner and shrugged his shoulders. "There's no answer," he said, holding the emergency red phone in his hand. "No one is picking up our line."

"How long until they engage us?" asked White.

"Thirty-two seconds," answered her major.

"What about our F-39s? When will they intercept?" asked the general, nervously twitching her fingers on the table.

"Intercept of the entire group in five minutes, twenty-one seconds, general."

"What about their ATAs? What air-to-air missiles do they have on them?"

"If they fired their AMRAAM missiles, impact would be in one minute, twenty-eight seconds, sir."

White looked at Ratner. "They wouldn't get there in time, Madam."

"Keep trying with the prime minister," said Ratner.

"Time?" asked White with beads of perspiration bubbling up on her forehead.

"Twenty seconds."

White looked nervously at her boss while Ratner looked out the window, searching for an answer.

"Other options?" Ratner asked, her voice level rising.

"We could have our pilots try to communicate directly with the squadron leader of the fighters," said the aide de camp in an odd outburst.

"Do it!" shouted Ratner.

White communicated the message to the USSA squadron commander and waited for the reply. She listened and then turned to the commander in chief. "No response, Madam."

"Time?" asked Ratner.

"Eight seconds."

White looked again to Ratner. "Madam?"

Ratner just shook her head.

Shanta knew what that meant. The decision would be hers and she would be blamed for any negative outcome.

"Prepare to fire on the targets," said White, speaking in as much of a monotone as she could muster into her transmitter.

"Madam!" said Minister Emerson, urgently, "I've reached the Canadian prime minister, and I'm putting him through."

Popping up on the screen was the blue-suited image of Prime Minister Francois Oligay from the independent nation of Quebec, a stern-looking man in his late fifties with dark brown hair, broken up by patches of gray around the temples and sides. It wasn't at all whom she expected.

"It's not MacDonald," Ratner said, haltingly. "What's going on?" But then, she put on her calm, political mask and said, "Put him on."

"You're linked, Madam," said the major.

Keeping her tone flat and her demeanor sedate, Ratner addressed the Quebecois leader. "Prime minister. I was expecting ..."

"Yes, yes. I realize you were attempting to contact Prime Minister MacDonald, eh?" said Oligay with a heavy French accent.

"Yes, but ..."

"It is critical that I reach you now, as you are aware, the Royal Canadian Air Force has entered your air space over Montana. I have been in contact with the Canadian prime minister urging him to withdraw his force ..."

Just as the Quebec prime minister was speaking, the red dots on the screen in front of Ratner and her team shifted their direction and began heading back north, returning over the border and into their own air space in Saskatchewan.

"... We have been in discussions for nearly an hour, and he has agreed to change the direction of his squadrons. However, he has not agreed to discontinue his intention to align Canada with the Republic. He stated that his country considers the actions of the USSA in downing the Air Canada airline a provocative act and, in fact, an act of war against his country. He wanted me to inform you that he intends to take all measures necessary to protect his nation from the aggressive acts of the USSA."

Ratner put on her showman's face and smiled politely. "Thank you, Mr. Prime Minister. We appreciate your involvement in this incident and assisting in obtaining a peaceful resolution to this misunderstanding."

The Quebecois shook his head. "I'm not sure you understand my involvement, then," he answered.

"Prime Minister MacDonald is not willing to acquiesce to this condition. He is only returning his force to Canada in deference to my pleading with him to delay such action at this time. He agreed. However, he has no intention of abandoning his position on this issue based upon the USSA's denials of its involvement in the airline matter. He was quite firm and direct about that point."

"I quite understand," said Ratner. "But you see, we will not admit to something of which we had no part."

Oligay looked exasperated at the comment, but did not address it. "I see," he said simply.

"However, I do believe that we may be able to work out an agreement with the nation of Quebec," she added. "I would like to send my minister of foreign affairs, George Lytel, to Quebec City to begin discussions on a mutually beneficial treaty between our countries."

Again, Oligay shook his head. "I am sorry, First Citizen. But we have adopted a position of neutrality with respect to the matter between you and the Republic and you and Canada. We wish to stay out of this conflict altogether. Therefore, I will have no more involvement in these issues. If there is an altercation between you and either of the nations, then so be it. Quebec and its people wish to be left alone and in peace. We will respect the sovereignty of all belligerents and will not take sides. Do you understand?"

"That is unfortunate, Mr. Prime Minister. I do hope that you and your parliament will reconsider. We will keep open our lines of communication. Please contact me or my foreign minister at any time. We do wish to work with you."

"Good day, Madam Ratner," said Oligay, coolly. And with that the screen went dark.

The First Citizen had never liked Oligay, believing him to be an arrogant and self-serving public servant much like herself. And like her, he had championed himself on saving his nation from the capitalistic evils of the rest of Canada. But because of the many social failures he had experienced, his Quebec had fallen on hard times as well. It was true that Quebec was in better shape than the USSA, but not much better. Oligay's country still depended heavily on the USSA and Canada for its well-being, if not its very survival. It was on life-support, much like the country Ratner led.

"What do you think, Madam?" asked General White, regaining her composure and again able to breathe normally without hyperventilating.

"F*ck him," said Ratner with the rough, brazen tongue of a nineteenth century sailor.

"Excuse me?" asked Holt, not sure he had heard correctly.

"You heard me just fine. F*ck him!" repeated Ratner. "He's nothing but a douche bag. We don't need him now and we won't need him once we take over both Canada and his little sh*t country of Quebec. He'll be shot along with the rest of them."

It was the aide de camp who spoke up next. "General, Madam, I think you should see this," he said.

"What is it, major?" asked the general.

"It's Canada, sir. It appears they've started amassing a great many troops on its border with us."

Indeed, the tabletop showed a lot of movement to the north, across the border where they'd just seen the Royal Canadian Air Force return back into their own air space.

"What do you make of that?" the major asked.

"It looks like we've got ourselves a two-front war now," said White.

*****

CH 65 To Launch

As the economy of the USSA deteriorated and its isolation in the world became more acute, its leader became more desperate. The support from the World Council had been a boon to the country's image with the developing world, but it was as fleeting as it was helpful. The third world was no more interested in offering economic or military assistance than it was in seeing America resurrected. It was just fine with an injured, staggering, has-been of a prize fighter who was cornered into the ropes and likely to collapse on his own to the floor of the ring.

Once Canada entered the fray, it was more difficult to keep the two fronts engaged. Supply lines became stretched and subject to bombing raids by both enemies. What limited military assets the USSA had diluted; almost two-thirds were deployed to the north to dissuade the Canadians while the remainder was scattered all over the country to keep up the pressure on the Republic.

However, it only took a few months of this stress and increasing casualties to force Ratner's hand. She was running out of repair parts for her air fighters, tanks and mobile howitzers and what was worse the citizenry was beginning to turn. Although unemployment had dropped some due to the war effort, the shortages and martial law crackdowns were proving too much. Combined with body counts on the news reports each night, the people were on the verge of revolt.

Ratner had never felt such pressure. As if locked in a commercial pressure cooker set on *high,* Ratner began lashing out at everyone and everything. Her personality was changing, and not for the better. If it were possible at all, her demeanor was becoming ever more Stalinesque.

"… with the latest casualty report showing that we lost 412 killed and 1233 wounded last week. This was up from 395 killed and 1187 wounded the week before. The toll on our forces has been great. We have five divisions operating at an average field strength of 74.2%. However, if this attrition continues, our forces will be reduced to a critical level, unable to defend the mainland, within eight weeks." General White then turned to the next topic. "Now, as for our offensive systems …" she began.

Ratner sat sour-faced and irritable. She was no longer listening to the briefing. Things were not looking good. It was becoming increasingly probable that her Administration would not survive all the factors that were pounding away at the very foundation of her power and her authority. She was losing her grip, and she knew it.

"Stop!" she finally shouted. "That's enough. I've heard enough!" she exclaimed, turning to the general as if she had suddenly begun shouting in the middle of a Catholic cathedral during mass. The room froze in silence. No one wanted to breathe; no one wanted look at their leader for fear they would be singled out.

"I don't want to hear any more about how we're losing. No more about the dead, the dying or the injured. No more about how many planes were lost, how many tanks were destroyed, how many ships were sunk. No! What I want to hear is how we're going to win this war! That's what I want to hear. That's what I need to know."

But instead of initiating any talk or discussion, her remarks only brought more silence.

"Well? I asked a question? I demand an answer."

Still no one was willing to offer anything.

Ratner stood up and slammed her fist on the table. "If you won't bloody give me an answer, then I'll give you one," she said angrily. Her eyes flamed with anger, and her jaw was locked sternly into place as she clenched her teeth in rage. "General? I want three B2c bombers readied."

General White looked at the First Citizen with bewilderment. "Uh, and what would you propose to do with them?" she asked. "I want them sent – one toward Ottawa, one toward Vancouver and one toward Cheyenne. Each is to have a complete escort of F-39 fighters, AWACs, and support craft."

"What is the mission?" asked White.

"None really," said Ratner, "except as a diversion. I want to distract their forces toward these, believing that they are AGM-161b AJASSM nuclear warheads. We will wrap up most of their forces dealing with these planes while we execute our real attack."

White shook her head. "I'm still not understanding, Madam."

"We will launch our ICBMs from Minot. In total, I want thirty sent up, covering all the major cities in Canada and the Republic. Do you understand? I want them all wiped out … every, last one of them!"

"But we mothballed all our LGM-118D Peacekeeper ICBMs, except for six that we have at the mountain," said Minister Emerson from defense. "That's all we have."

Ratner growled. "Damn you!" she said. Again, it was well known that both she and her predecessor had unilaterally dismantled nearly all the USSA's nuclear capability. "We only have six? Well, I'll have to address that later, I guess. For now, I want all of them fired off. Start with Ottawa and Cheyenne and work your way back from there. Pick-off the other four top targets we need to destroy."

"You're not serious," said Holt, sitting in on the meeting, "Are you?" It was a brave, bold question – one that was not intended to be threatening but that was exactly how it was taken.

However, instead of blowing up, Ratner calmed herself and smiled. It was unnatural and strange, and no one in the room felt comfortable with the climate or what might happen next. "Serious?" the First Citizen asked, lowering the shrillness of her tone. "Am I serious?" she asked again.

Holt knew not to ask her again. She was coming unglued and what he wanted least was to be the lightning rod that would set things off.

Ratner turned again to General White. "When can this be readied?"

"This will take at least seventy-two hours, Madam."

"Hell no!" screamed the First Citizen. "I want all launched within forty-eight!"

"You're not going to destroy half the population of North America, are you?" quivered Emerson.

Ratner looked her straight in the eyes and without blinking, said, "They are our enemy. They are dead to me anyway."

*****

CH 66 Domes

"What are our risks?" asked the president, clasping his hands behind his head, "and do they outweigh the benefits here?" Sumner's face

"Sir, there are always risks in anything we do. You have to ..."

"John, this is a serious action we're taking. Will this result in millions of deaths?"

"That is a possibility, sir," said Johnny.

Sumner looked to Shea but only saw her shrug her shoulders before she said, "We need to find out what those possibilities are."

"Dr. Lin. What are the probabilities of deaths and how many casualties might result?" asked the president, reconnecting with the two physicists he had on the phone.

"Mr. President," Dr. Lin began, his face now showing up on the screen, "our computers tell us that the most likely outcome is that fewer than 2,706 deaths will occur in the larger metropolitan areas."

"What are the numbers at 95 percent probability and 5 percent probability?" asked Sumner, trying to get numbers that he could assimilate into a plan.

"Just a minute, Mr. President," said Lin. A few moments later, he said, "I show a mortality rate of just 376 with the very high probability of 95 percent — these most likely from secondary causalities — and at the low end of the estimate of 5 percent, we get ... upwards of 1.87 million deaths in a city like New York City."

"What?" asked Sumner. "Oh my God. That high?"

"Yes, sir," said Lin. "But that would mean that the mission would have to be protracted over a five-year period. That is highly unlikely, if not impossible. There is little chance things would last that long, sir."

"And the 95 percent? How long would we have to employ this tactic?"

"It would be over within weeks, sir — probably less than three."

"I think that is much more likely," said Sumner. "But we'll still see some deaths?"

"Yes, sir. You will always have the errant incident that will result in someone dying. That's part of any military operation, sir."

Sumner looked at Shea, and her face told him all that he needed. "Then, based on that, the mission is a go."

"Yes, sir," said Johnny, with Lin nodding in the split screen view.

"I will alert General Moore. He will coordinate the deployment with your lab. We obtained the funding from the Canadians who agreed to split the price tag of the venture as long as we share the technology with them. It was a deal I was more than willing to accept. So, I think that's all we need, Johnny – Lin. Do you have any other questions?"

"No, sir. I think this is a good decision, Mr. President," said Johnny, nodding affirmatively.

"I hope you're right, you two. If not, history will not be kind to any of us," said the president.

"Shea, you'll call the Canadian prime minister and get back with the colonel. I would expect the entire mission to be completed within the next forty-eight hours, correct?"

"Yes, Mr. President. That's what Johnny said."

"Okay. Let me know if you need anything. Keep me apprised," his words stiff and anxious.

After the screen went black, Sumner turned to his attorney general. "Shea you need to contact the prime minister and inform him of the decision. We'll need his satellites to activate the hardware." After Shea informed MacDonald, his only words were, "So, when will the fireworks start?"

"Our assets are on the ground and ready. They will attack strategic areas where USSA forces are congregated. It's risky, but imperative. The show will begin by fifteen hundred hours tomorrow, when the heat of the sun will accelerate the polymer reactions."

"I will inform our Aeronautical Administration," answered the prime minister. "Good luck," he added, before hanging up.

Good luck is right, she thought. If this didn't work, the Canadians and the Republic would both be demonized throughout the world as exacerbating the situation and potentially causing more loss of life if things did not work as planned. That was always the bar by which other countries assessed the situation. Even one lost life was unfortunate – even for the most noble of causes. However, at the same time, Shea often wondered how the West would have won WWII with that type of mentality. The socialists would have shut down the war effort after the loss of the thirteen hundred men at Pearl Harbor. She was convinced they would have called for capitulation to prevent further losses of life.

However, when evil is not addressed and defeated, far more death and destruction results. France and others found that to be true after the Germans invaded in 1940. By the time that struggle was over, 20 million Chinese, 25 million Soviets, 6 million Poles, 1 million Slavs, 8 million Germans, 3 million Japanese, 500 thousand French, 400 thousand Austrians, 400 thousand British, and 400 thousand Americans had perished. Nearly 3 percent of the world's population had been annihilated.

***

Even as details of the new mission were being finalized, the battles raged on.

Although air-to-ground missiles pummeled their army positions from above, the Republic had deployed between three and five of Lin's "domes" in the field. These energy fields created giant protective umbrellas over nearly an entire division of men on the front lines. These mobile dome units were capable of protecting groups of soldiers from small and medium caliber armaments. As a result, most of the bombs that hit the energy shield exploded, rather than striking their intended targets. Although a very few of the missiles were able to penetrate the shield at a sharp angle, these burned up once they were inside the dome due to the tremendous friction exerted on their casings.

The results on the battlefield were stunning. The forces of the USSA could not penetrate the shields, and their offensive weapons became useless. Sheltered by the domes, the divisions of Republic troops and their mechanized counterparts were impregnable. Most turned the shields on and off at will, protecting themselves when fighters or bombers were overhead and then removing the dome when firing their own weapons at the enemy's assets. Quickly, the casualty numbers turned against the Administration with virtually no dead or injured on the side of the Republic, compared with tens of thousands of USSA soldiers. With yet another remarkable technological advantage, the Republic had all but castrated the forces of their enemy. Without a remarkable turn of events, the outlook for Ratner looked bleak.

"Colonel, this mission is a go. I repeat, Operation Invincible is a go," said General Moore from his command center just outside of Cheyenne.

After transmitting the order codes, the general watched on the large screen at the front of the center to see if the satellites would react as planned and designed. It wasn't long before the orbs received their instructions from the ground and relayed these to the hovering, saucer-like discs scattered over various targets within the USSA. Using miniaturized cloaking devices Johnny had created, the discs had not been detected by USSA radar.

For the general, the scenes on screen were vicarious; for those looking up into the azure blueness above them, the scene was real. Within seconds, bright orange lines cut ribbons through the atmosphere, stretching from just above the troposphere down to the surface. At first, they looked like misfiring fireworks that had gone off before their scheduled after-dark ignition. However, the scope and magnitude of the releases proved something far more deliberate.

General Moore watched his aerial feed that showed the radiant, tangerine plumes spreading from a single apex in a cascading fashion that looked like Niagara Falls on a warm summer evening when the colored spot lights illuminated them from both the USSA and Canada. Yet, instead of dampening the effort, this spectacle only heightened the mood in Cheyenne. One by one, the domes appeared – first in

Sitting Bull City, and then elsewhere throughout the USSA: New York City, Boston, Philadelphia, Chicago, Newport, Pittsburgh, Detroit, Minneapolis, Los Angeles, San Diego, San Francisco, Seattle and other areas marked by military installations.

Although civilian airports in the affected USSA areas had been warned in advance to halt travel on that day, most of these airports had ignored the admonitions. As a result, two commercial airlines – one lifting off from Dulles International, near Sitting Bull City, DC, and another, preparing for a landing at New York City's LaGuardia, slammed directly into the nearly clear wall of charged particles. At first, the dome's outer wall absorbed the intruding projectiles, but they did not burst. Then, as the skins of the aircraft reached thousands of degrees Celsius, the planes disintegrated, leaving only a showering of fire and wreckage.

All told, there were twenty-four domes planned, but only twenty-one materialized. The three that failed resulted from misalignment of the injector saucer over the city. The domes had begun to form, but failed to generate enough energy to cover the entire parabolic area. One of the three failures was problematic.

"What's happening?" Shea asked, finally making the call into Command Headquarters.

General Moore answered. "Overall, it's a success. We have twenty-one fully functioning domes of the twenty-four launched." Shea waited for the bad news, if any was to come. "Of the three that did not succeed, we only have a problem with one."

"Which one was that? Sitting Bull City?"

"No. That one is working well. The dome extends over almost all of the one-mile square of the District." "Then which one?"

"Schriever Air Force Base in Colorado Springs," said the general.

"Sh*t," said Shea. "Why didn't it work?"

"We don't know. But what we do know is that the bases there pose a very serious threat to us. They are only a few hundred kilometers south of Cheyenne."

"Yes, I know."

"We're trying to realign the saucer plate overhead, but now that they've been alerted to the tactic, they're sending up Hawkeyes to find the mechanism. I think they'll be able to locate it within a few hours unless we can reset the cloaking device on it. Otherwise, it will be a sitting duck for their F-39 fighters."

"What are your recommendations, general?" Shea asked.

"We're putting those together now, Madam Attorney General. We should have them for you within the next twenty minutes. We have already planned for this contingency, but we don't know how the USSA will react."

"By the time they react, I hope it will be too late, general. Let's go over those recommendations within the next ten minutes. I'll arrange a conference call with the president."

Shea hung up and got Sumner on the line, filling him in on what had occurred and what had not.

"Call me when the general gets a hold of you," said the president.

Exactly seven minutes later, Shea received the general's call.

"There hasn't been any sign of a response yet," he told the attorney general. "We've been monitoring all channels and all visuals. We really don't know what's going on. However, I have ordered the mobilization of two phaser brigades to the southern border with Colorado. We've also launched two new AWAC's units to circle overhead covering 160 thousand square miles within the state."

"Thank you general. I'll let the president know."

"Oh, and ma'am."

"Yes, general?"

"If I were the president, I would buckle in for a ferocious response from the First Citizen. She has a reputation of not liking to be cornered, if you know what I mean."

"I do, general. But are you suggesting that she might go nuclear?"

"That's always a possibility, ma'am. You just never know." answered Moore.

*****

CH 67 Secret Meeting

Without the ability to move goods in or out of the strategic targets now encased by the domes, the USSA had no choice but to dig tunnels underground which took time and money. Even with these access points, the effectiveness of the military bases, government offices, manufacturing plants, and distribution hubs was limited. Unless they found a way to destroy the domes, they could not survive as an industrial economy. The USSA was paralyzed.

Life under the domes was becoming more and more desperate. It had been five days, but the psychological effect of being "trapped" beneath an impenetrable bubble was more than some could bear. Runs on grocery stores began almost immediately, and virtually everything on the shelves was taken. When supplies began to run low, madness ensued. Mobs began smashing store windows and what remained was looted and ransacked. For those few cars still using gasoline, the lines were long, even though there was nowhere to go. Water was in short supply. Where water reclamation plants were inside the dome, the pumps lacked electricity and no water flowed through the pipes. Power transmission lines from nuclear power reactors located in remote areas of the countryside were severed by the gelatinous, translucent material that imprisoned everyone beneath it. Coal had been outlawed decades earlier. Wind and solar could not generate the amount of electricity needed, so nuclear had been the only option. But ultimately, the lack of power, food, gasoline and water had set-off a wave of civil unrest that no one had could have conceived.

"What do you want from me?" shouted Holt. "I know we've got problems.

"Screw the *Constitution*," said General White. "It hasn't mattered before. Why do you think it matters now?"

"If it doesn't matter, what are we left with?" asked Holt, looking around at the small group that had gathered in secret at the Ministry of State.

Lytel looked at Holt over the top of his glasses. "Anarchy," he said calmly. "That's what we're left with. You can expect total and utter chaos. The rule of law is quickly sinking, as we've seen, and the First Citizen is too preoccupied with her vengeance against the Canadians and the Republic to address her significant domestic problems."

"What do we do?" asked Sara Miller Emerson.

"I don't see we have much other choice but to surrender," answered Wanda Fredrick of the CIA.

"Surrender? Really?" said Holt, shocked by the suggestion. "The First Citizen would never allow that."

"My generals certainly wouldn't want to see that," said General White. "They would strongly oppose any effort to surrender to a bunch of half-weight rebels."

Lytel turned to White with scorn and said, "General, I don't think your generals are in any position to dictate the course of things – not when they've performed so poorly on the battlefield."

White did not take kindly to those remarks, and anger sparked inside her. "Excuse me, minister," she shot back rather savagely, "but since when is State the referee that decides who is doing their job and who isn't? I seem to recall that you failed to arrange a peace with Canada several weeks ago. Isn't that right?"

"Listen!" said Holt, stepping in. "We aren't going to get anywhere with this infighting. Sara, you're the one who wanted this meeting. What do you think we should do?"

Sara Miller Emerson rose from her seat. "Clancy is right. We're not going to get anywhere if we don't stick together and think things through. Our First Citizen is not addressing the anarchy in the streets under the domes. They have effectively cutoff all our ability to wage war against them. I suspect they will now implement a siege mentality – that is, just wait us out. Eventually, we will run out of necessary supplies and will be forced to surrender."

"What about knocking out those devices that are creating the domes over the cities? Can't we fire some cruise missiles at them from offshore subs to destroy them?" asked Conrad James, minister of Justice.

General White shook her head. "The Administration mothballed all our attack submarines five years ago. We don't have that capability anymore."

"What about missiles from other bases that aren't being impounded? Can't something be shot at them?"

"We've tried," said White, "but the Republic has mounted their phaser technology on satellites overhead. They shoot down anything that gets close to them. We've shot forty-three SRAAMs and three ASATs or anti-satellite missiles – all failed to hit the devices. We've also lost two F-39s in the process. The Canadian satellites are targeting our incoming too quickly and destroying them before they can even get close to their targets."

"So, we need a diplomatic solution," said Lytel.

"The First Citizen would not hear of it," said Holt. "I'm sure of that."

"Then perhaps the generals must take matters into their own hands," said White, pushing out her chin and straightening her back. "We're not afraid of a fight, no matter where it comes from."

"You're speaking of a *coup-d'etat* then?" asked Emerson, shaking her head.

"Yes," said White. "If it takes that to save the country,"

"Now, now," said Holt, trying to calm things. "I think we can find another way out of this. We just need to think about it. I do think that a diplomatic solution may be in order. George, do you think you could talk with the First Citizen about negotiating a peace with the Republic?"

"Me? Why me?"

"Because you're the minister of State, I suppose," said Holt. "Isn't that what you do?"
"Yes, but ..."

"Like I said," said White, "no one is willing to stand up to her. Everyone's afraid. Well, I'll tell you right here that the military is not afraid of anyone. We can and will stand up for what's right. I think things have gotten out of hand with the First Citizen. I don't believe she's thinking clearly anymore. Either we get her to understand that a different direction is needed, or the military is going to take control."

"I guess we should take that as a threat?" asked Lytel, staring at the general.

"No, it's what I like to call encouragement. You ministers need to work toward a civilian solution to this problem or we will come up with a military one."

*****

CH 68 Dealing with the Dome

Things were less calm at the White House. Although emergency communication lines had been reestablished, everything else was down. Power, which was generated outside the major metropolitan areas, had been severed as the domes had sliced through the huge power lines that were suspended from electric towers and that transferred their currents into the downtown areas. Water continued to flow through underground pipes, as did gas through the gas mains; however, since underground telephone lines had been abandoned and replaced by cell towers and satellites, all civilian communication was broken as electromagnetic waves from working cell towers became distorted passing through the plasma barrier. Unwilling to spend the money to reinforce these networks, the Administration had allowed them to go fallow and face threats from EMP pulses or other external dangers. It was true that some governmental com lines and hardened military segments were operating despite the wholesale collapse of everything else. Yet, even some of these high-frequency transmissions couldn't pierce the plasma-like mass that locked them into their newly-constructed prisons.

"What the hell happened?" shouted First Citizen Ratner, coming unglued. "Why weren't you able to get this out of Johnny when we were dealing with the phaser issue?" she asked her chief of staff. "We had no idea they had this capability!"

"No, we ..." began Holt before being cutoff.

"I want General White, all the armed force commanders and their second in commands in my office within the hour," she demanded.

As her Holt left her office, Ratner made another call. "Get me my senior ministers," she commanded.

By 14:30 all the military leaders and their seconds had arrived and waited to be ushered into Ratner's office. Not knowing what to make of the new and bizarre weapon that had been unleashed upon so many cities and military bases throughout the USSA, they scrambled to piece together any intelligence they could so they could present some options.

"The meeting will be held in the Ministerial Cabinet Room next door," said Chief of Staff Holt motioning toward the heavy, dark double doors. "But, you'll need to leave your side-arms out here," he added, pointing to the long table pushed up against the wall behind him and to his right.

The heads of the Army, Navy, Air Force, Marines, as well as the ministers from the Federal Bureau of Domestic Policing, the International Policing Agency, and the State Ministry, were all in attendance. They took their seats around the large, oval mahogany table which had once graced the grand house of Stalin's in Sochi, Russia, during the second World War. It had seen its share of atrocities over the years.

There was little talking amongst the leaders as they awaited the First Citizen. The apprehension was thick, but it only grew worse as the minute hand on the old-fashioned clock on the wall marched around the face. Ten, then fifteen minutes passed. The generals and ministers began to grow impatient, but had become accustomed to such power-plays by the First Citizen.

Finally, after forty-five minutes, the doors of the room opened, and Ratner entered with the minister of Domestic Policing attached to her hip.

"Be seated gentlemen," she said sitting down in the plush, comfortable chair that had been pulled out for her at the head of the table. "What I want to know is what is happening and how can we stop it!" she said sternly, her nostrils flared with rage. Folding her hands in front of her, she tightened her interlocking fingers enough to show the whites of her knuckles. Her jaw was taunt and rigid, unwilling or unable to release its tension. With a formidable scowl, she stared menacingly at all who were present. "Let's start with you, General White. What are we seeing here?"

"Well, based on what I've gotten from scientists who've been involved in research of this type of phenomena, I'd say it's a plasma dome. We didn't know it was physically possible to create one with current technology, even though it's been theoretically possible in the laboratories for years."

"A plasma dome. And why didn't we know anything about this project?"

"I don't know, First Citizen. They were very successful at keeping it a secret. No one we had on the inside of their operation or the government had any idea it was being actively pursued," said White.

"So, what are we going to do about it? I need to mobilize my forces. I need to do something! Right now, no one can get in or out unless they go through the Metro Underground for god's sake, and I'll be damned if I will *ever* use *that* proletarian means of transportation!"

No one in the room was willing to brave speaking up, as they feared being skewered by their commander in chief. There was silence, an awkward quiet that seeped deep inside everybody seated at the table.

"No one?" Ratner spewed. "There's *no one* here who has a god-damned idea of what to do?"

Everyone around the table stared at each other, hoping someone would come to the rescue and pop the straining bubble – the bulging, building pressure in the room. Yet, no one did.

"First Citizen, if I may," said White, trying to soften the blow. "We need time to analyze the makeup of this dome. We don't know what the energy type is and we are trying to locate the sources of each. The Republic may also be using some sort of cloaking device to conceal the machines that are creating these domes. However, we should be able to pinpoint the source quickly given time."

"Cloaking device? There is yet another invention that we knew nothing about? How is this possible? All of you in this room are responsible for this failure! All of you! You have failed miserably, and now it's going to be up to me to again find a way out of it. You're all worthless!"

Then just as suddenly as her outburst had come on, her face softened and a calm came over her. "Okay, then," she said before smiling and nodding to Clancy Holt who immediately left the room. Within moments, several armed marines came into the room carrying ornate boxes, made of rock-hard ebony wood with fine carvings around the edges. The soldiers positioned themselves around the table at intervals between the generals and their seconds in command.

"Each general is to open the box and choose a 'motivator,'" she said.

At that, the sturdy, sober, dispassionate sergeants opened their boxes, revealing one shiny chrome, short-barrel revolver and one black, ten-clip nine-millimeter pistol.

"If you fail to pick one, someone else in this room will be told to select one – to be used as commanded," Ratner said.

At that, all the generals chose a pistol and clutched it in their hand, wondering what was coming next. Although most had fought on the battlefield, this was something different. It struck a fear in them that was as unsettling and disturbing as anything they'd seen in war.

"Now, I want each second in command to take the other weapon from the case," said Ratner, with an eerie gleam in her eye.

As their seconds-in-command lifted their pistols or revolvers from the boxes, the generals looked quizzically at each other and their subordinates, wondering what was coming next.

Ratner straightened herself, pulling back her shoulders and folding her arms. "I want each of you to raise your weapon and point them at the head of the person to your right. If you fail to do this, the marine standing behind you has been ordered to shoot you. Do you understand?"

At those words, the marine sergeants in the room drew their weapons and pointed them at those sitting around the table.

"Only one of the two weapons in the box contained one bullet in the chamber. The other is empty. The revolvers will rotate into position to fire the bullet either on the first pull or the second. Of course the pistols, if they contain a bullet, will fire immediately. If anyone fails to discharge their weapon when instructed, then the marines will fire. Their guns are fully loaded, I assure you."

The marines cocked their pistols and stood at the ready.

"I don't understand," said one of the generals in a panic. "You haven't given us enough time to tell you …"

"Shut up!" Ratner shouted. "I asked for solutions – you gave me none. I asked for competent commanders – you've given me none that I can see. We're here because of your incompetence! My military and intelligence services are supposed to protect us from this sort of thing. You've failed! Miserably failed! I can't accept such stupidity!"

She sat back in her chair, obvious to all that she was enjoying the exercise. She took sadistic pleasure in witnessing the tortured faces writhe in intensity and angst. It was the rawness, the base animalism that drew her to this sort of ritual. Bloodthirsty and monstrous, her craving for such a macabre and destructive staging was only growing stronger. Watching her troops dying by the thousands on the battlefield had been vicarious and had only whetted her appetite. She now craved something more.

The tension in the room was so thick it couldn't be measured. Everyone feared for their lives, yet to break for the door or to refuse whatever she ordered meant instant death.

"On the count of three, all second-in-command are to fire their weapons into the temples of their commanding generals. Do you understand me? Those who fail to pull your triggers will receive a bullet directly into the back of your brain." The marines placed the muzzles of their guns at the brain stem of each second.

'This is madness!" said General White. "This must stop!"

Ratner smiled and looked at her Joint Chiefs chairman. "You're right, general. It will stop." The First Citizen rose, pulling something out from under the table. She pointed the pistol at the general's head and fired. The shot went straight through the general's forehead, sending a spray of brains, tissue and pieces of boney skull onto the back of her chair and the wall behind her. She immediately slumped forward, hitting what was left of her head on the table as blood poured down her neck onto the table's surface and pooled in front of her.

"Does anyone else have any questions?" said Ratner, menacingly pointing her gun at the group. "Good, then we shall continue."

"What do you want from us?" shouted another general.

"Nothing," the First Citizen answered. "You've already given, and you've failed."

She counted, "One, two, ..." then she paused to prolong the agony before finishing, "... three!"

Shots rang out throughout the chamber, and general's heads fell with a heavy thud onto the conference room table, carnage splattered everywhere from the massive wounds suffered at the point-blank firings. The blood began to flow toward the edge of the table and began dripping off the edge onto the crocodile green carpeting.

The *aid de camps* held their pistols in stunned silence as to what they'd been forced to do or witness. One wretched all over the conference table. There were only two generals still alive with their colonels; they sat petrified with the certainty of what was coming next.

"I see two lieutenant colonels are cowards. Well, we'll have to address that now," said Ratner, nodding to the marines behind them.

"I thought you said one of the two guns was empty?" asked one of the two colonels. "But they all fired?"

Ratner grinned. "I lied." Then, she motioned to the marines. "Shoot them both and their generals too."

Again, shots rang out and the two generals fell as did one of the colonels. However, one shot was not fired. One of the marines pointed his pistol at Ratner. "This is for you, Madam," he said.

But before he could get off the shot, a marine standing beside him pulled his trigger, firing into his chest and killing him instantly.

Although a fleeting show of terror came over Ratner's face, it quickly dissipated with the shooting of the rogue marine. The corners of Ratner's mouth inverted, turning from trepidation to pleasure as she watched the marine's body fall like an anchor weight to the floor.

"You see," she said, "you can't win against me. There is no way. So, what I command is that the seconds go back and figure out what to do against this new threat from the Republic. You're bosses failed me.

Make sure you don't. If you show any signs of treason or abandoning your position – you will be shot.

Do you understand?"

Others around the table nodded robotically, almost unconscious with fear.

"Good," she said smiling as widely and broadly as ever. She was relishing this – in full command and in full domination over all.

Suddenly, another shot rang out, reverberating through the room. It was as unexpected as all else had been, but coming after everyone thought the nightmare was over made it that much more surreal.

Ratner turned and looked at her chief of staff who stood pointing a gun at her, its muzzle still hot from the exiting bullet. Her eyes were opened wide with shock and surprise as she glanced at her unforeseen assailant. "Clancy? You?" she moaned, before collapsing to the floor.

A single red spot in the middle of her white blouse began to grow, turning more of the silk a rich, glossy red. It was over. It was done. The monster was dead.

The Chief of Staff looked on as stunned as did the rest of the military and ministerial staff. But none offered any reprisal or resistance to what had just happened. Holt, expecting to be shot outright waited too. Yet, nothing more happened. He too realized it was over.

*****

CH 69 General Simmons

After the death of the First Citizen, a vacuum formed in the government. There had been a deputy First Citizen, but he had died and the position never replaced. General White whom Ratner had shot and killed had been the next in line after the deputy First Citizen. Ironically, Chief of Staff Chancy Holt, was implicated as next in line; however, it was not clear from the new *Constitution 2.0*. No action was initiated against Holt, although the District Court of Columbia had been brought in to evaluate it.

In the meantime, details of the massacre inside the White House were slowly leaking out. Although the bodies and any news of the deaths of the First Citizen and other military leaders were buried in the darkness of night, those spotting an opportunity were seizing the chance. And for General Simmons, the former vice chairman of the Joint Chiefs, now Chairman, the temptation was just too great.

Amidst the chaos within the Administration and the infighting that was starting between ministers, Simmons contacted his generals and colonels at the Pentagon. "It is time to act," he had told them. "If you want another bloodbath like what happened in the White House, then do nothing. If you want to survive, then you'll follow my orders."

Within forty-eight hours of the shootings, Simmons ordered the marines to take control of every government ministry building. All ministers were arrested, as were their senior staffs. Only when the deputy minister signed a pledge of allegiance to Central Command and General Simmons, were the staff allowed back into their offices.

Simmons also placed trusted officers within each ministry to monitor minister meetings. The Red Shirts were redeployed to watch all senior officials and their comings and goings. Anything suspicious was communicated to the general and his staff. Usually, the person was immediately arrested and put in prison without a hearing or due process.

Military troops sequestered under the domes were sent out to battle rioters and given orders to "shoot to kill." Martial law was imposed, and the looting and other crime stopped almost immediately.

Simmons had Clancy Hold arrested too, just to be sure there was no challenge to his rule and power. He suspended the *Constitution 2.0* and declared that a new Constitution was needed – this one tentatively designated as *Constitution 3.0*. However, he remained ambiguous on when it would be crafted. He also stated his intention to hold open and free elections; yet, again the dates were uncertain.

All of this was sudden and shocking. And none of it resulted in any marked improvement for the citizens living in the nightmare of the USSA. The domes were still sealing off anything trying to get in or out and life was a struggle for all not powerful enough to have connections to food, clothing and electricity.

***

The general stood on the Ratner Porch of the White House, where the Truman Porch had once stood. He had ordered people to be brought in to the South Lawn so that pictures of the "throngs" could be streamed around the world showing the people's love for the general and their approval of his takeover.

Waving to the crowd and wearing his army-blue ASU or army service uniform with the row upon row of ribbons pinned across his left breast pocket, Simmons smiled effortlessly soaking in the pageantry and illusion that had been created for his benefit. Having taken off his blue beret, he stood with his bald pate shining in the diffused sunlight overhead. Beside him were several marines with rifles, standing at attention, but clearly there to underscore the fact that the military was now in charge.

"Thank you," said the general, feigning an attempt to quiet the group. He let them go on for several more minutes, chanting "Simmons is Our Savior! … Simmons is Our Savior!" which had been started by Simmons's staff.

"Thank you, again," said Simmons now trying to calm the masses. "As a great people, we have been through hard times and good times, but each time we have surfaced victorious and stronger. Now is a time when we face hardship – one caused by the ruinous policies and actions of a government that has ruled under the guise of wisdom, justice and equality for all. Corrupt officials drafted a constitution that gave them all the power over you. It was unjust, and it needs to be thrown out and rewritten so you, the people, can voice yourselves once again.

"I am here to take care you … my people. I am here to make sure the enemy is defeated! And I am here before you this day to declare that I will do just that!" he shouted, as the people erupted with cheers, whistles and shouts.

"But, we must use our power to destroy the Republic and those domes overhead. Power is not love. Power is what we use to crush our enemies. Power only comes from the end of a long rifle, and I am not afraid to use it! We must use war to abolish war; we must use the gun to get rid of the gun; we must use violence to eliminate violence. This is the only way!"

When the next round of applause died down, he continued. "We can only impose our system on others as far as our armies can reach. We can only use our armies if we have a leader willing to use all the forces at his disposal to destroy the enemy.

"However, you must be willing to fight too. As the great leader, Joseph Stalin once said, 'Those who want to live, let them fight, and those who do not want to fight in this world of eternal struggle do not deserve to live.' I agree with him. That's why every able-bodied man, woman and child must take up arms against the Republic. Once the domes are defeated, we will conscribe every person between the ages of sixteen and fifty into military service. You will be given a gun, a knife, or a pitchfork, but you will be expected to stand on the front line and charge the enemy when ordered. You will be required to stand by your nation and commit to our freedom. You must defend the Motherland."

This time the applause was more tepid, reflecting concern over the words being spoken.

"However, this is a great day. It is the dawn of the Third Empire of the America. Gone are the days of the USA and the USSA. Now is the rise of the New Third Reich of the American States. And I shall be your guide. With me and my generals, we will destroy the domes, defeat the Republic and crush the Canadian accomplices. We will restore America to its greatness. We will make the New Third Reich a model for the rest of the world. Everyone will be rich; everyone will have whatever they need. No one will need to work and toil. We will conquer other lands and other peoples to expand our nation and the empire. We will bring the rest of the world to its knees!"

As his speech went on, the more vitriolic and combative it became. By the end, he was fully bellicose, challenging every world leader and threatening to invade with the technology he claimed he had from the Republic already. Stating that his scientists had already developed the same weaponry as the Republic, he shouted that he would crush anyone who defied him – anyone who challenged the power and capability of the Third Reich.

The speech went on for two hours before the crowd began to grow restless. Although that didn't stop Simmons immediately, he soon realized he was losing his audience.

"And in conclusion, we are a great people. We have a superior culture and a superior civilization. It is our way that will conquer all others. And if they do not go quietly, we will use our forces to make them comply. We must never feel the threat of a foreign nation again!"

*****

PART VI – THE END IS NEAR

CH 70 Trust Factor

Even with martial law imposed, there were other problems under the domes. The bubbles were acting like greenhouses, and the temperatures inside were rising. Those with medical conditions were flooding the hospitals seeking relief. Cooling centers were setup in high schools where air conditioning was permitted. Local governments were warning people to stay inside and avoid the stale, putrid air, but for most -- without jobs and without decent places to live -- the air inside was just as bad as that outside.

Those with money and influence were able to get out through the tunnels, which were quickly turned into profit centers for the government. Charging thousands of United Coins for a one-way trip, the cities' transit authorities began gouging its patrons. Most couldn't afford it. Those that could got out to catch a plane to a second or third home in Europe or some other country. Even the political elite found refuge in their summer cottages or second home retreats.

As most of the government-run manufacturing plants were near the cities and under the domes, they weren't able to produce anything. Without power and workers able to get to work, all manufacturing and assembly efforts stopped. Nothing was being produced. There was nothing on the shelves and the prices of everything were skyrocketing. Lines of people waiting to get staples were long and getting longer by the day. In some cases, mothers and fathers waited in queues overnight to be first to see if the store had stocked anything during the midnight hours. Most times they left empty handed and increasingly desperate.

When cities began announcing the stoppage of trash pickup and sewage treatment as well as the closure of public hospitals and schools, the point of criticality had been reached. Disease began to spread in the more densely populated areas, particularly dysentery, were widespread. In two areas – Philadelphia and Detroit – there were outbreaks of tuberculosis. Some feared that cholera had struck in two other areas.

As a result, life under the bubbles was quickly becoming a living hell. And, unless something was done, thousands of lives would be lost.

***

President Sumner weighed the options. He didn't want to be responsible for such casualties, especially not civilians. Such losses hadn't been seen since WWII, when in a single night, eighteen thousand Brits lost their lives to German bombers in London. The same happened in the German town of Dresden -- that time under a curtain of charges dropped from British Lancaster bombers. He never dreamed that the leadership of the USSA would let it go as long as it had. Over a month had gone by, and still the White House had refused to respond to requests for a negotiated peace deal.

When Shea received the call from Thorne, she was puzzled by it. "So, why are you calling me?" she asked him.

"I still have contacts at the White House and in Congress, and I thought they may come in useful. I didn't want to reach out without the expressed approval from the president. I wanted to discuss the idea with you first." His approach was less direct and forward than she'd experienced from him in the past. It was odd, and it made her wonder.

"Are you asking for my approval? Because you don't need that, you know. It's the president that you need to talk to."

"Yes, but there are a lot of things going on in Washington – a lot of gossip and speculation. It's hard to know what's really going on, you know?"

"Well, we have heard that Ratner might really *be* dead. That she may have killed most of her top-line generals, and that there's an all-out fight going on over who will take over. Some say that the new guy ... what's his name?"

"General Simmons?"

"Yes, Simmons. He's come out and said he's in charge, but no one knows for sure. What do you know?"

"I think you've got it right, except that Ratner is dead and that Simmons has usurped control. But if I can contact a few people, I can confirm this."

"Confirming it is all well and good, but how is that going to get us to a negotiated settlement? We were expecting them to sue for peace weeks ago. Can't they see that their people are dying?"

"It doesn't matter to them. They and their families are safe. They have their homes, their fortunes and their concubines. That's all they need," said Thorne. "It's lousy, but it's true. You know it's true."

Shea sat back and listened to his voice – the intonation and rhythm. She watched his facial expressions and body movements. *He's telling me the truth,* she thought to herself. *Perhaps he has changed.* It was then that she realized something else. With all the trials and tribulations they had all gone through, she also saw another truth – that they had all changed. No longer was she the innocent, naïve business owner fighting with her husband for their little company. No longer was Sumner responsible to only a few thousand of his district's constituents. No longer was Thorne directing a self-serving behemoth of a company that only served the interests of corrupt politicians and greedy board members. No, these were different times and each of them had assumed larger roles within the promise of a new country – and perhaps within a new world.

Leaning forward and smiling, Shea said, "You know Thorne, I do. I know a lot more than I did just two years ago." She paused, comfortable in where she was and what she had to do. "I will speak to the president about this. He will call you with his answer."

Thorne hung up. Shea sat with a black screen in front of her. She knew they had to do something about the suffering in the USSA, but she also worried about doing something that would fuel the rise of this unknown general to power. If anyone would know what to do, she felt confident it would be Sumner. *He had led them this far – he would be able to bring them the rest of the way,* she thought. At least she prayed he would.

The red phone rang on the president's desk, and he immediately picked up. "Shea? What is it? Is everything alright?"

"I got a call from Thorne, JC. He confirmed what we thought about the death of Ratner and the takeover by a General Simmons. He said he still has contacts on the Hill and at the White House and believes he may be able to talk to people there to get us a negotiated peace settlement."

"I see," said Sumner, a frown coming over his face. He looked down at a short glass of Scotch that he was apparently nursing. "What do you think?"

"Are you still worried about trusting him?" she asked

"Are you?" the president asked, with an unusually quick response.

"I've thought about that question for a long time. I'm sure we all thought there was a chance that Thorne was the mole in the Underground Network, right? I'm sure you were thinking that the entire time."

"I have to admit that it crossed my mind, as I told you before. But I always thought that he wasn't the problem. For some reason I felt we could trust him. I told you that too."

"Yes, you did. Do you still feel that way?" Shea asked.

"I believe I do, Shea. I can't put my finger on it, but I think we can trust him."

"I agree. I feel that more strongly now than I ever have."

"What changed your mind then?"

"I don't know. It's just a feeling … just like you have."

"Do we want to risk the survival of a nation on a hunch?" asked Sumner.

"Which nation, JC – ours or theirs?"

"Both, I guess."

"I think we have to. There are thousands of people who could perish if we don't strike a peace deal soon," said Shea. "We could just lift the domes."

"Yes, but then how many more of our service men and women will die in battle? The war will continue. You know that. If this general seizes power or has seized power, then peace through him doesn't seem promising," said Sumner.

"No. If what Thorne says is right, then no. He is just a new dictator in a long line of dictators. Whether he is more-or-less barbaric, it's hard to say," said Sumner.

"So, how do we handle this? What do we want Thorne to do?" Shea asked.

"I have an idea," said Sumner.

"I knew you would, JC. That's why I called you."

Sumner spent the next hour going over what he wanted done. In the end, Shea understood.

"Are you okay with this?" he asked her. "I wish I was there with you right now."

"I'm fine. It will be hard, but we'll make it happen."

"I know we will," said the president.

Shea put the phone down and shook her head. It was her turn to pick-up a short cordial glass and pluck three ice cubes from the small refrigerator-freezer unit she kept in her office. Unscrewing the cap on the Petronas Gold bottle, she poured three fingers into her glass and swirled it around twice before taking a sip. Not satisfied, she lifted the glass and emptied the rest into her mouth, wincing as the biting sting of the tequila scorched her throat.

I just hope he's right, she thought.

*****

CH 71 Last Feast

As soon as he took power, General Simmons disbanded Congress and unilaterally declared the second USSA *Constitution 2.0* null and void and vowed to create a new version 3.0. Using the uprisings and riots as the pretext, he issued the military forces to seize control and place the nation – which was mostly under the siege of the domes – also under martial law. All rights of *habeas corpus* were suspended, and all travel restricted. His enemies were summarily rounded up and disappeared and anyone who voiced disagreement was arrested and imprisoned. Even Clancy Holt, the chief of staff under First Citizen Ratner, was taken into Red Shirt custody shortly after Simmons's power play and thrown into prison. Like his predecessor, the general was ruthless and sadistic. He felt it important that the murderer of the First Citizen be punished for the sake of his own credibility with the people.

"You *will* sign the confession," Simmons had said to Clancy Holt, who was in chains in his jail cell. Not having had food or water for days, Holt was corybantic for sustenance.

His eyes puffy from the repeated beatings he'd taken, Holt resisted, wiping the grimy black soot from his eyes and beard. "I will confess only to killing a despot. That is all."

Simmons shook his head. "I tell you what. You and I will have dinner together. It will be a nice feast. You will regain your strength and feel much better about yourself and about what we can do together. If you sign the confession, then I will, as the new Guide of the Reich, grant you amnesty. I think that's a wonderful deal – especially for someone who has murdered the leader of a great nation such as ours. Don't you think?"

Holt said nothing, only staring at Simmons with contempt.

Still, even without his declaration, Holt was cleaned, dressed and brought before the general into the glittering gold State Dining Room at the White House. There he found Simmons already seated, alone and indulging in a glass of Riesling and a dozen raw, Chesapeake Bay Virginia oysters served on ice.

"Ah, Mr. Holt. It is so nice of you to join me. I thought I was going to have to eat alone tonight. Please, pull up a chair."

The room was vast, but there was only one, large round table in the middle of the room. Big enough to serve at least a dozen guests comfortably, the table had a grand floral arrangement in the center with lavender orchids and bird-of-paradise flowers of rose and soft pink. Over the years, more and more gold had been added to the room making it, what many considered, the gaudiest room in Washington.

Holt walked over to the table, and although his ankles had been released of their bondage, his wrists were tightly bound by clear, plastic handcuffs.

"Oh, I don't think we'll be needing those tonight, do you?" asked Simmons, smiling as he popped another small, gray squishy oyster into to his mouth.

Before Holt was a series of plates, glasses and layers of silverware. He was familiar with how each was to be used, but he was not in the mood to go through each course as was intended. "I'm not going to play your game, general," said Holt, glancing coldly at his uniformed host who sat at the head of the table.

The general chuckled and finished off another oyster, motioning to one of the waiters to bring him another platter. "I didn't figure you would, Mr. Holt – at least not voluntarily. So, we will have to do this the hard way, I expect."

Holt braced for the worst.

"I want you to write down what you really think of me and what I'm trying to do," said the general, raising a finger to the attendant. The server rushed over to the table with a stack of blank papers and an old-fashioned ink pen for Holt to write what he wished.

Holt looked down at the white sheets and shook his mangy, disheveled head. "I don't understand. You want me to write what I really think about you and your little *coup*?"

"Precisely. Write whatever you wish to say about me. We will make sure that it is published. I welcome criticism of my words and actions. I've always been straight-forward about that. Please! Go ahead and provide us with your critique."

Skeptically, Holt took the pen and began writing furiously. He went on – page after page – and turned over each as he completed it. In the end, he had twenty-two pages of narrative when he lowered his pen. "There," he said, "I think that about covers it."

"Good," said the general. "Now, will you please sign it?"

Holt signed the last piece of paper and handed all of them back to the general.

Simmons smiled, his eyes flaming like he'd just won the lottery. "Wonderful," he said. "I think this is definitely something we can work with, don't you boys? I presume you got all that?"

There were words coming from others in a room elsewhere in the mansion, broadcast over speakers imbedded in the ceiling. "Yes, Guide, we have captured it all on film. Now all we have to do is complete our side of things. It should be finished within a few minutes."

Holt stared at the general with a look of surprise and concern. "I don't understand. What are they doing?" he asked.

"You will see soon enough," said the general. "Now, why don't we have a bite to eat?"

Food was brought out and placed before the general and Holt – platters heaping with roasted vegetables, poached salmon, quail, dozens of imported cheeses and fresh baked breads, as well as another bottle of the general's Riesling wine. Holt did not take anything and watched the general instead. Finally, the general smiled, and laughed. "Oh, I can tell you don't trust me, is that it? You want to see if I will eat anything before you take a bite. Well fine, I will help myself just to show you that I am a man of my word."

Simmons helped himself to some of each of the dishes that were on the table and began eating with abandon, not caring what was on his plate or what he had placed in his mouth. Comfortable with the safety of the food, Holt began tasting the morsels too – at first hesitantly, then with more gusto given that he hadn't eaten a solid meal in more than four days.

"That's good," said Simmons. "So, what is your strongest complaint about me? You and I have not worked together much. I can't imagine you would be against what I have to offer this country."

Holt wiped his mouth with his napkin and placed it back in his lap. "From those who know you well, they'd say your egomaniacal ... that you have a penchant for power and control and that you have complete disdain and disregard for rules other than the ones you create for others."

Simmons took another sip of his wine goblet and placed it back on the white, linen tablecloth. "Perhaps," he answered without yielding an expression one way or the other. "But perhaps too, they're just jealous. Don't you think that's a possibility?"

Holt took another bite of the quail. "Yes, but with that many people voicing their antipathy, there's something more there. Don't you agree?"

"No, of course not. I only want what's best for this country and my people."

"Your people? Really?"

"Yes, that's the way it's been. From Fourier to Ratner, they've taken a paternal or maternal approach to the people they serve," said Simmons.

"They didn't serve the people. The people served them, and you know it."

Simmons smiled. "If that's the way you look at it, then so be it," he said.

It was only moments later when Holt began to feel unwell. His stomach began to seize up on him and he became feverishly hot.

"You don't look well, Mr. Holt. Is everything alright?" asked Simmons without emotion.

"I ... I'm not sure," Holt said. Then, the energy began to drain from him. His face grew pallid and ghostly.

"I'm sorry to hear that," said the general looking over at someone who was just now coming into the room. "This is my colleague, Mr. Huan Yang. He's worked with the Chinese government for years and is on loan from the government there to help me with my transition."

Holt's eyes were glazing over and his head was spinning. "Chinese? Why are the ..." but his voice trailed off as he steadied himself, his hands on the table for support.

"The Premier there was kind enough to assist me with accessing their military technology and weapons systems. He's also providing critical information on biological and chemical weapons. But what was most intriguing to me was the toxins that they've created. Traceless and absolute – they have the ability to kill a man within minutes without anyone knowing the cause. Are you saying you don't feel well, Mr. Holt?"

Holt nodded, his head lowered and his arms, hands and fingers beginning to tremble.

"But before you go, you must see this," said Simmons.

The young man, allegedly Mr. Yang, held a small black device in the palm of his hand. He turned it on and a stream of light flashed from it, creating a 3-D holographic image in front of them. It was an image of Holt sitting at the table writing on pieces of paper as he had just minutes earlier. Then the picture changed to show Holt holding up his paper. The camera angle zoomed in and showed the details – a full confession of his act of murdering the First Citizen and accepting the punishment of death by execution. His signature was at the bottom of the page.

"But ... but I didn't do anything of the sort!" yelled Holt with a final burst of energy. "That's a lie!"

"Yes, it is. But you won't be around to defend it, will you. The paper you signed also holds me and my government harmless for anything that may happen to you. Convenient, isn't it?"

Holt's face began to pucker and turn red. His eyes began to cloud before he grabbed his throat. "Can't breathe," he murmured, a shock in his eyes that he'd been duped. "But how?" he gasped.

"You didn't have any oysters, did you? What a shame. I guess I forgot to offer them to you. After all they were laced with an antidote serum to prevent what's happening to you. Your airways will constrict and you will suffocate, just as if you're underwater drowning. You won't be able to find any air, and ... well ... that will be that. Too bad, though. We do have your confession and other footage that we created having your endorsement of me as the new First Citizen, or as I prefer, the New Guide. So long, Mr. Holt, and thank you for your service."

Holt gagged, struggling to breathe as Simmons got up from the table and walked away. Within minutes, Holt's body sat rigid and cooling in the chair, face down in his plate of roasted vegetables and poached salmon.

*****

CH 72 Abandoned and Alone

"This just in," said a newscaster in a rare break during a broadcast. "We have information that there is a mob of over one hundred fifty thousand that is marching with clubs and knives down Pennsylvania Avenue toward the White House. Domestic police have mobilized, but we're told there are only about three hundred police available to defend the grounds at 1600 Pennsylvania Avenue."

The general sat and watched the screen as the protestors descended on his palace. The ruddiness of his cheeks left his face, and the creases in his face became more pronounced. "We have to stop them," he said with resoluteness. "Where is the city's police commissioner? I want him on the line immediately!"

"He's vacationing in the Caribbean, sir. We don't have a number for him," said the general's assistant.

"Then get me the mayor. Get her on the line right now!"

"Yes, sir," said the major, and with that, he left the room and made a hasty retreat to the underground tunnel that linked the White House with a network that would take them out of the city. Several other staff members pulled over from the Pentagon also accompanied the major who had learned of the uprising earlier and had made plans to escape if and when it came to that.

Minutes passed as the crowd grew louder and more riotous, passing the Treasury building and making the jog in front of the white mansion. Police stood with shields and rifles ready to fire on the crowd when they reached the perimeter of the north lawn. When the multitude reached the White House gate, the police lowered their rifles and aimed them at the front line of the march.

"Destroy the domes!" the group chanted, along with "Give us back the USA!"

Finally, Simmons got the Washington, D.C. mayor on the phone. "Shanice, what are you doing to protect me?" he asked.

"We're doing all we can general. Things are a little tight in the city since you at the federal level cut our funding in half." There was a sharpness to her tone that was intended to be accusatory and crude.

"Am I safe?" asked the general, beginning to exude trepidation for the first time.

"Of course, your excellency," said Shanice sarcastically. "You don't need to worry. We got your back."

But worry, he did. As he looked out the White House windows, he saw the crowd growing by the thousands, encircling the grounds – both north and south.

"I want your police to open fire on them now! If you don't, then I'll bring in my army and have them do it."

"Yes, sir. We will do what we can. If you feel you need to bring in extra troops, then by all means, I encourage you to do that."

Simmons hung up on her. He was getting nowhere and he realized it. His second call was to the Pentagon. After reaching the new Chairman of the Joint Chiefs, he said in a threatening voice, "You'd better get your Apaches over here from Andrews as soon as possible. And I want tanks here too. Bring them in from Fort Belvoir pronto!"

"Yes, sir. I'll make the arrangements on the Apaches, but sir, we can't get the tanks in because of the dome. Fort Belvoir is outside the perimeter, sir."

"I don't care if they have to blast their way through the dome! Get them here!" yelled the general.

"Yes sir."

"Hold your fire," said the deputy police chief outside, watching events unfold.

They did – until the first protestor began scaling the fence line – then a single shot rang out, striking the protestor in the chest and pushing him back off the fence into a heap on the outside.

"I said, hold your fire!" shouted the deputy, aiming his pistol at the officer who had fired the shot.

Watching their compatriot bleed out on the sidewalk, the crowd stormed the front gates, pushing them over and rushing up the circular drive just across from Lafayette Park. The three hundred Washington policemen and those security guards inside held their fire. Instead of protecting the house and grounds, they raised only threatened the protestors if they came near them, then they merely motioned them away with the barrel of their rifles.

It only took minutes before they were pounding down the front door to the White House. Quickly, the guards inside were overrun, barraged by flying rocks and sticks. The general ran toward the emergency exit tunnel, pushing aside everyone else who was also starting to make their way to the underground escape. "Get out of my way!" he screamed. He got as far as the second series of doors when a guard pulled out his pistol. "I said, get out of my way!" shouted the general, indignant that anyone would prevent him from leaving.

"I don't think so," said the soldier calmly.

"I'll have you shot," said Simmons, curtly.

The soldier smiled. "No, sir. I'm having you shot." He fired one bullet that struck the general in the head. Simmons quickly collapsed like a glass house in an earthquake. It was done.

The crowd soon broke out the windows and pushed in from other entrances on the property, making their way down the hallowed halls of the White House. There they ripped priceless oil paintings from the walls, took statues, china, silverware, and small pieces of furniture as they ransacked the place. Nearly three hundred years of artifacts and cultural heritage was stripped barren. Even the silk plants were taken from their vases to beautify someone else's home.

The police outside stood helpless as the looters ran out of the building, clutching their treasures and many of the nation's. There was little they could do or even wished to do. There was no point in shooting those involved. They understood the rage. It was something they too had felt for years and suppressed. Now the valve had been opened and the anger had come pouring out. It was ugly and vane, not unlike the scene from Jackson's first inauguration in 1829.

Thorne watched on a private video feed as the events unfolded.

"What's happening?" asked Sumner, from his home in Cheyenne.

"It's all going according to plan, sir. The people are rising up against their dictator. I don't know what's happened to him at this point."

"And the mayor?"

"She played her part perfectly, sir. I wired half the money yesterday, all gold-backed securities. We'll need to send the rest today."

"And the police chief?"

"Same for him."

"Alright. So, all we need to do is contact the Speaker of the House and Senate Majority Leader to arrange a peace settlement. Will you handle this?"

"Yes, sir. I'd be happy to," said Thorne.

Thorne turned off the president's image and sat back to soak in the scenes of chaos and destruction that had befallen the once-great nation's capital. Yet, instead of feeling remorse or regret, he felt good. *This signifies a new beginning for the country – the entire country,* he thought, sitting back in his leather chair in the White House. *One I hope this time won't devolve back into a socialist or totalitarian state as had the other one. It had all started out so promising in 1787, and it had fulfilled nearly all of those promises until the early twenty-first century. Now,* he hoped, *it could be reconstituted, and once again regain its greatness and sense of importance within the larger citizenry of the world.* Ultimately, he prayed for a better future for everyone. But, only time would tell.

*****

CH 73 Negotiation

The USSA, or what was left of it, was in tatters. In less than two decades, the reconstituted country under first a socialist and then a totalitarian flag, had collapsed. It was yet another example confirming the failure of the socialist experiment. It was not the first time it had happened, nor would it be the last.

The mantra expressed by most of the socialists still in power was expected. *If only we had had more time, more money, more control, more ...* From the executive branch's ministers to those still in Congress, the feeling was much the same. Even with the cold reality their cities in flames, their economy collapsed, their government paralyzed, and their dreams were broken, they still held on to the belief that it was someone else's fault or that there were external factors present — not the flawed concepts imbedded within the construct of socialism.

"What are we supposed to do now?" asked Preston Brooks, the spineless House Speaker. He had supported whatever measures the First Citizens had presented him over the years. He was a survivor — blowing with the wind whichever way was most advantageous for him. But now, without a leader in the White House, he was uncertain which way to blow. What he feared most was being on the wrong side when the music stopped.

"Calm down," said Thorne, able to reach the speaker through backchannels he was so accustomed to navigating when he'd been the CEO of EG, Inc. "There is a way out of this. We both know that."

"First Ratner, now Simmons! I just don't know what's happening to this country. We can't leave — imprisoned by this damned dome over us. The people are rioting and destroying everything in town. They say next they'll turn their sights on the Capitol. We have the DC police, as well as the Hill police, but that didn't seem to save Simmons, did it?"

"I understand," said Thorne, trying to play diplomat. "Now, Preston, you have to work with me on this. I'm close to the president here in Cheyenne. He'll lift the domes as soon as he gets a signed surrender from Washington. Since there is no First Citizen, that job now falls to Congress. You and the Senate Majority Leader are going to have to bring your people around to approving something."

From the video call, Thorne could see Brooks staring at him in utter disbelief. "Are you mad?" asked the speaker. "There's no way in hell, we will turn ourselves over to the vultures of capitalism! We can't sacrifice everything we've so hard to achieve."

"What have you achieved?" asked Thorne, sarcastically. "You've got a nation that's disintegrating before your very eyes! Have you looked out the window lately? Your system has failed you. Your leaders have failed you. And most importantly, your ideology – that which you have been lured into worshiping -- has failed you. I realize you don't want to admit that, but it is the cold reality of where you are."

"It doesn't matter what I believe in and what I don't. You'll cart us off to prisons and forced labor camps. Our children will be enslaved by the factory owners to do manual labor, working in chains for cents on the dollar. That's the way it was during the last century. We won't allow that to come back."

"Tell me Preston. How are your children faring now?"

"Well, now, fine, of course. I'm talking about in the future."

"Alright. Then tell me how the children of families in your district are faring," said Thorne, challenging him.

"What do you mean?" asked Brooks somewhat confused.

"The people in your district ... you know ... the people you represent in Congress. How are the children of those families doing right now?"

"I ... I don't know. How the hell should I know?"

"If you don't know, then who does? Aren't you supposed to represent them in government. Isn't that the nature of a republic – for you to know what your people want -- need? How can the system work if you aren't connected with your own people?"

"We don't have a republic anymore, Thorne. Come on. That's an antiquated idea. That democracy crap doesn't work. That's the ideology that was tried and failed – not socialism."

"And this thing called socialism has? What is the state of your nation right now? How has it improved since you went down the path of socialism? Hell, more like Marxism."

"It's because of you -- the ATLAS Republic, as you call yourselves. It has nothing to do with what we did or didn't do," said the speaker.

"Really? The USSA was in steep decline long before the Republic decided to split from the Union. Your domestic national output *declined* every year during the last twenty-eight years. The average disposable income of your citizenry also declined, as did the standard of living. Unemployment rose by a factor of three during Fourier's and Ratner's time in office, and the cost of products rose by nearly 33% per year during their reigns. Is that what you call progress?"

"Yeah, but poverty went down. And so did the hatred of minorities, gays, and others not in the majority."

"Wrong! Poverty increased by 51%, with more welfare, food stamps, and other government handouts being funneled to the slackers from the people who actually worked. The country got poorer and more divided – not better. You believe what you want to believe, but if you want the truth, you have to look at the cold, hard facts."

"You're lying," said Brooks, crossing his arms in defiance.

"I have the numbers right here," said Thorne, turning to his computer display. "Computer, give me the GDP, unemployment, average standard of living, interest rates, and government debt numbers for the USSA for the last five years."

"Retrieving information," said the computer voice. Within seconds, she responded again. "Here is the information you requested."

The computer read the numbers, and each reflected exactly what Thorne had been saying.

"You're taking your information from a propaganda database of the Republic. Those aren't the real numbers."

"Dig into the numbers on your end. Go to the Ministry of Facts and Statistics and see what it says. You'll have to claw your way through the BS, however, and understand the detail. If you're willing to spend the time and do this, you'll understand the picture much more clearly," said Thorne.

"This isn't right," Brooks said. "These aren't the numbers we got up on the Hill."

"No, they're the real numbers," said Thorne. "The numbers you got were the same ones given to all the media outlets through all the ministries so they could coordinate their stories. It was all propaganda. Once you analyze things, you'll see that the numbers don't add up."

Brooks sat shaking his head in stunned silence. "I don't know what to believe any more," he said.

"You should believe what makes sense to you. If it doesn't make sense, then it's not real."

"What do you mean by that?"

"What do you see all around you? Do you see prosperity, optimism, a burgeoning middle class, a lot of working opportunities for people, and a general feeling of hope for the future?"

"Of course, not! You've put us under a dome, for god's sake!"

"Before that, Preston. Before the dome ever appeared – did you see any of those things?"

"It's because of the ..."

"Don't say it's because of the Republic. You know that's not the case. You and I both know that the USSA was in freefall well before the split. You've been around long enough to see it. People had checked out of the system long before then. When more than fifty percent of the public went on the government dole, it began to unravel. Voters elected people like you whom they knew would vote to give them more 'free stuff.' They elected socialists who only wanted to increase taxes on those who were actually working and creating wealth so they could give it away to get votes from the rest of people -- people only too willing to take it.

"It's far easier to take than to earn. People caught on quickly to the concept of 'free stuff' as they have for centuries. If you don't have to work for something and you still get it, most people will just wait until it's handed to them. They don't care if others must work their asses off to make it happen. And those who make it happen and work long hours to do it, only to see it taken from them. That works for a short time until they say 'Why the hell should I bust my ass, when I don't get anything for it? Hell no! I'll sit on my ass like everyone else and let some other poor bastard work his off. It's the nature of man. It's always been that way."

"But it shouldn't be that way. We should all look after one another," said Brooks.

"Just like you've looked after the people in your district? You haven't done it either. You've only looked after yourself and your own. You haven't given a rat's ass about anybody in your district – not for years."

"That's not true! I always think about my people!"

Thorne shook his head. "Now you're lying to yourself, aren't you? I don't have to tell you that. You've made millions, if not billions, in Congress, haven't you?"

"No! I've only made what I'm worth! And I'm worth a whole lot to the people of this country."

"You are? Why?"

"Because without me, the people would make stupid decisions. They need me to make the right decisions for them. Most are uneducated – ignorant of how things work, ignorant of what is required, ignorant of the politics and the horse trading needed to achieve equality for all."

"If equality is your goal, then why is the divide between the Haves and Have Nots greater than ever before? Why is it that you are a Have and the common man is a Have Not? Where is the parity?" asked Thorne.

"We haven't had the money or time," answered Brook, reverting to the age-old argument that has no possibility of being proved or disproved.

"And even before the ATLAS Republic, the people were better off than they were during the twentieth century?"

"Absolutely. The society today is much fairer and kinder than back then."

"Not according to the statistics on the standard of living I quoted," said Thorne.

"Well, they are certainly better off now than they would have been under your capitalism," said Brook. "Look at the miserable conditions people suffered under during the nineteenth century. Many starved to death!"

"There's a difference between *laissez faire* capitalism and that which we practice which we call *moderated* capitalism. Our Republic was founded under the premise that government does play a role in managing commerce, albeit a small role. It just doesn't intrude into every aspect of it or our personal lives. We want government involvement to be limited to four areas. First, it must demand transparency in business dealings. This includes periodic financial reports and prohibitions on insider trading. There should be equal access to information. Second, the government must ensure and vehemently defend active competition, promoting it at every level. Third, the government must work to protect American business from *unfair* foreign dealings. Just as it is their obligation to protect us from foreign invasions and attacks, it is the government's responsibility to protect us from foreign governments that engage in monetary manipulation, raising tariffs, national subsidizing of industry, and other restrictive practices. There must be an even playing field worldwide in which companies compete. Fourth, the government should remain neutral in issues between labor and management. They should be allowed to reach mutually beneficial terms that are for the good of the workers and the company or resolve them in the courts. And, lastly, the government should not permit business to influence lawmakers on the Hill. If the federal government largely stays out of over-regulating business, there is no need for special interests to get a foothold into the halls of the Capitol."

"The only way to achieve that is through socialism. That is the only *fair* way. Socialistic principles have been proved to be true."

"Where? When? Tell me where and when?"

"Scandinavian countries during the late twentieth and early twenty-first centuries. They had the highest standard of living in the world during that time. They enjoyed all the fruits of socialism, from free health care to free retirement benefits. Cradle-to-grave, as they used to say. Their people were taken care of."

"I'm glad you raise that point. It is, of course, a fact that those countries had the highest tax rates in the world – over 60 percent. Their governments began providing generously to their people after 1970, offering free services – from education, healthcare, food distribution, etc. However, your facts are misplaced. Sweden's per capita income dropped it from fourth in the world in 1972 to fourteenth in 1993. The crushing load from unsustainable welfare payments plunged the country into deep debt. As their economies faltered, they lowered their tax rates and reined in welfare spending. Still, the damage was done. From 1970 to 2000 job growth was close to zero during the period, even though the population grew by 30 percent. There were no new entrants into the top one hundred firm listing after 1970.

"But it isn't that socialism created their wealth and happiness. Scandinavian countries had the highest standards of living dating back to the nineteenth century. That continued through the 1960s under capitalism. It was only in 1970 that they moved to socialism and saw their standards of living fall. Yet, unemployment was masked by not counting people on welfare or reclassified as 'students.' Even people who were actually employed were often on extended, government mandated, sabbaticals – all paid by struggling businesses.

"By 2024 their economies collapsed. Like Greece, Spain, Portugal, and Italy before them, they had no means to support their generous handouts. Without businesses, there were no taxes. Without growth, there was no revenue coming in. So, they borrowed, just as we did in the USA in the late twentieth and through to the present.

And where they now? Broke. Just as the United Coin currency is worthless, so is their currency. Just as the people of the USSA are starving, so are theirs. Yes, indeed, socialism works everywhere it's tried? The evidence for that is nonexistent."

Brook shook his head adamantly. *There must be another answer,* he asked himself. *Socialism can't be wrong! It just can't!* "I'm sorry, Thorne, I just can't accept that," he said flatly, his arms crossed in continued defiance.

"It's not that you can't, Preston. It's that you won't. And I understand. You aren't the only one. Most of you in Congress and all the Judiciary and Executive Branches at this point would agree with you. However, you are where you are. Your country is destroyed. Your economy is in shambles. Your people are in revolt. You're in a no-win position. You can't hold on to your power much longer. The people are speaking out finally. They will bring your government to its knees. It's happening already. Do you really want to face another French Revolution? Do you want to be brought to the guillotine bound and chained and drawn behind a cart pulled by mules?"

"No," said the speaker somberly.

"Then, it would be better to negotiate a peace now, then to suffer a bloody, violent fate under the hands of your rabid people later. Don't you agree?" asked Thorne.

Brooks looked down at the floor. He shook his head in agreement, but said nothing. "When and where can we meet to work out a settlement?" he asked.

Thorne made the call to President Sumner, who was hoping for the communication.

"Sumner here," the president answered, aware that Thorne was being patched through by his secretary.

"Mr. President, it's Thorne. I have spoken with the leaders of both houses of Congress and their Chief Justice. They have asked that I convey to you their intent to sue for peace and settle this long-outstanding disagreement over the secession of the Republic from the USSA. They realize they are not in a position to dictate terms, but wish to negotiate something that is fair to both sides of the conflict. Am I granted the authority to negotiate on your behalf?"

"Yes, but I will have Secretary Ingram fly to Virginia to meet with you and them. I trust they will be able to get out of town through the tunnels?"

"Yes. They will make that arrangement."

It was two days before the proper arrangement could be made and Ingram and Thorne arrived in Lynchburg and traveled the twenty minutes east to Evergreen, Virginia. The old Baptist church there was off the beaten path and looked like it had just gotten a new coat of red paint during the spring months. The parking lot was small and there were already several black cars parked within it. Ingram and Thorne had also come with a team of two other SUVs and their own vehicle. It was more visitors than the church had ever seen, even those who routinely attended services on Sundays at eleven o'clock.

The men in black suits got out first and scoured the area, including the inside of the church. It took them nearly twenty minutes to complete their inspection before coming to collect the senior members of Sumner's staff.

Thorne walked into through the double white doors of the church front and was immediately in the long, narrow nave. The ceilings were low, white and flat, although the church was divided into three sections – two for the congregation and the last, in front, for the sacristy. Arched windows lined both sides with alternating clear glass and stained glass windows. The pews were of light maple with scrolled backs and wooden trays placed in the pew backs where red hymnals and dog-eared bulletins from the previous Sunday's service awaited their next usage. In the front of the church were a matching maple podium emblazoned with a cross, a long, high table, draped with white, cotton cloth, and a baptismal font – octagonal in shape with a brass bowl at its center which seemed disproportionately large for the stand in which it sat. Pictures of the Virgin Mary and St. Peter hung from the wall behind, each recreations of artisan master paintings from the galleries of Florence and Rome. And in the center, was a simple, wooden cross, not more than five feet high and three feet wide, hanging from the ceiling by thin, black wires.

"Preston," said Thorne, waking up to greet the House Speaker. Brooks nodded, but did not smile. He quickly glanced at Ingram to size-up the person with whom he was to do verbal jousting. "This is Secretary Ingram from the State Department. He will be the primary in our discussions."

Brooks extended his hand and after a brief shake, introduced his team. "… and finally, this is our Minister of State, George Lytel, and the Majority Leader, Manuel Perez. They too will have a say in how these talks proceed. Well, if we are finished with the introductions, let's get started. There is a room downstairs that has been prepared for us. It's austere, but then again, we don't wish to linger too long anyway, now do we?"

It was an odd comment, but Thorne and Ingram followed the USSA delegation to the basement and pulled up chairs around a round table with a green tablecloth. There were water glasses provided and pads of paper, even though everyone pulled out their computers to take notes.

"I'd like to advise everyone that we will not permit any recording devices in these proceedings. These are considered secret and confidential in all respects. If anyone is found to leak any information from today's meeting or any future meetings, it will be grounds for the discontinuance of these talks. Does everyone understand?" asked Brooks, sternly. "… Good. Let us begin …"

There was no small talk. The two sides outlined their positions clearly and directly. First, Brooks started with what his expectations were for the meeting and the ultimate resolution to the conflict. Then, Ingram introduced the positions of the Republic. Each took several hours, as each man elaborated on why each point was essential to reaching a mutually agreeable solution. However, almost immediately, there was a problem.

"What do you want?" Brooks asked hesitantly.

"We want peace, of course, but it seems we want something more than you're suggesting," said Ingram.

"We wish peace as much as you do," Brooks said quickly. "We believe that a truce is in order and that you should lift the domes. We will then sign a peace agreement that will leave things *status quo*. We will then promise not to threaten the Republic and expect the same in return."

"No. I'm afraid there is some misunderstanding, then," said Ingram, looking grimly at his counterpart. "We're looking for your surrender."

"Surrender? You've got to be kidding me?" said Brooks. "Surrender?".

"Yes," said Ingram, point blank. "We are looking to reunite the Republic with the old USA, reconstituting the country we once knew. We believe we can again become the 'shining light on the hill' as President Ronald Reagan once said. We can again be the leader of the free world."

Brooks shook his head. "That's not going to happen," he said flatly.

Thorne looked at the others sitting at the table to gauge their reaction. There was a softness in their faces, unlike those pasted on their spokesperson. Even Lytel looked despondent with the position being taken. Tired and gaunt, it appeared that he had already been through multiple wars in his lifetime. Not willing to engage Thorne's glance, he only sighed.

"Minister Lytel," said Thorne, calling him out, "what do you think about this? We are wanting to bring the country back together and will not take any measures that will punish you or your leadership in any way. It would be foolish for us to take any such measures, especially if we're looking to unify the country. Don't you agree?"

"This is a proposal that we should review and assess," said Lytel diplomatically, careful not to contradict his colleague.

Brooks cast him an angry glance but then quickly recovered his decorum. "What I believe the minister is saying is ..."

"I know what the minister was saying, congressman. You don't need to clarify," said Ingram, inserting himself before Brooks could regain control.

"I will tell you now, that we won't surrender – under any terms," said Brooks adamantly.

"That's a shame, then," said Thorne. "Because our military is moving into position around your major cities and around your military bases as we speak. We can and will choose when, and if, to lift the domes at each location. If we have to, we will force a referendum within each location and let the people decide whether they wish to continue to live under the current conditions of the USSA or to surrender and join the Republic. We will make the referenda binding, and we will enforce the decisions by military interdiction if necessary."

"You wouldn't."

"We will," said Ingram without wavering.

Brooks was quiet. He believed the Republic would be satisfied with living in peaceful coexistence with its neighbor, the USSA. It would allow the USSA to elect a new leader and fend for itself, allowing the socialists to 'refine' their methods to improve on their experiment. He believed that ultimately the USSA would become strong again and dominate the continent, again able to either convince the Republic of its ignorant ways and convert to socialism or to be annexed quietly by the power of the USSA military machine. Two countries occupying one land would eventually become one country again – the Greater USSA.

"So, you're willing to continue the war?" asked Brooks.

"No. We don't have to. And, neither do you," said Ingram.

"But that means that we will become servants or worse slaves to you and the Republic."

"No. We want a re-unified country," said Thorne. "A country that once again is founded on the idea that man was created with inalienable rights … life, liberty and the pursuit of happiness. That the people decide how they are to be governed and that their duly elected representatives are looking out for their benefit and interests. That the people have a responsibility under this arrangement to do their part -- to work hard to achieve their own happiness rather than rely on the government to take from others in order to give to them. That the people are right to expect their protections under the old *Bill of Rights* will not be eroded by liberal policies and practices and that they can depend on the government to protect those rights. That the people can expect the government to stay out of their business and ensure their freedoms under the original First Amendment to the *US Constitution*. That the people have the right to say what they think and not be thrown into prison for expressing their beliefs. That the family and God play an important role in the lives of our citizens, and that everyone has the right to believe or not believe as they so choose. That everyone is created equal under God, and that it doesn't matter if you're black, white, brown, red, yellow, green or blue. It doesn't matter if you are gay, straight, semi-gay or semi-straight. It doesn't matter if you're a man, woman, trans, old, young, fat or skinny. That you don't get special treatment just because you're a minority of some type, form or manner. That you are judged based on what you *contribute* to society and the world we live in.

"We want a country where it isn't a crime to be successful or seek success. We want a place where it isn't a sin to be better than someone else at something and to be proud of our successes. We want a society where those who are most capable are promoted to the highest levels and are viewed as models to others – that merit and success is rewarded and recognized and where those things become things toward which everyone strives. That is how you achieve a better society for everyone – not just the rich and well off, but the poor and struggling as well. For it is those who succeed who provide opportunities for those who are trying to succeed.

"At the same time, we want a nation that is compassionate with those who are truly in need -- those not capable of taking care of themselves. Those who are mentally or physically challenged where they cannot meet the basic requirements to sustain themselves -- we should be a nation who will support them. We seek a country that encourages assistance, not from the government, but from independent and religious organizations. And, by using these entities, we will allow the people to determine which groups offer the best aid most efficiently and contribute to them, rather than the wasteful spending and corruption that goes on within the halls of government bureaucracies. Our citizens are very giving; they are some of the most charitable on the planet. They have supported the right causes for centuries and they will continue to do so.

"So, no, Congressman Brooks, we can't accept a mutual peace agreement. We wish to be the single, greatest country that others turn to for help. We wish to be the leader of the free world, as we were after World War II. We wish to be the land of opportunity for others around the globe – the one place of safe-haven for the huddled masses. We wish to be one again – a unified country that will reclaim its rightful place as the greatest on Earth."

"That's some speech, Mr. Thorne," said Lytel, impressed with what he'd heard.

"He means it," said Ingram. "We all do."

"If these are principles that you can live by, then I think we can strike a deal," said Thorne. "If not, then, we will continue to live as adversaries in a civil war that may continue on as the world's second Cold War."

Although it was becoming evident that there was clear disagreement between Brooks and the rest of his coterie, it was also apparent that Brooks was calling the shots.

"Neither of us wants the people under the domes to continue to die needlessly. However, our president stands resolute in his determination that we have to get this right or we will have further problems in the future. The Civil War was not properly resolved and it caused bitterness for generations. WWII, however, was ended in a way in which both Germany and Japan became allies of the Allied Powers within a short time after hostilities had ceased. That is what we want between us. Can we work toward that end?" Ingram was pleading, and Thorne thought his offering perhaps too weak. But only time would tell.

"We will consider your proposal," said Brooks, his face Stoic and unmoved. "You will hear back from us."

"When?" asked Ingram.

"When we have an answer," said Brooks. "Thank you for your time."

***

"How did it go?" asked Sumner on a later call with the two diplomats.

"I'm not sure, Mr. President," said Ingram. "Either we made progress or there is no hope. How is that for an answer?" *****

CH 74 Jericho

Days passed and there was no word from Brooks or the others from Sitting Bull City. Plans to disarm the domes was suspended until peace terms could be reached. Now well into its third month, the heat, and pollution inside the domes was becoming unbearable. People by the thousands were dying from the lack of food, clean water, disease and crime. Murder and other violence under the domes became rampant, as people devolved into desperate animals fighting amongst themselves for life-saving medicines and basic life-sustaining needs for food and water. As the temperatures rose, panic was also building from rumors that the cities would run out of oxygen soon.

All tunnels out from under the domes were guarded by the military to prevent utter chaos from ensuing. A black market had appeared too, where those with money and power were able to buy their way out by paying off corrupt policemen or political officials to allow them and their families to get out through those subterranean pathways. As for anyone else, they had their orders to 'shoot to kill' anyone trying to leave without proper credentials.

In Chicago, there were only three such tunnels going from the main downtown area of Chicago to freedom in the near suburbs. Even though the dome extended out into the waters of Lake Michigan, the power of the energy was strong enough to slice through the blue emulsion. Although somewhat diluted, its intensity still dissolved anyone trying to swim through it to safety on the other side. Hundreds died this way until word of the danger got around.

Of the tunnels, one was intended to transport passengers from downtown out to the O'Hare airfield via underground rail. Some sections of the tunnel system had been destroyed by the Republic Underground during the war, and they had not been rebuilt. The second tunnel, built to the south side of town, had never been completed. Money appropriated for the tunnel had been pocketed by the mayor and his cronies. It was typical of the hypocritical and callous treatment of the poor on the south side by city politicians who only wanted their votes and cared little for their wellbeing. These politicians had been the first to escape the squalor once the domes were in place, leaving the rest of the masses behind to suffer in silence. The third tunnel linked the Loop area downtown with the north shore where those in power lived. This one had been seized by the mayor and his council aldermen who were the iron-fisted strongmen of the city. Graft and corruption in city hall had no bounds, and the tunnel was the one whose access had been auctioned off to the highest bidders – even in times of greatest despair.

A battalion of Red Shirts was stationed at the single, remaining open tunnel to the north, keeping everyone else inside the doomed dome, and although that size of force – some three hundred troops -- might have been enough during the first few days of the calamity, it grew precariously insufficient as each day passed.

Jackson White and his family had lived on the south side of Chicago for his entire life. He was the third-generation White who had taken up residence in the small, white, two-bedroom home left him by his mother after she died. Now, his two kids, Alisha, age seven, and Tray, age nine, were sick with cholera. They feverishly needed help, but there was none available. The hospitals were dens of disease and now, and all were overflowing with patients waiting for assistance for days outside in parking lots or in the streets. Doctors had no medicines on hand as supplies had run out, and sanitation was worsening as access to clean water and electricity was scarce. Clinics that once dispensed pharmaceuticals were ransacked for their precious inventories and left in ruin or burned to the ground by mobs angry that their demands for medicine couldn't be met.

Jackson turned to his wife, Lakisha, and looked lost. "I don' know what to do no more," he said, forlornly. "We gotta get help for our kids. I've tried everywhere but everythin's closed. There ain't nothin' open. Nothin'!"

Lakisha began to sob. She knew her children needed help and they needed it quickly. But she felt as hopeless as her husband. "I dunno either, Jackson. What about the tunnel? I can sneak out through the tunnel somehow to get to a clinic on the outside."

Jackson waggled his head. "No! You're not doin' that. It's too dangerous. You know they's got armed soldiers there night and day! They shot fourteen dead yesterday tryin' to get through there!"

"But we gotta try, Jackson. We really gotta! I can't let my babies die!"

Jackson was quiet. He sat down, looking defeated, as if he were the one who had been sent to death row. Then, he got up and went to the back room. He came out moments later carrying a snub-nose, blue steel revolver.

"Where ya goin', Jackson?" she asked him with alarm, her eyes seized with terror and apprehension.

"You're not gonna ..."

"We gotta try," he answered with melancholy in his voice. "I gotta go get some medicine for our babies, mother," he said.

She again began crying, burying her face in her hands. Tears flowed down her fingers and into the long sleeves of her soiled, pink blouse.

Jackson left the small, cramped house they'd lived in together for ten years. He tucked the gun into this waist belt and headed off in the direction of the tunnel. Both he and his wife knew that there was a good chance he wouldn't return.

***

Jackson finally arrived at the north side of town. It took him almost the entire day to walk there. There were no taxis, buses, trains or other modes of transportation. Without electricity or fuel most everything was shut down. When he was still three blocks away from the opening, he encountered a milieu of people lining the streets. They were loud, and many were armed with rocks, fire bombs, and other make-shift weapons they had pulled from their homes. The stores on both sides of the streets had already been destroyed – ransacked weeks earlier by people trying to find staples to survive. The scene was apocalyptic – taken from the pages Revelations and the End of Times.

But now, while some people were chanting angrily, beating their fists into the air in defiance, others sat quietly, holding prayer beads and either mouthing prayers under their breaths or out-loud. Emotions were high, and frustration and fear palpable.

"We want our lives back, now!" one young man said. "Give us our freedom!"

The mob was boisterous and unruly, and as Jackson pushed his way toward the entrance of the tunnel, he could see that the Ministry of Unity had stationed additional troops – military grade soldiers -- at the gates. Men were sitting in tanks and armored personnel carriers with those perched on top wearing smart, computerized helmets and gripping the triggers of their .50 caliber machine guns. Other soldiers were on the ground, their visors lowered and their rifles aimed at the threatening crowd.

"Stay back!" shouted a commander using a megaphone. "We have orders to shoot if you advance any farther!" However, his threats seemed to do little to lower the agitation of the crowd or to persuade anyone to leave the scene peacefully. "I said, stay back! We *will* shoot. We are authorized to use deadly force to guard this station."

The crowd began throwing rocks at the soldiers who raised their shields to deflect the projectiles. However, as more and more rocks were hurled, the soldiers began pushing the citizens back with the butts of their rifles, slamming them into heads, abdomens, or anything else that got in the way. Several protestors went down, bleeding, and were trampled by the advancing military. Caring nothing for those upon whom they stomped with their shiny, black jackboots, the ground troops overran those in the crowd who were the most aggressive in stirring the violence.

Then, as events continued to escalate, several shots were fired. Several in the front line of the crowd fell to the pavement unmoving. The commander did nothing to stop his men, instead choosing to sit atop his Abrams tank and watch as things took their course.

"They're firing on us!" shouted one of the protestors, who began a hasty retreat.

But for every one of those who ran in fear, there were three others who were only refortified by the danger. These were the brave ones who stood their ground and continued to roar their insults and grievances at their oppressors.

Then, several black sedans pulled up, forcing the crowd to part in a wave. Additional troops surrounded the cars and held a perimeter while a family of four got out and hurried to the tunnel. The man was a city councilman, and with his wife and two children he presented his papers to the commander who looked at them carefully before motioning him on. The gate was opened only slightly – a gap only large enough for one person at a time to shuffle through before it started to close once again.

But before the cars could drive away, the horde of people exploded. It was spontaneous and unstoppable as thousands of rioters ran toward the battalion, throwing more rocks and Molotov cocktails, swinging knives, swords or whatever else they had to use and overwhelming the force that stood in their way. Overpowered, the soldiers fell back, and the commander shouted the order for the machine guns to open fire. Loud roars sounded as blasts of gunfire ripped through the streets, mowing down denizens by the hundreds. Still, the masses came. They were willing to sacrifice themselves for the sake of their children and their children's children. It was the only thing they had left and they were willing to die for it.

More tanks moved into place, and the scene became a bloodbath. Thousands fell. Even scores of the heavily armored military personnel were killed too. Still, thousands of other protestors made it through the phalanx of resistance and reached the high, black iron gates. The gates were no match for the force and weight of two thousand people pushing and jumping on it. In minutes, it collapsed, opening the way to hope and promise.

As soon as the gates fell, the Red Shirts and many of the military began withdrawing, unwilling to kill any more of their own. The battle was over. The people had finally won.

Seeing the others dash for the opening, Jackson ran with the rest of those hurtling through the passage, yelling and cursing the powers within the USSA. The group continued into the tunnel where they were surprised by another, smaller band of Red Shirts which at first began to fire upon the lightly armed crowd. But after seeing the light at the tunnel opening darken as thousands flooded the aperture, they decided to lay down their arms instead.

Jackson passed through the gate and followed on the heels of the growing stampede. Finally, he was only a few yards from the railway tracks that would carry him outside the dome to find the medicines he needed, when another burst of fire came his way. He ducked and watched as the woman next to him caught a bullet in the skull. She fell backwards dead. He flinched, shocked at the near miss, but he kept running, praying there wasn't another bullet engraved with his name.

But Fate had other plans. Mounting the train, Jackson and the others crammed into every square inch of space they could find, and when the locomotive's cars were full, it began pulling away from the station. Slowly at first and then with more speed, the engine plunged into the darkness – an irony not lost on Jackson and the others. Darkness, yes, but it was merely part of the storm before the calm. There would be light at the other end.

For Jackson, he was able to find a clinic outside the dome and procure the antibiotics he needed. And as he walked back through the front door of his house, his wife rushed to greet him, throwing her arms around his neck and holding on to him for fear she would lose him again – this time forever. He smiled at her and kissed her softly.

"I love you," she said to him tenderly.

"I know," he said lovingly back to her. "And now our babies are going to be okay too."

Word of the violence at the tunnel spread throughout the city. Trapped under the dome, people began marching *en masse* toward all the government buildings. They broke down the doors and ransacked all the offices, pushing over computer server racks, destroying monitors, breaking furniture, and trashing electronics equipment.

In Sitting Bull City, the mobs that had attacked the White House regathered to set other government ministries ablaze. While after the assault on 1600 Pennsylvania Avenue many of their members were hunted down and arrested or outright killed, the incident at the tunnel in Chicago gave them renewed confidence – even in the city that was once the seat of world power. As a result, congressmen and senators fled through many tunnels under the dome to the suburbs of Maryland and Virginia. They had privileged access to the dozen or so Metro tunnels that branched out in all directions from downtown and the National Mall. But after hearing of the bloodshed in Chicago, they knew their clock was ticking and the escape hatch for them would soon close. Those unlucky enough to be in their offices on Capitol

Hill when the citizen posse showed up found themselves dragged out into the streets and beaten unconscious. Several died. But just as with the White House incident, the DC police turned a blind eye to what was happening – instead standing down and letting things take their own course. The legislators who were not flogged were arrested and led away in handcuffs. And as they were dragged away to the Capitol Hill precinct station, they cried out about the injustice of it all.

House Speaker Brooks and others were among those arrested and thrown into the DC jails. There they screamed for their lawyers and demanded to be released as an officer of the nation. But, instead, the iron bars of the cell were slid closed and the on-duty deputy only snorted his contempt at them before shutting and locking the main door to their new, gray-cement accommodations.

George Lytel picked up the phone to call President Sumner to make a unilateral surrender of the entire nation. He knew he didn't have the constitutional authority, but on the other hand, there was no one else left who did. He clicked the button to get a dial tone – but there was none. He tried the emergency line, the red phone, but it too was out. The backup generators were out of fuel and there was no other way to get a message out through the dome's shield.

Just as Lytel tried again to make contact, a Molotov cocktail came crashing through the front window of his house in Georgetown, spreading gasoline all over the floor and instantly spreading the flame across the carpeting. Within seconds it began spreading up the walls and over the furniture. Lytel jumped from his comfortable chair and, picking up the glass of brandy he had poured only moments before, he ran from the house and down the short flight of stairs to the street. As he turned, he saw the flames leaping up in the windows, consuming everything he owned inside. There was a deadness inside him as the hopelessness and terror of a world he had helped create finally came home to his address. Like the others in power, he had been above the fray, above the pain, above the hardships. Now, he was being given a taste of the wretched medicine he had forced on others.

Lytel took a sip from his glass. He was calm in his defeat. As the brandy dribbled down his throat, it burned his insides, much like the fire that was enveloping the rest of what he had once owned. He again put the phone to his ear. It was a hardened line, and he hoped he would be able to reach someone in Cheyenne.

Finally, there was an answer.

"Hello, I'm trying to reach someone there – anyone there. I'm George Lytel, the Minister of State for the USSA. I believe I am the lone, senior member of the Ratner Administration and Congress – perhaps the only one left to be able to make contact with someone in authority in the Republic. Is there anyone there with whom I can talk?"

"Yes," returned the voice. "I believe there is. May I ask what is the nature of the call?"

"I need to speak with someone about suing for peace. The USSA wishes to surrender. Is there anyone there with whom I may discuss this?"

"Me," said the voice.

"And who might *you* be?"

"President Sumner," came the answer.

It was over. The nightmare had finally ended.

*****

CH 75 Lifting the Domes

Shea walked into Johnny's barn, approaching him from behind and touching him on the shoulder. He jumped, as he'd had in his earphones piping music into his head while he worked on some new refinement to the phaser weaponry.

"Don't do that!" he said, trying to shrug it off.

"I came to tell you that we're almost there. Sumner got a call from the USSA. They're interested in a surrender," she explained, smiling.

"That's wonderful news!" said Johnny, breaking the first smile she'd seen in a long time. "Then no more GI's have to die on either side."

"Yes. Thank God. Now all you have to do is disarm the domes. How soon can you do that?"

"That's easy," said Johnny. He walked over to the console where there were scores of colored monitors and a few 3-D holograms of various domes, with full read-outs on their energy levels, pulsation frequencies, and other critical measurements. Lifting his arm, he thrust his hand toward a small red button in an obscure part of the cabinet. Without any label or other warning signs, it seemed to be just another switch – simple and innocuous. "All I have to do is push this," he said.

Shea looked at him with amazement. "What? It's just one little, red button? That's all it would take to turn off the domes and stop the war?"

"Yep. That's it," Johnny answered.

"What if someone accidently hit it and turned it off? Would all of them just shut down, just like that?"

"Yeah, pretty much. But you have to know the sequence to shut it down, not just hit the button," Johnny said.

"Sequence? I don't understand," Shea answered.

"It's an encoded key that only I know – something very deep, complex. Definitely an enigma in the world today."

"What is it?"

Johnny stiffened his lips and mouth and began his articulation. "Dot dot -- dash; then dot dot – dot dot dot; then dash dash dash – dot dot dot dash – dot – dot dash dot … that's all." Shea made a face at him. "Come on, Johnny. I'm not a computer. What does that mean?"

"It … is … over," he answered, slowly and deliberately.

Shea laughed. "Good one. So, what happens after that?"

"Well, in layman's terms, the disconnect switch will reverse the ionization of the plasma. Once the charge is reversed, the crystalline structure of the plasma will destabilize and begin to collapse. Gravity will do the rest."

"But will the plasma fall and hurt anyone?" asked Shea.

"No. The domes will … well … melt, I guess. The energy will be absorbed into the ground."

"What about contamination?"

"The plasma disappears almost instantly. There's no residue or anything else to worry about, if you're wondering."

"No, not really. As long as we don't have to sue you for polluting the land around our largest cities – I'm good." She laughed.

Johnny looked at her, but then got the joke and chuckled too.

"Okay, then," he said. "So, do you want me to …" and as he spoke he moved his hand toward the red button, "… push the button and shut it down now?"

"No! Not yet. Let me contact the president and see. We will let you know."

***

Shea knocked on Sumner's door. His office was quiet – something odd for the president of a nation that had overcome the odds to win a war against a superior foe. "JC? Are you here?" she asked, looking suspiciously around.

Sumner emerged from an adjoining room. He was still in his suit, but his red silk tie was pulled down and his upper button undone. He looked weary. It had been a long two years, and every minute of every hour of every day of that time showed prominently on his haggard face.

"Shea," he said with affection and a weak grin. "I think we've made it. We just received a written response to our demand for an unconditional surrender. Lytel has accepted the terms and we've made arrangements to sign a peace treaty." There was an attempt at a smile, but he was almost too worn out to manifest one.

Shea grabbed him, wrapping her thin, elegant arms around his chest and putting her head against him.

"Congratulations," she said softly. "You've done what only one other president was able to do – you and Abe."

"You're kind, but I'm not in the same class."

"You are to me. You are my hero," she said, cooing. She put her hand on his face and caressed it with her fingers. "You know, you're the most magnificent man I've ever known. You are the champion of freedom. You are the leader of the free world. You were the one – you are the one – who could pull this off. And you have."

"I had a lot of good help," he answered, now mustering a smile back at her.

"Can you pour me a whiskey?" she asked him.

"A whiskey? You never drink whiskey," he asked, puzzled.

"Well, I've been in Wyoming now for over two years. Don't you think it's time I drink whiskey?"

Sumner grinned. "Yeah, I guess I knew you'd be a cowgirl sooner or later."

Shea frowned. "Cowgirl? You're saying that about your attorney general?"

Sumner put his arms around her and began kissing her tenderly. "Yeah, you're my cowgirl, and I'm your cowboy. So what." It was corny, but it made her giggle.

She kissed him back, placing her arms around his neck. "Sumner, I don't know what I would have done without you being there for me. After Patrick, I mean Johnny, and all."

"I could say the same for you, Shea. After my wife died, I was devastated. You helped me pick up the pieces and put my life back together. I miss her, of course, and I always will. But, my heart is big enough for someone else. I know she would have been alright with it."

She planted her full, moist lips again on his, opening her mouth only slightly, and letting his tongue meet hers. They kissed deeply and passionately. It had been some time since they'd been with each other, and both needed it now more than ever.

Sumner ran his hands gently over her back and then to her breasts. Her eyes lit up, as if he'd found her secret switch. She smiled again and went back to kissing him hotly, wildly. As it heated up, he took her by the shoulders and pressed her down onto his desk, pushing away the papers and pens that were scattered across the surface. He reached for her blouse and began releasing the buttons, but by the third one, he merely pulled her blouse apart, letting the rest of the buttons fly off to find places in the carpet. She reached for his belt and unbuckled it, unlatching the catch on his trousers and unzipping his pants. She reached her thin, long fingers down his undershorts, where she found his crown jewels. He was already excited, and she could tell instantly that he was ready for her.

"I love you," he said to her, sweeping his hands over her nipples and then suckling on them ever-so gently.

She rolled her head back. The ardent emotions were flooding her consciousness all at once, overwhelming her senses. "I ... I ..." but she couldn't get it out. She was in the middle of a typhoon, and her mind was delirious with pleasure.

Sumner unzipped the back of Shea's skirt, and pulled it off with her panties. He could feel she was hot and moist and worked her toward a state of ecstasy. Together, they were one, giving each other the pleasure that each desired – craved – from one another. Their bodies too were joined as one, writhing and twisting – each movement only heightening the feelings of pleasure and love for one another.

It was their nirvana.

***

"Mr. President," said Oishi, calling Sumner on his intercom, "you have an urgent call from Thorne." Summer punched the button on the video screen and Thorne's face materialized; not far away, out of camera range and adjusting her skirt was Shea.

"What do you have for me, Thorne?" Sumner asked, situating himself at his desk.

"Sir," Thorne began, "Ingram and I met with Lytel in Evergreen, at the small church where we tried to negotiate with Brooks only a few weeks ago. We agreed on every point. The deal is signed, sir. We are at peace."

"Excellent, Thorne. Congratulations."

"We couldn't have done it without you, sir," said Thorne, tired but smiling.

"So, what are the details?"

"It's much like the Marshall Plan of WWII, sir. There is no punitive action in it, and they know that. We agree not to prosecute anyone for any war crimes or any other action taken by them. We will also not require restitution for the damage they've caused or the lives lost. They understand that we only wish to re-unite under a new country, a new USA – a nation based on democracy with capitalism as its foundation. They are willing to accept our constitution and have agreed to turn over their military command to you. But, they do insist on one thing, sir."

Sumner looked surprised. "And what's that?"

"They want the capital moved back to Sitting Bull City, sir. They don't wish to have the federal government in Cheyenne. Perhaps I was presumptuous, but I agreed. I didn't think you'd mind."

Sumner smiled. "I think that's fine, except for one point, Thorne. It must be renamed Washington, D.C. again. I won't settle for anything less."

"I don't think that will be a problem, sir," said Thorne.

"Is there anything else in the agreement that I should know about?" asked Sumner.

Thorne thought for a moment before answering. "There is one other thing, I think," he added.

"What's that?"

"Lytel actually said he was sorry for what had happened and wanted you to accept his apology on behalf of the people of the USSA."

Sumner smirked. "I accept, of course. But it isn't the people of the USSA who caused this calamity. It was the pinhead, social liberals who eventually morphed into totalitarian barbarians who did this. They are the ones who should apologize. And we will not exonerate them."

"Is that what you want me to convey to the minister?" asked Thorne.

Sumner thought for a moment, and then shook his head. "No, that wouldn't be appropriate. Just simply tell him that his apology was accepted. Would you do that?"

"Yes, sir. Consider it done."

*****

CH 76 Op Ed

Although the ATLAS Republic had won the war, the truth was that no one had. Both sides had suffered from death and destruction. If there were a winner, it was the spirit of democracy and the freedom of a once-great country, waiting to be reborn.

The headline in the *Republic Times* the next day read:

War is Over. Both Sides Sign Armistice.

But what was most insightful was the editorial page and a post from a regular contributor.

Is the Doctrine of Democracy Strong Enough to Prevail? by Silence Dogood

The war is over. The Republic of ATLAS has won. Totalitarianism has again been defeated. We are all again safe and content. Or are we?

History has not been kind to democratic institutions. Of course, the Greeks tried it beginning in the sixth century BC, with Licurgus and his first constitution called the Great Rhetra. The Romans also attempted the governing form from 509 B.C. when Lucius Junius Brutus took control from the Etruscans and setup the republic. It was from then until Julius Cesar usurped power and Octavian defeated Marc Antony and Cleopatra at Actium in 31 B.C. that the republic existed. England started down the road in 1215, when King John signed the Magna Carta under pressure from his noblemen, bestowing certain rights to the people and recognizing that the king was not divine after all.

Then there was the grand experiment with the United States of America in 1776 with its glorious separation from the chains of King George III, not realized completely until 1781, but cemented with the signing of the Constitution and its Bill of Rights in 1789. France's revolution in that year only overturned the monarchical rule of thirteen centuries, from Clovis I in 481 to King Louis XVI, which ended in a severed head. Other countries followed suit in one form or another throughout the nineteenth and twentieth centuries.

However, after World War II, many of these countries succumbed to human nature. No, the writer is not referring to generosity and munificence. He is referring to the basic, primal instincts that seize those who are in power, who then impress those predilections upon people who are not. In the ape society, the leader is referred to as the silverback – the one who commands authority and respect out of sheer power and cunning. The silverback is typically the eldest male ape of the clan – the one who's decisions and direction are unquestioned. In today's societies, the silverback may be male or female but is always the one whose rule is absolute.

But how does the silverback maintain that authority?

The lead ape can bully his opponents into obsequiousness. This lasts until the male leader ages to the point when a younger, stronger challenger usurps his power. It is inevitable. It is part of the society of apes. It is also part of the society of mankind.

Since the dawn of time, leaders of tribes, clans, and empires have arisen as those with the ability to outwit and out-muscle their opposition. So it is today.

Democracy is supposed to be virtuous. It is an ideal of what we believe society should be – what all societies should be. Yet, it is a veil that hides the true nature of man and often only offers a deceitful cloak under which that true nature of man may weave its malevolent web. Those societies, which have not evolved beyond a tribal status, cannot assimilate nor can they appreciate the benefits of a pure democracy. Lacking education and knowledge, they are easily manipulated by the tribal silverbacks and led unknowingly into a life of enslavement or servitude.

Is Democracy lasting or is it merely doomed to fall victim eventually to man's most basic instincts?

We have been through a terrible civil war. Although not as murderous as the one fought from 1861 to 1865, it has killed more than one hundred thousand of our finest young men and women. It was fought because the United States of America, which rose to power and strength between 1789 and 1941 and became the world's lone superpower until 2008, fell into the historic trap into which so many other countries have fallen victim—first socialism and then totalitarianism. America's core system of beliefs changed from personal pride and rugged individualism – our ability to work hard and rely on ourselves for our own successes and take responsibility for our own failures – to one of victimization and dependency. People no longer were responsible for their actions – they were mere victims of other people's actions or circumstances beyond their control. There was always someone else to blame – whether a murderer blaming an abusive father or a welfare cheat indicting a system of racism for her woes. As such, it was the obligation of government to fix all their problems – to cure the ills and to right the wrongs brought against society by these straw bogeymen.

Enter the role of big government. To this monster, these societal victims turned in droves. To this insatiable beast, comprised of individuals thirsty for power and riches, did the people put their trust and believe their problems would be solved. These elites, these beasts of ersatz intellect, had all the answers, the people were informed. "Trust us. We know what's best," they were told. "We will give you everything you need. We will make you happy. We will make the world a safe place for everyone, everywhere, all the time."

However, two little things corrupted those ideals. The first – money – only facilitates the second -

- power. And power is what both men and apes alike crave, whether they are silverbacks or First Citizens. The ability to force others to do what you wish them to do is what a cup of cool water is to a thirsty, hallucinating desert nomad or a gram of heroine is to an addict going through withdrawal.

But whereas the silverback rules by shear strength and power, the First Citizens of the USSA ruled by deceit and ruthlessness. The only thing keeping a dictator in power is the fear of his people, the power of his military, and the endless depths of his brutality.

Yet, the United States didn't devolve directly into a dictatorship. It first found a convenient escalator rooted in socialism to descend into the depths of humanity.

First, socialism provided a safety net for everyone. To pay for this, the USSA imposed usury tax rates on the productive workers of the nation. Therefore, a socialistic system requires unlimited amounts of other people's money to make it work. But when people stopped working because the tax rates were too high, funding for social programs dried up. The USSA then was forced to borrow more to maintain the inertia of the welfare movement. But as more people become unemployed, more welfare programs were needed by the socialists and the more money was spent. This required more and more borrowing until the country could no longer pay the interest on its debts. The cost of money skyrocketed as the risk of default grew – as neither the American people nor foreign banks believed the USSA would ever be able to pay its debts. As interest rates rose, fewer businesses could afford borrow to fund their businesses, so the economy flattened and then all but collapsed.

At first, the Administration tried to print money to pay its bills, but quickly, it only created rampant inflation. With more money in circulation, each bill was worth less than before. As the money's value declined, it took more bills to buy the same goods. As prices rose, people could no longer afford to buy those goods as their salaries or welfare payments could not rise quickly enough to stay ahead of the price increases. As purchases for the goods fell, production of those goods dropped. As that happened, factories laid-off workers. As people were laid off, they had no money to buy anything, which further reduced purchases and drove more plants to cut back. As people lost their jobs, they went on welfare and only increased the crushing burden of debt the government experienced to fund their food stamps and other giveaways. In the end, the economy plunged into deep depression and the government into a position of debt from which it could never hope to recover.

This is what happened in the old USSA.

But instead of changing course, the socialist Administration chose to double down. They declared that the reason their grand plans had failed was that they had not spent enough money and had not borrowed and taxed enough to save the country. As one of the oldest tricks in the book, this illogic can never be proved. One can always assert that their failure came from not doing, spending, taxing, repressing and oppressing enough. Had the civil war with the Republic not occurred, the USSA would have been forced to devalue its currency or reissue United Coins as United Dollars, a new denomination, to buy more time. However, without the ability to borrow or generate tax revenue, the government would not have been able to continue its welfare programs or, ultimately, continue at all.

But socialism is more than about money. It is fundamentally about control. Some control leads to more and more control – over people's lives and over their possessions. At first the rights sacrificed are small; however, as the malignancy spreads and control becomes an obsession, more civil rights are surrendered. In the beginning such relinquishment goes unnoticed; however, as momentum builds, the train of socialism becomes almost impossible to stop.

After civil liberties, the socialist beast seeks the very possessions of its victims. When the USSA government took control of businesses and property they controlled the entire economy. Unable to react to rapidly-changing markets, the government ministries created shortages of products that people wanted and needed as well as surpluses of things they didn't. Centralized planning as a model can never respond as rapidly as a free market to meet the needs of consumers. Consequently, unrest followed as society reacted to the long lines and empty shelves. In response to the signs of violence in the streets, the government tightened its grip on society to avoid social unrest. Eventually, the Red Shirts and military were brought to bear as a force to suppress the masses and keep them in their places. There could be no more threats to the leaders and their power – none could be tolerated.

At that point, that society drifted into totalitarianism – a form of government ruled by a dictatorial regime intent upon sustaining its power by all available means.

Consolidating power was the quickest way for Angel Ratner to secure her position as First Citizen. With the rest of the country imploding, she gathered her power from anyone who would yield it, and she found willing victims. First it was the media, which abdicated its responsibility of independent reporting years earlier, then the Congress and the courts. The states were a bit harder to bully, but passage of acts by Congress and the eventual nullification and redrafting of the Constitution solved that problem. As for the courts, they had been willing accomplices for many years – facilitating the takeover of society by enabling the socialist Left to get their way and achieve their ends. For them, like all on the Left, the ends justified the means. For years, university law schools had been pliant with hiring left-leaning law professors, along with the rest of their liberal faculty members. Indoctrinated in school, law students were eager to employ their trade to defend the liberal agenda. Once on the bench, they continued to support the righting of perceived injustices, particularly when it increased their own power and that of the Administration.

But the economy had become more than just a commerce of goods – it had also become one of information. And since information is power, control over that critical cog became paramount.

Consequently, those in power wished to manipulate information for their own benefit. It had been done throughout the ages and had been found to be a successful ploy. By rewriting history in the schools and inculcating these revisionist thoughts into the very youngest of minds, they were able to extol the virtues of socialistic thought and vilify the evils of capitalism. Continuing the filtering of information through selective news broadcasting or distorting the reports altogether, the government-media complex succeeded grandly in obfuscating issues that were morally clear-cut and clouding others that should have been more clearly explained. As a result, the Goebbels-like propaganda machine worked overtime to create the illusions the Administration wished the populace to believe.

As socialists always say -- the dumber, the less informed, the better. "Without knowledge, they'll vote with their hearts instead of their heads," said one prominent socialist of the times. He also said, "It is always easier to persuade someone who is either stupid or ignorant of the facts than to convert someone who knows the truth."

The end result for the USSA was tyranny – a totalitarian government not unlike that of the old Soviet Union during the twentieth century. True, this political power did not result in the deaths of over twenty-five million people, but it is not inconceivable that the death toll from the regime might have risen to several million over time had the war not restored democracy to its proper place.

So, it is now over. Democracy and capitalism are alive and well again in America. There is nothing more to worry about, right?

It is difficult to say, but the odds are against it.

Those in power will do anything and everything to maintain that power. Again, the silverback will not voluntarily step aside unless he is defeated in a direct confrontation with a younger, stronger ape. So too is man. Even with the obvious safeguards – divided government and separation of powers, term limits, balanced budget propositions, etc. – these would only be stopgaps. Man, as he always does, will find a way around them, and left unchallenged, his base animal instincts and motivations will grow and spread – like a malignant tumor – until it once again kills the host nation.

So, the answer comes down to the people. If the people are vigilant; if the people fight constantly for their freedoms; if the people stand up and resist anyone who tries to take away those freedoms for any reason, if the people show the kind of courage our Founding Fathers showed during the eighteenth century, then we have a chance. But that requires an educated populace with the capacity for critical thinking. This means we must instruct them on how to disambiguate information they are being fed by their leaders and the media. This means the people must embrace and relish independence and rugged individualism. This means that we can no longer take our freedoms for granted.

There is no guarantee that our new democracy will survive three hundred more years or even thirty. However, if we don't take our responsibilities as citizens seriously -- to stand up for those God-given rights enunciated in the Declaration of Independence – then it may not even last that long.

Sumner put down the paper. He picked up the phone. "Oishi, I want to know who wrote this editorial in the paper. Get me an appointment with him or her as soon as possible. I want to hear more about what they have to say."

*****

CH 77 Reunification

Bringing down the domes only required a phone call from the president, and once the rough terms of the armistice were agreed in Evergreen, Virginia, Sumner quickly contacted the Manhattan scientists.

"Drs. Lin, Tokarov and Johnny, you have shown fortitude and perseverance in creating a defensive shield to ensure we can keep our cities safe from outside harm. Now that the Republic and USSA have settled our differences, we will use it to keep all our cities safe from the aggression of foreign nations. Now, however, it's time to bring them down. Please disengage the domes."

"Yes, sir," said Lin. Standing behind him were Tokarov and Johnny, both of whom were grateful to see the pain and suffering ending.

Lin punched-in the Morse Code command with its series of dots and dashes to neutralize the plasma domes. Once completed, the Canadian satellite sent the signals to all the hovering generators to cease their operation. Instantly, the low hum of the plasma domes stopped and the view from inside the imprisoned cities outward cleared. It was as if days of perpetual smog had dissipated and they could see again beyond their municipal border. Normalcy began to return, as they could come and go as they pleased. But even more important, they had regained a sense of renewed freedom.

"Are they down?" asked Sumner, awaiting some sign from his Manhattan staff.

"Yes, Mr. President," said Dr. Lin, grinning.

Shea smiled too. "Finally, we have one nation again," she said to the president.

***

A reunification conference was convened in the renamed Washington, D.C. within the month, with representatives from the former USSA and the Republic present. No former members of the USSA Administration, the Congress or the federal court system were permitted to participate. Instead, the representatives were elected directly by the people in the former USSA states that had held fast to the doomed policies of the socialist nation. Two representatives per state were sent, much like those sent to the Second Continental Congress in 1775. Although powerless, these representatives listened and engaged with their counterparts from the Republic, arguing points and defending positions. Moderating the affair was Shea, as the president's representative.

When all points had been agreed, drafts were circulated, and a final, comprehensive agreement reached. It was referred to as the Unification Treaty of Grosvenor Hill, the place where the document was signed. In it, the former USSA states agreed to unilaterally accept the Constitution of the Republic as its governing document. As expected, Washington, D.C. was chosen to be the seat of government for the combined nation. However, as the federal government was shrunk to only 20 percent of its former size, many parcels of land and buildings owned by the government were sold to pay off debts. With vastly restricted powers, the new federal government was strong enough to unify the states, but not too strong as to dictate to the states. And like the federal government, the states too were forced to relinquish power to the cities and counties, rather than become the arbiter of all things.

In the final draft, as prescribed in the Republic Constitution, the federal government's purpose was solely to protect and defend its people by raising an army, negotiate with foreign governments, coin money, defend the rights and freedoms of its citizenry, ensure the states did not usurp power from their citizens, permit the armament of the citizens, regulate interstate commerce in a very narrow form, raise taxes, and declare war. And lastly, the assemblage agreed to restore the name *United States of America*. Gone was the additional word, the moniker for socialism. It was expunged to the dustbin of history – or at least so it was hoped.

In return, the Republic extended loans to the USSA states to help rebuild their neglected infrastructure and for businesses to recapitalize and reconstitute their operations and capacities.

Things were good. Life was getting back to normal, or at least more normal than they had ante-bellum. The economy was beginning to recover, unemployment was falling, inflation was contained, and there was an optimism that hadn't been seen in the country for generations. It was true that capitalism was the centerpiece for all that was going on, but President Sumner was determined to be sure that big corporate interests didn't unduly influence legislation or the direction of the new, united government. Term limits were enforced, and nearly all the provisions of the Republic's Constitution were adopted by the new United States.

Together with the elimination of interstate travel restrictions, the new, united country began to resemble what it had looked like during the two hundred years after the Revolutionary War, with the exception of the divisive issues of slavery and bigotry. Families were re-united, but just as the North and the South had continued to feud for years after 1865, so too did those from the Right and the Left continue to spar over the direction of the new nation. At many homes throughout the former socialist country, families still flew the green, orange and black flag of the old USSA on their flag poles and porches. Some in the south, particularly in Arkansas and Virginia, the Confederate flag was flown right next to that of the USSA – a protest, to be sure, but at least it was a protest that could be made in a free and open society.

Sumner, Shea and the rest of the Republic Cabinet set to work to ease the integration of the authoritarian USSA regime into the democratic one established in Cheyenne. But, just as the East and West Germans found unification difficult during the latter part of the twentieth century, so too did the Sumner Administration. Old mindsets died hard, and those who had grown up in a socialistic world were reluctant to embrace capitalism – even a bridled one. The distortion of the history books and continual drum of poisonous rhetoric spewed by the previous government had been strong. Prejudices and misunderstanding would not die easily, and it would take time.

In addition, Sumner knew well that *laissez-faire capitalism* was little better than unadulterated socialism. *Bridled capitalism,* on the other hand, was something that most could accept and support.

***

Sumner's plane landed in Richmond, Virginia, where his brother, Theo, and his wife Claire lived. It was a surprise visit to the extent that presidential trips were surprises. Out of necessity, safeguards were heightened and security tight as the president left Fort Lee for Tuckahoe, just north of the city.

Eventually, the black limousine and its entourage pulled up in front of a red-bricked, gabled home with two dormers, a front bay window, and a small flagstone porch covered by a colonial-styled awning.

It was a quiet, tree-lined neighborhood that had declined greatly from years of municipal neglect and the widespread abandonment of homes from the unemployed. As rich as the government handouts were, even they could not sustain the lifestyle of those living in the Tuckahoe neighborhood. Wild grass and a jungle of weeds had grown to nearly waist level in many yards, and garbage littered the roadside as trash pickups were only available by appointment and then only if paid in advance by the homeowner. Potholes pocked the street, causing the limo driver to take evasive action several times to avoid breaking an axle. As the car came to a stop, Secret Service jumped out from an advance vehicle and scanned the community for any threats. With sunglasses concealing their glances and thoughts, they opened the rear, patent leather-like door, allowing the president and his personal secretary to step out.

As Sumner planted his foot onto the pavement, he lifted himself out of the car and took a deep breath. The air was thick with pollutants that had not been scrubbed in decades making it more hazardous than that the dinosaurs of the Cretaceous Period, some 100 million years earlier, would have breathed.

Buttoning his subtle, gray plaid sport coat, Sumner pulled the cuffs down just above his shirt's sleeve line, and pulled up on his collar so that it rested above the lapel of his coat. He walked along the flagstone pathway that led to the front porch and stopped, staring out at what was left of his brother's house. When he had last seen it, some twenty-six years earlier, it had been beautiful – a two-story, four-bedroom colonial with a detached three-car garage. The yard had been lush and green with the pink azaleas in full bloom around the front and lining the driveway and the white dogwood blooms bursting from their pods on the trees next to the garage. It had been bright and happy place. Now, the brick was a dirty rust color with paint peeling on the eaves and the two shutters broken and askew guarding the lower windows on the front living room side of the house. Most of the landscaping that Theo had planted had perished during the harsh winters – with temperatures far below normal. Water rationing had doomed all but the sturdiest trees that had already established deep roots. And where a black mailbox stood by the roadside, now only a decapitated wooden post remained – the box stolen and presumably sold for scrap metal.

Sumner knocked on the torn screen door, the metal wiring ripped by Theo while he was bringing groceries in from his car one Sunday afternoon. Theo answered the knock, opening the forest green front door and peering out to see who was calling. He looked neither pleased nor unhappy. He was just there, standing in the doorway.

"Well? Are you going to invite me in?" asked Sumner, half-joking and half-serious.

"Come on in," said Theo, holding open the screen door. "I certainly didn't expect to see you ever again," he grumbled.

Theo was two years senior to his younger brother and had taken a different path in life. Unlike his brother, he had graduated from another Ivy League college, Dartmouth, and had gotten a job in Boston with MPAI, a major non-profit charity that worked with inner city poor and disadvantaged youths. Like most other charities, their contributions dried up as tax rates increased and deductions for charitable contributions were eliminated. Government groups were created and funded by Washington to take over the role MPAI had served, and Theo had gotten a position in one of these agencies.

Stocky and broad-shouldered like his brother, Theo's once brown locks had turned gray. His rounded face and pudgy cheeks gave him the appearance of a likeable, congenial neighbor. Indeed, when he wasn't fighting with his brother over politics, that was his normal demeanor.

Motioning with his short stubby fingers, Theo showed his brother and Oishi into his home. However, as the rest of his party began to come in too, Sumner held out his arm stopping them. "No," he said, "it's just my brother and me. You all can wait outside."

Claire was in the kitchen making noises, but Sumner couldn't tell exactly what she was doing and whether or not she would even come out to meet him. She and he had had words the last time they had seen each other which was more than a dozen years earlier. She was a staunch supporter of the former regime in Washington. Educated, but not in touch with current events or anything dealing with financial or economic issues, she had never understood how the economy or political systems worked. She had always just trusted her government to know what was best. But few could fault her, most had done the same thing.

"Have a seat," said Theo, motioning toward the faded, striped burgundy and gold couch. The cloth armrests were still intact even though one was badly worn.

"Thanks," said Sumner, undoing his coat jacket and planting himself on the sofa. He sat stiffly on the couch, but tried to appear comfortable. "So, how have you been, Theo?" he asked.

"Fine, compared with others," his brother responded. "You people sure screwed us up with those domes, you know."

"Yes. I'm afraid we found it necessary to prevent further bloodshed. Too many had already died on both sides. We talked about it quite a bit before we decided on it. We really didn't think the holdout would last as long as it did. We certainly didn't believe there would be deaths as a result."

"Maybe. But die they did. Thousands died because of your domes," Theo answered with spite in his voice.

He took out a pack of cigarettes and offered one to his brother. Sumner declined, waving his hand subtly. Theo tapped the pack against his hand and withdrew one. Cigarettes had been illegal in the former USSA. Getting them required the same skills as trying to buy heroin or cocaine. Theo's dealer looked to be one of the more sophisticated, Sumner judged, based on the type of European brand he was smoking. Theo struck a match and lit the white stick, sucking in the gray smoke and blowing it out through clenched teeth.

"We're sorry for that," said Sumner. "I'm sorry for that. It wasn't intended that way."

"Yeah, well the streets are paved with the blood of good intentions now, aren't they?"

"I guess that's been true throughout history, Theo. Some things just don't change."

"What else doesn't change, Sumner? Are you going to tell me that nothing is going to change with the unification of the two countries?" No, quite the contrary. I think there will be a lot of good things happening here now that we've reunified."

"Like what?"

"Like jobs. Like a currency that means something in the world." Sumner paused. "Like being able to buy something when you go to the store – something you really need or want."

"At what cost? The blood and soul of the worker?"

"Theo, we've had these discussions before. We've argued about these things over and over again. But now, I hoped you would see how your system just doesn't work – how it got you to the point you are in now. Don't you see it?"

"The way we're living is better than being herded into some capitalist's cubical coral like some domesticated animal working like a slave for pennies."

"But if that happens, it's a free country; you can go anywhere to get a better job. You can pick which company you want to work for, and if you have skills that people want, you will find other employers eager to pay you more for them."

"Hell no! Management always puts down the workers. It's only when there's a union that the worker has a chance to make enough to survive and feed his family."

"We didn't do away with unions, you know. They're still allowed. It's just that most companies find that it's to their benefit to treat workers really well. It's too expensive to have turnover and have to find and train people. That's why union influence declined during the latter part of the twentieth century and ever since. All the unions did was fight for higher wages and benefits and prevent improvements in productivity. At that point, companies went overseas to have the work done. That's when American workers lost their jobs."

"Rubbish! Company owners just wanted more money. They went overseas to exploit the workers over there! They paid cents on the dollar compared with what they would have paid here, and they didn't want their rich shareholders to suffer," said Theo.

"Did you ever stop and look at what those foreign workers were making before and then after the US and other countries began sending jobs to them? Yes, they were only making about twenty cents per hour, compared with thirty dollars per hour demanded by the unions. But before that, those foreign workers were on the streets begging or they and their families were starving to death. Even with twenty cents per hour, they could buy food for their families."

"Maybe, but they couldn't afford a house!"

"Must everyone have a house? Is that one of the unalienable rights? Life, liberty, happiness and a house?"

Theo looked away in disgust. "Of course not! But everyone is entitled to a place to live."

They have a place to live! Most live within an extended family. In general, they are happier and more satisfied than we are! We measure poverty in this country at a level considered to by upper-middle class in most other countries. Having a 4-D TV is not poverty!"

"It's still oppression. When the rich have so much and the rest of us have so little. It's about fairness! It's about inequality!" snarled Sumner's brother.

It was at that point that Claire came out from the kitchen. She was polite and extended her hand to Sumner. "Hello, JC. We didn't know you were coming. At least I didn't know you were coming," she said, looking over at her husband.

Theo shook his head. "I knew nothin' about it either, Claire."

Claire smiled, but uncomfortably. "Can we get you anything to eat or drink?" she finally asked.

"No thank you. I just wanted to stop in and see you two. We haven't been together for years, and I ..."

"... and since you won the war over us, you thought now would be a good time to stop by," she said, her hackles raised.

She was petite, only five foot three, and she wore her hair, brown with streaks of gray, pulled back sharply in a ponytail behind her head. Her face was thin, the wrinkles around her eyes and mouth revealing her true age of fifty-eight. But there was still a youthfulness in her eyes. They had been the window to her compassionate soul since she was born, and even though she had been raised in a once-wealthy family. Their fortune, or what had been built by her late father, had been confiscated by the socialist government, together with all their land holdings. Yet, Claire had supported the move, believing what she'd been taught in public schools throughout her childhood. She still clung to the belief that society is ever enriched when wealth is redistributed.

"Claire, it is always good to see you again," said Sumner, trying to keep the interaction civil.

"So, why have you come, JC?" she asked bluntly.

"I told you that I wanted to …"

"Cut the crap, JC! Really, why did you come?" she asked again, her mouth and lips tightening.

Sumner hadn't been talked to like that for many years; however, he was prepared for the assault.

"We aren't getting any younger, Claire. I really *did* want to see you both." He stopped and then continued. "I also wanted to assure you that everything will be fine. The Republic has no intention of punishing the former USSA or its citizens for the war or what was done before. There has been enough damage done that we don't need to create anymore. Both sides have suffered. I think both sides want reunification. At least I know that most within the Republic do. They would like nothing better than to be reunited with the other states."

"I wish I could believe you," said Claire, now folding her arms.

"Why don't you?" asked Sumner.

We could never trust a thing you-all said during the war. You lied to us! You killed thousands of innocent civilians. You put thousands more in concentration camps! You tried to create a mass genocide by installing those domes to kill all of us off! Those were war crimes! You should be convicted by the World Court and sentenced for that!"

Now it was Sumner's turn to be defensive. "I don't know where you got that information, but it's wrong. We did none of those things, except put the domes in place. We always had a plan to dismantle them, and never would have let civilians die inside had we known that …"

"Well, civilians *did* die!" she shouted at him. "I lost my sister!"

The shock stunned Sumner. He had no idea that the tragedy had directly affected his brother's family.

"I'm sorry," said Sumner. "I truly am. I know how much Lizzie meant to you."

"She was killed in a street mob that destroyed the town she was in. They burned her house down. She and her husband were inside."

"Again, Claire. I'm so sorry. It does sound like it was internal violence more than what we did with the domes that caused her death. Is that right?"

"Hell no! *You* were the ones that created the domes in the first place! You were the ones that caused the unrest and rioting. If you hadn't put those in place, none of it would have happened."

"Again, I'm sorry for your loss," he said. "It's important now that people in the USSA believe that things can be better in a unified country. We were once a great nation. In time we will be again."

"We just didn't do enough," said Theo. "The government should have done more, not less."

"I know you don't want to believe this, but your socialism will always fail you. You can rationalize it all you want by saying more should have been done or spent. Heck, you can take all the wealth away from the top 10 percenters and you still won't be able to live off it. Even from the top half! You simply cannot do it."

"Well, it doesn't matter, anyway. We didn't win," said Claire. "You did. So, we have to live with it. And, as a matter of course to the victors go the spoils, as they say. What is it that you've come to claim as your prize?"

"I not here to claim anything, nor do I wish to. However, I do wish that the people of the USSA give the reunification a chance. The Republic is willing to spend trillions to rebuild the decaying infrastructure of your country. We're willing to increase taxes on our wealthier citizens to help fund it. This won't be in perpetuity, but it could last for up to ten years. After that, we hope things will stabilize."

"I guess we have no choice, do we?" Claire answered, sarcastically.

"No, I guess you don't. And, we understand that it will take time to heal the wounds that have been opened up by this conflict. We know that not everyone will join us. But, I'm hoping that you two will."

Sumner got up and held out his hand. Claire turned and walked away, going back into the kitchen and not giving the president the courtesy of a goodbye. Theo stared at Sumner without emotion.

I want to believe you," Theo said to his brother.

"I know. And I know it will take time," said the president.

The president turned and walked to the door. He pulled on the handle and pushed out the screened door to journey back to the waiting black cars. He was half way down the path, when his brother called to him. "JC," he said. Sumner turned back to him, surprised by the response. "I really do want to believe you. But you're right. It will take time, and you'll have to be patient with us, especially Claire. You have to agree that taking care of those less fortunate is important. Can you do that?"

Sumner nodded his head. "I've never said it wasn't. We have differing approaches to accomplish that. I just hope you will see that mine works better than yours does."

The president got in his car and drove off. He turned to look back at his brother's place and shook his head.

"What's wrong?" asked his secretary. "It didn't go well, did it?"

"Let's just hope that others will eventually see the light," said Sumner.

"They will," she said. "As your brother said, you have to give them time."

"At least we have a fresh start. That must count for something," said the president, looking out the window at the other decrepit homes and overgrown yards flashing by.

"It does," answered Oishi. "To most of us, it means a whole lot."

*****

CH 78 Presidential Box

Sumner returned to Cheyenne. He seemed despondent for a few days after coming back but soon regrouped once he had sunk his teeth into the long and tedious project of reunification. There was much to do – not unlike what he faced when the Republic first split from Washington. In addition to that work, the president had announced that there would be a general election held the next year. It was overdue, he had said, but with the outbreak of war, the plans had been postponed. For the first election, only Republic states and their citizens could vote; this was because the USSA states would have easily swayed the election at all levels toward their pro-socialist candidates. Representatives and senators for those states would be appointed by the president until the next presidential election cycle.

But it wasn't all work for the president. His social calendar was also filling up quickly. He and Shea had become inseparable and their relationship common knowledge. Together, they had announced their intentions to marry before the general election over a year away. During that time, Sumner and his government also had to move their operations back to Washington, D.C. Everything took time.

Yet, the time passed quickly, and his relationship with Shea continued to blossom. The time was early spring, and the Japanese cherry trees along the Tidal Basin were beginning to thrust out their stunning white blooms too. It was the next day, when President Sumner was scheduled to travel to DC to reclaim the house that had been given to presidents for nearly two and a half centuries. Although the house had been defiled by the First Citizens, it had never given up its grandeur and dignity, waiting the day when true democracy would return to the land and a true believer of those democratic principles would once again reclaim the Oval Office to execute the responsibilities of the presidency. The time had come.

Shea's car pulled up in front of the governor's mansion in Cheyenne, and the driver stepped out to open her door. She got out, wearing a long, black, sequined gown with a v-neckline and one side slit well up her right thigh. She walked up the broad, white staircase to the wrap-around, front porch where the doorman let her in.

The house was beautifully appointed, with a large, round, black cherry pedestal table in the center of the entryway. On it was a Romanesque, bronze planter overflowing with fresh, scented flowers, ranging from brilliant coral colored bird-of-paradise to canary-yellow callas and lavender hydrangea. The walls were a light yellow with white trim. On the walls were rustic picture frames and photos of the president with friends and acquaintances he'd developed over the years. On an old, oak roll-top sat against the hallway wall, missing its desk chair. Sitting on the escritoire was only one picture bordered in a gold, wooden frame. It was that of Maria, Sumner's late wife. It was a beautiful picture, almost like a portrait, shot in sepia tones. She had been young then, and full of life.

Shea was escorted into the adjoining library where she waited, but it was less than five minutes before Sumner walked in, dressed in a tux and a black, string tie with a turquoise stone that he used instead of a black tie.

"Hey darlin'," he said, sounding like an old John Wayne movie. "You goin' the same place I am ta' night?"

Shea smiled broad and wide. She walked over to him and planted a big kiss on his lips. "I dunno, Zach, are ya' goin' to the opera or the stripper house?"

Sumner laughed. "That was the worst impression of Claire Trevor I've ever heard!" he said.

"Claire who?"

"Never mind. I'll take your comment as a *yes*, then. I am going the same way. So, what are we watching tonight anyway? Don't you know we don't do operas out here in Cheyenne?"

"It's good for you. It'll give you a little culture, Sumner. God knows you need a little culture," she said, joking.

"Very funny," he answered, enjoying the banter.

They left the house and got into the awaiting, black limousine to take them to the small theater in downtown Cheyenne where the opera production of *Tosca* was being performed. The theater was crowded, as it was seldom that operas came to the western town of Cheyenne. However, since the rise in importance of the small town after the war, many new production companies were scrambling to have the president view their work.

The president's box was draped in the original American flag with red, white and blue flower arrangements in flower boxes held in front. Below and to the right was the stage, a small area but large enough for the limited sets, backdrops and other props needed for the show. There were four floors to the theater – the orchestral floor, right in front of the stage; the mezzanine, which was raised higher behind the orchestral area; the first-floor balconies, where the president's box resided; and the second-floor balconies. Security was high, and metal detectors were placed at all entrances to the building. It had been soured by dogs and other experts prior to the president and his attorney general's arrival. Heavy anti-aircraft batteries were placed all around the theater, as were police snipers. No stone was left unturned,

The guest list was comprised of long-term supporters of the president. He knew almost everyone by name and was happy to share this last night in Cheyenne with them. After the production, Sumner was to hold a party of the opera-goers in a separate banquet hall located next door.

Act One started on time, and Shea curled up next to the Sumner, putting her hand on his as it rested on the arm of the leather, pin-cushioned chair. As the operatic soprano belted out her arias, Shea smiled to herself. She had missed this, living in Wyoming. It was something she had grown up with in Boston and again when she was on Capitol Hill in Washington. It was nostalgic for her, and it gave her a sense of security and oneness with life.

Shea watched Sumner's eyes as he absorbed the opera. He was mesmerized, soaking in every descant and verse as it touched his soul. His eyes were ablaze with emotion as he saw Tosca being manipulated by Scarpia, implying to her that her lover, Cararadossi, was cheating on her.

Shea squeezed Sumner's hand as the scene became emotional, a sense of overwhelming sadness being conveyed by the tenor that touched her heart. However, he didn't squeeze back. She turned to connect with him in that moment of passion and angst. However, instead of meeting his eyes and his gaze, she saw that his head was slumped forward on his chest.

"Wake up, JC! It can't be that bad," she admonished. But there was no response. "JC?" she repeated, shaking him. Then, she pushed on his arm, and it fell to the side of the chair, limp and lifeless.

"Oh, my God!" she exclaimed. Shea stood up and waved frantically for the Secret Service man standing behind her at the door. "Get help!" she yelled. "Something's wrong with the president!"

But even as events were unfolding in the presidential box, the orchestra continued to play and the singers on stage sing, as the crescendos and timpani overwhelmed the attentive audience. The Secret Service agent immediately radioed for a doctor as Shea clutched her husband's head in her arms, desperate to save him.

Secretary Ingram was in the box with his wife Simone, and he rushed over to where Shea and the president sat. "What's wrong?" he said, putting his hand on the president's neck to feel for a pulse.

"I don't know," said Shea. "I looked over and he was unconscious!" She was pale and shaking. Fighting back tears she added, "I don't know. I just don't know." Lost and in shock, she could only hold onto him until the doctor arrived.

"Ma'am, the doctor is here. You'll have to move aside," said the agent coming into the box with the president's staff doctor. Within moments the commotion in the box caught everyone's attention and the opera was halted. People gasped as they watched what was going on, uncertain of who was being worked on in the president's box.

Shea stepped back and let the doctor and two paramedics stretch Sumner out on the floor, administering CPR and taking vitals. One of the agents whispered in Ingram's ear, and the secretary nodded.

"The doctor said that they'll need to move him to the hospital right away," said Ingram. "You'll need to come with me, Shea."

She began to protest, but Ingram gave her no time. He pulled her away and led her down to the waiting limousine, where they were whisked off to the nearby Cheyenne Regional Medical Center.

"I need to know how he is!" she shouted to Ingram while they were driving to the hospital. "You need to call the doctor or the hospital or something. I need to know!" she said panicked. Her face was expressionless as her breathing got faster and shallower.

"You need to calm yourself," said Ingram. "We don't know anything right now. You're no good to anybody, especially the president, if you don't get a grip on yourself."

"You're right. I know you're right," she muttered. "How soon until we're at the hospital?"

"It's only a matter of minutes, Shea," said Ingram. "I'm sure the ambulance isn't even there yet. We'll have to wait a few minutes before it arrives."

Shea and Ingram waited in a private room until they heard movement outside in the hallways. A brigade of doctors and nurses stood by as the ambulance screamed into the emergency drive-through and stopped abruptly.

Shea ran into the ER lobby and watched as the paramedics unloaded her fiancé from the ambulance and quickly raised and locked the frame on the stretcher. With a clear, intravenous bag dangling from a steel rod attached to the gurney and one paramedic continuing to do chest compressions, they rushed the president passed Shea and Ingram and down the hall through two, automatic, double doors. He disappeared with the rest of his medical attendants, and she could only stand and worry about what was happening and how he was.

Shea rushed over to the doctor who came walking in moments later. Having also attended the opera, the doctor was dressed in a black tux, rather than any sort of white lab coat. "Doctor? What happened? Is he going to be all right?" she asked the doctor, cornering him so he couldn't move passed her easily.

The doctor looked at Ingram first with an expression of uncertainty. Then, he answered, "Attorney General, I really don't have any news right now. All I can tell you is that he suffered a major stroke. We are working on him as you can see. We'll just have to wait at this point. I'll let you know. Now, if you'll excuse me."

The doctor hurried down the hallway, pushing through the doors just opened by those working on the president.

Shea put her hands to her face and began sobbing. "A stroke?" she said, before looking into the face of Ingram. "No, this can't be happening! He's worked too hard for it to end this way. This can't be. It just can't be!"

Ingram took her by the shoulders and led her back into the private waiting room. There, he left her to see if the doctor would prescribe anything for her anxiety and distress. Returning, he handed her a paper cup and two small white pills. "Here Shea, take these. The doctor said they may help you calm yourself."

Shea shook her head, but when Ingram insisted, she took the water and pills and handed the crumpled up cup back to him.

The next hour was the longest of her life – at least the longest after she had discovered Patrick missing from her house and her life. Together she and Ingram waited, watching for any signs coming from the double doors of the critical care area.

Finally, the doctor, now clothed in his normal hospital garb, walked through the double doors. His stride was swift and steady, giving no clue to what he was thinking or what he was about to say.

The doctor entered the private waiting room and Shea jumped up to speak with him. "Well?" she asked, coming over to him. "How is he?" she asked.

The doctor looked at Shea and then Ingram, unsure how to respond.

"Doctor," said Ingram, "how is the president?"

"I'm sorry," he answered. "We weren't able to save him. He's gone."

Everything after that sentence was a blur to Shea. Her knees began to give way, and she nearly collapsed. Ingram helped her to the couch and sit down. "Shea," Ingram began. But then he stopped, not knowing what to say. "I don't know what to say. I'm so sorry. I know how much you loved him."

Shea sat on the waiting room couch without moving. She was frozen in time, hoping that the moment would somehow disappear and reality would be suspended. But the minutes passed and the reality didn't change.

"Shea, is there anything I can do?" asked Ingram.

She looked up at him, her eyes red, the corners of her mouth downturned, and the energy and life seemingly gone from a once-radiant face. "If only you could bring him back to me."

*****

CH 79 Epitaph

The shock of Sumner's death reverberated throughout the Republic, as governors of each of the states scrambled to make sense of the sudden change of events. Most wondered whether the new USA would survive without their leader.

As for the states of the former USSA, the reaction was predictably different. They quietly celebrated the passing of Sumner whom they viewed as a traitor to his homeland.

Still, the funeral was held in Washington, D.C., and he was buried in Arlington Cemetery. There was no eternal flame or other grand monument constructed to honor him. Instead, his plot was a simple grave marked by a plain, white cross. In the ground was a granite slab with the inscription:

> **Jonathon Crist Sumner**
> **1983 - 2051**
> **US Congressman 2035-2047**
> **President of the ATLAS Republic 2048-2051**
> **Father of a New Beginning – Timeless**

It was a fitting list, but Shea thought it lacked one epithet: The Moses of his people. It was sad that he had led his people out of bondage but had not lived to see them enter the promise land. That would be left to someone else.

Maria's body was transported from a cemetery in Cheyenne to Arlington where she was laid to rest beside her husband. Shea had no problem with that. She understood the deep love they had for one another and thought it fitting that they share eternity together.

As Shea walked away from the grave site, she looked back upon the freshly prepared earth and wondered how things might have turned out had he lived – both for her and the country. That, she understood, would be something that could never be known. She only hoped and prayed that the new USA would survive and that she would, at some time in her life, rediscover the happiness she had found with first Patrick and the Sumner. Only time would tell.

*****

CH 80 Election Night

... Nearly two years later

Under the new *Constitution*, elections for president were to be held every six years, rather than the four under the previous one. Four years was not seen as enough time for a president to institute his or her agenda given the complexities of the world in the twenty-first century. Presidential term limits were retained, with only two terms permitted – a limit of twelve years to reign. Similar term limits were imposed for members of Congress, and for justices of the federal court system, including the Supreme Court. A new fourth branch was instituted, which was independent of all other branches. It had little power or authority but provided the nation and other branches with statistical data on the country and the world at large. A fifth branch became the Federal Reserve – no longer a smoke-and-mirrors entity of illusionary independence. Strict rules were engaged for its operation and the appointment of its chairman and reserve board members. The electoral college was eliminated, so the total popular vote, rather than the 538 electoral votes, determined the winner. There were other changes of course, which were thought to improve on the old model. But only time would tell.

When the new *Constitution* was ratified, there were sixty-three states in the Union, including several partitioned states like California which was divided into three, and Illinois, New York, Oregon and Colorado into two. Hawaii was the only state permitted to opt out, as they had wanted to do for years. It was replaced by Puerto Rico, U.S. Virgin Islands and Guam. In addition, the western Canadian provinces of British Columbia, Alberta, Saskatchewan, Manitoba, and Ontario also petitioned to join the Union. After the USSA concluded its armistice with Canada, the prime minister had contacted Sumner to join forces. These Canadian provinces, while operated independently, would become part and parcel of the new United States of America with Prime Minister MacDonald acting as governor.

Everyone expected a good turnout for the first election of the new USA. It had been a hard-fought primary season – short, but intense. Neither side was taking anything for granted. The party of Sumner had campaigned hard against its primary opponent, House Minority Leader Evelyn Langley Burns, an opportunist who saw the chance to seize power from the party who led the country to prosperity and out of a bloody and costly civil war, just as Clement Attlee had done in 1945 to Winston Churchill after WWII.

By twisting the truth and casting the Freedom Party in the worst possible light, Burns had succeeded in gaining a following. She had charisma and a personality that attracted others to her cause despite the complete lack of wisdom or logic. She was a personality, and that was all it took to draw others to her.

With current technologies, the election results were instantaneous to the closing of the polls in each state. And unlike past elections, this one was being followed with great interest.

Shea, Ingram, Templeton, and White sat on a sofa in the Oval Office with their senior staff surrounding them. It was nearly seven o'clock in the evening, eastern time. The polls had closed an hour earlier in the east and had just closed in the Midwest. The results were coming in fast and were being displayed on the video screen as quickly as they could be projected.

"To summarize where we are ..." said the NNC news anchor, Brian Johnson, "... at this point, with 95.4 percent of the counts in from those states eligible to vote in the eastern time zone we have Burns leading Disone by 491 thousand votes. Burns has 8,355,037 compared with Disone at 7,863,564. The Independent Party candidate, Calvin Williams, has just 163,824. The total votes cast thus far, about 16.4 million from these southern states, suggests a very high voter turnout, which was expected. As we've said all night, all the East Coast states were not permitted to vote in this election cycle since they were still part of the USSA when the war ceased. Only those states that were formally admitted into the ATLAS Republic or those that had broken from the USSA prior to the end of fighting are permitted to vote in this election. Under our new constitution, all states will be able to vote in the next presidential election cycle in six years."

Looking up at the clock in the studio, Johnson noted, "States in the Central Time Zone will be closing their polls soon as well. Like the eastern states, many of these Midwestern states were unable to vote as well, like Michigan, Ohio, Illinois ... there were a few such as Indiana, Colorado and a handful of others that were allowed partial voting rights These states had some regions that had defected to the Republic prior to the end of hostilities."

"... Ah, yes," Johnson continued, "it is now six o'clock in most of the Midwestern states where, as I said before, less than half of their citizens were allowed to vote. But right now, we are watching as those vote tallies are posted on our board." Up on the screen came a graphic showing blue and red bars leaping up from the states where the vote tallies were taken. Then, there was a total shown at the bottom. "Right now we show -- with 97.1 percent of the votes registered -- Disone continuing to trail Burns in the overall count. The gap has actually widened with 45 percent voting for Disone and 52 percent for Burns. That would result in an increase in Burns's lead from 491,473 to 616,254, an increase of nearly 125 thousand votes and in an area where many believed Disone would be strong. I'm sure the Acting President did not count on such a big showing for Burns in the Midwest."

"Damn," said Ingram, shaking his head. Even he was surprised with the results in the Midwestern states where they had polled very well. "I just don't understand where all of this Burns support is coming from. It certainly never showed up in any of our polling."

"With the Central Plains states expected to go Disone," continued Johnson, "the current Acting President was expected to have a sizeable lead at this point. However, that is not how things are turning out here tonight. Now, she will need a significant showing of support in the Central Plains states to regain the lead and provide some cushion going into the western states and, perhaps, Canada. The Western states are expected to vote heavily for Burns, so Disone will need all the lead she can garner before the end of the night when the last votes from the West Coast are counted."

Shea shook her head. "I don't understand," she said in a daze. "This isn't at all what our polling showed. We should have a lead right now and be building on it through the Central states. There was no way we were supposed to lose the South and Midwest."

"Canada is a wildcard in this election," said Johnson from the broadcast booth, "as that group has never participated in an American election. Still, their history has swung between liberal and conservative over the last several decades. It's hard to tell which way that bloc of voters will lean."

Secretary White got up to pour herself a glass of Goldfield Chardonnay to calm her nerves. "Anyone else want some? It's a 2049," she said, studying the label. "I think that was a good year, wasn't it?"

"No, I'm afraid I need something a little stronger. What do you have over there?" Shea answered, looking over the edge of her overstuffed, leather chair.

White perused the line of liquors that were conveniently aligned along the edge of the counter, otherwise used for papers and binders. Her eyes jumped from the Macallen single malt and Glenmorangie Scotch to the Balvenie 40 which had been Sumner's favorite.

"Would you like the Balvenie 40?"

Shea's eyes watered as she thought about the former love of her life. If only he were with her at that moment, to help her through this trying night. But then a warm feeling came over her body and she smiled. *He is with me, isn't he?* she thought, looking up to the heavens.

"Yeah, that would be just fine. But remember, I need to be sober enough to make a speech at the end of the evening."

"A victory speech, right?" asked White.

"Of course," she answered, with forced optimism. She gave White a hopeful look but returned to watching the broadcast.

As another hour passed, the news anchor and his two political pundits filled the space with commentary and analysis on what all the voting to that point meant. After several more commercial breaks, Johnson presented another diagram of the old United States and Western Canada. Each state and former province was filled in with the potential votes and historic percentage splits by party.

"Here are the numbers we have thus far. To recap, the Southern and Midwestern states are showing support for Burns with 51.1 percent of the vote. This puts her in the lead by 616 thousand votes according to our computers. The question is whether this will be enough to stem the tide expected from Freedom Party regions in the Central Plains states that will likely be voting for Disone. But even if she gets this surge, Disone has to worry about the late-night numbers from the pro-Burns western states and the unknown support levels from the western Canadian provinces that are also presumed to support Burns. This looks like it will be a very interesting race as the night wears on. Please stay tuned to this … your *Election Night 2051*."

As the station cut to another commercial break, the White House media room was quiet. Templeton and Ingram were on the phone with campaign managers trying to figure out what was happening. The evening was not going anything like they had planned. Their numbers had shown that Shea should have been up on Burns after the Midwest tallies – as much as 850 thousand ahead or as little as 375 thousand, but not behind.

The broadcast resumed, but the anchor was immersed in a discussion with someone off camera, listening to the phantom voice in his earpiece. "We have just received news that the numbers from the Central region of states do *not* include votes from Texas or Wyoming. Apparently, the polling software in those two states was not functioning properly. We're told that the software was purchased from a company called Subrosa, Ltd. We will give you more on this breaking story when we have it."

Shea leaned over to Ingram. "We were all counting on Texas to help us clinch the election tonight," she said with angst in her phone. "Now we won't know? What is going on?"

"We will find out once they fix the glitch in the software, I guess" said Templeton, less than reassuringly.

"If there's something going on there, we need to find out what it is," Shea answered. "Find out everything you can on this Subrosa company." She was increasingly agitated with the newscast, but there were few options when trying to track the progress of the voting in real time.

"To repeat," said Johnson, "We were told moments ago that the numbers for the Central states we will be given *do not* include Texas, nor do they include Wyoming, which also uses the Subrosa company. Those numbers have been withheld from the totals thus far until they can be verified. We will get you those vote totals as soon as we get them."

"Althea, I think I need another one of these," said Shea, pointing to a glass that still held half-melted ice cubes. "Make this one a double."

The next hour dragged on, but finally, the old, hickory grandfather clock in the Oval Office struck nine o'clock. "Anything on Texas and Wyoming?" Shea asked. "What do you have on Subrosa?"

"Nothing yet. Our people are still working on it," said Templeton.

It was then that Johnson started in again. "We now have the numbers from the Central Plains states. These are substantial, as most of the states were early defectors to the Republic's cause. Therefore, most of the states from the Central region were permitted to vote in this cycle. Now, we see ..." The national chart changed instantly showing the added vote counts for the new set of states. "... Disone claiming 54 percent of the vote, compared with 45 percent for Burns. Nearly 5.8 million votes were cast there for Disone versus 4.8 million for Burns. That is a big win for the Disone campaign and brings the numbers much closer for the Acting President. As a matter of fact, it appears that Disone now leads Burns by 354,025 votes. This surge was, however, expected. Yet, it's not nearly as large as Disone had hoped for coming into tonight's contest. We're sure that her campaign is worried that it may not hold up going into the largely Burns-minded West Coast. We'll just have to wait and see." "

Templeton had been on the phone the entire time and was still mumbling to whoever was on the other line when the anchor finished the segment on the Central states results. For a time, the Defense Secretary was quiet; listening intently, he only uttered sounds intermittently, saying, "uh, huh" and "right." Then, he turned to the rest of the group.

"Well? What is it?" asked Ingram, glassy-eyed and standing nearby with his beverage firmly in hand.

"Subrosa is a company that is owned by Nathan Arnold. His mother is the sister of Burns's husband's step-father, Andrew Burns," said Templeton.

There was quiet in the room. Shea felt sick to her stomach. "How could that have happened?"

We don't know. Obviously, someone snuck it through the system. We're finding there were several other states that also bought the software — not just Texas and Wyoming," said the Secretary of Defense. "It looks like most of the Southern and Midwestern states bought it as well."

"Jesus," said Shea, shaking her head and sighing deeply. "And I thought the days of dirty tricks were behind us."

Johnson resumed his broadcast and the panel reviewed the results of congressional races in the House and the Senate as well as key governorships. On that score, the Freedom Party was doing quite well, capturing the majority of the races on all levels. Finally, the nine o'clock hour came, and as the grandfather clock in the Oval Office sounded its nine chimes, Johnson resumed his remarks on the presidential race.

"We've just gotten the vote count from the West Coast and Western Canada," said the anchor, reading off the invisible monitor in front of him. "With 97.2 percent of the votes in, it appears that Burns has received 68 percent of the West Coast vote, compared with only 28 percent for Disone. This is a *huge* development tonight. No one predicted that large of a difference on the West Coast either. However, the total number of votes will be relatively low, as California, Washington, Oregon, Nevada, New Mexico and Montana were not permitted to vote in this election. So, if we look at the tally, we see that Burns does again lead Disone by ... let me see ... uh, yes by over 1.1 *million* votes. That is an *enormous* spread. I really don't know how Disone will overcome that kind of a margin. However, we still do not have the votes in from

Western Canada. The votes I just gave were only from those Western states that were allowed to vote. But, stay with us as we await those important Canadian votes."

The screen faded again to another promotion of a product, while Shea let the last of her second drink, disappear down her throat. "How many votes are there in the western provinces of Canada?" asked Shea. "And how many of those do we need?"

"We're looking at 14 million of voting age in the provinces, but if only 40 percent vote, that would yield 5.6 million votes to be split amongst the candidates. If we get 52 percent, that would only cut the lead by 112 thousand votes," said Ingram.

"So we'd still need to find more than, what, 1 *million*?" asked Shea, increasingly alarmed. She shook her head, but said nothing more.

"Well, if we lose, we'll demand a recount," said Templeton, getting angry. "There's just too much smoke around Subrosa. The whole thing stinks."

"It may stink, but I don't think this country can take a contested election," said Shea.

"What? You're not going to fight?" asked Ingram.

"No. I'm not going to protest the results – no matter what," said Shea, her arms crossed.

"But ..." began Templeton.

"No, Josh. I won't do it. That's it," she said, adamantly. Shea shook her head. "Unless we find blatant corruption of the voting data, I'm not going to. It's too important for this country to heal."

You know we're not going to find anything easily. They don't fight that way," said White, taking another sip of her Chardonnay.

"Shea, come on!" said Ingram earnestly. "You're beginning to sound like those people who came before us and gave everything up to those pushing on the Left. '*We don't operate that way*,' '*We play by the rules*,' '*We are better than to stoop to their level*!' Have you forgotten who you're dealing with? These people are cut from the same cloth – living by the lies, deceit and treachery that have always come from their playbook!" Ingram was red-faced and animated – more so than anyone had ever seen. They didn't know if it was the liquor or whether Ingram had just reached his breaking point. "How many of our own had to die, Shea? How many more will die, if we don't take a stand right here, right now? For too long, we've taken the high road, believing that if we just stuck by our principles that everything would work out all right. That's not how the Left thinks. They believe the ends justify the means, regardless of what you need do to get there – beg, steal, lie, even kill. It's all fair game if they can bring about the totalitarian society they were able to build in the USSA. So, no! I don't think we can just stand by and wait for things to work themselves out. After our secession, the war, the dead, and the destruction – how can you believe it? We can't. I don't believe everything will turn out fine in the end." Ingram took a breath. He took another sip of his brandy and then put down the glass.

"Karma," said Shea. "What about karma?"

"Excuse me?" asked Ingram

"Karma. What goes around, comes around. You've heard of that, right?"

Ingram nodded.

"So, the evil in the world — doesn't it eventually come around to bring down those who create it in the first place?"

"Sometimes," said Ingram. "Sometimes it takes a while."

Shea grimaced, her brow crumpling like a piece of plastic wrap.

"You know this to be true, Shea," said Ingram. "History is replete with rulers, evil rulers, who governed their people ruthlessly for decades. Then, after they died, their descendants continued to rule for centuries or even millennia. How is that Karma?"

"I don't know," said Shea. "I think, at that point, Karma transcends generations. God has the final decision about a man's fate. The evil that one man imposes on others may not find a route back to the perpetrator in this life, but the Buddhists believe that through reincarnation the person will suffer in the next one."

"So, you're a Buddhist now?" asked Templeton.

"No, but at some point, you have to have faith. Don't you?" asked Shea.

"I think it's okay to have faith, but you'd better back it up with action just in case," answered Ingram.

"In case what?" asked White, sitting on the sofa next to Shea.

"In case God doesn't get around to punishing the evil doers in this life. We don't want to wait until the next one to find out, do we?" asked Ingram.

"For the sake of others suffering, we can't," said Templeton. "I think we have a moral obligation to our people to protect them from that."

"I agree that we should take action," said Shea, "but it is not our obligation to protect them from those things. It is our obligation to protect them from criminals and hostile foreign interests. Otherwise, you're just going down the same path as Burns and her party — to protect everyone from everything. We don't have an obligation to do that — not when it takes away people's liberties, their freedom."

"She's got a point," said White, looking at an empty wine glass and contemplating getting another.

"So, are you willing to fight back, Shea?" asked Ingram, looking at her beseechingly.

Shea sighed.

"I didn't want to say this, but you know ..." began Ingram.

Shea held up her index finger to shush him. "Don't say it, Lawrence. I don't want to hear it."

"I don't care," said Ingram. "I know you don't want to hear it, but I'm going to say it anyway. It's not what Sumner would have wanted. Is it? He had faith in you. Hell, we all still have faith in you, Shea. But you have to fight back. You can't let JC down. He would not have wanted that, and you know it."

Shea looked down at the carpeting, where the seal of the President of the United States was prominently etched into the threads. She knew he was right. She knew it was her time now. Sumner was gone, but his spirit was there – it was right behind her, giving her support. She had to have the backbone to stand up to the tyranny that was constantly in the shadows, constantly threatening them, constantly ready to seize the moment when it sensed weakness.

"You're right," she answered him. "We can never let this happen again."

The night dragged on with numbers from Western Canada coming in later than the others as they were using a different polling system. However, when their tallies were submitted, the networks were quick to pounce.

"Finally, we have the vote counts from the western provinces of Canada," said Johnson, looking somewhat haggard from the long evening he'd endured. "As we've been saying, Burns leads Disone by more almost 1.1 million votes, and a good turnout by the Canadians is desperately needed by the Disone campaign to have any hope of claiming the presidency tonight. So, let's see what the numbers look like."

Johnson stopped and watched the numbers as they came in from British Columbia, Alberta, Saskatchewan, and Ontario. The largest by far was Ontario with a population nearly three times larger than any other in the voting bloc, although the turnout was not supposed to be that significant.

However, when the numbers shot up on the screen, even Johnson was taken aback. "Wow!" he exclaimed, sitting upright in his comfortable studio chair. "I don't think anyone expected those kinds of numbers coming from our new partners to the north. It looks like Canada showed up today, registering nearly fifteen million votes – some four million more than we expected. It looks like Disone has made up a significant portion of the votes she needed in the Western Canadian provinces. They are giving her 52 percent of the vote to Burns 47 percent. But that still gives Burns a 607-thousand vote lead on Disone. The big question now is what is happening to the votes in Texas and Wyoming? It is taking a lot longer to sort out the problems than anyone thought. It will come down to that to determine who will be our elected president in January. Stay tuned as we continue our coverage of the presidential election cycle here at *Election Central 2051*."

But by two o'clock in the morning there still hadn't been any more information, and both the news outlets and the candidates' campaign headquarters were clamoring for results. The White House was putting tremendous pressure on the election officials in Texas and Wyoming to clear up the issue. Still, by early morning they'd made no more progress. Finally, Shea dozed off in her chair. The others in the room also curled up on their couches or in their chairs, waiting for some answer – any answer that would come out of the Lone Star and Cowboy states.

At 7:30 that morning, an urgent wire came in to the White House. The Texas results were finally in and would be announced at 7:55. Shea was already up and awake by six and took the time to shower and change her clothes so she could look presentable in front of the zoo of cameras likely to swarm her after the final numbers were released. She asked for a cup of black coffee with a lump of brown sugar from the White House kitchen, which delivered it and other morning coffees to the three Cabinet members still camping out in the media room.

Shea came down to join the rest of them at 7:50, and together they watched as the news broadcast came back online. A new anchor had taken the helm. No longer was it Brian Johnson; instead, it was now Erin Howard, a young woman of about thirty took to the screen. With long blonde hair and angular, goddess-like facial features, she looked like the perfect eye-candy the networks craved. But to her credit, she was not an empty suit. She was also smart and quick-witted, not allowing anyone to best her in one-on-one interviews and could hold her own easily during marathon broadcasts as this one was shaping up to be.

Across the bottom of the screen were the flashing words **Breaking News**.

"Good morning," Howard began, putting on her *serious* journalism face. "We have some breaking news on the election from last night. Although all the other races have been decided at this point, the presidential race is still in question, as the votes from the states of Texas and Wyoming were not correctly counted. There were apparent problems with the software that controlled the voting process in those states, and we were unable to get any vote counts. As for the congressional races, we do have final counts for the House and Senate. Both the House and Senate will remain in the control of the Freedom Party, although that party did lose its supermajority in the Senate. We are showing that the House will have 255 members of that party, as compared with 168 for the Democratic Party and 12 for the Independents. In the Senate, the Freedom Party has 82 senators while the Democrats hold 47 and the Independents one.

"As for the presidential election — let us recap the numbers as we had them as of midnight, Eastern Standard Time, Burns held a lead of 607,039 votes over Acting President Shea Disone. The lead between the two candidates oscillated back and forth all evening, with Burns at one point up 1.1 million votes. That lead was shaved by the flood of votes Disone received from the western provinces of Canada ..."

Howard stopped and listened in her earpiece. "This just in ... we have the final vote numbers from Texas and Wyoming. As of this morning, with 100% of Texas votes in, we show ..."

Shea sat on the sofa biting her lip. She hadn't slept well the night before, and she could feel her hands were cold and clammy, shaking ever so slightly from anxiety.

On the screen, a graphic popped up with the state of Texas prominently displayed. Inside the state outline were the percentages of the popular vote cast, with 52 percent for Shea and 47 percent for Burns; one percent was cast for the Independent candidate.

"Disone with 52% of the vote will earn nearly 5.6 million votes from this contest, while Burns will garner a little over 5 million. Therefore, at this point, Disone holds 26,617,082 versus Burns with 26,687,902 – a margin for Burns of only 70,820 at this juncture,"

The summary graphic displayed on the screen read:

Burn	**26,687,902**	**49.4%**
Disone	**26,617,082**	**49.3%**
Williams	**687,387**	**1.3%**

"Burns has just a tenth of one percent lead over Disone – 49.4% of the vote, compared with Disone's 49.3%."

Howard stopped the broadcast one more time, listening and nodding as she tried to understand what was coming next. "Okay, so I have verified that we do have the Wyoming results as well. These will decide who is our next president."

Shea wanted to look away but forced herself to stay focused on the moving lips of the anchor.

"Wyoming weighs in," Howard began, "with 232 thousand votes counted, we show Disone with 68 percent of the vote. That is a big number coming from former President Sumner's home state. We'll have to wait and see if that is enough to put the Acting President over the top."

They didn't have to wait long. The results flashed quickly on the monitor in front of the anchor.

Disone Wins Election ...

"It is official. With Burns getting only 31.5 percent of the vote and the other half percent going to Williams, Acting President Shea Disone becomes President-elect Disone. She wins the popular vote by a mere 14,004 votes."

Again, the summary screen flipped onto the monitor:

Disone	**26,775,111**	**49.4%**
Burns	**26,761,107**	**49.3%**
Williams	**688,549**	**1.3%**

"By the slimmest of margins, Disone becomes the first officially elected president of a reunited United States," said Howard without emotion or expression.

Shea put her hands to her face in disbelief. Then she looked up to the ceiling and mouthed the words, "Thank you, Lord. And thank you too, JC."

"We did it, Shea!" shouted Ingram, his face ear-to-ear with a grin. "We did it!"

Relieved and ecstatic, she felt vindicated for all that they had been through and all the sacrifices they and others had made. The election was much too close – closer than any of them had imagined, but she had still won. Now it was time that Shea work to reunite the other 50.6% who had not voted for her. In that regard, it was a defeat for her. She had hoped that she would win with at least a majority, but coming so soon after such a divisive war, it was perhaps too much to ask. She would take the win, and with it work with Congress and the people to better America.

*****

CH 81 A New Union Message

As forty-nine presidents had done before her, Shea Disone stood on the west side of the Capitol building steps to accept the office of President of the United States of America. It was a very different country than it had been 264 years earlier when George Washington had been administered the oath. At that time, he had been sworn in on the balcony of the New York Federal Hall building, overlooking Wall Street. The world was a different place then and so were the nation's challenges.

As the infantile country neared the end of a tumultuous century, it faced an uncertain future with tremendous war debts, foreign threats from Spain and the violent French Revolution, militia unrest over not being paid their war wages, and the inability to rein in states that resisted a strong central government.

Unlike the first time in 1789, a woman raised her hand, putting the other on top of the Bible and said:

"I, Shea Renee Disone, do solemnly swear that I will faithfully execute the Office of President of the United States, and will, with all my ability and probity, preserve, protect and defend the Constitution of the United States. So help me God."

The words to the best of my ability were replaced with all my ability and probity to reflect the importance placed on integrity within government. In addition, Shea added the words So help me God, which had been struck, but had been left open as an option for any president taking the oath.

The applause started immediately after she had concluded the oath, and Shea raised her hand to accept their adulation. Then, she composed herself and looked out over the sea of people who lined the Mall in front of her. The words of her address appeared before her on a teleprompter. She had been offered the same special contact lenses that the once First Citizen Fourier had used, but had declined.

Standing straight and tall, Shea was elegant in a midnight blue, double-breasted jacket with matching skirt. Her blouse was of white silk, with a medium-length, gold, link necklace around her neck. She looked both polished and presidential. And with confidence and assertiveness, she delivered her first Inaugural address.

"Today, I stand before you as your humbled servant, one who has worked tirelessly for the reunification of this nation – the new United States of America. Four years ago, it would have been uncertain whether anyone would be standing here now, taking the oath of office as president of this great land. However, by the will of God, we have survived, and, I believe, we are stronger.

"It was not the choice of the people of the USSA to enter into a conflict. It was thrust upon them by the tyranny that forced them into bondage and now threatens other parts of the world. It comes in various forms, many of which begin as benign hopes of a better future, only to devolve into the basest form of primitive man – one of greed and power. Power seduces even the most pious. It is the Siren song, one more deleterious than anything God has placed on this planet. For those without self-control and without a core of principled beliefs, it is a song that is not often resisted. It is that which has destroyed civilizations and has more than once destroyed democracies.

"As Lincoln said in 1865 at his inaugural address, both sides to this Civil War conflict invoked the name of Almighty God to help them against the other side. It was the same with our conflict, except that fewer of us believe in Him today. But in this regard, both could not have what they sought from Him. Both could not win the conflict. And, although only one could win, in the end, neither did. For in victory, Lincoln saw there was no triumph for the Union. Yes, the Union – the nation -- won with respect to the unspeakable evils of slavery; however, it lost its virginity and its innocence. It took decades, even a century, to recover from the devastation of that first, horrible civil war.

"Like 1865, we have the opportunity to start anew. Hopefully, unlike 1865, we will pursue a more productive path to unification and reconciliation. In 1865, a president was assassinated before he could see the Promised Land..."

Here, Shea paused. For a moment, she thought about Sumner and fought back her emotions. She knew she had to be strong. This was the part of the speech she most dreaded but knew had to be said. She only hoped she could get through it in one piece. Clearing her throat, she continued.

"... In his stead was a man, Andrew Johnson, who was not up to the task of unifying a torn nation. Impeached and relegated to the bottom of the list of presidential greats, he is the image of what we should not, cannot do to heal this country now.

"However, here I must insert my own feelings. President Sumner, whom you all know I adored, was a strong man. He wanted to see this through to the end, and he is with us as I am speaking here today. He was a great president of the Republic – one whom I can only try to emulate. Yet, for his sake as well as for that of the people of this great new nation, I must and I will.

"We must and we will join together to fight against the tyrannical forces that still remain embedded within our borders. We must be vigilant to ensure they are never released again to impose the destructive forces that were set free to impose their will on our people during the last decade. We must never let it steal away our liberties and our freedoms!

"Likewise, such tyranny cannot be allowed to destroy the engine that has always created the vast prosperity of this land, raising all boats upon the shores of liberty. Capitalism once enabled this nation to become the most powerful on Earth. It is true, that left to laissez faire practices, it too can succumb to the base-human attributes responsible for so much suffering in the world. However, when moderated by the hand of a just and righteous governor, it can become an indispensable partner with democracy to forge possibilities and opportunities to make our country that shining city on a hill for all the world to see.

"We must not dismiss the power of capitalism, and, we must not ban the use of the word profit, from our vocabulary. Although dictionaries have bastardized the word's meaning over the last several years, at its core is the idea of benefit and improvement. It is what drives mankind to greater heights, not lower lows. It is the drink that quenches the thirst of those who seek to improve their own lots in life. It is the warmth of a loved one that hasn't been seen in years. It is the yearning for something better that we all have inside us – to better ourselves and our lives, to better the condition of our families and that of our children, and to better the world around us through charitable donations of those profits to worthy causes.

"At the same time, we cannot forget those truly less fortunate. We will not abandon the people who cannot, whether physically or mentally, fend for themselves. It is the responsibility of those in society who can care for themselves to care for others among us who cannot. I did not say it is our obligation to care for others among us who will not care for themselves and their families, but rather those who truly cannot. I believe It is the responsibility of government to encourage and incentivize those within society to help those less fortunate. However, it is not the obligation of the government to help and, thus, decide who will and who will not benefit. We have already seen that when a government is offered the chance to make that decision, everyone qualifies regardless of their capability to provide for themselves. That leads to dis-incentivizing of those who work and ultimately to the financial ruin of the golden goose.

"Today, I conclude my remarks, with this. It is vital to the interest of this nation and the world that the United States of America, as reconstituted, again regains its leadership role within the society of nations and with its own people. We must heal. We must rebuild. We must regain and renew the trust and confidence of, not only the American people, but of our allies around the world. It is our duty to our citizenry and to those on this Earth who have always looked to the United States as the one source for defending the fragile concepts of freedom and liberty. We cannot let either down.

"Abraham Lincoln concluded his second Inaugural address, speaking to a group of several thousand from the east side of the Capitol, in this way. He said.

'With malice toward none, with charity for all, with firmness in the right as God gives us to see the right, let us strive on to finish the work we are in, to bind up the nation's wounds, to care for him who shall have borne the battle and for his widow and his orphan, to do all which may achieve and cherish a just and lasting peace among ourselves and with all nations.'

"God bless all of you, and God bless the reunited United States of America. Thank you."

At that point, Shea again raised her hand and over the renewed earth, she traced in space the outline of the dollar sign and then the letter V.

"What was that?" asked Ingram, as she stepped off the podium to go back into the Capitol.

"That was the future," she answered.

*****

CH 82 Who is Johnny G?

"Who is Johnny G?" asked the young student, raising her hand in class.

The sixth-grade teacher at the front of the room smiled but was puzzled. "That's an interesting question, Silvia, why do you ask?"

Silvia was a precocious eleven-year-old who was growing up in a disadvantaged home with both a father and a mother. It was an unusual arrangement, as most other children had one or the other or two of one or three or more, but not one of each. She had been pitied by her teachers, who worried about what kind of home life she might have, being burdened with a biologically male father from birth and the same as a biologically female mother. Psychologists at Harvard, Princeton, and other Ivy League schools had long warned of the damaging effects of such marriages and family units. Then too, Silvia was hobbled with a father and mother who believed in freedom and liberty for all people, as well as God's inalienable rights. There were many things going against the child, and none – according to the school authorities – were good.

Indeed, the civil war was over and the country was reunited, but many in the former USSA states still felt strongly about the role of socialism, political correctness and the suppression of contrary views. Political correctness was still alive and well in cities on both coasts -- towns and neighborhoods from Maine to Maryland and from Washington state to southern California. In this case, MLK Middle School just outside of Boston was a prime example.

"Well," continued Silvia, "my father said that Johnny G was a patriot and a hero. Is that true?"

The teacher laughed and leaned forward to address the child's question. "Well, there are a few who think that, I guess. But, most people do not."

"So, he's not a hero? Didn't he make a weapon that ended the war and brought the country back together?"

"He did make a weapon. That part of it is true," said the teacher. "But it was an awful weapon that killed a lot of innocent people. It was a bad thing, not a good thing. Many people died from what he did. And all he cared about was the money he got from it."

Silvia, scrunched up her face and put her finger on her cheek in thought. "But my dad said he only got a little bit from the government for it even though he worked two years on it."

"I'm sure that's not the case. I'm sure he made billions from creating that wretched device," exclaimed the teacher.

Silvia turned her computer screen toward the teacher and pointed. "I don't know. Right here, the government's page says he only received that amount. Is it lying to us?"

The screen showed the number *US $56,381.21*.

The teacher felt uncomfortable, but continued striking back. "You can't always believe what the government tells you," she said, matter-of-factly.

"So, what about all the other stuff we're supposed to look up on government websites for our papers? Are we not to believe those things either?"

"Well, that's different," replied the teacher.

"I'm confused," said Silvia.

"Listen," said the teacher, smiling again and trying to deflect the questions. "You're a bright person, Silvia. You need to understand that Johnny G was *not* a friend of this country. He was an evil capitalist." Again, the teacher grinned, knowingly using words too big for the sixth grader to understand to make herself sound authoritative. "A capitalist is someone who makes money at the expense of others. That is, the person made money because that person took advantage of other people. That's not the way we should treat people. Wouldn't you agree?"

Silvia shook her head. "But I just showed you that he didn't make any money. And, my father said that he was a great inventor and *aunterpenur*," she said with difficulty.

"You mean entrepreneur," said the teacher. "That's someone who creates a new business. They do that so they can make money, of course. They certainly don't do anything out of the goodness of their hearts or to help others."

"My dad said he started his own business with our president, President Disone. Then the government wrecked it. That's when they left the country. My dad said Johnny G went on to create that shield that kept out bad bombs that were going to blow us up. He said that's the same thing we use around our houses to keep us safe at night. It's what they use to zap garbage to keep it from piling up in dump sites, and it's what they use to get rid of junk floating around in outer space that could hit one of our rockets.

My dad said that ..."

"Yes, yes. We've used Johnny G's laser technology to eliminate nearly all the need for landfills and cleaned up most of the space debris that was threatening our space flights. There have been a lot of good things that have come from what he's done. But he's profited by it," said her teacher, growing more agitated. "And that is *not* a good thing."

"Why is that a bad thing?" asked the child.

"Because he gets money from it and other people go hungry."

"Huh? I don't understand how people go hungry from someone else making money," asked Silvia.

"Because *they* aren't making the money," replied the teacher.

"But my dad said Johnny G's companies make jobs for people. Doesn't that let *them* make money?"

"Yes, but ..." the teacher was getting more and more frustrated. "It's just not right that he has all that money and others don't."

"Why?" asked Silvia, being stubbornly persistent.

"It just isn't!"

"But why?"

"Silvia, do I have to send you to the principal's office?" said the teacher, having run out of patience.

"No, Mx. Assinova. I didn't mean anything by ..."

"I've had about enough of your smart mouth, young person," said the teacher, huffing and furious. "Go down and see Mz. Haywood. Ze/he will know how to handle you. You're just trying to stir things up, aren't you? You and your father. You two should be ashamed. We just fought a war over all this stuff and you want to drag us all back into it. This country is going down the toilet because of *your* kind! We were on the road to a great society before your President Disone and that Sumner fellow before her got involved. Now everything we've worked so hard for is going nowhere.

"You tell your father that he's a greedy person and he only thinks about himself. None of you care about the poor and homeless – the children who go hungry and die in the streets every single day. You don't care about the millions who need our help! You only want to make more and more money. The almighty dollar – that's all you want.

"You and your family will rot in hell for the way you think!" shouted the teacher, red with rage. "So, go down to the principal's office right now! You're just being difficult and disruptive to the rest of the class."

Silvia sat at her desk trembling. No teacher had ever yelled at her for asking questions. In fact, all her teachers had always told her to ask questions about anything to which she didn't know the answer. She thought she was doing that – what she was supposed to do. She was only trying to learn.

The hallway was dark and lonely, as no one else was out and about during periods. Silvia trudged down the long corridor lined with closed classroom doors to get to the principal's office. She reached the heavy, oak door that had **Mz. Haywood – Principal** written on the outside and pushed it open. Inside was one of three assistants who helped the principal on his-her daily business.

It was Mx. Daley who looked up from his-her desk first. "Silvia? What brings you down here? Are you not feeling well?"

Silvia was a straight-A student and had never before been in trouble, so it was easy to understand why the assistant would immediately think she were ill.

"Uh, I'm not sure. My teacher sent me down here."

"Why is that, Silvia?"

"She said I was being difficult and disruptive."

"Were you?" asked Mx. Daley, eying her over the tops of his-her glasses.

"I don't think so. I wasn't trying to be."

"I see. Well, you'll have to wait there in that chair until the principal can see you."

It was over thirty minutes before Mz. Haywood came out of his-her office. "Silvia?" he-she said. "Why are you here?"

Silvia recounted the entire story for the principal, not embellishing, twisting, or distorting any aspect of her conversation. When she finished, she looked up into the face of the principal, hoping to see leniency.

"I see," was the only answer Silvia received. The principal was not pleased. "Well, I think it is important that we send a note off to your guardians about this. I don't think it will do much good, though. We know your father and know how opinionated he is about things. Still, we hold out hope for you." The principal paused after filling out the paperwork and handing it to the young student. "I do need to tell you that if you and your father persist in causing disruption within the classroom, we will need to take more severe measures to deal with it."

"More severe?" asked Silvia. "What do you mean?"

"I mean, we may be forced to take you away from your guardians."

"You mean my mom and dad?"

"Yes! We may need to put you in a loving foster home where the people there can teach you the *right* way to think. It's obvious you're not getting that from the place you're living now. It appears that your guardians really don't love you very much or they wouldn't fill your head with those ideas."

Silvia shuddered. She was petrified at the thought of being taken away from her family – her home. She didn't want that. She wouldn't say anything anymore, ever. She would make sure she didn't cause any problems in class again – never saying anything that would get the teacher upset, regardless of what her father said to her.

"My lips are sealed," she said. "I will obey. I promise."

"Good," said Mz. Haywood. "We like to keep our children in control and in line. Then perhaps there is hope for you after all."

Silvia left the office clutching the threatening note from the principal. Are my parents really that bad? she thought to herself. Maybe it's best if I just stop talking to them about stuff. I don't want to get anyone else in trouble too.

Mz. Haywood watched as Silvia strolled back down the hall and opened the door to her classroom. He-she was smiling.

"I'm glad we have good teachers at this school," said the assistant, watching his-her boss. "I know our children are in capable hands to really learn the truth and what's right."

The principal nodded. "Not only what's right, but what's righteous. If you can't believe in the righteousness of our education and government institutions and the religion of secularism, what can you believe in?"

*****

CH 83 Always in the Shadows

The afterglow of the unification was still burning brightly even though there were pockets of firm resistance to the path chosen by the Disone Administration. Still, most were rejoicing in the reality that the Union had been saved. The Republic and the USSA were once again united with a new beginning and a new opportunity for greatness. The president of the new USA had delivered an eloquent speech, and afterward, reiterated her desire to exonerate those of the USSA of any wrongdoing in the civil war. The new president was quick to recognize the rebellious states and welcome them back into the fold.

Unlike the 1861-1865 Civil War, it was not decades later before the two sides began to work together again. The Republic made it as easy as possible for the reunification to be painless and reach out a helping hand to heal the old wounds. The better analogy was the Marshal Plan after WWII, which brought back Germany and Japan more quickly into the fold of world society. Everyone understood what was at stake, and the stakes were high. Too many had died. Too many families had been torn apart. Too much grief and sadness had been witnessed. Those in the Republic felt the fire and passion of their righteous cause. They volunteered. They were the ones who understood. On the other hand, those in the USSA were conscripted, threatened with incarceration if they didn't obey. Worse yet, in battle, if they didn't obey they were merely shot. There was no principle for which they were fighting. The use of terror was not a cause; it was a whip.

People from the USSA were weary from a war in which they wanted no part; an economy that had collapsed; oppressive restrictions on speech and travel; and rampant corruption at every level of government. There was no moral conviction about what the country stood for ... that had vanished years earlier. But once the war was over, reconciliation and harmony were in the air. It was a pandemic of relief and joy that swept the country. There was a new sense of optimism – a modicum of hope for the future. Under a constitution that reflected the conservative thoughts, religious values and democratic virtues espoused by the Founding Fathers in the late eighteenth century, the nation was poised to become great once more.

Life was good.

The economic engine of the country began bursting with productivity, sparked by low taxes, low interest rates and drastic cuts in regulation and red tape. Jobs were growing once again in the former USSA where most business had fled elsewhere to more favorable economic climates. The economy was prospering and so were the people.

It was only overseas that frictions grew. Support from socialist countries in Europe – those that had not yet converted to Islam -- began to wane as they saw the fast and determined rebuilding of the country under capitalistic rules. The old tensions crept back, as European countries began sensing the resurgence of US dominance and hegemony. The theocratic states had rejoiced when the USSA had been in its final death throes. Believing they had finally cut the head off the evil, capitalistic snake, the

Islamic states began plans for a major worldwide expansion which included the subjugation of unbelievers in Russia and China. But now, all that changed. And, so too, did their plans.

The fight was not over – it was only subdued. That was true not only in hostile, foreign nations but also at home. There were still those who were passionate about their utopian vision of socialism, and they would continue the struggle.

***

It was a cold, autumn night, one that foreshadowed the advent of winter, which was celestially only a few weeks away. In a dark, dingy and impoverished part of Philadelphia, lights glowed brightly in the basement of the First Baptist Church. Flyers had been handed out throughout the week, advertising that there was an important meeting planned and many were expected.

Anna Walling smiled as she watched the curious walk through the door. She handed out meeting agendas covering what would be discussed that chilly evening. At the top of the page were the words in bold, sixteen-point font –

The People's Government – Where has it gone?

After the many of the pews were filled and the clock struck the appointed hour, Anna stepped to the podium, nervous but determined.

She was short, slight of build, but a powerhouse of energy and spirit. Her father and mother had both been members of the US People's Social Democratic Party or the PSD during the Ratner Administration. She was the second of three daughters born to the pair. Each had been indoctrinated in the thoughts of class struggle and the subjugation of the less fortunate by those with more. They were told from a young age that it was only chance and luck that separated the wealthy from those who wanted and needed more. They had been privileged, and that was wrong.

The starving children, they had been told, were the result of the rich and ruling class – people who cared nothing for others but themselves. The rich were the ones who screwed others out of what they deserved. It was the working man who had enabled the affluent to get where they were, and they had gotten nothing in return. The rich fat-cats had also benefited from the country's infrastructure that was built on the broken backs of those blue-collar workers in the trenches and under the whip of their capitalistic bosses. Therefore, those Have-nots were *owed* by those who were considered to be Haves. There had been no skill or talent involved in the wealthy getting that way, only Machiavellian greed. It was "anti-Christian," even though her family had been atheist. It was just a convenient argument that her father used effectively against those with a religious backbone and conscience.

"I'm so glad all of you could make it tonight," Anna said, greeting the thirty or so who had ventured in out of the cold. "This is not going to be lecture or a sermon. I'm only here to tell you the truth about what is really going on in the world and what we, as citizens, must do to fight back against the tyranny of capitalism."

In front of her were several homeless people wearing dirty blankets wrapped around them. Their faces were smudged, their hair stringy and unkempt, and many had eyes that were glazed over from over-imbibing throughout the day. For the most part, they were there only taking advantage of the warm, open church and soon curled up on the pew bench and fell asleep. There was a man and woman there in the front row – he dressed in dirty, blue coveralls as if he'd just gotten off his shift at the steel mill and she holding their infant daughter dressed in a torn, pink loosely knit fleece. Others too were there, mainly blue-collar workers in search of a better life and higher-paying jobs. In the back were two union men watching her carefully and monitoring what she was saying to see if it was anti-union and someone they should add to their enemies list. Finally, there was a well-dressed, older man in the back pew, on the other side of the church. He merely sat and watched, his keen eyes absorbing everything that was going on and everything that was said and not said. His silver mustache was well-trimmed and he had the air of sophistication and experience about him.

"We, as a country," Anna continued, "were so close to achieving our dream of equality for everyone. But, instead, it was a rug that was pulled out from under us. We got embroiled in a war that drained us of our treasury and our livelihoods. If we'd only been able to spend more money on the citizens of this country – on you – we wouldn't be in this mess. Instead, we had to spend it on other things such as guns and missiles to defend ourselves against the slave masters of the Republic and their evil capitalistic ways. With so many children suffering and parents without the ability to feed them, it is wrong for the country to go back to those tragic and failed policies of the capitalists – they, the ones who broke the backs of our people just to have another Mercedes Benz in their garage. This is wrong! And it's time we rise up and fight back!"

"You deserve your fair share! You deserve to get a piece of what the rich people have. After all, they don't need all that money to live on. It's only right that they share it with everyone else," she said. "It's only right that they give some to you! But the problem is they won't. They want to keep all of it for themselves. So, it is and has always been the duty of the government to force them to give it to you. It's just like Robin Hood – except we're not taking from the rich, we're only getting from the rich what they owe us! We're demanding what is rightfully ours!"

The small crowd clapped politely in support. It was modest applause, but it was a beginning and that was her only goal. Most didn't really understand what Anna was telling them, but they liked the part about getting more from their government. They had all felt jealousy and resentment against those who had more than they, and they liked to hear someone else felt the same way. What was better was that it seemed to be someone who could do something about it – or at least wanted to do something. They didn't care about where the money and wealth came from – only that they got their *fair* share of it. It was the government's money or it was the rich people's money – it didn't really matter. They both just printed it. And, they felt they deserved some of it. To them, the government printed it and the rich stole it. It was that simple. They were sick and tired of driving their beat-up, fifteen-year-old car that had failing solar cells that needed replacing, and being passed on the highway by some brand-new, million-dollar Ferrari or Aston Martin. The rich had no right to that! They hadn't worked hard in the factories or in the mines to earn that. It had been handed to them.

Those in the pews began nodding their heads as she spoke. They clapped and then began cheering as she continued talking about the evils of the new USA and the great divide between the Haves and Have-nots.

Anna smiled. She was getting through to them. She was glad about that, and deep down, she knew that someday, the USSA would rise again from the ashes and reclaim the rights of those less fortunate. Hopefully, she would be one of those who would be in control and help lead those less educated and less privileged to a better society and a better life.

"So, join me and the socialist program, as we take on the big government and the rich robber barons. Sign up tonight as a card-carrying member of the Democratic Socialist Party. You will be one of millions worldwide who have seen the light of prosperity and the promise of a rich and glorious future for you and your family!"

After Anna stepped down from the podium, a few from the crowd stopped her to ask questions about the party and what it meant. Others quickly found the hot chocolate and left without saying a word. It was the older man in the back pew who waited until everyone else left before he approached Anna. He extended his hand and smiled. "I like what you said tonight," he told her.

"Why thank you," she answered. "Are you familiar with the Democratic Socialists?"

"I believe I am," he answered, leaning on his cane. "Is this your first meeting?"

"Yes, it is. Was it that obvious?"

"Oh, no. I thought you did quite well," he answered looking more keenly at her as if sizing up her potential and ability to influence.

"So, what is your background?" she asked him.

"I've done a lot of things in my life," he said. "I've seen things from both sides. I've experienced things from both sides."

"You've been poor before?"

"Well, I wouldn't say that," he answered.

"Then what?"

"I make it a habit of always being on the right side of an issue. In any debate, I look to see which side I believe will win and then I align myself with them. It's worked pretty well for me through the years, and I'm not about to stop now."

"So, you're interested in joining the party because ...?"

"As I said, I want to be on the winning side. And with my help, I think you can be on the winning side this time," the old man answered.

"Can you give a donation, then?"

"Perhaps. I'll give you a little now and then fund more as I see progress. You're not the only group I'm supporting you understand. I'm spreading out my investments to make sure I'm betting on the right horse."

"It doesn't sound like you have a conviction about this like I do," said Anna, indignantly.

"I don't. I assure you of that. But does that make any difference? Do you want my financial support or not?" he said bluntly.

Anna hesitated, but it didn't take her too long before she smiled and held out her hand. "Of course. Where do I sign?" she said laughing.

Instead of shaking her hand, the old man presented her with his card. "Call me," he said. "I'll see what I can do. You know there are always people like me who don't have conviction, but they are good to keep on your good side anyway. We come in handy."

Anna took the card and watched as the man put on his hat and coat and walked out of the church. She turned over the card in her hand. It read:

> MR. KILBY THORNE
> OPPORTUNIST
> 999-555-1789

#####

About the Author

The author has written numerous novels, many of which are trilogies or multi-volume sets that span different types of book genre from fantasies and murder mysteries to horror stories and allegories. He has been cited for his creativity and fresh approach to books written in each of these book categories. The ATLAS Trilogy is the only novel series Gregory Phillips has penned using that *nom de plume*. Books authored in each genre are inked using a unique pseudonym most fitting to that style writing.

Phillips lives with his family in the Chicago area.

Blue M Publishing

Go to www.blueMpublishing for more works by this and other authors.

Thank you

The author hopes you enjoyed this trilogy. The story and its presentation are not without controversy, but perhaps it is a starting point for dialog and discussion.

*****

www.ingramcontent.com/pod-product-compliance
Lightning Source LLC
Chambersburg PA
CBHW051434260626
47162CB00001B/83